THE DIAL PRESS
NEW YORK
1976

NOW PLAYING at CANTER-BURY

Vance Bourjaily

Excerpts from this work were originally published in different form in the following publications: *Boy's Life, North American Review, Phoebe, Esquire* Magazine, *Dude* Magazine, and *The Iowa Review*.

Copyright © 1964, 1969, 1976 by Vance Bourjaily

Manufactured in the United States of America

First printing 1976

ISBN: 0-8037-6450-2

Book design by Holly McNeely

Library of Congress Cataloging in Publication Data

Bourjaily, Vance Nye.
  Now playing at Canterbury.

  I. Title.
PZ3.B6672No [PS3503.07]   813'.5'4   76-24902
ISBN 0-8037-6450-2

In memory of
Diarmuid Russell
1902–1973

Acknowledgments

In the twelve years I've spent working on this book, off and on, many people have been helpful, and none more so than Tom Turner. Tom is the actual composer of the opera $4000, but is no more like Ralph Lekberg, the fictional composer in the book, than I am like Maggi Short—much as I might sometimes wish I were. Jim Dixon and Herald Stark let me watch their rehearsals and learn what I could from them. John Irving helped; so did Marvin Bell, Chase Twitchell, Bill Murray, and Leonard Michaels. So did Scott Barker, Rudy Galask, and Tony Colby. My friend Mickey Angel taught me a song, and my son Philip showed me a tower.

The University of Iowa not only produced Tom's opera (with a cast and crew totally unlike the cast and crew in the book) but has also underwritten my own work—not only with a couple of direct grants from the graduate college but also by giving me employment that provides time for what the university generously regards as research, making no distinction in its support between the scientific, the scholarly, and the imaginative.

The writing began in North Liberty, Iowa, in 1963, and went on in Oaxaca, Mexico; Sharon Center, Iowa; Barcelona, Spain; and is finally being finished back in Sharon Center, in December 1975. My love and thanks to my family for seeing me through it.

V. B.

. . . Now Playing at Canterbury

Dick Auerbach
Sidney Bennett (née Cindy Benesch)
Henry Fennellon
Debbie Dieter Haas
Billy Hoffman
Maury and Karen Jackstone
Ralph and Josette Lekberg
John Ten Mason, M.D.
Sato Murasaki
Beth Paulus
David and Susan Riding
Marcel St. Edouard
Mike and Mona Shapen
Rigby and Maggi Taro Short
Hughmore Skeats IV

&

Thoreau, William Cullen Bryant, Mr. Dawson.
Cops.
Gottfried and Gerhardt.
Marcel's Agent.
A Famous Soprano.
John Haroldsen, Ned.
Al Riker, Pill Donovan, Bert Tannenbaum, Poker Players,
    Harry the Paymaster, Sally Anne, Raymond Applegore,
    Norah Applegore.
Jane Lee Ransom, Old Lady Dove and Quail, Phyllis, Injoe,
    Piano Player, Earl, Parky, Mr. Beach, etc.
F. Scott Fitzgerald, Betty Cass Collins, Miles Hubbert, Petey
    Luther, Kevin Candlekirk, Eartha Hearn, Janssy, Jonesy.
Oog, Lady, Christine, Carolyn, Bud Jamison, Short Fat Man,
    Detective, Pete Erickson, etc.
Gomez the Fat Chileno, Appealing Blonde Girl.

&

Bitsy, G.I.'s, King Con, Garage Attendant, Thief, Millie, etc.
    Cindy Auerbach, Sam Auerbach.
Cougar Edwards, Mary Virginia, Earl Warren, etc.
Banjo Man, Dead Musicians, Ronnie, Accompanist, etc.
Daddy Jean, Mother, Uncle Fuzz Peach, Tuba Player,
    Half Brothers.
Warren the Turtle, Old Coach, Rabbit, Loveliest Maidens.
Dukey Woerber, Mrs. Woerber, Custard Dan, Soldier Cats,
    Old Beagle, Sheriff Ka, Billy Weedle, Fat Woman, etc.

    &

Charles, Maria Luisa, Corrinne, Jody Skink, etc.
Crazy Betty, Stoney, Little Rock, Spiro Agnew.
Fats, Tondelayo, Wholly Goosed, Marymary, Fidel Castro.

    &

Herve Gandenberg, Galdencio, Doberman Pinschers.
Two Undergraduate Girls with Shining Hair.
Lila.
B-52's.
Etc.

    Etc.

       Etc.

 Tuning Up

Here we go. The quest is on again. There's lots to do, many voices to hear and some to heed.

But let's start simple: Start with grass.

Now in June, in the pastureland around State City, it's waist-high—bluegrass and brome, orchard grass, timothy, reed canary. The roots have survived Antarctic winter, Asiatic rains, a day or two of treacherous Dalmatian spring, and now the weather's Panamanian.

We could ask someone in the botany department at State University what's going on with this grass, and be told that it's photosynthesizing, strong and true, and then he might write on the blackboard the great summary equation for the beginning of everything:

$$n\mathrm{CO}_2 + n\mathrm{H}_2\mathrm{O} + \text{light} = n\mathrm{O}_2 + (\mathrm{CH}_2\mathrm{O})_n$$

But what's really nice is that we can lie down in the grass and disappear, and look up at the sky.

The pretty black-and-white-streaked small bird darting past overhead, trilling, is a bobolink.

It was an unpopular, drab little rice guzzler down South in winter plumage, and sometimes called the skunk-head blackbird. But here, where it nests, the creamy patch on the back of the male's head seems endearing, and his song a wonder.

There are plenty of people around State City gentle enough to like bird watching—plenty rough enough to like bird shooting, too. The latter might just feel a little frustrated reading in *Birds of America* (1917) about the bobolink, protected now from their guns, that banqueters once fancied it as "reed-bird on toast." But lying in the grass out of sight under the big American sky, we might be more pleased with this passage, if we have the good old standard bird book along:

> The bobolink's song stands alone in the musical utterance of American birds. Thoreau caught the spirit and technique of the effort when he wrote: "This flashing, tinkling meteor bursts through the expectant meadow air, leaving a trail of tinkling notes behind."

Not one of Thoreau's best sentences, is it? But the notes do seem to trail and hang that way.

> William Cullen Bryant's oft-quoted poem contains . . . the refrain: "Bobolink, bobolink; spink, spank, spink," . . . a feeble effort to reduce its notes to spoken words.

Yes. Mr. Bryant may stand down.

> Mr. Dawson's transliteration, *"Oh geezeler, geezeler, gilipity, onkeler, oozler, oo . . ."*

Hey, Mr. Dawson, wow. Terrific.

> . . . really is a clever rendition of the opening notes . . . following which the bird is likely to become a sort of hysterical music box and to produce a burst of sound pyrotechnics which make one fear that the next second he is going to explode outright and vanish in a cloud of feathers. [George Gladden]

Okay, and now, half a century later, there are people with equipment in the sound lab at State University who could record that song, and people in the music department who could transcribe it in every variation. Not to mention gloomy ecologists who would have statistics for the decline of the bobolink population as pasturelands are converted to row crops, row houses, rows of parking space. Never mind.

Let's sit up, close *Birds of America,* stop hiding in the grass. Our company has started to gather in State City. Some of it's already there.

Look, as we walk back to the car: In those crop fields, beside this pasture, the corn is ankle-high and finger-fat, the fist-sized soybean plants are kelly green against black dirt. We had better wish them well. There's a tithe growing out there to keep big State University moving on its earnest, complicated mission—for a cup of soybeans, your kid can triangulate a star, for an ear of corn, memorize two lines of Lermontov.

Let me spread the strands of barbed wire so you won't get snagged crawling through the fence.

Here's an idea: Couldn't one of the student composers write a piece of music based on that transcription of the bobolink's song? Why not a ballet? *Skunkhead's Dance*: (I) Drab and greedy, hunted and reviled all winter, he escapes from the rice fields, North with spring. (II) Beautiful now, loved for his song, he mates and is adored by nineteenth-century poets. (III) But winter comes again.

What do you think? There'd be dancers here to dance it, stages for them to dance on, someone like old Debbie Dieter Haas for the bird and poet costumes, an affectionate audience—and no need to finance it with investors or beg patronage from some duke with tertiary syphilis or funding and approval from a mean bureau of the government.

Skunkhead's Dance is not this summer's project, of course, only an idea. Ideas grow like oats around here.

Debbie Dieter Haas is a fierce, kind, homely German woman, in the middle of middle age. Professor, if you like. She doesn't mind. *Professor's* nothing to be ashamed of to a European. She teaches theatre lighting and design, does sets and costumes for the major shows here, and will, in September, take charge as the first woman head of a major university department, Speech and Drama.

Just now she is the subject of an agitated phone call.

"Where in hell is bloody Debbie?" The Australian voice of Hughmore Skeats IV, head of the university opera guild.

"At the art museum, according to her office." Rigby Short, who is generally called Snazzer, is sitting at his office desk in the English department, drinking early afternoon whiskey and water from a coffee cup, talking with Skeats. Mr. Short's a professor, too.

"For God's sake, does she know we've lost our rucking director?"

They are talking about the latest crisis in the production of a new opera, for which Snazzer Short wrote the libretto and in which Skeats will appear. Today is Thursday. Rehearsals are scheduled to start on Monday.

"The police came and got her."

"The blinking what?"

Snazzer Short allows himself to enjoy a sip from his cup and Hughmore Skeats's confusion for a moment. "There were a bunch of paintings stolen from the museum last night, and no art historians around on summer faculty. Debbie's got enough art-history background to give them some idea of the values."

The secretary at Debbie's office said twenty paintings or more, but that seems incredible. It'll be big news by evening. Short's been wanting a reason to get over to the museum to find out what happened.

"I'll go look for her. What time's the meeting?"

"Three o'bloody clock, and everyone notified but Debbie. See here, Snazzer—"

"Oh, hell." Short has just realized why he's been so disturbed at learning of the art theft. There is—or was?—in the museum's permanent collection a lovely de Chirico of shadowed streets, strange forms, and long perspectives. It has meant enough to him so that, from time to time, he's felt a need to visit it. Now he visualizes an empty space on the gallery wall.

"See here, no use beating around the famous bush on this director thing. I'd like to propose to the meeting that I take it on myself. Your libretto, you know. It's such a bing-banger to work with, I don't see how it can let me go wrong."

The flattery comes nowhere near touching Short. He is wet-eyed suddenly with anger, a feeling of probable loss: Someone may have wrenched away, may even now be defacing, his de Chirico.

Distraught, remembering he must go and look for Debbie, he leaves the office and in it, faceup on the desk, the program proof he was to have taken to the meeting and has spent the last half hour correcting.

PRINTER'S PROOF   PRINTER'S PROOF

The State University Opera Guild)—(*Ital.*)

(*delete?*) *or* Hughmore Skeats IV, Chairman

Presents

[handwritten annotation: cap. ital. bold]

THE WORLD PREMIERE OF

$4000

[handwritten annotation: cap.]

An opera by Ralph Lekberg
Libretto by Rigby Short
The University Symphony Orchestra Conducted by Sato Murasaki
Production Staged by Robert Rosetti
Designed by Deborah Dieter Haas

[handwritten annotations: delete; name to come]

Just as there is one name lacking, a "name to come," so there is another so eminent as to be startling. That is the name of the conductor, Sato Murasaki.

Sato was on the faculty here for three years, in the late 1950s, on his way to becoming a world figure in music. He now conducts a European orchestra, and it's assumed that he'll be hired, in due time, by Boston, Philadelphia, or New York.

It was because Sato agreed, surprisingly, out of loyalty to this institution and old friends here, to come back this summer that the opera $4000 will be the inaugural production for the new, ten-million-dollar entertainment complex the university has just finished building, a sort of Lincoln or Kennedy Center for this region. The original plan had been to open the 2700-seat main auditorium by booking the Bolshoi Ballet.

Rigby (Snazzer) Short enters the museum, goes directly to the de Chirico, and almost weeps to find it still in place. He would touch it if there weren't so many police around. He goes into the next gallery to see if the little early Gauguin is missing, but it's still here, too, and next to it the lovely big Chagall. Dutch landscapes, British portraits, even the Rembrandt—if there has really been a robbery, the thieves went by a couple of hundred thousand dollars' worth of paintings.

"Sir, you shouldn't be in here. The museum's closed."

"But what's been stolen?"

"Who said something was?"

A second policeman is at Short's blind side when he looks, and, up the steps, through open double doors leading from the basement comes a third.

"I heard about it from Doctor Dieter Haas's office."

"That's the old lady prof."

"We better get his name."

They seem more ill at ease than hostile. Short gives his name and his errand, and is told that Debbie was here for half an hour, talking with the police lieutenant, but has just left. The police lieutenant arrives, is polite and uninformative except to say that he understands Professor Dieter Haas is now at the new auditorium.

"I hope she was helpful?" Short gets a funny look for that hope, leaves, gets into his red Volvo puzzled, relieved, excited. He drives out of the parking lot; when he's got a block between himself and that mass of State City policemen, he stops and has a sip to calm himself.

Short is not an every-day drinker, but now and then, having had one at lunch, and if there aren't afternoon classes to teach, he'll permit himself to keep it going, low key. And sometimes by evening the pitch will rise more than he means it to.

Now he drives slowly through the streets that cross the campus, feeling just nice, enjoying the place, indulging in a little meditation—delaying the pleasure of finding out from Debbie what in hell is going on. It's a warm, windy day, and the great, familiar physical plant of the university seems all his. The library, with its half-million books—and if they don't include one he might need, a special librarian knows how to get it from Harvard or Oxford or Roberts College, Istanbul. The Engineering Building, and in it the university radio station, broadcasting intelligent talk and serious music anytime you're lonely for such sounds. This ivory tower, covered with graffiti, scarred by rebellion, still stands, has survived to 1972, will stand, is still ivory as a carved tusk is still ivory. Short, wounded in the Second World War, a newspaperman after it, waiting for a place in graduate school, would not have it otherwise, likes it best in summer.

Classroom halls, Physics Building, dormitories, hospital complex, Memorial Union with its hotel and cafeterias, tennis courts, stadium, soccer fields, Center for Asian Studies, Center for . . . two hundred million dollars' worth of grounds and buildings and now, in the quiet summer of the year, with half the faculty and half the student body gone, Short likes the way it's kept productive: with summer workshops, exhibits, action groups, seminars, festivals, and clinics. For everything from majorettes to anesthesiologists, etchers to wrestling coaches. They come to State City. To learn something. Or achieve something. Or wonder at something.

Summer restlessness is not materialistic but an ethical dissatisfaction

(Short stops for a light); as the blood warms, one yearns for self-fulfillment and travels to State City, where an idling educational plant needs fools to suffer, not just gladly, gratefully, and if a wise administrator is one who knows that it takes a fool to suffer one, it might be claimed that everything redeeming in human life is rather foolish—heroism, tenderness, fun, art, pure research, and the different kinds of love.

Not to mention operas.

Brisk now, Snazzer Short parks the Volvo near the stage door of the new auditorium alongside the cars of the workmen finishing things up indoors. He strides in, and misses Debbie again.

The electrical contractor's foreman, who is supervising installation of stage-light fixtures, seems pleased to report to Short that Miss Teeter Horse has been here and gone.

"Listen, you know her? She comes in, grabs the spec sheets out of my hands, and everywhere she looks, she's going to show me a mistake."

"Is she right?"

The man grimaces. "She knows her stuff, I guess. But listen, this is complicated." To mollify the foreman, and because he's in a nice mood, Short lets himself be shown wiring diagrams that look like blueprints for spaghetti, all the time secretly rather thrilled to think that in a month this vast new theatre will be filled with people listening to words he wrote.

"Did Miss . . . Teeter Horse say where she was going next?"

She didn't. Short's nice mood is threatened as he goes back out to the car again; he's sorry he delayed; he wants so much to talk to Debbie before the meeting, to find out what happened at the museum. He decides to try her office, opens the door on the driver's side of the Volvo, and there she is in the other seat, waiting.

"So, Short. All over I have been looking for you. We have a meeting."

Short steps back, staring; then he deliberately closes the door again without entering and leans on the car window looking in at her, loving the big teeth, the wrinkles, the sheer radiance of her.

"You are a crazy old woman, and I'm glad they're making you head of Speech and Drama. You'll drive them right up the wall." Now he opens the door again, moves in under the wheel, closes the door, and takes her arm. "Come on, Debbie. The art museum. What happened?"

"Start the car, Short. We have to get a director."

"Don't tease. Were there really any paintings stolen?"

"Twenty-six, I think. Some very big, three-by-four, three-by-five. They come from the storage room in the basement, all Spanish religious by forgotten painters of a century ago. I have never seen them, but from the inventory I know exactly what they are. Terrible."

"But why? Who'd take them?"

"Somebody with a key and a truck. Who can tell? Maybe somebody fanatic from Religion, who wants to make a vulgar church."

Short is delighted. "Is that what you told the police?"

"I tried. All they want to know is how much. I said, from me, one dollar. But somebody wants them."

Short starts the car. "Fifty thousand."

"Please?"

"That's what the papers will say. When you have to have a figure, fifty thousand's always good. You want to stop at your office?"

"I want to stop at your house. To get Maggi."

Short nods. His wife is Maggi Taro, the actress, a genuine celebrity for State City. Kids, he knows, sometimes register for one or another of Short's courses just to see and hear the man she married. In getting this opera production past the deans and committees who wanted to book the Bolshoi Ballet for the inaugural, Maggi's been a powerhouse of reputation, energetic presence, cool authority. Now she will help them handle Hughmore Skeats.

"He still wants to direct. He just told me so." Short.

"That will be so bad? He has experience."

"With student casts and faculty colleagues. People he can bully. This is different."

There is a pause as they drive. Debbie: "Last year I went to give a lecture in Lamoni. You know where it is, Lamoni?"

"Down on the southern border, isn't it?"

"Afterward, people talk to me. They want to know if I know Mr. Skeats. Every summer these people come to State City for the opera. They have heard him sing such a villain. Iago. 'I believe in a cruel God.' "

"What?"

"What Iago sings. In Decorah, too. In the north they ask about Mr. Skeats after the lecture. One man cannot forget Mr. Skeats singing Rigoletto."

"Oh, Debbie, Debbie. What kind of God does Rigoletto believe in?"

"You shut up, Rugby. A hunchback God, I guess."

"My name is Rigby, Madame Chairperson." She won't call him Snazzer, thinks the nickname silly. "Sure. He's a star to our home-grown music lovers, all right."

"And what have you and I done that people speak of in Lamoni and Decorah, Short?"

"You think Skeats should direct?"

"No."

Maggi is waiting. Debbie called her.

Burly, bearded, faddishly dressed in tight pants and knee-high boots, Hughmore Skeats meets the three in a corridor of the Music Building outside the office of Ralph Lekberg, the composer.

"Hi, chums."

"Where are we having today's panic?" Maggi Taro Short asks.

"Ralph's office. Sato's with him."

"I'm to meet Mr. Sato Murasaki now?" Debbie is pleased. Sato's been here three days, working with Ralph on the score but not seeing many people.

"He's lovely," Maggi says. "You'll want to eat him up."

"Be sure to brush your teeth afterward." To Hughmore Skeats Japan is still the enemy.

Ralph's office is really a workroom, music manuscript in neat piles on the several tables, a small desk, a blackboard marked out in painted lines like music paper, some old music stands, and just enough golden-oak straight chairs for the six who are gathered: the composer himself, the Shorts, Debbie, Skeats, and—

Mr. Sato Murasaki. He is unexpectedly tall—five ten perhaps—slim and very elegantly dressed in pale, tan gabardine. He was, in spite of Skeats's dumb joke, born in California, but his manners and speech seem immediately eastern, Ivy League, fashionable. Ralph Lekberg looks like an old, fat farmer, rising beside his Japanese-American friend to make the only introduction necessary.

"Come in, Debbie. This is Sato Muraski, Debbie Dieter Haas."

"Professor Dieter Haas. How do you do, and congratulations."

"Oh!" Advancing to seize the slim and famous hand, the elongated fingers that are so often and so dramatically photographed for record album covers. "Of you I have heard so much about." When she's flustered, Debbie's English is a scandal.

"I'm so pleased we're going to work together." Sato.

"Yes, Me also."

"And I want to ask you—"

"Whoa, Joey," says Hughmore Skeats IV, baritone. "No one's going to work with anyone till we find a bloke to stage this bloody show."

"Sit down," Ralph says, and Sato asks:

"Is there really no other director here now?"

"Not with Rossetti gone."

"Steady." Skeats. "Not in the theatre department, that is. Unless Debbie's hiding someone from us."

"Mr. Paulding is retired," Debbie. "But would do it for us, I think."

"He's not well enough, Debbie." Maggi Short. "I saw him Sunday. He has that awful wheeze old smokers get."

"Emphysema," says Ralph, puffing on his pipe.

"What about the kid that did *Ubu Roi?*" Short.

"He is very limited still." Debbie. "One kind of thing he can do very well, but has still that wonderful contempt of the young people for everything else. Such as realism."

"What about doing it yourself, Debbie?" Skeats.

She shakes her head, without returning the compliment. "I have here letters." She reaches into her vast canvas shoulder bag. "From agents. From New York, Los Angeles. They represent professional directors who will come to work—"

"We haven't time for that." Skeats.

"Anyone loose might come quick, lover." Maggi. "Do you need someone who knows music?"

"Yes, certainly." Ralph.

"I don't think so." Sato disagrees. "This is such a difficult score. Someone with just a little musical experience would be no better off than someone with none at all."

Ralph concedes. "As long as you're helping coach the singers."

"But is it absolutely necessary that we bring in some mucking stranger? After all—" Skeats bristles his beard at them, bulges his eyes.

Short interrupts before the eyes can actually pop. "Yes. We all think so, Hugh."

"Let's see your agent letters, Debbie." Maggi. "There might just be someone who's been dying to visit State City for years and had a little trouble with the rent lately."

"I should bloody well—"

Ralph. "You have a long, difficult part to learn, Hugh."

"You know, I'm counting on you, Mr. Skeats," Sato says. "To help me with the coaching. Particularly with the students whom you know and I don't."

"Here's a good name." Maggi.

"A director?"

"Man I worked with once. Lots of credits, but how odd. His agent's down in Philadelphia. The same agency has a couple of women who are hot properties now—they must book into colleges a lot. But so many names I've never . . . well, lovers, Maggi's been away." She closes the file of letters, holds it out to Debbie. "You want these back, or shall I make some phone calls?"

"Now, look here, hold on just a bit—"

"Please. Make calls."

"Use my office, then." Hughmore retreats a little, rising to show Maggi the way. "We may as well find out there's no one available, and be done with it."

The meeting idles. Sato helps Ralph put music away. Debbie is showing Short yet another folder of letters and memoranda about people she might hire eventually for the theatre department. Hughmore returns, and begins to talk about Sidney, the feisty soprano, and Beth, the handsome young alto, who are coming to town, two of the young professional singers hired to play leads.

"But Sidney's been a student of yours," Snazzer Short remarks. "Not exactly a newcomer to your dreams, Hugh, or you to hers."

"Ah, but a year older, chum. More worldly, I'd expect. And young Beth, a wispy gauze of innocence with passion ready to burst through."

Debbie: "I think they come here to work, Hughmore. Very hard."

"Ah, but a cast must do something to pass the bloody time not spent rehearsing, mustn't it?"

"Sleep. Eat. More work."

"No, no. Strangers to one another in most cases, spirited men and women brought together by chance, mustn't they make love if they haven't time to make friends?"

But Debbie is hard to bait. She has a way of turning down her thermostat so that the usually constant transmission of warmth ceases, cessation made visible by mobility leaving the face, hands and arms going somewhat rigid, eyes staring flatly but not away. Skeats appeals from this to Short:

"Isn't it so, then, Snazzer, when a group of people's brought together by chance for a while? As in a school situation, or, say, a vacation place. How do they bloody well behave toward one another?"

"They tell lies," Short says, and Sato, finished now with tidying up, says almost simultaneously, "Miss Dieter Haas?"

"Yes. But I am Debbie."

"Is your brother the conductor?"

"I have got two brothers. The other a composer."

"I always thought they were the same man."

"Such a fearful symmetry."

"Excuse me?" Sato's smile would thaw a glacier.

Ralph supplies the familiar couplet: " 'Tiger, tiger, burning bright/In the forests of the night. . . .' "

"Of course."

"I always think that poem two tigers has. My brothers, Gottfried and Gerhardt." Her face is all motion again, though for the moment she speaks to Sato as if he were the only other person in the room. "Gottfried, the composer, lives in Santiago, Spain. Santiago de Compostela, a holy city like Mecca. Gerhardt in another Santiago lives or did live, Santiago de Chile, where you see when you look up any street, a mountain at the end of it."

"I met Gerhardt. Is he not in Chile any longer?"

"I do not know, but I tink now Gerhardt must have left another country. Who left Germany, Spain, France, England, Mexico, Costa Rica, Uruguay . . . who is old, now, for . . . for . . . burning bright."

She smiles her pain. "I think the forests of the night have got very deep for an old radical man—Neruda's friend he was."

"Gerhardt Dieter Haas was extremely kind to me in Chile," Sato says. "Ten years ago. He was associate conductor, I believe, and I a guest conductor for two weeks. A lovely man, your brother Gerhardt."

"No. A tiger. And Gottfried, too. Shall I tell you? But poor Ralph. He has heard me talk of this so much."

Ralph says, approvingly, "I like to hear it, Debbie."

"Do tell us," says Skeats, and he, too, is included now in the great, transforming smile, which lifts wrinkles, moles, bones, teeth into a combination so attractive and so strong one would rather look that way than young.

"Let's go," Short says. "To the distant deeps and skies. Where tigers are made."

"My father was a diplomat, but not a diplomatic man, so very strict and honorable, did always his duty and was sentimental only about music. He respected and obeyed von Neurath, the foreign minister who came before von Ribbentrop, and my father could not understand that these vons respected and obeyed Adolf Hitler. My father believed that the German aristocracy would use Hitler and destroy him, and when he learned that it was Hitler who used the aristocracy, my father destroyed himself.

"That was in Spain, in 1936, where he was on the German embassy staff. I do not know what it was that my father was required to do and felt he could not, but it must have seemed to him very wrong. He shot himself with his officer's pistol from the First World War, in a lonely place along the road between Madrid and Toledo, such a stern idealist.

"We had been five years in Spain then, for when he was sent to Spain, Paul von Hindenburg was president still of Germany, and Hitler only a politician. So my brothers, Gottfried and Gerhardt, and myself were not involved in Hitler Youth and such things. The boys had been both trained very strict by my father and by other teachers in music. Both could play the violin and the piano, and because we were in Spain, he permitted them to learn also the classical guitar. Himself, my father played upon the harp and would sometimes let me try the strings, but he did not believe women should become musicians. He would compare the life of Beethoven, who never married, to that of Schumann, who married a pianist, and say that without Clara, Schumann would have been as great as Ludwig. This offended my quiet mother, who said not a thing until after father was gone but then would say, 'You see? It is not his wife who stops a man, but his politics.'

"I was allowed only to draw and paint, and although I could yet play a little on the piano, it was only things my brothers taught me.

"It was music that was always how we had fun in our house. I remember gay times, for although I was not a pretty little girl, my brothers were so gallant to me. Gottfried would play while Gerhardt danced with me, and when Gerhardt played, how Gottfriend would swing me high. And mother would clap and father keep the time, and sometimes children from the other embassies would come to dance with us.

"After my father's death and before we could go back to Germany, comes the Spanish Civil War. A pension we had, and my mother and I went then to Portugal. My mother was loyal to Germany, and Gottfried too, who was of military age. A Catholic he became, and ran to join General Franco; a very holy convert, and before long he was with the German troops in Spain, the Blues, an officer and interpreter. He wrote to us in Portugal, and signed his letters 'A Soldier for Christ.'

"By Gerhardt, the younger nineteen years, it was to hate Hitler and the Catholic Spanish generals. From Portugal he got to France and then to Barcelona to join the anarchists, and never saw again his brother. Nor his mother either. To France he went, when the Spanish war was over, to be a partisan to the mountains, and after that a refugee, and became a Communist. And then to England, where the party helped him to study music, but he wanted to join the English army, as war was sure to come.

"The Germans knew where Gerhardt was and were asking for him; the English were afraid, and agreed to arrest Gerhardt, who tried then to go to America. He had no passport, but there was a man at the American embassy who wanted to help. I think that the American ambassador in London then was Mr. Kennedy, the father of the president.

"The man who wanted to help tried very hard. He was an intelligence man. I was staying then in London with Gerhardt, to go to school, and this man would be there often when I came home. He thought that Gerhardt knew much about how the fighting would come in Europe, or even might be useful for a spy, and there was much delay. The English made excuses to the Germans, and the Americans protected Gerhardt for some weeks—such a summer in 1939. Came the word then from Washington: Gerhardt was a premature antifascist, and could have no passport. The man at the embassy could only help him to go to Mexico, and the day before he left, in August, Hitler signed a nonaggression pact with Stalin, and Gerhardt told me now he could not be a Communist anymore.

"My other brother, Gottfried, had been decorated and wounded in Spain, and was next in the German army as an officer, and invaded France in a tank and was wounded again. And went finally back to Santiago de Compostela to live in 1941, with one arm only, so that he could not play music, but could write it. Such a devout man he is, who goes every day to mass in the great church from the twelfth century, who did not fight always, like his brother, but only once again, for the Portuguese someplace in Africa.

"From Mexico, Gerhardt, my younger brother, went to Costa Rica to be concertmaster of the symphony, but was persuaded to go into the jungle, across the border, into Nicaragua to fight against Anastasio Somoza. He was captured, and escaped then, and went to Uruguay, where the dictatorship was not so bad, and there were many socialists. I saw him there just after the war. He was then thirty-three years old, and not a concertmaster, playing just behind the first chair, and lectured at the university.

"After the war so far away, there came to Argentina and to Paraguay many Nazis, and there were agents, and Perón too had agents, and Uruguay was frightened of them. And so Gerhardt was told to leave. Back to Mexico he went, I think—I cannot remember exactly. He was, I believe, in some fighting that went badly in Peru. Later he was in the Caribbean, and then in some fighting against the American CIA army in Guatemala, so he could never get permission to come here. He was in Cuba with Fidel, then in Bolivia a little while, such a tiger, but now old for it, and reached Chile. And there he stayed from 1962 and found at last his friends, and his peace.

"Now, when I would write to Gottfried that Gerhardt has settled, Gottfried sends messages for him through me, from Spain, that they must forgive. But when I go to Gerhardt the next month in Chile, he ask that I do not tell him the message. He does not want to hear. Even when our mother died here in State City, five years after, Gerhardt does not wish to communicate with Gottfried, and by then Gottfried in Spain no longer wishes to either, not even through me. He is proud, too.

"You know, there are villages in Spain today through which that civil war was fought where the old people who were republicans sit on one side of the square and those who were Catholics sit on the other, and have not spoken one to the other for forty years, though the town is very small?

"But in Santiago de Compostela Gottfried has one rehearsal tape, I do not know how he got it, not a record, a tape only, of Gerhardt conducting Schumann's Concerto for the Cello, and sometimes he played this tape, and when it breaks, will have it mended.

"In 1968 I went again to Chile to see Gerhardt. His hearing had by then begun to fail, and the doctors said it was because of so much gunfire in his ears all his life long. He would no longer conduct. He taught a little, and had not a wife but a Communist lady friend and a pension then from the Chilenos. They lived in a stucco house in Santiago, Chile, far from and so different from Santiago, Spain. And often Gerhardt played upon an old, antique guitar from Spain, as fine and wonderful as a Stradivarius violin.

"In the garden he would sit, by thick stucco walls, under a small sweet-smelling, flowering tree, in the dusk, playing softly so as not to harm the instrument, just loud enough for himself to hear, but because he was a little deaf, I could hear too. I would sit close, and his lady friend, and perhaps some young students. We would sit, drinking tea perhaps as the evening came, and listen, and there was a vine of blue flowers growing behind him on the wall.

"And what he played, whenever one was published and arrived in the music stores of Chile, were the compositions for Spanish guitar of his brother, Gottfried."

There is a silence, and then Short says: " 'When the stars threw down their spears . . .' "

"What then comes?" Debbie asks.

" 'And watered heaven with their tears. . . .' "

"I think so," Debbie says. "Yes, I think so. But now the army officers have taken Chile, now where is Gerhardt? In what country and in what garden does my old brother play his old brother's music on his old guitar?"

In due time the door to Ralph's office opens, and Maggi is back from the telephone.

"Well," she says. "They laughed at me in New York, asking so late in the season. They don't answer phones this time of morning in Los Angeles. But the Philadelphia place specializes in campus jobs, and they've got people available."

"The bloke you worked with, then?" Skeats asks it belligerently; the talk of tigers seems to have fired up his Aussie blood.

"Other blokes." She looks at her notes. "A young one named Haroldsen. He's got some good credits. An old tramp director I've heard of, called Billy Hoffman. They think perhaps a third one they were being mysterious about. You want to bring 'em out to interview? I said I'd call back."

"Now then, you see? Nothing but second-raters on short notice. Come along, then, I should very much like to do the show myself. I really haven't heard a good reason why I shouldn't. What do you say?"

Skeats says this to Maggi, who smiles, takes a beat, and replies: "I think Ralph better say."

Gentle Ralph Lekberg apparently sees the answer on the tough toe of his work shoe and transmits it by a shaking of the head without looking up: no.

"Maggi," Debbie Dieter Haas says. "Go to Philadelphia, you. You and Rugby."

"Rigby," says Professor Short.

"Shitby," says Hughmore Skeats.

 **$4000**

PRINTER'S PROOF

PRINTER'S PROOF

Cast:

Sung by:

Members of the Crew:
Al Riker, a surveyor.................. Marcel St. Edouard, tenor
Pill Donovan, the foreman............ Hughmore Skeats IV, baritone
Bert Tannenbaum, Al's friend......... John Ten Mason, baritone
First Poker Player................... Richard Auerbach, tenor
Second Poker Player................. Maury Jackstone, baritone
Third Poker Player.................. Mike Shapen, bass

For the Construction Company:
Harry, the paymaster................ David Riding, tenor

On Their Own Behalves:
Sally Anne, a local beauty............ Sidney Bennett, soprano
Raymond Applegore, owner of
   The Fisherman's Hotel............. Henry Fennellon, bass
Norah, Applegore's wife............. Beth Paulus, alto

delete? *delete?* *delete?*

tr.

   "A stinker, baby. Stink, stank, stunk. A bomb in a briefcase, you could blow up Grauman's Chinese. Are you listening to me?"

   In Los Angeles the manager of Marcel St. Edouard wants to know if his client is listening.

   "Come on, wake up, willya, blimp? What'd I have to do, stick a pin in you? You're asking me to let you waste a month of your fat life on this crap show."

"Last spring you said it was a wonderful chance."

"Last spring we didn't have the Frisco festival, big butt. Three big concerts, star billing, twice the money and half the time. Look at this crap." He tears the title page off a Dittoed copy of Rigby Short's libretto, crumples it, and slaps the second page, with its list of names in the cast. "What is this Al Riker, some kind of eagle scout, blimpy? What'd he get, his merit badge in knife fighting, huh? What a jerk."

"You said it was right for me to get out of costume roles."

"You going to lie there on your carcass remembering what I said, or you going to wake up and do what I say? Look at him: our slim, sexy, tanned young fighting surveyor, right? Look at his big, scarred fists. Look at his granite poker face. You ever play a hand of poker in your life?"

Marcel, a huge, soft-eyed young man with the beginning of a double chin, shakes his head and feels miserable.

"I'll learn if I have to." A sexy knife-fighting surveyor and poker player is the kind of part he yearns for, but saying so will only get him more abuse. "You told me it was a sure thing for television, too."

"Oh, listen to my blimp, he's got a full house this time. Second Thursday of the first year, every century, at eleven forty-five P.M. they do a new opera on television. Look, honey, baby, I'm on my knees." And on his knees he goes. "Let's throw this little two-bit professor's Christmas pageant into the corner, okay?" Into the corner it goes, losing its staples, separating into sheets.

"Don't." Marcel gets himself out of the chair, starts picking up pages around the room. "He's not just a professor. He's got screen credits. You told me that." Stops in his gathering, holding the pages to his big chest, both of them on their knees now and facing one another across twelve feet of white carpet. "I'm not going to let these people down. They're nice people. I'm supposed to be there day after tomorrow."

"Be where?" Cajoling time is over. The little manager hops to his feet again and advances with his fists clenched, but he won't actually hit Marcel. "No place, U.S.A. Pig shit up to the ankles. What do they do in no place? You read the papers? They steal paintings. Their idea of fun, right, knife fighter?"

"I don't believe it."

"Fifty thousand bucks' worth. I read it this morning."

"I'm not going to break the contract this late."

"They've already broken it, don't you understand? We haven't seen the music, have we? That Australian character, right, he was going to have it right out to us, he was."

Marcel, soft and stubborn, keeps shaking his big head, struggles to his feet, continues picking up the pages till he has the libretto together. The part about the paintings was too much. His manager made it up. He's always lying to Marcel, always going too far, this time offending a mysterious nostalgia for the Midwest (where he has seldom been) that our big tenor has conceived. Life, he feels, must still have the glow of sanity and reason there, removed as it is from the violence and irrationality that has overtaken the cities of the two coasts. It's a lag, but not a cultural lag any longer. A barbarian lag.

Leaving aside the status of Hughmore Skeats IV, baritone (Pill Donovan), who teaches voice and performs for fees outside the university, Marcel is the only male professional in the cast of $4000. Henry Fennellon, the bass, cast in the small but nasty part of Raymond Applegore, sang professionally once, years ago, and he has done many other things since; now he lives on a farm near State City and would call himself a farmer.

But both female roles will be sung by outside professionals like Marcel. Beth Paulus, alto (Norah Applegore), is a very well-known young singer indeed. Sidney Bennett, soprano (Sally Anne), is far less so.

Sidney is a professional now because she had an engagement last summer doing light opera and musicals in the resort country of Minnesota. But she did her undergraduate work quite recently in State City, a classmate of the other students in the cast, then switched to Oberlin for graduate school. So it's to be a homecoming of sorts for Sidney; vindication is today's sweet dream as she sits at her desk in Oberlin, bags packed, writing a letter.

The letter is to Mr. Skeats, whose student she was, and who came to Oberlin in the spring and cast her as Sally Anne.

Dear Papa Bear:
    Before I see you in State City, I did want to write and say how sorry I am that I was so exhausted when you were here auditioning me for the wonderful part of Sally Anne!

It's a wonder you chose me for it, and I'm really grateful and will do everything I can to make you feel you were right. And I do wish I'd been able to just hippy-hop myself into your gorgeous car afterward to go to Cincinnati to dinner, but honestly. Exams! Recitals! Coaching! I was just so tired I wouldn't have been fun company, and I was a silly little girl besides. (But there's nothing new about that, is there? Do you think I'm ready to start growing up?)

Remember I told you the man I worked for last summer might offer me a job on the East Coast this year? And I said I'd never been to New England, and would probably accept if it came through? And you were sweet enough to say not to worry, that the part was mine if I wanted it, but you did have another soprano in mind, too?

Well, of course, the New England job did come through, just a few days ago, but you can tell the other soprano that I'm on my way to State City anyhow.

Honestly, I suddenly started getting telegrams and phone calls, and it was all I could do to keep the man from New England from flying out here to talk to me, which would have been so embarrassing. But you see, by then I'd read Mr. Short's wonderful libretto (is it true he's married to Maggi Jaro? I never knew them) and just fallen in love with the part of Sally Anne. Isn't she something? An angel to one man and a naughty little devil to the other! (Which do you suppose is me?)

A boy I know here wanted me to spend the summer making a movie, too, at a commune, practically the whole thing in the nude.

I do hope you can get some managers and producers to come and see us, like you said. (I could try writing to the man from New England, but of course he may really be mad at me now. What do you think?)

I'll see you almost as soon as this letter arrives, and please tell Dr. Lekberg I hope his music for Sally Anne isn't too difficult (it probably is, oh me). Such a long part, but it will be so much fun singing with you again — as bad old Pill!

As ever,
Sidney
(Sally Anne!)

Our third young professional, Beth Paulus, the alto, lives in Boston. She is the protegée of the famous soprano Janet Margesson, on whom she has come to call in the great diva's hotel apartment.

"Did you have a chance to read it?"

"Beth darling, of course, of course. Let me find it. Here, you see. Such a marvelous part for you, so strong. Sally Anne."

"No, it's Norah. Here. Norah Applegore."

"Of course, of course. And how shall you do her?"

"Well, it's so . . . so physical, isn't it? And fighting like terrible monkeys in the end. . . ."

"You must save yourself for that, you know. Don't give it all at first. Look, there are five scenes, aren't there? Five."

They look:

Time: 1949, the postwar economic recession.

Scene One: A construction camp in Georgia. 10:00 P.M.

Scene Two: A swamp. 2:00 A.M.

Scene Three: The Fisherman's Hotel. Next morning. 5:00 A.M.

Scene Four: Telephones. 8:00 A.M.

Scene Five: The Fisherman's Hotel. 10:00 A.M.

"You see. You must save yourself, darling, in those first scenes. I know my Beth. Gives everything, everything, always, but you must learn to build. . . . My word, a construction camp? You must be some sort of little whore, aren't you? I love to do whores."

There isn't much Beth can say, since she isn't in the first and second scenes, and isn't a whore.

"Did you bring the music, darling? Shall we sight-read some?"

"The music hasn't come."

"Never mind. When I was nineteen, I did a ghastly one-act by the most beautiful wop. The man was a dream, but the music—oh, my God! So I simply improvised every line of it, and the reviews called him a genius."

On the plane to Philadelphia to interview directors, Maggi Short sleeps, neat and sleek as a short-haired cat. Snazzer Short reads a book about F. Scott Fitzgerald in Hollywood, which he's been looking forward to and enjoys. These two haven't much to say to one another, though they are in no particular state of tension.

For further amusement the Snazzer plays a game. When the stewardess takes drink orders, he looks over at his sleeping wife, nods, and tells the attendant:

"One Scotch and soda, one Canadian and water, please." When they come, he drinks both; when reorders are taken, he says, first, "Just the Canadian this time"—waits till the girl has taken a step away, calls her back—"Afraid we'd like the Scotch, too, after all."

Twenty minutes later, meeting the girl on his way back from the rest room, he smiles; she smiles back:

"Is that, I mean . . . your wife?"

"Yes, it is."

"She looks so familiar."

"She's Maggi Taro." Shameless Short.

"Is it really? Ooh, I knew it."

"Miss Taro'd like another drink, if it's all right."

"Oh. Yes, of course." Though the airline rule limits each passenger to two. "Scotch?"

"And a Canadian." Short walks back to the galley, accepts two little bottles, glasses, and ice from the girl, and pays.

"Is she enjoying the flight?"

"My poor wife."

"Oh, what's the matter?"

"Drinking problem"—Short, solemnly, accepts a sympathetic hand squeeze and bears off his bottles—"Terrible thing. Terrible."

So by the time they get off at La Guardia Airport in New York to change planes for Philadelphia, he has spent nine dollars and knocked back six whiskeys.

Doesn't show it much, knows he does a little, gets no rise out of Maggi—but she makes a phone call between planes and tells him she has a dinner date in New York, if he doesn't mind staying alone in Philly.

In Philadelphia they have appointments at three, three thirty, and four in the agency's conference room. It's a neat, cheerful enough little room, with a conventionally handsome walnut oval table, lightly upholstered arm-chairs, and blue carpeting, quite like the rooms maintained for real estate closings and such proceedings by middle-bracket law firms in State City. But in place of a law library, there are bound playbooks on the shelves that decorate the walls; and instead of Gauguin reproductions, framed theatre posters.

"Here's John Haroldsen," the agency manager, a young woman, says. "I'll leave you three to talk."

Haroldsen is tall, curly headed, and reluctant to sit down. Standing at one end of the table, balanced on the palm of one manicured hand, he manages to keep his chin high so that the eyes look down at the Shorts in a way that makes the upper lashes noticeable.

"Well, first let me say that I've done opera and I love it," he begins. "I've done *Fledermaus* and *Butterfly* and even *Wozzeck,* which is such a challenge. And two Kurt Weills—*Three Penny* and *Mahagonny.*"

"*Die Fledermaus* is an operetta, isn't it?" Short asks.

"Well, I don't mean to say that opera is my absolute doggy bag, Professor, but I am comfortable with it, especially with a good conductor."

"We've got Murasaki, Mr. Haroldsen." Maggi.

"Oh, I know. I know. Please call me John, I think of you as Maggi already. Do you know my work at all?"

"I saw your *Moon for the Misbegotten.* It was very special."

"Oh, thank you, Maggi. I did love doing it. Sir, tell me about your show, please?"

Short does.

"It sounds marvelous. I'd love to read it. But, well."

"What?" Maggi.

"I just frankly don't know about going all the way out there to do it. I mean, it means practically spending the whole summer away."

"It isn't everybody's doggy bag." Short agrees.

"Shut up, Snazzer. Spending the summer away from whom, John? We'll pay accommodations for two."

"Well, I mean, where would we live and everything? And well, after all, State City?"

"People there'd pay no attention to . . . where you lived and everything." Maggi. "State City's all grown up."

"Oh, I should realize that, shouldn't I. I mean, if people like you and your husband . . . Oh, Maggi, that wonderful film of yours. Won't you ever do another one? Please tell her she must, sir."

His smile now is more than Short can resist.

Eventually Haroldsen takes a copy of the libretto, saying he knows he'll love it, but wants to be sure it wouldn't be like putting a left-handed catcher's mitt on a right-handed kid, he'll read it right away and phone their hotel room in the evening, so exciting to meet you, Maggi, an honor to meet you, Professor, and goes.

"Well?"

Snazzer. "Would we have to call him Ms. on the program?"

"He's an artist. His *Moon for the Misbegotten* was beautiful work."

"Would it be a little cruel to put him in the ring with Hughmore Skeats?"

"You can assume he's handled the big-ball laddies before. He'll have his ways."

"Debbie'd mother him. Sato's nothing if not civilized. What about this Marcel, the tenor?"

"What about him?"

"Hughmore says he's one of the boys. Would it matter?"

"Snazzer darling, in the theatre not only do they let homosexuals work together but they even let male and female thespians do their act together, right on the same stage!"

"Sorry. I never could do chemistry, but . . . Ralph and I tried to write a very virile piece. When we first talked about it, as a matter of fact, it was going to be an all-male opera. It was going to start from an army-camp poker game. But then we both found that we wanted women. . . ."

"How normal of you."

Short: "I suppose he could make it look like muscle beach, at that. Let's talk to the other two, anyway."

"There's only one. The woman they were being so mysterious about was named Barb Collins, who'd be marvelous. But they're all grinning over at the office now, because they got her summer rep in Cambridge. It's a Harvard group."

State University always gets euchred by Harvard. Also Yale, Princeton, Berkeley, and Columbia. We can play at the same table with the rest.

"Who's left?"

"Billy Hoffman." Maggi (Taro) Short gives the famous grimace a hundred new young actresses have tried to produce—not that she's such a very old young actress yet. The line that went with the grimace in the film was, "What the hell, baby, we've still got each other," but there was a facial expression and hand movement that made it into a Maggi-Taro take, adding, in effect, "You've got me, but Jesus, you mean all I've got is you?"

Billy Hoffman, in he shuffles. Big ears, ingratiating grin. He's wearing what's got to be the best sports jacket he owns, just as debonair as frayed cuffs and permanent-soil collar can get you.

"I'm Billy Hoffman."

("I could feel him deciding, an hour earlier"—empathy's cripple, Snazzer Short, will later report to Ralph Lekberg—"I swear, I could see a brown suit hanging in his closet, and see him get it out and put on the pants and take them off again, because he didn't want us to think he was so anxious for the job he'd overdress. And feel him looking at those cuffs on his sports coat and thinking, 'What the hell, you know, I'll iron it, it's clean.' ")

Short and Hoffman shake hands. "My wife . . ."

"I know your wife," Billy Hoffman says. "Margaret Taro. You auditioned for me once."

"Really. What show?"

"*Dangerous Crossing.* You got the part. I got canned before rehearsals started."

"What for?"

"Listen, when you're canning Billy Hoffman, any reason will do. I go in to ask for an advance, they give me a bus ticket back to Philly, you know. I saw you in it, though."

"We never played here."

"No. But I wanted to see you, Miss Taro. Believe me or not, I'm the guy that cast you. I went back up to New York to see if I was right."

"Were you?"

"What can I say? No. I was wrong. The part was too old for you."

"The notices weren't so bad."

"They were spectacular." It was after *Dangerous Crossing* that Maggi Taro went to Hollywood, made her one film, approached stardom, announced her contempt for movies and retired. *Movies are lies made by phonies to comfort cretins,* she'd said, getting some newspaper and television space for that opinion, and become, briefly, a cult heroine of the disaffected young. That was a couple of years before she married Rigby Short. "I'm not saying you were bad in the part, you had a lot of emotion. But you were girlish, and the part was a woman, am I right?"

"You're a jerk, Hoffman. Am I right?"

"All my life, Miss Taro," he says and grins, anticipating forgiveness like a dog. Sleek Maggi mimics it perfectly, and Short, in some wonder at the man, interjects:

"Do you know about our script?"

"I heard it's an opera."

"Have you ever directed one?"

"More musicals than operas. Do you know *Seventeen?* I've done it seventeen times. Some Gilbert and Sullivan. Once, in Cincinnati, *Madame Butterfly,* a disaster. Why does everybody want to do that show? Okay, opera, what do you have to know? Just, the conductor's in charge, am I right?"

"That's all you know?" Maggi asks.

"Once, off-Broadway, I did *Four Saints in Three Acts.* They went through four other directors first, and none of them could make sense out of it. So they get to me, and I can't make sense out of it either. I mean, Gertrude Stein, what is she, anyway? But what does it matter? I can make a show out of it. And I did. You want to know my point?"

"Jesus, you got one?" Maggi, tough, perfect looking, unbemused.

"My point is, if the conductor's got the say, then the conductor's going to do the interpretation, what the lines mean, how to sing them, right? I mean, this is real opera, no speech, okay? So what you want is a real dumbbell director, you know? Solid brick from one ear to the other, because you don't want him to understand anything, you just want him to make a show out of it. Give them something or other to look at. You gotta search the alleys for a real dimwit, turn over garbage cans looking—"

"You're overplaying, Hoffman," Maggi says, and they both laugh quietly.

"Do you two know one another?" Short is honestly puzzled.

"Saw the man once, according to him."

"I was going to offer you our script to read." Short.

"He's trying to tell you he can't read."

"Oh, I can a little bit." Billy Hoffman. "I put circles around the words I don't know, and look them up in the dictionary, and write them in a grubby little notebook, you know?"

This time Maggi laughs aloud. "You ass," she says. "We can probably get Haroldsen."

"The smartest. An intellect. Listen, Professor. How you doing this? I mean, when do you decide?"

"This weekend, I hope. We planned to start rehearsal next week. I still hope we can."

"It takes me ten minutes to get ready, and I go anywhere. I don't want you to get the impression I'm eager, but threaten me and I'll make it five minutes. That's my big asset. No, listen, I'd like to see your script, okay? But I couldn't tell you anything, not until I'd seen the cast and the hall and maybe heard the music?"

"Now give him the pitch," Maggi says.

"Yeah?"

"Yeah." She sticks her chin out at him.

"All right, Professor Short, I'm a hack. I've directed more shows in more places than I can remember, some good, plenty bad. But I'm a professional. Wherever I work, whatever I work on, whoever I work with, I give it all I've got. What I've got is the ability to stage a show so an audience will watch it and listen to it. Any show. And I think I can get performances out of people. I worked just once on Broadway, it was a bomb, but what I want you to know is that I don't work any harder or think any harder or even care any more, doing that one Broadway show, than I do if I go out to Station City and do your show, even if it turns out to be *Seventeen* for the eighteenth time. Okay?"

"Here's the script." Snazzer Short is still in wonder.

"I'll call you this evening," Hoffman says. "A privilege to meet you, Miss Taro. I really mean it."

"How would you like a big wet kiss on the ear?" Maggie Taro Short says, and the back of the nubbly man's head lights up with embarrassment, finally, as he walks out, slightly bowlegged, the tops of the ears as moist and red as the lining of a possum's pouch.

"Well, baby-boy." Maggi pleasantly to her husband. "Were you had?"

"I don't quite know." Snazzer.

"You want him, don't you?"

"Yes, but how did he do it?"

She must still feel like kissing, for now she cool kisses the Snazzer on the temple. "Noble brow and sparkling eye," she croons, and it is accurate. Short, when he is not depressed, is a rather handsome, lively-looking man, and it's the brow that does it—that and the wavy chestnut hair, quick eyes, and slight, distinguished limp with which he walks. His mouth is nice, too, maybe a little sensitive; he's of middle height and was an athlete long ago in school—before the limp.

Hoffman can get pretty silly. Holding up the manila envelope Short gave him like a piece of music, he glances around his shabby, furnished room, commanding silence and attention from the furniture, and sings:

"This is an opera, ra, ra, hahhaha."

Bows, acknowledging the bed's applause, and prepares for an encore by opening the envelope and extracting the libretto:

"It is called . . . huh?" What it's called is $4000. "If you dig *Pigoletto,*" Hoffman mutters, "you'll think four thousand bucks is real moolah." Grins, puts the libretto down on the bedside table, which is also the chair-side table—the chair is quite a comfortable overstuffed, mohair number. Rubs his unkissed ear, bows again, hornpipes over to where his jacket's hung to get a cigar.

The furniture smiles. Hoffman hasn't been in such a good mood lately. He joins old mohair now, turns past the title page, and reads: "A construction camp in Georgia. 1949, the postwar economic recession."

"What's Maggi Taro like?"

"Formidable," John Haroldsen says. "Terribly talented."

The apartment is furnished with flair, not luxury. Inexpensive things combined with taste, and a nice eye for what's dramatic, in the living room, where John will do his reading.

"Have you ever worked with her before?"

"She's not in this, Ned. Her husband wrote it."

"The libretto?"

"Yes."

"Oh, what's he like? The husband?"

"Half-sweet, half-hostile. Lovely eyes, but I think he'd been drinking. Don't you remember? He's the university professor she married, after she blasted off."

"What was it she said? That jingle?"

" 'What are little movie stars made of?' Only I doubt she said it. 'What are little movie stars made of? Piss and moan and silicone, that's what little movie stars are made of.' It doesn't sound like her, really. She seems more tough than bitchy."

"I'm dying to meet her. State City . . . how's the money?"

"Enough to help. Twenty-five hundred for three weeks' rehearsals and stay through the opening. About a month, with traveling back and forth, and they'd pay expenses except meals."

"We could drive."

"Yes."

"Let's do it. We need the money."

"I know."

"The bills are incredible this month."

"They always are."

"Shall I read along after you?"

"Yes, please, Ned. Here's page one."

" 'Four thousand dollars.' "

Scene One

A construction camp in Georgia. 1949, the postwar economic recession. 10:00 P.M.

 Six members of the construction crew are playing poker around an outdoor table by the light of gasoline lanterns. A dilapidated sign off to one side reads:

> To Be Built Here:
> GEORGIA MANSION HOMES

Looming behind the poker players is a power shovel. Its cab, over and behind the men's heads, is dark. Its boom crosses the back of the stage. The poker players are: AL RYDER, the surveyor. PILL DONOVAN, the foreman. BERT TANNENBAUM, assistant foreman. And three others. They are in work clothes. They use their hard hats to hold chips. Pill is dealing five-card stud.

 PILL [*Deals the down cards. Starts around with the up cards.*]: Four of diamonds. Nine of spades. Ten of clubs. Two of hearts. Another ten. Five for the dealer. First ten bets.

 FIRST POKER PLAYER: Check the ten.

 THIRD POKER PLAYER: Bet a dollar.

 BERT: I'll see.

 PILL: Dealer folds [*Whacks his cards angrily on the table*].

 AL: I'm in once.

 SECOND POKER PLAYER: Not me.

 PILL [*Deals around again*]: Five on the four. Eight of spades. Big black jack. And a red one, too. Jack-ten bets.

BERT: Another buck.

AL: I'm still with it.

FIRST POKER PLAYER: Not me.

THIRD POKER PLAYER: Raise you five.

BERT: Jack-deuce raises? Okay, once.

AL: I'm still with it. Deal the cards.

PILL [*Deals to the three remaining players*]: Two-four-five, possible straight. Two-jack-trey, no help. Ten-jack-deuce, not much better.

BERT: Check to the power.

AL: Bet ten bucks.

THIRD POKER PLAYER: Think it's comin'? Raise you ten.

BERT [*Folds his hand*]: Too rich for me.

AL [*Seeing the raise*]: Deal the cards.

PILL [*Deals to the final two,* AL *and* THIRD POKER PLAYER]: Caught your ace—ace, deuce, four, five. And a lady—deuce, jack, six, queen. Ace bets, boys.

AL: One hundred dollars.

THIRD POKER PLAYER: That says you've got it? Where you from, Al? Colorado? They got high bluffs there. I think you're bluffing, boy.

AL: That information will cost you a hundred bucks.

PILL: Call him, damn it. Let's find out.

BERT: Play your own cards, Pill. We're all big boys.

THIRD POKER PLAYER: Well, I'll tell you now. What I got here ain't nothin' but a pair of ducks [*Folds his hand*]. I never seen two deuces worth a hundred bucks.

[*Now* AL *collects the cards and rakes in the pot. He is winner, and next dealer.*]

AL: Ante a dollar. Same game. Five card's the one that treats me right.

PILL: I'd like to know the one that treats you wrong.

FIRST POKER PLAYER: I'll bet you got a grand in front of you.

PILL: Yeah. Wanta count it, Al?

"Can the audience follow it, John?"

"The poker talk? It may not matter. It's very rhythmic. It should sing well."

BERT: Let it go, Pill. You're winning just as much as him.

PILL: You think so? Countin' last night and the night before? I'll be lucky to get out of this damn swamp with a gallon of gas to drive home on. Twelve weeks in here, boy, buildin' streets to nowhere. Georgia Mansion Homes! Twelve weeks in here, boy, they ain't marked a drive or dug a cellar.

SECOND POKER PLAYER: Hell, you can't dig cellars here.

THIRD POKER PLAYER: Maybe for water skiin' in the basement.

BERT: They haven't sold a lot yet.

FIRST POKER PLAYER: Where's the model home they said was goin' up? Hell, where's the carpenters?

PILL: The only building here's the tool shack. Pickax mansion on bulldozer square.

AL: They got some streets. The streets that we put in are here to stay, by God.

PILL: Yeah? Let 'em stay. Maybe the gators from the swamp will use 'em to take sunbaths. I ain't staying. Not another week. I'm going crazy here. Working weekends. What else is there to do? Slap at mosquitoes. Watch my money go.

AL: Why don't you ever go to town when we do, Pill? Hell, it's your home.

PILL: That town? We know what *you* like there. What's there for me? I've spent my whole life trying to bust out of it.

SECOND POKER PLAYER: Why'd you go back when the war was over, Pill?

PILL [*to* AL]: For Chrissake, deal the cards.

AL: The eight of spades. Jack of hearts. A trey. A deuce. A ten. Seven of spades. Jack bets.

FIRST POKER PLAYER: Bet a buck.

[*All stay except* BERT]

BERT: I'm out.

AL: Club king. Heart seven. A pair of treys. Club queen. Spade four. Treys bet.

SECOND POKER PLAYER: Make her ten.

PILL: I smell a big pot acookin'. Raise you ten.

AL: Dealer's in [*All stay*]. A pair of eights. No help. A deuce. A five. Black bullet, boy. Eights bets.

FIRST POKER PLAYER: Make it fifty. Let's get the ribbon clerks out of the game.

THIRD POKER PLAYER: I got nylon, silk, and satin. Any color ribbon that you want [*Folds his hand*].

SECOND POKER PLAYER: Fifty? Okay. One more card.

PILL: It's gonna cost you. Up a hundred.

AL: A hundred, Pill? What have you got there you're so proud of? Five-queen-ten? I'll see you.

FIRST POKER PLAYER: So'll I.

SECOND POKER PLAYER: I wonder: If this was real green money, like you spend at bars and grocery stores, would I be in or out?

AL: It's just the same as money.

PILL: Good old scrip. Cheap damn company. Won't send no armed guard in with cash. They pay us with company paper, good at company stores for company marked-up candy bars and beer.

BERT: You trade it in at Jacksonville, it's money.

SECOND POKER PLAYER: It still don't feel like money when I bet with it out here.

AL: That's why poker's played with chips.

SECOND POKER PLAYER: I'll stay. There's a week's pay.

PILL: Deal 'em. Be good now.

AL: A seven on the pair of eights. Six with the treys. Big ace for Pill. A little spade for me.

PILL: Four spades.

AL: Eights bets.

FIRST POKER PLAYER: Check.

SECOND POKER PLAYER: A hundred.

PILL: A hundred on a pair of treys, huh? Let's see how good the flush is over there. Up a hundred.

AL: I'll see. And I'll raise another hundred.

FIRST POKER PLAYER: That's all for me [*Folds his hand*].

SECOND POKER PLAYER: Maybe you got it, Al. Your luck's too good. Two hundred dollars, scrip or no scrip . . . nope. I'm done messing with you, this hand.

PILL: Somebody's gotta keep him honest. Okay, Al. You're seen. You got a spade?

AL [*Turns up his hole card and shows it*]: That's right, Pill. [*Rakes in the money*]

PILL: There's fourteen hundred dollars in that lousy pot.

SECOND POKER PLAYER: The way he's winning, we don't work for the company, we work for Al.

FIRST POKER PLAYER: I gotta borrow, Al. Or quit the game. Two hundred?

AL: Sure.

THIRD POKER PLAYER: You shouldn't do that. Make a guy play against his own dough.

AL: It's okay. [*Pushes over a pile of scrip*]

FIRST POKER PLAYER: It's just a game. Something to pass the time.

PILL: Yeah? With fourteen-hundred-dollar pots? That ain't a game. That's a month in Miami.

BERT: Or a year in engineering school, huh, Al?

AL: Well. Be kind of a tight budget for a married man.

BERT: Married?

THIRD POKER PLAYER: The little blonde girl?

AL: Sally Anne.

PILL: A little girl? Man, that's not little nor a girl. That's woman, female woman.

FIRST POKER PLAYER: That's the only sight in town.

BERT: You really thinking about getting married, Al?

AL: Yep. If she'll have me.

PILL: You ever talk to her about it, sport?

AL: Yes and no. We kid the idea of getting married. Make jokes. Talk about places we might see. But that's a question you don't ask seriously until you're pretty sure the answer's yes.

And I don't know. I only know I think about her all the time. I see her in my transit, when I'm sighting. I see her in my whiskey, when I'm drinking. I see her in the clouds, the dust, the water. I even see her on the dozers and the cats. Can't you?

"Oh, look, John."
"Yes."

[AL *gestures toward the cab of the shovel. It lights up, with an unreal, romantic glow. In it, demurely, sits* SALLY ANNE—*and* AL *sings to the shovel as if she were really there.*]

Can't you see her, living in my trailer? Would she? Would she have the strength to love adventure? Building in jungles, leveling mountains. Oh, yes. There's Sally Anne. Smiling in my trailer. Waiting in the hotel rooms of tropic cities. Clean when I come home dusty to her. Gay when I'm discouraged. Soft, soft when I'm tired. Can't you just see her?

"It's a kind of aria for the tenor, isn't it?"
"Not strictly speaking, John. An aria's got repetitions, and a structure. But it could be a lovely solo."
"I'm glad you can help with the music. Ned, did the Baileys call?"
"Remember when you did *Wozzeck?* It could be *Sprechstimme.*"
"Did they call?"
"Yes. They can come Sunday. John, shall I do shrimp and sour cream? And then something in the chafing dish?"
"Suppose we have to leave for State City right away."
"Oh, I hope. We can put the Baileys off. Kirk will be nice about it, and who cares about Norman?"
"You wouldn't hate it, Ned? It's not exactly a summer paradise."
"I know I'd love it. Away from these hot streets and all the meanness for a month. Oh, let's. Maybe I'll learn to play poker."
"Well," John says, smiling and tapping the libretto page. He starts imitating the voice of a familiar sports broadcaster. "This is some kind of solo passage. I mean, this is one of the match-ups we've been waiting for."
"In addition, I want to make it utterly pellucid"—Ned does the voice even better—"that the young man who sings it must be possessed of a truly exceptional vocal apparatus."
They begin fantasizing what Ralph Lekberg's music might be like.

Happy, the meanness of the Philadelphia summer streets held off by the humor and affection they've begun to feel.

"Maybe it's country music. The orchestra like a big guitar. These wonderful, rough men."

BERT: Take it easy, Al.

FIRST POKER PLAYER: It ain't all that exclusive yet.

PILL: I seen that piece of fluff a hundred ways. Including diapers, lollipops, and the look on her face when she took her first drink of corn liquor. The only way I never seen her is the way Al's tellin' it. . . .

AL: Soft, sweet . . . living in my trailer . . .

POKER PLAYERS [*Together*]: Come on/
   Let's play poker/
      Deal the cards.

[*As another hand is dealt and played, the lights fade on the poker table, except for a mild spot on* AL. *The romantic glow in the cab of the power shovel intensifies on* AL's *vision of* SALLY ANNE.]

Al's Vision of Sally Anne

"Whither thou goest, I will go. And where thou lodgest, I
   will lodge. And thy people shall be my people."

You see, I went to Sunday School, and know those pretty
   words.

Because I fool around with men, and drink their beer
   And like to dance and flirt, it doesn't mean I couldn't live
   By words like those. Put girlish things aside and be your
   woman.

It's a small town. So little here to do. Show me the world,
   The deserts and the jungles. Find your adventure there
   And I'll come, too.

Love is the great adventure of a woman's life. Love is the
   Adventure, the jungle, the glory that a woman searches
   for. Yes, I'll be gay when you come dusty from the job.

Proud of you, strong for you when you're discouraged. Soft, soft when you're tired.

PILL [*Slaps the table loudly*]: I'll be damned [*Lights up on table, down in cab, as* PILL *collects the pot*]. A pot at last. A pot. Now, boys, let's play. You better cut the mooning, Al. I'm out for blood now, too.

THIRD POKER PLAYER: Thinkin' about the blonde too, Pill?

PILL: Me? Hell no. He can have her. That's just hometown stuff to me.

SECOND POKER PLAYER: For sure, Pill? I heard you used to like her.

PILL: Damn sure. But I'll tell you this. If I was goin' after it, it wouldn't be for playing Tarzan in the jungle.

Those little shoulders could wear mink. That neck could wear diamonds. Those hands. I can see 'em holding tickets from the pari-mutuel—for luck! Screamin' the winner home. Out to the beach after, huh? in the Cadillac.

[*As he describes his vision of* SALLY ANNE, *a more brilliant light appears around the big shovel.* SALLY ANNE, *in the cab, shrugs off the chaste housecoat she wore during* AL's *vision, and shimmies out along the boom in a bathing suit with a diagonal ribbon across the front reading "MISS WINNER."*]

I'll tell you what, she likes old Pill all right. Not that I'd ever try a kid like that, hell. . . . You shoulda seen me when I come home from the war. Ribbons on my chest. She was fourteen. I seen her grow.

Fill out. And buddies, I mean fill.

POKER PLAYERS [*Together*]: Come on/
    Let's play poker/
            Deal the cards.

Pill's Vision of Sally Anne

Friday at the races. Sittin' in the clubhouse. Juleps, bets and cheerin'. Gotta see him win. Let the fun begin.

Saturday the parties. Yeah. Flirtin', gin, and jokin'. Party clothes and dancin'. Keep the music goin'. Keep the liquor flowin'. Let the big wheels see. Pill and me.

Sunday at the beaches. Like the new bikini? Rub my back with lotion. Let's fly out to Vegas. Look at California. You bet. Deal around New York. You can make it, Pill. All you need's a stake. Smarter than a crow. Tougher than a snake.

Take me with you, lover. Did I say no before? Let's leave this town behind us. Just ask me one time more.

[Lights down on shovel]

Grinning, Hoffman relights his cigar. It's a Miami cigar, almost like a real Havana. Hand-rolled by resettled Cubans. Expensive. He bought it out of the excitement of meeting Maggi Taro. For the fifty-five cents, he could have had half a dozen of the factory twists of which he generally smokes three or four a day. Hoffman's head is full now of plays remembered: There was a power shovel in the set of *High Tor.* There's a poker game in Puccini's old wheeze, *The Girl of the Golden West.* He can see lantern light now in the pages in front of him, bright yellow plastic hard hats, dramatically unshaven faces—but this is not conception yet, only accretion of images from stages past. Nothing will interrupt the process, no knock will come, no phone ring. Damn phone's out in the hall and a flight down, anyway, pay phone. Hoffman's hand goes into his pocket to check that there's a dime there for calling Professor Short when he's done reading. But thought hardly accompanies the feeling fingers. Thought is focused through the eyes, on the page in front of him, where the old plot's thickening up just about the way you'd expect, you know?

AL: What's your bet, Pill?

PILL: There's two hundred in the pot. Pot's the limit. That's what I'm bettin'.

AL: On a pair of threes?

PILL: And whatever's in the hole.

AL: I'm gonna see it, Pill, and raise it, too. Who else is in?

THIRD POKER PLAYER: Me. I got too much in there now to quit. I got queens showing, and that beats his threes and beats your eights. I just believe I'll raise it too, another hundred. And that's all I got.

PILL [*Matching the new raises*]: That's damn near all I got.

AL: Let's see it, then.

THIRD POKER PLAYER: Queens over deuces. There they are. Two pair.

PILL: Yeah? I got two pair, too. Aces high. Read 'em and weep, friends.

AL: Don't reach, Pill. Three eights aren't very good. Just good enough.

THIRD POKER PLAYER: Man. Man. Man.

PILL: On a case eight you beat us. A case eight? Where do you get 'em, Al? These cards you're drawing?

AL: What are you trying to say, Pill?

PILL: I only asked a question.

BERT: It don't deserve no answer.

FIRST POKER PLAYER: I want to hear one.

SECOND POKER PLAYER: All week this guy's been lucky.

PILL: Too lucky.

AL: There's not much luck in beating guys who play it stupid, Pill.

THIRD POKER PLAYER: I'm quittin' anyhow. I'm clean.

FIRST POKER PLAYER: He's got all our pay.

BERT: What do you want him to do? Give it back?

THIRD POKER PLAYER: Come on, Pill. Let's quit. We got machines to run tomorrow.

AL: You'll get your chance to win it back tomorrow night. Now if you want.

PILL: Win how much back?

BERT: Shut up.

FIRST POKER PLAYER: You got a wad there that would choke a cow.

SECOND POKER PLAYER: It's chokin' me, boys.

FIRST POKER PLAYER: That's for damn sure.

THIRD POKER PLAYER: What *are* you winning, Al? That is, if you want to say.

[AL *smiles, shakes his head.*]

PILL: About four grand, I figure. Cut me high card for a grand?

AL: No. I'll play you poker.

PILL: Cold hands?

AL: That's sucker stuff. I'll play when there's a game.

PILL: When is a game not a game? When it's a fix.

AL: You're kind of old and fat to talk like that.

BERT: Let me have him, Al.

[*On their feet, the men shift, some toward* PILL, BERT *toward* AL.]

FIRST POKER PLAYER: What do you say, Pill? Does he keep our dough?

SECOND POKER PLAYER: We're with you, Pill.

FIRST POKER PLAYER: I worked my butt off for that dough.

SECOND POKER PLAYER: Let's get it back.

[*Only* THIRD POKER PLAYER *remains uncommitted.*]

FIRST POKER PLAYER: Damn right.

SECOND POKER PLAYER: How about it, Pill?

THIRD POKER PLAYER: Take it easy, for Chrissake. Nothin's been proved.

AL: Why don't you all sit down? You want to play, we'll play.

PILL: I'm all done playin' poker with you, sport.

AL: Suit yourself.

FIRST POKER PLAYER: Come on, Pill. Let's take 'em.

SECOND POKER PLAYER: Let's get the son of a bitch.

FIRST POKER PLAYER: Come on. Come on.

THIRD POKER PLAYER: What did you see, Pill? Are you just shittin' us? If you really seen anything, why don't you tell us?

PILL: It's okay, boys. Leave it to me. Relax. I'll handle it.

AL: You'll handle what?

PILL: Relax, Al boy. Forget it. I got hot. Let's hit the sack.

AL: All right. Suits me. [*To* BERT] I'm goin' to the tool shack, Bert. Gotta clean my instruments for morning. [*To the rest*] I'll see you guys [*A steady look at each of them, and* AL *goes off*].

SECOND POKER PLAYER: He's carryin' four thousand bucks.

BERT: It's his dough. I lost, too, you know. A pile in fact.

FIRST POKER PLAYER: How come you're standin' up for him?

BERT: That guy's no cheat. He just plays good poker. Better than the rest of us.

PILL: You're stupid, Bert. You don't know when you been took.

BERT [*Stepping right in*]: You want to call me stupid once more, Pill?

PILL: I call you any goddamn thing I please, *stupid*.

FIRST POKER PLAYER [*Still watching after* AL]: Hey, Pill! Did he say he was goin' to the tool shack?

PILL [*Dropping the affair with* BERT. *Alert*]: That's what he said.

FIRST POKER PLAYER: There ain't no light up there. No one went up that hill.

PILL: He's cut out, then.

SECOND POKER PLAYER: That rat.

FIRST POKER PLAYER: An honest guy would stay. That proves it.

BERT: Proves nothing. A guy with that much dough'd be nuts to stick around, the way you big deals are actin'.

SECOND POKER PLAYER: What are you sayin', Bert? You think we'd hurt the guy?

BERT: I don't know what you'd do. I sure don't blame Al if he didn't want to sit here and find out. When Pill says, "Just relax. Forget it," that's a damn good time to move.

PILL: We're goin' after him.

BERT: You're crazy, Pill.

PILL [To his cohorts]: You take the pickup. Check the road to town. Take lights and shotguns from the shack. [FIRST and SECOND POKER PLAYERS run off. To THIRD POKER PLAYER] You stick with Bertie, here. See that he stays in camp.

BERT: Here's where I'm stayin', Pill. Al's in the swamp by now where he surveyed. He knows it there like no one else.

PILL: Oh, yeah? I know that swamp too, pal. I was raised right here.

BERT: I'll be waitin' here to laugh when you come back.

PILL [Getting a key from his pocket]: Look at this, wise boy. Key to the swamp buggy. I can move on land or water. Let him go where he wants. I'll follow faster. That's for damn sure. [PILL runs off.]

THIRD POKER PLAYER [After a moment]: Bert?

BERT: Yeah? What do you want?

THIRD POKER PLAYER: He didn't cheat.

BERT: God, no.

THIRD POKER PLAYER: Maybe we better stop Pill. He'll get rough.

BERT: Don't worry. Al's plenty rough too, when he needs to be. That won't be tonight. Nobody finds nothin' in that swamp at night.

[Sound of motor starting, vehicle driving off]

THIRD POKER PLAYER: There goes Pill.

BERT: If Al's not back by morning, we'll take the other buggy and go out. But he'll be okay.

THIRD POKER PLAYER: Pill's crazy and he's stubborn.

BERT: Al's smart and stubborn. That swamp's like one big hidin' place.

THIRD POKER PLAYER: Hey, look! [*Offstage lights draw their attention to the direction in which* FIRST *and* SECOND POKER PLAYERS *went off.*] The guys that started into town. They've got him!

BERT: They sure got someone.

THIRD POKER PLAYER: It ain't Al [*As three figures appear behind flashlights*].

BERT: The paymaster!

THIRD POKER PLAYER: What's he doin' here?

[FIRST *and* SECOND POKER PLAYERS *reach* THIRD *and* BERT, *with* HARRY, THE PAYMASTER.]

HARRY, THE PAYMASTER: Where's Pill?

BERT: He's in the swamp. I doubt that he'll be back till morning.

HARRY: You're assistant foreman?

BERT: You know that.

HARRY: I got instructions for you. You're all done.

BERT: The whole crew?

HARRY: Job's canceled, and I want the keys.

BERT: The keys to what?

HARRY: All the machines. The bunkhouse, tool shack, everything.

BERT: For what? To protect the company's property from us or something?

HARRY: It's not the company's. There's no more company. I lock it for the creditors.

SECOND POKER PLAYER: The outfit's busted?

HARRY: Yeah.

THIRD POKER PLAYER: We got pay comin', Harry. For the week.

HARRY: You'll have to line up with the other creditors. Me too.

BERT: Of all the crappy deals.

FIRST POKER PLAYER [*Showing scrip from his pocket*]: What about this, Harry? What about this scrip that we been paid with up to now?

HARRY: Who knows? It'll be redeemed. Part of the settlement. So much on the dollar.

SECOND POKER PLAYER: Yeah? How much, half?

HARRY: I don't see how they could.

FIRST POKER PLAYER [*Laughing*]: And I was sweatin' about losing mine.

BERT: None of *us* has much of it left. So much on the dollar. How much on four thousand dollars? Jesus Christ.

[*Curtain*]

End of Scene One

"Well."

"It'll play."

"I think so, Ned, depending on the music."

"I hope they know enough to know you can make it play."

"Let's go on."

"I was going to start supper."

"Let's finish reading and go out for pizza."

"Let's get pizza in."

"Do you mind going out so much, Ned?"

"It was those boys in the car, yelling at us. I'll get over it."

"They were white boys, Ned. I'm sure of it."

"I thought they were black. It doesn't matter. When they went off around the block and then came speeding back at us, yelling again . . ."

"It isn't like you to be so frightened."

"Not young anymore, John. Worn a little thin maybe, after the winter here."

"We'll go to State City."

"It's starting to sound heavenly, let's do read on. Read on. He's in the swamp next, isn't he? Al, the winner."

"The lover."

"The student engineer."

"The tenor."

In his hotel room Snazzer Short sips Calvados, wonders if he's hungry, wishes Maggi hadn't gone to New York, waits for phone calls. Judgments? Not likely. Directors don't sign on as critics, do they? They're teachers, brick makers with or without straw, enthusiasts. Swamp runners.

Scene Two

The Swamp: 2:00 A.M.

Creatures unseen move about. AL *enters, trotting, out of breath. Pauses to look back and listen carefully. Turns, shines his flashlight at a spot on the stage. Jumps back.*

AL: Snake! Water moccassin. [*Picks up a stick*] Get out of the way, boy. I need that grassy place to rest on. There you go. Give my love to Mrs. Cottonmouth. Don't hurry back. [*Shines his light around, checking. Throws himself down.*] Oh, God, I'm beat.

[*Now, for the encouragement he needs, a new vision of* SALLY ANNE *appears, an entrancing will-o'-the-wisp, glowing—her face perhaps—here and there in the night*]

SALLY ANNE, AS WILL-O'-THE-WISP: Keep movin', Al. Keep movin' through the swamp for Sally Anne. Four thousand dollars and Sally Anne. Find your way, man. Get your breath and move. Isn't it worth a struggle, if she'll go with you?

AL: Let me rest a minute.

SALLY ANNE, AS WILL-O'-THE-WISP: No, move. There's a little town out there that you can phone her from.

AL: I'll phone her and she'll come.

SALLY ANNE, AS WILL-O'-THE-WISP: Can you be sure she will?

AL: Oh, yes. Money or no money, Sally Anne will come. This is the kind of thing you know about a girl without her saying it. Better to have the money, though. Why start out poor?

SALLY ANNE, AS WILL-O'-THE-WISP: This is the kind of thing you know about a girl. She'll come. She'll come. [*Disappears*]

AL [*Stands to assess the situation*]: Let's think it out, old buddy. Back to camp's two hours. Is Pill in camp?

[*The will-o'-the-wisp vision reappears at a different place.*]

SALLY ANNE, AS WILL-O'-THE-WISP: Pill's in the swamp buggy you can hear from time to time, more likely.

AL: Yeah. Sure he is. And I could wait for Pill and take him, if I knew he wasn't armed.

SALLY ANNE, AS WILL-O'-THE-WISP: And leave him lying in the swamp . . .

AL: No. No, I wouldn't do a thing like that. Nearly an hour since I heard the buggy, saw the lights.

SALLY ANNE, AS WILL-O'-THE-WISP: He may be comin' without lights.

AL: I know that there's a little town, northeast by east. A little place, but there'll be phones there. If I go right on, I'll hit it, or the road that leads there.

SALLY ANNE, AS WILL-O'-THE-WISP: If you go back to camp, or go to Sally Anne, Pill and his crazy-headed boys will find you. And there'll be someone lyin' in the swamp.

AL [*Resolved, glancing at the stars*]: Stick to the high ground. Guide on the stars. Northeast by east. I'll find the little town and when I get there . . .

[*Something catches his attention. The image of* SALLY ANNE *disappears abruptly. Sound of the swamp-buggy motor. A beam of hard light sweeps the stage, goes off.*
AL *considers his direction; acting on an idea that occurs to him, he goes smoothly and quickly out, circling toward somewhat the same direction from which the light came.*
Sound stops as motor is cut off. PILL *enters with flashlight, searching.*]

PILL: Was there a noise? Gator? Or a gator-skin wallet full of dough, running off on two legs? Tracks! Hey. Boot tracks. Goddamn, he was here.

[*A totally different swamp vision of* SALLY ANNE *appears; if the first was white magic, this is black, sensual, writhing, even a little malevolent*—PILL's *vengeance.*]

SALLY ANNE, AS VENGEANCE: He might be resting now. He must be getting tired. He's got the money Sally Anne wants, Pill.

PILL: Oh, yeah. She'll go with money, Sally Anne.

SALLY ANNE, AS VENGEANCE: Little ol' girl you always wanted, huh? You better have her.

PILL: He's got the dough. He's maybe not too far from here. Turn off the light. Don't tip him off. [*Turns off his flashlight.*] The kid's no patsy.

SALLY ANNE, AS VENGEANCE: Now that you're close, go after him on foot.

PILL: Four thousand bucks.

SALLY ANNE, AS VENGEANCE: Get it for Sally Anne.

PILL: Get Al.

SALLY ANNE, AS VENGEANCE: Get Al.

PILL [*Flourishes a hunting knife*]: Get Al.

SALLY ANNE, AS VENGEANCE: Don't let him leave this swamp alive.

PILL: For Sally Anne and Pill.

SALLY ANNE, AS VENGEANCE: This swamp has seen dead men before. A perfect place. The snapping turtles eat the meat. And gars. And foxes carry off the bones. Ever kill anybody, Pill?

PILL: That guy near Rome, back in the war. That Sergeant what's-his-name?

SALLY ANNE, AS VENGEANCE: That said he'd turn you in for selling food?

PILL: You're damn well right I did. I killed him. No one knew.

SALLY ANNE, AS VENGEANCE: Nobody checks ballistics on the wounds in war.

PILL: Eaton his name was. Sergeant Eaton. Fresh from camp. Replacement. What a Holy Joe! I never will forget old Holy's face. He turned and saw the pistol and he knew I'd shoot . . . that's one I never told.

SALLY ANNE, AS VENGEANCE: You could tell Sally Anne.

PILL: To the music of four thousand dollars, I could tell her anything. I bet I could. I know I could. Then it won't never again be: "Go 'long, Pill. Go on, now, Pill. Don't bother me. Pill honey, I'm so sorry but I'm busy every night this week."

SALLY ANNE, AS VENGEANCE: Give her a chance, Pill. Try to understand. She was so young, there when you first come back. Roughtalking, in your army uniform. And when she did go out with you, three years ago, you lost your head. Yeah. Tried to go too fast. You got to talking foolish, Pill, wanting to carry her off to the moon or somewheres, without a dime . . .

And that slick cracker in the Oldsmobile. It wasn't him she liked, but you that scared her to him.

But now, Pill. Now's the time. Now you'll find out what those sweet blouses have got under 'em.

Now she won't mock your belly, Pill. She'll want to curl herself around it, just so close . . .

[*Shatteringly, just offstage, the swamp-buggy motor starts, interrupting this tender thought. The* SALLY ANNE *image vanishes. Headlights flash and disappear, and the machine can be heard going away.*]

PILL [*Leaps toward the sound. Stops*]: Hey, damn me for a fool. You sneaked around me, did you, bastard? All right. Go on. Take it and damn you. You think I can't track that thing through the night? You think I'll quit now? Baby, you don't know Pill.

[*Curtain*]

End of Scene Two

Hoffman grunts and turns the page.

Scene Three

The Fisherman's Hotel: 5:00 A.M.

Lobby of a seedy little hotel, so called. Really, it's a fishing camp. Far edge of the swamp.
Empty at rise. Beat-up furniture, and a lot of fly-specked, comic signs about check cashing, credit, and the habits of fishermen. Into this comes AL, *dirty and tired from the night's flight. But now exhilarated. Sits in a chair to rest. Gets up to gaze out the door. Smiles, goes to the registration desk and rings the night bell on it loudly.*

AL: I shook him. I shook him nine miles back. I left his buggy for him, but I took the plugs. [*Takes a handful of spark plugs out of his jacket pocket, drops them in a wastebasket*]

Sure like to see old Pill, trying to start her up. The big mechanic with the weak flashlight, checking his motor out.

Hot damn. I came on through the water. Not a track. Got lucky. Found a boat.

Nowhere for Pill to go but back to camp. [*Rings again. Gets wad of scrip out, and starts to count and straighten it.*]

Fifty. A hundred. Two, three, six, a thousand. A hundred forty, there's three forty . . .

[*Enter* NORAH APPLEGORE, *a handsome, discontented brunette. She wears a dressing gown over nightclothes.*]

NORAH: Yes?
AL: Sorry to wake you. Got a room and bath?
NORAH: No bath. You're out of season, mister. Water's off.
AL: I'm pretty muddy, lady.
NORAH: Wash up in the kitchen. I'll heat water if you want to shave. Four dollars, in advance. Room number nine. I'll get your sheets and towels. . . .
AL: Look, never mind. I'll use cold water and I'll get some rest. Call me at eight?

NORAH: That's much too late for fishing.

AL: Call me at eight, please.

NORAH: Are you planning to stay long?

AL: A day or two. Can I buy clothes and shaving stuff in town? I mean, when things are open?

NORAH: What town? When things are open here, the town's still closed. Bus stop, post office, and a grocery store. They might have work shirts at the grocery store. And fishing hats. Oh, lots of fishing hats. Big visors, little visors, wide brim, and no brim at all. Cute little emblems on the bands of some. And bait. Red worms, black worms, corn worms, and crawdads. Minnows and crickets—God, I spend my life with worms for neighbors. At least worms can't talk. I never had one tell me of a fish he caught.

AL: Yeah. Worms don't do much to liven up a place at that.

NORAH: A place! A penitentiary for bass. A crazy house for addled bream. A prison where they lock bad gars away. [*She bares her shoulder*] Look at me. Have I started growing scales?

AL: Why do you stay?

NORAH: You haven't seen my husband. He's the jailer here.

AL: Yeah. Well. [*Can't help yawning*] It must be better in the season when the guests are here. The kitchen this way?

NORAH [*She intercepts, and makes him listen*]: The guests. Old men with fishy hands. Young creeps that do their drinking in a boat, watching a float that hardly ever moves. Come in for supper and go straight to bed. To be up early for the morning rise. And not too many of them, either. Three's a crowd.

AL: That's tough. But I'm tired.

NORAH: Did I ask for sympathy? Come on. Four dollars in advance. The only pleasure that I've got is sleep, and I'm losing that.

AL: This money's scrip. Mansion Construction Company, across the swamp. It's what they pay us with. Here.

NORAH: A ten? This piece of paper?

AL: Look. You turn it in, at any company office. Hell, discount it if you want. I'll pay the ten just for the room.

NORAH: I'll have to get my husband, mister. I take this, he's apt to kick me half across the room.

AL: He is, huh?

NORAH: Sometimes the foot. Sometimes the fist. Oh, if I'm lucky, just the open hand. You want to see a bruise? [*The bruise she has in mind is up on the thigh.*]

AL: Thanks. I've seen bruises. But I'm sorry, anyway.

NORAH: I told you, buddy. I'm in jail for life. And nothing off for good behavior. Hell, where would I find a chance for bad behavior in this dump? [*Calling offstage*] Hey, Ray. Raymond. Wake up and come down here a minute, will you? [*To* AL, *suddenly pointing to wastebasket*] Hey, mister. You dropped your spark plugs. [*She laughs rather wildly.*] What goes on? You rob the payroll over there, and run the swamp? You look like dogs are after you.

AL: One dog. The money's mine. The dog thinks he can bark it out of me.

NORAH: Oh, sure.

AL: Why would it matter to you, lady? I'm a passing customer, that's all. Let's say I'm one that's sorry you're unhappy—but knowing my story wouldn't make things any better for you.

NORAH: No. Don't tell me. Listen, let me help you if I can. When Ray comes, just forget about your scrip. Hang onto it. You've got a watch—give it to Ray for room and board. I'll sneak you some shaving stuff in the morning, and a shirt.

AL: I need a little money for the telephone.

NORAH: There's no phone here, except the pay booth in the yard. All right. I'll find some change, and let you . . . shhh! [*Calls offstage*] Come on, Ray. I want to get back to bed.

AL: And I'll help you. When I get out, I'll send . . .

NORAH: Shut up. The water's off, I said. [*As* RAYMOND APPLEGORE *comes in, wearing pajama pants and a hairy chest*] Hey, Ray. This bunny wants a room and breakfast for his watch.

RAY: No dough, young fella?

AL [*Offering his wristwatch*]: This is a Benrus. Cost me sixty bucks. One or two nights, a little cash to boot?

RAY [*Takes the watch*]: One night, one breakfast.

AL: We're talking about sixty bucks.

RAY: Here, take your watch back and get out of here.

AL: You win. I'll take the room.

RAY: Make up the bed, then, Norah. Snap it up. I'll see you in the morning, buster. Pleasant dreams. [*Goes out, admiring his new watch*]

NORAH: You'd better register. Here. What name you using?

AL: Al Riker, Bridgetown, Colorado. Yours is Norah?

NORAH: Yes.

AL: I want to thank you, Norah. If things go right, I should be leaving later on this morning. But if you want me to, then I'll come back. With money and a car. To get you out of here before the week is done.

NORAH: Kiss me, and I'll believe you. [AL *hesitates, complies. She moves her head away.*] You kiss like a man with his mind on someone else. Whose waist are you holding when your hand's on mine? Did you close your eyes and think some other name than mine? Who are you pressing now? What color hair got in your face?

Tell me and I'll write her an I.O.U. for one kiss, borrowed. Or stolen. I don't care. I need it more than she does. I'll take whoever's kisses I can get. Begging and choosing never went together yet. [*Presses against him until he kisses her again*]

All right. [*She breaks, goes to the cash register.*] You've done your duty. Phone her in the morning. Here's your dough. [*Rings cash register to open drawer*]

[*Curtain*]

End of Scene Three

"Oh, I love Norah."

"Isn't she wonderful? Poor Norah."

"It's building, isn't it? To Sally Anne's real entrance."

" 'Phone her in the morning.' Yes, it must be. The next scene's called 'Telephones.' "

"What a part for the soprano—up to now she's been singing two opposite characters. Now we find out which man's right about her."

"I'll bet I know which."

"Well, of course. This is opera, sir."

"I wonder if the composer has that in the music—two kinds of Sally Anne music, and then a resolution?"

"Oh, he must."

"I wonder who they've got to sing it."

"Her name is on the front. Sidney Bennett."

"Have you heard of her?"

"No. Marcel St. Edouard's the only one I've heard of. He's supposed to be the size of a football player and have a beautiful voice."

"Be fun to have someone big like that in the swamp scene, with weird lighting and special effects."

"Won't it?"

"It's a brand-new auditorium, Ned. Enormous new stage, electronics, special acoustics."

"It'll be beautiful."

"And you can help me on the music."

"I wish I could see a score right now."

"I wonder where we'll stay?"

"Oh, someplace quaint. John, I'll phone for the pizza. Shall we have a drink?"

"Let's do. Make margaritas, all right? Then we'll go on."

"I'll hurry."

"Scene Four. Telephones, Ned."

"Don't start till I get back. Wonderful telephones. How nice to go someplace and do a show and have some fun again."

Hoffman, in his room, has already begun to read,

Scene Four

Telephones: 8:00 A.M.

Center stage remains dark. At stage right a phone booth is lighted. AL *goes into it, can be seen putting coins into the box. Ringing, as the coins go through. We hear the ringing of a telephone at stage left, where a small area lights up, showing a table, a phone ringing—and* SALLY ANNE *in negligee steps into the light to answer.*

SALLY ANNE: This is Sally Anne, speakin'.

AL: Hello, darling. This is Al. Good morning, love.

SALLY ANNE: Why, Al! So early. What a nice surprise. [*Up behind her, grinning broadly, comes* PILL. *He stands with his arm around* SALLY ANNE's *waist, caressing her lightly, to which she responds with naughty pleasure as she talks with* AL *on the phone.*] How come you're callin'? Don't you work today?

AL: I left the job last night. I've come across the swamp. Sally, darling, can you get a car?

SALLY [*Wriggling, as* PILL *kisses her neck*]: Why, whatever for, darlin'? What am I to do?

AL: First, will you marry me?

SALLY: Why, Al! Why, lover. Now? Get married? Al, you take my breath away.

AL: Sally Anne, I won a lot of money. Four thousand dollars. Listen, you know Pill?

SALLY: Why, yes, of course I know him. Old fat thing. Know him since I was little.

AL: He chased me all night long. I got away. I'm at The Fisherman's Hotel, in Anchortown.

SALLY [*Repeats for* PILL's *benefit*—PILL *nods*]: The Fisherman's Hotel, in Anchortown.

AL: Sally, I want you to get a car and come for me. We'll go to Jacksonville and cash this scrip. Then we'll be married, if you'll have me. We'll go back West. We'll have the money. I'll go back to school.

SALLY ANNE: Oh, Al. It just sounds wonderful, it's like a dream. Just let me keep my feet from running to you, while I try to think. [*Covers the mouthpiece. Whispers to* PILL. PILL *grins and nods vigorously.*] Oh, Al. I accept, darling. I accept. I'll get there. I'll be there by ten o'clock.

AL: I love you, Sally Anne.

SALLY ANNE: Me too, darlin'. Me too.

[*She hangs up.* AL *hangs up and steps out of booth.* AL *stands alone, singing his next phrases, while—miles away, on the other side of the stage—*SALLY ANNE *and* PILL *converse.*]

AL [*Alone*]: I love you, Sally Anne.

PILL [*With* SALLY ANNE, *embracing her*]: Are you Pill's baby now?

SALLY ANNE: I'm Pill's four-thousand-dollar baby, ol' mean thing. [*Kisses him*]

AL [*Alone*]: And you love me. It's too damn wonderful.

PILL: It was a long, cold night, Sally, in the swamp. I knew I better get on over here when morning came. He had to call you, didn't he?

SALLY ANNE: The schoolboy had to call. You smart, mean thing.

PILL: The other jokers, they gave up, it looks like. No dough for them.

SALLY ANNE: Mustn't we get one of 'em out to help?

PILL: And split the dough?

AL [*Alone*]: Gay, when I'm discouraged . . .

SALLY ANNE: No, sugar, no. Not that.

AL [*Alone*]: Soft, soft when I'm tired.

[*Curtain*]

End of Scene Four

Short's bottle of Calvados is a third gone. He waits, half-forgetting what he's waiting for, half-remembering a long-ago spring. It was June and her name was June. She pitched a softball to him. He was on his last home leave, after basic training, with orders to report for embarkation. He was strong from the training, stronger than he'd ever be again, and he hit the ball hard and high and it disappeared in the dusk of the sky, in the heart-stopping smell of lilacs . . .

Scene Five

The Fisherman's Hotel: 10:00 A.M.

[AL *and* NORAH, *waiting*]

NORAH: Fishing. Every day he's fishing. It doesn't bother him that I'm alone with you. It doesn't seem to bother you much, either.

AL: Norah, I got engaged this morning. You're so much woman that I'm damn-near sorry.

NORAH: You will come back, and get me out of here?

[*Sound of a car.* AL *grabs* NORAH's hands, quickly]

AL: Come or send someone, Norah. Soon. [*Drops the hands, moves toward the window.* NORAH *stops him.*]

NORAH: Stay back. I'll look.

AL: Is it her, Norah?

NORAH: There's a cute enough blonde getting out—with half a figure. Yes.

AL: It's Sally! [*Door opens.* SALLY ANNE *stands there.* NORAH *stays by window, looking steadily out.*] Sally Anne!

SALLY ANNE: Oh, Al. I hurried so. I look a mess.

AL [*As they embrace*]: Most beautiful mess I ever saw.

SALLY ANNE: Let's go quick, Al. Are you ready, hon?

NORAH [*Who has continued watching out window*]: Wait!

SALLY ANNE: Who's she?

AL: Norah. Wife of the man who runs this place.

SALLY ANNE: It's nice to meet you, Norah honey. Look, we gotta run. Good-bye.

NORAH: You're Sally, are you?

SALLY ANNE: 'Bye now, Norah. Thanks.

NORAH: Just what I thought you'd be. [*She moves to block* AL *and* SALLY ANNE.]

SALLY ANNE: Well, who cares what you thought?

NORAH: A little butter-brickle ice-cream cone. You'll melt in the heat, dear.

» 55 «

SALLY ANNE: Well then, I'll go and leave the heat to you.

NORAH: You'd taste good to him, but he'd find his face and hands all sticky with the sweet.

SALLY ANNE: I hope he's got you all cleaned off him, anyhow.

NORAH: That's a laugh. Saving himself for you is even funnier.

SALLY ANNE: Hope you enjoy your laughin' when we're gone.

NORAH: Hope he enjoys his lovin' when you're gone. But girls like you—all get, no give. I know your kind.

SALLY ANNE: I don't know yours. Leastwise, not when I can help myself. Now, let us by.

AL: We have to go. I won't forget my promise, Norah.

NORAH: You might not have much longer to remember it. Maybe a minute. Maybe five.

AL: What do you mean?

SALLY ANNE: You fulla swamp juice, woman, this early in the morning?

NORAH: *I mean there's someone hiding in that car.*

SALLY ANNE: You're crazy.

AL: There's what?

NORAH: There's someone in the back. I saw him move. Under a blanket. . . .

SALLY ANNE [*Pressing against* AL]: Come on, darlin'. There's a blanket there. You know what for.

NORAH: I'll go first and have a look, Al. Watch me out the window.

SALLY ANNE: Come on, lover. I can't keep the car forever. It's not mine.

[AL *starts for door with* SALLY. NORAH *pushes them back.*]

NORAH: You'll have to knock me down—or watch me go out first.

SALLY [*Leaps at* NORAH, *pushing* AL *aside*]: You crazy woman, let us by. You hear?

NORAH [*Meets the attack, throws her off and down*]: Murderous little bitch.

SALLY ANNE [*From the floor, screams*]: Pill, in here. Pill, here.

AL: What, Sally? What?

SALLY ANNE [*Screams*]: Pill! Hurry, Pill!

AL: Sally Anne!

[PILL *enters, pushes* NORAH *out of the way, moves past* SALLY ANNE, *hunting knife in hand, grinning.*]

PILL: Morning, old buddy. Believe you have a little something there belongs to me.

AL: You know damn well it doesn't, Pill.

PILL: I got an eight-inch blade that says it's mine.

AL: You can try it. I've seen guys with knives before. [AL *picks up a straight chair to swing.*] There's lots of knives in Denver, Pill. Mexican boys. Handle them quite well.

PILL: That right? This sounds like fun.

[PILL *moves in.* AL *hits at knife hand with chair. They circle, feinting, thrusting—but before they can close again,* RAYMOND APPLEGORE, *coming from kitchen door, steps in behind* AL *and grabs* AL's *arms.*]

RAYMOND APPLEGORE: Just what the hell is this?

PILL: He's got four thousand bucks of mine, friend.

RAY: Yeah? Been stealing here, too. Gonna steal my wife. "Norah, I swear I'll send to get you," huh? [*To* NORAH] Thought I was fishing, did you? How stupid do you think I am?

NORAH: Pig-stupid. Skunk-stupid. Stupid as a fish.

RAY [*To* PILL]: You like him with his chair, or shall we take that from him? [*As* RAY *shifts his grip to try to get the chair,* AL *breaks away, throws the chair at* PILL *who was moving in, vaults to behind desk, where* NORAH *stands, and turns to face his adversaries.*] Now we've got them both together, friend.

PILL: So we do, friend. So we do.

[*They move up, one toward each side of the desk, as* NORAH *pulls a handgun from the desk.*]

NORAH: Here, Al. Take the gun. It's loaded.

AL: No. There's nothing here worth having, Norah. Gun or no gun. Nothing here at all. [*Pulls the wad of scrip from his pocket*] Here you go, Pill. It's all yours. [*Steps out from behind desk, extending wad*] Take it and make the girl happy, if it's what she wants.

NORAH: No, Al.

PILL: And when we leave, you call the sheriff up and say I took your dough? Oh, tricky, boy.

RAY: There. That's the spirit, friend.

[RAY *pushes* AL, *from behind, violently, into* PILL, *who steps forward to meet the impetus, blade first.* NORAH *screams.* SALLY ANNE *watches, big-eyed.* RAY APPLEGORE *laughs with relish.* AL *falls.*]

NORAH [*Screams again, and shoots* PILL. *Shoots again and again.* PILL *falls.*]: Oh, my God.

RAY: Good, Norah. Very good. Four grand!

NORAH: I killed him. God, I killed him.

RAY: Here, Norah. Better let me have the gun.

NORAH: No. Never, never.

RAY: Come on, Norah, Now, don't get me sore at you. . . .

[*Limp,* NORAH *turns over the gun to her husband, who laughs again, as* BERT *and* THIRD POKER PLAYER *enter with shotguns.*]

BERT: What's goin' on? God, are they dead? [*Kneels by* AL]

THIRD POKER PLAYER [*Raising shotgun at* RAY APPLE-GORE]: All right, mister. Throw your cannon down. These things don't miss.

[*With a shrug,* APPLEGORE *drops the gun.*]

BERT: There's two men dead. [*He stands.*]

SALLY ANNE [*Points to the scrip spilled on the floor*]: The money. Look, the money. . . .

BERT: Both of them meant for you to have it. Pick it up. [*Angrily, threatening her with shotgun*] Down on your knees and pick it up. Go on. [*As she kneels, her hands going into the money*] It's two cents on the dollar that they're paying, girl. Easiest eighty bucks you'll ever make.

[*Final curtain*]

Telephone.

The telephone is ringing in Snazzer Short's hotel room, where he has been entertaining himself with masochistic doubts about the quality of his libretto. It's too melodramatic; but isn't opera always melodramatic? Over a hundred operas, Ralph told him once, from Shakespeare, but some of those must be comic. Short doesn't really know very much about opera . . .

Answer the telephone.

. . . and there is very little additional information in the bottle of Calvados he's been working down. What he really feels, he supposes, is guilt, not doubt, about his libretto, because it took him only a few weeks to write, while Ralph has spent nearly three years finding a particular note of music to go with each word in it. Each syllable. A sung note, a played note, finally an orchestrated note.

Hey, it might be Maggi.

"This is Rigby Short. Hello."

"Well, this is Billy Hoffman, you know? This script of yours is okay."

"Thank you. You liked it? It can't be changed at all, you see, because every note is orchestrated. I mean every word, well, you can't—"

"This isn't the first thing you ever wrote."

"I publish scholarly stuff," says Short, who hasn't recently. "But the closest I ever came to anything like this was some movie continuity. Additional dialogue by . . . me."

"No kidding? You get a credit?"

"Yes, but the picture hasn't ever been released." Feels relieved now of the guilt or doubt, and chatty. Hadn't meant to make such a drinking evening out of it, but what the hell? "It was from a Fitzgerald story, 'Diamond as Big as the Ritz,' and I was in Hollywood to be a consultant but also to help with production, I mean promotion."

"Yeah."

"They wanted the college audience, of course, and they were worried about how to approach the academic community, and when I read the script, I was talking to this man, and . . . what a wild place. One day I was a little old professor and the next a bright young writer and the next, well, forgotten, I imagine." Short realizes he is having a little trouble controlling his speech. "Have you been there?"

"I did a play at Pasadena once."

"Well, let me . . . listen, Billy. What are you doing? I mean, tonight?"

"I don't know. Smoking a cigar."

"I'm having a drink. Listen, Maggi's gone to New York. Can you, how about having dinner with me? And we can talk about the play. The opera. Listen, the university pays, we'll have the best dinner in Philadelphia. You name the place, any place at all." That speech seemed to go better. He pours just a touch more in his hotel water glass.

"Sure. Okay."

"Hey, Billy, you do want the job don't you? I mean, have I got myself a director hired?" Did he mean to say that? Now that it's said, he feels quite sure he did.

"Did Maggi say I'd be okay?"

"Hell with her. She's gone to New York, Billy, my friend. Friend in Philadelphia."

"You hiring a director or a friend?"

"Come have a drink, Billy."

"Okay, I will. I mean, I'll have the drink and take the job too, if you're really offering it to me, you know?"

"Absolutely, Billy. Meet me over here, okay?"

"Fifteen minutes, Professor."

"Hey, call me Snazzer. Everybody does. My friends, anyway. My enemies, too, listen, there's one son of a bitch you'll meet, his name is Skeats. Mr. Hughmore Skeats, Fourth. He calls me Snazzer, and one of these times I'm going to ask him not to. Very politely. I'm going to say, 'Hughmore, Four, my name is Rigby, One.' " This is incredibly funny, and Short breaks up over it.

"See you in fifteen minutes. What's your room number?"

Short has barely hung up the phone before it rings again.

"Rigby, One, here," he cries.

"Is this Professor Short?"

Well, of course. It's the curly candidate. The fag. J. Wellington Fag. Short is not unsympathetic, but he is not sober, either.

"The music. Well, I'm dying to hear the music too." Short. "Everybody is. I think even Ralph is. Ralph Lekberg. They're still copying parts. He's a, a master of serial music, and every time he says it, I think of snap, crackle, and pop." That old joke gets a pretty good laugh. "Twelvetone, yes, but Ralph says this is eclectic. He says it's more like Alban Berg. Very, I don't know, atonal? *Sprechstimme* . . . that's a word Ralph says, but frankly I haven't the slightest idea what."

Short half-listens while the curly one explains that the term means speech, half-sung, half-spoken, with pitch left partly to the performer. What Haroldsen goes on to say is pretty dazzling stuff, probably. Probably so. Compositions, lines of action, focus. Probably so. Some dazzler, this J. Wellington Fag. Probably if Maggi were here . . .

"Well, that's fine," he says, realizing that the analysis is over. "That's very . . . impressive. I mean, you obviously know, know your trade, all right, Mr. Wellington."

Charm comes over the phone.

"She went to New York. I mean, I'll call you in the morning."

Little more charm.

"Oh, yes. Tonight, well, I'm already. I mean, tied up, but that would have been. I'll call you in the morning, Mr. Wellington, for sure."

Hangs up, has a drink.

"John? Johnny?"

"I guess not, Ned."

"But what did he say? You were wonderful on the phone."

"He kept calling me Mr. Wellington."

"That doesn't need to be serious."

"He was drunk, Ned. He said he'd call in the morning."

"Well, then . . ."

"But he didn't wait for me to tell him my number."

"Oh."

"I guess he's going to use Billy Hoffman."

"That impossible little man."

"No. Billy will give him a show."

"Not the kind of show you could give him."

"No. Or the kind you'd have given him once, Ned. The doorbell."

"Yes."

"It must be the pizza."

"Let's not answer, John. I'm not hungry."

"Neither am I, but we have to answer, Ned. It's all right. I'll do it."

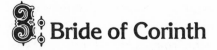# Bride of Corinth

Friday afternoon in Los Angeles: Marcel St. Edouard, tenor (Al Riker), is returning a score to the music collection at the public library. It is the score of a woodwind quintet; earlier this week he read through it with some friends who sometimes meet at his apartment to play chamber music. Marcel did the clarinet part. This particular score interested him because it is an early work of Ralph Lekberg, a little-known American composer in whose new opera Marcel has been signed to sing the lead.

Tomorrow he will leave for State City.

The quintet turned out to be a twelve-tone work of considerable melodic interest, which pleased Marcel, though it was too difficult for the bassoon player in his group. The flautist loved it.

People recognize Marcel in the Music Collection Room, and smile at him or point him out to one another. Anyone who has ever seen him, and most of the musicians and serious music lovers in this community have by now, does not forget his appearance. Marcel feels uncomfortable about this recognition, fearing there is a certain amount of amusement in it, because he is so oversized. He is six foot six and weights 280 pounds. But he hopes there is some admiration in it, too, for the quality of his voice and his musicianship.

A teen-aged girl asks him for an autograph as he goes out. It takes forever for Marcel to think what to write, in addition to his name, when he signs autographs. If someone is nice enough to ask him, then he ought to try to say something special and personal. *To Greta,* he writes, *I'm glad you liked the recital. Your friend, Marcel St. Edouard, June 1972, Los Angeles.*

Friday evening in State City: Hughmore Skeats IV, baritone (Pill Donovan), is entertaining. He has invited Sato Muraski, conductor; Debbie
Dieter Haas, designer; Ralph Lekberg, composer; and Josette Lekberg to
cocktails. Afterward they will go out to supper. It would be ungenerous to
think that Hughmore issued his impulsive invitation to his colleagues on the
opera staff as part of a never-give-up campaign to be permitted to direct the
opera. It is true, perhaps, that the Australian has not lost hope. But it is also
true that he is a gregarious man who enjoys entertaining and who feels
restless and eager for social action in his wife's absence. She is touring
Europe. In particular, he wants Sato to meet his acquaintance John Ten
Mason, M.D., a young surgeon-baritone who will sing the small, featured
part of Bert Tannenbaum. He feels Sato and Johnny Ten will like one
another.

The group is on its third drink, and old Debbie, who loves a drink and
hasn't much head for it, is starting to get raucous when Johnny arrives.

"Sorry I'm late. Making rounds."

"We've had a few bloody rounds here ourselves." Hughmore.

Debbie finds this hilarious. Josette Lekberg, who is Basque, says something to Debbie in Spanish. The doctor, who is from Texas, adds something
or other in the same language, with a Mexican accent. Ralph and Sato both
spent time as young men in Mexico City. Ralph and Josette were married
there. Sato was their best man. So they can participate in the Spanish somewhat, and suddenly Hughmore feels an outsider at his own party. "Bugger-
ing hell," he cries. "Time for a bitchering bellyful, isn't it? Is Henry
coming?"

"I'm sorry." Josette Lekberg. "I was to tell you. Henry is delivering a
goat."

Henry Fennellon, bass (Raymond Applegore), holds the muzzle of a
chrome-barreled .22 calibre pistol an inch away from the head of a just-born
kid. It is the second of a set of twins, from his Nubian milk goat, Candy.
The first twin was huge, and Henry finally had to reach in with a loop, made
for the purpose, and pull it out of the mother. It took considerable strength,
and was hard on Candy but necessary to save her life. It was even harder on
the following, much smaller twin kid. The firstborn will survive, Henry
thinks; he has it up and nursing. But this second, damaged and its birth
delayed too long as it waited in the passage behind its well-formed brother,
cannot hold its head up. There is something wrong with the spinal cord.

Henry shoots. There is a small explosion, a plopping sound. The deformed kid barely quivers as it sinks into death. Henry picks it up by its legs and carries it to his pickup truck, puts it in the bed behind the cab, keeping it out of Candy's sight.

He goes into the farmhouse and cleans the gun. He does not think of it as a gun, but as a tool of farming. Using this tool, as he must several times a year to dispatch an animal, always saddens Henry. He goes into the house and has a drink of moonshine whiskey, which he brought back earlier this spring from a visit to relatives in Kentucky.

He thinks of showering and going to Hughmore's cocktail party; he'd like to meet Sato; finds Debbie congenial, though he's not well acquainted with her; he sees the Lekbergs daily, for they are next-farm neighbors; and supposes Hughmore invited him for that reason. He and Hughmore don't like one another much. He decides to stay home.

Friday evening in State City. Among the students, Davey Riding, tenor (Harry, the Paymaster), has managed to reserve a university tennis court and is playing mixed doubles in the late June light. Davey's partner is Mona Shapen, who will be stage manager for the opera. Davey's wife, Sue, who had a day off from work, is partners with Mike Shapen, bass (Third Poker Player). The Ridings are both good tennis players, and nice to watch, both fair, tall, slim, both graceful. The Shapens are small, dark beginners—hence, the pairings. But Mike is extremely quick, covering the court, hawking the ball, seldom missing, though he slaps and punches his shots rather than stroking them. Good little athlete. Mona, who is lovely and sometimes intense, hasn't brought much emotion to the tennis court yet, beyond a feeling of helplessness, so Dave plays for both of them. His wife, Sue, tries to hit easy shots to Mona. Sometimes Mona can get them back, and then everyone laughs and applauds and congratulates her. All four seem to be having quite a good time, anyway.

Davey is, certainly. He is serving hard when it's time to serve to Sue; she is cracking the ball back in good style. But he is serving to her strong backhand, an almost classic, low-bending slice, which she hits beautifully; if Dave wanted points, he would serve to her forehand, which is quite strong but sometimes erratic. Dave doesn't care a thing about winning points. What he cares everything about is getting back into some sort of rhythm with Sue, any sort, for their marriage is failing. His own fault. And he can almost lose the awful, low-key perpetual consciousness of it in the rhythm and sense of communication of the long, cross-court rallies between himself and Sue, with Mike and Mona Shapen almost standing aside as each supposedly plays up at the net, until eventually Sue, trying to bring Mona back into the game, will tap an easy one toward the beautiful little dark girl—at which Mona, having become absorbed in watching the Ridings hit back and forth, is invariably surprised.

"Mona? Hey. Here it comes." Sue has started calling the shots that way.

Friday evening in State City. Dick Auerbach, tenor (First Poker Player), is with his friends Karen Jackstone, the rehearsal accompanist and vocal coach, and Maury Jackstone, baritone (Second Poker Player). Dick has brought his part over, and Karen has started teaching him the music. Dick doesn't read as well as an M.F.A. musician ought.

Maury, who is black and a genius, reads better than anybody, even Karen. Maury can sing Dick his cues, regardless of which character in the opera has the line. Maury does this at sight the first time through, and from memory thereafter.

The Jackstones' phone rings.

"Maury Jackstone here."

A voice tinkles at the other end. It is the voice of Sidney Bennett, the soprano who will sing Sally Anne. Sidney has drawn away from this group— they were undergraduate music majors together—and is doing her graduate work at Oberlin. "Sweet, sweet, sweetheart Maury! Do you love me still?"

"Mush as ever, just exactly, Sidney. You want Dick?"

Sidney and Dick both come from a small town named Dueyville, a couple of hours north of State City.

"Is he there? But it's you I want, fiend. Why are your torturing me this way?"

Maury to Dick, covering the mouthpiece. "Hey, farmer. Your heifer's back in the barn."

"In Dueyville?" Dick seizes the phone. He's been trying to call Sidney, and left word where he'd be. "Hi. Hi. You home?"

"Dicky, lamb, I'm at your house."

"How's Sam?" Sam is a baby.

"Marvelous. Everybody's fine. Can you get me?"

"Don't you want to stay up there a day or two? How about I'll come up, and we'll stay a day or two?"

"I can't, Dick. I've got to get started. Is Karen coaching?"

"When did you get in, Cindy? Sidney."

"To Dueyville? I've been here for hours."

"You have? I've been trying to . . . it's overnight from Oberlin. Did you fly, or what?"

"Don't be like that, Dicky. Just a boy I know. He was nice enough to drive me."

"Yeah? What's he being nice enough to do now?"

"Dick! He dropped me off, and turned around and went back to Marquette to sleep. At a motel, I suppose. The poor darling was exhausted. Dick, we drove all night."

"You must be tired, too."

"No, I'm ready to leave. Can you come for me?"

"Tonight?"

"If it's not convenient, I'll call the motel and wake my friend. Would that be better?"

"I'll come. I gotta put the carburetor back on the bike, but that won't take long."

"The bike? Dick Auerbach, are you planning to come for me on your Honda?"

"Don't you want to? Ride down like we always did?"

"Oh, darling lamb, of course I do. But I've got heaps of stuff, and I'm really too tired to hold on, even to your lovely waist, all that way. Dick, shouldn't I just call the motel?"

Maury to Dick. "You take my car, wrassler."

"I've got a car, Cindy. Sidney. Listen, I'll be there soon."

Night in Boston. Beth Paulus, alto (Norah Applegore), dresses carefully for dinner. It will be a rather formal dinner, given by some Boston friends of music, patrons really. It is some indication of the regard in which Beth's talent is held that, while the dinner is being given her for godspeed and good luck, most of the other guests will be both older and better known than she. For example, if Sato Muraski were in Boston, his presence at the dinner would surely have been sought, even expected. Janet Margesson, the world-famous soprano and Beth's professional patroness, will be there.

It should not seem strange, as these worlds within worlds go, that Karen Jackstone's parents will be among those attending. The host and hostess know, of course, that poor, plain Karen's husband, that marvelous, tall neegruh boy, did you meet him? will be singing in the cast with Beth. Messages will be proposed tonight from Boston to State City; will Beth remember to deliver them?

Night in New York. Maggi Taro (Short) is at the theatre with a friend.

Maggi, by the way, knows Janet Margesson, Beth's patroness, mentioned above. This is more significant than those not-to-be-delivered family messages.

Night in Philadelphia. If Hoffman had twenty dollars, he could get Short laid. They are walking the night streets together after a long dinner, and Short seems just halfway between wanting a big night out and wanting to go to sleep. A nice lay would satisfy both wants, wouldn't it?

There's a young woman Hoffman used to work with—hasn't seen her for a month or two. Hasn't felt amorous lately, for some reason. She's Greek. He'd just halfway like to see her before he leaves, and she has this friend. . . .

("Ever been in this joint?"
"Gower Club, huh? Can't say I have, Professor."
"Let's get a drink and see what the music's like.")

The Greek girl's friend, Hoffman understands, will turn a friendly trick now and again, reasonable rates, quite pleasant—in fact, if this good-looking, fine-boned Professor Short were less sodden, the nice friend might reciprocate, not just accommodate. And Hoffman wouldn't have to be holding a possible, covert twenty bucks.

("This isn't bourbon and water. It's cold tea and water."
"Yeah, they don't put much tea in, do they? You want to go
up to my room? I gotta bottle.")

The bottle is Wild Turkey. The Greek girl, who got him the job where they worked together, gave it to him for Easter. Easter is big with Greeks. The seal of the bottle's unbroken. Hoffman hasn't been drinking much lately.

In Hoffman's room, Short gets pretty animated. Maybe all the man really wants is not to be alone away from home.

"The big excitement when I left was an art robbery."

"Yeah? They get important stuff?"

"No. A couple of dozen big canvases, worth nothing. They didn't even slice them off the frames, the way art thieves usually do. It was a great and daring robbery, Billy, truck and loading dock, and the thieves walked back and forth past five little paintings worth a quarter million."

"Funny taste in art, huh? Fix yourself another."

"Mind if I use your bed?" Short does. "You live a roving life. Where'd you work last?"

"I didn't. Not since a year ago, I did summer stock in Vermont. Last winter, nothing. I ran an office for a car-rental outfit here, you know? Small-timey car renters, boy; there was a chick worked with me there. She had us some buttons made for Easter: 'We're number thirty-seven.' We'd sight-read plays to pass the time. I never worked in your state before."

"It's no different. I go around the country lecturing; they're all the same, aren't they? The states. Interchangeable parts, molecules breaking—"

"No." Billy Hoffman has to get himself together, brighten up, say something in the pause. "No, I like your phrase, you know. But I can't agree with you."

"Nobody can agree with me."

"Oh, come on." Billy Hoffman.

"Right. Sorry. Sorry for the self-pity. Tell me what places? What's different?"

"Shit, they're all different." Hoffman finds energy. "Take the South. Take your own libretto here, you know? It's South. Take this girl, Sally Anne. She's South. I mean, she's flirting with Al and any of the other guys because that's a girl's duty, you know? It's the moral thing to do, she's raised to flirt. There wouldn't have been any malice there to start with. How'd she know Al was going to come up with four grand? Or Pill was going after it? But it's just the way they are down there. Any man walks by, it's your duty to give him a little whiff of the good stuff and see if it turns him on."

"You've been burned by a gallant southern lady."

"No. I got burned by a raunchy western one. My wife came from Montana."

"An actress?"

"Tried hard to be. Then she outgrew it. Then she outgrew me. She's raising our two little girls with a third husband by now. I can't even find out where—not that she'd let me see them if I could."

"Billy?"

"Yeah?"

"This Wellington. I mean Haroldsen. Is he supposed to be a real hotshot?"

"Sure. Wonderful details, good discipline. Knows theatre. Listen, there was a southern lady, Snazzer. But, boy, if she burned me, it was the kind of burn you get from dry ice."

"Deep . . . deep South?"

"All the way, boy. Biloxi, Mississippi."

Biloxi, Mississippi (Hoffman says, and Short's eyes stay with it, wherever his mind may be), is one of those crazy places you've got to see to believe.

I mean, it's sleepy-time Southy, with the grits and salty ham for breakfast at the motel restaurant, but you look out the window, where are we now? Vegas. "Show Time." "Girl Time." "Action." Only the neon's pale and jittery from being up all night. So you look out the window on the other side. Asbury Park, boy. Piers. Boardwalks. Sand, seagulls, salt water. All the way South: the Gulf of Mexico.

Take a walk on the streets, it's South again. Nasty South, this time. A car goes by with the Alabama license plate on the back, you know? He stops for the light. You cross in front and catch his front plate, something extra he bought for himself to advertise his sentiments.

Or maybe it's a dignified family car, then it might just have a nice Confederate flag, made to fit the space in three colors. Buy it at the service station for eighteen bucks, or you can get George Wallace and Mrs. George, cheek to cheek, gently smiling, and it says *Wallace Country*. The gentlefolk, boy.

You buzz in someplace for lunch: Vegas again. I mean it's lunch time, chopped liver and cheesecake on the menu, but the bunch that hangs there isn't eating the chopped liver. Not yet. They're forking up the eggs, still, and they'll surprise you. Like, you've seen them before, but you never expected to see them here, outside the gangster show on your motel TV. But here they are, with the scars and the Panama hats, and I promise you never heard them before, not this mixture.

These are hoods with southern accents, out of Birmingham and maybe Atlanta. Half of them. The others, though, sound just the way they look: Jersey City, Times Square, longshore. And here they are, all mixed in friendly, doing a little business over the eggs and grits. The new South, huh? Hospitable to northern industry.

What do you want, cheap labor? Look, this is a part of the country where we go out and pot civil rights workers on Sunday for fun. It won't cost much to have a job done weekdays in the line of business.

Service guys walk the streets there, quite a bit. Government payroll for the gambling, I suppose, though a game's not what I look for. Anyway, I was busy nights. I was there doing a show for the Little Theatre people; it's one that likes to have professional directors in.

Booking out of that office you were in today, I see plenty of country, but never anything like Biloxi.

You understand, of course, the Biloxi Little Theatre is a different element from the late-breakfast set. Business, professional, and a few old families, upper middling along, not paying any attention to who else is using their town—unless maybe they get together for one of those Sunday shotgun frolics sometime. The young bloods, anyway.

But I couldn't prove that, and they were certainly nice to me when I got there. Disappointed, but hiding it, because I wasn't your curly-headed friend, Haroldsen, who'd been down to do their play last spring. There's two kinds booking out of that office, young ones like him, filling time between real shows, and the rest of us a little bit seedy—pros, you know. With maybe a Broadway show or two back in the credits. But chasers. Boozers. Lungers. Sour guys with the big juice squeezed out, but enough tricks left for Biloxi. Guys that can give you a show.

Anyway, I wish you could see that town, the honky-tonk, the beach and the boards, and Jefferson Davis's big, beautiful mansion that he retired to after his career of public service.

Like I say, it was winter. The place was only halfway operating. It's a summer place, for God's sake. Stop and think, there've got to be places like that down there, in spite of the heat. Where southern people go to the beach in July. You know they're not on Cape Cod or Fire Island or Wisconsin or Colorado. They've got to leave Birmingham and New Orleans and go someplace.

Biloxi, Mississippi, for salt air and honey children.

But that's not to say they close down in winter. Everything stays open, and the neon never lets you forget it.

Of course, for our little show there was no neon. It was the genteel, amateur posters in the store windows, announcing an evening of wit and sophistication: *Blithe Spirit.*

Blithe Spirit, by witty, sophisticated Noel Coward, huh?

Why do those people always want to do comedy? Give me that cast and Tennessee Williams, I could show you something.

There's this girl cast as Elvira. Woman, I ought to say. Remember the play? Elvira's the first wife that died. She gets materialized in a séance, and then she sticks around trying to bitch up the new marriage, right? Jane Lee Ransom.

She's who I'm telling this about, Jane Lee.

She was a foreigner in Biloxi, just like me. She came from the North, this isn't a joke, North Carolina.

Those people considered her a Yankee. Pretty, big-eyed, dark-haired little thing. About thirty. I mean, one night the woman that's going to play the second wife, the live one, this was a woman named Phyllis.

Willowy piece of stuff, boy, with the short yellow curls and the melted-butter voice, but fast. Phyllis would never let anybody finish a cue before she'd have her own next line going. Talk about pace. Phyllis doesn't need a stage, she needs a drag strip.

Anyway, I'm giving notes one night after a run-through, she's been popping along like Chinese New Year, so I say: "Phyllis, please. Let Jane Lee finish her speeches. Those are good lines. We want the audience to hear them too, not just the actors."

And this Phyllis says, "Well, I'm sorry Mr. Hoffman. I sure am. I just can't tell when she's going to get done. I'm 'fraid I have a little trouble understanding how you Yankees talk."

"What do you want me to do?" I asked. "Resurrect Jefferson Davis and put him in the show in drag?"

But I couldn't get over her calling little Jane Lee, with the big boobs and orphan eyes, a Yankee.

So I asked. It was Jane Lee's turn to drive me home to the motel. See, I didn't have a car down there. I was kind of excited about riding alone with Jane Lee, you know? But I'll be frank with you. I rented a car when I first got there, but I didn't dare keep it.

What happened was, they weren't quite ready to start rehearsals. There I am, a little bit unwelcome, feeling kind of empty the way you do, and don't meet anyone except the old lady who's president of the theatre outfit. She's going to play the medium in *Blithe Spirit,* the fat comedy part, guess who chose the play?

Anyway, she asks me to dinner the second night. Colored cook, big butler in uniform. Yassuh. Lots of booze—not juleps, come to think of it. Out of season, I guess.

There are two or three other guests, older people, and I don't find myself communicating too well. I sit there after dinner, listening to the old gentlemen talk about dove shooting and quail shooting, and if a dove and a quail flew in the window, I wouldn't know which was which.

We join the ladies, it's horseback, dogs, and when to prune the roses. Wow. My cast has got to be younger people, maybe I can find some of them to talk to. I admit it, I'm a talker, but I can't get my mouth around the first word with this older bunch. So no more booze, thank you, ma'am, I'm tired, excuse me.

Down the road and I see a barbecue place. It makes me feel like I'm still hungry. I park the car and it's nice in there, friendly and jukey and comfortably vulgar, you know. There's a cop sitting at one table, and he gives me a smile. I kid with the waitress, and she's a cute kind of high-school thing, and kids back. I eat the barbecued pork on a bun, and drink a shot and some beers, and I feel better. I could be what? A salesman, coming in off the road after a long day. I act it up. More kidding. A dollar tip for the two-buck check, so Miss High School Tightpants won't forget me. Stroll out, puffing the Antonio and Cleopatra recommended by the blonde cashier.

Well, I was this salesman, see, looking for a little fun in town, so naturally I drove to a night club. End of the line. Everybody out. As I parked the rented car, the friendly cop from the barbecue joint pulls alongside and says: "C'mon. I gotta book y'all for drivin' 'roun' drunk, mistah."

I don't know. I don't think I'd had enough to flunk a blood test, but that wasn't really what he busted me for. He hauled me in for being smartass North at a funny time of year. Midwinter non-Confederacy, I mean, that's a bad charge in Biloxi. I could see why. It's a hell of a place for cops, especially at night. They go screaming up and down the street along the beach in squad cars, three to a pack. Because of the toughs, you know? There's a lot of beating up and a little shooting, and the cops like it kept reasonable.

They had to figure I might be in town for some of that, and they wanted me and them to be acquainted.

The most efficient way to place me was find out who cared about me: Was there some local person who'd go my bail? Once I answered that, they could make the other connections. It's funny. I didn't want to tell them. I didn't feel connected with those dove shooters and rose pruners that had me to dinner. I did explain about being there for the play, and then the cops still had to pretend it was a big drunk-driving thing, but they had me pegged. So they said they'd let it go if I'd turn in the car and not try to drive in Biloxi, okay? The high school auditorium's just six easy blocks from the motel, they said, you know what? I was sitting there chatting with them with a three-year-old, expired Pennsy driving license in my wallet, and they never asked to see it. I never owned a car in Philly, you know? I never drive.

I didn't want anything but love and understanding from those big Biloxi cops, so I said sure, yeah, be glad to walk, exercise do me good . . . what was I going to say? Get me a lawyer, give me a blood test, and I'll be back tomorrow for my driving test so I can have a legal license, too?

I thanked them for their many courtesies, and got the hell out of there.

So when rehearsals started, somebody'd generally drive me back to the motel afterward. Everybody in the cast has cars, and it's Jane Lee's turn the night this Phyllis called her a Yankee.

"What, was Phyllis kidding you or something?" I asked. Jane Lee was driving along slow, frowning a little frown. I could see the look on her face every time we went by a street light or traffic light, so the frown was different colors, red, white, green, blue. It was a tense, tight-lipped face, and the skin was stretched tight over it and smooth. I was thirty-six then. She wore the dark hair fluffy, and everything she said she tried to make it sound as if the world was a nice, kind, laughing place, and she was personally having a ball, but all Jane Lee's laughter was in her mouth. The rest of the face was wary to frantic to wild, except when she kept the expression off it altogether. Sometimes she could look amused, but that was one she'd practiced in the mirror, and did on stage.

Not that she was much good on stage. None of them were, but those southern women are bad in a different way. Whatever happens, you know, they've got to be charming. It's the upbringing. Like, there's a cockroach in the soup, they're supposed to say, "Why, Mr. Cockroach. I sure didn't 'spect to see you here today."

Their house is burning down, they got to learn to say, "Oh, I jus' love an open fire."

You know?

They're not easy to direct. Criticism doesn't get through, because they're, they're automated to answer anything a man says with some kind of flirtation. I mean, what could be greater socially? But if you're working with them, you stop being charmed after a while. You start wishing when you say something like, "Phyllis, take that second-act entrance much slower," you'd hear a good, gawky, girlish, northern "Shit. Okay, man" just once. Instead of, "Why, Mr. Hoffman, I'd just do anythin' to satisfy you, I surely would."

You try to answer tough: "All right. Just skip the sorghum and watch the pace, will you?"

When they get on stage, they're as bad as any amateurs, like I was saying; but they aren't unattractive about it. That's the difference. There's some kind of poise and appeal, so the audience keeps liking them even if they're blowing your show to bits.

Well, I asked Jane Lee Ransom if they were kidding, calling her a Yankee, and she said:

"Oh, Phyllis doesn't mean anything by that. Just don't pay her any mind, she's havin' fun, that's all. I believe she thought she ought to be Elvira, 'stead of me, don't you think she'd be good?"

"Play's all cast, lady," I said.

"Y'all from Brooklyn, Mr. Hoffman, or what?"

"Pennsylvania," I said.

"I just think the way people talk from up there is the cutest thing." Like I was Leo Gorcy or Maxie Rosenbloom. We're arriving at the motel now. "That doesn't get you mad, does it? I'm just havin' a little fun, too."

"Help yourself," I said.

She stopped the car in the motel parking lot, just past the big lighted sign. "You like this town, Mr. Pens'l-vainya man?"

"It's a job," I said. "It's all right. Why?"

"I just love it when you talk mean to us," she said, forgetting to look amused. Her shoulders were trembling a little. "We don't bluff you any, do we?"

I shook my head, and didn't say what was in it: If you bluff me, you'll never know it. But I'll bluff you, because that's the essence of directing. That's what my own lousy nature likes about it. Being powerful to people.

Being right in the center of all that intensity and artificially stimulated energy that builds and lavishes through four weeks' rehearsal. With a group of people that might be more attractive and stronger and brighter than you are, but all exposed to you, through their vanity, boy, you get into their dreams.

I said, "No, Jane Lee. It's okay. I think I can get a performance out of you people."

"Oh, I know you can."

"I better be able to. It's my trade."

She was sitting there, staring out the windshield. It was a misty evening, so the lights were a little blurred, but I could see how tight her hands were on the steering wheel. They showed pale. Blood squeezed back out of the fingers. I wondered what it had to do with me, and that kept me from getting out of the car, of course. You see, it was wrong, it was too soon, we hadn't been rehearsing long enough for her to have a big feeling about me. She was a woman, wasn't she? Couldn't she smell the failure in a man, the way women can, here in this first week, before her nose got all stopped up with adoration?

"I hate this town," Jane Lee said.

"Yeah? Why should you?"

"I hate these people."

Then she turned and looked at me. Her head came darting at me, and before I knew it, she'd caught my mouth with hers in a queer little sucking kiss, like she was eating spaghetti. In goes my upper lip, into her mouth, and her tongue darts under, in and out between my teeth, all too fast for me to respond. I guess my arms were halfway over to her when she threw back her head laughing, and cried: "You'll give it to them, won't you?"—the kind of thing a kid might say that's been beat up at school—"You hear me?"

And then her laughter changed in what? Midpeal, huh? From something frantic into just a plain laugh, like it was all one of those nice jokes the kindly world was so full of.

She gave me a tissue from her purse: "Y'all better get my lipstick off you, Hoffman honey, and I better drag my little tail home to my big, strappin' husband, hadn't I?"

That sounded awkward, not quite natural for her to say. I figured she was trying to talk some cute-dirty, to turn me on.

The fact that I figured it doesn't mean it didn't work. Those women have an instinct for where the switch is, don't they?

You might imagine I was looking forward to seeing Jane Lee next night at rehearsal. I was, but I should've known better. Bitchy? Boy, you know that play? She's the spirit of this dead wife, she can float around like Peter Pan. Perch on stuff. So I'd blocked her up on what was going to be a tall bookcase, only now it was a tall pair of sawhorses, with a board across them, you know?

Would little Jane Lee please perch on it? Huh-uh.

"Oh, please, Mr. Hoffman." Then she'd whisper to Phyllis, like they were the two best goddamn friends in the world, and they'd giggle together. Poor Jane Lee; too bashful to say it, and needs a bold spokesman, spokeswoman, so Phyllis would whoop and say:

"Splinters, don't you see? You gonna pick all those little splinters out of her, after she sits up there all evenin', Mr. Hoffman?"

"Get a cushion or a coat or something," I said.

Jane Lee whispered again to Phyllis, and Phyllis jumps down off the stage and comes to where I'm sitting, in the second row of seats, and tells me sweet and low:

"Don't you see, that puts her so high off the stage. It's like sittin' on a swing. Next time you let her know, so Jane Lee can wear slacks and be decent."

"Next time I wish you'd both wear bib overalls," I said. "Let's go to work on this play, huh?"

"Whah, Meeyistah Hiahfmun . . ."

"Look," I yelled, so everyone could hear it. "Anybody want to rehearse? Because if not, there's a movie I want to see downtown."

So then they shut up and we ran through a couple of times. One of the actors lifted Jane Lee onto her board, and she made quite a show of turning her legs sideways, pressing her knees together, and tucking the skirt around and under. As if I'd try to peek at her pants.

Jane Lee had pretty legs. I peeked every chance I got. That made me mad at myself, and I took it out on them that evening, the way you do. Interrupting rehearsal instead of taking notes. Chewing on them. Nearly had Phyllis in tears a couple of times, and wore them all down—all except Jane Lee. She kept playing me with the blank, innocent, offended looks, and saying her lines in a blank, innocent, offended voice that made our witty, sophisticated play into something very, very weird.

What I see now: I was like a log in the sawmill by then. I might have a couple of knots in me that would make things bumpy for the operator, but I was on my way to the blade.

But that night I told myself, oh hell, Hoffman. Jane Lee's just passing the time according to her nature, last night and tonight too. I shouldn't let it get to me and make me petty. Forget that item, boy, and try to shoplift something else.

So I turned down my ride and walked home, thinking these old-enough-to-know-better thoughts, and next morning the two-day rain that started the night she kissed me was over. I'd stayed up drinking and getting to know the guy that played piano in the motel bar. He was a guy from Tennessee and he had a car and a few contacts, he said, over in Mobile. He said Mobile was Sweetmeat Town, and why didn't I give my cast a rest, his next night off, and we'd go try to *pur*loin us some of that *tender*loin. I liked the way he talked, you know?

So I got up late, relaxed. Looked out at the beach, all washed clean like a rich kid's sandbox. Made some coffee with one of those wall-bracket coffee makers they hang in motel bathrooms. Felt good, felt hungry, grinned at myself in the mirror and said, "Buddy, this morning you're man enough to try the grits, okay?"

I, well, what I did was stroll forth, yes. Jauntily. Out of my room, swinging down the motel corridor, past the desk, big good morning to the sourpuss behind it, beautiful day, sir. Twirling my cane, song on my lips, boutonniere, ready to buy the first dog I see a T-bone steak, and out onto the street.

And there was Jane Lee, waiting in her car.

One of those halfway expensive, not too new, slightly crushed convertibles. Even the sag in the roof looked classy, you know?

Little strip of tape on the rear plastic window.

She was pulled right up there, fresh and bright. Lipstick perfect, shining her face in my eyes.

"Come on," she called out, as if we'd done it a dozen times before. "Let's go ridin' down the beach."

And a big wave came sweeping up from the sea, over my little pile of resolutions about saving up for Mobile.

I got in the car. She started chattering away as if we were good old friends that hadn't seen each other for a week or two. She'd reach over and pat my hand as she drove, and say something like, "I was actin' so silly last night, I swear. I don't know what got into me."

Or, "Mind goin' fast?"

Christ, she was doing ninety on a two-lane highway. I was scared and trying not to show it. Finally she slowed down and pulled off toward the beach and around back of an empty stucco building so it stood between us and anyone going by on the road. And there wasn't anybody to see us from the beach.

"There," she said, cute and pert. What am I going to do? I reached for her. She came toward me. We did the look, you know? Solemn. The trembly smile, both of us. And then the first big long kiss. She was the kind of kisser eats all around at your mouth and then she'll let hers go wide open, all of a sudden, as if she was going to swallow your tongue. Wild.

She sank against the back of the seat, half-lying-down, and pulled me over her. If we hadn't had clothes on, we'd have been off to see the wizard, then and there, but four layers, boy. I moved her skirt up out of the way and made it three layers. She did an odd thing I never knew of before. She hooked her fingers onto the front edges of my pants pockets, one on each side, to hold me tight against her. There was more of that loose, lovely kissing, and some loose, lovely squirming along with it, and then I raised up.

"Come on," I said, and tried to get a hand on her. She permitted that, right up until the palm was tight against the crotch of her underwear. Moist, warm, but guarded by elastic and when I tried to move the hand up and over the waistband she suddenly said,

"Oh. Not that." With about as clever and cataclysmic a wriggle as you'd ever hope to see, I mean a real athlete's move. How could she be over under the wheel with her skirt down so fast? I'm practically still grabbing, but it's a handful of air. "We can't do that, Hoffman, darlin'."

She didn't sound so much offended as surprised, like we'd been getting ready in her mind for something altogether different—crochet a little, or play a hand of gin, huh?

"I'm sorry," says Jane Lee. "I was lettin' myself get carried away so." She was looking at me very closely, studying me. "But oh, darlin', I'd get killed. I sure would."

She went back to her studying another minute, and then she moved toward me, slow and steady, smiling, and took my ear into her mouth. I mean this whole, damn, big, thick ear slowly into her mouth, and worked around with her tongue, hand on my chest, pushing me back against the seat. Christ, I about starched myself. Then she takes one of my hands, and starts working over the index finger with her mouth, and throws herself against me, and we start kissing more or less the way we had before, only now she's on top. And this time she pretty much put herself onto my hand, and the rule seemed to be that I could move the fingers in under the thigh elastic as long as I didn't try to go up and over the waistband.

It's funny. All the time there on the beach she wouldn't let me so much as unbutton the first button on her blouse. Like, if someone had come along, you know, she was completely dressed all the time, all over.

She smelled good. She had the best woman smell I ever knew. Moaned and clutched me, and then I tried to get her pants down again. Right about hipbone high she did her amazing Olympic wriggle again, and there she is, sitting coolly under the steering wheel, saying, "Honey, honey. I've just got to go now. I just have to, I'm meetin' Earl for lunch." Earl's the husband. "Oh, I wish I didn't."

She was busy getting things straight under her skirt, filling my eyes with those lovely legs, then pulling the white skirt back down again. She sort of shook herself, and combed her hair, gets out the old tissue, where would love be without Kleenex? Just once she interrupts herself, stops the fixing. Her hands stay up, as if she'd forgotten them, her mouth opens a little, and she gives me this frantic, breath-caught look, oh boy, you've got to see this.

She, she swiveled slowly around toward me, shoulders squared, chin in and up, head back, and the hands, as if she'd remembered them again, moved down and out with the palms open. A position of total exposure, the shine all gone from her face, eyes very wide, and she said:

"You feel anythin' . . . like hittin' me, Hoffman?"

Was she asking for pleasure or punishment, or was it maybe an inquiry into my character? Or all three? I couldn't tell you to this day. I only know she looked so lovely and so vulnerable . . . all I could do was gulp. And say no. No, I didn't feel anything like hittin' little old her. Jane Lee.

If she hadn't done that, maybe I would have felt like belting her one, but now I started feeling this desperate, mysterious sadness for her, and aching because she might be way beyond my help.

She started the car, pulled back onto the highway, and drove much slower going back to town, but pretty soon the chatter began again. Almost like nothing happened, as far as her tone went, but she kept talking about the little interlude behind the stucco building.

"I love to neck and fool that way," she said.

And, "I don't mean anything by it, I don't guess. It just makes me feel young, does it you?"

"It makes my nuts hurt," I said, but I wasn't really cross. Already I had to think carefully to remember where I'd touched her and in what sequence and what she did back—I mean, it was clear enough but it somehow wasn't vivid, and still isn't. What still is, is the moment when she asked if I wanted to hit her, and how I felt beginning then.

The other thing she said on the way back was, "I gotta get out of this town, Hoffman. I'm goin' plumb crazy in this town."

First time anybody used that particular word, *crazy*. It stuck in my mind like a stone, and a lot of stuff started ricocheting off it, from then on, and not just about Jane Lee.

Starting that night I took rides again, after rehearsal, as you might guess. I wanted it to look natural when it came up Jane Lee's turn again. I could hardly wait for it, but of course I had to. Somehow I didn't quite dare call her in the morning, or do anything but leave the initiative up to her. It felt like something springlike and young and, I don't know, *pretty* might happen. Imagine me, between my big ears, feeling that way. I didn't want to louse it up.

Rehearsals were going pretty well. Jane Lee could do the comic stuff when she felt like it, and when the bitch Phyllis would feed her cues right. Sometimes the bitch Phyllis would. The old lady who played the medium was going to be quite good; she'd had years of amateur experience, and gave the others a quality of control to shoot at. Once she had something right, she'd keep doing it right until she got something better, the way real actors do.

Well, it generally happens with amateur casts that the women are the ones that come along first, learn their lines in time to get some work done.

The men are the problem. Either they're regular-fellow guys, who've let themselves be flattered into doing a play, so they're good-natured but treat the director like he was the strict-old-lady teacher back in school—hell, they figure they'll know the crumby lines in time for opening, what else do you want? Another kind is an older guy, usually in a character part, who's a steady local-color item on or off stage. Whatever the part's supposed to be, this guy wants to do all the same stuff for laughs he did in the last show and the one before, you know? The same stuff he pulls all day long behind the counter in his drugstore or photo studio. Sometimes there's a young fag, who may not know he's a fag yet, who takes the whole thing as seriously as the women. You're lucky when you get one of those. You can work with him.

Maybe the second kind, the old local-color boy, is what the young fag grows into if it so happens he never does learn he's a faggot, huh?

Anyway, that's what I had, the middle-aged town clown, in my big male role in *Blithe Spirit*. A little bald for the job, he told me he had the local franchise for some kind of sewing machine. I wonder why I remember that? A store downtown, anyway, and business with the ladies, could give sewing classes—there's my lover-boy husband that the dead wife comes back to fight the live wife for, huh? In the play he's supposed to be a writer, maybe that's realistic. Most writers look like guys that could handle a sewing-machine franchise, don't they?

A night or two after the beach grapple, I keep this guy late. I want to coach him to play just a little bit straighter, and okay, he takes it pretty well, and then he's driving me home. There's something on his mind, you know? It so happens he's usually talkative, but not just now, so what is it? Something about the play? I ask.

"No, suh. I did wonduh if you were findin' suitable injoemint heah in ouah town?"

Sure. Fine. What kind of mint was that?

"I find great pleasuh in conductin' you 'round a few places for injoemint, most any evenin'."

Sounded like something to turn on with.

"I don't mean to pry, but are you a fam'lah man, Mr. Hoffman?"

Divorced, I told him, and about then I got it. He was saying *enjoyment,* for God's sake.

"I wouldn't like for you to get cravin' injoemint so bad you'd get yo'seff into some kinda mess 'round heah."

"What kind of mess?" I asked him.

"Oh, we have some very pretty messes, Mr. Hoffman," he said. "Like any little town. We sure 'nough do. I don't believe you'd injoe gettin' tangled up in one at all."

I thanked him. What else could I do? Tell him my mess had already slid by the injoe stage, somehow, starting when the lady spread her fair white hands and asked did the gentleman wish to clout her one?

I wanted to see her alone, if only for a moment. I mean, boy, I was on my way out of my skull. I mostly wanted to hold her still, and tell her things were all right.

But don't get me wrong. I had the old connecting rod in mind, too, of course.

The following night we had a private word together. She said it: "To-morra."

But she wasn't out there in the morning. I decided she meant the same thing I'd been counting on, her turn to drive me home from rehearsal. Still, I moped all day. Like a kid. Couldn't eat supper for excitement.

Showed up at the auditorium so early there were still extracurricular high schoolers there, practicing some kind of music program. I listened. They were pretty bad.

Then the building was deserted for a while, no cars in the parking lot when I wandered out to see. It got dark. And my cast started to arrive: Injoe, the sewing-machine writer. Old Lady Dove and Quail, with her car-poolful. And finally: Phyllis, with a message:

"Mr. Hoffman, poor little Jane Lee, she's got such a bad cold. She asked me to tell you, could she be excused tonight?"

"Okay," I said. God, I'd let myself get so tense about it, what I actually felt was a kind of cowardly relief. "The rest of you probably need the work more, anyway. We'll polish some spots tonight."

That got Miss Phyllis upset to a point where I really started getting something out of her for a change. We'd reached the time in rehearsals where the cast is pretty much stuck on the director, and I found myself wondering why I'd been overlooking Phyllis? I'll be frank with you, I usually get hooked up with something or other when I go out on those jobs. It's one of the things that makes them interesting, I'll admit that, and Phyllis was all free, divorced, rational. Like me, huh?

But it didn't happen to be her turn to drive me, and I didn't want to join the old lady's car pool. When rehearsal was done, I said I'd walk. Stayed on a few minutes, talking with the set and costume crew. They left, and I locked up. I went out through the back door, as I always did, and into the parking lot, and there it was.

The shabby, classy convertible.

I damn near broke into a run when I saw it, but I managed to control that boyish impulse, and walk up from behind the car. I saw the window was down on the driver's side, and I thought I'd lean in and kiss her, but as my head lowered, it was a man's face looking into my puckered lips, and the man's voice said:

"Get in, Mr. Hoffman."

"Oh, hello." I jumped back. "You must be Earl."

"Get in, suh." I saw by the parking-lot lights that he had two other men in there with him. Earl was a good-looking, boyish man around thirty, with wavy hair and hands like a pair of unabridged dictionaries. Big, thick, strong—you'd have to be Mr. America to raise a pair of hands like that high enough to straighten your hat.

"No thanks," I said. "Awfully nice of you. I decided I'd walk tonight." I got back another inch or two. "Hope your wife's not too ill, Earl, uh, Mr. Ransom."

The man who was sitting in the right-hand seat beside him got out of the car, and came walking around it till he stood behind me.

"Come on, now, Mr. Hoffman," he said. "You know we wouldn't let you walk all that long, long way. You might git lost."

"Might tire yo'seff and git sore throat and double pneumonia," Earl said.

" 'R slip on something, an' hurt your sacroiliac."

"Git snake-bit—git in the car, you hear?"

"Listen, buddy," I said. "I don't know what this is all about."

"We gonna let you guess what it's all about," Earl said. "Can you git him in all right, Parky?"

Parky grabbed for my arm. I jumped away, yelling, "Look, you got something to say? Say it, goddamn it."

"Don't go cussin', Mr. Hoffman," Parky said, tenderly.

"I'm not getting in that car." I ran backward a few steps till I felt safe. "You think I'm crazy?" That word.

This time Parky moved fast, had my sleeve as I was turning to dash off, grabbed me, spun me, and pinned my arms from behind. He wasn't more than twenty inches taller than I was, and his arms would hardly have reached around me twice.

Earl said: "If he doesn't wanta get in the car, let him start runnin'. I just as soon see kin he play Dodge 'Em?"

"Why sure, Earl," Parky said. "That's a right nice idea." And he hauled me out in front of the headlights of the car. There were no other cars in the lot. There was cyclone fence on my left. "Wanta start youah motor?"

"Aw, Parky, that wouldn't be sportin'," Earl said. "Let's play like skeet. Now, pull."

With that, Parky turned me and gave me a great shove, straight away from the car, and I heard the starter grind.

I stumbled forward, recovered, and started running toward the far edge of the parking lot, toward the nice quiet residences a hundred yards away. The fence was on my right now, and, loping along at my left, ten feet away, Parky, and I heard the motor catch. I was out of breath immediately, scared as I've ever been. The car moved after me. I could hear Parky laughing. Earl came slow. I ran.

I knew I had to circle, get inside his turning radius, and I turned toward Parky, who backpedaled lightly away. And the car followed.

When I thought there was room, I swerved, back toward the fence, darted between it and the car, got behind it and started back along the fence the other way, and Parky yelled,

"Whoo-ee. Look at 'im go," and then Earl slewed the car around, and I was in the headlights again and saw that I was out of running room, for the fence turned a corner twenty yards farther down, and I fell. The car came swelling toward me, and the bumper was over my legs when it stopped.

I damn-near started throwing up. Grace under pressure, boy.

"You like that Dodge 'Em?" It was Parky. Christ, he couldn't have said it in a pleasanter, more courteous voice.

"Ask him, does he want to try again?" Earl called out. "We got time f'another."

I got up, trembling, walked to the right-hand door and got in the shallow rear seat, next to the third man who hadn't said a word. I tried to remind myself that these weren't the open-town toughs, or rednecks from the country. These were young businessmen, the nice people, you know?

"That's Mr. Beach there beside," Earl said, turning toward me and grinning. "I don't expect we going to need him after all, but hell, we heard you were mighty tough."

"You can't ever tell, Earl," Parky said, getting in. "He might not have showed it to us yet."

Earl started the car.

"Must we go to the beach or the golf club, Parky?" Earl asked.

"Why, I don't know. You like to play golf, Mr. Hoffman?"

"No," I muttered. "No, I don't do that."

"We going to teach you, then," Earl said. "Don't you think that's the kind, Christian thing to do, Parky?"

"I think that's altogether Christian," Parky said, and Earl drove on out of town.

There's pretty grass where we stop. There's a nice twinkle, twinkle of lights from the clubhouse, I suppose it was, in the distance.

"All right," I said. "What do you want with me?"

"Want for you to git out," Earl said, cordial as ever, and Parky stepped out, opened his door, and made room for me.

I thought of hanging in, grabbing a piece of automobile, trying to kick and scream. The one they called Mr. Beach discouraged that. All he did was gently press a knuckle into my side. Mr. Beach never did get out of the car or say anything. But I did. I got out of the car and said: "You're making a mistake, Earl."

"Why, that's all right," Parky said. "Anybody can make a mistake, can't he?"

"I just make mistakes all the time," Earl said. "Don't y'all, Parky?"

"Why, sure I do," Parky said. "Mr. Hoffman doesn't have to feel bad about that." They'd guided me out onto the grass now, away from the car lights, and Parky asked: "Want I should tee him up for you?"

"Just kind of tilt him and turn loose," Earl said. "I'll see can I play him to the green from heah."

He pulled that big mass of fist way back into the middle of the night somewhere. Parky pulls me up straight, tips me toward him, and gives a mild push.

It was like being hit in the chest by a sackful of rocks. I went down, with my rib cage feeling as if it was going to come unsprung, wire by wire, and let the bird out. I hadn't failed to weasel out of being hit for years, not since my old man used to punch on me, Saturday nights in the kitchen. I thought my old man had a hand on him, but that Earl could hit harder. I heard myself scream going down.

"Topped him," said Parky.

"Listen here, Mr. Hoffman," says Earl. "Jane Lee wanted to be in yoah play, and she is going to be in yoah play. Jane Lee is also going to act crazy and want y'all to touch her because she is a crazy lady. But you not going to touch her anymore, because you not a crazy man. Isn't that right?"

"Okay," I said. "Okay."

"Come on. Stand up heah, now." He helped me up.

"Maybe it'd be better if she left the cast," I said.

"No, suh. She is not going to leave the cast. I am not going to have people sayin' she left the play, when she is finally in it, just like she wanted to be."

"Look," I said. "I can't do this. I can't direct like this." And Parky hit me. He could only hit half as hard as Earl, so he made up for it by hitting twice, on the shoulder and in the stomach, and down I went.

"I'll call my agency," I yelled. "To send someone else."

"No, suh," Earl said. "You will stay right heah, and not cause talk of any kind, you hear?"

I tried to roll and felt a terrible, sharp pain. "You've broken my rib."

"We might break you some other little things 'fore we get done," Parky offered, in that same pleasant way. "Gimme drink, Earl." Earl handed him a pint of something. "Maybe we oughta whop on him with a tire iron, Earl, and see how many little things we *could* break."

"Maybe so," said Earl. "Save me a swallow of that, now."

They were in no hurry. They were going to have a little visit about things now. I lay there hurting and thinking a wild, irrelevant, professional thought. No kidding, I really did: Wouldn't they be something onstage?

Now Parky squatted by my head and said, in a nice, soft, sly voice: "Hey, Mr. Hoffman, you love niggers?" I heard something in the question I'd never heard before, though I'm perfectly sure of it. I heard that he didn't give a damn what my feelings were, you know? But that he assumed I'd believe it mattered to him a lot.

That was a little bit crazy, too. North and South, boy, they drive each other crazy. That's what I think. They can't understand each other in any way. Put them together and everybody starts to spin out.

I didn't answer, and they both laughed.

Earl was squatting at the other side, and he took my chin in his big hand: "The gennulman asked you did you love niggers, son," he said. He squeezed his thumb and forefinger against my jaw so that the inner skin of the cheek went between the molars. Then he shook till my mouth was wide open, and lifted me by it to my feet. You ever get lifted by your cheek skin pressing up into your molars? "Love 'em?"

He let go.

"I love myself," I said.

"You know, I think you a lyin' son of a bitch?" Parky inquired, and gave me another little whack. This time I staggered, but didn't fall. I was hurting, but I was feeling some kind of stupid strength to endure it, because my friend Parky was quite right. I was lying when I said I loved only myself. I loved, and that was the moment I knew it for sure, Jane Lee.

I knew I loved her, because I was going to stand there, or lie there, and take whatever blows these maniacs were going to deal me, and then I was going to get her away from them. Somehow. Sir Billy the Chicken-hearted, boy, with the busted rib, I was going to rescue my wistful lady.

The rib was cracked, I guess, not really broken in two. But I was in enough pain so that the scene was pretty confusing for me from there on, you know? They were drinking their pint and having a big time tramping around in what they supposed was this big area of northern sensibility about Negroes. There was something about invitin' me back down for Juneteenth, when they'd let some of the caged ones go, and hunt them on horseback.

I think I remember Parky saying, "You might think we eat them after the hunt that way, but hell, that was granddaddy style. Nowadays we give those wild ones to the orphanage."

"They so gamey tasting," Earl said.

"The ones we eat, that's what we call a meat-type nigger," Parky said. "Little short blocky ones we raise, out ahind the levees, kind of like a Aberdeen Angus. . . ."

I fell about then. Neither of them touched me. I just fell.

"Looky there," Earl said. "Y'all shouldn't have told him, Parky."

"Aw, me and my big mouth," Parky said. "Now he knows, he knows the ultimate secret of the old South, don't he, and we gointa have ta kill him."

"Reckon we will," Earl said, regretfully, and they lined up beside me. "Drowndin'?"

They were law partners, those two young bloods. God.

"Drowndin's best, they say. Don't hardly hurt at all." I couldn't see what they were doing, but I heard it. They were unzipping their flies. Do I have to tell you what my two young friends did next? They walked away laughing after doing it, and I lay there drenched and steaming, and the reek of whiskey after it had been through those two healthy sets of kidneys was awful.

I waited until the car drove off. Then I crawled toward a hole in the ground that looked like it had water in it. It did. Something to do with the game of golf, I guess. I rolled over the edge of it and lay in the shallow water, moaning and shivering, and you want to hear something ridiculous?

Glad Jane Lee couldn't see me now. Why she might have lost confidence in me.

I was miserable as I've ever been in my life, but I wasn't even going to stumble to town and catch the bus and get away from there. Nope. And not just because I pretty much imagined Mr. Beach and some of his colleagues were going to be charged with watching the bus station and the used-car lots, either.

What I'm trying to say is, now my ♥ was in Dixie, and I didn't want to get my aching 🐴 out of there.

A cracked rib, there's nothing much you do about it. You stay out of certain positions so it won't twinge. Most of the time, if you walk around stiff from the waist up, it doesn't hurt, and pretty soon it gets well by itself. I found that out from my friend the motel piano player, who'd got kicked out of Tennessee medical school as a boy.

He made a pretty good nurse, anyway. Brought me my meals. I halfway wanted to tell him, so I halfway told him, you know? Made myself a little more the gay dog, a little less the ugly loveling. Made Jane Lee a little more the hot number, a little less the troubled, big-boobed victim. Damn relationship seemed to make a certain kind of sense the way I revised it, so I could go on and admit I'd got beat up. So my piano player took four bucks out of my muddy pants, went out to the hardware store, and came back with a sheath knife. He cut off the top of the sheath, where the belt goes through, stuck the knife in what remained, and Scotch-taped the sheath and handle together. He told me that way I could carry it cased in my pocket but it wouldn't, in his opinion, be a concealed weapon. He'd been kicked out of Tennessee law school once, too.

He offered to sneak me out of there, over to the bus station in Mobile if I wanted, but I said no, I had to stick till I got paid part of my fee, dress-rehearsal night. I was broke, and had asked for an advance, but it was slow coming. He didn't have any suggestions about raising the cash.

I was pretty down when I got to rehearsal. Reaction, partly. Partly starting to believe, because it felt more comfortable, the lies about me and Jane Lee I'd told the piano man. A profligate who gets caught playing around can turn it off, so he won't be caught again.

Consequently I judged Jane Lee's appearance quite plain when she walked onstage that evening. Too small for her eyes, I thought. Too short for her teats. Lacking in grace and laughter.

That welcome state of disaffection lasted about twenty minutes. We came to a place at the end of Act One, and what Jane Lee did was to blow a line, a line she'd never missed before. It comes at a moment in the play when the ghost-wife turns off the comedy for a couple of beats and plays pathos, a moment Jane Lee always did well with. It looked quite natural for her to seem not to remember the next line, and look at me from the stage because I was prompting, and to say in the same tone she was using for the scene:

"Help, me?"

"Sure," I said. "Sure." And gave her the line.

She said it, but not before she'd given a small, clear, serious nod. And I felt all released, you know, and wonderful. She wanted my help. She'd sent a message. Everything was okay now, and suddenly I became brilliant.

I didn't need to bully anyone. I didn't need to shout. I got very witty, in a mock-pleading way, and made them laugh. Or blush. If I only knew how to reach the part of myself that can be that way whenever I wanted, instead of its being accidental. . . . What I did that night was to let them run each time to a scene break. Then I'd gather them around and get them laughing, tell them apropos anecdotes they wanted to hear, from the big time, New York and Hollywood and, Christ, Elizabethan England. I made half of it up.

There were positions I could get my body into that stabbed the flesh around my rib, but I was good. Good as I've ever been at any rehearsal. I had their confidence, their complete attention. They were doing things for me they'd forgotten my telling them to do. Even my sewing-machine man, you could almost believe he was some sort of classy dilettante writer, doing research on the occult.

He and Phyllis drove me. He babbled away those few blocks going to the motel in his friendly, Abyssinian dialect, and Phyllis, sitting between us in the dark car, took my hand secretly between hers for a moment, squeezed softly and said:

"Mistah Hoffman, I just don't know when I ever spent a more excitin' evening."

You know how stuck I was on Jane Lee by then? Instead of suggesting that we keep the excitement rolling, I patted Phyllis's hand instead of squeezing back. Boy.

Went to my room, stripped to the waist so that I'd look fierce to myself in the mirror, and practiced with that silly knife. What I'd do, I'd pull it out fast from my pocket, flip the breakaway sheath away, and go into a knife-fighter's crouch.

Once, I directed *West Side Story,* so I knew what the moves were supposed to be. You come in underhand, and low, knife fighting. I drank and pranced and finally went to bed with a big grin on my face. Crazy.

So next night Jane Lee rewarded my fidelity by coming to rehearsal drunk. I didn't know at first just what the matter was. Her eyes were bright, and she was tart with me. She giggled with Phyllis a lot when they weren't onstage, and the two would run off to the rest room together when I'd give the cast a break, and belt a couple, I imagine. At least Phyllis was looking pretty bright-eyed too by the end of the evening. I remember once when I asked her kind of sarcastically if she wanted me to put down a chalk mark for her position in one of the scenes, she said, "No, but I'd like to put me a kiss mark on the bald spot right on top of yo'ah head, Mr. Cuteman."

That sent both my girls into spasms.

I wanted to talk to Jane Lee. I wanted another message, huh? Sure. So I stopped the rehearsal early, and said I was going to spend a few minutes with each of them in turn tonight, giving notes, instead of speaking to the cast as a group.

I sat in the back of the auditorium, and called the medium lady. I called the sewing-machine man. I called Jane Lee back third. She came sauntering up the aisle, shoulders back, smiling, and the rest sat down front, waiting their turns. She slid in and sat by me, forward on the seat, head turned my way.

"Well, Mr. Hoffman?"

"Hi, Jane Lee. Are you all right?"

"I'm just fine," she said. "Got some little notes for me tonight?"

"No. Not really."

"Haven't I been doin' anything wrong at all?"

I shook my head.

"Well, then, what in the worl' we doing back here?"

"What's the matter?"

She stood up. "Bet y'all got plenty of notes for Phyllis," she whispered spitefully. "Hateful."

And flounced away down the aisle.

You know?

The next night, the night before dress rehearsal, she was drinking again, but different. Big-eyed, yearning drunk, but at the break I wasn't looking for her. To be frank with you, I was confused as hell, and wanted just to get away from all of them. I told them to take twenty minutes, went downstairs quick to the men's room and then on to the sanctuary I'd found myself. The boys' locker room. It smelled of soap and sweat, and it always seemed to me the quietest place in the high school building. It was full of the ghosts of yelling, scuffling, towel-snapping kids. That made it quiet. I wasn't doing anything there, walking along between the locker rows, looking at the empty benches, swinging a discarded football helmet I'd picked up, imagining myself a young, southern, T-formation quarterback, when I heard her call:

"Hoffman? Hoffman?"

I turned and went to the door. She slipped inside the dim room.

"Hoffman, what y'all doin' with that helmet?"

I shrugged and put it down.

"I'm sorry," she said. "The way I been actin'. Earl's got me so nervous I don't hardly know what I'm doin'."

"You'll be very good in the play," I said.

"Bein' in this play is what's savin' my life," she said. "Just to get out of the house and be away. Not just Earl, ever'one of them. Phyllis and Mizz Carter and all. When you get 'em on the stage, they're not themselves. You don't let 'em be Biloxi, Mississippi, anymore, Hoffman."

"Why don't you leave here, Jane Lee?"

She didn't ask how she could. She just looked at me. So what did I do? I nodded, and said:

"Okay. Night of the play. Right after the performance."

And she pulled me to her, against the half-glass door, with the word BOYS curved over the top of her head backward, ƨYOᙠ, like some kind of dark halo. Spread her legs, pulled me between them, and began to move her hips so our scrota rubbed. If that's the plural. They weren't plural very long.

"Don't kiss me. Better not to kiss me," she whispered, sticking her tongue in my ear.

Then she got deft with her hands, down there in scrotumville, and I could hardly believe what she was arranging. My arms were around her, and squeezing made the rib hurt, but I squeezed.

She got me unbuttoned and hauled out, never missing a grind. Then she hitched up her skirt, and she'd left the pants behind this time, maybe in the ladies' room when she stopped off, huh? I could feel her soft fingers firmly guiding me to the opening. Then she started scrunching for an angle, and of course I scrunched too, and I'm trying to look through frosted glass with the letter Y right about eye level to make sure no one's coming, but they couldn't have got the door open if there had been, and anyway, I couldn't really see anything out there, not even shadows.

She found our angle then. I could feel myself slip up into her, that easy slide and close. Hell, I don't know. It was a strange fuck, if it was a fuck. Of course it was, but, well, those muscles in there were quiet, receiving only, not grasping. Do you know what I mean? It was no whore's counterfeit, but external excitement and a sad, involuntary, inner indifference. . . . Oh, I came all right. But she was still drawn-away, up toward the womb, so that I can't say I felt her. You know, in England, in the war, they say girls did it standing up and felt it didn't count that way? I don't know. We hunched and wiggled, and whispered and clutched, till I was done, but there at the center it was a strange, cool, dusty little fuck.

"I don't ever mean for you to hurt, Hoffman," is what she said, and then we had to get ready to hurry back up, by separate flights of stairs, one for girls, one for boys.

In the morning there was a letter, delivered by hand, I never knew by whose. There it is, under the door of my motel room when I get back from breakfast.

She reckoned I could get a car. She knew where I ought to have it parked. After the curtain calls, instead of going to the dressing room with the others, she would slip away and come to me. Would I want to go to Arkansas? She knew people there. It was a good state to get a divorce in. If we drove all night, we could be in Arkansas in the morning.

I'd got my advance by then, two hundred and fifty dollars. I went and woke my piano-playing friend and bought his car from him for a hundred seventy-five.

At dress rehearsal I found a way to tell her it was all set. And the next morning I settled up with the motel. It left me with about twenty bucks getaway money, and I knew I'd never dare try to collect the rest of my fee. I figured Jane Lee to bring a contribution. That would make it easier.

I couldn't tell you how the play went. Like any other, I suppose. I couldn't keep my attention on it, though openings are generally my big cathartic. I had the car stashed, my suitcase in it, and just at the end, as the applause started, I ran out to it. It was in an alley between the school building and a little brick service building.

I had a drink for courage. I got the sheath knife out of my pocket, and kept it in my hand. For more courage. I'd thought I would be able to hear it, laughter and applause diminishing from the auditorium so I'd know what was happening. I kept the car window down, but I couldn't hear a thing.

After a while, I decided they must be dressing. In a minute I'd start to see people leaving, or hear the cars start up.

She wasn't coming. I began to feel sure that the calls were long over, there just didn't happen to be people going by where I was parked, and Jane Lee wasn't coming. It would be the final, brilliant twist in the mysterious game of Screw Hoffman they were all playing. Any moment now that convertible would drive slowly past the end of my alley, with her and Earl in it, and she would stick her head out the window and laugh her gayest, most relaxed laugh and call out:

"Y'all comin' to the party, Hoffman?"

I decided I would start the car and drive away before anything like that happened. I put a finger on the ignition key and tapped it. I would tap it a hundred times. Then I would start the car and drive away. Somewhere. I might even make Philly and sell the car. And I could send for the other half of my fee, and to hell with them, all of them, and then I saw it.

In the rearview mirror. Something white. Moving along the side of the school building. Fluttering softly toward me.

It looked like a ghost.

I opened the door, turned and leaned partway out of the car, and looked directly at it. It still looked like a ghost. The ghost of Jane Lee Ransom, Daughter of the Confederacy, you know?

Makeup. It was makeup, of course, because she'd run out the back door and around here straight from the stage, the writer-guy's dead wife: grey-white dress and pale face, with a little greenish luminescence in her hair, and she ran almost up to me, spooky, and then around, to the other side of the car, pulled the door open, threw herself into the seat, and whispered:

"Let's be free."

So we started.

It was a strange trip, boy.

I wasn't going to say anything too solemn, but I didn't want to say anything absolutely trivial, either, like, you know, think the play went all right? or, Bet you're tired. I silently passed her the fifth of Calvert I'd opened, and she had some. Then I had some more, and we were going through the outskirts of town before I knew what I wanted to say: I wanted to tell her about how I was in love with her. But I didn't quite dare. Not cold turkey. Right out flat. So I gave it a little romantic buildup:

"Bring any dough with you?" You know?

"Dough? Oh, money. I couldn't even go by the dressin' room for my purse. I just came quick as I could."

We were clear. We were on the highway, anyway, and she put her hand so lightly on my shoulder I could hear it, moving against the fabric, more than I could feel it.

"Yeah," I said. "Sure. I love you."

"Oh, Hoffman," she said. "Y'all better love me, hadn't you? I better too."

So you see, we got that topic pretty well explored in depth, and had to turn to something else, which worked out to be more silence for a while. Silence and cowardice, boy, on my part. I went as fast as that heap could go, in a state of low-key terror, not just because of Earl but because of my old friends the Biloxi copsies. See, I still didn't have a license. I wanted out of Mississippi so bad, I kept scrunching forward in the driver's seat, as if that could speed us up.

"Hoffman," she said, after a while. "I wish y'all could know my daddy. Could have known him befoah."

What was this? Now things are serious, you'll have to meet my family? I might just have met all the relations of Jane Lee's, natural or by marriage, I'd ever want to meet, and I might just have the throbbing rib to prove it. But when she didn't go on, I said:

"What does your father do, Jane Lee?"

"Nothin' now. He just sits home, in a cane rocker. But he used to be one of the biggest tobacco growers in No'th Carolina."

"Is he old now, or what?"

"Oh, no. He jus' couldn't stand it."

"Come on," I said. "Couldn't stand what? Isn't growing tobacco a big southern thing?"

"No. Not now. Not anymore, well, oh, sure. For some it is still. It's big for money still. But since the cancer, Daddy feels like he spent his life growing poison. And folks act, they don't like for him to feel that way. He's got his different farms in corn now, and peanuts, but he won't take an interest in it. He was so proud of his tobacco, always, always topped the auction."

I said he must be a righteous man.

"When I was a little girl, ever'body was always so nice to ever'body else. Now tobacco families are mad with Daddy, and the righteous ones, the Baptists and that kind, they're nice enough people, I reckon, but. I couldn't stand it there. 'Case y'all wonderin' how I come to marry Earl."

"Earl's pretty," I said. "Strong. The strongest."

"I met him in college. I was a verra popular girl in college, Hoffman. But to me, you the pretty one. You believe that?"

"No," I said.

"It's true, though. You got more expression in yoah eyes than most men in their whole face. And yoah voice. Got a beautiful voice, Hoffman, sends chills. That's the first thing I thought, that man's got a beautiful voice."

I remembered when she thought it was just like Maxie Rosenbloom's, too, but I couldn't grin.

We crossed the border into Louisiana then, and the tail pipe celebrated our escape by dropping halfway off. All through the state, that damn pipe scraped and bumped under us, and Jane Lee kept striking her cheerful notes in counterpoint. Once I stopped and tried to knock the thing all the way off, but I only burned my hand trying that, and all the garages and filling stations were closed by then.

The pipe scraped along, and the old engine roared away unmuffled, and Jane Lee kissed my burned hand, and said what lovely, strong fingers I had. And I thought, pretty soon now the Louisiana cops are going to get us for the noise, and ask to see my license, reasonable enough. What, no license, suh? Well, we goin' to havta check back to Mississippi, then, make sure the car's not stole, and, whut's that you say? Warrant for *abduction*? No wonduh she's so pale lookin'.

I never knew a woman like Jane Lee, who'd try her hardest to be sweet and gay when things were tough.

I drove slow, to keep the noise down and save gas, and we made it into Arkansas.

Just before dawn, in a city called Arkadelphia, I picked a cheap-looking motel on the outskirts and stopped. The man was already awake there, feeding his chickens. He walked over and he saw Jane Lee, still pearly-white with greenish hair, and he wanted to know as I went with him into his living-room office whether my wife was sick. I said no, she was fine, buddy, a little tired if it's anything to you.

We went into our cabin and didn't need to turn the lights on by now to see. Jane Lee didn't want me to, anyway. She saw herself in the mirror, and didn't want me to look at her at all, with the white greasepaint and greened eye sockets, and no cold cream to take it off with. She cried.

"Soap will do it, doll," I said. I put my arms around her, and she sagged into me. "Good old motel Palmolive in the postage-stamp size. Look, it's the greatest."

"Oh, Hoffman," she said. "I'm so tired. Let me rest a minute, darlin', will you? All right? 'Fore I take my bath?"

"Oh, yes," I said. "Oh, yes." And helped her to the double bed, and stretched her onto it, you know? I undid her clothing and covered her, and she dropped right off to sleep. I took her brassiere off and slid her gown down for a moment, because I'd never seen her bosom. There was nothing false there. The breasts swelled out, just as they promised to. But they were very white. As white without makeup as her face and neck were with the greasepaint. I touched a breast, to see if she'd happened to make them up too, but she hadn't. It was cool, pale, natural skin.

And that's the way I remember Jane Lee, white-skinned, blue-veined, and still, nude to where the covers reached around her waist, with the big eyes closed and green bruises painted around them. That's the way I remember her because that's the way she looked when I last saw her, you know. Because I lay down beside her, so deep asleep after our long drive from Biloxi to Arkadelphia that I listened to be sure she was still breathing. She was, very softly, and so I covered us both and went to sleep myself.

When I woke up, it was evening and she was gone.

The car was gone, the sheath knife and half the money. And there was a note, and I think I can quote it exactly, or at least not be too far wrong:

Dearest Hoffman: This is so you'll have a chance to came after me in Little Rock, or be shed of me if you don't want to.

Then it gave some woman's name and address, and went on. But it's the last line that kills me.

Earl's going to be coming after us, you know that, and it's going to make it harder for him if we go you one way and me another. I'm sorry I have to take the car and part of your money. I just don't know any other way. You came after me if you want, but when you think about it, I don't believe you will. I'm so very sorry, Hoffman, I was always a good tease but a bad lay.

Love ya,
Janey

You know what it was, that last line? It was the same moment we had on the beach, days before, when she asked me if I wanted to hit her. Only this time I thought I better not follow. Because what she was saying was, she'd let me catch her. Any number of times. So she could run again, and be caught and hit again, and run again.

By the time I carried my bag to Pannsy's Arkadelphia Lunch, I had four dollars left. No car, no woman, no job. Nothing but a cracked rib.

I went to the north edge of town to start hitchhiking to Philly.

Thanks for your honesty, Jane Lee. You are trying to tell me about something that goes way beyond frigidity, into a country no man ever heard of, let alone explored, can't fight in no matter how he wants to . . . are you? There was even a minute, as I stood there on the road, waiting, when I felt desperately sorry for poor damned Earl.

I won't say that lasted very long.

All I really knew, it seemed to me, was that I wasn't allowed to blame her, any more than you can blame a wild animal for getting out of its cage any way it can.

Even if you've got it caged for its own protection, it'll get out if it gets a chance. Or can make a chance. And that brought up the fascinating question: Just who directed whom, anyway, and in what part?

I was still in love, you see. It was just that when I read the last line of her note, I'd suddenly turned old and tired enough not to want to push myself any farther on.

A long time it took me, getting out of that town. Cars went by, fast and slow, and trucks, before one stopped. I climbed in, and as we pulled away, I looked back down the street, through the rear window, watching it recede.

Where North leaves South, Arkadelphia, boy: City of Arkansas love.

4. Fitzgerald Attends My Fitzgerald Seminar

"That was a pretty wild story you told me last night."

"I didn't know if you heard it all."

"Yes."

"Here's your wallet."

"Thanks."

"It was tangled up in the blanket when I made the bed this morning. Must have slipped out of your pocket, you know?"

"God. I hadn't even missed it. Did you bring me here?"

"Yeah."

"Thanks."

"'S okay. Feeling rough?"

"Kind of."

"Well, I'll leave you. You know where to reach me."

"Thanks for bringing the wallet, Billy."

"Snazzer?"

"Who, uh . . . Maggi."

"You still in bed?"

"Back in, back in bed."

"What did you find to keep you up late in Philadelphia?"

"Hello, Maggi. Uh."

"Have a good time?"

"I was at Hoffman's place. Where are you?"

"New York. You've got my plane ticket."

"Yes. Yes, I guess I do."

"Are you ready to go back?"

"I hired Hoffman."

"So I gathered."

"Will he be okay?"

"I think so."

"I thought maybe you thought we should get Haroldsen."

"It's done now."

"Would Haroldsen be better?"

"More brilliant. I don't know. Billy Hoffman's stable. Rolled with every kind of punch there is. Maybe he's the boy to take it from Skeats, who runs the opera guild. He's one producer. Hoffman will have the auditorium people and the university administration. They're producers, too. And Sato in charge musically, and Debbie in charge morally, sort of, and Ralph and you."

"I made the stodgy choice, then."

"Safe, anyway."

"You've made me feel a little better. I think I'll get up. The plane leaves Kennedy at one thirty. Will you meet me out there?"

"I'd like to stay a day or two here. I called home. Mrs. Warren can hang in, so you won't have the kids around your neck."

"Oh."

"Mrs. Warren says everything's fine."

"Uh-huh. What about your ticket?"

"Why don't you take Hoffman out on it? He ready to go?"

"All right, Maggi. Yes."

Somewhere over Ohio, on the long leg of their flight between New York and Chicago, where they must change again for State City, Rigby Short confides in Billy Hoffman, not quite natty in his only suit, this fantasy, illustrated for Hoffman by the dappled top layer of clouds that he can see, down under the plane at eighteen thousand feet, from his smoking-section window seat:

It is a frequent, not a favorite, fantasy of mine [Professor Short says] that one Tuesday afternoon when I arrive at Building UTBF to teach my graduate seminar in the work of F. Scott Fitzgerald, he is there, a pale, nominally handsome man, waiting for the class to start. He sits, I imagine, facing the desk where I will sit, as if he were to be one of the students, in the next-to-last of the five rows of seats in my small, plain classroom.

"Yeah," Hoffman says. "Yeah, I can see that. What happens?"

Like all repeated personal fantasies, it changes. As it usually goes, two of the dozen graduate students enrolled in the course are already there with Fitzgerald and me—a neatly dressed boy, a tall girl, who came together. We are all three (all four, of course) a little early.

"Hello, Mr. Short," says the boy, whose name is Miles Hubbert, and the girl smiles blandly.

The intruder, no, the auditor. The auditor has placed himself as far away as is tactful from the student pair—not in the farthest seat to the left (left as I will face the class), but one seat in from that final, next-to-last file, in the next-to-back row. I have noticed that students in a small classroom always tend to group toward my right, and I wonder if he didn't realize this when he chose his chair?

I knew who he was at a glance, of course, though my student pair, as well as those who will be along in a few minutes, do not. They are less accustomed than I to pondering his photographs; seeing him, I wonder again if the word *handsome* would have attached itself to this man had he not himself asserted that such was his appearance.

I am speaking, you understand, only of the appearance as pictured. I was sixteen when he died, and never actually saw him, nor is there any reason why I should have. But the man in the photographs has never seemed a handsome one to me. A masked man, rather, even in that young picture where he and Zelda and Scottie are all kicking out their feet in a dance step—the mask is debonair, merry, appealing, saved from smugness only in being somehow tentative, but only ordinarily good looking. The bones that stretch the mask are grave bones, and their marrow is pain. Or is this the aftersight of somebody brought up just after the twenties, on America's Monday morning? No matter. Surely one would rather look like the young Hemingway. As one would rather look like Clark Gable than—could I cite these to my students? hardly—Leslie Howard or Lew Ayres.

(Not, no, that I look like any of these; in my photographs I look bright-eyed and appalled, like a raccoon caught in the headlights of a car.)

As I turn to sit behind my desk, my eyes meet his (not a raccoon's but a wild bird's); he seems to be asking me not to make known who he is. I could not refuse him anything, not today anyway, for he looks ill, incipiently middle-aged, drawn, painfully sober—but less out of place than you might think, sitting in a scratched oak classroom seat with armrest for writing. Yes, he could be just such a curious older visitor as we sometimes have— someone from another department of the university, an out-of-town guest of mine—to the students' incurious human eyes. They will register white shirt and quiet tie, but not the odd cut and wrong color of his business suit. It is the creamy grey flannel, which did not become unfashionable until I myself was in an Ivy League college, and in the shoulder-padded shape of the late Depression. By it I know which period he is in—post-*Crack-Up,* Hollywood, *The Last Tycoon,* Budd Schulberg, Sheilah Graham, Arnold Gingrich. The last month. He is already, fatally, forty-four. The final period.

Immediately I am confused at thinking of him in this way, in his presence, confused because although it feels cold to me, I concede that he might like to contemplate the institutionalization of himself that the division into periods connotes. In the twenty-three years since he died, this way of describing his life as if it were merely a career has become a convenience universally used by teachers and their students. There is not a youngster entering the classroom who could not (and as the most obvious kind of literary information) tell you the order of publication of his books, describe the critical and popular reaction to each one, and tell you how things were going for him when he wrote it. Yes, it would please him; it's a kind of attention he died believing he would never get. Nor even merit.

Yet only six more years—all he'd have had to do would be to get past fifty, as Hemingway and Faulkner did, to see the processing start up: an emotional preface here, an M.A. thesis there, brief learnèd articles, larger ones, fictional treatments, studies at the doctoral level, whole books: an American become subject matter.

Four more students are seating themselves, Petey Luther among them. I wish this particular bright, harsh boy—my best student—had cut today. I hear his impatient voice arguing, and it causes me such alarm that I suddenly consider dismissing the class. Fitzgerald and I could get a beer. Well, no, some coffee. Yes, fine, Mr. Short. Just what he's come here for, the privilege of watching you drop saccharine tablets into bad coffee. And would you offer him a Hershey bar? The condemned man's last meal retasted. (It was a Hershey bar, you know, that Sheilah Graham reports she gave him when he asked for something sweet, sitting there calmly in the Hollywood apart-

ment, reading the *Princeton Alumni Weekly,* thirty seconds before his heart
quit.

(Almonds? That was a prep-school joke: male or female Hershey? I suppose he must have known that one.

(Ah, footnote writer; ah, diseased; ah, ghoulish; ah, Short; what a
grand fellow and wise teacher the world has in you.)

"Will it disturb you if I attend today, Professor?" He asks it softly,
placing his question under the clamor of youthful declaration. His voice is
cultivated, easy, touched with a protective whimsy to make it possible for
me to say he must leave. From this I can guess that it is not my teaching of
his work that he has come to hear, but what the young men and women will
say. How could I not have known it?

"You'll be very welcome."

"But if you'd prefer that I leave?" Painful courtesy, extending the anxiety of his moment, for it would destroy him if I were to say, "Yes, go."

"Please stay."

The students are paying very little attention to this quiet conversation,
for they are having a loud one of their own, a real bickering I know-his-god-
damn-batting-average-better-than-you kind of conversation about George
Orwell's *Burmese Days.* Petey Luther thinks it's the finest novel of the twen-
tieth century. Kevin Candlekirk, tricky debater, is leading the Luther kid
on:

"Don't you think British colonial matters are a little old hat? That's a
topee, of course—Maugham's old pith helmet, Conrad's elegant white cork."

"Pith on you, Candlekirk," says Petey.

"And Orwell was an officer, too, Petey, we'd better salute."

Such classroom manners, and with girls present, have startled my auditor, ending our own small discussion. Only the first boy, Miles Hubbert, has
followed it, and he looks at the visitor rather closely. I have seen Hubbert on
campus several times recently with this same tall, bland girl. She is not his
wife. She has a magnificent figure. She does not belong in my course. She is
vapid.

Hubbert looks at me and back at the pale man so seriously, with such
open curiosity that—no, I'm in charge of this fantasy. I shall not let him
guess. Hubbert, by the way, has three children, back in a Quonset hut
across the river. Before the tall girl, whose name I can't remember (it is still
early in the semester, the third class meeting, but now I do remember: Betty
Cass Collins), before her, Miles Hubbert used to be seen on campus with a

cute, medium-tall girl called Janssy. I enjoy Janssy, who has taken a number of my courses, and would have expected her to be in this one. I feel that Hubbert is to blame for her not having registered for it. He must have changed extramarital girls just at registration time. Since his contribution to a class session is to listen aloofly for two hours, not quite smiling, saying nothing, I resent him just a little. Two hours is a long time to keep things going, and an alert, provocative girl like Janssy can be a great help. Hubbert's new girl (Betty *Cass* Collins; why *Cass,* for Christ's sake?) is as quiet in class as he is; but not *like* he is; the quietness of cows is not like that of foxes.

"Who's asking you to repudiate Orwell?" Kevin Candlekirk cries, still teasing Petey Luther. "All I'm asking you to do, leaving Orwell out of it, is name one first-rate novelist, just one, who was also a first-rate thinker? How about Dostoevski, say, on politics? A czarist! Or religion?"

"All right, he was a bum. Does that make Camus into a bum, too?"

"No, but it doesn't make *The Stranger* into *War and Peace,* either."

"What about Joyce?" Petey's tone isn't really angry, but if you didn't know him, you might think it was.

"I don't think I'd want Joyce to tutor my sister," Kevin says, and they all laugh, even Petey; but not Miles Hubbert, who only smiles slightly. And not the cow girl, who cannot be presumed to have understood.

I glance at the auditor and see that the irreverence both pains and excites him. Joyce was a hero to him.

"We'll wait a minute or two," I announce. Petey and Kevin look at me, startled, I suppose, by the nervousness in my voice. "For the others," I explain. "The rest." My students are not prompt. Nevertheless, all are here, probably, who will be—eight out of the twelve—except for a girl named Eartha Hearn who is characteristically the least prompt and the most eager to be on time. Eartha is due to read us a paper today, and will wheeze in, distraught, apologetic, from a useless run through the parking area, which I will wish she had spared herself. And here she is, hesitating at the door now, panting—smart, disheveled, overweight Eartha—and is that another girl behind her? Yes. Yes, by God, it is: Janssy!

"Pro*fess*or Short," Janssy sings, gaily and all in a rush, pushing past Eartha Hearn and standing, legs apart, on the balls of her feet, pink hand on the desk, leaning at me. "I registered late, okay? I mean, I read *This Side of Flapdeedoodle* and Petey and Kevin told me what you said and they said, and the book for today, so I'm all caught up and I've got a surprise, okay?"

I wince at *Flapdeedoodle*. I cannot see past her to know whether he does. She blocks the view with soft sweater and open, corduroy overcoat, and I can't speak. I have always liked to look at Janssy, and whether she knows this or not, she does know that I'll agree to let her join the course. I nod, cannot speak, and try again to look past her at the pale man.

"But you have to sign my slip," she scolds and smiles and leans, all high coquetry, as a girl might demanding a kiss in public.

"After. After class, Janssy," I say, and she tilts her head, executes a ravishment, and slips into a seat between Kevin and Petey, ignoring the vacant one by Eartha Hearn, with whom she came in. Nor does she so much as look at Miles Hubbert, her former—what? boyfriend, lover, escort? Hubbert's face registers nothing more than its usual amused caginess.

"Let's settle down, please," I say, more crossly than I mean to. "We have a lot to cover." Kevin's hand goes up. "Yes, Kevin?"

"Something from last week," he says.

"All right."

"Just for perspective. We were talking about *This Side of Paradise* as if it were an undergraduate's novel," he says. "As if Fitzgerald were some kind of boy wonder. But look, he was twenty-three. Grad-student age, not a college kid. He'd been in the army already. He'd even written one book and had it turned down."

"Yes," I say. "Of course. But you realize this was the same book, don't you? With a new title and some further revisions. A good deal of it *had* been done while he was still at Princeton. As we were saying, portions of it had actually been printed several years earlier in the *Nassau Lit.*"

"So much the worse, though, wouldn't you say? I mean, can you imagine a real boy genius like Rimbaud having the kind of ego where you're going to reuse everything you ever wrote, instead of the other kind of ego where you keep tearing it all up, trying for something perfect?"

"He didn't need Edmund Wilson," Petey Luther says. Apparently he and Kevin have been rehearsing this. "He needed a wastebasket."

I hardly dare look at the visitor, but I do. He seems—oh, quizzical, I suppose. Realizing that the young are never generous in making allowances for youth. Very well, then, I will be tactically cautious in opposing class opinion for the moment; I will wait for a better opening, later in the period.

Still, I must establish that concession is not to be my posture at any point today, so I say: "You know, a novel's a good deal harder to throw away than a poem. It's several years of work, not just a couple of days. And remember the form itself, the novel as an American expression shaped to the times, wasn't all laid out for him as it might be for one of you. It still had to be developed. It had to go through the hands of men like, well, like Fitzgerald himself, as he'd become by the time he was writing *Gatsby*."

"Anyway, Petey," Janssy says. "Different people mature at different ages."

"You were speaking of perspective," I say. "Perhaps it would be better to come back to this point later in the course."

"Rimbaud was probably a boring old man at twenty-three," the girl insists, and this is apparently for Miles Hubbert to hear. "Who'd want him?"

"Let's get to today's work," I say, but then I'm reluctant to say what comes next. I know the visitor is going to be dismayed, but there's no way around it. I avoid looking at him and stare at beauteously insipid Betty *Cass* Collins. There are two sorts of girl one looks at in class. The Janssys, whom one enjoys intensely and tenderly forgets. And the Betty Casses, whom one sees with low-key irritation, but whose coeducated bodies and sorority group-photo faces stay on in the mind. You feel you could do anything with such a girl, not because she seems sensual but because she seems stupid. Bluntly with bland blonde blended—yes, Short, sure. And sometimes you realize that an aura of such stupidity is something they wear to attract, like perfume.

I continue to stare at her and say what I have to say:

"Today, as you know, we will discuss the second book, the short-story collection *Flappers and Philosophers*." But neither the clear-skinned alphabeta face nor plump knees of Miss Collins can hold my eyes away from his: They are stricken, the bird shot down. Why, on his only visit, must we talk about the least of his books? Why can we not be celebrating the great, achieved works, *Gatsby* and *Tender Is the Night*? Or discussing the tragic self-appraisal of *The Crack-Up*, in which everything is revealed but the one essential thing: How does genius survive the remorseless plots it makes against its own fulfillment? Hell, *The Last Tycoon*, or even one of the other story collections.

"Yes, Eartha?" It is odd about this bright girl, with her good mind and bad teeth, that she alone raises her hand when she wishes to speak and will not begin until recognized. The rest in my undisciplined class push their way in and out of discussion at will. New York subway manners.

"Yes, Eartha?" But Eartha Hearn is from New York, and is polite; Janssy is from a little town in Oklahoma, and steps on my feet whenever she feels it's her stop. Petey and Kevin are New York boys, true to type. Miles

Hubbert? The East. I do not know where cow girls come from, only that any time one goes away, another appears, mirages in the middle distance of the wasteland.

"Yes, Eartha?" There are others in the class, as indicated, but let them stay out of focus; they will get their C-pluses and B-minuses when the time comes. "Yes?"

Have I said, "Yes, Eartha?" once, or four times? Does the visitor sympathize with my uncertainty or hold it in distaste? But I'm a scrapper, Scott, really I am, capable of rudeness, too—no. Ten years of practicing the false tolerance that covers up uncertainty, to obtain the social and financial comfort of tenure, stand between this present and my scrapping days. I have become a fraud, who risks nothing but a hopeful good humor, practicing a restraint that permits many impositions.

"Professor Short, about my seminar paper." Oh, boy. Here we go. Eartha's excuse for not having done on time the paper she's supposed to read now. Some unanswerably drab, female medical excuse, I suppose. And then what shall I do with two hours? Lecture? Without notes? Well, maybe—yes; yes, it could be best at that. For me to lecture spontaneously, out of the feeling I have, letting the words and ideas come as they may—this is something I haven't done since my instructor days when, sometimes, I was so full of a subject (yes, in a sophomore-lit. survey, even there, talking about *Tom Jones* or *The Scarlet Letter*!)—so full of it, notes would have been too confining, a hindrance. Hooray for menses, I will save the day.

"Professor, we made a change," Eartha says. "If it's all right?"

I frown, insincerely.

"I mean, Janssy wanted to share the paper with me. So I have a general paper on the book, and she'd like to discuss one particular story in it, afterward. I mean, since she's just joined the course? And . . ."

Oh, all right. Let Janssy save the day, then. The girl's always been a dervish for extra work. All right. I find a smile somewhere and present it. "Which story will it be, Janssy? 'Bernice Bobs Her Hair'?" The best story in the book in many ways; the auditor has a smile, too. But Janssy shakes her head. " 'The Cut Glass Bowl'?" A failure, but interesting for its ambition. Janssy smiles, and shapes a "no" with her shiny lips. Three guesses, is that what we're playing? "Well, 'The Ice Palace' is a good story, and 'Benediction' very interesting indeed—one of those two?"

" 'The Offshore Pirate,' Mr. Short," Janssy says.

"For heaven's sake, why?" There are worse stories in the book perhaps, one or two worse anyway.

"I think I can show it's important," Janssy says.

"Oh, come on, Janssy," says Petey Luther.

(There's no reason you should know that story. It's about a flirt on a yacht, which is boarded by a young man who represents himself as a lower-class rebel and fugitive, bringing along his own jazz band. And woos the discontented heiress, and finally discloses that he's top-drawer eligible, just as she is—oh, hell, it's preposterously bad.)

The auditor's face is with me all the way, and yet resigned, disturbed by and resigned to whatever bumptions the young care to inflict upon us.

I nod to Eartha Hearn that she is to go ahead.

Her paper, which she reads carefully and not quite loudly enough, is what I've come to expect from her: thoroughly researched, critically conventional, a dull A. Yet last week I hoped: so often, when one is finished talking over with a student what he or she means to do in a paper, one does hope. The things they say they want to write about ("Perhaps try to get at what the flapper personality really was, was it different from a flirt?") sound so much more interesting than what they actually come back with ("Malcolm Cowley assures us that it was the flapper stories that made Fitzgerald's reputation as a popular writer.")

It takes Eartha forty-five minutes to read this scintillating stuff, and I must pay close attention to distinguish the words from the mumbles, so I miss the detailed reactions of the visitor. I can sum them up, though: beginning with intense interest, next twitchiness, then a suppressed desire to interrupt and correct something—God, I wish I knew what—then a wandering of attention. By the time Eartha's paper is done (". . . leads us to anticipate the recurrence of these themes in later works"), he has actually, quietly, gently, gone to sleep.

Petey Luther's opening observation to Eartha wakes him up:

"You say there are two good stories in the book. I disagree."

"Hang on," says Kevin. "Petey disagrees."

"What is your disagreement?" I ask, straight-man Short, patsy of a bright grad-student's dreams.

"I don't think there are any good stories in the book. I like it even less than *This Side of Paradise*. Well, why? First of all, the book is full of race prejudice. I don't just mean the word *nigger*—I mean that Fitzgerald was so taken in by Alabamans at the time, he was actually trying to be like one. Second point: There's an absolutely inverse relation between how serious a story tries to be and how successful it is. When he gets serious, he's embarrassing; or obviously tricky; or sententious. When he's not serious, he may be slick, but he's still a snob, and a would-be Alabama dandy at that. Now—"

"The man was desperately in love, for God's sake," Kevin says.

I am shivering.

"May I finish, please, Kevin? Thank you, Kevin. Now it's true that two of the lighter pieces come close to being good stories. And in fact each of them—'Bernice Bobs Her Hair' and 'The Ice Palace'—has one beautiful line in it. Here's what I think is significant: Each one of those lines is spoken by the chief female character, after a scene of catharsis. Right?"

I try to wrench myself out of my interior trembling to fit into the first role that occurs to me, and one I never play very well, the sarcastic teacher: "And what two special lines do you find up to your exquisite standards?"

The auditor's eyes are wild; the bird was shot down but only wounded, and is now crouching, hoping the dog will pass its hiding place.

Petey Luther is opening his book:

"All right. One: in 'The Ice Palace.' Sally Carrol has been driven back down South by the ice and snow and the ungracious northerners. And this cracker, or whatever he is, comes driving up to take her swimming, and he asks her: 'What you doin'?' And she says, 'Eatin' green peach. 'Spect to die any minute.' All right. Now that's a beautiful line. 'Eatin' green peach. 'Spect to die any minute.' All right? Now in 'Bernice,' Marjorie has conned her cousin into having all her hair cut off, thus ruining Bernice's appearance. So Bernice sneaks in and cuts off Marjorie's hair in her sleep—I mean, it's a real *Rape of the Lock,* okay? Bernice is on her way out of town, now, and as she passes this boy's house, she throws Marjorie's hair up on the kid's porch. Listen to this: ' "Huh!" she giggled wildly. "Scalp the selfish thing." ' That's a beautiful line, too. Why? Each of them expresses perfectly, without Fitzgerald having to explain it, the return of self-assurance a little tease would feel after she's failed to measure up to a situation."

Miles Hubbert laughs out loud. Miles Hubbert!

"Let me answer him, Mr. Short," Kevin says, grinning excitedly. "May I?" This is not really courtesy, but only a device for assuring himself the floor.

"Go ahead." I pin my wings on the slippery shoulders of Kevin Candlekirk. The auditor looks at him gratefully.

"I've heard Petey make many absurd statements," Kevin says. "But this one's got them all beat. He's asserting that somehow, very nearly out of context, a line—that is, a moment—in fiction can be beautiful, more or less by itself. He discounts the author's preparation for it, as if aptness were a characteristic of the line regardless of its function in the story."

"You're willfully misunderstanding me—"

"May I finish, Petey? Thank you, Petey. I mean, it's like asking us to believe that 'Eatin' green peach. 'Spect to die any minute' could go into the language, like a great epigram. Fitzgerald never wrote a great epigram in his life. In fact every time he thinks he's got one, and tries to slip in one of those polished, thought-out phrases, he ruins his tone—like, look, how could anything but a really sharp story survive an opening line like the one to 'The Ice Palace'?" He flips pages. I want to yell at him that this isn't necessary, but can't. He reads: " 'The sunlight dripped over the house like golden paint over an art jar, and the freckling shadows here and there only intensified the rigor of the bath of light.' That's not part of the story. That's part of the notebook."

"You're not disagreeing with me, you're talking about something else," Petey says.

"But the lines you picked are wonderful because they're wonderful character lines. How can you have a wonderful character line if there isn't a wonderful character to speak it, and therefore a pretty successful story?"

"*I'll* speak about those stories," I suddenly hear myself cry out above the opening cough of what would have been Petey's next contention, and the room goes quiet. I am appalled. What was I going to do? Claim these stories are great works? I mutter: "After, after Janssy reads her paper on what story, what story? 'The Offshore Pirate'?"

A boy might have a difficult moment trying to follow an outburst like mine—not a girl; a girl's sympathies are seldom general, and Janssy is quite ready, composed. Nerved up. She improvises a little preamble: "Petey calls Fitzgerald's flappers 'teases.' I suggest there's no way of knowing whether that's true or not. We don't know what the word *kiss* stands for in those stories. Anyway, what I want to show is that his understanding of immature relationships wasn't one-sided." She begins to read in a bold, take-charge voice, and the auditor's face grows bright with hope:

> If Fitzgerald exposes the heartlessness of shallow flirtation as
> practiced by his flappers, he also provides one of the most telling
> examples in literature of the male counterpart, the snow job. "The
> Offshore Pirate" is a story about a snow job so elaborate that we are
> actually disappointed to find out that the boy, who has been pre-
> tending to be a penniless wild man abducting the rich girl, is
> nothing but a nice, safe rich boy, after all. He was fascinating,
> sympathetic, worth our attention in the rebel character he assumed
> to snow the girl; he is unbelievably vapid, a perfect creep in fact,
> when we find out what he's really like, and no more than the flap-
> per deserves. So well do these little morons deserve each
> other . . .

I could groan aloud. She is after Hubbert, of course, though it's the
cow girl who's blushing. By God, Betty *Cass* really is embarrassed, and if I
could only explain the background to the situation somehow ("You see,
Scott, this one girl . . ."), he might be very interested. (There's no way. The
students caught the teacher passing notes?)
Janssy reads on.

> The girl in the story is not even a true flapper. She's not like
> Marjorie or Sally Carrol or Bernice, who will at least put some
> energy into their flirting. Ardita is passive, selfish . . .

Whispering now. Betty Cass Collins to Miles Hubbert. Hubbert back
to Collins, nodding. Recomposed, and with a dazzling smile for me in lieu
of any spoken apology, Miss Collins simply stands, gathers her books, and
walks easily out of the room and away. Mr. Hubbert? He's grinning now; I
cannot say how comfortably, as Janssy, prim and grim and just a little
shaken, reads on.

And, in fact, it is Hubbert's hand that goes lazily up the moment she is
done reading. Should I ignore him, this first time he has deigned to speak? I
look at the auditor, as if for permission, and see that he has understood and
is fascinated.

"Yes, Mr. Hubbert?"

"Well, to borrow Petey's phrase, surely this is an example of willful
misunderstanding," he says mildly. "The story is simply pleasant, isn't it?

This is taking a joke seriously. That is, the peg's round, but I think the hole is pretty square. . . ."

"Hubbert!" I yell, furious. "What the hell makes you think you can use offensive language in my classroom?"

He looks at me amazed. "I'm sorry, sir. What did I say?"

I look at the auditor—he, too seems amazed. I look at Petey and Kevin and Eartha Hearn. They are all staring. Even Janssy is staring. Is it possible no obscenity was intended in his talk of hole and peg? It is too late to consider the possibility that Hubbert's was the first sensible comment in a twisted hour. I force my anger up a notch and rage on. "This has been the most extraordinary, stupid collection of misreadings, misinterpretations, snideness, and bad criticism I ever heard!" I shout. "How can you people be in graduate school and not have learned to read yet? Well? Do you think I'm asking rhetorically? I want answers, I may even want nine answers in writing. Well?"

Kevin's hand goes up. This time it's neither manners nor strategy but sheer precaution. He will get them out of having to write extra papers if he can.

"Perhaps these stories mean something different to your generation than they do to ours, Professor Short," he says, his tone pure placation. He is offering me an out for an unwise loss of temper, if I'll take it. The auditor (oh yes, I can tell) wants very much for me to take it. But I must refuse him now.

"Listen," I say, feeling triumph. For it is the exposed, the angry, the injudicious teacher railing at his students who is giving them something of himself. "Listen you're talking like a miserable publisher. *Generation!* That's not a critic's word. That's a word to sell books, and I hate it. Do you think I'm his age? Where's your arithmetic? I was born the year this book was published, and he was twenty-four. My father's his age, for God's sake.

"Listen, one winter in prep school, in the middle nineteen thirties, long after his name had gone dim—when I was fourteen and Sinclair Lewis was about the only writer I'd ever heard of—I was caught smoking and given a punishment. The punishment was called Five O'clock Study Hall. It was for stupid kids who weren't passing, so that they'd spend more time getting their work prepared. They had to study there, under supervision, in the school library. But I was never behind in my work. I was a disciplinary case. So the man in charge would let me read.

"When I'd finished all the Lewis, and whatever they had of Logan Pearsall Smith, I found Fitzgerald on the shelves, all green cloth and dusty. Three books were what they had: *Tales of the Jazz Age, Flappers and Philosophers,* and *The Great Gatsby.* I read *Tales* first. God, how I remember sitting in that dim room, lost in a big leather chair, prevented from putting on my uniform to play short-stop for the school baseball team, which was my chief athletic skill. I'd been looking forward to it all year—the sting of the ball when you go left and get the hard grounder, one hand, and the way your arm snaps when you throw hard to first. That feeling of being part of something with the other players, and the smell of clean uniforms on game day. And there I was, off the team, lost among the stupid and the slow, and I read a story called 'The Jelly-Bean.' I was too frail and snotty a little short-stop to let myself cry, but I sat there staring across the room when I'd finished that story with a stare so sad that the man in charge came in alarm to ask me what was wrong.

"I don't know if 'The Jelly-Bean' is a good or bad story. I only know that it still moves me to reread it—and it's Alabama, Luther, Alabama. And I know that if you can't keep yourself open to being moved that way by literature, then you are doing yourselves an unbearably grave disservice in committing your lives to the study and teaching of it. There's no critic worth reading or teacher worth hearing who's not a lover."

(I falter. There is a writer Petey loves, George Orwell. I shift my attack to clever Kevin. One does not speak successfully to a class, only to a student in it, letting the others overhear.)

"Let me tell you something foolish: As a boy, there in the prep-school library, I scorned reading *The Great Gatsby.* The title, I thought at fourteen, implied that it would be about schoolboys—about a particular one with a grandiloquent nickname, as in Owen Johnson's Lawrenceville stories, which you've probably never heard of. But we do read that way, don't we, even titles, self-centering the world upon ourselves?

"In 1936, eleven years after its publication, I do not believe there was anyone on the faculty of a famous prep school who would have told me *The Great Gatsby* was worth reading.

"So I passed it by. And by the time I knew my error, couldn't find a copy for seven years. Out of print. Unavailable. *Gatsby* out of print! It was on a troopship going to Africa in 1943 that I did read *The Great Gatsby.* I borrowed it from the company clerk, read it once, straight through, missing a meal and a roll call or whatever the hell they called it, wouldn't get up and fall in with the book unfinished, and told the sergeant who came looking for me to screw himself. Got myself on K.P. that way, and took the book with me, and started through it again in the nauseous galleys where we washed trays and cups and slopped out food—and was the only man on K.P. who didn't get seasick. I wasn't paying enough attention to the galley and the sea to be sick. Word by word I read it, page by page, moved by everything: '. . . boats against the current, borne back ceaselessly into the past.' Is that out of the notebook, Kevin? No, boy. That's out of the blood in his veins.

"I was wounded. I suppose you all know that, and it doesn't matter. I cannot tell you how bitter I was when I learned that, the way my shin was shattered, I would never be quite a whole man again, but I can tell you when it started not to matter. That was when a friend brought a copy of *Tender Is the Night* to me in the hospital in Italy. He was not even a particularly literary friend, but he knew I'd been searching for that book, through the bookstores of Casablanca and Algiers and Palermo and Naples—for over a year, every time I got to a city big enough to have bookstores with a few titles in English. It was an Armed Forces edition, paperbound, with the cover torn off, and Jonesy told me he'd traded a souvenir Luger for it, though he hadn't cared for the book himself when he tried to read it. I won't try to describe completely how it affected me then, but it was still affecting me two years later when I married my first wife, taking her for the image of Nicole. I can't—I can't get away from that book. My second wife, Mrs. Short, is more of a Rosemary, I suppose . . ."

I am starting to maunder. Maggi is not really a Rosemary. I catch myself up, and finish quickly, not very pointedly:

"Shall we be biographers? There are two events in literary history that have made me swallow tears. One was the death of Dostoevski's daughter, learning of it first and unexpectedly while I was reading through his letters; and the other the death of Zelda Fitzgerald by fire. That happened late in the forties, when the asylum she was committed to burned down. I was working for a newspaper on Long Island then, hadn't decided on graduate school, and you'd been dead—excuse me, he'd been dead. Long years. The telegraph editor took it off the AP wire and brought the copy to my desk. . . ."

No, I am not teaching, nor even railing any longer. I am only pleading, and have said nothing to them, after all. But to him, perhaps—I have always wished there was some way I could let him know.

"Dismissed," I yell at the class. "Dismissed. Get out of here."

But my fantasy is not always that easy to end. There are various endings, to fit the different moods in which I let it play.

The abrupt one I have quoted is the one that satisfies me best.

In another, I look for him when I am finished speaking, but he has disappeared, evaporated in disappointment before he could hear me out.

Then there is one in which he goes off with Janssy, whom, of course, I love in a way which is remote only because it has to be. Thus, between them, he and she tear me neatly in two.

But in the worst of my endings, he is still there, apparently waiting for me to pack up my books, when Janssy comes to the desk to get her slip signed. While I am diverted, I can tell only that he has strolled across the room. And when she steps aside, thanking me, I realize that he is walking off, smiling, ignoring all the rest of us, friendly and at ease with Miles Hubbert.

The plane flies on, over the rotating earth, which has already spun State City east of Saturday's sun, spun Denver east, Los Angeles, given a taste of summer noon to Anchorage, is moving the office workers of Honolulu now toward coffee-break time. Away from the city, out in the pineapple fields, the great-grandnieces and grandnephews of Polynesian kings are eating lunch already.

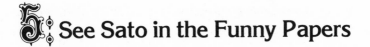

5 : See Sato in the Funny Papers

To Sato Murasaki, as to Debbie Dieter Haas, art is grown-ups' play.

Like Babe Ruth, both would confess to some continuing astonishment at being paid to have fun. Naïfs like the Babe, they are sort of sorry, but lack the comprehension to feel real sympathy, for those who find creation agonizing. Exuberance is Sato's way with an orchestra, Debbie's at the easel.

Certain athletes paid to play football or baseball think of relaxation as a game of pool or round of golf. Sato, when he has time to while away, likes to draw in pen and ink and to practice calligraphy. Debbie, pausing in her studio, fools endlessly with a harpsichord, at home sings *lieder* in a harsh, true voice, and has written songs. They sound like bad Kurt Weill, she will concede with a fine big laugh, but they are not meant to be performed or published. They are for recreation, though she may spend weeks working one out before she sets it aside.

Debbie and Sato have discovered one another almost instantly, not as a couple—that one is an early-middle-aged man, the other a somewhat older woman, is almost irrelevant to their games. What they are is fellow players, like new friends equally matched and equally enthusiastic at tennis or chess, who want to play together every chance they get.

Yet to call our conductor and designer well matched is not to say they are similar: Sato is inventive, faceted, light. Debbie is more scrupulous and more thorough. Sometimes Debbie will absorb, absorb, contributing mostly her happy concentration of attention to the game.

To be an audience is grown-ups' play, too, for those who will have it so, and if there be transcendental possibilities, it is possible that some pass as truly into ecstasy from exhilaration as do others from high, holy seriousness.

I have been thinking, Debbie, that a life, after all, is only one of those solemn comic strips we all love secretly, except that instead of a handsome doctor or soldier or meddling old woman to make sure it comes out all right we have natural irony, to make sure it comes out oddly. So you could draw, and I could letter—my calligraphy is disgraceful for a Japanese, but all right for an American, I believe.

So you must draw, for 1932, when we begin, a very thin hobo named Red. Have him sit with three others on stumps in front of a whitewashed chicken house on a California prune and walnut ranch. They sleep in the chicken house with their bedrolls. They are helping Sato's stepfather with the harvest. Give them a fire to cook on, and show small-boy Sato hiding to watch them cook. Red has a cigar-box banjo. Can you leave me space to letter what he sings?

The natural irony is that Sato is curious about fathers, and believes Red, the hobo, to be singing about his own.

Golden Grain was tobacco, which came in small cloth sacks. Bull Durham tobacco still comes in such sacks, I believe.

Using Golden Grain, Sato's mother rolls twenty cigarettes each morning for Sato's stepfather. She has been an artist's model, but you would make her fingers longer and more beautiful than any artist has ever drawn them before. She finishes the twenty perfect white tubes, of paper and tobacco, and Sato's stepfather puts them in a pigskin case, with his four initials on it in silver. *O.O.G.J.* He has a flask to match, which his parents gave him along with the case when they sent him from the East to go to Stanford University. He has strong hands, with blond hairs upon the fingers.

There is no way to show that his voice is a strong, caressing baritone, so I would letter another speech, aside:

I LOVE YOUR STEPFATHER'S VOICE, SATO.

LET'S GO, KIDS. IF THE OLD MAN KNEW I WAS GOING TO VOTE FOR ROOSEVELT TODAY, HE'D RECRUIT A FIRING SQUAD FROM THE NEW YORK RACQUET CLUB, AND THEY'D SHOOT ME DOWN WITH THEIR PURDY DOUBLES.

IN THE SQUASH COURT?

WEARING WHITES. READY, AIM, SERVE.

WE HAD LUNCH AT THAT CLUB, SATO, BUT YOU WOULDN'T REMEMBER, WHEN WE WENT TO NEW YORK TO MEET OOG'S PARENTS.

DID WE, MOTHER?

She is so beautiful. Today Sato plays squash at that club sometimes, but that is a much later installment and a more ordinary irony. Sato's stepfather has his own Purdy double. It is beautiful, too, in its way. Sometimes he will shoot ducks for them when food is short, cinnamon teal that come off the shallow lake in front of Oog's dog, in the tule weeds. Small ducks. They are beautiful, too. And the dog as well.

FETCH, JIMBO, FETCH. GOOD BOY.

Now I would have to letter a synopsis, "What has happened in our story so far":

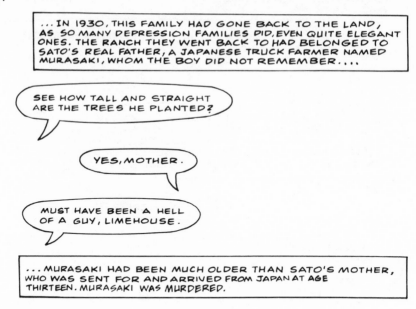

> ...IN 1930, THIS FAMILY HAD GONE BACK TO THE LAND, AS SO MANY DEPRESSION FAMILIES DID, EVEN QUITE ELEGANT ONES. THE RANCH THEY WENT BACK TO HAD BELONGED TO SATO'S REAL FATHER, A JAPANESE TRUCK FARMER NAMED MURASAKI, WHOM THE BOY DID NOT REMEMBER....

> SEE HOW TALL AND STRAIGHT ARE THE TREES HE PLANTED?

> YES, MOTHER.

> MUST HAVE BEEN A HELL OF A GUY, LIMEHOUSE.

> ...MURASAKI HAD BEEN MUCH OLDER THAN SATO'S MOTHER, WHO WAS SENT FOR AND ARRIVED FROM JAPAN AT AGE THIRTEEN. MURASAKI WAS MURDERED.

I believe.

> THE YOUNG GIRL-WIDOW RENTED OUT THE RANCH, AND TOOK BABY SATO TO SAN FRANCISCO, WHERE THEY LIVED WITH HER BROTHER-IN-LAW, A COMMERCIAL ARTIST, AND SHE BECAME A MODEL....

> THERE IS NO SHAME IN THIS. IT IS A PROFESSION, LITTLE SISTER.

> BROTHER OF MY HUSBAND, I OBEY.

I think she was very popular, young, exotic, and exquisite. In one painting she had eight arms, like the Buddha, but even with eight chances the painter did not get the hands right. It was an innocent art in San Francisco in the 1920s.

> SATO'S STEPFATHER HAD A BLOND MUSTACHE, A STRONG NOSE, A BASQUE BERET, AND A SET OF STONE CHISELS. HIS NAME WAS ORRIN OWENS GANSEVOORT JAY.

CALL ME OOG.

HE HAD BEEN KIDNAPPED AS A CHILD AND RETURNED AFTER RANSOM WAS PAID. HIS PARENTS COULD NEVER AGAIN TRUST AN OFFSPRING WHO CAUSED THEM THE WORRY AND COST THEM THE MONEY OF HAVING BEEN KIDNAPPED.

I believe. He was never serious as a sculptor, and meant to study architecture. He was a man's man all his life, perfectly created of received male wisdom, which he transmitted to Sato with such easy conviction that it came out as precept rather than cliché:

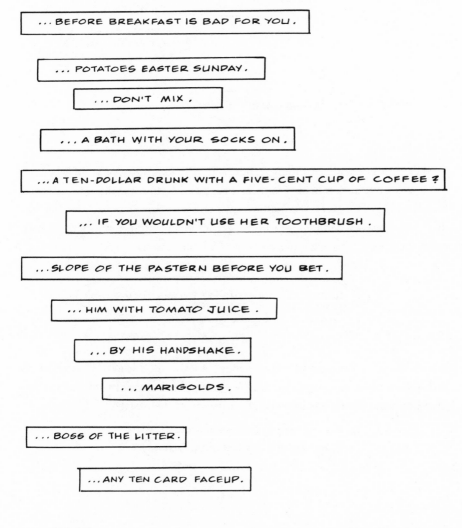

... BEFORE BREAKFAST IS BAD FOR YOU.

... POTATOES EASTER SUNDAY.

... DON'T MIX.

... A BATH WITH YOUR SOCKS ON.

... A TEN-DOLLAR DRUNK WITH A FIVE-CENT CUP OF COFFEE?

... IF YOU WOULDN'T USE HER TOOTHBRUSH.

... SLOPE OF THE PASTERN BEFORE YOU BET.

... HIM WITH TOMATO JUICE.

... BY HIS HANDSHAKE.

... MARIGOLDS.

... BOSS OF THE LITTER.

... ANY TEN CARD FACEUP.

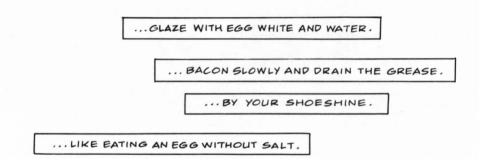

...GLAZE WITH EGG WHITE AND WATER.

... BACON SLOWLY AND DRAIN THE GREASE.

...BY YOUR SHOESHINE.

...LIKE EATING AN EGG WITHOUT SALT.

Oog is certainly welcome to ten-year-old Sato's part of Murasaki's ranch, and to anything else the boy has.

SATO, THAT VIOLIN IS BIGGER THAN YOU ARE.

OH, THANK YOU.

OH, YOU'RE WELCOME, KIDDO.

Sato is not really a prodigy, but will still look ten years old when he graduates from high school. From the prune and walnut ranch, Sato rides the red Trailways bus every Wednesday, two hours to San Francisco, for his violin lesson. Even when Oog can no longer afford to hire the migrants to help with the harvest, he finds money to pay for the lessons.

SOLD THE DRAFTING SET, LIMEHOUSE. I NEVER USE IT ANYMORE.

That year, Red and the other hobos come by. Red is even thinner, with a thin beard over his ragged collar. Oog, with his beautiful wife and twelve-year-old Sato, are trying to make the harvest by themselves.

COME ON, OOG. LET US GIVE YOU A HAND.

YOU DON'T HAVE TO PAY US. JUST LET US SLEEP IN THE CHICKEN HOUSE, LIKE BEFORE, AND GIVE US SOMETHING TO EAT.

YEAH, OOG. LOOK, SATO'S SUPPOSED TO BE IN SCHOOL.

They like Oog. Everybody likes Oog. They make wine with the prunes that year, many gallons of it, and one evening when the walnuts are in, Oog is sitting on top of the chicken house, singing soldier songs from the First World War, blond and strong and wonderful.

♪ THAT'S THE WRONG WAY TO TICKLE MARY... ♫

The livelier people in the town nearby, where Sato goes to school, treasure his mother, come to Sato's recitals, and Oog is very, very popular with them. They want him at their parties, and often he goes, and is sometimes wretchedly ill next day from hangovers, I believe. But everybody has a good time with Oog when he is drinking, Lady too, who has some talent for gaiety.

It is only that the prunes and walnuts do not support very well a life of horses and tattersall vests and large, European dogs.

I DON'T THINK WE CAN REPLACE JIMBO, LIMEHOUSE, BUT I'LL SURE MISS HIM.

SO WILL SATO.

OKAY. I'LL GET THE KID SOME KIND OF DOG. OKAY BY YOU, SATO?

OOG.

Once the phone rings at night. Some men from the East have come to play polo on the peninsula. One of them is sick, and the others want Oog to play. He has the polo boots and white breeches and helmet, still.

LIMEHOUSE, GOT ENOUGH MONEY IN THAT TEAPOT FOR BUS FARE, MY LADY?

GET YOUR THINGS READY, OOG.

She looks at Sato, and while Oog is busy, Sato slips away to get some money from a coffee can in his room without Oog knowing, money the boy has earned gardening. Sato is very proud to do this, and Oog goes to play polo.

He comes back, three days later, with another very virile, self-confident man, in a varnished wood station wagon, pulling a blue horse trailer.

They laugh a lot as they unload two polo ponies at the little ranch, and some mallets and balls and a saddle. The driver says Oog must practice now, and is in a hurry to leave. He gets quickly back into his station wagon and drives off.

Ten days later a green trailer comes behind a Packard convertible, with a different driver. There are reproaches. Sato stops practicing his violin and goes to the window to watch and listen. Oog is laughing it off and overwhelming the new man with charm. The man goes away, taking the beautiful, small horses on which Oog would have taught Sato to ride.

TOMMY WAS A NUT TO THINK WE COULD GET AWAY WITH IT.

THEY WERE NOT TOMMY'S HORSES TO LEAVE WITH YOU?

SO THE GENTLEMAN SAID.

WILL THERE BE TROUBLE?

In high school, Sato runs cross-country and hurdles, plays the piano at assemblies, and never asks for a date. There are no Japanese in town, except his mother and himself.

Several girls in high school are nice to Sato, but he does not know what they would say if he asked one for a date.

Oog has a high temper, and Lady does not like him to get into fights.

The next episode must be censored, not because of its unsuitability but because it is impossible to understand how it was done. *Why* is more apparent, though odd or at least illogical, referring to the foregoing exchange between Sato and Oog. The stepfather takes the situation harder than the boy, and retaliates. He does this by seducing the town's most cherished virgin, a high school beauty named Kitty Hamilton. Kitty is the school's other pianist, and accompanies Sato at his recitals.

They do not date, but work together often, sometimes very hard. Oog apparently just makes up his mind that to seduce Kitty will pay back the town, as mirrored by the school, for prejudice against Sato. What is illogical about this is that Oog's principles would never permit him to tell anyone about it. One afternoon he takes Kitty for a drive around the lake, charms her into copulating with him, who can guess how?, and drops her off at home afterward, with a kiss and a laugh to remember.

Sato, of course, does not learn of this from Oog, nor from Lady, who is uninformed and passive about Oog's infidelities, not that there are many, but from Kitty Hamilton.

They walk in the walnut grove, in bars of sunlight and bars of shade.

MY REAL FATHER PLANTED THESE TREES.

IT'S QUIET HERE, AND AWAY.

I COME HERE TO THINK. IT MAKES ME FEEL STRONG.

SATO?

YES, KITTY?

WELL, THERE'S SOMETHING I'VE GOT TO TELL SOMEONE. I DON'T HAVE ANYONE TO TELL THIS TO, SATO... WHAT KIND OF A MAN IS YOUR STEPFATHER, REALLY?

She tells him slowly, talking around and around what happened, until he understands clearly. He wonders if she is going to cry, but she doesn't. She seems more puzzled than hurt.

SATO GRADUATES IN 1940 AND GOES TO SAN FRANCISCO TO FIND A JOB TO EARN MONEY FOR HIS KEEP AT CONSERVATORY, WHERE HE WILL HAVE A SCHOLARSHIP, AND TO LEARN IRONY....

...WHEN HE LEAVES THE RANCH HOUSE, OOG BEGINS TO REBUILD IT. OOG IS A FINE CRAFTSMAN, AND HIS PLANS FOR REDWOOD WINGS, LARGE WINDOWS, AND A FLOWER GARDEN INSIDE AND OUT FOR LADY ARE ELEGANT....

...OOG'S PARENTS WILL NOT SEND MONEY, BUT AGREE TO PAY THE BILLS FOR MATERIALS.

IT WAS THE END OF THE DECADE, AND WAR HAD BEGUN IN EUROPE.

But we would not draw the tanks and roaring guns and Stukas. We would draw instead a bureaucrat in Washington who is already planning relocation camps for people of Japanese birth, to one of which Lady will be removed. He works in his shirt-sleeves:

THERE, THAT'LL TAKE CARE OF 'EM IF IT *DOES* HAPPEN.

And as we are now seeing a little of what will happen after tonight's episode, we may also draw Buck Sergeant Sato, in combat uniform of the Nisei unit in Italy, almost four years later, bayoneting an octopus to remove it from the stand of a Neapolitan fishmonger, for his infantry squad to feast on.

BANZAI! OCTOPUS!

GO FOR BROKE, SATO!

I THINK IT'S A SQUID.

And finally we would draw Oog, or Lieutenant Commander Orrin O. G. Jay, a PT-boat captain, on leave in Melbourne. But I do not know what he is saying to his new, Australian wife. But sometimes even Oog the powerful must miss his lovely, quiet, gay Limehouse Lady. All I know is what Lady says to Sato, on a day when he visits her in that dreadful camp.

Sato and Oog will not meet again. Can it be so late at night?

TO BE CONTINUED...

2.

Sunday-morning electronics in State City.

Maury Jackstone, *Second Poker Player,* isn't black; nobody is. Maury's skin tone is a dark amber in the summer. He has just finished turning a large Zenith color-television set upside down.

He takes out the eight screws that hold the protective metal grid to the bottom, and exposes the maze of tiny, interconnected parts that covers the underside of the chassis.

A middle-aged woman hovers at a respectful distance. She is a regular customer of Maury's ReeTeeVeePair, the fastest, best, and cheapest ree-teeveepair in town.

Maury's blue-eyed, blonde wife Karen watches, too; her skin tone is about that of vanilla pudding. It wasn't necessary that she come along on this particular service call to reassure the customer, but Karen likes to feel useful.

Maury plugs the set back in, and touches the leads from his Field Effect Multimeter to the first of many pairs of terminals between the little parts, starting from where the power enters.

Croons. "Mossy blaster's okay." Moving the leads. "Fictionator's just fine. Opalescer couldn't be better. Mexican Green prenuptializer. Cairo home-style fricassee, Organic gubbage eater—oh, oh. That's the rascal." He turns off the set, and gentles the tiny part out of its clamps, a blob of yellow ceramic with silver wire sticking out on each side. "Karen, get us a nice new gubbage eater out the truck, hon, will you?" Tosses it to her.

Karen catches the thing, not very deftly. It's a resistor, she thinks. Hurries out.

Maury first came to State University on a basketball scholarship. Went to Vietnam. Went to Harvard to study music and political science. Married Karen in Boston, and came back on a graduate fellowship to study voice here. Seems to like State City. His next Sunday-morning call's at the sheriff's department, where there's a squad-car radio to fix.

Bert Tannenbaum, Al's friend: That's John Ten Mason, baritone, M.D. He's a second-year resident in surgery, about to be appointed to staff in the medical school, who loves singing. He's the one on whom the older surgeons dote, really thinks out a case, they say, before he takes a patient to the operating room, and then his hands are smooth, his procedures bloodless, his way of preserving tissue really Halstedian. He declined a chance to make a fair amount of money doing a *locum tenens* this summer in order to be in $4000.

He is clearing his desk this morning in his small office at University Hospital—or rather was, until his attention was caught just now by a spec sheet from a biomedical-equipment manufacturer.

He moons over it like a gardener in January with a seed catalogue. This sheet describes a new, asynchronous, nuclear-powered cardiac pacemaker.

Johnny implants pacemakers as a subspecialty. He's had special training and, by now, quite a lot of experience. But every one he's put in so far has been battery powered, costing the patient, in addition to the surgery, no more than a thousand or fifteen hundred dollars, depending on the model.

Matter of fact, there's an old gent with a new pacemaker just out of intensive care right now whom Johnny will see shortly when he makes rounds with his students for the last time before his singing vacation starts.

Goddamn, wouldn't that be an ass full of cactus if a really rich one turned up needing a fast pacemaker job while Johnny's off going tra-la-la? Rich, that is, not because it would mean anything to him financially— Johnny's earnings are pooled with those of the other surgeons on staff—but because an old boy like that might be able to spring for five grand, for something like this deal on the spec sheet. Texas John sure would like to plant a nuke.

Harry, the paymaster—David Riding, tenor, tennis player, troubled husband, is in Ralph Lekberg's office, to which he has a key, tuning the composer's piano. Davey is Ralph Lekberg's star student composer, and much more serious about it than he is about his singing.

Davey earns $3.75 an hour, through a government-supported program called work-study, tuning the university pianos, and is provided with an oscillograph to measure the sound waves registered as each key is struck. He has the thing plugged in and turned on, and pays little attention to it. He has perfect pitch; occasionally, if there's a slight discrepancy between the oscillograph's version of the way a key should be tuned and Davey Riding's ear, he rules against the machine.

Sue Riding, his wife, is the fastest and most accurate check-out girl in State City, a Ph.D. candidate in mathematics, and has been fired by half the supermarkets in town. This is partly because wherever she has worked, the other check-out girls sooner or later begin to resent her, though Sue does all she can to subdue her intellect. On the job where she is now at work, one thirty-year-old woman in particular, a divorcee who talks endlessly to the others about which bars in town are good for finding men, has taken to jostling Sue in the room where they hang up their shop coats.

Another reason why Sue gets fired is absent-mindedness. While it hasn't much to do with the level of mathematics at which she is now studying, Sue has a phenomenal head for figures; when she was a child, teachers would show her off. The silly thing she falls into, again and again, is ringing up some customer's big basket, item by item, and then telling the customer the total before she totals it on the big (electronic) cash register. It makes customers suspicious.

"Hey, smarts," the divorced one calls over. "Where do I set the scale for baking potatoes?"

Billy Hoffman, newly arrived in State City with Short last night, is also operating an electronic machine, the self-service elevator in University House, which is like a big, four-story motel. Starting on the fourth floor, he pushed *1*. A graduate student named Mike Shapen, bass, *Third Poker Player*, is with him, delegated to show Hoffman around the campus.

Instead of going all the way to *1* the elevator stops at *2*. Someone else wants to go down. Door opens and there is a smallish, pert young woman, around twenty, with her light hair parted ruler-straight down the middle and pulled hard and tight down onto her head. The face is candy-box pretty, the lips pout at Hoffman, then smile at Mike.

"Michael, lamb. There you are. I can't believe it. I was going to call you. Look at your darling hair."

Mike Shapen isn't much taller than she, and wears his hair in a close, unfashionable crew cut, which the young woman is trying to get at to rub.

"Hey, starlet, lay off me, willya?" His voice is so deep it would be comic in a short guy if he weren't so plainly a hard little nail. "Mr. Hoffman, this is Sidney, uh, Bennett. Our—cut it out—soprano."

"Oh, yeah. *Sally Anne,* huh?"

Who ever saw a girl do what Sidney does? Curtsies! Curtsies, boy, to big-eared Hoffman, who tries not to let it distract him from driving the elevator safely down to the first floor, where Sidney is met by big, pink, muscle-bound Dick Auerbach, tenor, *First Poker Player,* whom she hugs.

At Trinity Episcopal Church, where he is choir director, Hughmore Skeats IV, baritone, *Pill Donovan,* switches on the new electric organ. It isn't just that he's paid to rehearse and sing with the choir, either; church suits him.

In his bed at home again, Rigby "Snazzer" Short, librettist, wakes, checks the time on his digital clock, and smiles to hear the sounds of his two children—by his first marriage—playing. There's a movie they'll enjoy today, and he'll enjoy taking them to it; their summer visits seem so brief.

The device with which Henry Fennellon, the big middle-aged bass who will sing *Raymond Applegore,* is working is not electronic, but mechanical. Henry lives on the family farm he inherited and returned to. He is engaged in discharging feed into pig feeders by means of an auger that he mounted, doing the work himself, on an old pickup truck. On the adjoining farm, which Henry also works taking a tenant's share, live Ralph Lekberg, the composer, and his wife, Josette. Nothing very electronic going on here, either, unless you count the controls on Josette's kitchen range, on which Sunday-noon dinner is almost cooked.

Sato is here to eat with them; he and Ralph are chatting. The Lekberg house is no place for the fastidious. You sit down and something sits on you—a dog, a cat, or a child. Sato is fastidious, but lets things sit on him at the Lekbergs'. He thanks Ralph, and says again that he won't be able to walk around the farm after dinner, nor meet Henry Fennellon today. He has an appointment. He doesn't say, though his mind is full of what comes next, that the appointment is for continuation of the story game with Debbie.

Maggi Short is still in New York, stoned this Sunday morning, zonked happily out of her sleek head on mescaline. She is in a seat in a small, off-Broadway theatre, closed this morning to the public, with thirty or forty other people. Someone is playing a Moog synthesizer. An automatic projector keeps changing slides of abstract color photos, which flicker over the bodies of nude dancers on the stage. The dance will conclude with intercourse, in which several people from the audience will join. Maggi probably won't be one of those; too happy floating and watching.

In Boston, Beth Paulus, alto, *Norah Applegore,* is still alseep, although it's late; in Los Angeles Marcel St. Edouard, tenor, *Al Riker,* is still asleep, but it's early.

And in State City, Debbie Dieter Haas is eating cottage cheese at her drawing board and drawing cartoon figures—Red the Hobo, Limehouse Lady, Sato as a boy. She hides them; they aren't ready yet.

3.

All right. We left Oog and Lady building the house.

Sato, let me see, gets off the red Trailways bus in San Francisco with eleven dollars, his high school class ring, and a beautiful little calfskin overnight bag with Oog's four initials on it. He carries his violin, too, and wears a white linen suit sent by the artist uncle, who is now living in Hong Kong.

He takes a room at the house of his music teacher, where he will serve meals, wash dishes, and practice. I apologize, Debbie, that this music teacher is a German, cruel and sloppy with a grey moustache, but we could put him in only once:

GOTT, SADO. DOT TRILL IS **SCHRECKLICH.**

Sato has washed out the white linen suit for the fourth time, and walked to every part of San Francisco.

SORRY, KID. TOO YOUNG.

DON'T LOOK STRONG ENOUGH.

JOB'S FILLED, EVERYBODY, CLEAR THE HALL, PLEASE.

NO JAPS, NO CHINKS, NO HARD FEELINGS.

WHY, YES. WE ADVERTISED FOR A SALESMAN. DO YOU THINK YOU CAN SELL?

Christine is shorter than Sato, with a cocky smile and a look of whimsical determination. She has light brown hair, and wears a tailored suit with the jacket open in such a way that the tailoring seems to frame her bosom, at which Sato stares.

STOP TYPING A MINUTE, CAROLYN, AND COME TALK TO SATO WITH ME. DON'T YOU LOVE HIS EYES?

YES, CHRISTINE.

THEY'RE LIKE ALMONDS EXACTLY, AREN'T THEY? OH, YUM. SATO, WHAT MAKES YOU THINK YOU CAN SELL?

Carolyn is sad and attractive, willowy, soft, a little taller than Christine and a little younger. Christine, who is twenty-five, looks unapproachably like a woman to Sato. Carolyn looks to be only an older girl. It may be the sadness, or it may be the pliancy of the green knit dress with cable stitching on the arms and shoulders. Carolyn is not tailored.

> SEE THAT SATO READS ALL THE MATERIAL. I'VE GOT LUNCH WITH BUD. BYE-BYE, ANGELS. SATO, LET ME GIVE YOU A HUG FOR LUCK. THERE NOW. `BYE. LET ME HUG CAROLYN, TOO. OH, HERE I GO.

Now Carolyn gives Sato a sandwich from a paper bag. He sees, after accepting it, that there was only a single sandwich, but she will not take it back. She says she has just been divorced. She says she is frightened living by herself. She says she is not hungry. She says her ex-husband trains dogs for a living. She says she does not know if Christine is a real friend or not. She stands with her buttocks resting against the desk top, and her hands flat on it behind her. Sato in no way understands how he suddenly comes to be standing on his tiptoes kissing Carolyn. It is the first time he has ever kissed anybody besides his mother.

> SATO, YOU CAN FIND SOME OTHER JOB. SOMETHING NICER. REALLY.

NO, I CAN'T.

Sato does not want any other job now. At one o'clock he stops kissing Carolyn because she says that Christine will be back now any time. Sato sits down to read about the Vito-Cycle Institute of America.

OH. I THOUGHT A VITO-CYCLE WAS SOMETHING TO RIDE.

NO, SATO.

Every human being! the material explains. Is born with a unique, personal, individual cycle of VITAL ENERGY, which begins at the instant of conception. This makes Vito-Cyclic charts both more exact and more risqué than astrology. Computations, based on the calendric studies of the Ancient Mayans! give us:

VITO-CYCLES FREE!
IT IS NOW POSSIBLE
FOR YOU TO HAVE YOUR
PERSONAL VITO-CYCLES CHARTED IN
ADVANCE BY THE
VITO-CYCLE INSTITUTE OF AMERICA.
FREE!
PREDICTS:
YOUR EBB AND FLOW OF ENERGY!
YOUR TIMES OF GREATEST EFFICIENCY!
TIMES OF BRAIN POWER! MAGNETISM!
FREE INFORMATION.
Just fill in Coupon.
Name _____ Address _____

This coupon ad appears in the San Francisco *Call-Bulletin*. Sato's job will be to call on persons returning the coupons.

He is to have a drawing account of twelve dollars a week, if hired, and, of course, commissions.

WE DON'T REALLY... SATO, I KNOW A MAN WHO HAS A STORE IN OAKLAND. HE MIGHT NEED SOMEONE IN THE STOCK ROOM. SHALL I CALL HIM UP?

OH, CAROLYN, THANK YOU. I'D RATHER WORK IN SAN FRANCISCO.

HERE'S CHRISTINE BACK.

HELLO, ANGELS. LET'S GET TO WORK. ARE THE LETTERS DONE, CAROLYN?

WHAT DO YOU THINK, SATO? SIT HERE AND LET ME SHOW YOU A CHART. YOU SEE? THESE REALLY DO HELP PEOPLE SO WONDERFULLY. IT GIVES THEM CONFIDENCE IN THEMSELVES...

Christine says this with the wiggliest part of her boson pressed against Sato's triceps, as she stands beside the chair she sat him in.

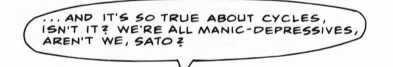

... AND IT'S SO TRUE ABOUT CYCLES, ISN'T IT? WE'RE ALL MANIC-DEPRESSIVES, AREN'T WE, SATO?

Sato realizes Christine is so absorbed in communicating that the contact between bosom and triceps is inadvertent, so he sits rather rigidly, flushing—possibly with pride at having learned what a true manic-depressive he is.

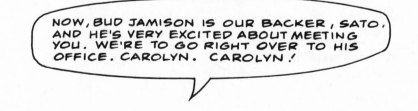

NOW, BUD JAMISON IS OUR BACKER, SATO, AND HE'S VERY EXCITED ABOUT MEETING YOU. WE'RE TO GO RIGHT OVER TO HIS OFFICE. CAROLYN. CAROLYN!

Carolyn stares sadly at them, and they get ready to leave.

BE A DARLING AND DO SATO'S VITO-CYCLE CHART WHILE WE'RE GONE.

A. J. "Bud" Jamison is sales manager for a large San Francisco metal-fabricating firm. As Christine's backer, he pays Carolyn's salary, the office rent, equipment rent, advertising, and, if he approves the new salesman, will pay for Sato's weekly drawing account. He is a heavy-browed, well-tanned man in a sharkskin suit with vest and watch chain, and his handshake hurts.

I LIKE THE CUT OF YOUR JIB, SATO. YOU'RE YOUNG, BUT YOU'RE KEEN, ALL YOU PEOPLE. NO OFFENSE.

NO, SIR.

CHRISTINE, WE'VE GOT TO PLAN THIS CAMPAIGN RIGHT. WHAT DO YOU SAY?

NOBODY KNOWS SALES WORK BETTER THAN MR. JAMISON, SATO.

LOOK, SATO. WHY DON'T YOU START BY WORKING CHINATOWN? GET THE HANG OF IT WITH YOUR OWN KIND OF FOLKS.

SIR...

SPEAK THE LINGO?

JAPANESE, SIR, A LITTLE.

HEY, THAT'S GREAT! YOU GOT SOME COUPON LEADS ON SLANTYTOWN, CHRIS? NO OFFENSE, SATO.

CERTAINLY, BUD. WE HAVE DOZENS.

GREAT, GREAT. THAT'S HOW WE'LL DO IT, THEN. SATO, DO YOU KNOW THIS WONDERFUL YOUNG LADY WON'T TAKE A SALARY? LOOK AT HER... AH, UNDERSTANDS BUSINESS. I CAN'T GET OVER IT... WHEN *YOU* START SELLING, THAT'S WHEN CHRIS STARTS EARNING. NO TICKEE, NO WASHEE, RIGHT, MY BOY? COME ON, SHAKE ....

He has a great deal more to say. All great American fortunes are based on sales. As soon as Sato has a following, A. J. "Bud" Jamison will put other men under him to train, and Sato will be the youngest general sales manager in San Francisco.

THIS IS MY DREAM, SATO. CHRISTINE. COME ON HERE, BOTH OF YOU. TO OWN MY OWN BUSINESS, SEND MY OWN SALESMEN OUT. NOW. THREE PARTNERS, YOU DON'T KNOW HOW MUCH THIS MEANS, PARTNERS.

Back at the office, Carolyn says she can't find any coupons returned from Chinatown addresses. Christine thinks they must be in a file drawer at home.

I MAKE GRAPHOLOGICAL ANALYSES OF THE PEOPLE WHO RETURN COUPONS, SATO. HAND-WRITING STUDIES. IT'S VERY SCIENTIFIC, AND HELPS ME LEARN THE PSYCHOLOGICAL PATTERNS OF THE PEOPLE WE'RE TRYING TO HELP.

Sato doesn't know much about psychological patterns, but is relieved that he won't have to start calling immediately on Chinese, whose country is being devastated just then by Japanese.

Actually, he begins by making calls in a part of the Fillmore district where American Indians live. A lot of them are Mohawks, families of men brought out from the East for bridge and high-building work, though there isn't much of it now. The people are surprisingly nice to Sato, though they laugh at the idea of anybody having an extra dollar to spend on Three-Month Preliminary Sample Charts. They paid no attention at all to what they were sending for when they returned the coupon. They are people who regularly go through the newspaper and send off all the coupons with the word *free* in them, generally pasting the coupon to a penny postcard. It is one of the amusements of poverty to see what will come back, and one of the more amusing things that came for some was the manic-depressive general sales manager of the Vito-Cycle Institute of America.

We have just noted Sato's only sale. He plays for an hour, by ear and from memory, the migrant songs he heard on hobo Red's harmonica. The Mohawk women get their change together and give him a dollar in pennies and nickels. They decide Mary Ann, who is a baby, should have the three-month sample charts.

By the end of the second week, Sato begins to find it difficult to persuade himself to make calls at all, yet feels duty-bound to try each morning. He goes to the office afternoons. Christine is seldom there. Most likely she is at home, doing graphology, for in the evenings, she has told Sato, she goes to classes. She is learning to be a psychoanalyst, and Sato understands that one reason he is not to come to the office in the morning is that Christine may be having a session with poor Carolyn.

On the second Friday, Sato feels that he has good cause to go to the office in the late forenoon.

Carolyn is wearing the green knit dress again, with the cable-stitched arms and shoulders. Carolyn is leaning back on her palms, half-sitting on the desk again.

Again Sato fails to understand how he comes to be kissing Carolyn. Besides kissing, they rub together, fully clothed but with a certain abandon. Comical as this may look, they feel very tender about it and toward one another.

It happens now most weekday afternoons. In the mornings, Sato conscientiously makes calls but never sales. At the lunch hour he goes to his room at the German (I am sorry) music teacher's house to practice. At about three o'clock he arrives at the office and eats Carolyn's sack lunch.

Carolyn goes to the ladies' room, takes off her lipstick, comes back, and latches the door with a complicated smile—it would have to include, somehow, resignation, invitation, desperation, and some fond mockery of Sato's innocence. She takes her position against the desk. They do only what they did before. We would not illustrate repetition but only say:

In the middle of the summer, Sato goes again to the office on a Friday morning. He has not seen Christine once all week, but has noticed different changes and combinations in the furniture, afternoons, which Carolyn would not explain. Today Christine is in the outer office.

Carolyn comes in from the other room, the smaller office, which is always locked when Christine is out.

Carolyn gets an envelope from her desk drawer and gives it to Sato. He opens it. Inside is a ten-dollar bill, and a note:

Christine grabs Sato's wrist and makes a ballroom-dancing move, a step and a half-twirl to place herself in front of and pressing backward against him, with his captured arm now coming down over her left shoulder, his hand squeezed in both of hers and held tight just below that bosom. She looks at Carolyn, Sato cannot see with what expression, but knows his own to be pretty much popeyed. Carolyn bites her lip hard.

ANGEL.

Christine springs away from Angel Sato's manic-depressive grasp and into Angel Carolyn's, squeezes the sad young woman, and seizes a shiny new purse.

I KNOW. HERE, SATO. HERE'S THREE DOLLARS MORE. TAKE CAROLYN TO LUNCH, YOU CAN BOTH HAVE THE AFTERNOON OFF, OKAY? BECAUSE EVERYTHING'S GOING SO WELL.

They do have lunch. Sato buys Carolyn a dry martini cocktail, tastes it, and feels rather drunk.

HEY, LET'S GO BACK TO THE OFFICE.

I CAN'T, SATO. NOT TODAY. I'D BETTER GO HOME.

PLEASE.

NO DARLING. I DON'T DARE. I'LL SEE YOU MONDAY.

It is the first time she has called him darling. It is said in a way very different from Christine's, which would be difficult to illustrate.

CAROLYN, I DON'T UNDERSTAND. ABOUT THE OFFICE AND THE BONUS, AND CHRISTINE SAYING HOW WELL EVERYTHING IS GOING.

She leaves, and Sato decides to go back to the office, to get some coupons from the file for Monday morning's calls. He is determined to make an extra effort, now that he has had a sip of martini and understands about public relations. People are already leaving the office building, going home for the weekend. They come bursting out of the elevator. Sato rides up in it empty, to the fourth floor. Halfway down the corridor, a short, fat man is trying their office door.

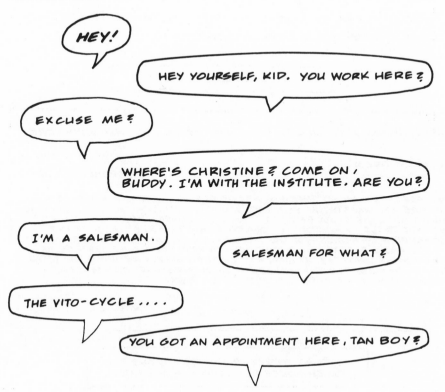

The short fat man has begun to look very angry, rattling the locked door. Sato, who has a key to the door in his pocket, walks quietly away.

...MEANWHILE, AT THE LAKE.

MRS. OWENS JAY   SOUTHAMPTON   LONG ISLAND   NEW YORK

DEAREST ORRIN:

JULY 4, 1940

INDEPENDENCE DAY!

SO SORRY I HAVEN'T TIME FOR A LONG LETTER, BUT YOU KNOW HOW THINGS ARE HERE IN THE SUMMER. YOUR REMODELING SOUNDS CHARMING, AND I HOPE WE SHALL BE ABLE TO SEE IT SOMEDAY. HOWEVER, YOUR FATHER FEELS THAT EVEN AT TODAY'S HIGH PRICES, $4,386.72 IS A GREAT DEAL OF MONEY FOR THE LUMBER, GLASS, AND STONE FOR TWO WINGS AND A GARDEN. HE WOULD LIKE TO HAVE YOUR SUPPLIERS SEND THEIR BILLS DIRECTLY TO HIM, RATHER THAN SIMPLY SENDING THE TOTAL TO YOU TO DISBURSE. I KNOW YOU WILL UNDERSTAND. OUR SINCERE REGARDS TO YOUR WIFE AND HER LITTLE BOY.

LOVE, *Mother*

...THAT WEEKEND THE REMODELED RANCH HOUSE BURNS TO THE GROUND.

FOR YEARS THERE HAS BEEN A HIVE OF HONEYBEES IN THE ATTIC IN THE OLD PART OF THE HOUSE, A NEW SWARM GOING OUT EVERY SPRING, THE OLD ONE FILLING MORE AND MORE OF THE SPACE BETWEEN THE WALLS WITH HONEYCOMB. LADY REMINDS SATO OF THIS WHEN SHE PHONES.

WHILE LADY WAS AWAY IN TOWN, SHE EXPLAINS, OOG WENT UP TO THE ATTIC TO SMOKE OUT THE HONEY BEES.

THE BEES CHASED OOG OUT OF THE ATTIC... AS HE RAN, SOME OF THE CHARRED, SMOKING RAGS FELL OUT OF THE SMOKER AND STARTED THE FIRE. OOG WAS ROWING ACROSS THE LAKE TO CONSULT AN OLD MAN WHO LIVES ON THE OTHER SIDE AND IS AN EXPERT ON BEES....

FROM THE MIDDLE OF THE LAKE, HE SAW FLAMES COMING OUT OF THE TOP OF THE HOUSE. LADY, DRIVING BACK, SAW THE FLAMES TOO.

WELL, LIMEHOUSE, I SURE GOT RID OF THOSE BEES.

ARE YOU BURNED, OOG? OH, ALL YOUR BEAUTIFUL WORK.

NEVER MIND. WE HAD FUN DOING IT. COME ON, WE'LL SLEEP IN THE CHICKEN HOUSE.

MIGRANTS, OOG?

WHAT ELSE, LADY? WHATEVER ELSE?

This is Sunday morning. Sato goes immediately to the bus station. There is a picket line of strikers. The buses are not running. Sato walks back to the German music teacher's house, walking along Mission Street, which is skid row. There are not so many hobos there now. They are going into the army and getting work at shipyards and aircraft plants.

Sato has read in the newspapers that midgets are getting work in aircraft plants because they can go inside the bomber wings during fabrication and rivet from inside.

Sato wonders if he is small enough to rivet on the inside of a bomber wing, but of course he was promised Christine that he will stay on with her.

When he gets to the office on Monday, going in the morning to pick up coupons because he was prevented on Friday afternoon, no one is there. He uses his key to get in. There is another new set of files in the outer office. Sato tries a file drawer, which is unmarked, but it is locked.

Carolyn arrives. She is not late for work. She has been in the ladies' room.

SATO! I'M SORRY THE DOOR WAS LOCKED. CHRISTINE SAYS WE'RE TO LOCK IT, EVEN IF WE JUST GO OUT FOR A MINUTE. THERE ARE SO MANY ROBBERIES....

I'LL BET I SAW ONE.

WHAT?

CAROLYN! I SAW A ROBBER TRYING TO GET INTO THE OFFICE ON FRIDAY. HE SAID HE WAS WITH THE INSTITUTE....

SATO, WHAT DID THE MAN LOOK LIKE?

SHORT AND FAT, WITH A VOICE LIKE A MOVIE GANGSTER. RATHER TOUGH, I BELIEVE.

THAT WASN'T A ROBBERY, SATO.

WHO WAS IT THEN?

SATO, DON'T YOU KNOW WHAT'S GOING ON?

SOME KIND OF PHONY-BALONEY.

KISS ME, DARLING.

Jobs are scarce in the summer of 1940 for girls like Carolyn, who is not a fast typist nor gracious on the telephone nor a midget. They are interruped in their tender swaying by, of all things, the telephone. It is a long-distance call for, of all people, Sato, who can hear what comes over the phone as Carolyn answers.

MY NAME'S ERICKSON, MISS. I'M THE INSURANCE ADJUSTER FOR THIS TERRIBLE FIRE HIS FOLKS HAD . . . .

MR. MURASAKI'S TIED UP, MR. ERICKSON . . . . SHHH, DARLING.

DO YOU SUPPOSE HE COULD CALL ME? YOU SEE, HIS ROOM WAS RIGHT UNDER WHERE THE FIRE STARTED, SO NOTHING WAS SALVAGED.

I'LL TELL HIM, SIR. I'LL HAVE HIM CALL YOU. GOOD-BYE . . .

Oog reaches Sato that evening at the German music teacher's house. He wants Sato to call Erickson, the insurance adjuster, and reminds Sato that Oog's double-barreled Purdy shotgun was in Sato's room. Sato has always loved to take that gun down and clean and oil it. A wonderful piece of machinery, and although Sato owns one himself today, he does not believe it to be the equal of the one Oog had.

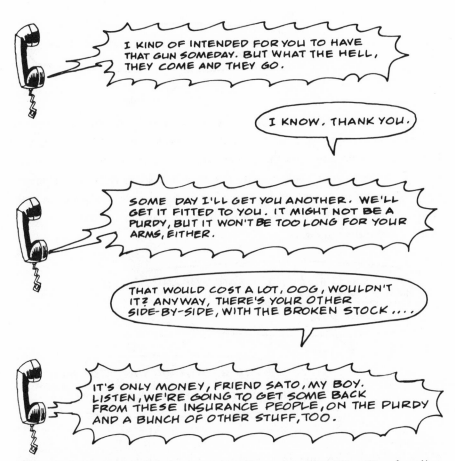

Next morning, Sato decides to go to the office early again. He will make a list, including the things Oog has reminded him of, and get Carolyn to type it for him. Then he will phone Pete Erickson, the insurance adjuster. He gets off the elevator. He starts down the corridor, so preoccupied he has his hand on the knob of the office door before he sees, in front of his nose:

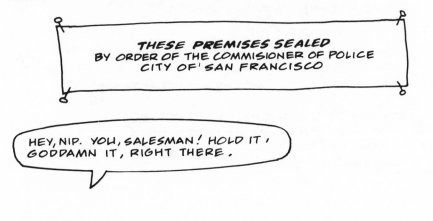

STOP KID. WE JUST WANT TO TALK TO YOU.

Sato runs from the short fat man and a much larger man, who is almost as fat. Sato moves very well, gets around the corridor corner, pushes the call button for the elevator, and then, knowing it won't be there in time, moves through a heavy door marked Exit, out to where stairs run up and down. Sato swings down, three or four steps at a time, rather exhilarated, and would keep going strong except that there is Carolyn on the street-floor landing, very distraught.

SATO, OH, IT'S YOU; I HEARD, HEARD, HEARD SOMEONE COMING... OH, BUT THIS DOOR IS LOCKED. SATO, WE CAN'T GET OUT.

IT'S ALL RIGHT, CAROLYN. IT'S ALL ALL RIGHT. COME ON. WE'LL GO BACK UP AND TRY THE SECOND FLOOR.

Hand in hand, tiptoeing in step, trembling together, they begin to steal back up the steps. Booming voices from above:

LITTLE SON OF A BITCH IS DOWN THERE SOMEWHERE.

YOU GO DOWN. I'LL TRY UP.

IF YOU GET HIM, WHAT WE NEED'S HIS GODDAMN KEY.

CAROLYN, SHHH, THEY DON'T KNOW YOU'RE HERE. GO BACK DOWN AND WAIT. SHHH.

NO, SATO, LET'S TRY TO GET BACK UP. LOOK, I'VE GOT A KEY TO THE LADIES' ROOM. WE CAN LOCK OURSELVES IN AND HIDE ALL MORNING.

This is about the naughtiest thing Sato ever heard in his life.

The short fat man gets them.

OKAY, SWEETHEARTS, COME ON. HEY, SERGEANT. I GOT THE NIP, AND THE LITTLE TOMATO'S DOWN HERE WITH HIM. WHAT A PAIR OF SWEETHEARTS.

YEAH? THE SECRETARY?

COME ON, DAMN IT. GET DOWN HERE. I OUGHTA KICK THE CRAP OUT OF YOU, SHOELEATHER.

DON'T, SATO. HERE, MR. ADEL. HERE'S MY KEYS. THE FILES AND CHRISTINE'S OFFICE AND EVERYTHING.

AWRIGHT, SISTER. THAT'S BETTER. COME ON, NOW. UP THE STAIRS.

He moves up ahead of them with the keys. As Carolyn and Sato get to the second-floor Exit landing, they lean together, very quietly, against the brass bar that opens the door. It isn't locked. They fade through it, and away,

Sato snapping the snap lock on the door, then both running across the building to the other elevator bank, into a down car, out, into the crowd on Geary Street, and away. They run for several blocks, and stop, finally, in a store entrance.

WHO ARE THEY, CAROLYN ? POLICE ?

THE TALL ONE MUST BE. THE SHORT ONE WHO TOOK MY KEYS IS MR. ADEL. HE'S THE BACKER FOR THE GRAPHOLOGICAL INSTITUTE.

BUT WE'RE . . .

THE VITO-CYCLE INSTITUTE. AND THERE'S THE GENETIC REBALANCE INSTITUTE, AND PERSONALITY RESEARCH, AND THE INSTITUTE OF POSTAL PSYCHOANALYSIS. FIVE, SATO. CHRISTINE'S GOT FIVE OF THEM.

WHY CAN'T SHE? HAVE ALL THE INSTITUTES SHE WANTS?

AND ALL THE BACKERS, SATO? BESIDES MR. ADEL AND "BUD" JAMISON, THERE'S MR. FARKINS AND MR. NARDOLINI AND MR. GELBER, WHO LIKES TO BE CALLED UNCLE PETE...

BUT WHY IS THAT WRONG ?

YOU LIKE CHRISTINE.

I LIKE YOU, CAROLYN.

SATO, WHAT'S WRONG IS THAT NONE OF THEM'S SUPPOSED TO KNOW ABOUT THE OTHERS. EACH ONE PAYS OFFICE RENT. EACH ONE PAYS CHRISTINE FOR MY SALARY. SHE MAKES FIVE COPIES OF THE PHONE BILL... THOSE POOR MEN. EACH OF THEM WANTED TO HAVE HIS OWN BUSINESS. AND THEY ALL THINK CHRISTINE'S A WONDERFUL PARTNER BECAUSE SHE WON'T TAKE A SALARY.

WAS EVERYBODY PAYING TWELVE DOLLARS A WEEK FOR ME, TOO?

NO. IT WAS JUST BUD WHO SAID SHE HAD TO HAVE A SALESMAN. AND SATO, SHE, SHE COULD MOVE MONEY AROUND IN DIFFERENT BANK ACCOUNTS.

SO IT LOOKED LIKE EARNINGS... BUT NOW I THINK SHE'S CLOSED THEM ALL AND HAS THE MONEY.... IT WAS MR. ADEL. GETTING SUSPICIOUS.

WHY, CAROLYN? WHAT WENT WRONG?

THE FURNITURE. SUDDENLY ALL THE BACKERS STARTED SENDING OFFICE FURNITURE. THEY'RE SALESMEN, SATO, AND THEY LOVE BARGAINS, AND THEY'D WANT TO SURPRISE THEIR CUTE LITTLE PARTNER, AND THIS STUFF WOULD COME. DESKS, AND FILES AND THREE WATER COOLERS. WE WERE GOING CRAZY. EVERY DAY OR TWO, ON THE FREIGHT ELEVATOR, UP WOULD COME SOMETHING, AND WE'D HAVE TO HIDE IT IN THE INNER OFFICE, AND TRY TO HAVE THE RIGHT THINGS OUT ON THE DAY THE ONE WHO SENT THEM MIGHT COME BY.

SATO, I'M AS DUMB AS THE BACKERS. I SENT IN A COUPON, FOR THE INSTITUTE OF POSTAL PSYCHOANALYSIS. I DON'T KNOW WHY. AND THEN I CAME, AND MET CHRISTINE, AND SHE SAID SHE'D HELP, IF I WOULD WORK FOR HER . . .

...BUT I'D HAVE QUIT WEEKS AGO, IF I HADN'T BEEN IN LOVE WITH YOU.

Picture Sato's confusion: A young woman toward whom he feels tenderly has said she loves him. But at the same time, he is forced to realize that he has not been earning toward his conservatory keep as a Manic-Depressive General Sales Manager and Public Relations Angel at all, only as a paid cuddler. Christine has needed all the hold she could get on Carolyn.

They walk quickly away—but who is this, waiting when they get there at the door of Carolyn's room?

ANGELS! OH, I'M SO GLAD YOU'RE BOTH HERE. LOOK WHAT WE HAVE. IT'S A BOTTLE OF SHERRY, FROM BUD! BUD JAMISON! HE KNOWS EVERYTHING, AND HE'S GOING TO TALK TO THE OTHER MEN AND STRAIGHTEN THINGS OUT.

CHRISTINE! HOW CAN HE?

YOU'LL SEE. JUST GIVE HIM TIME. DID YOU THINK CHRISTINE WOULD DO ANYTHING DISHONEST? OH, PLEASE. IT'S JUST A MISUNDERSTANDING. BUT YOU TWO, YOU HAVE TO HIDE A LITTLE WHILE NOW AND NOT TALK TO ANYBODY. NOT ANYBODY. WON'T THAT BE FUN?

NO, CHRISTINE.

CAROLYN. CAROLYN, LET ME TELL YOU SOMETHING. PRIVATELY. (whisper, whisper, whisper.)

ALL RIGHT, CHRISTINE.

Only later can Sato guess what the whisper was: If Carolyn lets things get to the point where there's a criminal action, Sato could lose his conservatory scholarship. Sato will make this guess because of what Christine says aloud to him:

Sato nods. He will do as Christine wishes, but he has not quite figured out yet what the whisper meant, so he is actually quite bitter and miserable—but of course, naturally inscrutable.

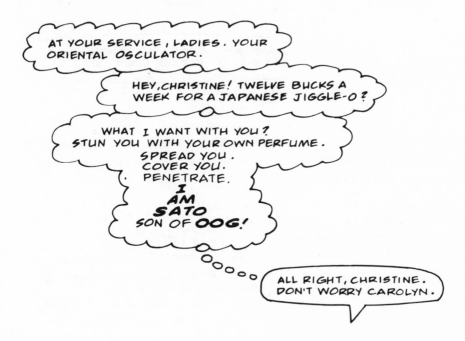

The buses are still on strike. He prepares to flee San Francisco in Carolyn's car. It is a little Ford closed coupe, which she began paying for before her divorce, but doesn't know how to drive. She has tried to sell it.

Sato leaves San Francisco, and this evening, Debbie, when I get back from seeing our director, Mr. Hoffman, we will meet a new character: Pete Erickson, the tough insurance adjuster.

Sato is still very young. In the final installment, he will be told to grow up. Sato is a good boy, and always does as he is told, I believe.

TO BE CONCLUDED.

Three small scenes of work, three little sex and drinking scenes:

Sato, calling on Billy Hoffman, so that he will have everything cleared away before evening. "Experienced piano coach."

"The black boy's wife?"

"Yes. Karen. She should have all those who sing small parts out of book by Wednesday."

"You'll coach the leads?"

"I'll help Karen, but she's very good."

Karen herself, working with Ralph Lekberg in his office, reading through the first scene in the piano reduction she will use as rehearsal accompanist. Ralph checking from his own manuscript to see that the copy Karen has is correct. Also, both Mike Shapen, the tough little bass, and his exquisite wife, Mona, slight and dark with gleaming hair. They are copying the rest of the reduction; they earn six dollars an hour each as music copyists, and are paid not by the university but from funds donated by a friend.

Concentration. A break.

"You've met Mr. Hoffman?" Ralph.

Mike. "Took him around campus this morning."

"How does he strike you?"

"Full of questions."

Karen, whose jokes are a little doughy sometimes. "Will he make our opera *Tales of Hoffman?*"

"Then he'd have to appear in it himself." Ralph's compulsive about information, a born lecturer. "E.T.W. Hoffman was an actual historical figure, and a very romantic one, born a hundred years before Offenbach used his stories for the opera, and made Hoffman a character in it as well. You see—"

Mona, thinking she has caught him out. "Shouldn't it be E.T.*A.* Hoffman, Dr. Lekberg?"

"Oh, no. He was born Ernest Theodore Wilhelm, and didn't change Wilhelm to Amadeus, in homage to Mozart, till he was thirty-seven years old."

Karen, Mike, and Mona exchange smiles and glances. They are very fond, really, of Ralph's almost legendary pedantry.

Josette Lekberg, feeding an orphan lamb from a baby's bottle.

Mischief, at the expense of Hughmore Skeats IV, who was having a little cocktail party. He invited the Jackstones and Sidney. Karen didn't come, of course—not that that mattered much to Skeats. But Sidney has brought along big, pink Dick Auerbach, who is very possessive toward the soprano.

"What'll it be?" Skeats, gamely.

Maury, with a straight face. "I'd like a soul martini."

Cheap gin on the rocks, he explains, with a dash of tabasco, and prevails on Dick and Skeats to try the preposterous drink with him. Sidney takes straight vermouth.

Skeats's party talk: "I feel bloody well convinced that the only animals that masturbate manually are male and female humans, you know. All the rest—dogs, cats, rhinos, what have you?—can lick themselves, can't they?"

"Oh, Papa Bear." Sidney. "What about poor whales?"

When the guests are ready to leave, Skeats draws Sidney aside to say he's got a couple of king hell fine steaks in the fridge, won't she stay for supper?

"Oh, but I promised to drive out with Dick and Maury to see the Ridings. We're taking Chinese food, won't you come?"

"Do stay, that's my girl. Let the big boys do the chop-suey run."

"Papa Bear." Whispers, a finger tickling just above the rib line. "I'm triple-jointed."

Johnny Ten Mason, M.D., a bottle of Walker Black Label Scotch, a red-headed radiology lab assistant named Tuttle. Powerful fornication, much relished by both, but sad for Tuttle, too, because she knows there's a piece of good-bye in every stroke. Her doctor's ready for a change, though she doesn't understand why.

Maggi Short is drinking, after an afternoon in bed with a man named Hervey Gandenberg, the world's most expensive cocktail. Gandenberg, as a matter of fact, is the friend of university music who donated the funds for Ralph Lekberg's copyists, so State City would be quite titillated to know that Maggi is in this gentleman's New York apartment. She has also been, from time to time, in his Chicago house, his Jamaica condominium, and his Wisconsin hunting camp.

The cocktail is called a Macedonia. Here is how Gandenberg's man makes it, and why it costs so much: An hour before serving, drip one quarter ounce of Framboise Grande Reserve raspberry brandy ($15 a fifth) over a single ice cube. Add ten drops Williams Pear Brandy ($17) from Switzerland; add ten drops good Calvados ($10); add ten drops aged Japanese plum wine (brand untransliteratable, $19 a small bottle); add ten drops Boissiere wild-strawberry vermouth (a bargain at $4.50); add ten drops Goldwasser kirsch ($8) and ten drops Arum Italian bitter orange ($10). Bring level to two ounces with good cognac, refrigerate for an hour. The ice should be hardly melted when you remove the cube. The ingredients will have mixed without bruising. Divide into two champagne glasses, and fill with well-chilled, vintage champagne.

Oh, and Marcel, in Los Angeles, is saying good-bye to Sheer Khan, a little redfin shark, and to Ruth and Amy, who are clown loaches.

4.

The drawings are wonderful, Debbie. You've done so many. Oh, I like your bureaucrat. He's so hardworking and righteous. Your Kitty Hamilton! I'm afraid she wasn't really that delicate, but how sweet. And this is Christine, of course. And Carolyn, yes, that's very much her expression, those big, sorrowful eyes. And the car, you must have looked it up? Carolyn's car.

Limehouse Lady did not live very long, after she was released from that camp. But those are her hands, at last. It's long ago now, Debbie. You haven't tried Oog yet, have you? I can't describe him, and I have no photograph. Well.

Sato arrives at the lake, and, to his surprise, he finds employment right away.

> THIS IS PETE ERICKSON, THE INSURANCE ADJUSTER, SATO. PETE, MY STEPSON.

Pete has square shoulders, big forearms, rough skin, and a rough tongue. Sato likes him. It is comfortable, after a summer spent with women, to be in a man's world with Oog and Pete.

Pete Erickson has a blackjack scar above his left eyebrow and a gun-butt scar on his jaw.

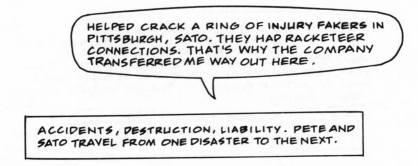

Pete always wears the same brown tweed suit, thin at the elbows, and scuffed shoes. Once Sato sees him hit a man, who has scuttled his own cabin cruiser, and with two valuable dogs locked inside.

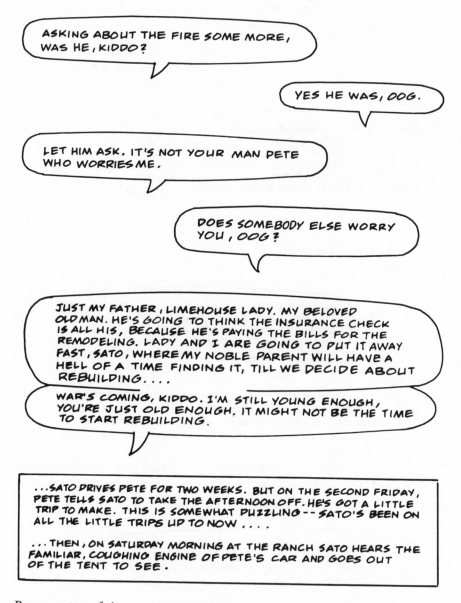

WELL, I REMEMBER HEARING HIM SAY HE WONDERED IF IT WOULD WORK.

Lady, Oog, and Sato are staying in tents on the ranch now.

ASKING ABOUT THE FIRE SOME MORE, WAS HE, KIDDO?

YES HE WAS, OOG.

LET HIM ASK. IT'S NOT YOUR MAN PETE WHO WORRIES ME.

DOES SOMEBODY ELSE WORRY YOU, OOG?

JUST MY FATHER, LIMEHOUSE LADY. MY BELOVED OLD MAN. HE'S GOING TO THINK THE INSURANCE CHECK IS ALL HIS, BECAUSE HE'S PAYING THE BILLS FOR THE REMODELING. LADY AND I ARE GOING TO PUT IT AWAY FAST, SATO, WHERE MY NOBLE PARENT WILL HAVE A HELL OF A TIME FINDING IT, TILL WE DECIDE ABOUT REBUILDING. ....

WAR'S COMING, KIDDO. I'M STILL YOUNG ENOUGH, YOU'RE JUST OLD ENOUGH. IT MIGHT NOT BE THE TIME TO START REBUILDING.

...SATO DRIVES PETE FOR TWO WEEKS. BUT ON THE SECOND FRIDAY, PETE TELLS SATO TO TAKE THE AFTERNOON OFF. HE'S GOT A LITTLE TRIP TO MAKE. THIS IS SOMEWHAT PUZZLING -- SATO'S BEEN ON ALL THE LITTLE TRIPS UP TO NOW ....

... THEN, ON SATURDAY MORNING AT THE RANCH SATO HEARS THE FAMILIAR, COUGHING ENGINE OF PETE'S CAR AND GOES OUT OF THE TENT TO SEE.

Pete gets out of the car with his briefcase.

Then Oog comes driving up fast, gets out, and does something abrupt and graceful with his hands, seeing Pete. Pete jerks his head. He and Oog walk down to the lake shore and sit on an overturned rowboat.

Sato joins Lady in her tent. She is ironing Oog's only white shirt. He lost twenty in the fire. After a time, Oog comes in smiling, and bows to her. He has papers for Lady to sign. She does, and he says he will now go to town with Pete, to cash the large insurance check before the bank closes at noon.

Oog leaves.

They almost expect that he will not return, but he does, for one last weekend of closeness and gaiety. But perhaps even Oog does not know yet it is to
be the last. Let us believe this, too.

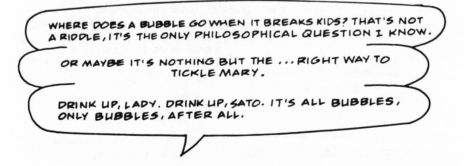

On Monday, Pete Erickson sends for Sato to come see him and bring
the title to Carolyn's little Ford car.

None of Oog's powerful graces, none of the airs that graces imply, about Pete, the working stiff, the tough, the undissembling. Sato knows where he stands with Pete, doesn't he?

Pete is busy writing down information from the title, and a surprising thought bubbles up behind Sato's naturally inscrutable face as Pete finishes and gets out his checkbook.

NINETY-FIVE BUCKS, SATO. STRAIGHT TO THE DEALER. HIS ADDRESS IS ON THIS TITLE.

SHE SIGNED THAT TITLE FOR ME TO SELL FOR TWO HUNDRED DOLLARS, PETE. I CAN'T TAKE LESS.

NINETY-FIVE DOLLARS'S WHAT'S DUE ON IT. LOOK, KID. YOU JUST HANDED ME THE GIRL'S ADDRESS. YOU WANT ME TO PHONE IT IN TO SAN FRANCISCO?

YOU'D PHONE THE POLICE?

IF I HAD TO. BUT THIS CAR DEALER WOULD HAVE THEFT COVERAGE. CAR'S UP FOR REPOSSESSION, PROBABLY. NO, I'D JUST PHONE THE INSURANCE BOYS. THEY'D HANDLE IT FOR ME. . . .

DON'T SIT THERE LOOKING RIGHTEOUS AT ME, SATO. YOUR BROAD'S A DEADBEAT, YOUR MOTHER'S AN ALIEN, YOU'RE WANTED FOR QUESTIONING.

AND YOUR STEPFATHER'S AN ARSONIST.

YOU CAN'T PROVE THAT.

YES, I CAN. BY A SHOTGUN HE DIDN'T FIND SATURDAY MORNING WHEN HE GOT WORRIED AND WENT TO REDEEM IT FROM A FRISCO HOCK SHOP. I GOT TO THE HOCK SHOP FIRST, ON FRIDAY AFTERNOON. HE SAID IT BURNED UP, DIDN'T HE? SO DID YOU, BY THE WAY. WELL, I'VE BEEN WAITING FOR THAT GUN TO TURN UP ON THE FENCE SHEETS -- I BEAT OOG THERE, AND I RISKED MY OWN DOUGH REDEEMING IT, SATO.

I think we will leave Sato now, walking in the grove of walnut trees, by the lake, where once he walked with Kitty Hamilton.

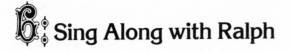 Sing Along with Ralph

Monday morning, 11:00, Billy Hoffman catches up with Sato Murasaki in the hall outside of Ralph Lekberg's office in the Music Building.

"Morning, maestro."

"Good morning, Mr. Hoffman."

"Time I met the composer, I guess."

"I'm just going in there myself," Sato says, and knocks on the door.

Ralph's voice. "Come in," and, as they enter, in Spanish: *"Aquí estamos trabajandos."* This translates "here we are working" but really means something more like "back at the old grind."

With Ralph are the two basses, little Mike Shapen, the student, and Henry Fennellon, Ralph's country neighbor from the next farm north. It's an industrious scene, Mike working away at his music copying, Henry doing some of the same on his own brief vocal part; Ralph benignly revising bassoons or something.

"You're not fussing with the orchestration?" Sato, smiling. "Ralph, this is Mr. Hoffman."

Ralph looks guilty of fussing, and says, "Sato, this is Henry Fennellon."

"How do you do?"

"I'm honored, Sato." What a speaking voice Fennellon has, not merely deep and strong but full of reverberation. Mike Shapen idolizes the man ("Christ, comparing my voice to his is like comparing a vibraphone plate to a big, old bronze bell.") Students have, from time to time, and for other than musical reasons, sought Henry out, become his acolytes. Mike is one of these.

That Henry Fennellon is to sing the villainous Raymond Applegore is a piece of cross-casting, for Henry is, in a way that grows more and more obscure, an heroic sort. Henry Fennellon, with his imposing shoulders, great greying tiger's head, and big voice, was a singer before the Second World War, a soldier during it, and then a network-television newsman. He left that profession near Selma, Alabama, in 1962, where he and his cameraman were hurt in a scuffle with some local white television critics.

Hospitalized overnight, Henry had appeared next morning in his head bandage, not to continue reporting the civil rights march but to join it. Then, no longer a newsman, he worked in the movement, knew Martin Luther King and the Evers brothers, Stokely Carmichael, Rapp Brown, and was useful to them for about three years—chiefly as a fund raiser—until black power and black pride rejected his big, sincere whiteness. After a strategy meeting one night a golden-gloves light-heavy-weight who was about to take a Moslem name and turn pro hit Henry and knocked him down for reasons no one there could quite understand.

Henry, a reformed country-tavern brawler, got up, butted the man in the solar plexus, hit him with an elbow in the throat, and then decked him with a clubbing left to the side of the face. Though the other blacks there congratulated him—a couple were close friends—Henry apologized for his loss of temper, left the meeting, and left the movement.

Now he's back on that farm from which he started, a magnificent recluse, although the Vietnam protest movement did get him involved again, locally anyway. Except for that, it would be hard to guess at any part of his past from the way he talks and dresses these days: hog prices and coveralls. He does withdraw a little into his natural dignity around Maury Jackstone, but Maury's such a nut he even affects older black people that way.

"*Aquí estamos trabajandos.*" Ralph. "How's it coming, Mike?"

"That's it, Dr. Lekberg." Mike relaxes, hits the page he's been working on. "You got a piano reduction."

"You still look the same size to me," Hoffman mutters to Ralph's upright.

"Thank you, Mike." Ralph. "Remember Gomez?"

Mike looks puzzled. Sato answers:

"Fat Gomez, from Chile," and explains. "A man Ralph and I knew in Mexico City. His favorite phrase was '*Aquí estamos trabajandos,*' but he never worked. The range for the paymaster is all right, Ralph."

"Not too high?"

"Riding can handle it. A nice voice."

"Have you started coaching?" Henry.

"Yes, with Karen's help. When shall you and I?"

"Early this afternoon? I can come back in after lunch."

"Mike?"

"I've got Dr. Lekberg's theory class in about twenty minutes," Mike. "Are we having class today?"

"All he did was eat," Ralph replies.

"Excuse me?"

"Our Chilean friend, Gomez. Was it 1954, Sato?"

Sato confirms that that was the year they met, with Ralph on leave in Mexico City, Sato there as summer guest conductor. Their friendship in Mexico led to Sato's having come here to State University for the following three years.

"Is that the whole lecture on Gomez?" Henry asks. The roomful of men is all tolerant smiles at Ralph.

"It's appropriate to what we did over the weekend, Henry," the composer says. Henry caps his pen and pushes the sheet of music manuscript aside. He has been standing at a lectern to copy; he has too much height and chest to write comfortably sitting down. Now he sits next to Mike Shapen and lights a cigarette. Hoffman sits on a small table. Sato takes the piano bench by the upright. "You see, one day I was with a blonde American girl when we found Gomez, eating at a table for one, in the café nearest the bullring, the Plaza Mexico."

"We all hated to eat out with Gomez." Sato. "He would always manage to be the last to order, and then somehow what came for him always looked better and more unusual than what anyone else had."

"Competitive eating." Hoffman. Henry chuckles, a big, rich sound.

"I hadn't expected to see Gomez at all. The girl had just arrived in Mexico City, and had come to me as someone who might know where to find that scoundrel on the piano bench." He points to Sato, who turns himself just enough toward the keyboard to reach his right hand around and play, in the treble, a couple of bars from *Der Rosencavalier,* of the passage in which the lecherous baron tells little Sophie how lucky she is to be getting him as a husband: *Mit mir, mit mir.*

"A sweet, eager girl." Ralph, in mock reproach, and Sato's treble quote in reply is from *Madame Butterfly* this time, a phrase from the Flower Duet of Cio-Cio-San and Suzuki.

"The young lady was named Pinkerton, of course." Henry. Mike grins, and Hoffman lifts his brows in incomprehension.

"I'd thought Sato might be in the bullfight crowd, and at the café after the fight. The girl and I hadn't gone that day. She wasn't able to make up her mind whether she wanted to. And I'd lost my *afición,* as the Mexicans say. Too many bad fights, too much exposure to the insiders' talk of shaved horns and slowed-down animals."

"I usually went, but not that day," Sato gives them a few bars of something even Hoffman recognizes this time, bullfight music, "La Virgen de la Macarena." "I never stopped admiring the courage of the kids who did it, but I agree. The exploitation of the kids is disgusting. And the conduct of the fights—but it's no better in Spain, Ralph."

"I asked Gomez what he was eating this time. And the girl, just being nice, said, 'Oh, it looks so good.' Gomez smiled at her and asked, in that atrocious English, 'What is the only part of the animal that we can eat while the animal is still alive?'

"What he had on his plate, you see, was some sort of whitish mass, and if the pleasant girl hadn't said the slow-witted, unresponsive thing she did say, then I might very well have said it myself.

" 'Eggs?' she asked. But unfortunately, she attempted it in Spanish, '*Huevos?*' "

"Oh, how Gomez must have laughed." Sato plays a tittering trill.

"Sputters and giggles and belches. Horrible." Ralph, shaking his head and falling briefly silent.

"Yeah, eggs scare the piss out of me, too," says Hoffman. "Don't they you, Mike?"

"Yeah, they do, Mr. Hoffman," says Mike, and Ralph, who asks nothing more from life than the chance to tell other people what he has learned, smiles.

"Yes. Well. *Huevos* does mean eggs in Spanish, of course, but proper Mexicans will usually call them *blanquillos*—'little white things'—because colloquially *huevos* means 'testicles, balls.' And that was exactly what Gomez had come to the bullring café to eat. Oh, how he urged her to try a bite, roaring with laughter, calling the waiter to bring a plate and fork."

Even Hoffman recognizes the next musical phrase: *Bring me food and bring me wine,* from "Good King Wenceslaus," to which Sato adds: "Poor Barbara. Was she offended, when she understood?"

"Well, I think only because Gomez intended that she be. And I was offended for her. She was an appealing girl, wanting only to have a little fun on a short vacation."

"We assume she did." Henry bows to Sato.

It was just/One of those things, Sato replies in melody on the piano, returning the bow.

"I don't suppose she had much of a first evening in town, though." Ralph. "I dropped her at her hotel, promised to get word to Sato of where she was. I remember feeling, as I drove out Avenida Insurgentes, back to my house and bride in San Angel Inn, a sense of small failure in a role I used to enjoy in Mexico City. I wanted to be the easy, wise, reassuring man—amusing but not insincere—who could show you that town and put a glow on your sight of it. The teacher through whom old hands and romantic newcomers might meet. The one whose house and parties and . . . personal spirit would somehow always be near the center when you remembered Mexico and good times there. Instead, with the eager blonde girl Barbara it seemed to me I'd been only the stranger who bungled his try at being of service, not even alert enough to protect her from a small, gratuitous unpleasantness. I remember passing a trolley car and nearly being hit by it as I made my turn off the avenue, because I was still absorbed in trying to think what reply I could have made to Gomez that would at least have lifted the passage to the level of honest bawdiness."

La cucaracha, la cucaracha, Sato plays. His brief musical contributions do not at all interrupt Ralph, but fill out his pauses. "Anyway," the conductor says. "She didn't take it all that hard, Ralph. She was always eager to see you and Josette."

Ralph looks at Sato thoughtfully and says, after a moment: "Those failures of role are never apparent to anyone but oneself, I suppose."

"How can they be?" asks Henry. "When the audience doesn't know what the hell the role's supposed to be?"

And Sato concurs, with a quote from *Pagliacci—Vesti la giubba,* the lament of an actor costumed for comedy whose heart is broken.

"Yes," says Ralph. "Well, I suppose Gomez's little sideshow had something to do with why a dozen years went by without my wanting to try eating . . . the balls of things.

"But I could have learned the taste any Sunday afternoon, after the fights, at that café nearest the bullring. Though I think the implication of its locality—that the meat course is supplied from the brave animals just now conquered in the ring—is probably false. Gomez's grisly riddle is more likely correct. . . . Come in, come in."

For there is a knock on the door. It opens, and Hughmore Skeats IV, very much the official Director of the State University Opera Guild this morning, stands aside to permit the entrance of an enormous, pink young man—a young man even taller than Henry Fennellon's six feet two, and fifty soft pounds heavier.

"Our tenor, chums." Skeats. "Marcel St. Edouard. Ralph Lekberg you met last spring. Sato Murasaki you've heard, of course. Mike Shapen. Henry Fennellon, who perhaps grew the last pork chop you ate. And this must be Mr. Hoffman, the stage director?"

Marcel, blushing, shakes hands, says how delighted, overwhelmed, oh my, calls the conductor "Mr. Murasato," apologizes.

"We're so glad you're here." Ralph.

"Oh, I certainly am, too. It's such a long trip from Los Angeles. Just one big airplane after another." The cadence is southern.

"Is your room all right?"

"Oh, lovely. Thank you so much." Marcel is quartered—as are Hoffman, Sato, and the women in the cast—at University House.

"The little motel on the prairie." Hoffman.

"I've given Marcel a rehearsal schedule." Skeats. "When do you want to get moving with him, Sato?"

"Tomorrow morning, I think. Shall I phone your room, Marcel?"

"Why don't you just rest up today." Ralph.

"Oh, thank you. You know, I looked up your woodwind quintet, sir, after we met last spring. I play the clarinet a little, and sometimes some friends and I just get together to read things, and we did yours, and it's simply lovely."

"Thank you. Would you like to see the campus? I'm not sure about getting into the new auditorium today, but the art gallery's open."

"Oh, yes, just to see where I am. Is it true that some paintings were stolen? I just read everything in the papers about State City this spring. Do you really have pigs?" The last is for Henry.

"About eight hundred." Henry. "Be glad to take you out to the farm sometime."

Marcel says he'd love that. Marcel asks if Henry has cows. "I love cows. I milked one, every morning and evening, when I was little, and I just loved her."

"Ours are beef cattle, I'm afraid." Henry. "Ralph and I have them in partnership. We have adjoining farms. And some sheep, too."

"It's all these peasants talk about." Hughmore Skeats. "Their blithering lambs and bulls and baby ducks. Am I right? That's what you were running on about when we knocked, weren't you, now?"

"To tell you the truth, Hugh, Ralph was discussing a riddle." Henry Fennellon dominates a person, a gathering, a stage sometimes, unconsciously, with an ease that makes certain others—Skeats is one—venomous. "Perhaps you'd like to try: Which is the only part of an animal we can eat while the animal is still alive?"

"Wait now. Not eggs." Skeats looks at him, picking up something from his tone, is not dumb. "Are you talking about the tickles, then? Good old outback oysters, is it?"

"Farmers around here always call them 'fries.' " Ralph. "You know, it turns out they're eaten anyplace animals are raised for meat and the young males castrated to be fed out. Such as barrows, or steers, or wethers. . . ."

"What about capons, then?" Skeats says. "Seen them done. Cut in through the back of the bird, just here." He points to Marcel's backbone just above the waist. "But what they take out's about half the size of your smallest fingernail. Not a lot of nourishment there, I'd say."

Ralph says: "What Henry and I learned over the weekend is that the ones from calves are quite a lot better than the ones you get in the big cookouts around here, which come from pigs. Or so Henry says, at any rate."

"Oh, dear." Marcel. "Do I understand that you and Mr. Fennellon . . . ?"

"On Saturday Henry and I penned fifteen calves," Ralph, "so the vet could cut the bulls and inoculate the heifers. These were last year's late calves and they had run all winter without being weaned, so they were rather large."

"Did you have to hold them?" Marcel. "Calves are so strong."

Ralph says: "The veterinarian brings along a squeeze chute. When an animal is in it, its head sticks out the front gate, with the neck held behind the head. Then the sides of the chute are tightened against the sides of the calf. Josette—Mrs. Lekberg—was in the pen, cutting out the calves one at a time. Then Henry would get behind and twist the animal's tail to get it to move forward."

"That how you hurt your hand?" Hoffman asks Henry, whose right hand is bandaged.

"I missed a tail, and the heifer caught me with her hoof."

Ralph says: "My job was to close the rear gate of the chute, behind each calf, and tighten the sides. The vet was across from me, with his knife for the bulls and his needles for the heifers. We were just ready to start when suddenly Henry said to Josette, 'Where's the dishpan, Josie?' My wife knows that farmer with the bandage, there, too well by now to say something dumb, like 'What for?', but I never learn. I said it. Henry and the vet said, 'Lunch,' together, and the vet got a clean bucket from his truck.

"It's odd, really. The heifers squirmed, reared, and twisted, trying to get away from the needles that would protect them from things like Bang's disease. But the little bulls stood rather placidly while the vet slit open each outer sac, pulled loose the membrane that covers the glands, and dropped them in his bucket. Apparently, it didn't hurt—"

"Excuse me," Marcel says abruptly. "I'm sorry, do you suppose? I would, well, I certainly would like to. Walk around the campus, I mean." With Hughmore Skeats after him, Marcel flees the conversation.

The five survivors look at one another, and Sato's right hand creeps back around to the keyboard, an operatic air from *Martha* which even Hoffman can recognize: *'Tis the last rose of summer . . .*

"Well, there's your tough young surveyor." Henry, sympathetically.

"He does have the voice," Ralph replies.

There is a moment's pause, and then Hoffman reminds them softly, "The balls."

"Are in the bucket." Sato.

"Did you eat the damn things?" Mike Shapen has been quiet for so long that his normal, aggressive voice sounds almost hostile.

"We took them to the kitchen, Josette, Henry, and I. It was noon. We had a shot of bourbon all around. Josette is Basque, you know, and she began telling us that the testicles of pigs and cattle may be all very well, but the best come from ram lambs. We challenged, and Josette then proved it, out of *Larousse Gastronomique*. Under 'Variety Meats,' we found that the French word is *animelles*. The book seems almost disapproving, saying that in France and Spain the taste for *animelles* has at times become so popular as to be almost faddish. And of course Josette was right: The faddists preferred testicles from young rams and then the book gives, I believe, six recipes for preparation—in cream sauce, fricasseed, fried, fried in batter, fried with mushrooms, and . . . and *à la vinaigrette*."

A few notes from Sato, which Mike identifies for Hoffman. "The prelude to *L'Heure Espagnole*."

"I'd like to vinaigrette the editor who wrote that entry." Henry. "There's only one way to cook fries."

"Which Henry was kind enough to show us Saturday noon. Josette, I could tell, was delighted. She'd been afraid she was supposed to know how. But Henry called for a very sharp knife and, since he couldn't manage it himself with an injured hand, directed me. He had me take each testis, slit the membranous inner sac very carefully from end to end, and pop the gland out through the slit. Each one was about three inches long and two inches through, oval-shaped, of course, pinkish, convoluted."

"Sounds like a brain, you know?" Hoffman.

"Well, a sweetbread perhaps."

Un Ballo in Maschera is the next prelude quoted.

"Henry had me slice them in quarter-inch slices. Flour, and season lightly, and sauté in butter. We'd castrated nine bull calves, about eight months old, and they produced two pounds three ounces of dressed meat. More than Henry, Josette, and I could have eaten alone. But then there were two student members of the cast. Did they tell you, Mike? Davey Riding, Sato, the Paymaster you've just been working with. And Dick Auerbach, who'll sing one of the Poker Players, another tenor, though not so high as Davey. The two were working for me, painting the barn.

"They came to the door, and asked Josette's permission to get some sandwiches they'd brought for lunch out of the refrigerator. And Henry said we had something a good deal better to offer them for lunch. It seemed natural not to tell them what, until after they'd started eating."

What is this thing/Called love?

"Actually, the boys were quite enthusiastic when they found out." Henry. "The things are damn good."

"What are they like?" Mike asks.

"Again, like sweetbreads. But the grain is finer and the meat perhaps a little firmer and richer. Though in no way strong.

"Another thing that seemed natural was that all four of us males should watch Josette when she was ready to start eating—she'd been busy while the rest of us began, putting our baby granddaughter, who's visiting, into a high chair and pouring fruit juice into the child. But I can't say Josette gave us much to grin about.

"She carries off that sort of thing in good style. Two weeks ago, for example, an old gentleman who rides horseback with her came back from a trip to Missouri, and presented her with a certain country artifact that's obviously related. It was a whiplike piece of cartilage a yard long, with a tuft of hair and dried skin at one end, to use as a riding crop. The old horseman watched her flex it, let her remark that it would almost do for a dressage whip, and then told us: 'That's what runs the length of a bull's penis, Mrs. Lekberg. They say it makes the only whip in the world that will turn mules.' And Josette, quite unruffled said, 'Now Ralph will have to buy me a mule. Thank you so much.' "

Incorrigible Sato thinks of a musical phrase from *Samson and Delilah*: *Amour! viens aider ma faiblesse.*

"Josette said she thought the fries very good indeed, so of course Henry had to push the next inch: 'Why don't you let the baby try a bite?' Our granddaughter is fourteen months old; she was messing up a plate of hamburger and rice, and I confess Josette did hesitate. But Henry and the two boys were ready to start grinning. Davey and Dick. And the baby was definitely interested, holding up a spoon, the way they do, waving it, cooing. She's accustomed by now to eating whatever we eat, you see. So Josette chopped her up a taste of fries, which our granddaughter ate with relish.

"I said, 'That might be something for a girl to talk over with her analyst twenty years from now,' . . . but you know, that was the wrong kind of joke? A weak, city sort of joke for a country matter.

"Our two graduate students stayed in character quite well, I thought, when Henry and I went out after luncheon to watch them getting back to their barn painting. They were up on ladders, stripped to the waist in the June sun, and they got on Henry.

" 'Hey, Henry,' Davey said. 'We were wondering how you cook a basketball.'

"Dick said, 'He'd have to shoot a basket first, wouldn't he?'

"And Henry said sadly, 'We fed those boys too many fries.'

" 'They're full of something,' I agreed.

" 'I believe they'll recover with time,' Henry said. 'But you know those young heifer calves we inoculated this morning? I wouldn't let one of them walk under a ladder with these boys above her this afternoon.' "

Henry grins. Hoffman grins. Mike grins.

Take me out to the ball game.

Ralph sighs. "I'd be happy if it ended with that variation of the Visigothic fallacy—it was the Visigoths, wasn't it, who ate a captured enemy's heart if he'd been a valiant man? I'd be happy to agree that Chief Henry had struck the right tribal note for the experience. Then I could put it aside to contemplate from time to time as a lesson for me in my current role: man about the farm, you see? Except that just this morning, two days later, Josette told me a dream.

"There is among our horses one named Echo. Born on the farm to Josette's favorite mare. A three-year-old now. Josette is very attached to Echo and protective of him, but is sometimes impatient with him because he is so gentle in the pasture that, though he is very big, he lets the other horses bully him. Because of this, we let Echo go as long as possible last year before we finally had him gelded. We hoped the delay would give him a little more muscle, a little more fire.

" 'In my dream,' Josette said this morning, 'I was eating fries again, but they were Echo's.'

"And in my role as husband, I didn't know how to reply."

Ralph's eyes go down to his music manuscript. Henry looks at him gravely, Hoffman with curiosity. Mike Shapen looks at his own worn denim knees.

From Sato at the piano there comes no melody at all, not even a concluding chord, but softly, after an interval in which they wait for it, a drifting arpeggio in the antique Phrygian mode, moving up the white keys, with a note here and there of recapitulation, and down again, back to its starting place on E.

# 7: First Reading

Old Biology Hall is one of six buildings, standing among maple trees, spaced by lawn, that made up the entire university campus at the end of the nineteenth century. It is four stories high, built of big blocks of yellow stone, and is disfigured now by black iron fire escapes, like moustaches drawn on the stone façades.

Inside, its halls are wider, its worn marble staircases far grander than the linoleum and elevators provided in the new brick Life Sciences Center, to which the laboratories were moved. There are still glass-fronted showcases of fish and fossils on the first two floors of Old Biology, and half of the third floor is still a museum of natural history, with habitat groups of birds and animals.

The other half of the third floor is occupied by what was once the university's principal auditorium. It, too, has been superseded—by the great ballroom at the Union, by the university theatre, by a number of smaller and more comfortable auditoriums in the newer buildings. With the coming of the big entertainment complex, Old Biology, third floor, is no more than a rehearsal hall. But for fifty years every cultural event of consequence took place here. Helen Hayes appeared on its stage in *Twelfth Night,* and Katharine Cornell in *The Barretts of Wimpole Street.* Lawrence Tibbet gave a recital here, Joseph Hofmann played. Congressman Richard M. Nixon lectured. Once Robert Frost read poems in what is now called Old Biology, and there were students sitting on the floor in the aisles and all around the poet on the stage.

Snazzer Short, propitiating, arrives thirty minutes early and thirty degrees hungover, sits on a folding wooden seat in the first row of Old Biology auditorium, waiting for the cast, and even more for Billy Hoffman, to appear. He feels something like the anxiety of a man required to present an uncouth relative to elegant acquaintances. Nor can he doubt that Hughmore Skeats IV is at work.

"Ralph, old boy. Walk you to the auditorium?"

"Good morning, Hugh."

"Have you had a talk with this odd little chap Snazzer found?"

"We've met."

"Doesn't know beans about music, so far as I can judge."

"Sato says it doesn't matter, Hugh."

"I heard that. You agree?"

"Whatever's on your mind, Hugh, I think you should speak to Sato."

Ass dismissed, eh? "Very well, old boy. If you'll excuse me I'll do just that."

"I have the authority in theory," Sato, on the telephone, agrees.

"Well, you see, if anything's to be done about it the time is now, isn't it? Before the poor blighter gets started."

"Mr. Skeats. My authority is, as I say, unfortunately quite theoretical."

"But you see, otherwise the cast will be confused . . ."

"I would feel quite helpless to assert it at this time, while I am only a visitor. Of course, if something were to happen—thank you for advising me of your doubts. We must keep an eye on things."

A slanty eye. "We'll watch him this morning, what?"

"I shall have the pleasure of seeing you shortly, at the auditorium, then?"

Ballocks.

Debbie then? Not much of a chance, but a chance. "She's doing what?"

"Sketching." Debbie's secretary.

"This morning? Are you sure? We've our first reading . . ." Debbie is sketching just across from the auditorium, the secretary explains, in the Natural History Museum.

"Heigh ho, Debbie. Not one to waste time, are you?"

She's on a folding canvas stool, in front of a showcase of dusty ducks.

"Teals. I am drawing teals, they are so small."

"Jolly good. Time to report across the way, isn't it? What sort of costume will you give me?"

"I think workman's clothing." She's packing up.

"Britches and boots?"

"Ach no, Hughmore. Maybe for the tenor."

"Do give us a bit of style, love. The bloke I'm playing's been in the army. Might look a soldier still. Met the director?"

"I meet him now."

"Here, let me carry it. Odd little gnome, all ears and a big cigar. I'm afraid it was Snazzer's whiskey did the hiring."

"Hughmore, stop. This man Maggi said would be very good."

Doesn't weasel, anyway. Let's see how Snazzer's dwarf does with the cast, then.

The first sight and sound of a cast he had nothing to do with choosing is crucial to Hoffman, so he pays no attention as they gather in Old Biology. He asks Ralph Lekberg where's a good place in town to get his shoes half-soled. He asks Snazzer Short when Maggi's coming back, anyway? He thanks Sato Murasaki for offering to go through the score with him after rehearsal, and says:

"You might as well try to teach me Hungarian, but I'll pretend I know what you're talking about, okay?"

He tells Debbie Dieter Haas he's glad to meet her.

And all the time he's looking covertly at the people in his cast, muttering, irrelevant, shuffling, finally pausing to look up at the old bare stage, while the singers find battered seats in the first two rows.

Behind his back he hears Skeats's voice:

"Here she is. Welcome, Beth. Sato, Beth Paulus."

Instead of turning to look, Hoffman walks up the flight of seven steps onto the stage. Already he's got a lot of stuff tucked between those unseemly ears. He has talked enough with Ralph and Sato to know what to expect from the singers in the way of vocal qualities. He has confidence in Sato, and Christ, one look at the old German broad is enough to give anyone confidence in Debbie. And as for Ralph, as for Snazzer, too, they're off the board now; they've been jumped. 'Bye, composer. See ya, librettist. It's our show, starting now, Sato's, Debbie's, Billyboy's, you know?

He turns to look at Beth, expecting the squared-back shoulders and deep bosom, and is shocked. Nothing prepared him for the face—strange, planed, chalky, the eyes more Mongol even than Sato's, with the expression, guiltless but not innocent, of a passionate twelve-year-old.

He walks back down the steps again, looking at her, watching Hughmore Skeats, the faculty baritone, beside her, acting proprietary, noticing Johnny Ten Mason (this kid's a doctor?) having a good look.

Time for the parade. "Uh, I think we better go up on stage. Everybody got a book? There going to be enough chairs up there?"

He sits by Snazzer and watches them move, go up the steps, find chairs, settle themselves.

Sidney/Sally Anne, the little soprano, up first and eager. Pretty. Any color hair you want. Straight back. Moves on the balls of her feet, deft, neat. Boobs artfully separated. Chin up, making the third ball-point of a perky triangle. Knows she's okay to look at. Will take every possible advantage of it; you can tell from the way she sends your look back to you. Presence. Will learn. Did summer musical stock. Studied here. Good student. Ralph says her voice is true; Sato says it's small. Ingenue, comedienne. She'll do the flirt and fickle, the changeable parts okay at the top of the show. Where will she get the power for the closing melodrama?"

"You always rehearse in bare feet, Sidney?"

She replies by lifting a foot and pointing toes at him, bobbing her head: "Yes, sir, please." It takes battalions of Sidneys for the national showbiz effort. They draft themselves, reporting for induction by the hundreds every month in New York and California. Curtain fodder.

See who's next: Al, our hero—Marcel. The lollipop ox. Ralph and Sato agree, great voice. He waddles just a little going up the steps, and there's a nice, unintimidating, friendly look about the way his size makes him slouch, which will put things a couple of bubbles off plumb, won't it? Probably have to hold him still. Don't let him mince. Every move something very definite. Try to use the size for authority. Toughest engineer that ever planted a flag, you know? Plant him. Keep his feet apart. Stand Sidney up against all that bulk, Beth, too, maybe you'll make a point; he's even going to be enough bigger than Skeats, the villain, old Pill. Natural match-up; when meatball meets cream puff, one gets dented, one gets smothered. Watch out when it's Marcel and big Henry Fennellon, though.

"Got a match, Marcel?"

"Oh, I'm sorry. I don't smoke."

"That's all right. This is a lousy cigar, anyway." Big puff looked all right making his turn, listening.

As for the Pill, Hughmore, our villain, taking Beth's elbow up the steps, how do we hold you down, baby? There's not enough ham in this country, we gotta import it from Australia? No wonder the pig farmers are tear-ass. Look, foot meets stage and already Skeats's movements enlarge. Exaggerate. His smile's good; big white teeth show bright, framed by the beard. Beard dyed? Hair dyed. Teeth capped? Makes him look like an actor. Experienced man, anyway. Takes charge. Playing captain.

"Who's got a blooming match for Mr. Hoffman?" Not too many of these singers smoke. "Davey? Mike? Thank you, here Billy. Catch." Deliberately bad throw, which sends Hoffman scuffling. "Now. Shall we have the chairs in a semicircle?"

Moving now to the chair Skeats holds for her, the extraordinary-looking Beth. Moves slow—serene? Systematical? Smouldering? None of the above. She moves in the way powerful men move and the sea, the way Fennellon moves, flowing, with that relaxation that usually originates in knowing one's own strength and that implies certain threats. But Beth's appearance is not muscular; the power in her movements is emotional, for Christ's sake, emotion moves that body the way muscles move other people's. Emotionally idle now, she idles. And that unnaturally girlish face. If the voice is all Ralph says it is, then she'll deliver passion in performance, won't she? Goddamn, what else does she use that passion for?

"Take the chair by Henry, Beth. Henry Fennellon, the big guy." Henry raises his hand. What a stage couple they'll make, Raymond and Norah Applegore.

As for the rest, the kids, just one tiny problem: Here's this fine construction crew of tough, bulldozing Georgia rednecks, big and little, okay, voices certified, student-looking bunch for now, but makeup will help, right? Lights. Costumes. Debbie's German hand will age and toughen them enough. Except. Except right in the middle of them we got one extra-tall, grinning, wavy-headed, gorgeous banshee of a basketball player, one brown face sticking up a foot over the white ones. Fine voice. Incredibly bright, according to Ralph and Snazzer. But just what in the hell is he doing in a white construction crew, in Georgia, in 1949?

"Uh, what's your name again?"

"Maury Jackstone, Mr. Hoffman. Your Second Poker Player. Poke 'um and play 'um, number two. Sir."

"Yeah, okay Maury."

"Understudy every part you got up here. Even Sidney's."

Sidney shows him her teeth.

"'Specially Sidney's. Sidney, you can go on home."

Hits him on the arm with her little clenched fist. Maury staggers, almost falls, his pain nearly fatal. "You can stay, Sidney. I give up."

Seem to be acquainted.

"The piano thing, what do you call it?"

"Reduction," Skeats says.

"The piano reduction will be here tomorrow, and we'll have a rehearsal pianist. That's Maury's wife, you know? You'll be coaching with her. And we'll have a stage manager to give you your calls for the week—that's somebody's wife, too."

"Mine," says Mike Shapen. Hoffman looks at the little bass and feels like giving him a wink. So he does.

"Today let's read it through and talk it over. Maybe you people can explain some of these lines to me."

Snazzer Short winces. 'Bye, librettist. Here is what Snazz, Ph.D., may never understand; Ralph, Ph.D., either; Sato and Debbie were born knowing it. A director may start as some kind of crumby literary critic while he has the luxury of considering whether to do a script, some sort of finicky judge of acting talent when he's casting. At that stage your director might have looked at Professor Short's work and said what the Snazzer knows perfectly well, but wishes someone would tell him different: That he's got a workmanlike little melodrama here, with occasional nice language, much of which won't be distinguishable when it's sung. Starting now, Hoffman must start working with the libretto as if it were the most profound and eloquent dramatic piece ever written. Sato must treat the music with the attention and care he would give a newly discovered score by Beethoven. Conductor and director, with Debbie in support as she designs settings and lighting and costumes, must work with the cast in the conviction that every member of it is capable of deathless performance.

Scene One

"You don't need to project," Hoffman says. "Just read the lines for meaning. Most of you've been working on the music, you know the script by now, but if there are any questions about what a line means, interrupt, okay?"

And remember, Billy, no cuts, no changes. All these words are set inalterably to music.

"Mr. Hoffman, I'm afraid I just don't understand much at all of this opening," Marcel says. "I mean, I just haven't ever played any poker."

"Yeah."

"I'm sorry."

"I don't think we'll stop and teach you now," Hoffman says. "But maybe we better have a game tonight. How many of you play?"

Skeats, Dr. Mason, the thick-necked pink kid, Maury Jackstone. Not Davey Riding, not Mike Shapen, not Marcel.

"We can do it at my place," Skeats offers. "If everybody will help clean up afterward."

"Everybody knows where our place is, Mr. Skeats," Davey Riding says. He and Sue live in a one-room, remodeled schoolhouse outside of town. "And it's a mess anyway."

It's agreed they'll gather at the Ridings'. Mason is tied up; he promised to take emergency tonight, for a friend.

"Okay, Al." Hoffman to Marcel. "We got a game. Just don't plan on running off into the swamp afterward with all the money. I got to get my shoes fixed."

As they start the first scene, Hoffman reading stage directions ("*Six members of the construction crew are playing poker . . .*"), Debbie rises quietly and leaves. She has seen what they look like now. She will be back when Hoffman has them on their feet, to see how he blocks them, how they group. What they sound like means little to her, and she has much to do.

But as she leaves, she can hear Skeats naming the cards in his deal, hear Dick Auerbach, as First Poker Player, say, "Check the ten," and hear Skeats again—out of character—say:

"I'm the bloody dealer, Dick. You address that to me."

And Hoffman: "Let's save the poker lesson for tonight, Mr. Skeats, okay? Start again."

There are not many interruptions: a discussion of scrip, a form of payment with which the younger members of the cast aren't familiar. A definition of transit. A bawdy suggestion from Skeats as to how Sally Anne might be costumed for her song when she's transformed from Al's vision to Pill's—in reply to which, Hoffman has an anecdote for them:

"Stage nudity in New York these days, boy, you can't believe it, like if you haven't got a nude scene, maybe you can't raise money for your show. So I saw this play off-Broadway, it's a drab little domestic number, you know? No way to bare the body, but they figure they gotta be up to date. So the play opens, there's the overworked wife at the ironing board, in the wrapper and pincurls, doing the list of what's gone wrong. She leans over for the next damp shirt and whoops, the actress has to let the wrapper fly open and show beaver. Some nude scene. Take it from 'Friday at the races . . .' "

They finish the first scene: the accusation of Al, Al's flight to the swamp, Pill's pursuit; the arrival of the paymaster saying the scrip is worthless.

"That's a blasted long scene, shall we have a break now?"

Hoffman stares at Skeats, turns to Mona Shapen. "Stage Manager? Want to give the cast a break?"

Intermission

Sidney leads Beth to the rest room and, as they come out again, says: "Hey, Beth. I want to show you something."

Takes her into the museum, three dozen cases of old-fashioned taxidermy. Polar bears, puffins, flying squirrels.

"Isn't this great? I run in here every chance I get." Stops in front of a case displaying a family of timber wolves, facing a snarling lynx. "I'm always for the cat."

"Oh, God, it's beautiful," Beth whispers. "Oh, God."

"Huh?"

Scene Two

They have just started Scene Two, The Swamp. Marcel—Al—shoos off a snake.

"Now," Skeats interrupts Marcel's reading. "Who is this Mrs. Cottonmouth? Is it a bunny or something the snake is supposed to give his love to?"

"Oh, no." Marcel answers it himself. "No, that's a name for water moccasin, too. Well, what we do down home, we call them either one of those names. Cottonmouth, moccasins. They're just horrible snakes."

"I thought they were horrible rabbits." Skeats. "Carry on, old boy."

"I think you're a horrible rabbit," Sidney stage-whispers to Maury.

"All right, hold it." Hoffman's brusqueness brings a slightly startled silence. He lets them all look at him, and then says, mildly. "I'll answer the questions, you know? If I can't, I'll have to ask somebody else okay? How else you going to find out how dumb I am?"

Scene Three

". . . Baby, you don't know Pill!" cries Hughmore Skeats IV as Pill; the swamp scene is over, and Sato moves from the tenth row down to the second.

Listens to Hoffman read, *"Lobby of a seedy little hotel . . . ,"* and Sato, along with everyone else, in the house and on the stage, is waiting. He checks his copy of the libretto, though he hardly needs to, and confirms that Marcel/Al has half a dozen lines first—and then they will hear Beth speak.

They have seen her half-smile, her tentative nod, heard her low murmuring in reply to something Sidney said or Skeats; and now, as Norah, she begins, and something begins for all of them:

BETH/NORAH: "Yes?"

MARCEL/AL: "Sorry to wake you. Got a room and bath?"

BETH/NORAH: "No bath. You're out of season, mister. Water's off."

How did Sato know what would be there? He hasn't met Beth before, hasn't worked with her yet, has yet to hear her sing. Yet merely hearing the voice in reading, he is thrilled. Hears the hum and throb of an engine, running quietly for now, knows that it can rev, roar, thunder, without ever losing smoothness. And how extraordinary that such a sound should come from one not grown beyond the blushing stage. Hoffman stops her, and it jolts them all.

"Those fish are called *brim,* Norah, even if it's spelled *bream.*"

"Oh, I'm sorry." The blush shows mostly high on the forehead, through the sideswept shiny brown hair. "But what kind of fish are they, Mr. Hoffman?" The maiden's chance for happiness depends on the answer.

"I don't know. Let's ask our librettist." Even Hoffman seems shaken by this rising unabashed sincerity.

"Small, small." Snazzer Short. "Smaller than bass, smaller, but freshwater. Southern . . . term."

A hand, a respectful hand is raised.

"Yeah. Yeah, Marcel? Go ahead."

"I believe that's what they call a sunny-fish up North."

"Bluegills?" Henry.

"Oh, pumpkinseeds." Sidney.

"Rock bass." Stolid, pink Dick Auerbach.

Ralph Lekberg clears his throat. "It's all the sunfish family," he explains. "The biggest member is the largemouth or black bass. Then the smallmouth, both rather elongated. And next the white and and black crappie, less elongated and somewhat smaller, quite pretty fish. And then the bream, which include half a dozen kinds, which are mostly lumped together and called bluegills around here."

"I say, Ralph." Skeats. "There's the natural-history museum, just across the hall. Shall we have a tour?"

"I don't know that they have fish," Ralph says, seriously, and even his old friend Sato has to laugh. "Do you know we even have some of the true bass around here? The same family as sea bass. The white ones people call stripers, and the yellow"— Beth is listening, absolutely intent—"but I only know of one lake in the state where you can catch yellow bass."

Scene Four

"Now we got this crazy duet over the telephone." Hoffman. "Only I suppose it's really a trio at the end, isn't it? Even though Al's miles away, Sally Anne and Pill are singing with him. Should we call it a trio?"

The question is meant for Sato, but Skeats replies: "Not unless two and one make three, Mr. Hoffman."

"Okay, Pill," says Hoffman. "Let's hear it."

Scene Five

Dick Auerbach and Maury Jackstone, being First and Second Poker Players, could have left after the first scene; so could Davey Riding. Maury wanted to stay through, so all three have. Third Poker Player (Mike Shapen) and the only named poker player, Bert Tannenbaum (Dr. Mason), stay for their reappearance at the very end.

Now, as the final scene is read, Dick watches Maury annotating his playbook. Dick can read the words easily enough, but can't solve what Maury means by them. Dick often finds Maury hard to solve.

Maury has his libretto in a legal-size binder. He's gotten two copies, so that he can paste each separate eight-and-a-half by eleven-inch page on an eight-and-a-half by fourteen-inch one. But the margins are trimmed off the Dittoed libretto pages, so that there's quite a lot of room for Maury to write. Dick thinks Karen probably did the cutting and pasting for Maury. Karen is very neat. There are extra sheets in the binder, too.

What Maury has written on one of the extra sheets seems to refer to the final scene, but even after his friend has finished crossing out and substituting and has copied the whole thing over, Dick still doesn't get it, beyond recognizing the names:

ALaphone, ALaphonse, ALabammy. Whammy.
IgNORAH, UggNORAH, atchaperil. Bammy.
SALLY ANNEtic going frantic
PILLie, Pallie, Pillo.
HooRAY, ataway, arma little dillo.
THIRD PLAYER, hold the gun
And BERTIE FLIRTIE TANNER BUM.

Hey, Dick Auerbach.

Dick looks away, caught, to Sidney, who catches him looking.

The climax has come. Al lies dead, Pill lies dead. Four thousand dollars in scrip lies scattered on the floor. Henry Fennellon and Beth, as Ray and Norah, are reading now:
(RAY): "Good, Norah. Very good. Four grand."
(NORAH): "I killed him. God, I killed him."
(RAY): "Here, Norah. Better let me have the gun."
(NORAH): "No. Never. Never."
(RAY): "Come on, Norah. Now don't get me sore at you. . . ."
Hoffman, reading stage directions: *"Limp, Norah turns over the gun to her husband . . ."* Looks up, and is shocked again. Everyone is. Beth is crying.
"Come on, Bert," Hoffman says. "Bert Tannenbaum, your line."
But Johnny Ten Mason, M.D., is still staring at Beth. It's Maury Jackstone, finally, who reads the line:

(BERT): "What's going on? God, are they dead?"

And now Mike Shapen. (THIRD POKER PLAYER): "All right, mister. Throw your cannon down. These things don't miss."

"Sorry," says Johnny Ten Mason. But now he and Maury read together. (BERT): "There's two men dead."

Hoffman grins. "Okay. That's enough of the choral reading," and Sidney goes on with Sally Anne's line. (SALLY ANNE): "The money. Look, the money. . . ."

Maury won't quit. Again he reads in chorus with the Texas surgeon. (BERT): "Both of them meant for you to have it. Pick it up."

Hoffman reads: *"Angrily, threatening her with the shotgun."*

Maury and Texas John, together. (BERT): "Down on your knees and pick it up. Go on."

"All right, cut it out, Maury. You know?"

Nope. Again Maury reads with Johnny Ten, two baritones but with speaking voices a minor third apart, so that it sounds like church. (BERT): "It's two cents on the dollar that they're paying, girl. Easiest eighty bucks you'll ever make."

"Curtain," says Hoffman. "Thank you, people. That was really weird."

"Splendid discipline, Mr. Hoffman." Hughmore Skeats, loudly, enunciating each of the five syllables distinctly.

🔖 Sympofo Sidnobet

Exeunt, mostly to lunch.

Sato Murasaki and Billy Hoffman go to Ralph's office in the Music Building, where the conductor keeps his copy of the score. It measures eighteen by twenty-four inches and weighs twelve pounds. Parts have been distributed, now, to ten singers and seventy-eight musicians. Karen Jackstone has the completed piano reduction; Sato will spend the early afternoon with her, working through it.

Sato will spend the late afternoon with Debbie and Mona Shapen, with the full score, in the new auditorium. Mona, as stage manager, and Debbie, as lighting designer, must be ready to prepare a copy of this huge score technically, adding to it, when the time comes, all the cues for lights and effects.

Tomorrow morning Sato will meet the orchestra, with Ralph.

Now he is giving Hoffman a preliminary idea of what the music will sound like, playing an occasional passage on the piano, singing here and there. It is a very intensive, no-nonsense hour or so of work by a couple of professionals, at the end of which Hoffman says:

"Boy, I'd like to hear it, you know?"

"So would I." Sato, with a smile. "So would Ralph."

It will be a couple of weeks before they start putting it all together, orchestra, singers, stage.

"You guys already can, can't you? In your heads."

"Perhaps to the same extent that you can see it."

"You mean, it's a jumble?" Hoffman grins. "Oh, shit, you're right. The jumble's slowing down. Like watching your clothes through the glass window in the dryer, at the laundromat. It's slowing down. You start to be able to tell the shirts from the underpants."

"Now we begin to take the clean clothes out and fold them neatly."

"The music comes last for me," Hoffman says. "But I've done musicals enough. After a while I get first one song and then another in my thick head, then I'm okay."

Sato hesitates. "My friend Hoffman," he says seriously. "With this score do not listen for songs. Think of it all, if you will, as one long, interesting, sustained song, telling its story with many voices and strings and winds and drums."

"Jesus."

"Is that discouraging?"

"Oh, no. Maybe I'll learn something. Listen, I want to hear you rehearse the orchestra when I haven't got a conflict, okay?"

"Of course. But listen to Karen. She is mechanical as a pianist but very accurate. And to your singers. They can teach you."

"Yeah. Which ones?"

"Henry, perhaps. Marcel especially."

"Marcel. Not Beth, huh?"

"Marcel is the best musician, I believe. He is well trained and very gifted. Beth, I don't know yet. Maybe no one will know for several years. She seems a very large talent."

"But talent's cheap."

"Oh, yes."

Yolande Janscombe Auditorium is the imposing center of the new entertainment complex. Cast and functionaries meet there after lunch to have a look, and there it is: the great new stage. The banks of lights, the ropes and cables, and, out where the audience would be, no seats yet.

"Wait till Sato sees the pit," Ralph says. "It's bigger than Chicago or Minneapolis."

"*Scusateme,*" Hughmore Skeats stands at stage center forward, singing. "*Me de ma sol presente. Io son il prologo.*"

"Somebody turn the stage on," Sidney cries, from somewhere. "I want a ride."

"Look." Debbie. They are all suddenly hyperactive, children on a brand-new playground. "Right here we can build such a steam shovel. How practical must it be, Billy?"

"We don't have to dig any holes with it." Hoffman. "But I'd like the girl to be able to wiggle all over the boom, you know?"

"A very real shovel."

"It should look like you drove it onto the stage."

"We ought to be doing *Aïda,* with elephants." Short.

"*E casta al par di neve,*" Skeats is on a *Pagliacci* kick, and Sidney runs up to sing the reply.

"Come, Mona." Debbie to her stage manager, Mike Shapen's wife. "We must see the light board."

"But it's so strange without the seats." Beth to Davey Riding, Mike, Johnny Ten Mason. "I can't help but see us all on stage, singing. And an audience, beautifully dressed in evening gowns and stiff shirts, sitting down here, two or three thousand, looking up at us from the floor."

"Let's get organized," Hoffman cries. "Come on."

"Everybody on stage." Mona Shapen, the stage manager, knows her job.

And when he has his cast, Hoffman says: "I made one of my best mistakes at Yale University, one summer, doing Sophocles' *Ajax,* in the Yale Bowl. It's a terrible play to begin with, and the guy who thought of putting it in a football stadium willed his brain to veterinary school, right? Well, the only way to do it would have been like a football game, you know? Ajax is murdering sheep, I oughta have had fifty sheep running up and down and Ajax after them with a sword, and maidens running around in togas and panty girdles, warriors throwing the javelins back and forth the length of the field. It might have worked. But we rehearsed indoors first on a stage, then in the gym, and my actors and I never did get the idea of how much space we had to use.

"Another time I did *Seventeen* in an airplane hangar, out in Colorado, and I'd have to say that of the two, that wretched *Seventeen* was the better show. At least we knew the size of the floor.

"Now, we can't rehearse here. We won't be in here till the last three days. But when I start blocking you, there in Old Biology, I want you to try to remember how goddamn big it is over here, okay?

"So now let's read it again and this time walk around, all over the stage. Anyplace you feel like. This won't be blocking, this'll just be trying it for size. Maury, what the hell are you doing?"

"Laocoon." Maury, who has slipped a headlock from behind on strong Dick Auerbach, and holds Dick immobilized.

Hoffman pauses, nods, and says judiciously: "It's an idea."

Zap says Maury's magic finger, and Dr. J. T. Mason, walking with Hughmore Skeats fifty feet in front of the four graduate students, turns into a column of titanium steel and rolls into the State River. Davey (the Paymaster) Riding has pointed out in the past and does again that the river is getting so choked up with titanium columns it's hardly safe for canoeing anymore.

"I'm sorry, Dave." Maury. "I forgot."

"You keep forgetting."

"Fats." Maury's diction transmogrifies. The cast is on its way to beer, after work. "Fats don't like for me to be no Second Poker Player."

"What Fats want today, man?" Dick Auerbach's impeccable, small-town, midwestern ghettoese is always at Maury's service for the Fats number.

"Fats want him. Medicool." Mason is cool indeed, walking along up there, neat, sufficient, not large but with such an appearance of perfect balance that he seems physically formidable. "Fats want me to be him, Bert Tannenbaum."

"Tell Skeats about it, Maury." Mike Shapen. "Don't tell us. He did the casting."

"Fats gonna loose the fateful lightning on Skeats, one of these high-noondays."

Those who follow Big Ten basketball remember Maury. He was the shortest man ever to lead the conference in rebounding—jump his own height, jets on his gym shoes, talons on his elbows.

Dick likes to tell about it. "He was plain hell on the boards, but he's such a nut. Sidney and I were there the night he sank the free throw that beat Illinois, after time ran out. It was during Christmas vacation; we were undergraduates and never thought we'd know him, but we rode down from Dueyville on the motorbike to see the game. Anyway, the game was over, Maury'd been fouled, tripped trying to drive for what could have been the winning basket. It was a one-and-one, but of course if he made the first free throw, it didn't matter about the second. And if he didn't make the first, the game went into overtime, and Illinois has been red-hot the last five minutes, catching up ten points since two of our starters fouled out. Anymore, this big black nut stands at the free-throw line, with a big smile, and at first the crowd was yelling for him. He was always their darling, putting on a dunking show for them before the game and things like that. They got very quiet so that he could shoot, and he did, and in it went, without even touching the rim. Swish.

"We started going wild, then, but Maury held up his hand. We thought he was asking for silence because he had a second shot coming, so the hush came back, and Maury lowered the ball between his legs like he was going to make a Granny shot, and then suddenly up it went, straight up as high in the air as he could throw it, and he whooped and started to sing: 'We're going to fight, fight, fight.' His voice filled the field house, and twelve thousand people picked up the words, and Maury led the team dancing off the floor."

After that, Maury went to Vietnam, to Harvard for a nondegree year in political science—he had the fellowship and wanted to hear some of those Kennedy staff people lecture—got married, and is now back here with a graduate assistantship in the music department (fix your television set, too, phone 682-1767).

It is Mike Shapen who knows what Fats looks like: "One day last spring, a couple of student radicals came around to try to get Maury to integrate a barbershop. We were sitting in the Gump, with Karen and Mona, our wives, drinking beer and talking music gossip.

"These two radicals both have beards—a little one, and a big, mangy one. They sat down, and told us that Coletown, a little place eight miles out from State City, needed to be shaken up.

" 'I suppose it does,' Maury said. 'Most places do.'

"Little Beard is a well-known character. He supports his political activity dealing speed, and he reminded us that this barbershop proprietor had been in the paper for refusing to cut hair for a black living out there somewhere.

" 'That redneck won't say no to you,' Big Beard said. 'Not if we all go.'

"Karen, Maury's wife, objected. 'I always cut Maury's hair.'

"Big Beard ignored her, and said, 'We got wheels. Let's drive on out there. We can phone the *Collegiate* from here, and get them to send a photographer.'

" 'I don't know,' Maury said good-naturedly. 'The barber said he didn't know how to cut woolly old black heads. He's probably right. I'd wind up with a ridiculous haircut.'

" 'Come on,' Little Beard said. His was a sharp Van Dyke job, and he lifted his chin to push the point of it at us. It was a lot easier to look at than the other beard, which was full and matted and dirty. 'Come on, man. Let's move out. This won't take half an hour.'

" 'I could shape it for you afterward,' Karen said anxiously. She's never sure what to say that will mesh with the gear Maury's in; he's got ninety-nine different forward speeds, but she knows the one she likes: Maury as the reincarnation of Paul Robeson, all-American athlete, leader of the orthodox left. Karen's one of those raised-Catholic rich girls from Boston, and what she can see is her parents watching the TV news one evening and there's their only daughter, sitting proudly on the platform, while Brezhnev pins the Order of Lenin on Maury's modest breast.

"Maury looked up past the ceiling, listened for a moment—Karen winced when she saw him do it—and then nodded. He had his message and he looked back at the beards. 'No, bossmens,' he said. 'Fats don't like for me to integrate no barbershop today, and what Fats don't like, I dassn't do.'

" 'Come on, guy, don't do it to us,' Little Beard said. 'We're in the club.'

"Big Beard said, 'Who's he talking about? Fats Waller, huh?'

" 'Ain't you ever been to Sunday school?' Maury said. 'Fats so thin you can't see 'um, so white he hurt your eyes. He 'bout nine feet tall, got him a real good hook shot, probly play pro ball, but he not much of a team man. Run and gun, and never passed off but once before in his life. Got him a starch blue warm-up suit, carry a live snake to whup bad black asses—'

" 'Oh, crap.' Little Beard was getting pissed.

" 'Fats don't have to. Tell you, boss, Him and his begot son, Tonde-layo, sure do like a boy like Mauryboy. 'Course Tondelayo don't like me quite as much as Fats do. I 'spect Tondelayo a little bit jealous.'

"Poor Karen was close to tears, Mona was halfway amused but comforting Karen, squeezing the girl's arm, and I was just pleased myself. The Gump's a special place, and I was glad to have Maury drive the beards out of our temple."

It has been Maury's reasonable contention while the casting of the opera was being worked out that Ralph ought to rewrite the tessitura of the lead part and let Maury sing Al—be just the right thing for the music department, the university, and, of course, the show. Failing that, he'd been willing to sing the small, featured part, Bert Tannenbaum.

"That medicat," he says, walking along the riverbank with his friends, from Janscombe Auditorium toward the Gump. "Seven, Eight, Nine, Ten Mason. Ol' Doc River . . . Don't transplant kidneys/Don't transplant femurs/And them that plants 'em/Is not redeemers. . . ."

Mike and Davey grab him, even Dick getting into the scuffle, which moves across the grass toward the water as Sidney and Beth pass.

& Sidney says, "Look at the hunks, Beth. Aren't they gorgeous?"

"You were singing in Minnesota last summer?"

" 'Bye, hunks. See you at the Gump," Sidney calls. (Dick has taken Maury down, Mike and Davey are sitting on the legs.) "Like a darling little bird, Beth."

"I heard. Was it your group that did the Brel show?"

"Oh, boy. Thanks for reminding me."

"Was it so bad?"

"Wonderful. We were just wonderful. The musicians kept passing around this Jamaica grass. They should have had enough for the audience, though. Poor darlings got terribly confused. Beth, you know Maggi Short?"

"No."

"She told me something about you."

"Who's Maggi Short?"

"Wife of the gimpy dude. The librettist. Snazzer. She was Maggi Taro, the actress."

"Of course." Beth smiles slowly. "Yes, I did hear that Maggi Taro lived here."

"From a mutual friend, right?"

"Oh, yes, Sidney. A friend."

"My, my. Janet Margesson." To speak so famous a name silences even Sidney.

Behind them come Hoffman, Debbie, Marcel, and Mona Shapen, talking lights. Ahead, but stopping now for a traffic signal, so that Beth and Sidney will catch up, are Skeats and Dr. Mason. Straggling up from the riverbank, the boys.

Surveying this line of march from a slow-moving car driven by Henry Fennellon, Ralph and Snazzer.

As they go by the rear group, Ralph says:

"Your man Hoffman, Snazzer. Are you sure he's going to be right for this?"

"Seems fine to me." Fennellon.

"Maggi thinks he'll do." Short. "Debbie seemed to like him."

Ralph. "Lake Biona. I wonder how the yellow bass got into it? Perhaps the people who wanted to build a resort stocked them."

With which Snazzer's attention becomes hopelessly fixed out the window, on the rear cleavage modeled by Sidney's short, short shorts. There's an obscene little flounce around the hem. Beth wore a blue-jean skirt to rehearsal. Look at Beth.

The car stops for the same light as the pedestrians, and Short, in back with his window down, hears Beth say:

"Where is Gump's?"

Then the car starts, and Short, being driven home now, hears, instead of the reply, "It would have been quite a nice place for a resort."

"Over by the drive-in bank," Sidney says. "We have to cross the river. But not Gump's. It's really called Hamel's, but Maury named it the Hamel's Gump."

"Maury. The black boy?" The light changes, and they start across, walking with Skeats and Mason now, but continuing their own chatter.

"The hunk. We always went to the Gump when I was a student here. I couldn't stand it if we didn't still."

"Does Maggi Taro go there?"

Skeats looks at Beth quickly, and is listening for Sidney's reply. "Not that I know of," Sidney says.

"You've been away," Skeats says. "Maggi doesn't exactly go there, but sometimes about closing time Maury will point his famous magic finger at the coatrack, and it'll turn into Maggi Taro, collecting chums along the bar for a party."

By the time Sidney and Skeats reach the glass door of the Gump, Johnny Ten Mason and slow-walking Beth are somewhat behind.

"It's up to us, my girl." Skeats, at the door.

"What, Papa Bear?"

"This director problem. Snazzer must have got drunk and hired him, and you can see: no control. Favoritism. He lets Maury walk all over him. He's bloody mesmerized by Beth. He'll be of no help to you, Sidney."

"All the men are mesmerized." Wistful smile. "I don't blame you. Isn't she something?"

"Gives me the creeps, frankly, but look here: No one's taking charge. If it were me alone, he'd be on the bus right now, on the way back to Philadelphia. But I'm afraid if anything's to be done, it will have to come from the cast, straight to bloody Sato, won't it?"

"What kind of creeps?" Lightly pinches the flesh at the base of his left thumb. "Let's go in."

"Can I count on you?" Feeling the after pinch, Skeats opens the door and stands aside for the soprano to enter. Squeal meets squeal:

"Bitsy, Bitsy."

"Cindy, oh honey." Squeezing out from behind the bar, with a great smile, comes the proprietress of the Gump. "I mean, Sidney. Let me look at you. You look wonderful."

"You've lost it. You've lost the twenty pounds!"

"Oh, I know, honey. It'll all come back."

"Not if you stay away from your own pizza. Bitsy, here comes Beth. Beth, come here. We're going to do Dr. Lekberg's opera."

"I know, I know. I've got my ticket."

"Bitsy has classical records on the jukebox."

"How wonderful." Beth.

"Bitsy, we need a table for jillions. The whole cast's about to arrive."

"How many, dear?"

"Jillions."

Apple

"Do you know a lot of people who work on Broadway, Mr. Hoffman?" asks Sidney Bigeyes.

"I know a guy named Moe Astenberg. He generally works on the east side of Broadway, around Forty-eighth Street. He's got a sign says, 'Help the Blind.' "

"I mean, oh, stars. Producers. People in the theatre."

"Well, Moe was in the theatre, you know? He was an usher in the Winter Garden, till he got canned for moving people into better seats than they paid for."

Sidney comes off it: "Mr. Hoffman's being such an amusing love. Isn't he being a love, Marcel?"

"I don't know how in the world he does it." Marcel smiles.

"Constant practice." Hoffman. "We got beer coming?"

Below the word *Apple,* on a blank page in his playbook binder, Maury Jackstone, having appointed himself scorekeeper, writes *Core Scooper. Half-man, whole point. Sid Knee No Cap, O Greatest city in Africa. Hoffman 1.*

"Dreaming of the bloody apple, are you Sidney?" Genial Skeats.

"The Bloody Apple. God, that's good." Mike Shapen, boosted into speech. "That's just right." Mike, smallish, often belligerent, deep, often reticent. His wife, Mona, looks at him with a touch of surprise.

Beth's eyes turn toward him. "Are you from New York, Mike?" Low, passionate girl voice.

"Born, brought up, and broke out."

"Ah, yes, of course." Skeats again. "That's the tale. Flight from the Bronx. The great, blistering fight to leave to bummos back in Brooklyn. And then, next chapter, the yearn to return. A beautiful myth. Bitsy, beaucoup beer!"

"But it is a beautiful myth," Beth says. Firmly murmurs. "Beautiful myth."

Beddiful Beth. Skeats shoots, Beth moots. Mascot Mike moves, Onion of Bermuda. Skeats 0, Mike 1.

"On my block you had three choices. Join the crooks, join the cops, or check out." For Mike, this is an oration. "Now there's only the last choice left."

"Mikey, what's got into you?" Sidney asks.

Whatever it is, it gets into Maury, too. "Read your physics, Michael. Black and white aren't colors, just degrees of light. You got a few less degrees of light in your neighborhood? Black kid there still has the same classic choices. Cheap punk. Chesty pig. Or chug off. See, you're still right? Blood's the only color in the apple."

"Mine's the same goddamn color as yours, Maury," slow Mike says; but nobody's as fast as Maury, who now, grinning with concern, lunges across, seizes his small, fierce friend from the side, under the arm and around the waist, lifts him out of his chair, rocks and hugs as Mike flails.

"But that's my point, my man, my Michael. That's the only point there is. Bitsy, bring a bathtub full of beer."

"Put him down, Maury." Mona Shapen.

"Put him down, Maury darling." Sidney. "Or I'll have Marcel darling punch you, very, very hard."

Certainly Cidley. Mike turns in puniform. Maury reprimanded by commissioners. Mother of Pearl of the Caribbean. No score.

"Dirty." Skeats has the floor. "I suppose there are dirtier ones, but New York's the first really dirty city I ever saw. Australian towns are quite clean.

But when I got discharged from your army, I knew no better. Went straight to the daffy apple."

"You were in our army?" Hoffman, drily.

"Yes, quite. I managed to join the Useless Army during the Second World Difference of Opinion. Bit young for the Australian Expeditionary. Barely fifteen, to be factual, but I was fairly tall, and my voice changed early on. Used to sing at a club in Perth, where the Yanks on R and R came. One night there were some Air Force wallers having a great drunk up—do you want to hear all this?"

"Yes, please." Sidney, and to the proprietress, Bitsy, who has just put down beer in pitchers and is collecting money from Hoffman, Skeats, and Johnny Ten Mason: "Bitsy, please bring Mr. Skeats some cashew nuts. Here." With childlike care counts out twenty cents from her purse in nickels. Sidney likes to give men little presents. Likes to give Skeats little presents, in return for his having taught her, in Diction for Singers, to replace the midwestern accent with something like standard English. "Were you a brave little soldier-bear?"

Dolling. Little wommekin. El Hughmore meets la tora delicia en rodillas, Lion of Denmark. Skeats 1, Mike out, Maury NLGBL, Hoffman 1.

"A brave little entertainer, in any case. It was a rowdy evening at the Coolgardie Club, and there was this one enormous T-corporal who kept shouting how he'd heard Aussies liked a good fight, where was a damn Aussie to fight? Finally he came weaving up to where our brave little singer had just finished doing 'I'll See You Again,' for about the fifth ballocky time, and pulled me off the bandstand. Young Master Balls pulls loose and hits the corp a lucky punch—but the big boy was probably ready to fall anyway from too much strong beer. The corporal sat there on the floor, laughing and hugging me around the knees, and then the other Yanks carried us both off to their table and proceeded to get me potted as a hare-o.

"About five A.M. off we all went to the airstrip, and they flew me right off with them to Guam. Well, I was ready for leaving home right enough, but we raised hell's own fuss on the airy plano, and I suppose the pilots must have radioed ahead; there were sixty bloody MPs surrounding the plane when we got off. Took in the lot of them, except our boy, Skeats, H., IV, wearing civvies, asleep on the plane, not quite six feet tall, weighing I suppose eight stone—that's one hundred twelve pounds?"

"That's how we say it in the Colonies." Hoffman.

"Thanks so much for straightening me out, Billy."

Everyman for herselves. Entry not elegant, but elicits, effluent of the cottage industrial revolution in England. Hoffman (cumulative) 1½.

"But you had your little 'stache," Sidney prompts, apparently no stranger to this farce.

"Oh, yes. I looked a bit older than fifteen. Wearing certain G.I. cast-offs, which were all the rage with Australian schoolboys. Didn't know what to do when all my friends went off in the paddy wagon, but the big T-corporal had said something about a recruiting office, so I set off to find it. Well, you can imagine that wasn't the busiest place on Guam in 1945, but they did have a man from each branch assigned to it, to handle reenlistments chiefly; on detached service they were and liked it bloody well. All four of them, army, navy, air force, and marine wanted a scalp—signing men up was the best way to stay on detached service, you see?

"They shared the same office space, and when I walked in and said, 'I'd like to join up please,' there was a great auction. The air-force bloke offered me his Zippo lighter, the marine and navy ones were actually into it with money at the three- and four-dollar level, till they found out about the age difficulty. They decided their regs were too hard to evade and dropped out. It was the army man who had the wit to guess I was hungry, and whispered that he knew a mess tent where we could still get brekker, so I signed on for a plate of fried Spam, some powdered eggs, and the most fearful cup of coffee I'd ever tried to drink. I can still taste it. Pure acid."

Fee, Fifi, fornicate, fumigate. Olefacts of life, Treasury of France. Hughmoring along, Skeats 2.

"Grabbed our saucy Aussie boy, gave him a doctored record to show training and past assignment, and goosed him off to the good infantry. A week later, and he's carrying forty pounds of ammo belts around his neck, crawling after a BAR man across a beach at lovely Okinawa. Couldn't have told you the BAR man's name, but it didn't matter for long; bloke crawled into a little Jap antipersonnel mine and went up in Skeats's face. So I picked the guts out of my collar, moved up to the gun, couldn't see anyplace safe to crawl to. I set the machine up on its bipod and commenced firing. Got half my platoon chewed to bits, because, you see, the automatic weapon is what draws the most return fire. But the other half made it to the bottom of the cliff under young Skeats's erratic fire, took the bunker with grenades and a flame thrower, and do you know what? Our hero had a bronze star, just like that. Hadn't even been sure how to fire the gun when he started across the beach; all he'd really learned was how to load it."

Garrulootes strong and long, no gadflies, Lifeline on the Palm of Grenada. Skeats 3 .

"Honorable-discharge time, and here we have Master Yankee Doodle Skeats, new citizen. His records are so hacked and bungled that the army assumes he's got the same time in as the rest of the few survivors in his outfit, gives him that many points, that much back pay, and asks him where he wants to be let out? There's only one place in America he's ever heard of, so he says, 'New York, please' and they say, 'Right, we'll start you off from Carolina.' "

Skeats stops to empty half the little cellophane sack of cashew nuts that Sidney bought him into his mouth, and Hoffman says:

"What were you in the war, Beth?"

"Oh, I suppose I must have been a bit of . . ." Beth blushes, "spermatozoon?"

Heartstopper stops Halfmoon, Number One of Herzogovina. Skeats rolls on: 4. Hoffman no score, still 1½.

"I find New York just plain irresistible," Marcel says. "All that incredible music, night after night. I just can't believe there's another city in the world with so many really impressive singers and recitalists and instrumental groups performing all the time—"

"I know." Skeats impatiently.

"I loved it there." A new voice is heard, twangy but not very, Texas John Ten Mason. "I didn't have a lot of time for music, but the choice of things when I did was almost impossible. I'd generally buy tickets to two things the same night, and change from one hall to another at intermission."

"It's a problem, you know?" Hoffman. "Here are all these producers and performers Sidney wants to hear about, getting up shows, movies, concerts, TV specials, ballet programs, and you know the trouble? It's inattention. Too few media, too much going on, a lot of it good, but who's going to know? New York's the biggest talent graveyard in the world."

So many impresarios, so little information. I was came, I was sawed, I was bonkered, Rouser of Ireland. Hoffman 2½. Mason, late entry, ½. Does Marcel want in? (½)

"Tell about the journey, Papa Bear. Marcel, it was very wicked of you to interrupt."

"Well, all right, then. We have Skeats in the North of Carolina, right? Money in one shoe, discharge papers in the other, and a train ticket for the Juicy Apple in his hand. Waiting on the station platform, Skeats falls into conversation with a nice, well-dressed character in a maroon felt hat who says he's a New Yorker; now, I have to admit I was all over the fellow. I was still sixteen, and badly wanted a line on where I was going. I won't try to do the conversation, but even at sixteen I ought to have been a little more suspicious, of course. Before long I truly believed that this man owned a lovely Packard car that was delayed for repairs in a local garage. That the man was desperate to be in New York on business, and had to leave his car. That the man believed Skeats trustworthy and would therefore take Skeats's train ticket in exchange for the car keys. The repair bill was paid in advance, 'twas said in honeyed wordos, and Skeats, on delivering the car in New York at a hotel address, would be reimbursed his expenses, be paid twenty-five dollars, and have had a lovely jaunt through the eastern part of the country by luxury auto.

"Now Skeats knew his train schedule, poor fool had written it in ink on his wrist, stops, stay-overs and all, so he'd know where he was in this big, new, ugly country. All he'd have had to do was consider that the train would take three and a half days, before it got to New York, to know the man was lying. But Skeats hadn't the foggiest that the driving time there from Carolina would be a day less than the roundabout war train. He blithely saw King Con off on the chugger in his red felt hat, and went whistling to the garage to find, of course, that the car was a stolen one and the man earnestly wanted. So now New York was Jaundice City in the boy's mind. . . . Beth, I say Beth. Have you been there, then?"

For Beth's look of concern for sixteen-year-old Skeats would stop a jet.

Jugger naut that you be not juggered, Rabbi of Jerusalem. Skeats laps the field, 5. (Doth Boes Lap?)

She has a way, even when she has been intently listening, of answering as if a kiss were interrupted. Startled, she smiles uncertainly, gathers: "Oh, yes."

Skeats smiles, lets her go on.

"I'd heard . . . I'd been. I'd been in Europe, where the concrete scratches so at the sky, and I was coming back to a job in New York, and

Paris and Madrid and Rome were so busy and full of little cars . . . I wasn't eager. I thought New York would be like that. And then New York was just what I'd imagined European cities would be. Enervated, tired, a kaleidoscope with the little flakes changing so slowly you could see the trick, muted colors in the fading light."

Listen to Beth.

"In Boston I'd been doing practice teaching, before Europe, and I'd wanted that, to teach children music, but we couldn't, of course. Teach. Only try to protect ourselves and the weaker children and the buildings, and New York uses up its bustle that way, doesn't it? Old and cold and once—"

"Once?"

"Listen to her, Maury." Mike. "Yeah."

"I can't hear the words for listening to the voice, you know?" Hoffman.

"Once, when I lived there with another girl, the summer after Europe, working at a concert agency—so vicarious for me, like watching a royal wedding on television—and my roommate went on vaction, and I was very lonely in New York then. Like being a sheep in an enormous flock, and all of you have lost the power to see or smell or hear each other."

Beth lonely? Beth melancholy? With that softly full figure, that mysteriously half-dark complexion, that helpless, naughty streak, that stirring voice, all those promises, lonely?

"Yes, I was, in the slowness of the city; it was summer then. Sometimes I thought New York quite lovely in its slow, sad way, capital of some ancient country that doesn't exist anymore, and once I was, a little bit . . . in love? We were to meet for lunch, and I wanted to buy just, oh, a new bra to look special for a special date, and left for my lunch hour early and slipped into a very famous store on Fifth Avenue, like going underwater. And then a quarter hour had gone by before a clerk came floating toward me, and I picked it out and tried to bustle to a dressing room to change, but I couldn't move any faster underwater than the others somehow, and when I came out, the clerk was going out of sight, slowly, too far away for me to catch, and I waited and I waited, and then she came drifting back to take my money, and then away again for change . . . and finally when I got up again to the surface and out the door, forty-five minutes was gone, and of course my boy was gone from the corner we were meeting at. And of course he was hurt with me, and I didn't know his phone, and I never saw him again to explain."

"How Viennese," says Sidney. Some of the men smile tartly with her. Mona Shapen and the other men stay tremulous with Beth.

"Oh, gingerbread lady." Maury. "With your shiny, raisin eyes."

"Me, Maury?"

"Now, hell," says Johnny Ten Mason. "We better open negotiations for some more of this underwater beer if we're going to talk about Kleptopolis. That's what my Dad called New York. City of Thieves."

Maury tries to remember the Arabic characters for *qisma,* "lot or portion," but his Arabic is rusty. He writes, instead, *kismet, mongrel English derivate, it bites. Kan guru woo? No. Kid Kockalot kicks it, thou Door to Fort Knox. Maury out of the game again, x. Nother half point for Hoffman, makes 2. Big point for Mason, 1½. Skeats lead still comf., loafs with 5.*

"London, Lebanon." Hoffman. "That's where the New York hustle always came from, and what's left of it still does, huh? You find yourself scrapping for a buck with a guy, he's got New York clothes, what Snazzer Short calls New York manners, the thickest goddamn New York accent you ever heard, but he comes from Lebanon, Pennsylvania, or London, Ontario. The boys from the provinces."

"What about Australia?" Skeats. "When I tell you—"

"Lick it." Johnny Ten Mason. "When you come in from out of town you know you can lick it, that's all. Whatever it is that's there, why, you just don't even consider giving in. I spent three months at Bellevue, couple of years ago, on some kind of surgery exchange. They wanted a city boy here to see what happens when a farmer runs his arm through the gears on a corn picker, and I was going there to work on cuttings and shootings. What I did was carry an umbrella, rain or shine. I'd drag that steel tip along the sidewalk, keeping it nice and sharp. I went through bad streets, night after night, but I never had to poke that umbrella out. What I learned is, New York's vicious, but it's feeble."

"Like winter." Beth. "Taking the easy victims."

Hoffman says, "No place would take you for an easy victim, Doctor. Not if you were naked in a shower bath with soapy hands, you know?"

"I saw them all the time, those victims. I patched and tried to comfort them, night after night. What they were typically were old women with elastic leg bandages who'd been hurt, generally around the head, trying to hang onto vinyl purses for two dollars and change. But I sure liked the eating in New York."

Lu Chow's Chinese Restaurant. Featuring Yangtze Doodle and Pekin Tom, 0

Tongue of Lichtenstein. Hoffman ball-handling, another half. Mason strokes, pulls even, both now 2½, tied like ribbons.

"We went to New York for our high school senior trip," Dick Auerbach says. "I sure thought it was all right, except Cindy couldn't go."

"Who was Cindy?" Sidney asks.

"Sorry," Dick says.

"I don't think she'd have liked the trip anyway, do you?"

"I said I was sorry," he looks away from Sidney, and then, shyly, to the others. "We had a real good time, except it wasn't long enough. We'd run from one place to the next to make it last longer. The city the rest of you are talking about must be somewheres else." *Le miserable Dick. Second movement: Now we know/Why Cindy Sidney couldn't go, Bosstown of Massachusetts. Dick strikes forever out.*

The narrative of Young Skeats resumes:

Mona. "What did you do, Mr. Skeats, when you got to the garage and found out the car was stolen?"

"Well, the garage owner had a good laugh at me, and then turned out to be quite decent. There wouldn't be another train till next day, and every room in the town was booked. He showed me the car, a long, sleek cherry-red machine, fit for a nabob, and said I might sleep in it if I liked. It wasn't to be moved until the state police could send a man to go over it, so I had the back seat for my bed, and very comfortable, too. There I was, safe in the arms, about eleven P.M., when I realized that someone had opened the front door of the car.

"I came wide awake, and kept still, saw in the dark a form get in the front, under the wheel, and commence fiddling about the dashboard, holding a torch on it. So I sat up and said, 'Hi.'

"He put the torch on me, and said, 'Oh, it's the young soldier, is it? You got the keys for this?'

"Well, I still had a set, as a matter of fact, and still not able to see him, thought it was my friend the garage owner. So I handed them over, he put off the torch, and then I could tell it was someone else.

" 'Wait,' I said. 'I thought this wasn't to be moved.'

" 'Stop thinking,' he said. 'This is your lucky night, soldier,' and he backed us out of that bay with the lights off, backed carefully around into another bay, and got out and closed the door. So I got out, too.

" 'Black-out curtains are mighty handy,' he said, turned on the lights, and I saw it was one of the mechanics.

"And we were in the painting bay.

" 'Here.' He tossed me a roll of masking tape. 'Start with the other headlight.' And he began taping the left one.

"Now up to that moment I'd thought whatever was going on must be part of getting ready for the state police, and I still wasn't sure about the situation until the mech got out a hunkering great slicer of a knife to open up a new case of tape with.

" 'I'm glad you're a smart soldier,' he said. 'You wouldn't like what I'd have to do to a dumb one.'

"You may surely believe that I confirmed his impression of my intelligence. That was one bloody-awful-looking knife. I taped like a maniac. Then I stood back while he turned on his airbrush, and in about an hour and a half the cherry-red Packard was a rather oily brown. The mech changed the license plates, and said we'd be in Roanoke before morning, where it would be sold and on its way, didn't I think I'd better come along?

"The car supply was very short just after the war; there simply weren't any to be bought, and a good one like this was quite an item.

"The man was putting out the paint-shop lights, clearing up, and told me to get in and start the engine.

" 'I'll open the door fast and close it faster,' he said. 'You drive it out quick, and then scoot over.'

"I'd never driven anything with more acceleration than an army truck, and even that not more than twice or thrice. I was utterly confused and a bit frightened. Consider that I knew nothing about that country out there, had known some infantry blokes under fire, some army bureaucrats who'd sent me along, my red-hatted con man, the decent garage owner, and now a thief mechanic. I had one other reference: gangster cinemas. As far as I could tell, I was in the mob, whether I liked it or not, and I certainly knew what the mob did to squealers.

"I started up, the door flew open, I pulled into gear, floored the pedal, and went flying out the door full speed, smash into a great iron lamppost.

"There was a ballocky great crashing of grill and glass, and most of the windshield fell into my lap.

" 'You goddamn fool,' the mech yelled. 'You'll bring the goddamn sheriff.'

"Just then a pair of headlights showed up down the street, and off ran the mobster mechanic into the night.

"I sat there. I'd bumped my head and wasn't altogether able to think clearly anyway, and watched the headlights crawl down to me, and right on past me, and then the bloody taillight, going away. Well, I didn't want to be where I was, and had no other way of getting elsewhere. I backed my shattered Packard off the lamppost, made sure one headlight was working, drove it out onto the highway, and turned north toward New York.

Now, once upon a time, in a small town called Dueyville, there was a star-nymphlet named Cindy Benesch (twice upon a time, she hasn't changed a bit). At the age of fourteen, freshman year in high school, she was the youngest and prettiest starter in the state girls' basketball tournament, Horse of Nairobi. Skeats apparent winner.

"Outside of town I picked up my first hitchhiker, a wild, ginger-headed Jew Marine named Oligarski, on the road, mustered out and happy-drunk at midnight.

"From there on, it was one howling odyssey. We stopped for soldiers, sailors, marines, and sometimes girls, all along the road, and carried them with us.

"About four A.M. Oligarski was driving; ran us into a ditch and over on one side. It's hard to believe, but we all climbed out the windows on the up-side, pushed the car back up onto all fours, and drove it on. The doors on the right wouldn't work, was all, but some of my mates smashed the windows out with their booze bottles, and on we went.

"It was a roaring trip, all the way. We'd slow down going through the smaller towns next day, whoop and cheer, sometimes let off a passenger, and often as not acquire another. Took turns driving, singing, eating, and for one stretch Oligarski and another Marine and a pharmacist's mate were making a bed with their laps in the backseat for a wild country girl to lie on and take the flesh from anyone who offered it as we drove.

"We sang and drank and screwed and ate, and the only difficulty was not letting someone keep us over in his town for the party to settle there. But Young Skeats insisted—it was his wreck of a car, after all—that we keep going to New York, even after he himself backed it into a fence post on some blithering Virginia farm and crushed the trunk lid. Since there were duffles and whatnot back there that had to be got in and out, we decided the best thing to do was pry off that trunk lid altogether and throw it away.

"But I had the train schedule written on my wrist, and I kept us at it day and night, an hour or so here and there for sleep or resupply, till we approached New York. Oligarski was still with me; he was a New Yorker, and the big boy took the wheel again when we got to Washington Bridge and found ourselves on time. It was him and me in front, several more in back, and we were clattering down the West Side at nine thirty, with the old chug due in at ten."

Older by a year, Cindy dropped basketball as a sophomore for cheerleading, at the age of fifteen. It was partly because her father, who owned the local radio station, held athletics in distaste, partly because Dick Auerbach, the strongest boy in school, liked her leading cheers for him at football games, wrestling matches, and baseball. O Tail of Oxford, will there be a prize?

"Perfectly frankly, I wonder that we got there at all, with the mess that car was in, but it never occurred to me to question at the time. Oligarski was roaring and rocking at the wheel, blasting through one-way streets the wrong way, stampeding other traffic out of the way. We bounced off a mail truck just before we got to Pennsylvania Station, went by, careened around the corner of Thirty-third Street, onto the avenue, and Oligarski certainly didn't stop then. Up he went, over the sidewalk pavement, up the steps, and right in the door of the station, and stopped in the lobby, where we all piled out into the crowd around the information desk.

" 'Penn Station,' Olig yelled. 'All bloody change.'

"I took that as a compliment.

"And while MPs and station guards chased our buddies and called city police, Olig and I went pell-mell down a level to the incoming gates.

"Simple Skeats had grabbed the keys from the ignition. The two paused at the incoming board, got a gate number, and Olig says, 'I'll lay back and bush him.'

" 'No, lay back and follow us up,' says Skeats, who had a plan by then. I don't know what the odds were against it, but I still had a trusting heart, never doubted for a minute, and it happened just that way: Along came the passengers, and stepping smartly along, pushing old ladies out of his way, the red felt hat.

" 'Hi,' I cried, smiling. 'I got your car here all right.'

"King Con stopped, not quite recognizing me, and said, 'What do you want?' "

" 'Here are your car keys,' I said. 'I just made it in time.'

" 'Oh, yeah,' he says. 'Well. You did, huh?'

" 'Sure,' I said. 'There wasn't anybody at the garage when I left, but you said the bill was paid. It's all right, isn't it?'

"He kind of half-smiled, and said, 'Yeah. Yeah, swell.'

" 'Thanks a lot,' I said. 'I had a wonderful trip.'

"Finally he took the keys I kept holding out and said, 'Okay. Where is it?'

" 'Oh, it's parked,' I said. 'Come on. I'll show you.'

" 'Where'd you get gas to come all the way up here?'

" 'You left your ration book, right in the glove box,' I said. That was true. The book was in Olig's pocket by then, and we found out later it was counterfeit. But no matter.

" 'The car better be in better shape than you are, Jack,' he said. I was looking pretty scroungy in my uniform by then; it had bits of vomit on it and come and grease, and I had a three-day growth of childish beard.

"I looked at my feet, and said, 'Golly, it does have a few scratches, sir. But . . .' I gave him a big, shamed smile. 'Please, let me carry your bag?'

"He started to smile then, too, and handed over the bag, saying, 'Scratches, huh? Well, I'll tell you, Jack, that twenty-five bucks I was going to pay you might just cover a few scratches. Fair enough?'

" 'Oh, yes,' I said. 'Fair enough. Thank you. Come on, I'll show you.'

"I had his suitcase by now, and I bounced on ahead of him. He didn't realize, of course, with all the other men in uniform around, that Oligarski was bouncing on close behind him.

"And by the time we had him up to street level and going through the lobby to where a crowd was gathered, including fifty cops or so, it was too late. He saw cop and the car in the middle of the station and tried to come after me for the suitcase.

"I ran right up to two boyos in blue, and cried: 'It's his car. He's got the keys right in his hand.'

"Olig closed in from behind and held him long enough for the blues to have an arm each. Then Olig turned loose and yelled, 'The bastard gave us a ride and tried to rob us,' and then Olig and I both ran like riptide, one each way."

Presently Cindy was sixteen. It was junior year. She had the boy under control whom all the girls wanted, but that hardly satisfied her appetite for conquest. There was a school rule in Dueyville against school girls getting married, so she took Dick over to to the county seat one lunch period, and they got a marriage license. They needed her father's consent, but that was not a problem for Cindy Benesch. She just said she was pregnant, whereas in fact she was still a maiden and remained so for some weeks after her marriage, Lap of Peloponnesus, is there laurel for a wreath?

"Quick." Sidney. "Tell about the suitcase."

"Well, I still had it, of course. We went on to Oligarksi's family, and slept for almost a day before we opened up the bloke's satchel."

"And the shirts fit," Sidney. "Some were bloody handsome, too."

"Jingling about in the bottom was almost two hundred dollars in nickels, dimes, and quarters. Olig thought the King must have been jimmying pay phones in the discharge town, where all the men were constantly calling home."

"But Skeats didn't care for the garish colors and ballocky patterns of the hand-painted silk neckties." Sidney.

"Quite right, and do shut up, my dear. Olig and I went up to the observation deck of the world's tallest with them next day, and drifted them off toward Wall Street, one by one, in the prevailing wind."

Quixotic Benesch, Cindy's father the broadcaster, fought the school board to get his married daughter back in for senior year, and won. What could the queen of Dueyville do next to cap the insolence of strolling about the halls on the arms of a husband? Costarring with him in the senior operetta at Christmas, insisting that her name in the program must be Cindy Auerbach, got her through the fall of her seventeenth year of have it and eat it. Winter dream of Quebec, is there loving for a cup?

"Say what you like, New York was the place for a roaring boy to roam. By the time I'd come of age there, I'd gone through Juilliard as Hughmore Skeats and Hunter College as Skeats Hughmore, and got checks each month from the Vets Administration for both. Not my mistake, all theirs, but a remarkably prosperous situation for a growing boy."

"Hunter College?"

"There were fifteen or twenty of us rollicky young male war vets plunged in the middle of that young female student body, ah yes. And there was Greenwich Village. And upper Broadway, where the students from all those campuses met in the Chinese restaurants and music bars. New York was the city of rosy lips, and a lad might learn how roguishly to redden them."

"Protect us, Marcel," Sidney says. "I think he's being naughty."

Right in the middle of spring, Cindy Benesch Auerbach achieved the unacceptable. As the other senior girls chattered of cap-and-gown measurements, or sewed frocks for the trip to New York, seventeen-year-old Mrs. Auerbach began attending classes in maternity gowns, perhaps a month or so before the garments were strictly necessary. She was barred from all school activities, except classes. She received her diploma at home, giggling because President Dick of the Senior Class, in noble protest, stayed out of the graduation ceremony, too. Earl of Rochester: Take a letter to Pyrrhus.

"In serious need of tutoring, of course, at Hunter. Vets Admin sprung for that, too, and naturally the tutors were all upperclassmen, aha, from the college itself. You should have seen the math tutor they hired me at four dollars an hour. Smashing. Sometimes we'd go up to my place and do the most sincere differential calculus for two and three hours at a stretch. Most grueling, you can imagine.

"Then about two o'clock one morning my landlady caught me having a sensational tutorial in Beowulf with a darling English major. This was one of the luckiest things that happened, because the landlady was a thoroughly grasping old bitch, and very chafed because the little apartment I had was rent-controlled. She threatened to report my study habits to the dean unless I'd accept a male roommate, so that she could double the rent, you see.

"Had me by what little was left of the ballocks it seemed, but that was before I met my new roomy. Landlady's nephew he was, and the old bitch did sincerely believe the boyo was a student too. Wasn't at all. New chum was one of the most gifted young burglars in New York. Once we started getting on, I'd simply give him my shoplifting list every morning, and we did live sumptuously, though at first the wine and liquor was a trifle uncertain. That was before my roomy found that just a few changes in our spare key made one that would fit the landlady's door quite perfectly, and old aunty had quite a prewar cellar down there, bless her stingy, hoarding soul."

Born a son, Samuel B. Auerbach, to Cindy and Dick in July—or perhaps to Dick and to Cindy's father; Cindy and Dick lived with him. Little Sam has never lived anywhere else. By late August the baby had already been left with the grandparents for almost three weeks—half his little life—while Cindy took Dick off to music camp. Dick hadn't realized he wanted to be a singer; he'd thought he wanted to be a wrestling coach. White Hand of Sicily, advisor to the loveshorn. Eddie Turd/Dear Ed:

"New York treated you pretty damn well, then." Johnny Ten.

"But a terrible thing happened." Sidney. "Really it did, didn't it, Papa Bear? Love."

"Yes. Love. New York is no place to be in love.

"There arrived in Tough City," says Skeats, "one of your bleeding people from the provinces, a certain Millie, of State City, born and raised right here. Who became, with just a little New York hustle on her part, the first Mrs. Hughmore Skeats."

"A hostage." Maury, softly.

"First of all, she was very righteous. No more two checks from the VA, no free rides of any sort. Work. Be proper. Be ambitious. To please Millie I had to have a job—singing in one of those awful choruses that hums behind the singer on sick ballads. And she started learning about recitals, debuts, all that. We hadn't been married six months before she started asking why not book me into one of the Carnegie recital halls. I wasn't ready, of course, hadn't the audience experience and all that. Tried it in a small way—not Carnegie—and nothing happened, good or bad. No reviews, no audience except friends. So then Millie agreed I needed preparation, and next thing I knew she had me an instructorship right here. I don't know how in tearing hell she did it."

Tentatively, clinging to Dick, leaving baby Sam at home of course, Cindy began her freshman year at State University. When she found that in an environment of twenty thousand, no one was especially aware of her situation, she left her husband living in married-student quarters, and actually moved into a freshmen-women's dorm, second semester, where she told the girls that she wanted to be called by her maiden name, informing them that it was Cindy Bennett. Dick took every course Cindy did, and dated her, forced to observe rules and hours, when she would consent to it. Sun of Tanzania, if there be no gold or silver, of what shall the coin be struck?

"I can understand Millie now that I've been an American." Skeats. "But my old Aussie's mum's uterus didn't have me awash in ambition vitamins for nine months. Not that I didn't catch a good enough dose of it from old Millie."

"Went back and had your recital, did you?" Johnny Ten.

"That must have been marvelously exciting." Marcel.

"Marvelous waste of marvelous time and money, far as I'm concerned. You've no idea the things you've got to pay for—rent, tickets, advertising, programs—and then, with all the other things going on, who's going to come?"

"That lovely bald manager with the Hungarian accent who was too busy to see the young artist at the beginning of the movie?" Marcel, smiling. "He didn't come up afterward in tears to say he'd been wrong?"

"Nobody but Millie's bastard of a brother from Long Island and his wife, saying let's go celebrate at the Russian Tea Room. Dutch. Well, of course, having a New York recital gave me a few reviews, did me good in this place. I suppose it's why I was hired back."

"What happened to Millie?" Beth.

"Still in New York, third husband, third recital coming up. This one's a smuggering cellist."

"People say there's no success except New York success." Hoffman. "But there's no failure except New York failure either, you know?"

Skeats glares.

"You can live your life and do your work without reference to it, can't you?" Johnny Ten Mason. "Buzz in, pick up a little technique if that's where to go to learn it, and leave when you're ready."

"I hope you can," Hoffman says.

Up to sophomore year Cindy Benesch ("Bennett") Auerbach had felt perfectly sure of Dick. Living separately but not legally separated, and feeling most guilty toward her, Dick began to see another girl, a biology major. Cindy had to seek the biologist out and tell her that Dick was married, which ended that. Cindy then chastised Dick by refusing to go out with him for a month, and dated several others in the interval. These dates were not very successful, however, since Dick would follow the automobiles in which Cindy was being taken out, on his motorcycle. Cindy was unsuccessful in getting him to stop this practice, as was he in getting her to resume living with him. Yet when they went home to Dueyville, they went together on the motorcycle, and stayed together at the Benesch house with their son who became, that summer, two years old. United Nations Nation, if there be not stone or marble, in what shall the sculptor carve eternal likeness?

"Millie was your first wife." Hoffman. "What about your various others?"

"Oh, come on now, let's drink up. I've talked too muckering much."

"He marries his students." Sidney. "Don't you, Papa Bear?"

"Well, twice then. The second lasted just long enough to tie up half my salary in alimony for the rest of my bleeding life unless the vicious little twup remarries, how I hope."

"I thought Vickie was sweet." Sidney. "So did Davey, didn't you lover?"

Davey Riding, who has said very little but listened in a rather alert way, says: "I always thought Vickie was probably what my grandmother called a baby vamp."

Sidney. "But she was a very good baby vamp."

"She's enough to give varicose veins to a bleeding centipede, if you want my opinion."

In reply, Sidney reaches over, picks up the half-eaten plastic envelope of cashews from in front of Skeats, and solemnly places it in front of Hoffman.

Hoffman, apparently not precisely aware of where the bounty came from, grins at Skeats, friendly and surprised. "Hey, thanks."

"But I did not give them to you, old boy." The words are dangerously spaced. "May I have my nuts back, please?"

Sidney's giggle is awful, primal, some kind of little scream.

"Goddamn," says Marcel, about as meekly as that particular word can really be said.

In junior year, vivacious Cindy managed to see a lot of people, including her Diction for Singers teacher, whose third wife she might have become had she wished to. She did not, nor his mistress either, and the man married yet another student. As for Dick, she informed him that year that she considered them formally separated, though they could neither afford to go through the appropriate legal procedure nor to stop giving the appearance of marriage when they went home to Dueyville at vacation time. However, in the summer, she managed to find a professional engagement. Dick took, on shares, a rather large hill farm near home, which had been set aside for some years to conform with a government conservation program, used his father's farming equipment, and grew on it a tremendous crop of buckwheat, on which he made quite a lot of money. Cindy, whose stage name now became Sidney Bennett, was unable to attend Sam's third birthday, in July, which Dick, though by now somewhat estranged from the senior Benesch, did manage to celebrate with the child. Merchant of Venice, if there be no victor, to whom do the spoils belong?

"Whoa, Sidney. Really. Whoa." Dick.

"I thought you wanted me to come up now, hoss."

"Why don't you gallop off and break your dear little neck?" Skeats.

"Aren't you going to tell about your wonderful third wife?"

"Who wants to go get something to eat?" Hoffman.

"Let's get a pile of hamburger and cook it out at the schoolhouse." Davey Riding, standing up. "We're playing poker out there afterward." Some stand to go with Davey. Sidney clings to big Marcel.

Skeats asks Beth to supper, but she says her parents are coming shortly to drive her over to Illinois for the evening. She'll be back tomorrow with her own car.

Whereas Cindy Benesch Auerbach has applied to this court—the legal name change to Sidney Bennett was accomplished, with the help of a smitten young State City lawyer, in her senior year. Papers for a legal separation were also drawn up, but not signed. She sang the lead in Pagliacci that summer. It is apparent that she avoided an affair with Skeats, who directed and sang Tonio. Dick tried out for, but could not make, the chorus, and so, having taken time in May to plant his buckwheat land in corn, spent the summer riding back and forth from State City to Dueyville to do his field work. Sam was four, and was brought down to Dueyville by the grandparents to watch his mother on the stage at Old Biology. Columbian District of Washington, if there be no granite for an arch, 'ware wounded bear.

The ex-schoolhouse on German Road, where Sue and Davey Riding have lived for five years, plays as much a part in recent music-department tradition as the Gump—yet for all its reputation for pot parties and X-rated concerts by topless tubas and bottomless basses, the schoolhouse is a gentle, unrepressive milieu.

Gentleness permits many things.

It is a faded, clapboard-sided one-room building of nineteenth-century design, with no windows in the east wall, where the blackboards still hang. This was so that the children, facing blackboard and teacher, would not have morning sun in their eyes. On the south is the entrance, the warmest wall in winter, and since the January sun at this latitude shines from the south from 10:00 A.M. to 2:00 P.M., more or less, there are no windows here giving directly into the schoolroom, either; there were, however, what might today be called thermal heat-collecting units—windowed cloakrooms on either side of the entryway itself. The Ridings have taken out the partition that formed the girl's cloakroom, for kitchen space, and converted the boys' equivalent into a bathroom—sink, toilet, and stall shower. The windows on the west wall are low; low winter sun would filter in, to warm the children's backs, but by the time the high, hot sun of spring reached this set of windows, school would already be out for the day. The north wall has tall windows; perfect north light. Logically enough, an easel now stands near the big windows, belonging to the Ridings' friend Charles, with a half-done painting on it just now of grotesque animals in procession. Charles sleeps on planks laid across the beams in the attic, in a sleeping bag, and complains much, in winter, of the cold, and of having to climb up to his bed by ladder. But you can't beat zero rent.

The poker game, with its seven players, is taking place around a white wooden table that has been moved out of the kitchen space into the center of the twenty-four-foot square room. There is a double bed, partitioned off in the northeast corner, where Sue Riding, exhausted from her day at the supermarket check-out lane, is already asleep. A wood stove. Nondescript chairs. An upright piano, which Davey tunes himself, at least once a week. He can't get it up to pitch, but can tune it with itself, which means that other instruments must be tuned down to it or transposed, to play with it.

Hoffman deals around, one card down, one card up. Five-card stud.

"There, Marcel. You got a queen. You bet."

"Mr. Skeats has one, too."

"You got the first queen. First queen bets."

"Couldn't he do it?"

"If you don't want to bet, you say, 'Check.' "

"Oh. Check."

"But you got no reason to."

"How much should I bet?"

"I don't know. I don't know what you got in the hole. Why don't you try a nickel?"

"All right."

Crisscross stories. One started in New York, with Skeats, the other's moving there with Sidney. The true Xanadu.

"Yes. He may raise a dime." Hoffman.

"Too terribly true. If we're playing poker, let's play poker."

"What am I to do?" Marcel. Maury folds, stands, and moves behind Marcel to see his hole card.

"Stay, tenor."

"That's enough of that." Skeats. "Let the man play his own cards."

"Yesmore, Hughsir."

Cards are dealt, the fifth and final round. To Marcel, Skeats, Hoffman.

"But what shall I do now?"

"No help. This is for money."

"Look." Hoffman. "Consider your cards, you know. You've got us both beat on the board. Why not bet and see what we've got?"

"Is that what's called bluffing?"

"No, if I bet and know you're beating me, that would be bluffing."

"I'm sorry to be so very stupid. I better check."

"All right. Just to show you what I mean." Hoffman. "Suppose I bet a quarter. There it is. I'm trying to scare you into folding, even though I know you've got me beat. Okay? A quarter raise."

"Oh, yes. Then I see it, don't I? I see your quarter!"

"No more raises, huh Hughmore? I already told you . . ."

"Raise a quarter." Skeats, promptly.

"Boy, you're really putting it to me, aren't you Hugh?" Hoffman sighs and pays.

Young Sam is five now, the separation legal—Sidney prefers that to divorce. That there has been a marriage is a fairly well-kept secret still around here, at her insistence. Our condolences now to the winner, to the loser our sincere congratulations, Sapphire of Yellowstone.

Johnny Ten Mason arrives now to zip up the poker lesson. With him, the young doctor brings Sidney, whom he found at the Gump, wondering where everybody was. Johnny'd stopped there to get pizza to contribute to the poker game.

"I'd forgotten you were all going gambling." Sidney. "Marcel, darling, have you won enough to buy me something pretty?"

When it's time to leave, Hoffman is driven back to University House by Maury Jackstone and Dick Auerbach, with the little soprano snuggled between the two big graduate students in the front seat. At Hoffman's suggestion, he sits in back by himself. He's got another of his bad cigars going, and this way the summer air can wash the smoke away through open car windows.

"He wouldn't put out his old cigar to sit with me, Dick," Sidney says. "Help, what am I doing wrong?"

O far, false Zanzibar.

# The Fastest Jeep in the World

"The first thing: It was no jeep at all. I don't know just what you would call it. On the sports-car tracks it'd be a Volkswagen Special, I reckon. But it sure wasn't meant for tracks."

John Ten Mason, M.D., smiles his small, significant smile; even his teeth are small, as if this could deprecate their perfect, even whiteness. Like the diffidence of pearls.

He sips beer at the Gump, after the Wednesday rehearsal, and Maury, Dick, Skeats, Short, Marcel, Hoffman—and especially Karen, Mona, Beth, and Sidney—sip back at him. It might be dangerous to interrupt the doctor.

"The chassis was a Volkswagen, but my bad buddy, Cougar, modified it in ways I couldn't name. Cougar had his own ideas about suspension. The whole rig was Cougar's idea. Except, deep down at the bottom, the boss idea that all the others came from, that was out of a book."

"What book, Johnny Ten?" Beth.

"It was a book by Erich Maria Remarque, about Germany after the First World War. These guys in it had a souped-up car. Looked like a heap of iron but ran like a chased cat. In the book they like to go coughing along and have a big new car pass them—then pass him back, and race.

"How a stud like Cougar came to read it, I can't say." Smiling, Johnny shakes his head. "He said the sex wasn't much in it, but he loved that ugly car. Cougar's book report."

"On the VW chassis, Coug fitted an old army jeep body, the worst one we could find. We went looking for that thing like hunting treasure, and that's the way we found it.

"We'd been searching the dumps, the salvage companies. And an old boy one place said there was a one-time army jeep out in the woods on the edge of the swamp. Maybe some duck hunter'd left it sit there when it quit. Cougar and I went out looking three days in a row, all through the pin oaks where they flood in high water. Once we thought we saw it, hidden in some willows out across the marsh.

" 'We'll never get it out,' I said. "Not even with a crawler.'

" 'I'll borrow something with a winch and a big roll of cable, and I'll winch it out,' said Cougar.

" 'Let's get us some hip boots, then, so we can wade out and look at it first,' I said.

" 'Don't need no boots, Johnboy,' Coug said, and he went off into the mud in his sneakers and jeans, right up over his knees. I stood there chewing grass, watching him heave his way across. It must have taken Cougar twenty minutes to go fifty yards, and mostly I wasn't thinking about how to get the jeep out—I was thinking how to get Cougar out when the mud got up to his waist and he couldn't move.

"But he made it, over to where metal showed through the willow branches. And I watched him hardly bother to look around, and then work on back, so bitten by mosquitoes his face swelled up.

"I offered him my hand to pull out on when he came near, grunting and puffing, but he wouldn't take it. He just looked up at me like I'd put them out there myself and said, 'Oil drums. That's a pile of Sinclair oil drums.'

"I looked over, and it was just as plain as anything you want that the metal was drum. On the bottom, one was turned toward us and still looked just a little bit like a wheel, but on the others I could almost read the letter-ing, now I knew what it said.

"Well, nothing ever looked more like a jeep when we first saw it. Maybe it would have looked like oil drums if we'd have wanted to make a raft."

"We finally found the jeep on the third day, close to the same place.

"I said, 'Cougar, if it's a mess of jeep-shaped metal that you want, you've got it.' That thing was stripped buck naked—no wheels, no bumpers, no spare-tire rack, even the mirrors were gone. I don't believe Cougar could have been more pleased if we'd found gold.

"We carried it out on a tow truck Cougar's daddy owned. Cougar's daddy had three filling stations and a spare-parts store. Cougar was supposed to be running one of the stations that summer, after he got out of the Korean War army, waiting to go to North Texas State Teacher's College—I don't know what kind of damn teacher Cougar's folks thought their boy would make, but he sure couldn't get into Austin, where I'd started pre-med—nobody ever got worse marks in our high school than Cougar Edwards.

"Anyway, he near killed himself with that old jeep cadaver, toting it out. I was driving the tow, babying the thing along across a field, with the jeep body swinging back and forth, just off the ground. Coug was sitting back in the bed, watching how his jeep rode, and suddenly he yelled at me to stop. I did, and got out, and saw him jumping off—one of the chains he had the jeep slung with had slipped, and the rear end was slanting off. I hollered I'd lower it so as to take the weight off the chains while he tightened up, and he said not to. The big fool was going to hold the weight of the chassis on his shoulders while he fixed the chain.

"When he got under and moved it, it lurched and knocked him down, and came sliding at him—he threw up a hand, and he was holding just about the whole weight with it. He really was. I skinned back into the cab and yelled 'Roll, Cougar,' and hit the takeoff to jerk it up sudden into the air. I guess he rolled in time before it totally upended and hit the ground, right where he'd been lying.

"He had a Porsche Carrera motor," Johnny says. "It was a going piece of machinery, that old Porsche racing motor. Cougar rear-mounted it on his VW chassis, with the Cougarized springs and steering, and then he just cut a hole in the floor behind the seat on that old jeep body, and lowered her over. Covered the motor with a homemade hatch, and threw some paper sacks of dairy feed on top to hide it. All that was left of the jeep, then, was the outer shell, the two raggedy front seats and cracked windshield, and a hood with nothing under it but cinder blocks for ballast.

"It took a long time to get it together, weeks. Months. Sure, it was months, because I went back to college just a night or two after the first run. I remember we finally had everything sealed up and tight and greased about two in the morning. We decided to fire up the motor and tune it, there at

Cougar's station. It wasn't muffled, of course, and Coug put the plugs in and said, 'Okay, kick it in the tail, Johnboy.' I got in the seat and tromped the button, and she caught right now, with a scream. And we grinned at each other and nodded—couldn't hear each other talk over the noise. Coug started to adjust something or other, and it seemed like it caused that motor to make a ringing sound along with every other kind. We didn't realize it was the telephone until the town cops stopped ringing and came over to see what the hell was going on.

"We cut off, but even so, the state cops were there too, maybe ten minutes later. Hell, I guess we'd violated about every ordinance they had except maybe cattle rustling, before we even ran the car. About three o'clock, we pushed it by hand out of town and way on down the road before we started it again, and drove, and broke whatever laws they had left.

"And the cops didn't have a car in all east Texas could catch Cougar's jeep, once he got it off straight roads."

What started this was Beth driving over here from rehearsal in the pretty car she picked up at home in Illinois last night, a red Ghia. It's parked right in front now, for everyone to see through the plate glass on the door.

She came up to the table saying, "Look out there, Johnny Ten. How about that?"

"Glorious," cried Highmore Skeats.

But Johnny looked very serious, leaned back just a little, folded his hands in his lap, and said:

"Beth, when I look at you and see that car, I start to shiver. My toes curl in and my stomach quakes and my heart goes tearing around crazy, looking for the way out of my chest." His neat, handsome, dark-haired self-containment is misleading. He is not a slight man, but his bones are so fine, his head so nicely modeled, his eyes so bright, his hair so thoroughly trained, his hands so delicately articulated, that he seems less than his size—and his voice is light and low, but not weak, with constant changes of tone and pitch and throb, but all controlled, never wild.

"When I got back from college for Christmas vacation, Cougar hadn't been away after all. He'd persuaded his daddy he wasn't ready yet for college, and he'd spent that fall driving the jeep. Coug and I were off-and-on friends, and that vacation we were altogether on. Maybe I ought to explain just a little bit—back in school, you see, we'd ridden bikes together—motorcycles—in the same bunch. I left that bunch. They were getting, well, kind of sloppy. Got Cougar mad at me; he was captain. Then after a while he left the club, too, and we were friends again, riding around on our own. Cougar had fights with some about it."

Johnny lets that lie a moment; then he says:

"Cougar was terrible in a fight. Wild and cruel and never knew when he was hurt. I remember once I told him, 'Next time, Cougar buddy, I'm not with you. I'm getting on my bike and leaving you to it.' Then we weren't buddies anymore. He *liked* to fight, that was the trouble. I never did. Long as there was a way out, I'd take it. . . ."

He breaks off, and looks at Beth with quiet menace. What do they learn to do, up there in the locked classrooms of the medical school? He would transplant an ostrich gizzard, down at the end of your esophagus, and give you a handful of grit to load it with before he felt free to knock your teeth out.

"That jeep could run by Christmas." He says this in a low, firm voice, directly to Beth, as if she'd been so careless of her personal safety as to doubt the fact. Then the nice smile: "We took a One-fifty Jag one day, and I knew the boy had it; that thing was tuned to race. Started with him even at a stoplight, and he knew what Cougar had. He got us in first. We came even in second, and passed him in third. We got to the straight, and he went back ahead—had him an edge in straightaway speed, I'll bet he was turning a hundred and ten, but I don't know for sure. We didn't have a speedometer on the jeep, not even a tach. Now, there's a diving turn two miles out of town, down into a big gully and out again, and the Jag came to it and chickened. We saw his brake light flash, and Coug yelled, 'I got him,' and around we went—I was never so glad for a seat belt.

"Another time we were lugging along, maybe thirty-five or forty. Coug liked to hold back the traffic, kind of get people behind a little irritated with him. There was big, strong Pontiac tailgating, and finally the driver saw clear road to his left. He pushed his horn and came up even, gaining speed. Cougar looked over and waved to him and floored the pedal and—there's no other way to say it—we shot. We went from forty to a hundred like the pin hit the primer. I looked back, and there was the Pontiac, maybe turning eighty-five or ninety, still on the left hand side of the road, and you never saw such a look as there was on that man's face.

"Well, I'd been home for Christmas just a day or two, when Coug started talking about running down to Mexico. It's just over a hundred miles from where we live to the border, and I tell you, I liked Mexico a lot. So much, I wasn't sure I wanted to go with Cougar. Still, he kept after me, and one night, when they closed early at the only bar we liked—and look here, we were right where you've got half a skin full and the other half feels empty—Coug said, 'I'm going there, Johnboy. You coming too?' And I said, 'Bueno, Bwana, let's buy us a jug. . . .' "

Johnny pauses. Then he says, almost solemnly: "Christ I wish I'd said no. Cougar wouldn't have gone by himself."

Sidney tries to break the spell: "I don't know about you, Johnny Ten. What do you think, Maury?" Maury shakes his head. "Marcel?"

"I think hush." Marcel pats her hand.

"Well, it was all desert and moonlight when we got down close to the border, and we didn't have much to say by then. Might have been two or three in the morning, and we'd half-killed our quart, but I don't recall that I was sleepy. I was all bright and alert and, well, ready for something, and just before McAllen, there was a great big billboard, said Impeach Earl Warren. So I was letting that one play in my head, 'The Impeachment of Earl Warren.' Warren wasn't a beefy Californian, the way I cast it. He was a frail, St. Francissy sort of old guy, and I was defending him against a whole Texas bar association of John Birchers, and when I lost it, they were going to shoot my old, holy man into little bits with their Smith and Wessons, so there wouldn't be anything left of him to bury, and I told them: 'You are termites in the house of civilization, rust in the wheat of justice, cutworms in the cabbage of the heart of man.'

"I was still playing this show for myself when we went by the border station, so I'm not too sure, but I don't think they even took our names. I know we didn't have tourist cards, but Coug shouted we were only going into Reynosa, and they waved us on.

"But we went on through Reynosa, out onto desert road again, and Cougar and I suddenly started laughing and joking and having a great time. Sometimes it takes the air of a different country to wash the crap out of a man's lungs.

" 'Cougar,' I yelled. 'Are you a termite in the house of civilization?'

" 'Nossuh, Johnboy,' he said. 'But I'm a damn big rat.'

" 'Let's ride it, rat,' I hollered. 'Let's get on down where the music plays.' There's one hundred twenty-five miles of desert and mountain before you get to a town I like, Montemorelos. Now also, there are three or four little official check stations along the road—places where a couple of uniformed guards flag you down and wave you on—I'm not sure why. It was at the second one of those—I was joshing with one of the guys, getting the moths out of my Spanish—when we saw headlights coming, way down the road behind us, coming fast.

" 'Let's go, John,' Cougar shouted. 'I'm not for eating anybody's moon dust out here tonight.' He swung out and took off. We were a mile down the way before I noticed the other car stop in at the checkpoint, and they didn't hold it long. It came swinging out, and by the time we had a two-mile lead, it was traveling just as fast as we were. And we weren't going slow.

"You know, it gets disturbing after a while, having someone follow you, well back, keeping the distance even. After a while Cougar noticed it and speeded up, and the car behind speeded up. Then Coug floored and cut loose for a couple of miles, bumping and jarring where the road got rough, but the other car never fell back a foot. Coug looked over at me—hell, it was bright enough so I could see the look on his face—and said, 'What in hell?' He slacked off, but we couldn't judge whether the other car really tried to slow down, too, because just then we came to another checkpoint and had to stop.

"We didn't waste a whole lot of time with it, but when the car behind us got there, it didn't either. It was much closer when we took out across the desert, and suddenly Cougar said: "You know, I'm kind of forgetting what this jeep was made to do, Johnboy. Follow what I mean?' He grinned, and we dropped the speed way down.

" 'He already knows we're fast, you can't fake him,' I said.

" 'He'll get all confused. Think it was some different car out in front—hell, he just won't believe it,' Cougar said.

"The other car didn't slow this time when we did. It came slurring up behind us, headlights getting brighter and brighter, and then whipped past with a rush of air felt like it could have spun us. Cougar's timing was off. He'd misjudged how fast that car was coming, and by the time he had his pedal down, it was gone by and running off.

" 'Three-ninety SL', I yelled. You know what that is? The beautiful old Mercedes, the last real sports car they made. Gull-wing doors and fuel injection and, by God, one that's in shape just doesn't have a top speed.

" 'Damn. Oh, goddamn,' Cougar said, and he hunched forward and I could hear his right heel grinding floorboard. We only hit that road from one bump to the next.

" 'It's no disgrace,' I said. 'That's a car.'

" 'It's not the car,' he said. He was going to be able to keep it in sight for a while, but we'd gradually for damn sure lose it. 'It's the driver.'

" 'You know the driver?'

" 'Know who she is,' Cougar said. 'So do you.'

"I hadn't seen it in the dark, that it was a girl driving.

" 'You hang on, John,' Cougar said. 'We going to get her in the mountains.'

"I have the feeling now she waited for us. It was a good thirty miles, and no checkpoints between, before the desert ended and the road started to climb. I don't mean she went slow, but I know she could have gone faster. She could have had a five-minute lead and gone on out of sight if she'd wanted.

" 'Who is it?' I said. 'What's her name?'

"Cougar spoke between his teeth. It wasn't just that he was mad: You daren't let your jaw loose, the way that car was jolting, for fear of biting off your tongue. 'She did that to me once before. Mary Virginia.'

"Then I did know who she was, but I hadn't thought about her for years. Her daddy was a rancher and an oil man that the tax boys put in prison. But before that I remembered her as a little girl, ten or twelve, who'd come to our town now and then from a ranch fifty miles away, and do exactly what she wanted. And always looked grim about it. Pretty? You'd have said she was a pretty little girl, until she smiled—no, this is the exact truth: She had a smile that darkened her face.

"Mary Virginia was a famous girl around home when she was in her teens, but I never knew her. She was East in school, or running around with guys her father did business with. No kidding, when she was fifteen, some wheel wanted to give her an oil well—that's what they said—and her daddy let her take it. Nobody claimed the wheel got anything more than a dark smile for it, but of course nobody really knew. A little after that her daddy went to prison, her mama was dead, and I guess she had all the protected income for herself.

"There's a kind of sport down home—pistol-shooting rattlesnakes. You go to a real snaky place, and try to kick them up and get them moving toward you. . . . I wouldn't try it now for the Taj Mahal, but it's what we did. Mary Virginia's the only girl I ever heard of doing it. I heard she took bullfight lessons—that would be after Pop was back and going in and out the front door of the bank again. It's true, there was a little private bullring on the ranch, I'd seen it driving by, illegal as hell to use it, but Mexicans used to come up and do private shows. So the word went.

"So maybe she did try that, too.

"You know, I would have hated the way Cougar was driving, would have been crying with him to slow down, let it go, stop breaking up the jeep—I wouldn't have known which to like worse, the jolting or the fright—but I wanted to see that girl. I wanted us to catch up, and run beside her on the mountain road a way, and then maybe fall back if we had to, but let me see her face.

"I kept imagining that face pure white, with a glow beneath the skin, and a kind of wild, unfurrowed, intent look, like an animal clear in its mind that it's going to attack. I thought maybe the mouth would be pulled in a little tight, but the hair would be swept back easy, the shoulders set loose, the hands firm and sensitive with all that Mercedes power under them. I wanted to see all that, and when Cougar held out his hand for the jug, I gave it to him gladly.

"Let me tell you about drunk driving: There's a point. Any amateur ever drove a hot car knows this. An amount of liquor that makes you drive better, because the car can do more than you dare sober. Listen, most cars can. Of course the pros don't need it, but next time you're in a real hurry, try a couple of drinks. I don't mean to sound perverted, but that'll make a driver out of you, and I was glad to see Cougar finish off the jug and throw it up in the air and drive on out from under it. There was just a far-back tinkle when it fell.

"And except for one thing, it went as I imagined. She was into the mountains, climbing maybe six turns up from where we were, and we started to make inches. You should have seen Cougar go after her, up through the curves. He'd take left or right in little, pure strength jerks on the wheel, tires going freep, freep, freep, so as not to lose a hair of speed he didn't have to lose . . . but she, she flew her gull through smooth, and didn't take an extra inch, drifting it when she had to, she could drive. But we caught her. She hit a rough stretch, where the pavement was broke up, and she backed off some, and there we caught her, soaring from bump to bump that way, smacking down, bucking into the air again, we inched up by her rear fender. We were high on the mountain now, working toward the summit, sheer drop-offs all along and no guard rail, but I'd forgot how to be scared, I was straining so to see her face. Our hood was even with her door, I could see the back of her head, but I still couldn't make out hair. Just shape. Then there was a little downhill run, just before the final turn and climb to the top, and Cougar took it crazy. I could glance forward and see the curve rushing at us at the end of the run, and Mary Virginia started backing off for it, we got even, door to door, wheel to wheel. And I looked. She wasn't four feet away, but I couldn't see her face.

"She had a scarf wrapped around her head, and the moon was behind and over to the right, throwing shadows from the mountain. It was like a woman with a cloth head driving, and just then, while I was willing that she'd toss her head back and the scarf might fall away, Coug hit the brake. We went into a long, screeching skid, and he wrenched the jeep in behind her, just in time to be able to drift the curve.

"We started the final climb, the steepest, and Coug got up wheel to wheel with her again, and he had some climb in that thing, too, and as we came along to the last upcurve, at the very top, he was inching ahead. There was hardly room for two cars—I could have reached over and touched her fender, we were that close. I could read her speedometer for a second, and it was near one hundred. We went over the top together and down the next slope, Cougar inching and inching toward a right curve, and WHAM. No. Not quite. She'd let her rear end drift, maybe just a fraction further than she needed to, and for one black second I thought it just might graze and flip us over the edge. If we'd been one foot farther back—but Coug got her. Whether she'd done it on purpose or made an error, it gave him his chance, and he came out of the curve and plunged on past, just a split better than she could. He held it easily enough around the next curve, which went our way, left, and in the straight that followed he cut to the middle, out in front. Held her while he chose to, then he grinned and sighed, and moved right, into lane. And don't think she didn't take it, that Mercedes had the horses, she came out on the left, going straight and a little downhill and went by us—she must have had the outside edge of her left-hand tires over nothing to do it, it was that narrow. Little Girl Guts.

"That was the last time the lead changed, though we were right on her when we coasted into Montemorelos, and as soon as she passed the first speed sign, she throttled down and idled on through town.

" 'Damn, Coug,' I said. 'That's a driving woman.'

"Cougar was puffing a little, but he grinned: 'What about Old Cougar?' he said. 'And doesn't Miss Mary Virginia know it? Two more miles of mountain, I'd have beat her again.'

" 'Give her a ring,' I said. We were passing a cantina that looked pretty nice, and I could hear guitar music coming out the door. 'Maybe she'd like to switch off and burn a little high-octane tequila with us.'

"So Cougar beeped what horn he had. She pulled over to the curb, but she didn't really stop, and as we went along slow, side by side, she was looking over at us. But I still couldn't see her face. All I saw was eyes, big, no-color eyes. Then she gave her car a shot and pulled away again, toward the other edge of town.

" 'Yeah, baby, let's go,' Cougar shouted, taking out after her. 'Bigger and better mountains where you're headed.'

" 'And narrower roads,' I said. 'Worse pavement. Half-mile drops.'

" 'She wants a race, she'll get it,' Cougar said. 'Winner take it, loser shake it.'

" 'Don't be a fool, Coug,' I said. Call my friend a fool? But I swear I knew it: 'She wants to kill us.'

" 'That would take a great heap of killing,' Cougar said.

" 'I'm getting off, Cougar. Set me down.'

" 'Johnboy,' he said. 'I don't aim to be inhospitable, but that was exactly the idea.'

"He stopped the jeep. We were right at the southwest edge of town now, and Mary Virginia was drifting along, out ahead, the white car flashing moonlight. 'Mind walking back?' Cougar asked me. 'That up there's something Cougar doesn't want to lose the sight of.'

" 'She won't play rules,' I said, and undid my seat belt. 'Come on, Coug. Let's hit the cantina back there. I heard music, Coug. There'll be girls.'

" 'You got a head full of weevily cotton,' Cougar said. 'Hell, yes, she'll play. I'm going to drive her down, Johnboy, when we get up there. I'm going to rush on by and get me a real lead, and then—there's no traffic now. Not any.'

"I shook my head. We hadn't seen another headlight, all the way down. 'Somewhere up there, there's a long, pretty straight,' Cougar said. 'When I'm past her and I've got my lead, I'll find it. And I'll stop, right in the middle, I'll swing out and block the road. And when she stops, I'll walk back to her car, and open the door and say, *Princess, will you ride in my fast jeep?* And she'll come with me, without a word.'

"I looked up ahead, and the gull was perched, half a mile up the road, waiting for him.

" 'You see?' he said.

" 'Yeah,' I said. 'Yeah, prince. I do.'

"Coug revved up, blasted, and left me there. I thought about his tires, his oil, the damn brakes, and I saw the white car start and take the road ahead, flirting out, and I yelled, 'Cougar, come back,' but of course he didn't hear me.

"I couldn't leave and go to the cantina, not just then. I watched the Mercedes waiting, flickering, flashing away when he came up close, and Coug right after it. I watched the two sets of lights climb the first part of the grade. I must have stood there twenty minutes, seeing the lights go out of sight and then come back in again, higher up. For a while I could hear the motors. Then there was no audible sound, and all I could do was see lights, appearing and disappearing. Twice, when they reached real switch-backs, the lights would be pointing right back toward me, but higher and smaller than ever, and of course I didn't know what was happening, who was leading.

"Sometimes those faraway lights were running right together, and I knew they were wheel to wheel up there, dueling. Twenty minutes, skidding at forty, bursting to a hundred, call the average sixty. They must have been twenty miles away by road, then, after twenty minutes, but ten or twelve from where I stood on straight trajectory. Almost invisible, but I swear I saw: one little set of lights come sliding, diving off the road, falling, rather slow, turning over and over in the air. And over, and maybe bumping once, bouncing off, falling again, still falling when they went out. And the other car, God, I never saw it. But I think it stopped a moment, just a moment, and then went on south.

"Then it was very, very quiet, and I ran. Back into town, all the way to the cantina that we passed. I'd seen motorcycles outside. I talked. I never talked such Spanish. I had to have a bike, had to, and I was showing all the money that I had, twenty bucks or so, pleading to rent one. Finally one said okay, take his, take it for ten; he'd hold the stuff I carried in my pocket, license, stuff like that, for security.

"I jumped on. It was an old Indian without much compression left, and

I went into the hills. But I never found the place. There was no way of telling where it happened, no skid marks, no guard rail to be broken, nothing. And places all along, when I was far up over town, where a car could fall, and fall, and disappear, down in some deep and narrow canyon, with a floor of trees to hide it for weeks or years or ever.

"It was around five in the morning when I rode back, light enough to see that there was nothing to see. It was going to be a hot day, but I was cold and fearful as I rode. I didn't know which car had fallen, but I knew which one I didn't want to hear coming down behind me. I didn't want to be caught running down that mountain road on a tired Indian motorcycle by a white Mercedes, slurring out of the dawn with its appetite up.

"I reached Montemorelos. I found the motorcycle cat, sleeping it off in front of the cantina, and traded his ignition keys back for my stuff. And then I walked to the police barracks.

"What was I going to say? There I was, a hundred miles deep in Mexico without a tourist card, almost out of money, no visible means of transport, but I went to the cops anyway, and tried to tell them what had happened in a way they'd believe. But of course I didn't really know what had happened, or to whom, and I could tell the cops figured I must have been on an awful drunk. I think what they decided was that there probably was a girl and a car, that I must have ridden down this far with her, that she chucked me out, and now I was telling a story to try and get them to chase her down for me.

"They were perfectly polite. They even drove me into the mountains in a cop car, but of course I couldn't show them anything. I was half-sick by then, from no sleep, no food, the heat, and what I knew . . . probably I was babbling, and Spanish got harder and harder to speak and even worse to understand. Anyway, the cops took me to the bus station when we got down: 'Go home to your country,' they told me, and asked if I had money for a ticket.

" 'Yes,' I said. 'Yes. There is a dead man up there, or a dead girl, who will never be found.' They made sure I bought my ticket. They smiled and went away."

Johnny stops, takes a sip of beer, and holds it in his mouth as if not certain he could swallow it.

"Johnny Ten," says almond-eyed Beth. "Oh, Johnny Ten." She puts a hand on his arm, and he looks at her quietly for a moment, swallows the beer, and shakes his head. Careful, Beth—she lowers the hand. If she didn't? He might whip her butt to compost, plant feather seeds, and sail her off into the air to float forever on the updrafts.

"Jesus, Johnny," Hoffman says. "I can feel the slats on that bus-station bench."

"I sat dozing, sick, scared, waiting for the bus. I couldn't eat, but I got a pint of tequila and an orange drink, and I sat there, I don't know how long, all alone, watching the door. Then the station started filling up with other passengers, coming to take the bus, and I felt reassured and dropped off asleep, and what woke me was silence. The hum of voices stopping.

"I looked up, and there she was. She stood in the doorway with the nice, helpful young policeman. Nobody spoke. The people looked at her. She looked at me. I cringed.

"Then, for one absurd instant, I felt triumphant: 'She's been arrested. Thank God. They've got her for it.' But it wasn't so. She stood there waiting for me to get up, and I felt I had to, couldn't stop myself from going to her.

"That scarf, pale blue, was still around her head.

"When I reached where she stood, she said, in beautiful Spanish: 'This officer suggested that I offer you a ride home.' She tossed her head then so that the scarf fell back, and the hair was as I'd imagined it, soft, light brown, in easy waves. The eyes were dark and a little sad, but the smile—it was a pure, calm smile, without amusement in it, not unkind, but distant. Inward. 'May I offer you a ride?' she said in English, as if perhaps I hadn't understood, and the voice—I don't know if it had invitation in it, but I felt so trusting when I heard it. There just wasn't any reason at all not to say, 'Yes. Yes, thanks, I surely will,' so I bolted.

"The bus had just pulled up outside the station, and the door was open, and I ran to it in panic, pushing past the people who were getting off, finding a seat on the side away from her.

"Crouched by my window, watched her walk to the white car without looking over my way, and the cop opened the door for her with a bow. It was the right side of that car facing me, so if there was any sort of scratch or nick on the left, I couldn't see it."

"Was she beautiful, Johnny Ten?" Beth asks. "Or ugly? What did you do?"

"Nothing. There wasn't anything to do. I doubted Cougar's daddy would believe me, and if he had, well, he was just like his son. He'd have got his deer rifle off the wall, and gone out for Mary Virginia's father, I suppose. So I just said Cougar'd gone on south and left me, and, well, it was pretty much expected he'd be taking off. And not too likely to write letters. I knew there'd never be a law case, and she knew it, too."

"But was she ugly? When you saw her face at last?"

"Oh, no," Johnny says. "She was more than I'd imagined—pale, glowing, perfect. But not tense. Serene. Almost holy, like a nun. Shall we try your car, Beth?"

He gets up. She follows. He stands aside at the door. She goes out.

"*Mes amis,* I think you have just seen the trick turned before your very eyes," says Marcel, reflective. Skeats seizes and drinks down an entire glass of beer not his own.

"Shut up, Marcel," says Sidney.

And Johnny's voice drifts back through the slow-closing door: ". . . she was Mummy Death's own little rascal, wasn't she? Death's own sweet girl. . . ."

10: When Fate Was on the River

In Old Biology, Sato addresses the cast with what Maury has begun to call the mad-glad smile: "Now! What a schedule we have, everybody. Still coaching, still learning parts, and already Mr. Hoffman must begin to block. For him, we should be out of book already. Soon, Billy. Tomorrow, perhaps. All right, Karen. All right, Mr. Hoffman."

The cast smiles madly, gladly back, and Sato and Ralph are off to orchestra rehearsal. Everyone else is here except for Henry Fennellon and Beth, whose scenes come later. Karen Jackstone opens piano music, ready to accompany.

"Okay." Hoffman. "Let's get this snail pacing."

"Places for the top of the show," Mona Shapen cries. *"Scene One. A construction camp in Georgia."* And Hoffman shows his poker players how he wants them seated.

"You know how much stage we got over there." Hoffman. "When you're at this table, concentrate. When you get up from it, move. These are very physical guys. They aren't working very hard. They still got energy in the evening. Burn it. Dick and Maury, you're the two young bucks on this crew. Figure you finished high school together, learned to drive machines. This might not be your first job, but you're fresh, okay? You're buddies. I don't know how in hell that happened, but you're a couple of athlete buddies—it was basketball and wrestling, right? When you move off this table, give me some of both."

"Excuse me?" Dick.

"Listen to the Hoffman man." Maury.

"What I'm trying to say in my semiarticulate way is something like this. Poker is an interesting game—"

"Oh, I agree." Skeats. "Let's do play again soon."

"—but the interest is kind of intellectual. You're going to have three thousand people out there, and a hundred of them will follow what's happening on the poker table, you know? We got to give the other twenty-nine hundred dumdums something to watch. Now, I don't know any way to make poker into a spectator sport, but let me give you the image of using athletic moves to express the emotions that come out of playing a poker hand. I fold the cards, right? Relieved to be out of that one, okay? I show the relief with something physical—a high jump. A cartwheel." Hoffman shows them a big-eared leap and freeze.

"Poker's a game of aggression, faking, power, deceit—and our little game of poker's going to occupy about ten percent of our stage space. Now, as long as cards are being turned, we got to be absolutely focused in that ten percent. But as soon as a hand is over, or there's a pause, we're going to bump and run all over the other ninety percent of the stage. Dick and Maury mostly, but we'll find stuff for all of you. We're going to have a beer cooler here, okay? And a garbage can over there for the empties. You can wrestle each other to the cooler, you know? You can take basketball shots with the empties, over the other guy's guard, huh?"

"Perhaps Pill, the foreman, should get to the cooler and sell them the beer?" suggests Skeats, the foreman, riffling cards.

"No. Listen, leave the cards alone, huh?"

"You've stacked them? Wicked bugger."

"Yeah. Every day Mona will have both decks fixed the way the cards go in the scene. All right, now. You got the game pretty clear in your head, Marcel?"

"Oh, I hope so."

"However, we'd all be glad to have another of your smashing lessons this evening." Skeats, who was into Hoffman for seven dollars by the end of last night's demonstration. "Perhaps at higher stakes?"

"Sure, you know? You're dealing, Hugh. Deal. Everybody watch him. Dick, you play with your knee on the chair seat, half-standing. Maury, lean way back, far as you can, till the round is dealt, then rock forward. Everybody else, forward, over the table, then rock back. Nothing moves but the dealer's right hand, and you can lift it high, Hugh. That's through the fifth line, 'Dealer folds.' Then you whack those cards down, stand up, and freeze in that position. Try it to there."

Karen plays. Song begins.

Beth, raisin eyes sleepy, candy-stripe mouth smiling, comes quietly into the rear of Old Biology and sits to watch.

"Okay, Al's got a line. Next line, Maury, you fold. You say, 'Not me'—roll off your chair, come up with an empty beer can, take a shot at the garbage can, turn back to the table, and freeze. Try it." Maury nods, puts aside his book.

Marcel sings, as Al: "I'm in once."

Maury sings, "Not me," flips the cards one way and himself the other, and is into a drive, double pump, over-and-under shot, pivot, and turns back to the table again.

"Jesus," Hoffman. "Can you do that with a beer can in your hand?"

"Do it with three at once if you want," Maury says.

Debbie makes a note. She knows before he does what Hoffman wants. *Long-sleeve T-shirts different colors & blue jeans tight like dancer's tights for some, and wide for others with stripe shirts?* She can take Hoffman's athletic extensions of the poker game further, do something that will suggest, subliminally, different teams—Al, Bert, and Third Poker Player against the rest. *White leather athletic shoes to move, protecting hats of different color shiny plastic? On one young boy, even, a shirt with numbers? For the captains, ornamented belts, very wide. Marcel boots.*

"Okay. No movement while Pill deals the next round."

"Standing?" asks Skeats/Pill. "Shouldn't I sit again?"

"No. Stand. Look, what we're doing is dispersing bodies, and then letting the cards pull them in again. Okay, run on down to Third Poker Player—that's Mike, huh? The thing about high bluffs in Colorado."

Music. Voices sounding something between speech and song.

"Okay, on your high bluffs, Mike, you can pick up your cards, walk them around, thinking, and then turn back to Al when you think he's bluffing. The rest watch Mike. What's he going to do? Then, Al, you react. You got, 'That information will cost you a hundred bucks,' and rock your chair back, slap your old friend Bert on the shoulder."

Marcel tries it, almost goes over backward; Johnny Ten catches him.

"The old poker face," says Skeats.

At the end of the hand, while Al collects the money and gathers the cards, Hoffman has all the others up, Dick trying to shoot a beer-can basket, Maury frustrating him, others egging them on, until Al calls them back to the table for a new hand.

"Got all that in your books? Okay, take it to there again from the top."

At break, Beth rises quietly, lingers long enough to be sure she's seen, and fades. Johnny Ten finds her in the natural-history museum, in front of a case of bald eagles, male, female, and young.

They exchange the fond, dazed smile of new lovers, and hug quickly.

"I've got to see Sato," Beth says. "But late this afternoon, after rehearsal?"

"Let's shop and cook supper at my place."

"There's somewhere I want to drive to. Could we? Instead?"

Hugs her. "These baby eagles look like they're trying to grow fur."

"Now there's a change in tone, you know? Bitching about the company not building. Afraid for your jobs. Say it all to Al. Make him your scapegoat."

"It's hardly his bleeding fault. He's just the surveyor."

Hoffman stops the rehearsal. He pauses until everyone is quiet, and then says with devastating mildness: "We got a lot to do. Let's move along."

"You do want questions, don't you?" Skeats.

"No. You know what? I don't want any more." Hoffman's problem, as expected, is Marcel. He wants him up, solid, using his size to brush the others away. The rest, as he goes along blocking, can move, some better than others, and he finds himself inventing business now to suit their aptitudes. But the main build now is toward the first confrontation—Pill to Al, Skeats to Marcel, eyeball to eyeball—and the big tenor is just so soft, so amiable, so clumsy.

Al says he's thinking about marriage to Sally Anne.

Pill sings, "You ever talk to her about it, sport?"

"Grab him by the shirt front." Hoffman. "Try it. Now, Al, just look down at his knuckles until he takes the hand away. You wouldn't mind hitting him, but you care too much about what you're going to say. It's like you're defending Sally Anne's reputation, but you do it with a song, not your fists. You're giving him a straight answer to a crooked question, shaking him with it."

Skeats, shaking Marcel's shirt front laughs. Marcel, looking at the hand as instructed, blushes, hears the notes of introduction for his first extended solo, and suddenly everything changes. Dropping his book on the chair beside him, Marcel sings, an outpouring of song, Al's Vision of Sally Anne. He sings it out full volume, notes cascading, words beautifully articulated, paying no attention at all to Skeats's hand, which, after a moment, falls away. The huge tenor's chest swells, the voice fills the room, catches everyone, holds them, thrills them. Debbie, Sidney, and Short watch transfixed. Henry Fennellon, who has come up to the auditorium door, pauses so as not to interrupt, stands in the doorway listening, whispers: "Magic time."

" 'Bethie,' he used to say. 'I was playing when Fate was on the River.' Do you know what that means?"

"No, Beth, I surely don't."

"I'd say, 'Old Man Banjo,' and he'd say, 'Little Miss Melody'—it was corny and sweet as a small-town parade. Oh, Johnny, I love your hands."

She has brought Johnny Ten to the Banjo Man's place, not the house he lived in but a cabin on a bluff, above the Mississippi River, on the Illinois side, to which he used to come evenings or weekends, often bringing children and friends. It belongs to Beth's father now, who was one of the friends—as Beth was one of the children—but has not been much used since the Banjo Man died. Out across the River, over Iowa, the sun is setting, setting the particles of summer dust that fill the sky all aglow. "I used to think the sky was God's brain, full of strange ideas He had, like storms and fireflies. The first time I came here I wasn't much bigger than a cartoon mouse, and we saw bald eagles. The Banjo Man said this wasn't a fishing shack or a hunting shack, this was a looking shack, and often you can stand here on the screen porch high over the river, and watch the eagles intersect the sky. . . . We lived inside the Brain, but they could fly little tunnels through it."

"That's why you stood there."

"What?"

"Why you stood in front of a case of eagles, there in the museum today, to ask me to come out here with you."

"You see right into me, don't you? Right through my skin and skull and funny membranes. He was an albino Negro."

"Who, Beth? God, or the Banjo Man?"

"Fate. Fate Marable. He was a piano player, and he led bands that played on the riverboats, and if a jazz man was really there at the beginning, when ragtime turned to jazz, they would say that he was there when Fate was on the river. That was even before the First World War. The Banjo Man was big and bald and kind as one of those big, happy dogs that grows up in a house full of children. I mean, whatever happened, the first thought that ever came into his head was how to do a kindness. He didn't play with Fate Marable, because the bands weren't integrated then. He played on other boats that stopped here at Rock Island, and at Davenport, across the river. They say jazz music came from New Orleans, but the men who played it came from all along the River, Johnny. Here and Memphis and Mound City, they were just boys who walked onto the boats, with their horns and strings. One was Bix Beiderbecke—"

"Believe I've heard of him. He was a boat man?"

"No, but he grew up in Davenport, right across from here and upstream twenty miles. But that's what I mean. He wasn't here when Fate was on the River. He was just a little boy, whose father was in the coal business. But the Banjo Man was here."

Can't keep his hands off her, any more than she can keep from presenting her body to the hands. An hour back, driving over from State City and only halfway here, they'd got too excited to wait, pulled off onto a gravel road, then onto a dirt one, to copulate on the front seat in a breathless lap-sitting tangle of clothes, sweat, and dust. Now they are at one another again, in the cabin, on a cot with flat springs and a thin mattress, Beth's denim skirt up around her waist, John's denim trousers down around his ankles, arms wrapped, fingers digging.

Now they are eating take-out fried chicken, which they bought along the way, and drinking Seven-Up. It tastes wonderful.

"Let's burn the dishes," Johnny says, and builds a little fire in the fireplace with very dry wood, while Beth lies back down on the cot, her head on what is not a pillow but a sofa cushion in a mildewed pillow case.

"Johnny, am I crazy? I look at someone like Sidney. I can't control myself like that."

About to lie down beside her, he checks the impulse, gets another piece of wood, a small log this time, adds it to the fire, and sits quietly on the raised stone hearth.

"What is it, Beth?"

"I love your voice. Don't wear a rubber glove on it."

"All right."

"I've never told before. Like when you're little, and your mother is angry and orders you to clean up your room, and you can't because she won't help you, and you lock it. . . ."

"Is it about the Banjo Man?"

"Oh, no."

"The Banjo Man is before and after, but Johnny Ten, don't you know who it's about?"

"No, Beth."

"Janet Margesson."

"I see." Johnny keeps his voice unimpressed, but he's got a dozen of the great soprano's records.

"Are you trying not to sound surprised?"

"What about her?"

"She's so immense, isn't she? Like a great, fierce angel and a tender nurse. A sorceress, I think. Did you see that movie about Italians? I think she is The Godmother. Have you heard her sing?"

"Not live."

"The Banjo Man didn't have his records, not one. We didn't know that he had been someone in history. Even modest history, like the first light bulb. He didn't know that himself, so big and plain as an oak bucket. Let a smile be your umbrella, Beth. Keep your sunny side up. But I mourned when I was little, because my parents had seen him before I was born, long before, years and years, at a YMCA show, playing his banjo for children, and at bedtime I would ask my mother to tell me the story of the Banjo Man playing at the YMCA, and she would say: He held his banjo straight up, by the neck, with his fingertips somehow across the strings, and swung it back and forth like a big pendulum on a grandfather clock, and said, 'Listen to the clock strike twelve,' and his fingers and the swinging banjo would make it play like a chime, back and forth, one, two, three, and sometimes I would be asleep before she got to twelve.

"And when I got older and he was so very kind, kind as a warm melon, one day I asked him if he would get his banjo out and show me how it could be a clock. I had to talk and talk describing it, and finally he smiled and said, 'Oh, yes. I'd forgot that trick. I used to know a lot of banjo tricks.' 'Please do it, Banjo Man,' I said, and he smiled, and said, 'Miss Melody, those are just tricks, not music. My banjo doesn't work any more, and neither do my fingers, I'm afraid.'

"But his health was very good because he was sick. He was diabetic and drank only tomato juice, and all his friends from when Fate was on the River were drinkers and were gone. But he hadn't played for years when I was little, not since the YMCA shows before I was born that I mourned like a dove, and he sold bricks for a living and was a great trapshooter and fisherman and a trainer of dogs, and would do anything for anyone, and anything for me, except get his banjo from the attic. I found it there one day, and opened the case, and it was all mother-of-pearl and dust, and spiders lived in the case like an old hotel.

"But you mustn't be jealous of Ronnie, please, because he wasn't at all important, just that he was the first English boy I ever knew, I met him at college, so sweet and distinguished, like imported chocolate with hazelnuts, are you jealous of him?"

"No."

"He knew about jazz, oh, his records were as scratchy as a daddy's beard on Sunday morning, but when I said the Banjo Man's name, this nice old, bald brick salesman who liked to get things wholesale for his friends, who could get Ronnie good prices on cases of English cigarettes and whiskey, Ronnie's face turned to borscht, all red with blobs of white, and he stammered so, 'Not *the* Banjo Man, not the Banjo Man,' for Ronnie said that everyone in England knew his name. He'd been, Ronnie said, the banjo player in the first great white jazz band, oh, with Emmett Hardy and George Brunies and Leon Rappolo, and I said, 'Bix Beiderbecke?' and Ronnie said no, no, no, of course not, Beiderbecke was a kid who *listened* to that band and learned from that band when they played in Chicago, like a little boy watching carpenters, and then, when I took Ronnie—really, he's not important, I'm so sorry that you mind about Ronnie—when I took him home to meet the Banjo Man and my parents, Ronnie got to tell the Banjo Man who he'd really been.

"Ronnie said, 'I have your records, not all of them, but didn't you play on this? and didn't you play on that?' and the Banjo Man sometimes could remember and sometimes couldn't, he just hadn't thought about it in years.

"And I said, 'Then you were a famous musician,' and he said, 'Not your kind of music, Bethie,' and Ronnie said, 'But why did you stop playing, sir? Everybody in England thinks you died,' and the Banjo Man said, 'Blimey, old boy, tell them that's one sin I 'aven't committed,' and he said that so good-naturedly we all laughed. And Ronnie, but it's all right, please, I'll be through saying anything about Ronnie in just a minute, but he made this little speech, he said, 'The only reason that the guitar replaced the banjo in the fundamental jazz orchestra was that so very few men had the ear to play it as you did, sir. It's a much less forgiving instrument than guitar, but played right, it gives a more precise beat to the rhythm, and there's considerably greater purity in the solos, but so few men ever could play them as you did. The guitar never was as good an instrument, it was only more forgiving.'

" 'Well, well, well,' said the Banjo Man. 'Three holes in the ground,' but he was pleased, and only sorry that he couldn't let Ronnie come back to record him, because he said he'd put the banjo away in 1930 after the Crash, and then he was too old to play semiprofessional football anymore either, and all that was for young fellows, and couldn't he see about getting Ronnie a heck of a price on a case or two of Guinness stout? But I know he liked hearing that he was famous among collectors of old jazz records, because when I came home he'd ask questions about, well, Ronnie, shy as a country robin with a city sparrow, but then he told me he'd begun to get letters, too, from a man in New Jersey, a collector who was an engineer and wanted to record him, and Marcel plays and has heard of him, did you know that?"

"Know what?"

"Marcel, the tenor. He's heard of my Banjo Man. Marcel knows his name and who he was, and Marcel plays jazz on the clarinet from New Orleans, for fun, but when I broke up with Ronnie, it was because he drank so much, like an animal that's been starved and always overeats, Ronnie drank that way, do you drink a lot? I know you don't, you have to keep yourself steady as a corner post, but, I felt hurt and went home and did a mean thing. I made him get his banjo out. I was persistent as wire; I always liked singing folk songs and I just budged and budged my Banjo Man to give me lessons, until finally one day, because I almost cried, well, I did cry but just a few tears, like dew on a desert morning, and he said, 'All right, all right, let's see if she'll still tune up,' and I kissed his bald head—like kissing a basketball right on the seams—and said sit still and ran up to his attic, I was always free and familiar in his house, and got the spider hotel and brought it, and he took out mother-of-pearl.

"I was such a little bitch about it, I just made him do that, and it made him sad at first, handling that banjo like a picture of the first girl he ever kissed. But he gave me some lessons, and then I started thinking I'd been mean and said he didn't have to give me lessons anymore, so he gave me *Un Ballo in Maschera,* with Marian Anderson singing Ulrica, because he wanted me to have all the records of operas with good contralto parts so that I wouldn't be unhappy about not being a soprano, like wishing you were taller or your eyes were blue, but most people can control themselves, cool as cream. Why can't I?"

"I'm not a psychiatrist," Johnny murmurs.

"Of course not, darling, how I would hate it if you were, so poky and prying like those combination tools with little augers and gimlets and cork-screws folding in and out and none of them ever does the job it's supposed to do but only cut you and pinch you and prick you when you try to use them, Johnny, do you want me to stop telling you about it?"

"Whatever you want."

"Could we have a drink now?"

"That's a good idea."

Johnny has a shot of straight tequila and mixes some for Beth with orange pop and Rose's Lime. There isn't any ice.

"Turn off the lights again, I do want to tell you, please."

"All right.'"

"About Janet Margesson, unless you really don't want me to."

"It's all right."

"Are you cold?"

"No."

"You're sitting so close to the fire."

"It's a small fire. Do you want another drink?"

"I've never been so proud. I was the special one, the gifted one, the swan. I was a senior, and the best, and still living in the apartment that I'd shared with Ronnie, that's the very last time I'll say his name, but by myself, and didn't tell the other students that I was the chosen person. Janet

Margesson was coming to sing a concert at the university, and it was I who would drive the university car to Logan Airport, on the other side of Boston, to meet her plane, and drive her to the guesthouse.

"I never thought of how she'd have an accompanist with her, such a pig of pride, I thought I'd have her in the car to myself for nearly an hour, and we would talk, and she might want me to sing for her as I drove along, and I would tell her how the wall of my room was papered with her pictures, I bought twenty copies of *Life* magazine with a big picture story, 'American First Lady of Italy,' and she was on the stage at San Carlo, and with a count, and a film director, and an Italian man who made racing cars, and in different costumes and all her faces, repeated over and over those twenty times on my wall, and I colored them with transparent inks after Ronnie moved, and lighted them to glow.

"I was an hour too soon at the airport, early as February spring, and of course the plane was late, and I nearly cried because it might have crashed and brought the world to a stop, but she arrived.

"Gino, the accompanist, was with her, and photographers met the plane, and there were many pictures of them and of her alone and of me greeting them, but I was too excited to remember to be proud. It was like meeting God at the airport.

"She looked taller and a little older than I thought she would, but more marvelous, that New England patrician look, she's a lobsterman's daughter from Maine, but she is dame of the world, sensitive and sensual and strong-willed, and I had never seen such clothes. The fur was real Russian sable, I wanted to kneel and put my forehead in it, and the suit she was wearing was an original, made for her for love by that Roman fashion designer who was so in love with her and killed himself.

"Then the photographers went away, and we had to get the luggage, it was late and no porters, and the first words Miss Margesson said to me at all were, 'Gino has a bad back, darling. You're such a lovely big girl, can you handle the bags for us?'

"I felt like I could pick up Logan Field for her if she asked me to, even when I saw how many bags there were. I'd have had to make three or four trips to the car to get them all, and I would have, but two sailors saw me struggling and came and helped. They thought she was a movie star.

"I drove the car up, and we loaded the luggage in the trunk, and she gave the sailors her autograph. Then Gino opened the back door for her, and she got in by herself, and he closed the door and smiled, and got in front beside me.

"'Thank you, darling,' she said. 'Beth? Was that it? Are you a singer, Beth?'

"'Yes, Miss Margesson. Oh, yes.'

"'So young.' She leaned forward and touched my hair, and my scalp jumped and prickled like popcorn. 'Always, the lovely little girl singers they send for me.' Then she took a little handful of hair and pulled it hard enough so that it hurt, and I turned to liquid like an aquarium with crazy little fish swimming around all over, bumping the glass.

"'Better than bigga boy singer, I think,' Gino said, and she still had her fingers in my hair, tugging and teasing, and I'd think she was about to let go, and she'd tug again instead, and I didn't know what to do, so I started driving, and she pinched the back of my neck.

"She said, 'We know what you think, Gino,' and then something in Italian, and they both laughed, and she slipped a finger around under my ear and pinched the lobe quite hard and then settled back. I could see in the rearview mirror that she was still smiling, but she'd closed her big, famous eyes, there was a lot of light in the airport parking lot, but it didn't stop Gino from just keeping on with what she'd started, they must have felt something about me or seen something or heard something, because they started right away.

"By the time we were on the belt highway going around Boston, it was darker, and at least people in other cars couldn't have seen what was happening, but there weren't so many other cars, it was late as crickets, and the night air was moist with New England smell, all tree roots and clamshells, and I was sweating and out of control already. Why am I that way?

"He started with his left hand on my neck where hers had been, and his right hand stroking my side under where the right arm was raised to the steering wheel, and the fingers kept half-circling my breast, and he said, 'We teach you Italian, lovely Beth,' and then all the rest was in Italian after that.

"Other men, even ones I had affairs with, always treated me like a nice girl who couldn't be expected to consent to certain things, certain ways of being touched and handled, but Gino treated me like a slave girl who'd have no way of refusing anything that might amuse him to do to her, he knew he could, and so did Miss Margesson, but I didn't realize about her. I was mostly worried that she would hear and understand the things he was saying, such caressing, dirty-sounding things, so I was trying to say shh! to him and move his hands away, but I wasn't trying hard enough, was I?

"And I think I said, 'Please stop,' when he undid front buttons on my dress, but I was thinking too that I didn't want her to open her big eyes and see, and I imagined he was her lover and she'd be terribly jealous and there'd be an awful scene right in the car about it, but at the same time I was a little bit triumphant because he liked me so, and she'd made me carry bags and pulled my hair and been so patronizing, so I, I pushed his hand down but not away.

"And I was driving sixty-five miles an hour on the belt highway, but thank God there wasn't any traffic by then, lonely as a winter beach and you're in a sleeping bag and the pale, white sun comes up and wakes you and you pull the bag so close around you and can't keep your knees together and don't even want to; anyway, you have to move your feet around when you drive.

"So he had my skirt up in just no time and started to arrange my underthings so that he could play, and I gasped and said, 'Oh, Miss Margesson,' it was like a cry for help. 'Don't you want Gino in back to, to talk to, talk to, talk to?' and she said no, she'd like to rest, and I sneaked a look back, she was lying across most of the back seat, still smiling, but her eyes opened, and she looked at me and said, 'Eyes on the road, darling,' and Gino slid my panties right off, down to my knees.

"And oh, I thought, *Thank heavens she's lying down and can't see,* and oh, that son of a bitch was so skillful with his fingers, he knew every little way to tweak and push and stroke, so busy, like I was a keyboard, both hands, bass and treble, and of course I could have stopped the car, but then she would have wanted to know why, and anyway, by then I didn't altogether want it to stop, and of course Gino knew that, and knew just what to do, didn't he? It was naughty and awful and secret, and I couldn't ask her to make him stop, mile after mile, and I do wonder how fast I was driving, and then, about ten miles before we reached our interchange, oh, I couldn't help it anymore and didn't want to, and it's a wonder I didn't wreck the car.

"So then he let me go, and pulled my panties back up and kissed me on the neck, and patted my knee like I was a little girl, and said sweet things in Italian instead of dirty ones, and I got them to the campus. But I was soaked. Can anything help?"

"We use drugs when sexual compulsion's a real problem. But mostly with men."

"Oh, I know, and it would be so much better if I were a man and in prison and . . . am I saying really crazy things?"

"Relax. Say whatever you want."

"I'm sorry that you minded about Ronnie, and it made you miserable, but now you're being sweet as waffles about what Gino and Miss Margesson did, and it was just the beginning. But we were met at the guesthouse by all the music-department important people, and the only thing she said was, 'Beth, you can come turn the pages for us when we rehearse tomorrow if you like.' Calm as an empty tennis court.

"And I rode home on my bicycle, oh, this is awful, and got all soaked again, riding home and thinking about it."

"I don't mind about your bicycle either." Silence and a gasp. "Go ahead. I'm sorry."

"Was it because I was dramatizing myself? Did I deserve it?"

"Go ahead."

"Don't feel you have to be professional if I sound silly."

"Okay."

"Maybe it's a funny story."

"Not really."

"When I got in bed I didn't know. Whether to feel ashamed or in love. And I was still confused when I woke up, but Gino was quite good looking, and I told myself nice lies, that he'd probably just been madly attracted to me, and Italians were passionate as pigeons, and that made it all right that I'd responded. I thought he'd probably call, and decided when he did, I would say no and make them get someone else to turn the pages, and then when he didn't call, I decided I'd say yes. Then I made up another fib for comfort, and decided to be angry at Janet Margesson because probably she suspected about what happened in the car and wouldn't let Gino call me. I was dying to see Gino by then, but I wanted him to evade her and come to see me, or even defy her if it meant enough . . . so I called him.

"Isn't that awful? I just had to.

"But he was mild and friendly, nothing like a lover, and said he'd just gotten up, and if I was coming to help them rehearse, would I please bring him a quart of buttermilk on the way? So I said I only called to explain that I had a headache and couldn't come to turn the pages, and instead of saying he'd come see me in my apartment, he said, 'Janet wants you to,' and I said really, no.

"Then in about fifteen minutes the phone rang, and I thought, happily, it would be Gino, begging me, and I'd change my mind, but it was the head of the music department, such a difficult man, autocratic as a stallion, but he was scared and upset. Miss Margesson was raging, he said, I simply had to come to rehearsal, and I said I simply couldn't, I was very firm with the nervous stallion, and I just started to feel like being difficult. But then, the head was just capable of coming over and trying to order me to do as he wished, and I thought I'd better be in my dressing gown if he did. And my landlady lived across the hall in another apartment, so I changed, and told her, because she might be out in the front rooms and stop him.

"So I drank some lovely hot potato soup, and put on Galli-Curci singing 'Obra Legere' and other arias, and I decided later I'd get dressed and slip into the concert, I had my ticket, and I did so want to hear Miss Margesson sing. But I knew I didn't want to have anything more to do with her or with Gino, I was cured. And do you know, I had my eyes closed, and the old Galli-Curci record suddenly seemed to fill out with new sound and come to life, I thought it must be a dream, and didn't want to open my eyes it was so beautiful, and then I opened them, and then there was Janet Margesson herself. Right there in my room, singing to me, Dinorah, along with Galli-Curci.

"And she finished, and shrugged off the sable, and turned off the record, and the next thing I knew she had her arms around me and was kissing me on the mouth. And I'd never had a woman's kiss before. Then she started to stroke me and whisper not to worry. The landlady had let her in, she'd said she was my mother, wasn't that fun? And the landlady was just going out, we had the place to ourselves. She kept laughing and petting me, and kissing me when I tried to say anything, putting her tongue in my mouth, and I did try to resist, and she acted like it was a joke we were having, but when I finally did catch one of her hands by the wrist with both my hands so she couldn't put it under my dressing gown, she called, 'Gino.'

"And he came in, I realized he'd been watching through the door open just a little bit, and he had his quart of buttermilk, that Italian son of a bitch, and was drinking it right out of the bottle and watching. Then they had me alone in the house, and I wasn't strong enough to keep them both away, and even, when Gino was there, I didn't, you know, resist quite so strongly, and he held my wrists, such warm cuffs, while she petted, and they just kept undressing me together, and that bastard, he had buttermilk around his lips when he put his face down between my legs and did me for her to watch."

"Okay, Beth. That's enough."

"What, Johnny?"

"Frankly, you're beginning to make me squirm quite a bit. Let's call it a session."

"Oh."

"Oh, hell, go ahead. Do the rest of it." He has gone halfway to the tequila bottle. Now he returns to his perch by the fire, stirs it, and repeats, "Go ahead."

"But there isn't really anything more. Not very much. Except that I couldn't control myself anymore, and let each of them do what they wanted to. She did first with her mouth and fingers and, you know, and then he did with, well, the regular way, sort of, and I was all excited for them, and let them, and then I realized afterward that of course she'd known all about it in the car driving from the airport, and they were sharing me like two bad children with a toy that doesn't belong to them. Is it all right, Johnnie?"

"God, you got any more to tell?"

"No. Only I don't want to make them sound like monsters, all green and scaly and fire ears, because I did let them, and didn't really feel upset until she, afterward, she, well, she paid me."

"What?"

"Oh, don't sound so shocked. I mean, with tickets. She gave me two tickets, she said they were much better than my student seat, she wanted me to bring a friend, she said they'd take us out somewhere after the faculty reception—but you see, it was her first concert after Italy, and everybody wanted to see it, out-of-town people were buying from students, like great owls swooping, and those tickets might have been worth a hundred and fifty dollars."

"And so?" He gets the tequila this trip.

"You're tired, aren't you? Poor doctor. So I tore the tickets up, and still had the key to the university car. I found it, in the parking place, and I drove myself to Logan Field, and left it there and flew to Chicago, and sat on a chair in the airport until morning, and took another flight and came here. And I was expelled from school, so uncooperative, such a car thief, but I didn't care."

"To this cabin?"

"My father had a key. I felt bruised and depraved and frightened, and I came right here, and rested. And along toward evening, one eagle went across the sky and disappeared, and the Banjo Man came. I was on the screen porch, and I heard his car door bang shut, and I knew who it was. So when he came in, I had a smile all ready for him.

" 'Hello, Miss Melody,' he said. He had his banjo case with him. 'That landlady of yours in Massachusetts called and said you'd run off. Don't know why she called me, but I'm glad she did.'

"I blushed, because when I'd gone back to school that fall, and I'd filled out an off-campus-housing permission form, there was a place to write in whom to notify in an emergency. And I hated my poor parents so and wrote in my Banjo Man's big, bald, kindest name, but never thought.

"He said, 'What is it, Beth? Is it that Ronnie boy?'

"So I nodded, and said yes, that's what it was, so deceitful.

"And he said, 'Well, I just came to tell you to keep your chin up, honey, and say thank you, thanks a million.'

"That caught me, and I said, 'Me?'

"He sat down, and opened up the case, and said, 'I didn't make much of a teacher, did I? But if it hadn't been for you, I'd never have got started playing this old box again.'

" 'You're playing?'

" 'Better than I ever did before. Some ways, some ways not. There's things my fingers can't do anymore, but then there's things I know about the world I didn't know.'

"He chatted along that way. Sometimes a friend's good fortune is desperately depressing, isn't it? If, from far away you hear about it, but if you're with that friend and if the friend is happy and unassuming and expects you to be pleased, then what can be more pleasing? My Banjo Man was back in practice for the first time in forty years, and playing publicly and loving it. He'd even been to New York, where the jazz musicians came to hear him at the club they gathered at, and all wanted to play with him, even the modern ones, wanted just once to play his music, too, with the Banjo Man, like a modern poet meeting Whitman might rather recite from *Leaves of Grass* than read some little poem of his own. My Banjo Man was having a wonderful time, and of course I said, 'Oh, play for me,' and of course he did.

"I think it was 'Tiger Rag,' very fast and cheerful, and I walked onto the porch and stood listening, looking down at the River, and it was as if 'Tiger Rag' was coming up from there, too. As if a riverboat were going by, with Fate at the piano, those chalky fingers flashing, and Bix Beiderbecke—but that was an anachronism, wasn't it?—and Joe King Oliver, and all of them were playing 'Tiger Rag,' with the Banjo Man laying down a beat that never stopped, and the boat was churning past down there, all lights and gay on the water.

"But the banjo beat did stop, of course. And there wasn't any boat then. And the Banjo Man said behind me, 'That's not it, is it Bethie? Well. How about this?'

"And he started to play just a simple, slow, pure air—it was 'Aura Lee,' that song college boys used to sing. He played it single-string, with no vibrato, every note rounded and separate, just lovely, simple notes dropping like warm rain from the banjo, around me and out into the soft evening, drifting west across the Mississippi, over Iowa, after the sun.

"Now the Banjo Man is dead. There are no players like him anymore, and that engineer from New Jersey never came to make records . . . but if I could, I would rather hear the Banjo Man once more play 'Aura Lee' single-string than Bach doing fugues on the organ or the boy Mozart at the clavichord."

Now Johnny goes over and lies with her, just holding her for a time, and at length says:

"We better go, hadn't we?"

Driving back to State City, she starts to speak again of Janet Margesson.

"I don't know as I want to hear any more about her," Johnny says.

Beth is surprised. "Why, Johnny!"

"What, did you see her again?"

"Not while the Banjo Man was alive. But we leave footprints. . . ."

"You see her again?"

"My life moved East again, after he died. I've just come back here, been away so long, like a lost cup from a matching saucer. . . ."

"Uh-huh."

"I spent a week with her in Bermuda this spring, Johnny."

She wants to go to his place. He says no. Then he gives in, and once there, bangs her like a Caribbean drum. Bongo man.

11: The Greatest Sopranos
Who Ever Lived
Were a Couple of Studs
Named Carl and Guy

Hoffman presides at a production meeting on the stage of Old Biology, prior to the blocking of Scenes Two, Three, and Four. Looking at the people he can count on makes him optimistic: Debbie Dieter Haas, with the sketch pads. With the piano music, Karen Jackstone so tireless, such a perfect reading and teaching machine, he has begun to love her lumpy, unexpressive face. With the cue book, Mona Shapen, small, dark, beautiful, committed—she'd walk through fire for this dumb show. Also present are Professor Lekberg, fifth wheel, and Professor Short, snow tire.

Scene Two
The Swamp. 2:00 A.M.

"See, it's one thing to turn the poker game into some kind of dance. We got all those agile young bodies to throw around, and the scene's long. But the swamp's different, you know? It's short, the music's more musical, and the setting can be interesting."

"Yes, I think so," Debbie. "I will give you such a swamp, they will watch the scenery, we move the lights around, and the girl, to keep the look of dancing, they hear the singing, and it's over while they are still wanting more."

"Then you don't worry about the men's bodies this scene?" Short is fascinated.

"We got the tenor on stage alone." Hoffman. "We'll just let him collapse on that foam-rubber backbone, up on one elbow and sing."

"And when Pill comes in?"

"Oh, we'll let him march around with the big, stiff gestures, but he'll only be half-lit."

"Like a dangerous, jerky silhouette of moving." Debbie. "And the colors and the interesting lights going on behind him, on the vision of the girl moving smooth and the swamp looking like it's going back forever and forever."

"Counterpoint." Ralph approves.

Scene Three
The Fisherman's Hotel. 5:00 A.M.

"In this third scene, we got an important entrance to set up. They been looking at their programs, they know there's somebody named Beth Paulus, and they haven't seen her yet."

"You make it simple?" Debbie says. "It's five in the morning, a little bit dark. Al comes in, he rings a bell, still dark."

"Yeah. He sings, rings, sings, rings—and there she is, turning on the lights, standing there to look at him, and we got to look at her."

"And outside the window we keep bringing up some blue lights, whiter, because it is getting morning, so we can change the modeling if you like the bodies to hold still while she sings it about the fishes."

"It ought to be a pretty interesting set, Debbie. We're going to use it twice."

"I understand. It will be a very shabby, interesting fishes camp. Yes, that will be fun, with much detail."

"And Karen, don't take it too fast, okay? We want to be damn sure the audience knows what's going on."

"Have you talked to Sato about that?" Ralph asks, suddenly stiff.

"I got a note to talk to him. Ralph, if they don't get the words in this scene, we got a dead play."

"It isn't a play, it's an opera."

"I can't do anything with tempo the conductor doesn't want."

"We have our two finest voices in a scene together." Ralph. "I think that should be enough."

"Nothing's enough." Hoffman. "We still got a story to tell, and a dance to keep going."

"I think Billy's right." Snazzer Short. Who asked him?

Scene Four
Telephones. 8:00 A.M.

"This one's going to go on sex." Hoffman. "We squeeze the tenor into a phone booth, he's out of sight. . . ."

"You want a real, four-sides phone booth?" Debbie.

"What the bloody hell?" Unheard in his arrival, Hughmore Skeats IV stands at the apron of the stage, his beard just bristling at the level of the stage floor. He looks decapitated down there, but isn't. "What's in progress up there?"

"Just a get-together, Hugh." Billy Hoffman.

"We're having a production meeting." Primly, Snazzer Short spills the beans.

"That's what I ballocky-well thought. What's this about a bloody-great four-sided phone booth?" Skeats climbs the stairs, approaches the table, and picks up Debbie's sketchbook. "Phone booths. Furniture. Bloody-great power shovels. Who's to pay for all this?"

"I will be inside my budget." Debbie.

"You've got enough budget to furnish the *Queen Mary*," Skeats says. "I thought we'd agreed we could get some back for the out-of-town advertisements?"

"Hey, Hughmore." Hoffman. "I'm the guy to yell at, all right? It slipped my mind, you know? That you were supposed to come to production meetings." Skeats is head of the opera guild. "Next time you're invited."

"I should think so."

"We'll serve crumpets, okay? Come on, Hugh. Sit down. I'll tell you why we want the phone booth. We stuff the tenor into it, and let the audience watch you going after the girl, on the other side of the stage. Do you waltz?"

"I don't see—"

"We're going to have the dirtiest little waltz ever staged."

"But the music?" Ralph begins, and checks himself.

Hoffman ignores him anyway, for the problem at hand. "It's the Harlem grab and the Viennese wiggle, Hugh. Listen, here they come." Karen rises, gathers her music and goes to the piano.

Sidney and Marcel arrive. So does Beth. So does Henry Fennellon, who will make his own first entrance, too, in Scene Three, as Raymond Applegore, proprietor of The Fisherman's Hotel. Henry doesn't carry a book. His part's short; he's known it for a week.

And who else is where? Maggi Short is still away, though she has reached Chicago by now. Josette Lekberg, Ralph's Basque wife, is bottle feeding the lamb again. Maury Jackstone, having fixed the squad-car radios again, is advising his friend the sheriff to replace them all.

"Your bad radios are my good business," Maury says. "But look, when I put on the badge . . ." Maury is going to work here when the show is over. A sort of internship.

Mike Shapen is in the library, Xeroxing pages from reference books that he needs for his M.A. dissertation in musicology. Sue Riding, not due at her supermarket until late afternoon, is with Mike and helping; she takes a mathematician's interest in the problems of music theory.

Sue's husband, Davey, was drafted right out of bed, quite early this morning, by Sato Murasaki, who, finding himself with a free morning, got together a foursome for tennis. They are on the courts right now: Davey, who is a well-trained tennis player, and Dick Auerbach, who is strong and competitive, so that he overhits a lot; against Sato and his partner, Dr. J. T. Mason.

The doctor was got out of bed for this, too. The doctor, a bit red-eyed, is about to serve. Sato, because of the speed with which Dick hits the ball, has elected to play back rather than at the net when his partner is serving. Davey Riding has enough control, probably, to defeat this strategy with drop shots, but is too polite; Davey wins his own serves—Sato and Johnny Ten take all the other games.

Dick is tying his shoe.

"Sato," Dr. Mason asks, as they wait a moment. "Have you ever worked with Janet Margesson?"

"With Janet? Well. Nobody works with her. You stand there humbly and admire her, I believe, and hope she won't murder you. A marvelous woman, Doctor, who always has her own way, and sometimes deserves to."

Johnny Ten Mason double-faults viciously.

The blocking, meanwhile, goes off without pain or glory, but with at least one pleasant surprise for Hoffman, who hadn't heard Henry Fennellon sing before. What Henry has is nothing like Beth's throbbing talent, nor yet like Marcel's extraordinary power and polish; Henry's quality is innate, a matter of vocal size. The three together, in their first hotel scene, will need to be challenged, not cushioned.

"Karen," he mutters to the accompanist. "Forget what I said about the tempo, you know? I was wrong."

And wrong again, Hoffman, just a little, in offering Skeats the opportunity to maul Sidney. Although it's exactly what the Australian must represent when performance time comes, he's far too frankly in the spirit of it for rehearsal purposes.

"Oh, Papa Bear, don't." Sidney. "I'll have to bring bodyguards to rehearsal." It's enough of a threat so that the red of anger or embarrassment shows at the roots of Hughmore's beard.

About forty-five minutes later he retaliates.

This happens in Ralph Lekberg's office, where the hired hands—Sidney, Beth, Marcel, and Hoffman—have gone with Skeats, Ralph, and Short, after blocking. There are payroll forms to be filled out; a music-department secretary has been sent to get them. Sato, of course, is a hired hand, too, but his appointment is a summer professorship, and is handled differently.

"When I arrived here that first day," Marcel, "you were sitting here, talking about castration."

"Quite so." Skeats. "Noticed you didn't take it very well."

"No. I've been wanting to explain my rudeness to Dr. Lekberg. You see, my poor old crazy stepfather had his heart just set on raising a castrato. My stepbrothers and I really just narrowly escaped, one after the other."

"Was he a choirmaster?" Ralph.

"He rebuilt clarinets, too."

"Must have been remarkably devoted to baroque opera," Skeats suggests.

Short: "That's hard to believe."

"Once he got to do an oboe."

"In Louisiana?" Hoffman asks.

"All the little parish high schools have marching bands."

"You're in good company." Ralph. "The same thing almost happened to Joseph Haydn. Kapellmeister von Reuter from St. Stephen's in Vienna, where the boy was singing, wrote to Haydn's father recommending castration. And old wheelwright Haydn came hurrying over to protest, thinking, however, that it had already been done to his son. 'Sepperl,' he said. 'Are you in pain? Can you walk, Sepperl?'"

"Who's Sepperl?" Hoffman.

"The pet name Haydn's family used. He was seventeen before his voice changed, and von Reuter thought he could have a great career."

"How old were you, Marcel?" Hoffman asks, with the grin that makes it so difficult for anyone to take offense.

"Oh, much younger. It isn't really anything to talk about, well, in—"

"You mean with young ladies present?" Sidney. "Oh, Marcel, how lovely."

"But I don't understand about poor Haydn." Beth. "Had he done something bad?"

"Only if it's bad to sing gloriously." Skeats, in his deepest voice. "I'm sure Herr von Reuter, of whose splendid intentions I had not previously been aware, felt that to sopranize the lad might make him another bleeding Farinelli."

"What would that be?" Short.

"Some kind of Sinatra," Hoffman guesses. "Bing Crosby?"

"The castrati were quite the biggest stars of their days. Farinelli was bigger than Sinatra, Crosby, and Pinza put together."

"It might have been a favor to Haydn." Ralph Lekberg, in a general way. "He had a miserable sex life."

"Really, Marcel? You?" Beth puts a warm hand on his arm, and Marcel says:

"Oh, of course not. I mean, well. Just the intention."

"But how terrifying to be threatened with not growing up, or is that wrong? Perhaps it could be reassuring, like illness on a school day."

"I wasn't at all terrified." Marcel. "To tell you the exact truth I was twelve years old, full of morphine, and lying in a blissful tub of hot water. . . ."

"Yummy." Sidney.

"But anyway, it was prevented."

"Dreadful little bitch," Ralph says, no reference, it turns out, to present company. "Haydn's wife. If I'm not mistaken, it was Palutinianus started the whole thing."

"Please, Ralph," Short.

"No, it's so. He manufactured quite a large group of castrati, shortly after A.D. 200, all boys from nice middle-class Roman families, to sing at his daughter's wedding to the emperor, Caracalla."

"It's sweet what a bride's father will do," Hoffman, "to give his girl a nice wedding."

"Of course, Palutinianus was an African. Africa's quite a center for the operation even today, we're told. Harem guards. Always be a need for them."

"And what was Caracalla?" Short means to tease.

"Oh, he was a Gaul." Ralph. "He got that name from a kind of native duffel coat that he always wore."

"Of course, the wedding caper was strictly a one-shotter," Hughmore Skeats observes. "Not nearly as consequential as what old Eudoxia laid on. She was an empress when, Ralph?"

"Around A.D. 400."

"Quite. Well, then, pagan choirs were extremely popular in Byzantium at the time, and Eudoxia was a most pious Christian who simply wanted to compete. She could see that her church group, of virgins and little boys, weren't much competish for the blooming pagans, who had grown-up women singing at their bashes, but St. Paul had made it clear that grown-up women were to keep their mouths shut in Christian churches."

"I don't suppose they sounded like genuine angels." Hoffman.

"Once she got her kid choir operated on and trained and started getting the music crowd away from the pagan outfits, Eudoxia wouldn't book anything but castrati. You understand, if you castrate a young male, you keep his larynx boy-sized, but the chest and diaphragm go on growing. Castrati could sing soprano with more power and flexibility than any woman born or yet to be."

"How high, Papa Bear?" Sidney is a secret mezzo.

Skeats. "Far higher than you, and much more easily."

Ralph nods. "I'm quite certain the greatest soprano who ever lived was Carlo Broschi, called Farinelli, of whom we were speaking. 1705 to 1782. His only rival was a man called Gaetano Majorano, called Caffarelli."

"They must have been ravishing in duets." Sidney.

"They made contraltos out of little boys, too." Beth.

"Absobloodyloutely." Skeats. "And fine ones, too. Off with the ballocks and on with the dance."

"That's why contraltos get to sing Orfeo."

"Who was the greatest contralto?" Short.

"Young fellow, oh, a smashing lad, we may be sure, called Frank."

"Francisco Bernardi." Ralph. "He was billed as Senesino."

"What were they, like bullfighters and ballplayers?" Hoffman. "With the nicknames?"

"My stepfather really preferred Caffarelli to Farinelli." Marcel. "You know how people will become absolute fans of some historical figure? Well, Caffarelli was apparently terribly lazy and bitchy and conceited, and Farinelli was a very nice, responsible man. Daddy Jean liked the evil temperament."

Ralph says, apparently in reproof of Marcel's Daddy Jean: "Farinelli was such a decent man. He was singing in England, you know, and didn't really want to leave when the queen of Spain sent for him."

"At least we've left Eudoxia," Short says to Hoffman.

"There are some quite readable books if you're curious, Snazzer," Ralph says. His tone is only slightly reproving, and he pauses considerably to let serious students take notes as he specifies: "Tompkins's *The Eunuch and the Virgin,* for one, and then the standard work, Heriot's *The Castrati in Opera.* Both extremely well done."

"What the hell happened to my queen of Spain?" Short.

"It was the king," Marcel clarifies. "He was terribly sad."

"He was a bloody psychiatric case of melancholia." H. Skeats. "What the queen did was to send for Farinelli from England, and when the blighter arrived, put him in a particular room, right? Then it was arranged that old Philip Five wander by and hear this flapping incredible soprano music, as if by accident. Philip was so enchanted he kept Farinelli there ten years. Let him produce his own operas."

"And he sang the girls' parts?" Sidney demands.

"Why, of course."

Ralph. "The men's parts were very often higher than the women's. They did use some women."

"But bleeding old nutless Farinelli had to sing for the sad king every night. Exactly the same four songs."

"Farinelli acquired great political power." Ralph. "Which he used very wisely—"

"*E pur questo dolce amplesso . . . .*" The song seems to tear itself out of Marcel, in a somewhat glorious falsetto. He looks surprised at himself, and then, seeing smiles, sings on strong. When he finishes, there is applause. He smiles, slightly embarrassed. "That was one of Farinelli's four. I had to learn them all. The next 'Palido el Sole,' from Haase's opera about Artaxerses—"

"Do it." Beth. "Please."

Most performers do not have to be begged, and it's Marcel's morning.

The falsetto flows again, and the music-department secretary, coming in to report a further delay in the papers, stands in disbelief.

"I thought it was a woman," she says.

"Marcel, darling, you're historic." Sidney matching his last phrase. "Even without the operation."

"No." Ralph. "Bring the papers as soon as you can, Connie." She goes. "No, they tried it early in the sixteenth century, when women singers were once again banned in church. There was great emphasis on training falsetti. But that all ended when the castrato Hieronymous Rossinus joined the papal choir in 1562. Compared to Rossinus, the falsetti squeaked."

"Return of the son of the Eunuch." Short.

Hoffman to Skeats: "How come you're letting Ralph do all the dates and facts and funny names?"

"Ah, I shan't try to compete with the musical aspect, but there's some beauteous political stuff. For example, a monorch, one vowel removed from a ruler, is one testicle short—as alleged, you recall, about Hitler in song and story. Then there is the spado, which is a chap with the whole works removed, the usual for harem guards. King Solomon started that, noting that a horse that had merely been gelded would still sniff a mare."

"But how do they go to the bathroom?" Sidney, in a small voice.

"On two feet, if they're able to walk," says Skeats, and guffaws. Then he adds: "But once there, my dear, the spado is still able to avoid the undignification of the female squat. How? Style. Style is what results from making elegance out of necessity, right? Those black gentlemen, who often attained great wealth and power in the happy Moslem past, and may again today as the oil flows boomicky up through the sands, carried a quill stuck rakishly in the turban. And with it they could use urinals of whatever sort, simply by removing the silver nail that plugged the urethra, and inserting the quill for direction and distance."

"But they dripped." Ralph, keeping things balanced. "In dynastic China, the spadones had terrifying power, but there were jokes about their smell."

"How romantic."

"An elegant castrato, on the other hand, assuming he was cut, not simply pinched, would often take his, ah, fruits to Venice, where the glass blowers would, for a sum, encase them at the end of the branch of a cunning glass souvenir cherry tree."

"Men do have their little problems, don't they?" Sidney says, and it seems to be the cue for which Skeats has been maneuvering, for he turns on her now with the mixture of venom and relish with which a sentimental rattlesnake might prepare to strike a particularly plump mouse.

"Among the holiferous Skoptsy, my dear, you too could find the true way. I'm not sure what it would do for your voice, but for your soul's sake you could get to be a Skopet, just like Georgi Malenkov."

"I heard that about Malenkov." Hoffman. "But I never believed it, you know?"

Beth looks puzzled, and Short says: "He was the Russian dictator after Stalin."

"Oh, that strange-looking man?"

"Exactly." Skeats. "Look at him. Hear his voice. He must have been a Skopet. We know the sect still flourished, and made common cause at the time of the Russian Revolution, when Malenkov was a young man."

"That's something I don't know about at all." Ralph. "What are Skopets?"

The opportunity to instruct Ralph diverts Skeats for a moment. "I'm surprised at you, Ralph. I think this is all in the Tompkins book you mentioned. Skopets belong to a very wealthy, persistent Russian secret religious order that believes in castration. It starts from the New Testament somewhere: 'There be eunuchs which have made themselves eunuchs for the kingdom of heaven's sake. He that is able to receive it, let him receive it.' And that is reported as being Christ's own word on the subject. Now, elsewhere in the holy blooming book, you will find—in Revelations—that it will require the existence of 144,000 male virgins to bring on the last judgment, after which we all go under the celestial knife, and paradise begins. So the Skopets are trying to save us all, and I believe Malenkov might easily have been one—and then, in the grand Byzantine tradition, become Stalin's Great White Eunuch and taken over, as they often did when the old tyrant died."

"He didn't last long," Short observes. "Khrushchev sent him off to manage a power station or something, didn't he?"

"Anyway." Sidney. "All those self-sacrificing virgins have to be male, the darlings."

"But Skoptsy women have trashy little redeemable souls, too." Skeats's teeth flash, his voice bludgeons. "On your celebrated tour of Russia, if you make the right connections, they might just take you out to the campfire some night, my dear. Where they'd begin by slicing off your nipples, sweetheart. And then move the sanctiferous razor down to just below the navel, and slice! Off comes your pretty bush, and the nice mound under it, and then your clitty, and your big outside labeys, and then your dear little inside labeys—"

"Hey, shut up, Hugh." Hoffman, and Ralph at the same time:

"For God's sake, Skeats."

For Sidney has gone a little pale, and Beth looks sick. It's the open sadism as much as the words themselves. "Please don't be dreadful," Sidney says, and then Hoffman, in his kindest, most cajoling voice:

"Hey, I thought of something funny. No, listen, this is funny, you know, not dreadful. I mean, I'm in South Dakota and a guy drives me past this big field of seed corn and it's full of pretty girls. So I say, 'What are they doing?' You know? And the guy says, 'Detasseling the male plants.' 'So what's that for?' I say. 'It emasculates them,' the farmer says. 'So they won't breed the female plants.' But what gets me is who's doing the job—all these sorority girls, all the sweethearts of Sigma Chi, it's their traditional summer work, how they get their fall tans and earn the dough for the football-weekend wardrobe, so they can marry the sons of the farmers that grow the seed corn, huh? Going through, tearing the nuts off male corn plants."

Sidney still looks stricken. Beth does manage a smile. Locked into the subject matter, for to change it now would be to leave the breach that Skeats created open for the rest of their work together, the males can only hope to try to restore some sense of general amusement. Ralph mentions that the castrati were so popular in baroque opera that producers who tried introducing actual girls saw their charges howled offstage. Short recalls that it was the ugliest black harem eunuchs who brought the highest prices, and that they were given names like Rosebud and Hyacinth.

But it's Marcel who finally retrieves the situation, speaking in his soft, effeminate voice with some traces of Louisiana still, in the diction and the cadences, resigned to performing a curious kindness. Though Sidney has been his self-appointed tormentor, and the tale he tells can do nothing so much as expose him to more particular torment, it is for Sidney's comfort that he tells it.

"Well," he says. "My poor old crazy stepdaddy did believe the castrato voice must have been the very finest instrument ever created. He couldn't quite have heard one. He was born in France, toward the end of the last century, just a few years after the last castrato in the Vatican choir died. He had two natural sons, as well as me, and he had us all memorize what one Italian critic wrote about that old survivor in the Vatican.

"I mean, imagine being an old man and having somebody write like this about you:

"Imagine a voice that combines the sweetness of the flute and the animated suavity of the human larynx—a voice that leaps and leaps, lightly and spontaneously like a lark that flies through the air and is intoxicated with its own flight . . . and when it seems the voice has reached the loftiest peaks of altitude, it starts off again, leaping and leaping, still with equal lightness and equal spontaneity, without the slightest sign of tiring or the faintest indication of artifice or effort—not the least mark of passage from one register of the voice to the other, no inequality of timbre between one note and another."

"I'd like one of those." Ralph.

"Are there bathtubs in the Music Building?" Sidney is recovering.

"Daddy Jean was going to be the man to make one. He'd talk about the hundred and fifty years of great music written for that kind of voice, and nobody around to try to sing it but a few straining countertenors. He wasn't just going to make a castrato, he was going to train one and conquer a musical world that had rejected him somehow, I'm not sure just how. But I know he dreamed of living back in France again, and us being triumphant.

"What he did for a living was repair instruments, especially clarinets. He always had a couple of dozen around the house in different stages of repair, and when he found one he liked, he was just absolutely unscrupulous about switching it for another one of the same model.

"You see, a lot of the castrati music has the vocal part written doubled with a solo instrument, so the two will start in unison and the singer improvise and embroider anywhere he likes while the instrument keeps the melody going. Daddy Jean felt like he deserved to have the best clarinet for me and my youngest stepbrother, Bucky, to sing with, while he played it.

"Remember, we were talking about one called Caffarelli? He was the kind of bitchy, conceited one that got so famous. Well, Daddy Jean had us on the same schedule Caffarelli was raised on. My stepdaddy lived in total fear of every kind of authority, 'cause he was an illegal immigrant, but training us was so very important to him that he bravely told the school board he was schooling us at home, and he did. In the morning we sang for an hour, difficult passages while we were still fresh. Then we did school work and

French grammar. Then we had to get in front of a mirror and do singing exercises in Italian to learn not to make ugly faces."

"I must try it." Sidney.

"In the afternoon he taught us theory for half an hour, and then came the part Bucky hated and I just loved, which was improvisation. I was almost two years younger, and Bucky had real good understanding, but I surely could improvise. I was half-scared of Daddy Jean, but just dying to please him, and that improvising was the way to do it."

"You mean, like jazz musicians?" Hoffman.

"One time." Marcel. "It was just before Farinelli went to England and Spain—he was the nice one, but this time he was a little bit mean. He had this famous contest with a trumpet player up on stage. They were working up and up, higher and higher, till finally they were both holding onto the same note, one singing it, one playing it. And Farinelli, he let his volume off just a little bit? So of course the trumpeter thought he'd won, and quit playing, ready to take his bow, and right on the same breath Farinelli brought his volume back up again, and rose up higher and higher in flourishes for another whole minute."

"Soap, soap." Sidney. "And a squishy washcloth."

"Sidney, honey, you've never seen a bathtub like the one we had." Marcel. "It was a very poor little farm Daddy Jean ended up on with us, though he said he'd been rich when he left France. He'd been a choirmaster, and he had to leave on account of some woman there. 'Fact, I believe he was a bigamist 'fore he ever got married to my poor mother, but anyway, this tub: It was a galvanized metal, kind of oval thing, about five feet long, and my mother had to heat the water in a big black iron kettle on the wood stove. Then we'd carry that to the tub together, and then I'd carry pails of cold water to fill up with, and after, I'd have to dip it out. Daddy Jean took a bath every day, and I sure carried an ocean of water for that man.

"Well, we'd go back to our school work after improvisation, and Daddy Jean'd go down to the post office. He went there every day in the buggy, about two miles, and he'd do his correspondence standing up, with a post-office pen. He wrote to people in France a whole lot, but he never got many letters back.

"And it was there he got helped out by a man we called Fuzz Peach. That was the only man outside of France and Canada who knew where Daddy Jean LaViolet was hiding. Y'understand, my mother's very sweet, but she's not real bright. I just love her, I want you to know that, but she doesn't have good understanding. I think by the time he married her, Daddy Jean was just plain scared of women, but nobody could be scared of my mother, and she raised the garden and the chickens and a pig, and fed us, and a neighbor farmed the few little acres she had on shares, and gave us all the cash ever came in the house except for instrument repairing.

"It didn't take much cash. A little flour and salt, and postage stamps to France, and kerosene for the lamps, was all. Sometime I'd help her chore, but Daddy Jean had her believing that studying music was all I ought to do—that and help fix his bath—and she did love to hear the music. So mostly what I'd do, when Daddy Jean was at the post office, I'd turn on the radio and prop open the window, and play the clarinet to her while she worked around in the yard, along with whatever music was coming on the air—country blues, and those nasal songs they sing.

"Bucky wouldn't generally stay and practice; he'd sneak off and play baseball, if he could find some kids to do it with, or go fishing if he couldn't. Now Bucky, his real name was Carlo, after Farinelli; and his big brother was Guy, after Caffarelli. That was the first son, and it was like you might name your first son Ty Cobb and your second one Babe Ruth, 'cause you liked Cobb's meanness. I told you about Farinelli and the trumpet player, but Caffarelli, he did the same kind of thing to woman singers. Once he was singing with a prima donna named Tara, and he started doing his improvising syncopated so she'd lose the beat. So when it came time for her cue, and she didn't start, Caffarelli just flung up his hand, right on stage, and started like he was conducting her and singing little snatches, prompting—Daddy Jean did love to tell that story. And sometimes he'd cry over telling about a young castrato, I forget his name, who was too successful in some girl's part so he got knifed to death by hired assassins, 'cause some cardinal's soprano mistress was so jealous."

"I'm glad somebody finally forgot a name around here." Short.

"Oh, cardinal." Sidney. "The diamonds are lovely. There's just one more thing I need to make me happy."

"I haven't quite got it about your stepfather's two boys." Hoffman.

"Well, I think when he first got to New Orleans, he met this Fuzz Peach in the music business. And Fuzz Peach said all he'd have to do was get married, and he'd be a citizen. So he married right away, some woman Peach found, and then after two or three years he tried applying, as a citizen's husband. But then he got scared they'd find out about his wife in France, and then that Louisiana wife died, and he had these two little boys. I used to imagine that maybe she didn't die natural, but that I don't really know. Anyway, later on he found my mother shucking oysters, or Fuzz Peach found her maybe. And we all moved back to St. Edouard parish, where she owned the little farm and I took my name from. Guy and Bucky and me. That's where Daddy Jean was going to raise up a castrato, if he could just keep hiding from the immigration people, and then we'd go on back to France and just astonish the whole world.

"We didn't see much of anybody from outside the parish except this character Fuzz Peach, as he called himself, who'd come up from New Orleans every now and then. Uncle Fuzz was a roly-poly, little bald promoter, and what he had was a hall in New Orleans and a band of quite old black men, who he said had been great jazz stars in their younger days. Maybe some had. Some of the rest I know hadn't ever been anything but amateurs, but all they had to be for his imitation of Preservation Hall was old and black and maybe a little bit crazy-acting. They could play just enough to fool the tourists, and he called them the Rampart Street Original Whoopee Band. Well, the year Bucky was thirteen, Uncle Fuzz Peach looked around and saw integration was the big new thing, and he thought maybe he better feature some of that. He'd put him a little white angel in, playing clarinet in front of his old black saints, and that would bring the tourists marching in. He figured little old Bucky looked the part.

"When he came driving out to the parish and stopped in to suggest it, I thought Daddy Jean would burst from holding in his anger—of course, Uncle Fuzz didn't know about the secret castrato plan, he just knew Bucky and I had a whole lot of music training. Daddy Jean made excuses the best he could, and Uncle Fuzz left a few roly-poly threats and went away, giving us time to think it over. Luckily enough, Bucky's voice started changing practically that night, almost like his hormones got the message. First Daddy Jean was in despair. Then he calmed down, and when Fuzz Peach came on back to St. Edouard to claim his boy, we had Bucky all ready to go, clarinet packed, hair grown long, and even a new dark suit that Fuzz Peach sent the money for.

"I knew Bucky didn't want to leave, but he wasn't much of a talker; all he said was he didn't like Fuzz Peach 'cause the old boy smelled like chewing gum. But he showed what he could do, reading off the clarinet parts from some of those little combo-orch Dixieland arrangements Uncle Fuzz brought up, and he sounded all right.

" 'Now cut loose,' I remember Uncle Fuzz saying, but Bucky just smiled then, and laid down his horn, and Daddy Jean said,

" 'Carlo can memorize that music. That's easy for him.'

"Uncle Fuzz Peach said that wasn't exactly the idea, but he was in a hurry, and it was going to be wonderful, he'd be sending money up from Bucky's pay, and away they went in a big shiny car with a big shiny driver.

"Now Daddy Jean LaViolet was frantic. I don't think my own voice was anywhere close to changing, but that little possibility was what was causing the panic, and I admit he had me worrying about it, too. I mean, he'd been telling me ever since I was big enough to hear talk, about the money we were going to make, and the fame and adulation, and I sure didn't want my voice to change before he'd got me fixed. I didn't understand just what the fixing was, but it seemed like I was real lucky he could do it for me, 'cause otherwise this voice changing was going to happen, and that would displease him, even if it wasn't my fault, and maybe break my mother's heart.

"The only argument in the household, now that there was open talk about when and how and everything, came from my biggest stepbrother, Guy. He was fifteen, and he hated his father, my mother and me, too, I think; he'd been halfway close to Bucky, and when Bucky went to New Orleans, Guy moved out of the house and commenced sleeping in the woods. But then he'd come in for meals, and he and Daddy Jean would start having these violent arguments about me, and in just a couple of days of that, I woke up one morning and heard from my mother that Guy was gone. He'd stole a good Sohner clarinet, which he couldn't play very well, and gone off to New Orleans to look for Bucky.

"I was most pleased to have things quiet down, but Daddy Jean was most alarmed. He must have figured the word would get out now, and he hadn't any more time to wait. He had my mother get him all spiffed up for the big evening—washed him and powdered him and curled his hair into long grey ringlets, so he looked like a Molière actor.

"He called what he was fixing to do *la chirurgie,* and that didn't sound bad at all, and he explained there wasn't anything to it but a little pinch. He borrowed the pincher from the veterinarian who took care of our cow and pigs, and he had a crony who was a Czech pharmacist and played the flute, and just about as crazy he was, come over and inject the morphine.

"He and the pharmacist were sitting in the kitchen, watching my mother boil up this thing like a big pair of pliers, only with the jaws running crosswise, kind of slightly curved and blunt, and I was lying in that hot tub one room over, in the washroom. I mean, that was a real privilege right there, a whole tub full of hot water just for me—not one of the other boys had used it first, they weren't even there.

"The door was open so they could keep an eye on me, and I could hear them talking in the kitchen, and after a while the pharmacist who was timing the boiling, said okay, that was good, and he better go now.

"Daddy Jean got up and bowed him out, and they talked a little French there at the door, and the man left.

"I felt just wonderful with the morphine. I mean, I felt like the center of the world anyway, and I remember very clearly now how it started taking effect by making my toes feel good, and then my ankles, and came creeping up my body, just a slow, warm wave of pleasure. I couldn't been more ready to start getting rich, I don't suppose, so my mother'd have her a black woman to slop the pigs and I'd be much more famous than Guy or Bucky, just from a little magic pinch, and a car drove up outside.

"It was Uncle Fuzz Peach, hustling Bucky back. I heard him storm into the kitchen, I don't think he knocked, and I could hear Bucky squealing that it wasn't his fault. They'd rehearsed that morning, after a couple of bad performances, trying to get going, Guy even showed up and tried out, too. And he'd have brought both the little frauds back, Fuzz Peach yelled, except Guy ran away.

" 'This boy can't play a damn note that isn't written down,' he yelled. 'I can't have him up there on the stand reading, when those boogies don't know one note from another, can I? I told you that, LaViolet, don't you listen good?'

" 'He plays well, he plays well. . . .'

" 'This ain't the one I heard playing with the radio. Now admit it.'

"I didn't know I'd been overheard playing with the radio, and admired for it, and it just made me smile all over.

"Daddy Jean tried to say that must have been Guy. I couldn't understand why he didn't want to give me credit, but I lay there in my hot tub forgiving him for favoring his natural sons, as it seemed to me, and then I realized my mother must have come back into the kitchen, 'cause Fuzz Peach's voice changed out of shouting to honey talk, and he said to her:

" 'Well, howdy, Mizzus LaViolet. Come right on in now, you ain't interrupting a thing. Now, you tell me, ma'am, when we was sittin' on the porch that time, waiting for your good husband to come back from the post office, you recall? And there was a boy inside playing the clarinet real pretty with the radio? Which boy was that?'

"I don't know whether my mother really recalled anything particular, but she said, 'Marcel plays pretty music, Marcel.'

"I started smiling again at that, proud as could be.

" 'Where is Marcel?'

" 'My good boy takes his bath,' Mama said.

"Into the washroom came Fuzz Peach, with his little ring of hair like a tonsured monk. I'm sure he hadn't any idea what the apparatus boiling on the stove was for, but he surely did recognize the hypodermic in the wash-basin.

" 'Hey, LaViolet,' he yelled in a terrible voice. 'You got this little fella under the influence of drugs?'

"Daddy Jean ran out of the house at that, and hid in the corncrib. Uncle Fuzz Peach and my mother got me out of the tub and dried me off, and kind of snatched off Bucky's new suit and put it on me, rolling up the pant legs, and fifteen minutes later I was on my way to New Orleans in the big shiny car.

"The only advice I got from my elders on going out into the world came from Bucky: 'Keep away from the tuba player.'

"Bucky didn't know about Uncle Fuzz Peach.

"I played in public the same night, and it might have been the first time New Orleans tourists ever heard eighteenth-century improvisation on the clarinet with a Dixie background, but it kind of worked out.

"I even got some reputation, after a while, as some kind of a jazz prodigy. That part was really pretty much fun.

"It went all right for a few months. Then Fuzz Peach got to fussing with the tuba player, and he turned him back to the parole board. He was kind of jealous about me, and he took me off the stand and got him a new attraction—a girl blues shouter. She was all right, as a matter of fact, but then it was me got jealous of her, I mean, this is later on, so then he sent me off to military school, and on to the conservatory. . . ."

"What about your stepfather?" Hoffman. "He still down there on the loose, looking for little boys to cut?"

"He found one." Marcel. "A little colored boy. To be honest, I think Daddy Jean bought him for cash when he was seven or eight. Bucky was back home then, and the way he told it, the boy's daddy got the money and the boy's mama got to join in dreaming the big dream. When he got ten, that little boy did have a wonderful soprano voice, I heard him once in colored church. But afterward, I tried to tell Daddy Jean not to do it to him,

I said the idea was crazy, and Daddy Jean promised me he wouldn't ever try the *chirurgie* again.

"Then a year or two later I ran off to Los Angeles, and finished training out there, and got out of touch, except for going back to get my mother when I started earning a little money, and put her in a comfortable home out near me."

"Who did you run off with, darling?" Sidney. "The tuba player, after all?"

"I can't tell you, Sidney," Marcel's tone is still perfectly kind. "But you've seen his movies. Anyway, about three years later Bucky came to Los Angeles and my friend helped him get a job in a studio orchestra, where he's doing extremely well. He told me the rest of it. Daddy Jean went right ahead with the operation on the little black boy, of course, and the boy's mama was real pleased. They were starting to talk about leaving soon for Europe, and the mother knew her boy was going to be a star, and he wouldn't be able to mess with bad women like his runaway daddy did. Bucky said the black mother was just about as daft as Daddy Jean himself, and as Jules got bigger and his voice stayed high, they put out that he'd had some kind of farm-equipment accident.

"But of course there were rumors around the parish, and when the runaway daddy came running back after seven years gone, he heard 'em. And he went straight over to the farmhouse and broke Daddy Jean's poor old neck. Just like that. Picked him up by the feet and broke it over a sawhorse. That's when Bucky took off, and I guess the place is deserted now, but you know what? A southern white jury let that black father off? They said a man had a right to revenge his son on a pervert. That was the way they understood it. So then the father took off again, and the mother moved onto our farm with her little castrato, Jules."

"But you said it was deserted." Hoffman. "That spoils my picture. I was seeing them down in Louisiana. Sitting and rocking on the cabin porch. The old mammy crooning spirituals to this big, black twenty-year-old, and he's crooning right with her an octave higher."

"Oh, no." Marcel. "No. Daddy Jean was right. Jules is already rich, and he'll soon be world famous."

"Huh?"

"A singer?" Sidney sounds shocked.

"You'll hear him." Marcel. "He's nineteen now, not yet twenty, and singing rock, and listen to me, he can do things with that voice you can't get with a Moog. High and strong and, well, he turned out very smart. He made enough on just two records to buy the record company, and listen here, he's abroad right now. Just like Daddy Jean predicted. He's gone big in London, and he's in Rome, taking more training. He's going to make Italian movies, and all the jet-set people just love him. He goes everywhere, he goes on yachts, he's getting ready to come back here for a big television special."

"Wow." Sidney.

"There's just one part I don't understand. It's Bucky keeps me up with news of Jules, and Bucky insists the boy is just madly attractive to women. He gets them all, black, white, and heliotrope, rich and poor, any girl he wants—but, I mean, Bucky says he does want them."

"Blooming hell you say?"

Short: "Maybe for playing with like teddy bears."

"But see here." Ralph. "The Italian castrati in the great period had all the women they could handle."

"Blooming hell."

"What'd they do with them?" Short.

"Why, the whole thing," Ralph says. "I'm surprised at you people. Especially if they'd only been pinched, they could take advantage of precisely the same misconception you all seem to have. As long as they believed in their own capacity, you see, they could have erections perfectly well, and orgasms—the only difference was the fluid was sterile."

"Are you sure?" Marcel asks. If it were anyone but Ralph, he'd be scoffed at.

"Oh, yes. Your man Caffarelli, for example, was a great Don Juan. He fought duels with jealous husbands—actually, he was a first-rate swordsman."

"Blooming hell."

"I can see those tombstones." Hoffman. " 'Killed in a duel with a soprano.' "

"Ah, Jules, Jules." Hughmore Skeats again. "Imagine him in Rome, about to return to us—the true man of the future. In a teeming world about to hump itself to death, a toast to the high-voiced hedonist, the ecological Casanova."

Beth knows where sympathy should go. "Oh, Marcel," she says.

"Tough, kid," Hoffman agrees. "Damn shame it didn't work out."

12: Her Sighed of the Story

How many jobs does Maury have, anyway? There's the television and radio repair. There's his music-department assistantship, which has teaching duties during regular semesters. He's got a real estate license, and is sometimes called in by a local firm, run by a couple of former university athletic figures, to show houses—they say he's potentially the best salesman around if he'd work at it, but he doesn't seem to care about money much. With the wife he has, maybe he doesn't need to.

What Maury does is help out. He'll fill in on drums for the best of the rock groups hereabouts and play with a little jazz combo when they need him. Accompanied by Karen on piano or guitar, he will sing certain evenings at the Gump, and occasionally at political rallies. He's a playground director weekends, does radio commentary on high school basketball; one Saturday morning Mike and Mona Shapen found him in the children's room at the public library, telling stories to very little kids. For most of these functions, it seems likely Maury volunteers.

He's about as well known and highly thought of as a young man can be in this electoral district, and will be going to the Democratic Convention in Miami later this summer as a young, black delegate committed to Shirley Chisholm on the first ballot, likely to switch to George McGovern thereafter. It's no surprise at all to find Maury wearing a bartender's apron at the Gump as the cast comes in from rehearsal, taking care of things for Bitsy, who has a dentist's appointment. Maury's present customers are Dick Auerbach and Davey Riding, who, like Maury, were free right after the first-scene run-through.

Now Sidney enters, sees Maury behind the bar, stops, makes a tent of her hands in front of her face, and does a geisha dip.

Maury acknowledges with bar towel, streaming it once, like a banner.

After Sidney come Hoffman and Skeats, the one chewing on a dead cigar, the other expostulating: "You must understand, to do a high passage I must have my bloody feet firmly under me. Marcel can tell you."

Following and appealed to, Marcel stops in the doorway, fills his lungs, demonstrates foot planting, and sings from Scene Two: "Stick to the high ground. Guide on the stars. . . ."

It's a nice, virile, open-spaces fragment of melody, and Maury, with a martial wave of the bar towel: "Major Nelson Eddy, isn't it? Will you have a beer today, Major?"

"If that makes me Jeanette MacDonald," Sidney, "I quit."

"I don't believe it." Hoffman. "Those shows were made twenty years before either of you was born. I was a little boy."

"Old movies at the union." Sidney. "We had *Naughty Marietta* and *Rosemarie,* and next Thursday's *The Chocolate Soldier.* Will you take me, Mr. Hoffman? I'll hold hands."

"I don't think I could stand the giggles." Hoffman. "I loved those movies, you know? I mean, I wouldn't want to go and start giggling myself."

"I promise to be nostalgic." They sit, others enter, beer is poured.

"Thursday nights I do the launderette."

"I'll come fold." Her chin grazes his nubbly cheek.

"Sidney, let the man alone." Dick Auerbach.

"Sidney is sensitive today," Maury observes, bringing additional glasses, for the beer comes in pitchers. "What is it, Miss MacDonald?"

"This show. It's so chauvinistic it's quaint."

"Really?" Short.

"I'm sorry, Professor, but really." Tosses back her head and sings, sweetly satirical, from Scene One: " 'Love is the great adventure of a woman's life.' Oh boy."

"Hey, Sidney." Hoffman. "You know what you got?"

"What have I got?"

"My glass of beer, but that isn't what I was going to say. You got a way into your part. You hide some feminist murder under Sally Anne's sugar, and she's not joining up with either guy, is she? It's a three-way duel—she'll let Pill kill off Al for her, and take care of Pill later."

"Beth and I are going to take care of all the gentlemen." Sidney shifts ground. "When we have our lovely catfight, won't we Beth?"

"Oh, Sidney."

"We are going to steal the opera, right there. The audience will get up and leave after it, completely satisfied. I'm sorry, Marcel. Sorry, Papa Bear."

"I shall have to hold my hand over your mouth."

"I'll sing a hole right through it."

"Sidney." Maury. "Let's get a basketball and go up to the gym."

"One on one." She pops up, approaches with a swagger, and stops in front of him. Her chin isn't much higher than the third button of his shirt. "I've studied your game, Jock. I'll put some moves on you you never imagined."

Maury opens his big hand over her shiny head, as if he were going to palm it, and says gently: "You got a reverse lay-up? I'm an all-day sucker for that shot."

"I didn't know you played girls' basketball." Short.

"She would have been a star." Dick. "She started for our school team freshman year."

"It's a big thing out here." Short to Hoffman. "A kind of mania. They get real crowds at the girls' games, and the state tournament's on television."

"They play six on a side." Dick. "Three forwards, three guards, each group playing half the court. Two dribbles, and then you have to pass or shoot. We had an all-state forward who did the shooting the year Cindy, Sidney, played. But Sidney took the free throws, and just about always made them."

"How come you quit?" Hoffman.

"Her dad." Dick.

"He didn't like sports." Sidney.

"Tell me about him."

"He runs the radio station at home. Poor Daddy, generally works evenings at the station, but the year I played he came to see me in the district finals."

"Proud of you?"

"No. I begged him."

"Sidney's father will do anything for her." Dick.

"He came to see me in this game, only he got there late and had to sit with the other team's fans. We were winning, when he sat down next to this big farmer that had a daughter playing guard for the other side, just when I stole the ball from her. So the first thing Daddy heard was the farmer yelling, 'Kill the son of a bitch, Becky.' Daddy hated that."

"Ugly fans at the girls' game." Maury.

"Your father wanted you to be feminine?" Hoffman.

"Let's not talk about me, let's talk about you."

"Her father bribed her to give up basketball." Dick.

"Did your mother want you to be masculine, Mr. Hoffman?"

"What'd he bribe you with? What kind of place is Dueyville, anyway?"

"Oh, it's just . . . I always used to want to be on the radio, and he had the station. But he's old now, he had a stroke. He can't come down for the opera."

"How about your mother?" Hoffman.

"Dueyville's just an ordinary little town, Mr. Hoffman. It isn't very interesting."

"What about this bribe? That sounds interesting."

"Two blocks of little stores, ten blocks of houses, and a lot of gas stations. Did you grow up in a small town, Mr. Hoffman?"

"Are you going to tell us about the bribe?" Hoffman.

"It really wasn't anything. He wrote a piece for me to read on the radio."

"Cindy wanted to broadcast the weather." Dick.

"Who was Cindy?" Sidney.

"I'm sorry." Dick.

"Yeah, who was Cindy?" Hoffman, enjoying himself.

"All right. I'll do the piece for you."

"The radio show?"

"It's about a turtle and a rabbit."

"Come on, Sidney." Dick. "Don't."

"Well, you may leave if you don't want to hear it."

"She did it at school too, for elocution."

"It was my standby," Sidney says. "I did it in the State Elocution Contest."

"You win?"

"The judges didn't like my story, did they, Dick?"

"I'd surely like to hear it." Marcel.

"Oh, poopsie. You could be the rabbit, couldn't you? Here." She takes Maury's bar towel off his arm, rolls it lengthwise, and sticks it under the headband Marcel wears to control his long wavy hair. Faintly like ears, the ends of the bar towel stick up now on either side of Marcel's head. "Can you hop? You're the hero of the story."

"I'll hop if you'll tell the story."

"No kidding." Dick. "It's not . . . . I mean. It's just a kind of a kid's story Sidney's daddy wrote. Heck, let's just have a beer."

"Dick's the turtle. He doesn't even need a costume." She pauses. "Of course, I shall have to have my feet under me for the high passages." Stands and recites, miming, indicating Marcel, Dick, sketching landscape features with her hands:

In a glass case, in the Tortoise Hall of Racing Fame, there is a claw cast in gold.

(She makes a claw.)

It was broken off the left front flipper of the immortal Warren in a cross-country race, by a yellowish, Allegheny snapping turtle who hipped Warren into a rock.

(She hips.)

Warren, awkwardly finishing the race on three flippers, kids laughing at him, and far behind the field, picked up the claw in his beak and brought it all the way to the finish line, eight yards away, to show to the judges.

But the judges had left by then. Only Warren's old, grey-shelled coach waited there to say:

"My boy, there is more honor in this defeat than in any victory." He feared Warren might never race again.

Spring went on, the flipper healed, but the claw did not grow back. Secretly Warren worked out, trying to train himself to run without the traction of the missing claw.

(One hand is a claw, the other a pathetic, scrabbling fist.)

Day after day in lonely places he worked, loping, a little off balance, climbing, practicing starts, even sprinting sometimes, until one day he felt ready to show the coach what he could do.

("Cut it out, Sidney," Dick says, as she tries to raise his arm.)

Warren was on his way to the practice field when he saw a small hillock, covered with stones and difficult tufts of grass, and decided to test himself once more. He drew a starting line with his beak, crouched, counted, and hurled himself uphill. Imagining runners beside him, he put on pressure, he dug, he strove, he called on his reserve for a final, devastating kick, flew across what he'd decided would be the finish—and off into space. Just past its crest, the hillock dropped two sheer feet, straight down.

Instantly Warren flashed into his shell, alarmed by the danger to the newly healed, clawless flipper. Buttoned up securely, he felt himself complete the fall, right-side up and with a surprising clank on an unexpectedly hard surface.

Stranger still, the surface began to move away with him.

Bewildered, Warren relaxed his front hinge slightly and peered out without extruding his head. Wind whistled in through the crack and stung his eyes. Sonic boom seemed imminent. There was only one thing to do. Stout-hearted Warren thrust his head bravely out, looked over the edge of the speeding platform, and realized he had fallen onto a cast-off roller skate.

His tumble had set it rolling at mad speed down the incline.

Below, he could see that the incline would level out, the skate slow down and stop, and he began to enjoy the speed. Now he extended his legs and head, and pretended he was running. Stalks of grass whizzed by, and the great notion was born.

The skate stopped. Warren slid off and inspected it. It was a smallish skate. With the clamps removed, his body would hide all but the wheels. And, seeing that, Warren sounded the stirring Shout of Clovis, the classical runner who had, in olden times, beaten a hare: "Slow and steady wins the race!"

Off loped Warren to see the coach, who was working with some dashing turtles on the practice field.

("Mr. Hoffman has to be the coach." She moves behind him and megaphones her hands.)

"How's that flipper, boy?" the old one bellowed, seeing Warren.

"Feels fine, sir," Warren said.

"Well, work in easy. A few push-ups, some hinge work, and jog ten laps. . . ."

"Coach!" said Warren. The old one was dedicated to his sport, and a scholar of its history. "Coach, whatever became of hare and tortoise racing?"

"Well, heh. Well. Fell into disuse, you know? Only a medieval event, you know?"

"But Clovis—"

"Ah, Clovis the Bunny Beater. The Rabbit Router. Clovis Magnificus."

"He really beat a hare in a match race?"

"From scratch," said the coach. "But Warren"—his old eyes clouded—"you're tough enough to know the truth. The following year, well. There was a return match with the same hare. At least they claimed it was the same."

"Cheats." Warren was appalled. "They used a ringer?"

"How else explain it? According to rabbit records, the hare completed forty-seven round trips between start and finish, insultingly carrying the winner's tape in his teeth after the first, while Clovis was covering the first five yards. Of course, this was before the days of the saliva test."

"Of course."

"Then, perhaps realizing the poor taste of such a performance, or perhaps simply growing tired, the hare quickly collected the large bets he'd made on himself—"

"Gambling!"

"—impoverishing some of the finest turtle families of the day."

"Cheating, disrespect, bad taste."

"Clovis retired with the series even. But there were others who thirsted for glory, and for many years the hare and tortoise race was a splendid annual event. Banners, music, turtles in gleaming armor. And the loveliest maidens in Turtledom waiting to crown the winner with the Wreath of Clovis, should a turtle win."

"And the rabbits?"

"Always won," said the coach. "And . . . and ate the wreath. They took it as a comic festival, I'm afraid. Grew bored with it even so. Finally had to be paid to enter. Came one year with a, heh, baby rabbit. And the next, Warren, with a mouse. A mouse! With long ears pinned to its head."

"Cowards, track bums, bad sports. Coach, find me a hare to race."

"Heh?"

"A rabbit. I want to race a rabbit."

"My boy. Oh, my boy. Did you ever clock a rabbit?"

"I don't care," said Warren. "I know a way to win. Come on, coach. I'll show you."

"Practice dismissed," cried the coach, and off they went to the hillock.

When he had watched Warren's demonstration, the old one said earnestly: "For my phys.-ed. Ph.D., I annotated the ancient *Reglaments for the Grande Coursing of Tortues Agaynst Coneyfoots*. My boy, there is nothing in them that forbids the use of roller skates. No, no, not a word. Yes, yes, let's find a rabbit."

That evening they stationed themselves in a mowed hayfield, along one edge of which ran a clear, swiftly dropping stretch of thirty yards or so. The wily old coach, a master of opponent psychology, hid himself in a pile of waste hay where the slope ended. He had decided this slope was to be their track, his hiding place the finish line. Sticking up from the hay, the coach waved a tuft of dried dandelion to represent a rabbit's tail.

It was Warren's job to hide where the starting line would be, and, when a rabbit came along, to bark like a dog.

"Fiercely, very fiercely," said the coach. "The rabbit will be terrified! It will look about wildly! It will see our decoy tail, and dash for what it takes to be the safety of its kind. Thus we will watch it run the course, and make a preliminary time check. Fiercely now."

Warren waited, growling. A wren landed, and flew off when Warren practiced his bark. A mole shuffled by, started to dig, and Warren's fierce yips made him dig faster. Two snails crawled past in low, moist conversation, and Warren could hardly resist the impulse to leap out and run a couple of circles around them. Then there came a rapid thumping behind him, and Warren turned to see a rabbit hurtling toward him in unbelievably great hops.

(She hops. And Maury is seen to put a shot of whiskey down for Dick.)

Trained reflexes took over. "Grrrr," Warren snarled. "Hey there! Woof!"

The rabbit stopped short. It looked around. It snickered.

("Now, Marcel." The big tenor wags his head good-naturedly. Sidney sucks her cheeks between her teeth and makes a rabbit face.)

"What are you supposed to be?" the rabbit asked in a friendly way.

"Grayrf, snurf, burfer-rowwowrow," Warren howled.

"Very clever imitation," said the rabbit. "Is it a birdcall?"

"No, of course not."

"Let's see . . . Marlene Dietrich? I know, Humphrey Bogart."

"Look," Warren said. "Down there. In the hay pile. Look!"

And as the rabbit looked, he gave a great "SNURF!", for true competitors never give up.

"Well, I'll be a candy carrot," said the rabbit. "There's another turtle down there, waving a dandelion tuft. Practicing signals?"

"He's supposed to be a rabbit," Warren shouted, getting angry.

"Charades. What fun. I'll do a turtle." And the rabbit jumped straight up into the air, tucked his chin in tightly and drew up his feet. In that position he flopped rigid back onto the ground, twitched his nose, and darted his tongue in and out.

This is one brainless bunny, Warren thought, and said as casually as he could: "Ever do any racing?"

"Me? Can't beat my grandmother down a row of radishes," said the rabbit. "I'm no athlete. But say, can I ask you a question?"

"Sure," said Warren, always ready to talk running.

"When you pull your head in, where does it go?"

Warren groaned, and the coach arrived to whisper: "Won't he make the time trial?"

"He won't make anything but jokes," Warren whispered back.

"Secrets, secrets," said the rabbit. "What's it going to be, generals? War or peace?" He snapped to attention and saluted. "Ain't fair. You guys got the tanks."

"Listen . . ." The coach smiled.

"You even got submarines."

"Now listen." The coach was charming, simple, and sincere. "How about a friendly little race against my boy Warren here? Would you? Just to help us out?"

"A race? Oh, okay. Go ahead, Warren. Take a start."

"No start," Warren snapped.

The coach said: "From here to where I was, down the hill."

"You want me to run backward, or what?"

"That's enough of that," Warren yelled. "You going to race or aren't you?"

"You really mean it, don't you? Okay. Let's go."

"Not just like this," the coach said. "We have to get organized. Starters, timers, judges. Publicity. There'll be quite a crowd. And"—he looked at the rabbit's soft pink belly—"I presume you'll want to train."

"Hoo, boy," said the rabbit. "No lettuce juice. No parties. Cut down on the sugar beets. Chugchug, choochoo, clackety, clackety. Me training."

He worked his forepaws like pistons, and rotated his haunches.

("Cute," Dick mutters. "Say something, Dickie?" "Nothing.")

"Haven't you ever heard of hare and tortoise racing?" Warren asked.

"Ah," said the rabbit. "Ah, dawn. Ah, sunrise. Ah, lovely light of day.

The old fable, of course. A reenactment. Well, why not? That could be fun, lot of gags—"

"I knew you were a sportsman," the coach interrupted. "Two weeks from today. Right here. Three P.M."

"But rabbits nap—"

"Of course, of course," said the coach hurriedly, as if the fact had really slipped his mind. "Five P.M. Five P.M."

"And no reenactment," cried Warren recklessly. "You be ready to run."

That very evening a crew of mechanics began to work on the skate. They chewed off the harness, battered down the clips, polished and lubricated the wheels. By night they tested it over the course, sometimes with Warren riding, sometimes rolling free, once with three fat turtles piled one on top of another as a stress study. On the final evening, they fitted it with a tortoise-shell skirt, flared to conceal Warren's legs, though just at ground level his feet could be seen to move as if running.

"If there's any question . . ." the coach said, approving the way the top line of the skirt was cut and chiseled to fit the worn, irregular bottom circumference of Warren's carapace.

("Wow," says Maury. "How could she have lost with a line like that?")

"I know what to tell him," Warren said. "We'll win it fair and square."

"Slow and steady!"

"Name of the game!"

"Desire!"

"Hustle!"

"Fight!"

"Hundred and ten percent!"

"Or die!"

They were ready.

At three P.M., on the day of the race, all the runners in the district stood in ranks to see Warren lifted onto the skate. A thin layer of clay was spread across its platform, and into it Warren settled, waiting patiently for it to dry and hold him firmly. At three thirty the honor guard formed and began slowly to push him out to the track, chanting the antique "Threnody of Clovis Purissimus," with which all major events, of course, begin. A great holiday throng of turtles was on hand already, watching the prelims, to cheer when Warren arrived and was rolled to a shady place.

By four thirty Warren was growing nervous. He was glad he had not eaten, and grateful to see the old coach arrive and wave the honor guard away. Time for last-minute instructions: "Keep your legs moving. Don't let him psych you out with his cornball act. You're in great condition. You're prepared."

"Yes, coach."

"And Warren, I wasn't going to tell you but, heh, well. The track committee. We've been talking contract and, well, it seems we've got to win today or . . . or I may not be coach . . . much longer."

Stoutly Warren held back the tears.

"Push me into place," he choked, bringing back the honor guard. There were massive cheers as he appeared, almost immediately followed by hoots of laughter; the rabbit had arrived.

He wore a Lehigh University T-shirt, scarlet Bermudas, and a black and white checked cap. "Hi," he cried, seeing Warren roll up. "Let's get larrapin', terrapin. How come they're pushing you?"

"Don't want to burn myself out early," Warren said shortly.

"You've put on some weight, haven't you?" The rabbit was looking at the skirt. "Or is that a turdle-girdle?"

"Haven't you ever seen track shoes?"

"You really got the fans out," said the rabbit. "How do we split the take?"

"Charge admission?" Warren was offended. "An affair of national honor—"

"Sorry, general." And the rabbit went into his saluting stance.

"And where are your supporters?" Warren couldn't help sneering.

"My brothers wanted to come along and sell pop," the rabbit said, sitting down. "But Pop hid in the closet."

The starter called: "Runners, get ready, please," and they moved and were pushed over to where the lanes were marked.

"Take the smooth one," the rabbit said. A crew had been dragging the right-hand lane all the previous night. "There's grass in the other, but I can hop it."

"Home runner always get the right-hand lane, Coneyfoot," said the starter, who was actually the coach wearing a false moustache.

"Haven't we met before?" the rabbit asked.

"Take your marks."

"Do we have to give them back?"

The honor guard settled Warren's off-front wheel against a small turtle painted stone grey, placed to hold him even at the starting line.

"Judges ready? Timers ready?" The crowd hushed. "Ready. Set."

The rabbit scratched some grass together, nestlike, and squatted.

Bang, went the starting gun, and with a flip, the small, grey-painted turtle cleared the wheel, the honor guard gave a hard, covert push, and Warren was rolling.

"Slow and steady," Warren cried, instantly coasting into the lead.

"Fast and funny," replied the rabbit, and went somersaulting past.

"Illegal start," came the coach's shout. "Go back to your starting position. Other runner, continue."

"Kind of unfair to tumble bugs," said the rabbit, strolling back out of sight, and Warren, knowing that races are won by taking advantage of the breaks, thrashed his legs as if sprinting. The crowd yelled. Perhaps the miserable hare was beaten already. But no, here he came, ambling up his lane; he bowed, rolled his eyes, and began to dance along backward, just ahead of Warren, and to sing:

"Now once there was a lizzard
Caught in a blizzard,
Crawled into an igloo
That froze to his neck—
The very first turtle, by heck."

"Cut that out," Warren roared. "Run, will you?"

"Oh, all right," said the rabbit, and turned back out of sight toward the starting line again as Warren rolled evenly on. The next he knew, the rabbit, streaking past, four or five hundred miles an hour, charged three or four feet ahead, dug in his feet, and skidded.

"Red light!" he cried, holding up his paw as Warren rolled toward him. "How's your brakes, snake?"

"Let's save our breath, fella." Warren stared past him, moving his legs powerfully, eyes on the finish line; he was halfway there. Then peripheral vision showed him something he couldn't for a moment believe: the rabbit's head, sliding along the ground, into his lane. The creature seemed seriously to be trying to peer up under his skirt.

"Get out of my lane."

"Just checking your skate."

"My WHAT?" Warren blustered.

"Thought one wheel was wobblin', dobbin, but I'm wrong. Rolling smooth."

"I'm finishing this race under protest. Lane violation."

The rabbit sat back and scratched his ear. "You really don't care for my jokes, do you?" he said. "I'm sorry. Don't mean to spoil your big day. Tell you what, I'll go back to the beginning and wait till you're a length away from the finish, okay? Then I'll take off and see if I can beat you."

"Run your race any way you want," Warren growled, and rolled on. Again the rabbit disappeared. Warren lengthened his stride. Cheering, louder and louder. Three yards to go. Time to start the sprint, that grueling test of character, and Warren began to dig his legs through the air more sharply. A perfectly paced race—he had something left.

Way behind him he heard the rabbit talking to himself: "Set. Now. Go." So he must be coming, charging, but Warren was gliding, rolling, closer, closer to the tape.

What?

Something was wrong. The skate. It was slowing.

Grass in the wheel? Or a low spot? There were groans from the crowd. Slower. Slower. Inches from the finish line, the skate was stopping. Warren could almost touch the tape with his beak. He stretched his neck forward till he heard vertebrae creak. Not quite. He strained at his legs. They wouldn't touch the ground. He heaved his whole body, trying to break away from the mud that held him. From behind now, emerging from the rhythmic groaning of the crowd, came the dread thumping of the rabbit, till, with a final leap, the intolerable creature stopped just beside him.

"You seem," the rabbit remarked as they stared together at the tape, "to have overestimated the gravity of the situation."

Cut wind resistance, thought Warren desperately, and snapped into his shell, though forward motion had completely ceased. And as if it were the force of longing, or even the hand of the god to whom all winners pray, he felt a soft nudge just above his tail, felt the skate lurch forward, and heard a roar of jubilation.

He had done it!

Popping every hinge at once, Warren thrust his proud parts into the sun.

"Warren Purissimus, Warren Magnificus," chanted the crowd.

"Nobody saw me push," murmured the rabbit.

Push what? Warren wondered briefly, but he was too elated to try to solve this last joke, whatever it was. The coach was coming, the crowd moving toward him.

And the loveliest turtle of them all, stately, train bearers pacing behind, all walking with slow grace, advanced, carrying the verdant clover wreath.

"For me? Oh, you shouldn't have," cried the rabbit, bouncing into action again—reached her in a single hop, seized the wreath, ate it, and was gone with a final, gay salute for them all.

But not even this could spoil the moment. Warren held up his clawless flipper for silence, and the crowd grew still: "Fight fair," he told them, his voice low and booming as a chipmunk's. "Play to win. And remember, slow and steady. . . ."

The coach was undulating with impatience.

"Warren," he said. "Ladies and gentlemen. Heh. The record. The winning time. Thirty yards in two minutes eleven point six seconds! It will stand forever."

But to that Warren shook his head. Down in the gravel pits and sand flats, he knew, there were already young turtles practicing with different model skates, with skate boards, with pull toys, push toys, wind-up cars, even batteries. Oddly enough he did not mind this thought, for, he thought grimly, up in the meadows, among the daisies, there were sure to be young rabbits grinning, loafing, indolently inventing new and more frivolous modes of atrocious disrespect.

18: The Man-eaters of Dueyville

"Now you know all about Dueyville, don't you, Mr. Hoffman?" Dick, to whom compassionate Maury has supplied a second shot of whiskey. "I know a damn animal story, too." Musuclar Dick is flushed, ponderous insofar as one so young can be, guileless but no longer taciturn. Dick is educated but not cultured; he and his M.F.A. in music are headed straight back to the farm.

"Oh, please." Sidney.

"Dueyville was in the papers for a week when we 'uz in high school, but that reporter never knew what really happened and I wasn't about to tell him."

"Please, Dick. I hate that ignorant story."

"Someone say you have to stay and listen?"

She does, though.

One time Dueyville was called Deauville, after some French city. Up in Northeast, 'fore the Scandinavians, there 'uz Swiss, and did you know Dvořak wrote the *New World Symphony* in an old stone tower up there? There was clock making, and before that New Englanders and Kentucky boys that dared to settle on the west side of the Mississippi, but first of all were French trappers coming through the portages in Wisconsin, down from Canada in those long canoes. They were the ones gave French names to the posts along the river where they traded with the woodland Indians for furs, and then went off and let the Indians be, just leaving names like Marquette and Prairie du Chien and Dubuque and Deauville.

Anybody can say Marquette and Dubuque, but can't nobody up there say Deauville, so they changed the spelling, and as for Prairie du Chien, anymore they call it Prair'de Sheen.

The man who's the main part of this story had a little education once, though we always treated him like he was slow, Duke Woerber. Dukey used to say the name was just right, the way it got changed, Prayer du Chine, because, he said, you didn't have a Chinese prayer once you left there. You see, it's on the Wisconsin side, and for a long time it's where men from Dueyville would go to drink, 'fore we got liquor over the bar legal in this state. Even after that, men would go to Prair'de Sheen to drink because they always had and there's where their favorite places were, and Duke Woerber was sure as hell one of them.

Just often enough to keep him in trouble, the state police would catch Dukey coming back from there drunk, driving along real slow in one or another of a half-dozen old junker Pontiacs he kept around his trailer, along with a bunch of iron-wheeled farm machines no one wanted.

Duke was a scary-looking guy, big and gaunt, but jowly, and a kind of prison-grey color that has got to make sense, because he spent quite a bit of his time down in the Fort, that's the state prison, on his drunk-driving charges. He always wore grey coveralls, in or out of prison, and he worked in the mechanics shop when he was staying at the Fort. But he wasn't the kind of mechanic you take work to. He seemed to know enough to keep a junker going, robbing parts from one Pontiac to fix another, but it wouldn't have been right to take Dukey anything to fix. Slow or not, jailbird sometimes, he was some kind of gentleman, and not in business.

What he lived on was the cash rent from the cropland his mom turned over to him. Different ones would rent it to grow corn or beans on, like I did myself one spring in high school. It's an eighty, mostly second bottom. Good land once and could be again, if you tiled it out and built up the soil. Anyhow, Duke's trailer stood in what used to be the farmyard before he burned off all the buildings that evening, and left her bare as the county road.

But I don't want to forget to tell you that there wasn't any harm in Dukey. He looked scary, and most people stayed clear of him, but nobody ever thought Dukey'd ever hurt someone else, and he didn't. I don't think he had the strength to hurt someone else, either in his mind or his body. He was more like a shell, like a pea pod you pick up in the garden, that still seems green, you can see the row of peas outlined, but you pick it up, it's light, and then you see it's been split open and the halves separated, and then closed itself back together again, maybe a bird robbed it or a small digging animal.

One night, the summer after the burning, I was driving back from a ball game at Marquette with a couple of friends and Cindy, when we saw Duke's car in the ditch along a gravel-road shortcut. Generally speaking, when one of the farm people does that, gets drunk and runs off the road, he'll have sense enough to leave his car and walk home. See, if the sheriff or the state police find a car like that with no one in it, it's an accident. But if you're right there drunk, sleeping under the wheel, 'course it's some kind of charge and fine and maybe lose your license and even go to jail. Anyways, in the country you always stop by a car like that and see if you can help out, and so we stopped, and there was Duke Woerber, passed out cold, smelling of liquor, and gasoline where it sloshed out of a can he carried in back.

We tried to get him to walking so we could drive him home, but he was too drunk to walk and seemed too big to carry, so I said I'd just drive his car with him in it. The others could follow me, and I'd leave the old Duke parked at his trailer, where they'd pick me up. Anybody'd do that for a neighbor around Dueyville, when we 'uz in school; anymore they might be too busy or too mean or just not care.

So I drove Dukey home, and I recall there wasn't any key for the car, just a wired ignition, and that Pontiac wouldn't shift into high, I went all the way in second. Just 'fore we got to the trailer, Duke half woked up, and made out I was stealing his car and kidnaping him. I heard him mumble and try to sit up, and I looked over and saw he was getting a rusty old penknife open to stick me with. I was never so un-scared in my life. I didn't laugh or say anything—I just pushed his arm away a couple of times. It was a light arm in spite of the size. Pretty soon his mind had wandered somewheres else, and he was thanking me, but I don't suppose he knew what for.

Then he asked me could I talk French? I said no, but I'd like to hear him, so he talked some French for me, or maybe it was Latin. Back in his good days, Dukey's education had been his proud point. People said he'd had quite a gift for languages, and that someone at the college where he went used to send him church articles to translate.

Dukey'd gone away to college for two years, some said, some said only one, and while he'd always been a little bit strange, he seemed to have been able to learn all right. He didn't have the kind of sense it takes to farm, but his mom never wanted him to, and I guess his grandaddy'd been a big farmer, there's some Woerbers around the county still have good land. But Duke grew up liking good clothes and whiskey, and it was drinking got him in trouble at the college. It was one of those church colleges and they threw his butt out of there, and he come on back to Dueyville, spouting a little French and Latin, and when I was little, he lived with his mom at the home place, and talked about going back to college and studying law or else theology. Even then they rented out their farmland, though a lot of it was sold off already; they lived on the cash rent, and anything extra was Duke's to spend.

The house had been very grand once, a fifteen-room big frame house in the old front-porch style, with parquet floors and bay windows in the living room and dining room. It was built about 1900, my dad said, and that was the first house in the county to have real central heat. But when Duke came home from college, it needed work; he started to paint it one fall and quit when it got cold, and when I was little, I remember how it stayed half-painted year after year. We used to call it the two-tone house. But by the time I was twelve or thirteen, it was pretty hard to tell which was the part Duke Woerber once put paint to.

By then Dukey was living in town at his cousin's, renting a room and boarding, 'cause his mom run him off. She got the idea it was time for him to be back in college, and never understood he wasn't allowed there. She thought any college be proud to have her Duke in it, so he moved on into town where she never came. Once a week he'd drive out to take supplies to her, all shaved up and wearing a suit he once had custom-tailored from Chicago, and she'd think he was home on a daytime visit from college or maybe law school, but I guess she didn't ask. She'd give him money out of a coffee can, and two dozen eggs as presents for his teachers.

Then she got older and stopped keeping chickens, and what she had for company was a bunch of cats. Twenty or twenty-five, all sizes and colors. I guess she started with three or four farm cats, and then took them into the house to live. Then, of course, kittens started coming and growing up indoors. Dr. Niebelson, the vet, said what worked out was one of the most interesting examples of inbreeding you could want to see. There'd been just one tom to start with, a big yellow cat. I remember seeing him when we'd drive out, before she locked herself in, to buy our own country eggs from Mrs. Woerber. When we stopped seeing him, I thought maybe the old tom-cat'd died, but I asked about him—I was still a kid then—and she said he was a bad boy and had to stay shut up. Then she began to keep them all shut up, and then herself too, and stopped the egg business. We started keeping chickens again on our own place; a lot of farmers won't bother. But Mrs. Woerber lived then in the dining room and kitchen of the old wood house, and heated with the kitchen wood range. The other thirteen rooms she got Duke to nail off when he was spending what he said was college vacation out there one time, and selling off walnut trees for money. They got the logger to trim up all the limbs for stove wood. Duke said he piled it right in the kitchen and what used to be a pantry. After the wood was in, nobody ever saw Mrs. Woerber, except Dukey and Doc Niebelson, she'd have him come out and give shots ever' time a there was a new litter of kittens born. Dukey didn't carry tales on his mom, but the doctor said it was about as evil smelling a place as you'd ever find. Mrs. Woerber had what used to be the bathroom for the cook and farmhand downstairs, and she lived in the two rooms with her radio and cats. Every week Dukey'd come on out bringing cat food and bacon and bread and coffee and the week's papers, the *Register* and the *Gazette,* for her to read through, and then put down on the floor for cat litter, right over last week's litter paper and the week before. Maybe there were a couple of hundred layers of it after a while.

Doc Niebelson reported that the old yellow tom did finally die, and he said there was congenitally blind cats there now, all bred down from the same sire, and cats with short front legs, and cats with hump necks. There was extra-big cats too, he said, and extra-little, and one so creamy he looked like custard, with one black leg, the biggest of them all.

"He's really a beautiful animal," the doctor said. "I'd like to have him. He must weigh near thirty pounds, and he's the big boss out there now. I expect there's other toms could do the breeding job on their mothers and sisters, but I don't think Custard Dan lets them. A couple more generations, if he sires them all, and there might start to be some real monsters, with manes and extra limbs and claws like knitting needles."

Now in a town like Dueyville, people'd care, we'd never figure if someone's worth caring about or not, because we'd know each other's all we've got. That's the way it used to be.

So when Dukey got back in jail one week, right now people thought about his mom and what she'd do for food and cat food and newspapers. This time it was the state police got him, and sheriff didn't quite dare to do what he'd usually do, which was give Duke the key to the jail on Wednesday and tell Duke to go on out and take care of his mom, and if everybody'd gone home when he come back, Duke was to let himself back into the jail, and he'd find his supper on the radiator in his cell, and he could just pull the cell door to and then toss the keys out through the bars onto the hall floor where the night deputy'd find them when he came on duty.

Now Sheriff Kalonis, he'd 'uv took what Mrs. Woerber needed on out there himself, but he had to do something or other else right then, so Sheriff Ka, he called my father, and Daddy said, Hell yess. Dick could take it. Sheriff thought of me because of the time I farmed the land, and figured Dukey'd trust me with his money to go to the store and get the stuff his mom needed.

That first part wasn't any sweat at all. I went down to the jail and talked to Duke through the bars. He couldn't understand why he wasn't being let out as usual, but he gave me fourteen dollars, and told me what to get.

"Dick, you be careful going in the house, now," Duke told me. "You got to go in through the front door. *Oui, oui.* Then you'll be in the salon that my mom doesn't use. Close that front door, though, 'cause there might be a cat or two get out when you open the next one. You better have a flashlight then. Wait, I got a flashlight in my Pontiac, I better come with you."

I reminded him that he couldn't come along this time, and he started mumbling then. It was awhile before I got him back on the subject of how to make my delivery. From the salon—the living room—I was to open the next door, into a short hall that had the stairs in it. Don't worry too much about cats, because the door at the head of the stairs was nailed shut, but try to get that hall door closed behind me 'fore I opened the next one. Did I know what a *salle à manger* was? he asked, and told me it was the dining room, where his mom slept, and it opened off the little hall I'd be in, and then the kitchen opened off that. So I should close the hall door behind me, and then knock at the dining-room door, and call who it was. Then probably I'd better leave the stuff, and let myself out, closing doors, but she might come to the dining-room door and she might not.

"If she does, Dick, you look out for them cats. They'll come streaming out all around you, but if you have that second door closed, the son of a bitches can't go no wheres. Then they'll follow Mom back when she picks up the food, and you skin out of there. Look out for that custard cat, Dan, he laid my thigh open all the way to the knee one time when I tried to kick him out of the way. If he'd wanted to jump higher, he could have knocked me down, *oui*. He's got knives on his feet and a ass full of quicksilver, I swear it to God.

"Probably be all right if she doesn't come right away. Then you just set things down and leave, all right? She gets sitting in the bathroom, and doesn't hear so good." And then he started in giving me the same instructions all over again, especially about not letting any cats out: "I fear she'd lose her mind if one got loose, Dick."

I thought of her the way I'd seen her last, a short-limbed, sad-faced, wrinkled-up lady, and I did wonder how much mind she might have left by now to lose. She was strong, though, in the neck and the back, you could see that, and I heard she dug the grave herself by hand that she buried Dukey's father in, six feet into the clay, her digging and him dying. He was the last dandy in the Woerber line, and quite a man. He was sick in bed, and she was too busy digging the grave to take care of him and reach his medicine, that's what was said. But you know how people talk, and anyway, that's 'fore I was born.

I didn't much like the sound of my errand. I called a friend or two to get someone to go out with me, but I couldn't. Then I thought, oh, hell, it's just an old lady and some cats, so I went on to the Safeway store and bought the stuff. Seemed like all she lived on was bacon and bread and canned applesauce, but the cats had it fancy. Puss 'n Boots, all different flavors, liver and chicken and fish of the sea. I got them at the Safeway to mix me up a case, and went by Dukey's cousin's to pick up the newspapers, and I asked the cousin would he drive out with me, and he said he never went near that house, didn't even like to drive by it. He was an old man cousin, from Duke's father's generation.

Then I got in my car, stopped by home for a flashlight, and ran on out. It was an overcast summer evening, hot and damp, the kind where you can smell the clay from where the banks are cut along the road if you're driving slow.

It's easy enough to say afterward about a thing that you felt there was something wrong. *Oui, oui,* as Duke would say.

I drove up the driveway, and thought I could see there was a weak light on at the back of the house, but when I got right up there, maybe it had got turned out. I packed the car so the headlights would shine in through the dining-room bay window, and show there was someone coming, and I left the car lights on.

Then I opened the trunk and got out my case of cat food and my pile of papers and sack of food, and put it all on the porch. It was a little more than I could carry easy holding a flashlight, so I made it in two stages. I took the things into the living room, put them all down, and shut the door like Dukey'd said to. I shone my light around the living room. There was stuffed furniture in it, and little mildewed piles of stuffing all over the place where the mice had pulled it out to make nests. The place smelled powerfully of mice, and I thought of those cats, getting out sometimes at least into the hallway one door off from this room, and smelling and hearing mouse, all that fresh meat, and how it must be a cat's dream to get through the door and into this room to hunt, like fishermen dream of lost lakes where no one's fished in a hundred years.

I listened at the hall door, and couldn't hear a thing.

Then I picked up my stuff and moved it on into the hallway, and closed that door behind me, too. It was very dark.

I shined my light till I saw a switch, and tried pushing it, but it didn't want to turn anything on. It was stuffy in the hall, and through the stuffiness I began to smell something else, coming under the door of the room where the old lady and her cats stayed, a smell of droppings and decay so strong I wanted to run. I thought, God, she's got old dead cats in there, too.

I stacked up my things then by the dining-room door, and got up my courage and knocked, and there came the goddamndest noise I ever heard. It was mewing and yowling and almost roaring, and bodies started thudding and scratching against the door on the other side.

"Hey, Mrs. Woerber," I called. "It's Dick Auerbach, with your food and papers. Did you want me to stay?"

The answer was more roaring and thudding—I even found myself holding the doorknob, so it wouldn't accidentally turn and let the animals out. I knocked once more, and the cat energy got so violent in there I felt sure they'd fight their way through the wood panels and get to me, and just then far away I heard my car door that I'd left open bang shut in the wind, and it scared me.

"Is anybody there?" I yelled, and maybe I heard a voice say back, kind of moaning:

"Custard Dan, Custard Dan . . ."

I thought she must be in there, but she didn't come. I made myself walk out; closed every door between me and the old woman and the cats, but when I was out in the damp night, I started running.

I looked again after I got in the car, cut my headlights, to see if there really was some kind of dim light on back where they were, and I still don't know. I kind of thought it turned on. Slow and weak.

I drove home a lot faster than I'd come out.

I stripped off at home and took as hot a shower bath as I could stand, and went downtown to the Dairy Queen, looking for whatever company I could find.

That was Wednesday, and on Monday Duke got let out of jail. That same afternoon, I saw him on a bench, in front of the courthouse, sitting by himself, and I had to stop my car and park and go over to him.

We weren't on any terms where I'd ever have done that before, but I had to, and I asked about the light.

It took a minute for him to get his connections made, and then he said, well, if there was a light in back, maybe his mom was in the bathroom, maybe. That made me feel better, and I was ready to move on.

"You should have told me about the noise," I said, starting off. "Those cats scared hell out of me."

He caught my arm with both hands, getting up.

"What noise?"

"All that yowling and screaming they make when you knock on the door," I said. Duke looked wild.

"They never done that."

"Done it the other night."

"Something's happened, then," he said. "Something's happened to my mom."

And he ran off to where his Pontiac was. I watched until he'd managed to get the old car started, and he came lugging out of there and back past me with an awful look on his face.

I couldn't think what to do for a minute. Then I ran into the courthouse, and found Sheriff Ka in his office, and told him what it seemed might have happened.

"Well, hell yes, Dick," he said. "That old lady could have died, couldn't she? We better go out. You coming?"

I didn't want to, but I got into the patrol car with him, and we drove on out, Sheriff Ka being cool, driving along normal, talking about baseball and things. But he did ask me:

"You sure there wasn't somebody moving around in that dining room?"

I said I didn't know at all, except for cats, one way or another. I didn't say anything about there might have been a voice, moaning, "Custard Dan." How could I have heard such a thing over the cat screams?

We'd almost got to the Woerber place when the old blue Pontiac came tearing back at us, almost out of control, so that Sheriff had to swerve out onto the shoulder of the gravel road to save being hit. We could see Dukey, bolting past at seventy miles an hour in second gear, the transmission whining like a siren. His mouth was set like a closed trap and his face was bleeding.

"What in hell, Dick?" says Sheriff Ka, and we went on up the drive. We got out of the car, and we could hear the cats, prowling and screaming like crazy in there, all through the shut-up house, see them at windows, leaping. Looked like they'd got out at last into the living room, and some must have found the back stairs. Sheriff ran to the bay window outside the dining room, and I saw cats jumping up against it inside, spread-eagling for a second and falling away. Then Sheriff got up on his toes to look in, he's not too tall of a man, and then he stumbled back like one of the cats had come through the window and hit him in the face, but of course it didn't.

I started over to him, he was turned away from the house now, and he said: "Don't look in there Dick. I'm going to be sick."

And he was. I went past and did look, of course. At first what I saw was seething cats, all over the floor, and then, in a chair, halfway sitting up, a dress with what was left of an old woman in it. But her face was gone, and the flesh off her arms, and I heard Sheriff moan:

"They've ate her. They've ate her halfway up, them starving cats."

And the last thing I saw was the case of Puss 'n Boots cat food I'd left, where Dukey'd kicked it in through the dining-room door, and the bag of groceries spilled out. Two cats were fighting to chew the bacon, and others were scattering around the bread.

"Sheriff." I caught him by the arm. He stopped heaving and was standing there panting and sweating like a horse that's been run too much on a hot day. "Sheriff, could she have been alive when I came last Wednesday?"

He said, "Oh, good God no, Dick. The bones on that arm are bleaching already. She's been dead for days and days." Then he said: "Jesus God, what a mess. I got to go back to town and get the doctor for a report and I don't know what all. I'll call the judge and the funeral home, I guess, and listen here, Dick, you better stay, would you do it? You don't have to go near the house, just if Dukey comes back, just keep him from trying to go back in there till we come. Just be with the poor, crazy bastard; he trusts you, Dick."

I begged him not to be gone long, and maybe to call my father to come stand with me, and Sheriff promised he would. I went out on the road where the driveway turned in toward the house, and stood by a cedar tree. I rubbed some needles between my hands and breathed the clear smell off my palms.

Sheriff hadn't been gone but five minutes 'fore I heard the transmission wail, far down the road and then coming closer, and Duke's car into sight. I stepped into the driveway where he'd see me, and then dived back out of it when it seemed like he didn't. He went on to the house, sixty, seventy yards, and stopped.

I started walking after him, saw him get out of the car with his five-gallon can he had for gas, and began running. But before I was halfway to him, he'd poured out the gas, all over the porch and on the grass by the house, thrown in a match, and the flames sprang up so fast they caught his hair on fire for a second.

Duke backed away fast, turned to his car. I was close enough to see that his eyebrows were gone, leaving little charred lines, but Duke paid no attention. The old wooden house was catching fire right now, and by the time I reached him, Duke had a sixteen-gauge Winchester pump gun in one hand and a box of shells in the other.

I stopped, seeing the gun, and Duke saw me.

"Stand back, Dick," he said. "Them son of a bitches . . . you stand back," and that's just what I did, too.

Duke loaded in his first five shells, and stood waiting, watching the house. Came the wind and wrapped the flames around the lower part of the house, and as it started burning upward, the cat screams got horrible. Then you started to see how the heat inside was bursting out panes of glass upstairs, and the first things to get away was pigeons from the attic. Probably thirty of them came out, and then the bats, fifty or a hundred. They were pretty well asphyxiated, because they'd fly into the light and then drop back down, some into the fire, and I don't know if any bats got free.

Then the first cat. It came out the broken panes in a dormer window, stood on the roof, a grey-striped little cat, and Duke's gun went boom, and the cat collapsed. Two more came then, and Duke shot them both, yellow cats. Duke pushed three more shells into his Winchester.

There was a mess of cats came after that, eight or ten at once, fighting each other to get out onto the roof, but of course they couldn't get down, and Duke started picking them off as they scattered around. One took a big jump for a pine-tree limb, got his front feet on it, but the branch broke away under him, and he fell, screaming, into the fire.

And I swear, all that time I was standing there trembling, because it seemed to me sure I kept hearing that voice from the house calling or moaning, "Custard Dan, Custard Dan."

Then he appeared, the big custard cat with one black leg, stepping out through the broken pane, kind of calm, and stopping to look down at Dukey. Duke gave a yell damn near like a cat screeching himself, raised up the gun, pulled the trigger, and the gun misfired. I heard the click. Then it was a minute before Duke could get her unjammed and shooting again, and it was like the cat knew just how long he had. He strolled to the edge of the roof, crouched, and took off through space toward the same pine-tree limb the other cat had broken, but Custard Dan was a lot bigger. I watched him sail through the smoke to the thick part of the limb, grab it, and disappear where the needles were heaviest. Right then Duke got his gun going again, and he was shooting hell out of the pine tree, but you couldn't see Custard Dan anymore. There was a cat fell out of the tree into the flames, but there was so much smoke I couldn't say what cat it was, might have even been a squirrel or a crow with a nest up there. Duke was yelling that he'd got the bastard, but I knew he wasn't sure either, because he kept reloading and shooting into the tree, and while he was doing that, I saw three or four other cats come sneaking out a cellar window and run off into tall weeds. Then the tree caught fire. Then the corncrib. Then the barn. Then I could hear the sirens of the volunteer fire truck, and Sheriff Ka, coming back with my dad.

They sent Duke down to the Mountain, that's the state mental hospital, after that. He was away six months, and then came back in the spring and moved the trailer out to the home place to live in. But it wasn't until summer that I went to see him, that was a few days after we helped him home out of the ditch.

He was living pretty solitary, with his old cars and tractors. Nobody'd wanted to rent the land that year, it was all up in foxtail and pigweed.

Next thing to the Woerber place is the Yellow River Forest; it's a state park, with a creek running into it off the Woerber place that the conservation commission stocks trout in. Little Paint Creek. Duke had his part of Little Paint posted, and it seemed like some of the state's fish ought to be up there. I went out to ask him did he care if I fished it sometime.

I found him at the trailer, two or three dogs lying around, Duke looking about the same. But his eyes had less light in them, and he was vague enough when he said he didn't care if I was to fish so I wasn't too sure he'd remember it. He made fair sense, though, and I could tell a time came that he recognized for sure who I was, because he suddenly stood up and said— well, he looked around first, and said it in a fierce whisper:

"Dick. Yep, Dick. I got him, didn't I? That custard cat? You seen me get him."

"*Oui, monsieur le Duc,*" I said. I'd been taking French and thought that would tickle him. But he answered, kind of heavy:

"There's something been killing neighbor's ducks and chickens."

"Raccoons?"

"I seen nothing. Neighbor said cats, but, Dick, I got them bastards. Dick, he burned up in the pine tree, didn't he? Fell blazing like a star."

"You don't need to worry about cats, Duke," I said. "Not with these dogs."

He didn't say yes or no. He looked at his dogs and patted one, like he was studying them.

Just a day or two later, Sheriff Ka told me Dukey's dogs were killed. He said fighting among theirselves, or maybe something came out of the woods, but it could have even been the neighbor; it might have been those dogs killing the ducks and chickens after all. Feral dogs do get to be a problem up home sometimes. They're apt to be lost hunting dogs that pack up together, and run lambs and sheep. I'd helped to hunt them, it's all you can do. They say once one has pulled wool from a sheep and tasted the lanolin and felt the crunch of wool tearing off in his teeth, he never wants to run anything but sheep, it's that exciting.

I was going to go out and see Duke, but I was busy. I'd just got back from music camp and had my corn to plow. Then it happened.

Just in the next week two kids busted out of the reformatory at Anamosa, stole them a car, and came heading our way. They got in a chase with the state police, wrecked their car, and one was caught, but the other crawled away into the Yellow River Forest, near Little Paint Creek. His friend said he'd broke his ankle and couldn't move too well, and he had a gun, too. Well, the state police and the sheriff figured they'd best keep the place marked overnight. It'd be safest to get him out by daylight.

We heard about it at the Dairy Queen, of course, and right now everybody started to drive out there and see what was happening. When Cindy and I got there, there 'uz five state-police cars, Sheriff's car, two deputy cars, and all playing spotlights into the woods.

There was a big bullhorn operating off one of the state-police cars, and every few minutes an officer would say into it:

"BILLY WEEDLE, come on out. Come on out, Billy. Throw down your gun. We got a doctor here."

Right from the first time I heard it, I wanted to leave, and I wanted to stay too, but I was scared, because it was like there was an echo to the bullhorn when it stopped, an old woman's voice whispering *Custard Dan Dan, Custard Dan,* sort of scolding and regretful.

Then a scream came, a couple of wild shots, and a most awful scream. Somebody yelling help, and it stopped much too damn quick. Cindy screamed too, at the suddenness, and grabbed me and started sobbing, and over her shoulder I saw the police look at each other, and start turning on their hand flashlights and drawing their guns and leaving into the woods.

But they didn't find him till morning. When they did, it was Billy Weedle all right, and he'd been kilt by animals, kilt and partly ate up. He'd been on his back, fighting, the gun no use that close, and his throat was tore open and Sheriff told me his hands was full of cat fur, mostly custard color.

"But there had to be more than one cat, didn't there?"

He'd called me in to tell again about the fire and Mrs. Woerber's cats, and Doc Niebelson, the vet, was there for the closest we could come to a cat expert.

"House cats generally hunt by theirselves," Doc said. "But I guess in nature the big ones, like tiger and lion, a pair will hunt together, maybe cubs too. Maybe a family."

"This don't seem like nature," Sheriff said.

A week later, the cats got a woman trout fishing in Little Paint Creek. It was a fat woman from a farm near Clinton who'd come to fish just at first light in the morning, fishing with cheese bait, setting on a folding camp-stool at the edge of the bank about eight feet above the water. Looked like the cats had come down on her off a tree limb and drove her over the edge into the water, where she drowned, and then floated down to where the stream gets shallow, and she caught in the rocks. They'd fed off her quite a bit and left before she was found.

The big hunt started then. The creek and picnic grounds 'uz closed, reporters came, and every one of us that owned a gun got formed up for a big drive, all coordinated with walkie-talkies and they even had a spotting plane from the highway patrol. Half went through the woods, and the rest had stands, some close in with shotguns and number-four buckshot, and some with rifles and scopes, farther out. My stand was on a bank over a country road, with a plinking gun; I was part hid, waiting to see what would come out in front of the drivers, and there was plenty of life—deer and foxes, and even some wild turkeys and grouse came out, but no sign of cats.

Then I realized there was someone had come up to stand behind me; it was Dukey Woerber, and he said: "They'd have to fire the forest. Them cats are in the trees."

I said that made sense.

"I killed him once," Dukey said. "I'll kill him again."

"No ghost ever done that to Billy Weedle, Duke," I said.

People just stayed out of that part of the Yellow River Forest then, unless they were armed and in the daytime. The cats weren't heard of for a while. Then they took to killing baby pigs. They'd find a sow out in pasture with a litter, and some run her till the rest could cut a little pig off and run it under a fence, and that was seen. First by one man, then another. There were six cats, they said: three plain soldiers, and one that had short front legs and hopped like a kangaroo, and one short-tailed bobface cat with weak eyes. He'd run into bushes and logs, but he moved like light, and seemed like he could hear a man sneaking up, and warn the rest, so they'd all run. And of course, the boss, a big, creamy-yellow cat with one black leg.

Sheriff hired some of us to try to hunt or trap them, work at it regular, and I started going out there in the dark every morning. But they 'uz a lot harder than a pack of dogs. They were smaller, and faster and quieter, and they could hide and climb. But what we all knew and didn't say was the worst of it—feral dogs'll run just from smelling a human, but the cats could hide and look it over, and if it was someone old or lame or a child, and no one else around, the cats had showed what they could do.

First cat killed was the sentry, the half-blind one. A farmer got him with a shotgun; it was caught in a hog-wire fence that the others went right through. Then one of the soldier cats in a fox trap, that was probably luck; Sheriff Ka picked off one other soldier; and it was me got the kangaroo cat. They begun staying away from the farms, and I saw him one day, but it was a her, watching at a ground-hog hole. I was almost four hundred yards away, downhill, and got down prone and adjusted my scope and shot her dead.

Then we thought maybe Custard Dan and his last soldier had moved out, deep into the woods. And then it happened that the two attacked a little boy, and got run off when the boy's daddy came up in a pickup truck, but the last soldier ran straight down the road, and the man was able to run him down and squash him dead.

So Custard Dan was alone, but Doc Niebelson told the reporter and it came out in the paper that people'd better be careful yet. Maybe more so. The daddy of the little boy said looked to him like the big cat was hurt in one leg, maybe by a trap, and Doc said that would make him that much more dangerous. He said if Dan couldn't move good enough to get wild game, and didn't have the help he'd need to work little pigs, then when he really got hungry he'd have to get hisself another human, they're the slowest prey around.

He did it too. There was an out-of-state truck driver came through at night, didn't know the park was closed, pulled into the camping area to wait for morning, when he'd make his delivery, and laid out in a J. C. Penney sleeping bag with a bottle of Four Roses to put him to sleep. Custard Dan got him. The man's arms were trapped in the sleeping bag, and Dan crept onto his bag, sunk his teeth into the back of the man's neck and his claws into the shoulders, and what killed him probably was his heart, while he thrashed around the empty campground in such terrible fear and pain, trying to get rid of something he couldn't even see. Dan fed off him four days before a ranger went through there and seen the body, but of course he never seen the cat.

About that time, Sheriff ran out of budget to hire hunters, but I said I'd got my corn plowed, I'd keep going out. There was something I wanted to try.

I was in his office again, and Sheriff sighed, and said: "I'm glad you can, Dick. Listen, if you see dogs roaming, you shoot them, too. There's sheep killing out there again, too. Real bad."

Seems like while we'd been hunting cats, a new wild-dog pack formed up. Listen, someone says "beagle," you think of a cute, floppy-eared, brown-eyed dog like Snoopy in the funny papers. Something adorable. But Sheriff said there was a sag-bellied bitch beagle led that pack, and it was one of the worst ever.

"Don't go out of your way looking. Deputies'll find 'em after a while for sure. Dogs ain't like that cat, living in the woods. They got to have a place to lay up under cover. We'll check the old abandoned farm buildings and the cellars, and we'll find 'em."

"All right," I said. "Just if I run into 'em."

"Imagine you goin' to see Duke, ain't you?"

"Well," I said. "When the custard cat comes out, it's always somewhere around Duke's place."

"Duke's cousin come by. Said Duke's drinking some, not going away
but sitting drinking beer at his trailer, and gets to stumbling
around. . . ." He didn't exactly say it, but we both feared it. "Be all right
if Duke was to move back with his cousin, least till the cat's dead, Dick."

"I'll tell him."

That afternoon I got me two iron stakes, like you used to pitch horse-
shoes at, and fastened light chains to them with a couple of U-bolts and
snaps on the other end of the chains. I cut up some two-by-fours, and took
out a hammer and nails, and on my way to set up I stopped by Duke's. But
he wasn't interested in moving back to town, and he didn't offer me a beer,
though he had a can in his hand, or ask me into the trailer either. Now, I
didn't want a beer, nor to go inside the trailer, but it seemed like Duke was
different. Usually he'd get real friendly, just about climb on me to stay and
visit when he got me recognized. Like I was his one friend in the world, and
he wanted to talk and talk. But this time he called my name all right, but
he made less sense than usual except for that, and he didn't seem to have any
of that warm-handedness to him.

Like he had another friend, that he might be able to talk to.

The place I went to from there was probably sixty rods away. That's
what? Three hundred yards and a little. There was a big burr oak, and the
biggest part of the trunk was out of sight of the trailer, behind a small rise.
But from the first big limbs I could see the trailer all right, and have it in
range. Now, that wasn't part of my plan, but one more reason for choosing
the tree, that I could see the trailer through my scope, but Duke couldn't see
what I'd be doing. I'd figured he wouldn't want me to. And I figured Custard Dan had to be getting hungry, back there in his forest hiding place.

So I built me a tree stand. I nailed my two-by-fours to the trunk of the
burr oak in steps, and then enough of fence boards to sit on across two low
limbs. I used old board, nice and grey, not shiny new ones. I had a pruning
saw, and cleared me three fields of fire through the tree limbs, one toward
the trailer, one toward the forest, and one down a little dry waterway that
seemed like a natural trail for a hunting animal to use. Then I made a rail of
two-by-fours, so I could shoot sitting with the barrel bench-rested.

In the waterway, and on the forest side, I drove my horseshoe stakes
with the chains and snaps, each one just eighty yards away. I had a box of

fresh pig manure, and I scattered that around, too. Then I went back to our place, and worked with the scope setting till I had it just right for eighty yards, and knew just how many turns to take to run it up to three hundred and a little.

I set out two groups of new lath at eighty yards, one left and one right, and down the center at three hundred and thirty yards I put a third group. Then I practiced till I could split first a right lath at eighty, then a left, then make my turns on the scope adjustment and hit one far down, all in about ten seconds. Then I put nose rings in two little pigs from a litter we had, and went early to bed.

I got up at three thirty, sacked my baby pigs, and drove out toward the Woerber place, turning off my headlights when I was still three miles away. About a mile off I stopped and parked, behind a row of Osage-orange hedge, got my pig sack and my rifle, and put on a miner's hat, with a strong lamp, but didn't light it. I took out southeast for my burr oak.

I found the first stake in the waterway without a light, got out a pig, and hooked the snap into the nose ring. As soon as I turned loose, he ran out to the end of the chain, felt the ring pull, and squealed, good and loud.

I hoped it wouldn't wake Dukey, but I needed that squeal. Then I tramped around in the dark till I busted my shin on the other stake, reached in and got bit on the hand by the other pig, kept myself from squealing, and hooked him up, too. By the time I climbed up and settled into my stand, it was almost five, and still too dark to see. I settled the miner's hat.

I listened. I'd hear my pigs squeal, now and again, and small animals moving. There were night birds, and tree frogs, and the air was so clear I could smell my pig manure, too, when the breeze came up a little. The scope was still set for eighty yards from the day before, like I wanted it.

The east sky lightened, over the trailer, the morning got even calmer, and for a few minutes I went off to sleep. I was dreaming that I saw the big, dark, wood Woerber house still standing over there, and then I saw it blaze up, and opened my eyes, and it was sunrise. My left pig let out a bellow, just then, and I turned, sighted, and nearly shot a red fox. He heard me move, and though I'd lots of time if I'da wanted to, I was glad to see him run off.

Crows came out of the woods, the first day birds up, and then all the little songbirds started waking, and a half hour went by. I hadn't counted on the cat, of course, not the first morning, but I was going to be in that stand every morning till he showed.

Then I heard a familiar sound in the morning stillness, and couldn't place it for a moment, because the last time I'd heard it, I'd been so much closer. It was a car, a Pontiac, moving slow in second gear, and as soon as I knew that, the car appeared.

The first thing I did was feel silly, if Duke had been out all night, maybe even off drinking again, and I'd taken all that trouble with lights and noise. Then the car stopped, and Duke got out, carrying something, and didn't look at all drunk.

I raised my rifle so I could see through the scope what he had with him, and it was a lamb, or a lamb carcass anyway, all limp and bloody. He closed the car door, looked around, and then he threw the lamb into the trailer. Then he opened the car door again, and the next thing that got out was a beagle, an old-looking, heavy-looking beagle, with sagging teats and a waddle. And after her seven or eight more dogs, all dancing, and licking at the blood on Duke's hands and arms, and then running for the trailer where their meal was.

I sat in my tree stand kind of shocked, knowing now why he hadn't seemed to want me to stay. He was hiding those sheep killers—no, it was worse than that. He was taking them out, wasn't he? One night to one lonely pasture, one night to another, and picking up their kill, which made it harder for anyone to know when and where, and bringing them in again.

"My God." I said it aloud. "He's joined the pack."

They 'uz all inside the trailer now, the door still open. One dog ran out with a piece of lamb, and the old beagle went after him, not too fast, and he slunk back in, in front of her. Then nothing happened for about five minutes, and then Duke came out in the yard by himself with two cans of beer, and while I watched through the scope, I saw him pour one can over himself, wetting his grey coveralls with it, and drink the other halfway, and pour the rest on the ground near the open door of the Pontiac. Then he got out his gas can and sloshed a little gas on the ground, put the can away, put his finger down his throat, and the beer he'd just drunk came up again. I remembered the smell from the night I carried him home, and that was Duke's mixture all right.

Then he laid himself down, right in the middle of the slosh he'd made, by the open car door on the driver's side, and it looked just exactly like a man home from Chinese prayer, fallen drunk out of his car, not able to make it to the house.

The beagle came out of the trailer then, jumped into the open car above him, and out of sight.

Twenty minutes went by. Then I saw the cat. He came out slow and quiet from the Yellow River Forest, forty yards from the trailer, big as the fox I'd seen, creamy yellow, and he was favoring the one black leg just a little, just a little, but not dragging it. Do you know, I sat there with my scope on him, admiring him, the way he carried hisself, the way he stood and then crouched, and I forgot to change my sights. I was fighting my admiration, ready to squeeze off, and suddenly remembered I was still set for eighty yards. Then he started moving, and it was too late to lower the gun and change. He was going forward in a crouch, getting closer and closer to Duke, and I tried just raising up at a guess, led a little, and fired.

And the gun jammed. I heard the click.

Then the cat started moving in bounds, leaping toward Duke. I yelled, but of course Duke couldn't hear me. Nothing moved but the cat, closing on his prey, and I kept the scope up and saw him go into his final leap that would have landed him on Duke's shoulders, and get met in the middle of it by that beagle bitch, making a small leap of her own from the hiding place in the car.

The two animals met in the air, over the bait, and landed on it, a blur of fighting, silent to me, and she had Custard Dan by his black leg. He turned and was raking at her to get loose, the pair swirling in the dust away from Duke, when the other dogs came out. They poured out of the trailer, and now I could hear, and they were all over that cat, fighting over him, tearing him to bits. It didn't take long. Then it quieted. There were dogs sitting down to chew, some spitting out the bitter cat meat, and then the old beagle, holding the black leg, started waddling toward the woods. And the other dogs picked up whatever they was chewing, and followed her away.

There wasn't much cat carcass left when I got there, just some of the fur he'd worn, and a head with the face chewed away, and Duke, sitting on the ground by his car.

You know what that hollow-headed man did? His coveralls 'uz ripped at the waist, and he was part laid open there, bleeding, but he smiled.

"You can go fishing now," he said.

Then he looked around for his can of beer, and I went and got him one from the trailer. When I came out with it, he said:

"We got him, Dick, he'll stay dead this time. *Nous l'avons tué finalement*. Listen, if you get some, want to cook 'em here? Was you goin' to shoot the fish with that, Dick, where's your pole? Bet you could, though, you a good shot; *oui, Monsieur*."

I tried to listen to his wanderings, tried hard, for I didn't want to hear the other, the old woman's voice, sighing and regretful, sifting back from the woods, "Custard Dan, Custard Dan . . . Dan . . . Dan . . ."

14: A Chorus of Poker Players

"Custard Dan." Maury. "Oh, Custard Dan."

"Bastard Dick." Sidney.

"Have a drink, Cindy." Dick, flushed and truculent.

"No thank you, Muscles."

"Bring Miss Benesch a brandy Alexander."

Maury smiles. "I just went off duty."

Sidney, saved. "Ick. Did I really used to drink those things?"

"Yeah." Dick, sadly. "Yeah, you really did."

A waitress, bringing fresh pitchers of beer. "Anybody here named Wigglesby Short?"

Rigby Short, grimacing. "Debbie calling."

"It's Professor Short, Miss." Hoffman.

The waitress, laughing. "It's the phone."

Short comes back from the telephone, nods at Billy Hoffman. The two go off to a booth, followed by Maury's question: "We're going to get pizza. What do you want on yours?"

"Peppers." Short.

"Anything special, Mr. Hoffman?"

"Sausage, onions, black olives, ham, capers, pepperoni, extra cheese, keep it simple, you know?"

The two sit down.

"We got another production meeting." Short.

Hoffman, glancing at the table where his stage manager and the opera guild chairman sit with the others. "All right. Mona and Skeats are here."

"Sato wants it. He and Debbie. Seven o'clock."

"Mona can call Karen. We don't turn a page without Karen."

"I don't think it's a big crisis. Plans for technical rehearsal."

"That's not till next week."

"I think Sato likes careful planning."

"I can see it: Sunday morning he writes on the calendar which tie he's going to wear for every day of the week."

"Debbie wants me to have supper with her afterward."

Hoffman, grinning. "While your wife's out of town? Hey, Snazzer."

"Call me Wigglesby, and moan my fate. A meal at Debbie's . . . well. What she wants to talk to me about is you."

"Me?"

"Now who's wife is out of town?"

"Okay, okay."

"Listen, Debbie's incoming chairman of Speech and Drama."

"I know."

"Which she deserves. But it's for political reasons. They've got to have a woman head. Federal money."

"Slush, boy? Most powerful fluid known to man."

"Positive action. University can't get by any longer saying, 'We got women heads. Look. Nursing and Girls' Phys. Ed.' Or they start losing slush. So they got to hire from the only minority in history that's ever been a majority."

"That where I come in?" Hoffman. "I'm a real minority."

"It is where you come in, Billy, if you'll listen to me. Debbie's in the only strong position anyone ever reaches in this screwed-down world. When they've got to have you, and you know it, then you can make conditions before you accept."

"Is Debbie tough?"

"Enough. One of the first things she's got to do is hire a director. She wants the appointment approved before she accepts the chair. She wants to talk to me about appointing you."

Hoffman stares.

"It'd be someone to teach directing, Billy, as well as to stage shows."

Hoffman, slowly. "There's things about it I could teach."

"You got any academic background at all?"

"Scranton High School, North Branch. Half a semester at Penn State. I couldn't remember where the classrooms were. Good-bye, job, huh?"

"Maybe not. Debbie wants to make a difficult appointment, I think. One to ram through, like it or not. Tenured, Billy."

"Does that mean what I think?"

"Once you've got it, you're here—as long as you don't indulge in too much rape and murder—till you decide to leave. She could bring you in as a visiting lecturer, no problem, one-year appointment."

"That'd be okay. More than I'm looking for."

"Not Debbie. It's more than just a show of leverage. She wants her own people. You'd be a test."

"Jesus. I'm a pretty sorry test."

"Let us worry about that. You've done it all—street theatre, children's theatre, Broadway, off Broadway, and the Yale Bowl."

"But I'd like the job. Jesus. You know, to stop traveling and live some place. To have a plant to work in, and a company to work with? I'll be frank with you, it'd be better by a hundred times than back to Broadway."

"I'd like to have you here. I really would."

Hoffman can't stop saying "Jesus." "Jesus. Throw my suitcase away, huh? Buy some clothes, hey, a gabardine suit, and hang it instead of fold it up?"

"All right." Short. "I'll go pay for your clothes. Debbie's the worst cook in town."

"Jesus, get stuff dry-cleaned instead of wash it."

"Health food, German style. Low-starch noodles with noodle sauce. Liver and apples for dessert."

"You're a friend, Wigglesby."

"She's fun to drink with, though. Outrageous. Hey."

Hoffman, rising, checks.

"What d'you think's going on between our ingenue and the home-town boy?"

"Some ingenue," Hoffman says.

Maury's wife/Hoffman's rehearsal pianist/Sato's piano coach: Karen Jackstone arrives.

"God, Maury. I thought you were coming home for supper."

"Why, I had some pizza." Maury. "Want some?" Lights a match, picks up a slice of cold pizza, makes a serious show of moving the match back and forth underneath to warm it.

"I've got your supper at home."

"I've got your supper right here." Maury blows out the match, and offers her the slice. Karen stands on one foot, chrome-yellow hair brushed scrupulously back from her distressed forehead, her right hand gripping her left wrist. "Wait, I'll bless it for you," Maury says, making the sign of the cross over the anchovies. "Peace be on this pieca pizza, gonna be the unifoo for all mankin'. Fats say jus' foh'git 'bout manna, that manna for ol' test'mint squares."

"Oh, God, Maury."

"Say the Yukes gonna eat it in Yucatán, Mads be crazy for it in Madagascar, New Borns suck on it in New Borneo, mak'um nice, simple missionary pizza with extra cheese. Come on, Karen. Let go of your wrist. Sit down and have a beer with us."

Lumpy Karen looks almost grateful. Hoffman slides his chair sideways to make room for her.

"I was going to have Mona call you," he says. "We got a production meeting in half an hour, if you can make it."

"Good news, everybody. Davey. I just got fired."

Sue Riding, Ph.D. Math, our favorite check-out girl, unexpected at the Gump. She is tall, as her husband is, tiny-waisted, from Somewhere out West. Idaho? Dave doesn't have much waist on him either; willowy; Wyoming. They met in Moscow. Moscow, Idaho, at college there.

Those are points of resemblance in this slim couple, who might, if they stay together after this summer, have tall, willowy, Western children. But Sue's hair is fine and dark and her face thin and sometimes anxious; Dave's head looks thatched, and his face is round and pleasant. Maury once observed that since Dave has hardly any nose, the eyes and mouth are round, and the bleached hair cut Dutchboy style, you can mistake Dave's face for a child's drawing of a Tahitian hut.

Now he stands for his wife, reaches for her hands across the table. "That's good, Sue. I'm glad."

"A little dispute with a customer." Sue. "I was trying to give her breakage on three of a six for ninety-seven cents. She didn't understand."

"Bad scene?"

"The manager was all sympathy as long as the customer was there. Then when she left, he started telling me the store always gets breakage. I said, 'Except in the balls, Mr. Riley,' and that did it. Hey, everybody. Get six-packs and come out to the schoolhouse?"

"Hey, let's, everybody." Davey. "Mona, bring Mr. Hoffman out after your meeting, all right? Mike, bring your guitar. Okay, Maury?"

Dave's voice is higher than Sue's, rising almost to a squeak when he gets excited. Sue's is husky.

"Sure." Maury. "That's what to do."

Mona Shapen offers to drop off Hoffman, Karen, and Skeats. Then drop her husband off at the schoolhouse. Then return for the meeting.

"We can walk." Hoffman.

"Thanks for volunteering us, old boy." Skeats, taking Karen's arm.

"Oh." Karen. "I don't mind walking."

The three go out, turn left, start for Ralph's office in the Music Building. Short follows to the door, then excuses himself. He has had enough of being supernumerary at production meetings. It was tactful of Debbie, of course, to have made the call to him, as if he did have a place in this. But now the librettist will go home, visit with his children, suck up a drink, make a phone call to New Haven, maybe sneak a bite of something before German health-food time.

On the street Skeats keeps firm hold of Karen's arm. "Beautiful evening. Bloody beautiful. Will you go to the schoolhouse, then?"

"Maury's going."

"Pressing mulliggy close to Sidney, isn't he?" Arm around Karen's thickish waist.

"Oh. You don't understand about that." Karen trying to pull away a little.

"Tell us about the Ridings, Sue and Dave." Hoffman. "I liked her fire."

Karen slips nervously out of Skeats's grasp, wavers toward Hoffman. "Sue used to say. Used to tell. How Dave would sing all the time around the house. She said it was like living with some wonderful kind of bird."

"Didn't get on her nerves, huh?"

"Perhaps it's you that doesn't understand about your husband and bloody Sidney."

"Oh no, it never got on her nerves. Sue loved it. She could tell where he was and what he was doing and even what he was thinking about. They were very close, and the singing was just natural and unconscious. And spontaneous. Davey wouldn't even know he was singing."

"What about Maury, then? Does your bloke sing around the old household?"

"Not unconsciously. Not like a bird. Maury never does anything unconscious." Again Karen moves away from Skeats and against Hoffman. She and the director are now walking thigh to thigh. Does Karen ever do anything unconscious?

Her hand brushes the back of Hoffman's hand.

Hoffman registers hard—hand tingling hand, lumpy thigh against his nubbly one. Glances at the fine eyes, the pudding face—not unattractive in profile but bearing a certain fixed misery of expression—and past it at burning Skeats. Feels uneasy about this.

Karen could turn Hoffman on, of course, if she so chose; it wouldn't be much of a woman who couldn't. Hoffman hopes Skeats's lecherous moves will not force her so to choose.

"What happened with the Ridings, anyway?" he asks.

"It's this painter friend who lives with them, I think. His name is Charles."

A sort of race, oddly reminiscent of Sidney's turtle story: Davey Riding on his ten-speed bike, Dick Auerbach on his motorcycle. Dick reaching the schoolhouse, getting a joint and an ashtray from Maury, who was there first, roaring back to hand them unasked for to Davey.

Maury and Sidney waiting in the schoolyard by the aging red convertible that some alumnus gave Maury once, for coming here to play basketball.

Mona arrives, and drops Mike. Then Sue Riding, in the Ridings' Volkswagen van with fading daisies painted on its sides. Sue saw Marcel walking toward the Gump, his post-rehearsal rendezvous with some admirer or admirers ended; there are half a dozen boys who come daily to hear Marcel rehearse. Sue stopped for him.

Sue wants to fill the schoolhouse with everyone she knows tonight, to celebrate being fired. Invited Marcel, said there was a piano, Mike was bringing his guitar, maybe Maury'd get drums. So they stopped at State House for Marcel's clarinet.

As Sue and Marcel arrive, join Maury, Sidney, big Dick and little Mike outdoors, there is noise above the entryway of the schoolhouse, and a light comes on. Down a ladder leading through a trapdoor into the school-house attic comes a pair of feet in work shoes. Then patched denims. As the waist, with its cowboy belt squeezes down, Maury asks:

"That Charles?"

Sue, as the painter's work shirt comes into view, and then shoulders. "He sleeps all day on boards, across the attic beams."

The head comes last, bushy in two tufts, like an owl's. "Who's out there?"

"Come on down. We're going to have music, Charles." Sue, trilling low.

Charles descends, stands on the stoop, squinting. "I'm going into town."

"Oh."

"How come you're not working?"

Sue, gaily. "I got fired."

Charles. "Yeah? How we going to eat?"

"Stay for the music, Charles."

"I'm going into town."

"You already said that," says Mike Shapen, boy basso, not too softly.

"All right, then." Sue. "Shall I give you a ride in the van?"

"I want to walk."

"He wants to walk," Sue interprets.

"Glower, little glower worm . . ." Maury sings.

"Please, Maury?"

"Dimmer, dimmer. . . ."

They watch Charles disappear. A moment later Davey rides into the schoolhouse yard, no hands, smoking the joint, the ashtray balanced gracefully on his head.

Short hears the operator say: "I have a person-to-person call for Mr. Jethro Ffoliot."

"Speaking."

"Go ahead, please."

"Snazzer Short calling, Jethro."

"Ah, yes. How are you, sir?"

"Fine, thanks."

"And the delicious Maggi?"

Short doesn't want to tell his old classics teacher that Maggi and he are, for the moment, out of touch. "She's fine. Jethro, I want to ask you about a production there of Sophocles' *Ajax.*"

"Yes. There's only been one. It's a play I've never quite dared do myself. It's so doggedly anticlimactic at the end."

"This was supposed to have been in the Yale Bowl. . . ."

"Oh, no. No, not at all."

"Damn."

"It was in the outdoor ampitheater, but you see, it wasn't actually a university production at all. Does that dismay you?"

"Quite a bit."

"It was a new translation by some wealthy alumnus. A classics hobbyist, you know. He hired the space and paid the cast, I believe. But it wasn't much of a job."

"The production?"

"No. The translation wasn't much of a job. The production managed to overcome it, somehow. It was one of the most intelligent stage realizations of Greek tragedy I've ever seen. That long-winded debate at the end, you know? The man who directed had discus throwers and Greek wrestling going simultaneously, imitating the debaters' points. Girls with laurels, and others weeping. It was lovely."

"Thank you, Jethro. Thanks."

"One more thing, okay?" Hoffman. The meeting is almost over. "I'm going to see the kids at the schoolhouse tonight. I'll be the bad-news man."

"Type casting, would you say?" Skeats.

"This is for you, too." Hoffman.

"Oh, yes." Sato, rising, with a smile. "Yes, we have discussed this, Mr. Hoffman, Miss Dieter Haas, and myself."

"Discussed bleeding what?"

"What Mr. Hoffman will say. I endorse. I must go quickly to the orchestra now. And so, good night, Karen. Good night, Mona. Everybody. Are you coming, Ralph?"

Ralph stands, puts his glasses on, and follows.

"All right, bad news, old boy.

"Hair cuts," Hoffman says. "Short hair all around for 1949. And clean shaves, unless you want to keep a moustache."

"No. Absofuckingbloodyloutely not." Bearded Skeats.

"You must do it, Hughmore." Debbie. "Not that Mr. Hoffman says, but I say. I design, I costume."

"Sorry, Debbie old girl. I simply shan't. Look, this Pill is back from the army, might have raised a fine old beard, don't you see? Come along, now."

"It will not look so right, Hughmore."

"It'll just have to look jolly wrong then, won't it?"

Hoffman. "It's what we all feel's best, you know? Sato, Debbie, and I."

"Yes, my dears, but I'm your producer, am I not? It's not exactly a voting matter. Suppose it were? Karen, would you vote to have Maury cut his Afro?"

"I don't know, Mr. Skeats."

"Mona, then. Shall Mike cut his hair? Come, our stage manager—"

The pale ferocity of her expression stops him, yet on Mona Shapen even pallor and fury are becoming. She is a small, elegant, sephardic beauty, with gleaming hair, enormous eyes behind enchantress glasses, and a strange, crippled hand. "Mike will cut his hair, Mr. Skeats."

"Oh, please." Hughmore. "It's Hughmore, Mona. Come along, then."

"Maury will have his Afro cut, Mr. Skeats. Davey Riding will have his hair cut. Henry Fennellon will shave off his moustache if directed to. Dr. Mason's hair is short already, but he will shorten it further if required. Marcel and Dick will have their hair cut, Mr. Skeats."

"Well, oh, see here, Mona. You mustn't be all wrought up."

"The stage manager has to represent the cast."

"Well, of course, my dear."

"Do you intend to exempt yourself from what's required of the others?"

"See here, I have bloody-good reason. I've been up there with the beard in ten operas. It's a trademark, isn't it? Like the cough-drop Johnnies."

"I can't serve as your stage manager, Mr. Hoffman. Naturally, I'll stay to help with lights and props."

"Naturally you won't get paid, my girl." Skeats.

"Hey, Mona." Hoffman. "It isn't worth it, you know?"

"Please, Mona." Debbie.

"I'd like my name taken off the program."

"Okay." Hoffman pats her hand. "You're right. Good girl, Mona."

"I can't represent the cast if there is to be special privilege."

"Oh, allocky-ballocky, off goes the beardo. All right, Mona?"

"Thank you, Mr. Skeats." Beautiful Mona. "Would you like a ride to the schoolhouse with us and Mr. Hoffman?"

"Good God, no. Not bloody likely."

"Was that Charles walking toward town?" Davey, dismounting.

Sue. "Let's go in."

"I said 'Hi,' didn't get an answer."

"Come on, everybody."

"He's mad because your wife got fired." Mike.

Sue turns, goes into the schoolhouse. Big white globes of milk glass, suspended from the ceiling, turn on as the others enter. Dave wheels the ten-speed in with him. He had one stolen last spring; a cable cutter will handle most bicycle locks, and there are trucks that cruise the night, looking for unattended bikes on streets and country lanes.

"Oh, let's put a blanket on the poor thing." Sidney, patting the bicycle. "It might get a chill."

Dick laughs.

Dave says, "All right, Richard. At least I can bring my hoss indoors to pet. It doesn't blow back and leak oil on the floor like your monster."

"These noodles are very good, Debbie."

"Yes, I make them myself. I use whole wheat flour, powdered eggs for not-so-much cholesterol, and special oil, I forget the name."

"Safflower?"

"God bless."

Mona drives, Karen sits in the middle, Hoffman on the right. Karen's knee finds Hoffman's. Compassionate Billy gives the knee a pat, moves out of contact, and says:

"Maury knows, huh?"

"What, Billy?" Karen, boldly.

"All about Dick and Sidney."

"Please don't ask me. I don't want to get anybody mad."

Mona. "It's pretty obvious they were married, isn't it? Mike and I have known Dick and Sidney for three years, and they've never actually said so, but—"

"I wish we'd talk about something else." Karen.

Hoffman's guess. "My guess is they still are."

"Oh, Marcel lovekins, let's see." Sidney wrests the black leather clarinet case from the big tenor. No, she doesn't. The movement begins with wresting and resistance. But then she gets into position to push her whole, small trunk against his massive side, bosom to elbow, stomach to hip, pelvis to lower thigh with a wiggle. Marcel's grip on the clarinet case melts, and he moves away, leaving her with it.

Opens the case. "Oh, beautiful. It's so French." Holds up the mouthpiece, opens the packet of reeds. "Let me lick your reed for you?"

Beth. "Are you going to play?"

Maury. "What have you got for sticks, Davey? My cocktail drum's still here."

Dave at the piano, over his shoulder. "Pair of brushes, in the piano bench."

Mike. "Mona's bringing the guitar."

Johnny Ten. "Got metal washtub, Sue, and an old guitar string? We can make us a gut bucket."

Debbie, reporting to Short on the showdown over Skeats's beard. "But then Billy Hoffman says that Mona is right. Here, Rugby, is the brandy."

"I can see it. But as soon as Hoffman said she was right, then Skeats could be mad at Billy and give in to Mona."

"It was Mona who was not resistible. But Hoffman, how Skeats hates him."

To make a gut bucket: Take an E string. Tie it to the top of a stick about four feet long. Tie the other end to your washtub handle. Now wedge the butt of the stick into the opposite handle, with the washtub upside-down on the floor. Secure it in such a way that there is good tension on the string, which tension you can slightly increase and decrease as you pull the top of the stick into your shoulder with the left hand. With the right you will strum that string, and from the washtub sounding board will come a note—even a variety of notes as stick-pressure is varied—like notes from a primitive string bass.

Get Maury swishing on a cocktail drum, hope that Mike, when his guitar arrives, can play the changes, and that Davey Riding's left hand is strong on the piano, and you will be part of an almost respectable rhythm section.

Take no solos.

As Mona with Mike's electric guitar, Karen, and acoustic Hoffman enter, Davey is saying to Marcel: "That's the best I can do for an A."

Marcel: "I'll tune one tone high, and transpose down."

Accomplishing which mysterious feat, he begins to play a blues line with the same authority and ease Hoffman has relished in his singing. But this is play.

Maury starts the brushes moving; Johnny Ten, softly, the gut bucket. Davey a chord or two. Then they all stop, more or less at the same time, for Mike to set up the guitar.

"Marcel, that's pretty." Even Sidney's response is genuine this once.

"Karen," says Dave. "You play piano. I'm going out to the stash."

Karen. "Have you something I can read?" Dave has sheet music. "Angel Eyes." "Satin Doll."

Karen. "I'd rather hear you play."

Dave. "I'm going to the stash. Hey, Sue, walk me out?"

"I've got to make coffee. For Mr. Hoffman."

Hoffman would decline if he could. Dave goes. Hoffman turns over a brown bag full of canned beer to his hostess, and wishes secretly for nasty whiskey.

"We've got some fruit wine, if you'd rather," Sue Riding says.

But "Angel Eyes" doesn't sound bad, at all.

Skeats pushes his way to the bar at the Gump, between a short, morose man and a trim redhead whom he has observed drinking by herself.

"Not afraid all that beer will ruin your figger?"

"Are you speaking to me?"

"If you don't object, I should very much like to speak with you."

"Maybe I do object."

"Then I shall run out onto the street and throw myself in front of the first large truck."

"Oh, I know who you are. You're Hughmore Skeats. I've heard you sing."

"Thank you."

"You're in an opera with a doctor I know. Johnny Ten Mason."

"Quite right. Quite right. I know him, too. Will you tell me your name?"

"Everybody calls me Tuttle. I'm in radiology, up at the hospital."

"Well, Tuttle. Do you shoot pool?"

"A little bit."

"Shall we have a game, then? Cue sticks, balls, and pockets, eh, Tuttle?"

Dave returns, distributes pot, and, with his gentle smile, consents to replace Karen at the piano.

They play "Laura," and Mike takes an interesting single-string solo, then trades fours with Marcel's clarinet as Maury, using the hard rubber knobs at the ends of the brush handle, turns the rhythm section to stop time. Marcel doubles the beat, modulates, and segues into "Balling the Jack" at electrifying speed. He's too fast for Dave, who can hit only one chord a measure now, laughing about it, and for Mike—so Dave and Mike combine guitar and piano, alternating on the upbeats; Johnny Ten stays with it; and Maury tries to push Marcel faster and faster, until the whole thing dissolves in happy shouts of defeat.

"Regroup, group," shouts Maury, throwing the brushes into the air, and Marcel, the winner, hits a last wild lick.

"Sing one, Davey," Mike says. "Sing 'Summertime.' " This brings Karen back to the piano, and stands Dave up, singing so high and true and with such a lovely clarinet obbligato from Marcel that Hoffman can barely believe they are unrehearsed. None of them, he supposes, would play this music publicly—suddenly he recalls a party where actors were playing charades, none of them a specialized mime but all with enough training in it so that their skylarking had the charm of complete proficiency.

Then, in the second chorus, comes a change: Beth has been beckoned at, to join her voice with Dave's—they have very much the same range—and the session takes on the quite different quality of music being performed seriously. Slow Billy Hoffman, not until the chorus is almost done, almost part of his past, something to haunt the memory, does he realize why the change in intensity. He will wonder, on certain sleepless nights to come, why he didn't listen harder, concentrate on and absorb every never-to-be-repeated note, forgetting that he was somewhat distracted by Sidney, standing behind him kneading his shoulders while helpless Dick looked on, and somewhat more by watching the loveliness of Mona Shapen, who looks as if she has forgotten to breathe, so focused is she on the music.

The high male voice, the great low female throb, the clarinet:

"So hush little baby, don't you cry-iy-iy-iy-iy . . ."

Jesus, Billy, don't you see? Dave is singing, and with him Beth, and playing behind them Dave's friends, Mike, Maury, Karen (and perhaps Marcel's sensitivity, like Beth's, maybe even Johnny Ten's inclination toward healing, are engaged by this): for Sue Riding, for Dave's estranged fine wife. Melt your heart, Sue, melt your heart. Hush. Sue, don't you cry.

Hoffman wonders what can be so wrong that the proud, tall girl turns away, even walks a step toward the easel, where Charles's current painting stands, waiting for the artist to resume his work, before she turns back, looks at them all, mouth a little open, a dark look and sad.

Ralph Lekberg is in his bed asleep and dreaming. He dreams that a lamb is crying in the kitchen, but that he cannot find it. He dreams that he has taken a shower, and dried himself, and walked out to his car to drive to town, but preoccupied, so that he has forgotten to put on any clothing. Then he dreams that he is in Mexico, and that it is all right to be nude, because the Mexicans cannot see him.

"So, Ringby, I think you should go on the airplane to Chicago, and find Maggi. She will be at a hotel, you have only to go to each one and inquire."

"She'd hate me for it, Debbie."

"You think she is with someone, then?"

"I'd rather not think about it. She does this, Debbie, when my children come to visit. It isn't that she can't get along with them, but she doesn't feel related to them. And, you know, I think she feels she's being tactful in a way? Letting me enjoy them by myself."

"I think you are dreaming, but it is not my business, will I answer the telephone?"

"Yes, please."

"You want to talk some more about Maggi, I will let it ring."

"Please, answer it."

"Hello. . . . Sato! . . . Yes, I am drunk with Riggleby Short. You must come. . . . You must put me to bed and drive home Mr. Short. . . . No, Sato, you come now, you may have some port."

"He coming?"

"He has been rehearsing his strings. Don't tell him that we hire Hoffman."

"All right, Debbie."

"Don't tell anybody."

Sidney is taking a turn as chick vocalist, singing "God Bless the Child," and Dick a turn at the gut bucket. Hoffman, not one of the world's great heads, passes the roach Beth hands him on to Johnny Ten, who doesn't use it either, but passes it to Sue.

Josette Lekberg stops the pickup truck at the side door of Henry Fennellon's farmhouse, a couple of hundred yards away from her own, where Ralph lies sleeping. That other farmhouse is indeed Josette's, for her Basque parents, still in Europe (her brother has been jailed recently by the Spanish police), provided, in effect, a dowry with which this farm was bought. Josette's parents could understand buying a farm to raise sheep on, and visited here with pride a year ago.

Josette needs to borrow a hypodermic. One of her lambs seems to have pneumonia, and she wants to give it a shot of combiotic before she joins her husband in sleep. But sometimes, on a soft summer night like this, it is hard for Josette to see Henry Fennellon, with whom she has been in love since the moment she met him, and whom she continues to love steadily, fiercely.

Neither of them has ever spoken of it, or acted on it, and Josette thinks that tonight it will even be hard for Henry to see her. Maybe she will drive away, and look again for a clean hypodermic at home.

"Josette?" The door opens, and Henry stands there with the light behind him, wearing only pajama pants.

"Have you a needle for combiotic?" She slides across the seat, and looks at him, four or five feet away, through the open right-hand window of the truck.

"Yes. Do you want to come in?"

"Yes. No."

"Stay as you are. I'll get the needle."

Sidney wants to try the gut bucket.

Dick. "Let me show you how to hold it."

"Darling Muscles, I know how to hold it. I've been watching you for hours and hours, with unspeakable admiration."

Mike wants to play "High Society," so that Marcel can do the Alphonse Picou solo for them.

"What's the tempo?" Maury asks; Marcel answers with rhythmic snapping of the fingers, but before Maury can pick it up on the drum, Sidney disengages herself from the gut bucket again.

"I don't know what you gentlemen are going to play," she says. "But I think I'll play with myself in the moonlight."

"That means she's going out." Dick. "In case some of us dim males didn't get it."

"That is correct. I'm going to find a nice bush, and pee, under the stars. Marcel, honey, want to come with?"

Instead of leaving, she moves to stand facing Hoffman, her knees touching his, not much taller than a child.

"Here we are, Tuttle."

"What a nice place."

"It's yours."

"Don't you really have a wife?"

"I'm between wives, old girl." Mrs. Skeats is actually traveling in Europe. "Like to have a try at the job?"

Mike and Mona Shapen, with a baby-sitter to discharge, have left. Mike said he'd drop off the baby-sitter, nearby, and come back for a last beer and a good-night pull on the joint.

Sidney. "Mr. Hoffman?"

The background music, with Maury picking up Mike's guitar, is soft and wild.

"Sit down, Sidney."

"I can't."

They are playing something of Marcel's invention called "Whole Tone Rose." It requires playing four bars of "Honeysuckle Rose" and then, in place of the next four, running up and down the whole-tone scale. Back to the original melody for bars 9 through 12, and whole-tone it again. It's either exotic or decadent, Hoffman can't decide which; music to smoke pot by, he supposes, and understands why Maury is laughing as Dick and Davey supply strange arhythmics on gut bucket and piano.

On the sofa Sue Riding has gone to sleep.

Hoffman. "What's the matter, Sidney?"

"I've got to leave."

"I got no car. You want me to tell someone?"

"No. Please don't. Would you walk me back to town?"

"If you want."

"I don't know what I want."

Hoffman rises. Sidney moves, not toward the door but toward the big north windows. He moves beside her. The easel is between them and the stars.

"All these one-room school buildings are alike," she says. "I went to one when I was little. Is that me behind the hippopotamus?"

She points at one of the figures in the half-done painting. It is an attractive, rather romantic painting of strange, mythological animals in a starry night, a little Rousseau-like, but what the hell, Hoffman likes Rousseau. A bestiary. The figure Sidney points to is like one of those little Malaysian night animals, furry and shy, with enormous eyes.

"Is that how you see yourself?"

"I sat right here, by the window, in first grade. Where the easel is, hoping recess would never come. The other children hit me at recess. It was their favorite game. I was youngest, and they were all related to each other, cousins and brothers and sisters, but my family had just moved out to the country then, and I had to be in their school. Just like this one."

"Then it's strange for you to have it full of wild sounds, and people partying, no teachers keeping order, and those other little boys and girls gone from your life."

"Are they?"

She nods, pensive, then inches her feet apart, rises slowly onto tiptoe beside him, and whispers. "I still have to pee." Then she inhales, and exhales in a long hissing sound, so close the breath plays like water on his cheek.

"Look what I have made for you." Sato takes out a neat little package, and hands it to Debbie.

"Made it where?"

"At Ralph Lekberg's. He has fine tools for working wood."

Debbie opens the package. Inside are ten little squares of wood, each carefully polished, and with letters on them, on one side. Each letter has an accent: à á â è é ê ç ä ö ü

"Sato! And will they match it?"

"Yes. I took one of your pieces, to match the wood stain."

He puts an s down beside the pieces he has made, turns them all

» 329 «

over, mixes them up. There is no telling from the backs which piece is not new.

"Oh, we must play. Rugby, are you too drunken for Scrabble?" She burrows for her set.

"Debbie, I don't see how in hell you can play Scrabble even sober." Short, weaving.

Sato. "We may beat you, Mr. Short. After you make a word in English, the next must be German, and the next French."

Henry hands the hypodermic needle in through the truck window to Josette, plunger first, holding it so their fingers will not need to brush.

"Good night, Josette." Stands there.

"Good night, Henry." Drives away.

"I thought you had to go out?" Dick.

"Oh, I do. I do, very badly." Sidney, pressing her knees together.

Dave. "Our bathroom's in good order, Sidney."

"No, no. Outside, outside. So pretty, darlings. Marcel, come with? No, he won't. May I take your flashlight, Richard dear?"

Dick shrugs. Sidney picks up his key chain from the table; it has a penlight hanging from it, along with the keys.

Sidney turns it on, and gropes her way, holding her crotch with one hand, through the well-lighted room.

Beth. "Darling as a plum tree blooming."

Dick. "Hell. Let's play."

As they turn back to the instruments, there is a roar outside. Dick's motorcycle, starting. Dick runs to the door, but Sidney is away on the Honda and headed for town before he can stop her.

"Goddamn her."

"Just what I do to Pill in the opera." Marcel.

Dick. "Dave, let me take your ten-speed?"

"Sure, but why not let her go?"

"She's got my apartment key on that ring."

"Sleep here. Take the bike, the van, whatever you want."

"Beth and I are going." Johnny Ten. "Come on, we'll run after her with you."

"To hell with Sidney. Let her go." Dick, blustering, unhappy. "Got any more tea, Dave?"

"Plenty."

"Open up, Tuttle."

"God, it's so big."

"Open up, damn it. There, that's my girl. That's my girl. That's my girl."

Karen leaves with Beth and Johnny; wary Hoffman, though getting sleepy, decides to decline the chance to occupy the back seat with Karen, which leads to the following, curious, softly spoke exchange:

Maury. "She's rich, Mr. Hoffman. Very rich."

Hoffman. "Yeah? And tell me, do the nice young Auerbachs have any children?"

Then Mike is back. Dick, Marcel and Hoffman are still here. And Maury, and so, of course is Davey Riding.

Sue is, too, but fast asleep on the sofa.

"We better go." Hoffman.

"Oh, yes." Marcel. "So you can put your lovely wife to bed."

"Thank you so much for playing, Marcel." Dave. "You don't know what a privilege it is for us to work with you this summer."

"Why, thank you. Thank you very much."

"Will you sit down a minute, Marcel, please? And Mr. Hoffman? Will you have a drink. I have some bourbon. Never go to bed this early anymore."

"But your pretty Sue." Marcel. "She can't be very comfortable."

"She generally sleeps there on that sofa, and often in her clothes, and won't want waking."

Dave.

Tender and troubled, he covers Sue, nudges a pillow under her head, skillful in managing the great, dark stream of hair. She sighs, half-smiles, settles, doesn't wake.

15: A Bad Spring for Everybody's Wife

"My tired check-out girl." (Davey Riding, crooning rueful, stepping soft away from the battered sofa where she sleeps.) "That's a rock-and-roll thought, isn't it?"

(Pouring bourbon for Stubby Hoffman, Big Marcel; Black Maury, Swarthy Mike, and Dick the Roan, fruit-wine drinkers, lovers of maryjane, declining).

There's no way I can tell you, gentle friends,
The level of Sue's mind. She comprehends
Books at whose mere titles my mind wearies:
Axiomatic Sets, Undecidable Theories,
Topology of Three-Dimension Manifolds.
The Fifty-nine Icosahedra holds
Her close attention, one hour to the next,
I glance, and see her smiling at the text,
And wonder what it is she knows? My pride,
My joy, my wonder, my despair, my bride.

I'd heard of Susan. Everybody had
Who went to school in Moscow. Some were glad,
And others quite upset at what she did:
"She's disrespectful!" "No, a gutsy kid."
She was a junior, and declined Phi Bete,

The campus paper interview was great.
        Sue said:
"Should I accept? Join the pretense
That nothing matters but intelligence?
Phi Beta Kappa stands for vanity of mind—
What are the letters for learning to be kind?"

Sue's grandfather had been first president
Of that school, and its old establishment
Was generally resentful—but not me,
A student there from practicality.
They had a small bequest, a buck or two
To help an undergraduate composer through.
(And if my choice of college still seems strange,
There's lovely skiing in the Sawtooth Range.)

I saw her first on skis. "Hey, reckless Sue!"
Some guy who didn't know a ski boot from a shoe
Yelled at her. I could recognize control—
To turn she barely had to use a pole.
I watched her skim the crust. Followed her track,
Knew she was someone whom the snow loved back.

Snow understood her, and I wanted to.
But Sue found me. One day I got a blue
Memorandum asking my consent
To be the subject of experiment.
Did a composer's creativity
Involve numeric concepts? By comparing me,
For instance, with a physicist she'd try
The theory. Asked me to stop by.
She programed me with the computer Doris,
She tested me with a control named Horace,
Fed me to calculator X 7-4,
And read me out. It paid three bucks an hour.

"Did you find out?" "It's negative." She smiled.
"Except for random overlap. A child

Or idiot could test statistically
Within that range of probability."
"Will you have coffee with this idiot?" I said.
"Do what?" "You know. Black stuff. It comes in red
Plastic cups. At the College Inn."
She looked so serious I had to grin.
"Young males and females sit at tables there
And drink it. And converse." She touched her hair:
"Now you *are* thinking like a physicist
Only I find you harder to resist."

Stepped forward to be kissed. Soft eyes
Showing consent, and also some surprise
At my initiative. Later she told
Me she had planned some bold
Move of her own, if I had lacked the grace—
Our clothing fell away, there in the testing place.

(Rueful, walking to the window, looking out, turning, looking soberly at
dopey, sleepy, half-drunk Hoffman—as with the music earlier, it seems uncertain big-ears Billy can be hearing this, as it will seem in his remembering, fuzzing, fogging, fading.)

I wanted to be married quickly. No.
Sue's family is an old one as things go
Out West. Five generations down from homesteading.
Mine's only four. Both said the wedding
Must wait till all the generations met.
We begged, but they were absolutely set:
Grandparents should know grandparents. Dad
Should ride with Dad. Each mother had
Dinners to serve across state lines, and dozens
Of my young nephews to play with Sue's young cousins.

Are there degrees of such a sacrament?
If so, then we were married to the nth.
"That's an indefinitely large ordinal number, hon,

To go with your definitely large carnal member." Fun
Had to be made. With foolish jokes—
Whispered before we'd even left her folks'—
We mocked our own intensity to reach
A love too deep for other modes of speech.

So we came here. Sue for her Ph.D.
(*Where* didn't matter all that much to me.)
Pure math—if that means anything to you—
Applied math seems too easy to my Sue.
She studied for a year, and I began,
Then, quite expectedly, the money ran
Thin as a discount guarantee on an appliance.
Our families believed in self-reliance.
Sue said she'd drop till I had my degree.
Read Russian. Earn some kind of salary.
I countered: I'd work first for her. We'd save.
　　　　　Sue said:
"No. Your commitment's greater, Dave.
You have your goal so certainly in sight—
To teach young singers, sing yourself, and write
Music that only you were born to make.
My doctorate comes second. I can break
Off any time, and pick it up again
When we get settled somewhere. Then
I'll start my dissertation, have my turn
To make a contribution. Hon, I yearn. . . ."

There was no question what she yearned for so.
I did as well. In northern Idaho,
Up in the foothills, lies her family ranch,
Nine thousand acres, crossing it a branch
Of the Flathead River. Cattle, sheep and deer,
Grouse, trout, and grayling grow together there.
Timber and hay. See, my old family dig
Is twice as prosperous and half as big.
Sue would inherit. She's an only daughter,

Two brothers lost in the Korean slaughter.
It's still the only place for us. I clung
To thinking of it—till this spring got sprung.

(Dick looking at Mike, Mike at Maury, Maury at goofy Hoffman, Marcel
closing his great brown eyes, shy of the circle of contact, yet minding like
the others Davey Riding's hurting, haunting, husking.)

Sue joined the pool of talent, charm, and brain
Which this community of business men can drain
To get their donkey work done: Student wives,
Doubly selected. First: They choose these lives
As grubby internships in gracious living.
And second: They've *been* chosen—giving
The males who choose them (otherwise
Easy enough to mock and satirize)
This unfamiliar credit—I'll be indiscreet—
Grad students are your only young elite.
Preening, ridiculous; like it, friends, or not,
We're about all the future that you've got.

From an employer's standpoint, see our women:
Attractive, energetic, smart, and driven.
They really want to work, and do it well,
To help the husband (sometimes wife) excel.
This couple flames toward comfort and distinction.
If he can't make it, sorry girl, extinction
Of a whole catalogue of dreams, gone with a sob.
She works. She works. She will not flunk the job.

Still the employer bitches. Every second year or third,
This bright, remarkable young woman, whom he hired
To keep his swindle going at the rate
Paid to a high-school stenographic graduate,
Finishes putting husband through and leaves.
Curses. Excoriation. Ire. He grieves:
"Hey! Where's her loyalty? This is some crappy
Job market. Right?" As if this sappy

Real estate dullard, shingle man, insurance clown,
Could hire such talent in some other town.
And after underpaying, year by year,
For comprehension, vigor, and the clear
Thought of youth, this man of thumbs,
Who lives by hustling students, farmers, other bums,
Has to break in another lovely, overqualified
Young woman. In a week he can confide
The dull and grubby details of his life
Into the hands of this new, neat student wife.
Leaving him not much to do but watch,
Poor clown, and scheme to reach her crotch.
Somewhat abusive when she says, "No thanks."
Pities himself. Makes his collections. Banks.

Sue couldn't go for that. She tried a place
Or two. And couldn't bring herself to face
Those mute, crestfallen roosters. Made
A fast descent from office work to trade.
She was a waitress, then a check-out girl,
A seamstress. Then one month she took a whirl
At taxi driving, which she liked quite well.
I worried. Didn't say so. Sue could tell.
She quit. Pretended that my fear for her
Was her fear. That's how very close we were.

There's one more choice: a university spot,
Teaching assistants here aren't paid a lot.
Sue took a job up in the Children's Ward.
Mentally ill kids. And she took it hard.
Some women love hurt animals the best,
Sue wants to take stray humans to her breast.
That time I trespassed: "Please leave, hon." And then
Back to the check-out went my Sue again.

(Summoning, organizing, thought into word, word into line, caring, meaning, telling it to himself, and to Mike smoking, Maury smoking, Dick

chewing something, Marcel slumped and staring, Hoffman chewing something, too, a dead cigar, lipping, looming, liquefying.)

Now what I've got to talk about's the drones,
We little princelings, on our classroom thrones,
Crowned by our willing, drudging mates,
A curious reversal now takes place:
Because she's dressed to cool off Sir Clown,
Because she wears not makeup but a frown,
Because her days are long, her tasks routine,
Because her work's concerns are small and mean,
Because her mind gets little light or air,
The wife becomes the plainer of the pair.

Because he toils not, neither does he fret,
Because his clothing risks not dirt nor sweat,
Because he's cherished for his future role,
Because the way for him to pay the toll,
To compensate the drabness of her days,
Is to be charming, sunny, full of praise,
The husband blooms. His shirt is bright and new,
His pants fit slickly. Bottles of shampoo
Are more for him than her. Ah, what a jewel,
Trimmed down by handball, coming from the pool,
Humming of classroom time and preparation.
The daily hours of work at his vocation
Are one, or two, or three, and seldom more,
Even assistants teach no more than four.

There's lots of time for him (unless, like Maury,
He gets compulsive. That's another story)
To spread and lounge and polish up his wit
With other husbands. Beer goes well with it,
Or coffee in the morning. Visiting and chatter,
Billiard and Ping-Pong balls in swish and clatter,
And quite a lot of looking to be done
At girls less careworn than his wedded one.
Assistant? Then at twenty-two, our boy can strut

Into a classroom full of teen-age pretties, gut
Sucked in, beard trimmed, our shining blade,
To lecture, tease them, guide, and finally grade,
Or soothe their little academic desperations
In office tête-à-têtes. Such situations
Breed guilt, and guilt resentment. When it stops
He's got home duties: cooks, makes beds, and shops.
Weary to stir-fried dinner comes the wife,
He knows his soys and chiles, with a knife,
Can french a bean, or butterfly a shrimp,
She takes her shoes off, not inclined to primp,
She'd settle for a turkey TV dinner,
If only it were ready. She grows thinner.
"Honey, let's eat and hit the flicks," he says.
"You go." "We can meet Mike and Maury?" "Please
Forgive me but I'd rather sleep." She's dull,
Isn't she? Poor darling. Lovely fool.
If children come, it's different, but still—
After you've worked construction, paid the bill
At Student Health—she goes to work again.
You do some sitting, pay for day care. Then
The days begin again, hers drab, yours glistening—
So comes the weekend, and the listening.

Mike and I spotted the phenomenon.
This special listening goes on and on,
Follows a party to relax when Friday ends:
A small, serene affair with pot and friends,
A Friday sleep together. Saturday does come.
Now you are loose and private in your home.
She will not hurry off to heartburn, toil,
Nor you to class. Today nothing can spoil
The listening game. Perhaps her greatest pleasure,
It overtures the future you both treasure.
Here's how Mike put it, one December day:
"Mona's gone home for Christmas, but I've got to stay
And study." "Eat with us. Chip in for beers."
"Know what I'll miss? Those dusky little ears,

Those little whorled receptacles for guff
That I pour in them—that's the part that's tough."
"You too?" That's when we saw it first,
The well of young men's fancies, and the thirst
Their partners have to drain it to the sludge,
Each day-dreamed triumph, hope, each paid-off grudge.
Your voice goes on, your troubles, schemes, and thoughts,
So does the coffee, pots and pots and pots.
Daydreams. This cantata that I'm going to write,
This truck we ought to get. This really bright
Chance for a job out there. "This mean
Trio I want to write for slot machine
And eighteen instruments, and two old hags,
Instead of a conductor, hon, they're dressed in rags,
They fight each other in a kind of dance
To pull the handle next, and so by chance,
—Instead of fruits and bells and cards, intense
Interest develops in which three instruments
Will come up next to play the next twelve bars. . . ."
Stuff like that, friends, for narcissistic hours.

These wives are lousy candidates for lib,
They dig it, and they'll pay a certain glib
Lip service, but you know that it won't last,
After the years of hanging in, steadfast
As heads of households, what they want to see
Is what their guys will do to set them free.
They're ready to be hostesses and decorate
Nice homes. Rear pretty children. Stay up late.
Sleep in the morning. Buy stuff. Maybe roam
A little. Have a studio at home.
But now supported, moving up in class,
Their growth's been stunted, and it's time to pass
The old lunch bucket on to other hands.
Let husband work now, while the wife expands.

And Mike said: "Books. Professors. Friends. Great trips.
Uncritically spew from my self-sounding lips.

Speaking of which, you should have heard me rave
About that damn recital that I gave
Back home. We held four tickets for reviewers—
The bastards must have been inspecting sewers,
Or covering a rat show at the city dump.
None came. Some critic's head deserves a lump.
And when they do review, they don't know crap
From Christ, if it were sitting in their lap.
I'll write some music criticism someday. . . ." See?
Mike talked, she listened, just like Sue and me.

We started checking other married guys.
I asked a dental student. It was no surprise
To have him answer, "Yeah. 'Bout once a week
I'll start about an oral-surgery technique
That sounded dumb. About state boards and specialities,
Or joining a group practice with M.D.'s."
Mike asked a law-school friend whose wife had split,
"You know, I see I should have thought of it.
We kept on screwing, but the listening stopped.
I should have known that's when the bottom dropped."

We marry ears, belief. She wants to hear
Sounds from the life she's going to have next year.

Marcel and Mr. Hoffman:
            Maury, Dick, and Mike,
Might help me tell you what this spring was like.
Without loud fights, or scenes, or open strife,
It was a bad spring for everybody's wife.
I spoke of Fridays' parties. Saturdays'
Are different in a dozen kinds of ways.
Bigger, more strangers. Drunker, less rapport,
Especially when they're thrown by Maggi Short.
Along with Hughmore Skeats, she gave a blast—
About the time this opera was cast—
Each Saturday at Short's house. A ferment
Of spring excitement, breathless accident.

There was a perfume, and a reckless spirit,
Odd, fervent, public but intimate.
Music, and bodies pressing, tongue to ear—
Abandon chastity who enter here.
Play wastrel, is there something you might lose?
Not us, we felt, and Hughmore bought the booze.
   Maggi said:
"I haven't known this music school.
Hey, have I ever been discretion's fool!
You've got some wiggle in your boyish butts,
Not like the English-student putt-putt-putts.
The music's strong. Let's wiggle one tonight.
I've got a weakness for performers. I'm half-tight.
Kiss me, you ass, I'm weak."
     Snazzer would stay
Till ten or so, and then he'd start to sway
And disappear upstairs, bottle in hand,
Foxtrotting to some never-never band.
One week he left.
   Maggi said:
     "All gone
Off lecturing to Minnesota. I'm alone.
What can I do with him? His act's not bad.
He could charge fifteen hundred bucks, and they'd be glad
To pay it, if he'd get his new book ready.
His agent sends him screenplays. There's a steady
Demand for Snazzer Short. The lecture stint
Just takes publicity and management.
He sets his fee down at the usual level:
Three hundred bucks, a piece of ass, and travel.
To hell with him. Hey, Maury babe, let's shove.
Give me some pelvis." God, to see her move
Made Karen leave the party. That was it,
The first time Maggi did the standard bit
Of picking someone off quite openly
To dance, then, chuckling, off to privacy.
She'd never do it with the same guy twice,
   Maggi said:

"Sometimes an affair is nice,
But always quite emotional, and takes
Your time and thought completely, till it breaks
Off, messy as marriage; it can be a pile
Of sighs and thrills and laughs, if, for a while,
It's what you want to do with your sweet time.
But one-night stands for Maggi! They're sublime.
Gaspy, and sentimental, undemanding,
Fun, no harm done, if there's an understanding.
Nice memories of a mutual courtesy,
Charm of the unfamiliar. Mystery."
      Maggi said:
"But we protest the minute-dip romance
It's hardly been worth pulling up your pants,
And straightening your skirt around your hips.
At least insist, dear girls, on double dips."
(That husky voice that crawls around your pelt,
Tickles your stomach, loosens up your belt. . . .)
The other chicks. No. First time I've confessed
We were the women's chicks. Would you have guessed?
They were the wanton, bawdy, strong-winged hens,
There was a big, tough pretty one who drove an ambulance.
She made good money. Owned an Audi Fox.
She understudied Maggi. Got her rocks
Off with that lady once, so I've heard tell.
Sometimes a boy'd attract her, and Corinne would yell:
"Let's go, hero." Take him off to Davenport
For whiskey, and rock music and a little sport.
Grab all the checks. Get a motel room. Be
Back at the party about half-past three.
Maybe drop boy-chick home, with a goose and a wink.
Rev up and take off, laying rubber. There was Jody Skink,
A languorous, long southern girl, whom Hughmore cuddled.
Sometimes she liked him back, sometimes befuddled
Him with a hot, hand-squeezing intrigue
Behind his back, and one of us in league.
I think what she enjoyed was the snow job—
She'd meet you in the garden for a blow job,

All fast and sweet, say: "Hurry, darlin', mmmm,"
And Hughmore'd never know she'd left the room.
Maria Lisa, a big, bossa-nova coloratura,
Everything about her thoroughly bravura
(She's gone home to Brazil to sing down there),
Had energy to dance all night. Her hair
Smelled like cigars. She smoked them without cease,
And sang us dirty songs in Portuguese.
Those were the babes who heated up our lives,
Those, and some others, let alone our wives.
And samba was the beat. Your waltzing mate
Needing the weekend recuperate,
Couldn't forbid the Saturday affairs
And really couldn't stand them, either. Flares
Of temper might repel. The wife was trapped
Unless she opened parcels that were best left wrapped.

Technically, I stayed faithful. But one night
Went with Maria Lisa down a flight
Of stairs, into the basement bedroom, all
Sweaty, excited, ready for the ball.
We samba'd in the dark, tripped on the bed,
Fell down together. "Just a sec," I said.
Turned for a moment, just to lock the door,
And in that moment she began to snore.
Left her, passed out, half-naked, felt remorse
At coming close. Another night, of course,
I schemed with Jody, went outside and kissed her,
She knelt down in the garden. Hughmore missed her,
Came charging out. I hid, and then I ran.
Old Hughmore thought it was some other man.
When I got back, though, Sue had left the place.
I told myself that there was no disgrace,
That I'd done nothing, Sue had been a bore,
Stayed dancing, drinking, flirting there till four.
Woke with a smile, quite forgiving, lofty—
Susan was in the kitchen, making coffee.

We had a silly sadomasochist routine,
Verbal, with flourishes. I might say, quite mean,
In an Uncle Willie voice: "Say, wouldn't you
Love to be Mrs. Fields? Black and blue
I'll pinch you. Don't you touch this bastard.
I'll jump ten feet away and go get plastered."
Or: "Hey, now. You've just married Buster Keaton."
Give her the oogly eye. "You sit there eatin'
Strawberry shortcake. Yes. A sweet girl's dream,
Only it's garnished with my shaving cream."
Sue'd squeal, and try to hide. I'd stalk. We'd laugh,
And kiss and chase and pass all sorts of chaff.
That morning I said, "Howdy, Mrs. Groucho,
And how'd you like to play a game of oucho?
My big cigar is lit. Your tender tail . . ."
I stopped, dismayed there, seeing myself fail.
Sue shrugged and turned away to get a drink
Of water. Teardrops washed the kitchen sink.

Next Saturday I promised to behave.
Sue said, "I'm sorry. I'll go with you, Dave."
That was the night this painter, Charles, appeared
With his strange owl haircut and his scraggly beard.
We sympathized. The guy had been in jail
For sending marijuana through the mail.
Second offense. The first was stealing beef—
He's a good painter but a lousy thief.
He learned a lot of hate, there in the pen.
Sue hoped that we could get him straight again.
It's in her nature to adopt the blighted.
She offered him this studio, north-lighted.
I kind of liked him. At the school of art
They kind of hate him. Charles is not too smart.
He shows them his contempt. He curls his lip.
"Well, okay baby boy, no fellowship."
—No place to live. No place to paint. No bread.—
And Sue said, "Use our attic for your bed."

Good. Now she had an interest. I kept on
Hitting the pollen parties, went alone.
Came in at dawn one morning. There she slept.
I took my shoes off. Brushed my teeth. And crept
Into the bed beside her, nestled in.
When I awoke my arms were full of thin
Pillow, crushed against me. Sue was up.
Past the partition, I could see her hand, a cup
Of coffee in it. Then I damn near groaned
Aloud. Aloud. Because a man's voice droned—
Of colors. How to mix them true and lush.
Of how you couldn't buy a decent brush
Here in State City. It rehearsed in snarls
Injustices by teachers, done to Charles,
By God, he'd see that they were paid—
The spring is over, and I am afraid.

"Oh, no," says Marcel. "Oh, no, but why? It can't really be that
serious."

Hoffman. "Giving her ears. To the painter. Jesus."

And the phone goes off like an alarm clock. Davey Riding is up and has
it off the hook before the first ring ends, glancing at sleeping Sue, smiling
when she doesn't stir.

"Hello
        She's asleep
                I hate to wake her
What's the problem, Charles?
        Good God.
                I know you only get one call.
Talk slower, Charles. You're still drunk.
                No.
                        I'll come myself.
No, in the morning.
                Charles, I'm sorry. No.
                        We just don't have two hundred dollars.
She'd have to borrow it.
                I'll ask her in the morning, Charles.

No, I can't.
Good-bye."

"Drunk and fighting." Davey with a sigh, hanging up. "He's in the county jail. Charles."

"He hurt anybody?" Maury.

"I don't know. He wants bail."

"I can write a check." Marcel. "Do you want me to?"

"I think I want to talk to Sue first. In the morning."

Maury, muttering. "Recidivist . . ."

"What?"

"Third-time offender. Habitual criminal, if they've got a felony on him. Long time gone."

"Maybe it's just a misdemeanor."

"What is it? What was the phone call?" Now Sue is sitting up, looking at them wide-eyed over the sofa top.

"Charles."

"What's happened?"

"He's in jail, hon. He's all right."

"What did he do?"

"Got drunk. I think he threw a bottle at the bartender in Eddie's."

She has pushed up onto her knees, palms supporting on the sofa top. "What are we going to do?"

"There's not much we can do till morning. The bail's two hundred dollars."

Sue shakes her head. A tear forms. "We don't have it."

"It's all right, hon. I can borrow it, from the credit union."

"Please." Marcel. "Let me lend it to you. You'd have to pay interest at the credit union."

"Thank you, oh, yes." Sue jumps up, grateful, comes around. "Do you really have that much?"

"Not in cash, but . . . Maury, you seem to know. Would they take my check?"

"Not in this county. Hey, Sue. Won't hurt the man to sleep it off in jail."

"Oh, Maury."

"Let him wake up there scared. Every bartender in the county will want to buy you a drink."

"Stop it."

"No, I won't. Have you seen the bunks there in our jail? They're new. Foam-rubber pads. He'll have him a hell of a good night's sleep."

"Yeah, they're not bad." Mike suddenly coming into it. "We used to play cards for who'd get next turn on those bunks. They're okay—a lot better than a couple of boards across your attic beams, Sue. No kidding."

"Would they let me take him his sleeping bag?"

Maury. "No. Well, I could probably get us in. . . ."

"Come on, hon." Dave. "By the time we got there, he'd be sleeping. He probably is already. Charles is very drunk."

Sue allows herself to be sat down again on the sofa, Dave beside her.

"Hey, Mike." Hoffman. "You spend quite a bit of your time playing cards in jail here, do you?"

"During the demonstrations." Mike.

"When that girl flogged the sheriff with a dead rat." Dick remembering, laughing. "Boy, they got a couple hundred of us."

"The jail was jammed like a subway car."

Marcel, standing in front of Dave and Sue. "I'll meet you first thing in the morning there. Both of you? As soon as the banks are open. Please go back to sleep, Sue."

"Come on, hon. Lie down. Can I get you a drink?"

Sue is lying down, Dave has fixed her a light bourbon and water, the others are getting ready finally to go, when the phone rings again.

"Damn Charles." Mike.

"Oh, let me talk to him. Please?" It's Sue, fully awake again, stopping Hoffman with her voice. He was about to pick the obnoxious instrument up to stop its noise. "Please, Mr. Hoffman. Let me answer?"

They all stand back for her. The phone rings again. Sue picks it up. Discreetly, they pretend to turn away, not listen.

"Hello?"

Her face, composed into cheerfulness, falls puzzled. "Who? Oh, yes." Turning, holding the handset out toward anyone who might be willing to take it from her. "It's some man. For Maury."

"Yeah?" Maury taking the phone. "Maury Jackstone here." Then there is rather a long wait, while he listens, more and more carefully. "Is that so?" he says. Listens a while longer, thanks someone, and hangs us. "Well, Mr. David Riding. Got any controlled substance in your dungarees?"

"Huh?"

"Come on. Action. Get the dope out of this place, every shred. Butts, all of it. There's going to be a raid."

"What? What for?"

Maury isn't standing still to explain. He's emptying ashtrays into the toilet, but he calls: "My buddy, the sheriff. There's a patrol car on its way right now, with a warrant. To raid your happy home."

"Raid us?" Sue can't believe it.

"We're lucky the sheriff made the arrest. Not the State City cops."

"Arrest?"

Maury comes out, four or five empty ashtrays in his big hands. "Wash these, can you? Your man, Charles, Sue."

"What's he done?"

"Here take the ashtrays." Mike has taken over flushing. Mike is emptying his pockets of shreds. Dick has a whole tobacco pouch full, and waits in line for the toilet. Davey holds Sue's arms lightly from behind. Hoffman watches. "Sue, he's trying rather ineptly to bargain his way out of the slammer. He wants them to know there's a big drug party going on in this schoolhouse. Insisted that they write down all the names. Gave them mine—which was good. Hey, Sue?" The tears are starting from her eyes again. Maury's voice is careful, almost caressing. "Charles is a rat, Sue. Made them write down, 'David Riding,' for a dealer."

The tears roll now. Davey holds her.

"You better take my car and leave, Mr. Hoffman." Mike, done flushing, yielding to Dick, going for Dave's plastic envelope on the table; there's a cigarette-rolling machine, too, but Dave's too good a cowboy to need to use it. It's clean. "Mr. Hoffman? Charles wouldn't have known your name."

"I'll stick around."

"You sure?" Maury.

"Haven't been busted once so far this year, you know?"

"Nobody's getting busted," Maury says. "Listen to me now." Sue has left Dave's support and gone into the part of the room divided off by a counter for the kitchen, carrying ashtrays.

"He's not a rat, Maury. He's scared. You would be, too."

"You listen, too, Sue." Maury. "I know the guys who are coming. It's all cool. They'll know we got a call, all right? But they'll pretend they don't. And so will we, all right? Surprise, surprise, and let me do the talking."

"What about the stash?" Dave.

"Warrant's for the house and grounds. It won't stretch across the road into the cornfield."

"I think you'd better take me to see Charles." Sue, composed now, starting to polish the newly rinsed-out ashtrays, one by one. "He must be out of his mind with fear, and alcohol. And loneliness. He's afraid they'll hurt him."

"I hope they shave his goddamn tufted head," Mike says. Mike's the only one who would, and curiously, Sue permits him to. "I hope they bathe him in tomato juice to take away the smell of skunk."

The place is clean, even the floor's been swept. They are waiting, largely in silence. Hoffman strolls over to the piano, lifts the keyboard cover, peers under it, and is surprised and pleased by what he sees: piano keys. Looks at the others, showing them his discovery. Rubs his hands together, points to himself. Beckons Mike. Holds out his hand, demandingly. Mike gets it, and opens up the heavy music case he's been carrying around after the maestro. Offers Hoffman a piece of music. Refused. Something more difficult, Hoffman indicates, twiddling fingers dramatically. Maury gets it. Lugs over an even heavier music case. The three pore through it. Ah, this one. Mike and Maury together lift the heavy score up and arrange it on the piano rack to Hoffman's satisfaction. Hoffman mimes putting on glasses. They aren't strong enough. He crushes them under his foot, and gets out a stronger pair. No good. He hurls them to the ground and holds out his hand for more glasses. Maury gives him a telescope. Hoffman sits down, regards the score with the telescope. Mike takes it and holds it for him in order to free Hoffman's hands. Hoffman flexes. Maury claps silently for silence. Hoffman raises his hands above the keyboard, has to scratch his right ear—even Sue is laughing just a little, when the red light of the patrol car colors the odd animals in Charles's painting, by the big north windows.

There is a knock. Maury arranges a smile, steps to the door, opens it, and says: "Well, hi, deps. Hey, there. What brings you out this nice June evening?"

There are two of them in the entryway, a middle-aged one and a young one in uniform. They could be a farmer and his grown-up son, masquerading.

"Hello, Maury," says the older one. "What you doing here?"

"Shooting breeze, shooting baskets, shooting what's that stuff that comes in barnyards?" Maury's voice takes on some sort of generalized ghetto overtone; he could be a TV situation comic, couldn't he? "Blowing some music. Vic, you get a complaint from those neighbors two miles off the party's loud?"

"Maury, we got a warrant," Vic says.

"Too late, too late. I got it all eat, all drunk, all smoked away, man. Yes, I do."

Deputy Vic laughs. The younger one says: "We're not after users. We're after a dealer."

"These men never sold a flake, they too kind-hearted. Give it away faster than the girl next door. Come on in for a beer."

"We got a warrant."

"What made you get that?" Maury stands aside, and the two enter.

"Got an information."

"Where from? State narcotics?"

"Tell you the truth, Maury, no. Man named you all and stayed listening to be sure we called the judge. Two o'clock in the morning, and we had to go by and get him to sign the warrant in his nightshirt."

"There really isn't anything here, you know?" Hoffman.

"Who's he?"

"That my ninety-six-year-old daddy. Got no teeth, but he can sure gum those grits, hey pop?"

Both deputies laugh.

"I guess we better look around," Deputy Vic says. The younger one starts taking books out of the bookshelf and putting them back. Vic goes into the kitchen and solemnly inspects each newly washed ashtray that Sue hands him.

"You can't really get glass to sparkle with this hard water out here, can you?" he says to her.

The younger deputy sits down, opens a notebook, and begins taking names and addresses. When he gets to Hoffman, he repeats Maury's joke:

"How 'bout you, pops?"

" 'y name iff Biwwy Hoffmum—H.O.F.F.M.A.N.—wivvin' a' de State Houfe," Hoffman says, toothless.

Vic checks the bathroom, lifts the lid of the toilet tank, opens the medicine cabinet. He comes out and opens instrument cases, looks down the barrel of Marcel's clarinet.

"You go right on playing if you want," Vic says, handing the horn to Marcel, who appears slightly anxious for it.

"Thank you, sir. We just about played out heah tonight." Marcel's light, southern, epicene voice could be taken for that of someone mimicking, trying to horn in on the dumb gag. He gets a reproving look from the younger deputy, and a startled one when he adds: "I guess I'll just unjoint it."

Maury grins.

The raid is over in fifteen minutes. The two men shake hands all around, apologize to Sue for the intrusion, and Hoffman opens the door for them. Sue runs over to Maury and whispers, Maury winks at her and shakes his head. It's not hard to guess that she wants permission to ask for direct news of Charles.

"What about the ladder?" the younger deputy says to Hoffman. "You making some repairs?" He's asking about the ladder in the entryway, which Charles climbs to go up through the hatch into the schoolhouse attic.

"No, it's a friend of ours," Dave says. "He sometimes sleeps up there, but he, he isn't here tonight."

"We got to check it out," Vic says. "I'm sorry. When you got an information, the informant . . . well, you understand?"

Hoffman understands. "You got someone who tried to bargain for a dropped charge, there could come a time when the lawyer wants the judge to know how thoroughly you checked this information you say wasn't any good. Yeah?"

The younger deputy has started up the ladder. Dave stops him: "You'll need a flashlight. There's no lights up there."

Sue brings one. "Even in the daytime there's no light. No windows. The . . . our friend who sleeps . . ." Trails off.

"That's all right, Mrs. Riding," Vic says, accepts the flashlight from her, hands it up to the younger deputy, who resumes climbing.

"I'll just wait down here," says Deputy Vic. "Maury, there hasn't been a bit of trouble since you worked on the radio." And that's the last thing said before a muffled, incredulous voice from the attic yells:

"Jesus H. Christ. Get up here, Vic."

"What is it?" Vic is climbing.

"Paintings." The younger deputy's face appears at attic-floor level, looking down through the hatch.

"Our friend's a painter." Dave.

"Not of these he ain't," says the face in the hatch. "These are big old canvas paintings. Some of them must be a hundred years old."

"Jesus," says Vic. "The ones from the museum."

16: All Quiet on the Middlewestern Front

"You didn't know?" Davey Riding says it to his wife.

"Oh, hon."

Then Vic, the older deputy, comes partway down, the younger one passes a three-by-five painting to him, and Vic hands it on to Maury, who stands it on end against the entryway wall. Hoffman tilts his head to look at it: against a cracked, muddy background of browns and blacks, a big, smudgy bowl of fruit and flowers, with a crucifix behind them.

"School of Peter Paul Rhubarb?" Maury suggests to Hoffman, in a murmur. "Today we learn to render pear and peach, fuzz."

Deputy Vic comes down. The younger one comes down, and out comes his notebook. The entryway is pretty crowded. Dick and Hoffman move out, back into the room with Marcel. All three stay close enough to hear.

"Is that your property, Mr. Riding?" Vic asks.

Slowly, Dave shakes his head no.

"Did you have knowledge that it was on your premises, and others similar up there?"

Dave looks at his shoes, looks up. He nods his head this time. "Yes, sir. But Mrs. Riding didn't."

"Dave!" Sue takes his arm in both hands.

"I'll advise you of your rights, and meantime nobody goes up there, okay?" Vic says. "Sheriff's going to want to send us back out with a camera." He gets out a card from his wallet, and begins to read Davey a passage in legalese.

Maury lets him finish. "Let's not get fooled, Vic. This not the man we want."

"I took the paintings," Dave says. "I brought them out here in my van."

"Yeah?" Maury says. "How you supposed to have got into the museum in the first place?"

"I, I knew somebody . . . I had a friend that worked there on work-study. He got fired, but he had the keys copied."

"Stay out of this, Maury." Vic. "Now, Dave. What about the person or persons that sleeps upstairs?"

"He didn't know anything about it. It's so dark, even in the daytime."

"Yeah, you told us."

"Wait, Vic," the younger deputy says. "Look, this is the guy who said we'd need a light. He just about sent us up there himself—"

"I brought them here in my van. I've been feeling so guilty. I'm glad you caught me, really. Student prank that went wrong, because then I didn't know what to do with them."

"Davey Riding!" says Marcel.

"We'll have to take you in." Vic. "You can make whatever statement you want in the sheriff's office."

"In the morning," Maury says. "With a lawyer present, Dave, and after you've . . . thought things over."

Dave hesitates, and then says to Vic: "All right if I get my toothbrush and a sweater?" The early morning has grown chilly.

Dave goes inside, Sue hanging on. They start for the dresser. Dick intercepts: "Listen, I could say I helped you?"

"No, Dick. Thanks."

"Davey Riding," Marcel scolds. "What do you think you're doing?"

"He thinks I knew." Sue. "I should have. Charles told me so often how he couldn't afford new canvas. And likes old canvas, anyway. He's told me what kind of paint remover he likes, and had me buy it for him. He likes the discolorations after he uses it, and finds patterns in it . . . but hon, stupid as it seems, I never made the connection."

Dave hugs her. "I know. I'm stupid too."

She goes on. "Of course, Charles would have had his keys copied when he got fired. And he did borrow the van, even, when he went to get things from his old room. But he wouldn't let us help him move. Dave, that painting on the easel right now. . . ."

"Sure."

"Dave, tell them. We have to."

Dave kisses her on the cheek. "Take it easy, Mrs. Riding-person or persons."

They move together to the bathroom, where his toilet things are.

"You still think I knew."

"Not if you say you didn't."

"Then tell them."

"Let's see if I can work things out."

They drift toward the entryway, where Marcel is asking if he won't be able to bail Dave out by check. Deputy Vic says no, and calls out: "You ready, Dave?"

Maury. "We going to have to bail him tonight, Vic. We got to have him out and talk with him."

"You want us to wake the judge again to set bail? It'll be sky-high, and you won't have the cash."

"Property bond," Maury says. "Take him along. We'll get us a landowner, and be there in half an hour."

"What landowner, Maury?" Sue has finally turned loose her husband's arm, releasing him to walk out and stand, trying not to smile, between the two deputies. "Do we know someone?"

Maury looks at Mike. Mike nods and says, "Yeah. Henry Fennellon."

*

Mike and Marcel, Sue Riding and Billy Hoffman sit at a rectangular oak table in the sheriff's outer office, waiting for Maury to arrive with Henry. Dick was left at the schoolhouse, a ten-speed courier in case something should be needed.

Dave is booked and out of sight. The younger deputy is waiting, asleep on a bunk in an empty cell. The painting is locked up by itself in the next cell. Charles is in his own cell, too, passed out cold. Deputy Vic has gone off duty and home.

The sheriff himself has been here and gone already, quite elated. His country boys have solved one that frustrated the State City police, the state bureau of investigation, and the criminology professors who run university security.

*

Mike talks.

*

In this jail part of our war was fought, but we didn't know it was a war then.

It was hard to recognize, because it was between armed men with powers of arrest on one side, who had every kind of backing except the authority to kill. And on the other was a heterogeny of flakes. There were two dozen kinds of radicals and pacifists, some of them disciplined. Poets were some of the first troops and the best, and poetry readings some of the first engagements; the poets were mostly pacifists, as Mona and I were, but Vietnam outraged them as early as 1963. Every kind of crazy kid got into it finally, and middle-aged liberal crazies, and by the end of the sixties I remember some very old people picketing and standing vigils with us and getting arrested. Henry Fennellon said it was America's cold Civil War.

It was cold all right, sometimes.

Mona and I and Crazy Betty, the rat flogger, called it The War of the Ice Men Against the Snow Flakes.

*

The battles were in the streets of State City. There was one in front of the fire station, and a skirmish in the A and P parking lot. Bull Run was the steps of the Union, Fennellon's farm was our guerilla hideout, and I tore up my commission in a temporary prison camp in front of Former Territorial.

That's the fine little gold-domed building among the old soft-maple trees in the middle of the campus, where the Territorial Legislature met in the 1860s. When statehood came, they moved the capital west and left the university here in State City. The president's office was the governor's, in Former Territorial, and the faculty senate meets sometimes where the legislature sat.

Maybe the war was always to control that building.

*

We were all generals on our side in that war, of course, but some were more general than others, and Crazy Betty, the rat flogger, was the most general of all.

*

Mona and I grew up standing on a walnut desk in the university president's office in Former Territorial, led there by Crazy Betty, and with a dozen others. The door was barricaded on our side with bookcases, and we'd moved the desk against them for more weight.

Up to then Mona was a little married girl, pretty enough so that she had been on the cover of *Seventeen* the year she graduated from the High School of the Performing Arts in New York City. She played the cello awfully well, in those days, and was brought here to the university on an orchestra scholarship. I met her here and married her out of the arms of the richest kid in the best Jewish fraternity on campus. Then I was a little married boy who sang bass, until we broke into the president's office as pacifists, but we made the mistake of taking some radicals along.

The working day was over when we forced the door, went in and made our barricade. Then we called the local newspaper on the president's telephone and said we would not allow any more administering of the university until it canceled its War Department research contracts.

After about half an hour the president came to the door by himself, without any deans or aides or policemen. He was a tall, scholarly old man, who liked to think and talk about education. He was very much criticized in the state that year because he was not tough, and was not a negotiator, but he hadn't accepted the presidency of the university knowing that he would be expected to break strikes and enforce order.

He knocked on the door of his office and called:

"This is Lawrence Esterhart."

Then he knocked again and said:

"It's Lawrence Esterhart. May I come in?"

At that time several people were writing slogans and dirty words on his office wall.

I said, "Betty, let's talk to him."

Crazy Betty yelled: "All right, shut up, everyone. Mike's going to talk to President Esterhart."

He waited quietly out there in the hall while we shoved his bookcases here and there to make room for the door to open about a foot. Then, to be able to see him, I had to climb up onto the desk and look over the top of a bookcase, down at him. He was a humble-looking man with his face turned up that way, but he never lost his dignity, not even later when some of the radicals were yelling dirty words back at some of the things he said, and laughing, and drowning me out. Maybe they wouldn't have yelled those words if they could have seen him. I don't know.

*

Mona stood on the desk beside me. I could tell Lawrence Esterhart was struck by her physical beauty, as all men are, because he'd look at her from time to time and look surprised.

"With whom am I speaking?" he asked. He was a historian, and spoke rather formally.

"I'm Mike Shapen. This is my wife, Mona."

"Are you deputized to speak for everyone in there?"

"I doubt it," I said. "But I'll try."

"Mr. and Mrs. Shapen, are you holding any of my staff in there? I can't see in."

"Excuse me?" I didn't quite understand his question.

"Do you have hostages?" It was a time when deans and chancellors and provosts were being captured and held in their offices; blacks used that tactic at a number of schools.

"We don't believe in violence against people," Mona said.

"Neither do I, Mrs. Shapen. I'm very glad to hear you say that."

"Research that helps the war is violence against people," I said.

"I was thinking about that as I walked over here. Do you suppose, isn't there someplace we could sit down together? Might I come in?"

The radicals were pushing up close around the desk to hear what he was saying, and they started yelling and laughing at that, "Bullshit!" "Stay in the hall, Esterhole." They called him a fascist and a closet queen, and Crazy Betty pushed some of them away, and said,

"Let's hear the man. Let's listen to him." She was almost six feet tall and an athlete, had been captain of girls' tennis, a field-hockey star, and maybe women's Olympic calibre in the high jump, before she got started on politics and vodka binges and her rather original approach to sex.

*

Lawrence Esterhart said he had been thinking, as he walked over to meet with us, that perhaps we weren't familiar with how complicated the government research contract situation was. It supported so many activities that we would have to contemplate a much smaller and less diverse university if it were cut off completely. That might not be bad. But then, as far as he knew, none of the contracts had to do with weaponry. Many were for pure research of various kinds, even though supported by the military. Many had to do with space and oceanographic exploration.

"Bullshit, bullshit."

Would we consider a review procedure? If we could appoint a student-faculty board, he would be willing to ask the various department heads to review their contracts with us, one by one. Objectionable ones could be canceled; he'd favor that himself. Of course, he couldn't compel any department head . . .

"Bullshit, Esterhole."

"Go sit on the crapper."

Mona whirled around to face them with such a look of anger that they mostly shut up. "If you want Mike and me to stand up here, you keep quiet," she said. "If any of you want up here, I'll make room." Mona is tiny, but she shines like a light when she's angry.

*

When it was clear that nothing rational could be worked out in the circumstances, Lawrence Esterhart asked us if there weren't other conditions he could meet to permit us to leave his office.

Job interviewing by the armed forces and by companies like Dow Chemical was a big issue to us, and we said so. And what about ROTC?

Lawrence Esterhart said he was willing to consider all those things, but didn't think he should do so under duress. He asked if we couldn't at least agree that a university should be a place for reasonable discourse about problems, and joint learning, and said that he hoped that he could learn from us.

There were a lot of cat-calling suggestions about things our associates might teach him that I won't repeat, but I thought Mona was going to start kicking faces, so I cut it short, and said it didn't seem as if we could agree to much of anything right now, that we had food and supplies for several days and would stay. I also said I was sorry.

Lawrence Esterhart said, sadly, that he was in sympathy with so many of our views that he hoped we could reconsider our methods. He didn't want to have the civil authorities go over his head and order police or soldiers to come and evict us.

"Shouldn't a university be a sanctuary for students and scholars?" he asked. "With its own rules, and with entrance forbidden to civil authority? I've always liked to think that I'm on some kind of sacred ground here."

The radicals knew their answer to that clearly enough. "Screw sanctuaries," they shouted. "Screw you too, Esterhole."

Confrontation with civil authority was just what they wanted. They didn't want the university interposing its protection. They wanted the sacred community of students and scholars to see people beaten on by men in uniforms. That would bring polarization. Conciliation was betrayal.

Lawrence Esterhart could understand that historically, but it wasn't in his nature to know how to deal with it. He was an expert on the Russian Revolution, but he was personally Tolstoyan. That was why he'd believed that he could understand and deal with pacifists.

We shouldn't have brought the radicals along.

When he realized we weren't going to yield without being arrested and carried out, President Esterhart asked us, quietly, please to be careful of his papers in there while we waited for the police. The files contained the research documents for his intellectual history of Russia.

I said I'd be personally responsible, and he said, "Thank you, Mr. Shapen. Perhaps it seems petty of me to worry about it, but some of those documents go back forty years, and are not replaceable now."

Then he left, and one of the radicals pulled out a file drawer and dumped it and started skating around in the papers. Mona pushed him, and he pushed her back and I hit him twice. I'd have hit him three times but Crazy Betty told us all to stop it. Then I dropped my hands, and he hit me, but he didn't know how to punch, and it didn't hurt.

Mona put the papers back in the drawer. A lot of them were letters in Russian, and some of them were badly torn. Then she put the drawer back, and she didn't look angry any more. She looked sad and puzzled, like Esterhart.

We stood with our backs against the filing cabinet, and the others moved off, and Mona said, "Does it have to be all rude, ugly clowns on one side, and on the other, and decent people caught in the middle?"

"I don't know," I said. "Probably it does. Probably the clowns get uglier and more dangerous, and we do, too. You and me."

Mona didn't say anything to that, and Crazy Betty got everybody to sit down, and we started singing and feeling better toward each other. That was the first time we went to jail, but it was the State City police station, not here, and they didn't hold us long. President Esterhart wouldn't make the kind of complaint they asked him to make, and not long afterward he had his heart attack, and resigned, and died.

Mona and I would have visited him in the hospital, but the doctor we talked to said it wouldn't be a good idea.

*

Crazy Betty, the rat flogger, was married to a student pilot named Stoney. They'd got to know one another in ROTC flying class, where Betty was the token woman of whom the captain-instructor had been very proud.

The captain-instructor was very disappointed when politics made her resign, and with a certain amount of publicity. Then Stoney did the same thing, but there wasn't any publicity.

The captain-instructor said Betty could easily have been the first American woman astronaut. Apparently she was a lot better pilot than Stoney.

She was a strawberry blonde, with matching high-colored, freckled skin and one of those aristocratic, eastern-seaboard voices that could have got raucous and hee-haw when she got older; even at twenty-one, Betty's voice didn't have much music in it. She had a beautifully shaped oval face, high and tight in the forehead, thin, firm lips with a lot of bow in the mouth and perfectly white teeth. Stoney was Californian and shiftless, with a certain whiney charm to him. If I was a one-star, Mona a two-star, and Betty a five-star general, Stoney was our private and goldbrick.

When they moved in next to us at the so-called duplex, I didn't much care for either of them, but Mona was smitten with Crazy Betty, partly because Betty'd been raised a horse woman by parents who could afford it, while Mona's girlish love for horses only got indulged for two weeks a year, when she was off in Jewish summer camp.

My dusky, perfect, black-haired, tiny Mona, wishing she'd been born a raspy, six-foot, Ivy League blonde, in riding boots.

*

Betty came from Long Island, Mona from Manhattan, and I'm from New Jersey. It gave us more in common out here than you might think, in spite of the class differences between our fathers: a Yale Law School corporation counsel, an Antwerp diamond cutter, and a Kosher meat cutter. When we got to know each other, we used to talk about that, and about growing up in and around New York City, but the things that made me like Crazy Betty, eventually, were the high-spirited way she took living in our student ghetto, and the candor with which she lived out her energetic strengths and notorious weaknesses.

The so-called duplex into which she and Stoney moved next to us, when he got out of ROTC and into drugs (which moved them, like a lot of people, into protest politics), was a typical State City landlord deal. It was a sub-standard single-family house to begin with, a sagging, one-story frame with asphalt siding and a front porch eight inches off the ground, held up at the corners by broken cinder blocks. None of the windows opened, most of the wiring was exposed, and there were patches where plaster'd fallen off inside, letting the fuzzy lath show.

Your State City landlord knows how to remodel a place like that. He buys it cheap, throws a couple of sheets of plywood in here and there as partitions, cuts a second entry door, installs a cheap stall shower, a junkyard second toilet, and a two-burner range; thus he rents it as two apartments and calls it a duplex.

Half the Value for Twice the Rent is the first commandment for a State City landlord.

"May I look forward to a wallow in your bathtub some day?" is the first thing I remember Crazy Betty saying. They had the side with the shower in it. Mona thought that was an hilarious way of putting it, but at the time Betty's voice and accent still gave me a pain.

Practically our whole block, on Territorial Street, was either so-called duplexes or, on the corners, old three-story wooden homes, cut up into five and six apartments instead of two. Eventually that section of State City became our bastion as much as our ghetto, which was very uncomfortable for the few, elderly working-men's widows and welfare families who hung on to their own places in it.

*

While Stoney, her husband, was getting into drugs, Crazy Betty discovered vodka. She'd been in training for athletics so much of her life that, except for the wine on the family dinner table, she really hadn't known about alcohol.

"There's simply no sociability in pot for me," she said. "And anything else I don't understand. But doesn't vodka make one friendly?" She was too accustomed to thinking of her body as one of the best machines around to experiment with speed or hard drugs, but she felt perfectly able to handle eighty proof.

She was a silly drunk. She drank too fast, and was impatient for it to take. She didn't drink constantly—maybe a couple of times a month, for two or three days at a time.

These drinking periods often started when Stoney was away scoring drugs somewhere to bring back and deal, and when they did, Crazy Betty often did the other thing that got her a reputation and made people laugh at her. I think she'd been fastidious about sex, growing up, and needed to maintain that, and still be free like the rest of us were supposed to be. And never were.

Dave spoke of Jody Skink, who often did her love making with her mouth. But in Jody's case, as I understood it, it was an act of convenience and naughtiness, one she could perform quickly on the sly with an accomplice, Jody on her knees, the guy standing, the position in itself not irrevocably compromising, and his clothing barely opened, not removed. With Betty it was quite different and quite compulsive.

"I find I don't much like having part of someone else's body inside mine, not even Stoney's, to be frank. And I don't like the helplessness." She said that to Mona, her new confidante, indifferent that I was listening, too. "Stoney, of course, is free to do as he likes with others, and so am I theoretically. But I haven't much inclination to make a full test of the theory, you see."

She'd always liked to control things, horses and airplanes and sports cars and her own hard-driven body. She didn't wish to surrender it, but she liked very much indeed accepting a man's surrender of his body to her control.

"I like him lying on his back buck naked, offering his pride to my lips to tame and control as I see fit. God, why do I find that thrilling?"

But she mostly found it thrilling after half a bottle of vodka, and with a stranger, and when it became known in our section that she went into working-men's bars and picked up guys and found her satisfaction in that particular way, the freaks and hippie men resented her, the severe left-wing women said she was disgusting, the flower-children women laughed at her, and she got the name Crazy Betty. But Mona didn't laugh at her, and as I came to understand Betty's despair, I came to love her as much as Mona did. It was the despair of having too much energy and nothing worth spending it on, too much vulnerability and nothing worth exposing it to. Certainly life with Stoney wasn't worth what Betty had to spend.

One day she said to me: "Help me think, Mike. Please. I've got all this goddamn body and no head." Then she started laughing her raspy laugh at the double meaning, only suddenly I noticed that the laugh didn't sound raucous to me any longer, it sounded lonely and defiant.

She'd grown up thinking all the highly approved things she'd learned to do were as fine as her parents believed them to be, and started intensive-language training, meaning to become a diplomat; then she noticed that all the interesting and creative people in her generation were moving, however discordantly, in a totally different direction.

*

There was a rat that lived under our duplex. We called it Lyndon, and it was no affectionate nickname. We hated the dirty animal. It went in and out through a broken floorboard in the porch, and into our kitchens, but we didn't believe in killing it.

Stoney went away on one of his trips, and just before he left he bought some rat poison and sneaked it into Lyndon's hole, figuring it would work while he was gone and we wouldn't really know he'd done it.

While he was gone, Crazy Betty got raped. There was some action about to begin; Dow Chemical was sending interviewers the next day to offices provided by the university in the Union, to try to recruit chemical-engineering graduates. It may have been because she had taken herself out of things politically, after the radicals in the President's office, that Betty started drinking at that time.

She came to our side of the house, and we were talking with some others from the section, making plans; she listened and then she smiled, and said, in one of the pauses:

"To quote Joan of Arc, 'I don't suppose anybody here would rather join me in a drink?' " Then she went back to her side of the house.

Then she had quite a lot of vodka by herself, apparently, and went downtown and picked up a local strong man who's a house painter, and drank quite a bit more before she went off with him in his panel truck. When the house painter understood what it was she proposed to do for him, he thought it was perverted and got mad and raped Crazy Betty. She'd had much too much to drink by then to be able to get her own strength to work against him.

The next morning the guy must have felt proud as hell of himself. He opened a six-pack and drove through our section, and there weren't many people on the street. A lot of us were off at a morning meeting, getting ready to get between the chemical-engineering whizzes and Dow Chemical. They were due in the afternoon. We decided at the meeting that we were going to burn some dolls, about the time the recruiters finished their cocktails and expense-account lunches at State House with the nice university placement-office folks and came strolling back to the interviewing rooms, gently burping away the brandy. We figured we'd do a couple of dolls, to stand for the Vietnam babies Dow was in the business of burning, and try to see to it that the interviewers' postprandial dreams weren't interrupted by having any job applicants to talk to.

The house painter drove around several blocks and drank several of his cans of beer. He knew where Betty lived because he'd rolled her off there after raping her the night before, getting the address out of her purse.

Meanwhile, Betty had waked up, feeling lousy, come over, and borrowed the use of our bathtub in our absence, bringing her vodka bottle along. She'd had a long soak and a number of drinks, and wandered back to her side of the duplex to go back to bed.

Mona made a speech at the meeting: "Our rat Lyndon was an ugly pet, but lying dead in the garbage can this morning, he's even uglier. We didn't want to kill him, and certainly not with poison chemicals.

"We don't want to see these Dow Poison-Chemical-Company recruiters dead in the garbage can. We don't want to hurt people, unlike the Dow Poison Chemical Company.

"We just don't want their people dirtying up our university, any more than we wanted the rat Lyndon living under our porch like a pet.

"I mean, a rat's all right in the woods, it has a right to live. We should have blocked his way and maybe trapped him alive and got him out of town.

"These interviewers are just men, even if they're rats and work for a rat company. But let's not hurt them. Let's just block them from doing their dirty business here, trap them in the Union alive, and get them out of town." Her rhetoric was getting strident.

When the painter came around the block for the third time, he saw Betty flicker by, naked, out of our door and into hers. That proved that she must want him to rape her again. He parked his panel truck, finished his beer, walked across the yard, and put the rest of the six-pack down on the porch. Then he went inside and, finding Betty in a drunken torpor, did rape her again, trapping her arms with bed sheets.

Mona and I were walking, almost trotting, home, excited by the meeting. We hadn't seen Betty to know about the night before, and when we noticed the painter's panel truck parked in front of our place, I remember wondering if the State City landlord had finally been shamed into ordering our place painted. Then we saw the painter himself, sitting on the porch, sipping beer and looking smug. Then we saw Crazy Betty, stark naked, come stealthily out the door.

She had dead Lyndon by the tail, and the first the house painter knew of her being up and active was when she smashed the dead rat across his face. He screamed.

He jumped up, and Betty flogged him with the dead rat all the way to his truck. There were a lot of people coming back from the meeting by then, and a lot of jeering, some of it at naked Betty, I'm afraid; when the house painter would stumble and raise his hands to try to shield the back of his neck from the rat, Betty would give him shots in the ass or around the groin with her sharp, high-jumper's knees. He finally made it to his van and got in, and she threw the dead rat into the window after him.

That was the first rat flogging.

*

I guess it upset the house painter a little. I mean, this is what they call nonviolent protest, a man's sitting quietly on a porch, enjoying a morning beer, not in anybody's way or anything, and all of a sudden, without any warning, they start hitting him with dead rats? And then the ingratitude, here he'd just given Crazy Betty two wonderful rapings, at no small risk to himself, since his wife might hear of it, and this is the kind of thanks he gets.

*

Betty bathed again, put on whites, and went up to the tennis court. She said she needed to sweat it out, and asked us to come by for her in time for the confrontation. She'd been turned off to politics, as I said, but now the house painter had turned her on again.

When we went by the courts, a couple of hours later, was the only time Mona and I really ever saw Betty doing what she was meant to do. She'd found a boy from the university tennis team to hit with, and they were whipping the ball back and forth across the net with tremendous speed, Betty just as fast as the kid she was playing with. When one of them hit one into the net, it was generally the boy.

Then, I don't know what the tennis terms are for it, but she ran up close to the net, and he started hitting her these high ones. She'd drift back under them, get set, and crack them back at him overhand, from anywhere in the court. God, it was beautiful to watch her do that. Drift back, and crack, the bronze arm whipping, racket gleaming, legs set and strong—then she saw us, and came trotting over, smiling, and Mona'd brought her a towel and a pair of slacks.

*

Mona and Betty and I were sitting together on the steps in front of the Union door. The steps aren't very wide, and there were probably forty of us on them, the earliest to arrive. It was the best place to be, because you could see over the heads of the rest of the protesters, out onto the street. There were about three hundred protesters by then and, facing us from the street, maybe thirty or forty other people to start with. They were the chemical-engineering students who wanted to get interviewed, and some deans and university-placement officers, ten State City police, the sheriff and seven deputies, and the rest spectators.

A couple of the engineers had tried to push through by then; our people didn't do anything to stop them, except lock arms, and let their rank sway back against the next arm-locked rank. Only one got as far as the bottom of our steps, mostly by ducking under and doing some crawling, but at the steps our bodies were so piled up, there wasn't any place for him to put his feet, and he went back. We all cheered.

We had the Dow interviewers trapped inside the building, burping away that brandy in peace, and wouldn't let them out. We'd got lucky and caught some Marine Corps recruiters back there, too; the brave leathernecks had tried making their beachhead without an opening barrage of prior publicity. Now they were cut off, too.

Maybe the Dow guys could teach the marines how to make napalm while they waited, and the marines could show the Dow guys how to use it. We tossed them in a couple of our dolls to practice with.

Out on the street, the nice university-placement folks and deans were going up and down the front of our lines, cajoling, and the crowd that came to watch got bigger and noisier. Sometimes one or two would leave and join us, and we'd cheer, but mostly they were either against us or curious.

Finally one of the deans signaled the sheriff, and the uniformed boys started carrying our people away. But since the strategy was to go limp, it would take four of them to haul one of us and put him or her in the paddy wagon. With less than twenty of them, it was going to be a long afternoon, and every time they'd make a grab, we'd hum the funeral march as they bore the pall:

"Dum, dum, dedum, dum, dedum, dedum, dedum. Yea . . . !"

The fact that everybody they wanted to arrest did the same thing, going limp, was the kind of item they used to get a conspiracy indictment later. Crazy Betty, the rat flogger, and I were on it, but they missed Mona. It's five years, mandatory.

The way they fingered Betty was the housepainter again. He and some other local business aces, the kind that pay dough to hear the coaches and athletes talk at service-club luncheons and pick up a check for a jock's meals and wardrobe every chance they get, had taken their cars and trucks up to the particular dorm where the athletes stay.

They gathered up a bunch of them and brought them down to taunt us, maybe help out the uniformed guys with some body hauling, maybe even bust our lines.

One of them was the kid Betty'd been playing tennis with. Betty saw him from our high spot on the steps, stood up tall, and called out pleasantly, but in that loud, commanding voice,

"Hey, John. John. Come up and join us."

"Betty, what are you doing there?" he called, and then the house painter stepped to the front of their knot of men, saw Betty, and gave us the benefit of his psychiatric diagnostic ability:

"Pervert! Pervert!" Then he charged.

Some big jock yelled, "Let's go see the marines, come on."

We were pledged to resist passively, not to fight—another item for five years, mandatory—but they weren't. They started pulling the arm-locked ranks apart and hurling people aside; then they got their group wedged in, and the ranks couldn't close again, and they heaved and worked nearer, and of course the shouting got really loud on both sides, and there were other attacks. There were uniformed guys happy to give up the pretense of gentleness, and some hot ones on our side starting to lose their cool, but the hottest was Crazy Betty.

She had a metal can of tennis balls in her hand, and she stayed on her feet and got set for the house painter to fight his way through to her, laughing this Valkyrie battle laugh and pushing me back—I'd got up, too—to make room. Mona'd swore to stay seated, no matter what, and she stayed, locking her arms around under her knees and going into a little ball, and I tried to stay in front of her, but it was hard to manage.

Then the house painter got within range, and Betty let him have it with the tennis-ball can, right on the side of the head, her best forehand shot, she said later, racket-head up, wrist locked, and plenty of follow-through. He went back, and would have gone down except for all the bodies preventing it. There were policemen following the jocks in, and I saw Mona get kicked in the side by one, throw out her hand to brace herself, and I saw somebody's boot come down on her hand. Then I got a club in the head, but it didn't keep me from getting my body in front of Mona's. Betty was leading some kind of counterattack. We stayed.

Behind me, Mona said, "You're bleeding," and she was crying and said, "God, Mike, I can't move my fingers," and then we got Maced.

But Mona would have fainted anyway from the pain of her broken left hand. The fighting moved away from us, and I pushed and carried, getting Mona to an ambulance, and they took us both and a lot of others to the hospital. The house painter was in the same ambulance, with his ear swollen up. Just about the size of a tennis ball. There were deputies guarding us, and after the emergency treatment they brought us here, to the county jail, but they let the house painter go home.

*

Hello, Henry. (Henry Fennellon nods, goes through to the inner office. Maury drops off and joins them.)

*

During the next six weeks, Betty became a general. Her leadership when we sat in the president's office had been fortuitous—she had the loudest voice there and was among the biggest physically. Radical men tend to run kind of small. Besides, it had been Mona's and my idea, and she was ours to appoint.

But now, while Mona's hand was in the cast and my head bandaged, we would often stay in, and see Betty striding through the section, calling people out, leading them maybe to a draft-card burning, maybe to a vigil. She had pretty good control, and wouldn't allow trashing, and if some of the radicals were disgruntled by that, a lot of other people who'd laughed at her and even some of the ones who'd said Betty made them sick spoke of her respectfully and were proud if she spoke to them. She was like a good, virile team captain for the little guys on the squad who aren't quite sure their leader knows their names. But those are the names the captain's readiest to use, aren't they? With a flash of magnetism, an unexpectedly intimate smile, a familiar rub on the head. There was a lot of loyalty around to Betty.

The vodka drinking went on, more frequently now, but she didn't go downtown anymore. She generally brought her bottle over and drank with me and Mona. Sometimes Stoney was there, too. Often she'd get quite drunk, but never publicly anymore, and Stoney'd be nice about getting Crazy Betty over to their side and into bed.

We still went to classes at that time.

*

Six weeks and a couple of riots later, we all knew that Crazy Betty was pregnant. She'd already told Stoney about being raped, but he didn't believe her.

At least he said he didn't. I think he really wanted out. He was a strong-jawed, San Francisco boy, and he talked a good riot, but when one was coming up, he generally managed to be somewhere else. By now his wife and his closest friends and neighbors had been busted twice, and Stoney was afraid to be the fourth of us. Our State City landlord had seen a chance for a little new business. He said our arrest records showed poor moral character, and he had grounds for eviction unless we paid more rent.

He happened to say it to me and Stoney one morning, and Stoney was trying to signal me to go easy, and I said,

"We're through paying you any rent at all until you get this porch fixed and this house painted and the wiring made safe."

Then the State City landlord made a complaint to the State City police. The cops started hassling the place, one way and another, I got to our legal guys, and they drew up a countercomplaint, and Stoney hated the whole thing. He wanted to deal hash and speed, and it didn't seem safe to him now.

Mona, Betty, and I were drinking tea with milk, and talking about Mona losing her orchestra scholarship because she couldn't play cello with her hand in a cast, when Stoney came in:

"Listen, yew know the news about my dear little wife, don't you?"

"We know she's pregnant, Stoney," Mona said.

"We know why, buddy," I said. "And so do you."

"I just don't buy that," Stoney said, in this Northern California hot-rodder whine. "Who gets raped twice by the same man?"

"You're about to get your ass kicked twice by the same woman." Betty got mad.

"Did you make a complaint to the police?"

"Sure," Betty said. "Just the moment they got me in jail, ready for booking, I said, 'Hold everything, boys,' and took my pants down and showed them, hair by hair."

"You want to try making a complaint about something to the cops in this town, Stoney?" I asked.

"I'm taking off," Stoney said. "Betty can have the furniture."

"Stoney." Mona stood up. "Leave her some money."

"I got none."

Stoney'd been dealing hash. He had plenty. "Listen, Mona, you want to put me in the wrong because I don't like having my wife knocked up by some goddamn fascist house painter?"

"We know what you don't like," Mona said. "You don't like the fight.

You like the drugs and the bullshit, but when it comes to standing up, that's not for Stoney."

Her hand was still in the cast when that happened. Stoney left, and Betty tried to cry a little, but she wasn't the crying kind.

*

In the spring a new rat came to live under the floorboards. By now Crazy Betty voted to kill it, but we were two-to-one against. At first we called it Hubert. It wasn't until nearly election time that we started calling it Tricky Dicky.

Crazy Betty was Mona's and my dependent that spring when Bobby Kennedy was killed and the action was quieter because a lot of the political energy went into Gene McCarthy's campaign for a while. But there was still a war.

Stoney never sent a nickel, wherever he was, and Betty's family cut her off, to try to make her let them bring her home for an abortion.

But we could afford to support Crazy Betty as her time came. Mona was an administrative assistant in Internal Medicine by then, and I'd started getting a lot of music copying to do for Professor Lekberg. Money was not the problem.

We went to the war in Ann Arbor, Michigan, and we were in a bad battle in Madison, Wisconsin, where a lot of people were hurt, and we were afraid Crazy Betty would miscarry, but she had a reputation by then and had been in news magazines, and the Madison people had asked her to come. We also went to the big one in Washington, D.C., but we missed Chicago, because Betty was in her eighth month by then. And sometimes Mona would just sit there and cuddle this big, sensational, fighting girl with the awkward stomach and challenging eyes, and croon to Betty and rock her, and there was a helplessness in that that Betty didn't mind. She'd lie stretched out on the floor with her head and shoulders in Mona's lap, and Mona would rock and croon, and I knew it was partly because Mona wanted a baby so herself, but I couldn't have said whether it was Crazy Betty or the fetus in Betty's stomach that Mona felt was the child it would be wrong to bring into our torn world.

There were four years of that world, more or less, for us. You heard where the war was going to be next, and you decided to go or not, seasoned troops by then, in groups of two or three or ten, under your own command.

"What are we, Mike?" Mona asked me once. "War buddies who sleep together?"

*

We wouldn't let Crazy Betty put the rest of Stoney's poison out for Tricky Dicky. She had terrible visions of Dicky jumping into the basket with her new boy baby, so we got Betty a cat.

That was against the State City landlord's rules. He decided it was a good chance to evict us again, or raise the rent. We had a small, personal riot of our own over it.

A sheriff's deputy came in the morning to serve papers when Mona and I were in class and Betty was alone. Betty started shouting at him, and people came out of the other duplexes and apartments in the section and drove him away with shouts and threats. Then they settled in our yard and ate lunch there, on guard. The deputy came back with three others in the late afternoon, and Mona and I were there by then. The deputies drew their guns. They came into the yard with their guns out, and people moved back. Betty handed Mona the baby and went to meet them.

"Shoot me, boys . . ." she said loud, wild, and laughing. When she was excited, her whole face would get the color of her freckles, which would disappear. "Then, you won't have to bother evicting me and my cat. Much less trouble."

The lead deputy looked embarrassed and started to put his gun away, and the section people started laughing and calling,

"Rooti-toot-toot. Shooti-shoot-shoot."

I had a photograph of the rat Tricky Dicky that I'd taken by flash. I'd taken it one night when we heard him in the kitchen, and waited for him on the porch, aiming the Polaroid at his hole.

I walked out to where Betty stood facing the lead deputy; I had the photograph and a deposition about our housing conditions, made out with our legal guys. I told the deput we'd accept his papers if he'd accept ours and the photograph in exchange.

I signed his receipt, and he signed mine, and the section people yelled, "Signi-sign-sign," and the deputies got in their car to leave. Someone had tied some nylon water-skiing rope, four strands of it, to their rear bumper, and tied the other end to a big dead-elm stump. The deputies tried to pull out fast, the rope caught, skewed their car, and tore the bumper half off before it broke. The deputies came pouring out, and the section people scattered, and some got chased, here and there, but they didn't catch anyone and didn't know exactly who'd done it.

I sent a print of the rat photograph to the State City paper, and one to the campus paper. The campus paper used it, and the State City landlord stopped trying to evict us. And we stopped paying rent. We had to, anyway. Professor Lekberg hadn't finished anything for me to copy, and Mona quit at the hospital. She quit because there were still War Department research contracts, under the new university president, and the medical school was part of the university. The Internal Medicine doctors were very decent men, and liked Mona. They were all on our side, and some had started coming to our meetings. They were concerned about Mona's hand, because as long as she worked for them she would go every day to orthopedics, where a hand specialist would give her exercises for it. They asked her to stay, but by then she really couldn't.

*

Mona and Crazy Betty were pretty much blacklisted as far as State City jobs went. I drove Mona sixteen miles every day, out to a cattle-auction barn, where she did the bookkeeping. The men who ran it were Amish, wore beards, and didn't care about politics. Their religion didn't allow them personally to touch the electric adding machine, but Mona could use it, and worked cheap.

Then I'd drop Crazy Betty and the baby off at Henry Fennellon's farm, where she worked half-days, helping at the farmhouse, and theoretically studied during the other half until I'd pick up Mona after work and then we'd go by for Betty. Often Henry would ask us to supper, which Betty sometimes cooked. We spent a lot of time at the farm, and were comfortable with Henry. He'd gone along with us on the bus to Washington and been arrested there himself, on the mall, but I doubt he had been doing anything disorderly.

The boy baby Betty named Rock Junior, which was pretty forlorn. Rock was Stoney's given name.

*

When you'd say Nixon to me, I always thought of the rodent who lived under our porch, never of the President. Tricky-Dicky Nixon was a little smaller than Lyndon Johnson had been, and his fur was scrappy looking. I don't think he was a well rat.

Nixon the President we always referred to as the Prick, or sometimes Licky Pricky, if you wanted to give him his full name, but we didn't say it that way when Crazy Betty was around.

She was getting back into stride, into action, but people didn't follow her as readily as before. The baby, whom she often carried in a papoose pack on her back, reminded them that Betty was sexually irregular, and there were new leaders, jealous of their influence. The radicals were getting our side organized, and pacifists were less popular as things went on.

One Saturday morning Betty scaled the outside of the civic center, where the police station is, using handholds and toeholds between the bricks and window ledges. She got to the roof, hauled down the state and U.S. flags, and hauled up a peace flag she'd made herself—a nylon nightgown with a big peace symbol painted on it. It made the papers, but not many people had turned out to watch. Some said she was too much of a show-off, and others that it was just a prank, and not serious enough.

Mona said: "She's getting crazier, Mike. It was really dangerous, what she did and, well. Not exactly pointless, but not organized to have any real effect."

That night I got home late from chorus rehearsal and found Crazy Betty sulky drunk because Mona wouldn't go downtown with her, and Mona furious because Betty'd set out Stoney's rat poison. Mona'd found it and thrown it away, but they couldn't be sure whether or not Nixon had had any.

Then Betty got drunker, and wanted me to go downtown with her, or come drink with her, after Mona went to bed. It was the only time she ever came close to making me her particular offer; I found Betty awfully attractive by then, I'd even had fantasies, but there wasn't any possibility of my acting on them.

There was a signal for Cop Car in the Section—everybody'd start beating on garbage-can lids, and roll the cans into the streets to impede the car. The can drumming started then.

"It's me they're after," Betty said. "For the flags."

"Let's go," I said. "Come on, Mona."

We all ran out to the alley, where I kept our car, and drove Betty out to Fennellon's farm. When we got back, the people said the blue knights had been to our place, so Betty was right, even if she was drunk.

Mona and I sat up in the living room, with the porch light off, listening for Nixon, hoping he hadn't been poisoned and would come out.

After a while he did.

*

The spring of 1970, before Cambodia, was a lull, but not a truce. In Washington John Mitchell was leaking hints of his plans for a police state, Henry Kissinger was kissing actresses and presiding over an orderly transfer of baby-killing authority to himself, and Spiro Agnew was reassuring people that their children were their enemies. There was a sense, I think, that our side might be losing the initiative, and it resulted in a relatively well-organized plan to strike the university for a day and have a peace teach-in, in case anyone needed to go to class.

In Music Theory, Professor Lekberg had asked his neighbor, Henry, to come and talk to us about the Second World War, where Henry had been wounded and decorated, had a battlefield commission, been an authentic hero. Mona and Betty went with me. It was the quiet part of that strike.

Henry talked about a soldier's feelings. He said there was a succession, starting with belief, and then fear, and then anger, and finally weariness, barely counterbalanced by a survival reflex. He said that what was most dangerous was when the survival reflex wore down, and a soldier became careless of his own life. Then he'd be indifferent to other lives, friend or enemy; in that state of mind he'd commit atrocities, perhaps, or, as easily, go to sleep on guard duty and be killed. Henry said he was not sure a man was ever a full person again after he'd been through that succession, and that the big risk in what we were doing was that we might save the country and lose ourselves doing it. He urged us to love each other as hard as we could, and to cling to nonviolence for our own sakes, and to try to feel forgiving, even to the Mitchells and Kissingers.

We applauded him, on our way to seeing his prophecies fulfill themselves.

That day's strike was followed by an evening peace rally. Mona and Betty and I were monitors, as we always were. We put on white armbands, and we helped keep the violent kids, who wanted to break loose and trash stores and fight, separated from the hostile locals. New kinds of people were on our side by then; it was the first evening, for instance, when I remember high school kids joining us. Most of them had white armbands, too, or were working the first-aid tent, and the doctor there was a Vietnam veteran. We had a little squad of veterans with us, but I remember that by then the blacks had more or less dropped away from the peace movement. They said their own cause deserved more attention.

We were walking the street where the bookstores are, facing Former Territorial. We'd closed the street to traffic.

Down on Bancroft Street, less than half a mile away, where Highway 6 joins it to go through town across the State River, there was a blockade. The people running it had piled up some fairly flimsy stuff, but mostly were depending on their own bodies being there to stop all the through traffic, so that it had to wait, and the drivers join the demonstration or go around another way.

In the center of town, where we were patrolling, it was a soft kind of evening, and there were a lot of people watching but not ill-naturedly. Almost all the faculty were on our side by then, and tradespeople with whom they dealt had begun to listen and even sympathize for the first time. Betty was carrying little Rock Junior, and wearing her white armband, of course, and she'd put a little white armband on the baby, too.

Then, as we walked this circle around the crowd who were listening to speakers, keeping ourselves between them and the onlookers, I began to hear a strange, distant swelling of sound, a rumble from the direction of the river, which grew into a tumult as it came across the bridge from the blockade.

The voices outran the runners coming across the bridge, shouted words were picked up by closer voices, growing toward us, first a louder and louder sound inseparable into elements, and then even louder, but with distinguishable, hoarse, shouted phrases, until it burst around and buffeted us, drowning out the loudspeakers, drowning what Mona and I were trying to call out about keeping calm, crashing in and surrounding us.

Crazy Betty grabbed Mona, Mona grabbed me, and we all understood at once that men in a green pickup truck had run down kids at the blockade, and some were badly hurt. The crowd started to break. I found myself holding Crazy Betty's baby and watched Betty tear off her armband and start for the bridge, going into her big, athlete's stride, out to the front of the mob.

Mona and I, carrying the baby, ran back and forth, yelling at people to stay cool, not to play into the enemy's hands by getting violent, but we didn't have much effect. I remember a high school girl crying, and that a lot of the peace people we knew tore off their white armbands that night.

We followed until we were close enough to see the scene on the highway. The men in the green pickup had jumped out and abandoned it, going away in a car, and later the owner of the truck insisted it had been stolen and that he himself wasn't one of the hit-and-run team. I don't know. Whatever the truth of that, there were three victims, one of them with a broken back.

While the ambulance was picking them up, Crazy Betty and a dozen volunteers beat the pickup truck to death.

They used a lug wrench, a jack handle, and their bare hands. Betty stood up in the bed, just behind the cab, holding the base of the jack, banging at the cab top with it and directing the demolition.

First they broke out all the glass. Then they got the hood up, three guys got up on the left fender, and tore the hood off its hinges. They lifted out the battery and smashed it on the pavement. Some of them opened the tailgate and jumped on it until it broke away, and a couple more took off the spare tire and rolled it into the river. They ripped out handsful of wiring from under where the hood had been, and hoses, and they smashed plastic parts like the distributor and electric boxes, broke off the spark plugs, hurled away the air cleaner, beat down the carburetor, bent the fan blades. Then Betty got them all on one side, and stood up on the cab top, and they rolled it over. Betty rode it down, jumping gracefully off as it went. They took off the two wheels that were exposed that way, and rolled them into the river, too. They couldn't do much with the springs and shocks, but they got the torsion bars and steering linkage pretty well bent up, and pounded the chisellike end of the lug wrench into a universal joint to ruin the drive train. They they beat holes in the oil pan. The blue knights got through about that time, and Betty and her squad ran, leaving the beaten truck on its side.

The violence spread from there all over State City that night. Stores were trashed, windows broken, and an old wooden building belonging to the university was set afire and burned to the ground.

There were deputies brought in by radio from other counties, and state police came, and Mona and I both got arrested again. I had the damn baby, so I let them move me along, but they had to carry Mona.

At the county jail they took Little Rock up to the sheriff's wife, who got some county pay as jail matron, and then they beat on me some. The blue knights were scared and mad that night, and there were two who whacked on me, side-handed. They kept telling one another to hit me in the body where it wouldn't show, and Mona called out that she knew both their names, so one of them hit her in the body, too. He enjoyed it. You know how they are.

*

The jail was very crowded. That was the night we took turns on the cell bunks. Every cell had thirty or forty guys in it, before morning, and around two A.M. they decided to separate the women out and lock them up in a courthouse storeroom that the sheriff's department used.

When I saw Betty and Mona next morning in court—they charged more than two hundred of us—they were both bruised and both smiling. All the women looked peculiarly happy, and most of them faced the judge with their arms folded across their chests or stomachs. The idiot sheriff's department had left a packing box full of Mace in the courthouse storeroom where the women were locked up, and every one of them left the hearing with a can of it under her shirt or down her jeans.

*

When the Prick and Kissingass went into Cambodia, Mona and Crazy Betty killed Tricky Dicky.

They did it with the can of Mace Mona had stolen, spraying the stuff under the porch until the rat came staggering out, and then braining it with a boot. I was at school.

The boot was one Stoney had left, a rough-out Wellington.

Then Crazy Betty put her baby in its basket, covered it, picked up the dead rat, and went running down the street with it, singing out some kind of battle cry, Mona said. The streets were full of our people by then. And others, who came pouring out, all the ones who'd never poured before. The ones that bitched when we trashed the library, during the Dow riots, disturbing their studies. Foreign students. Even the blacks came back out.

When the Prick and Kissingass went into Cambodia, there weren't any neutral kids anymore. There weren't any now who didn't understand what was being done to us.

Mona saw Betty start off down the street with her dead rat, and knew someone was going to get flogged. Mona ran after Betty, pushing her way past people who were following and cheering Betty on.

"Stop her, please, stop her. Crazy Betty is crazy."

Betty was Mona's baby, and my wife got through the crowd of excited kids right to the scene of the flogging.

It was the sheriff, but not the one we've got now, who got Nixon in the face. That was probably what made him go back to his office in the courthouse and call the governor's office for help, but not before he hit Crazy Betty in the stomach with a club. Betty went down, and the son of a bitch ran for his life and jumped in his car. He only had three armed deputies to stand in front of it, protecting him.

Betty was crazy, but clubbing her in the stomach was the assassination of the archduke.

*

The kids went after the car, rushed the deputies, and Mona went to

Betty. That's how Mona got clubbed that time. The deputies were determined to arrest Betty, who was being sick on the ground from the blast in the stomach. But when the kids who were rocking the car looked like they might turn it over, and the deputies left Betty, picked up some State City police help, and rushed the kids with Mace. So the sheriff got away, and later ten men, armed and in uniform, surrounded our house and took Betty. The sheriff told the governor he'd been attacked by a girl with a shotgun, and all the deputies said that was true.

While they were surrounding the State City landlord dump we lived in, I was running home from the Music Building. Once I got away from the campus and the center of town, there wasn't anyone much around. On our street there wasn't anyone except two blue-knight cars, one of them pulling away as I came along, the other on the lawn, loading up men. I slowed down and walked. Finally I stopped, a hundred feet away, and watched them. They watched me back. I was ready to go through backyards where they couldn't follow, and I guess they understood that. Or maybe something came on the radio, because they piled in the car and left.

I went up to the house. It looked empty. Then I heard movement, saw something move in a big bushy juniper on the west, got ready to run, but it was Mona.

"Mike," she said, and I hugged her. "God, listen. They've got Betty."

"I saw the car," I said.

Mona told me. "They were waiting for us to enter the street. They knew her, and knew where she lived. They had one car hidden, and it came out after us from behind a house, and chased us down the street. Then they had the other end blocked. We split two ways, but it was Betty they wanted."

"You were in the alley?"

She grinned. "In a garbage can. But the thing is, they had Betty before she could go inside."

"The baby's in there?"

We went in and gave him his bottle. It was hard to think what to do, but pretty soon he went to sleep. We both yearned to be out on the streets.

Mona said: "You go first. We'll take turns."

I said she could go, and just then, of all things, Stoney walked in. He was on his way East. He'd left his car at the blockade and come over to find out what all the excitement was.

We told him. He said he'd probably come out and demonstrate later, right now he was beat. That was all right with us. We told him to go to sleep, and not to leave the kid, and we went out. We told him the password for our section, and that if it got overrun, the reassembling place was the A and P parking lot. It was a good place to run to, because it was nearby and usually full of cars to dodge around if you were being chased.

Mona and I left, and trotted up our street, across Bancroft and over to Main where the bookstores face Former Territorial. Someone had built a bonfire, and Mona said:

"Goddamn, he's in Cambodia. After all the lies and all the promises, Licky Pricky's in there."

"We'll run his runny ass out," I said. "His Kissingass, too. We'll close this country down. It's happening." I'd heard some broadcast news. "It's happening all over."

There was a kind of thrill to it.

"I'm going to take it off." She meant her white, monitor's armband. "I'm going to burn it."

She was right. I burned mine, too.

*

A demonstration is a funny kind of battle. It has no real objective except disruption. We surged through the civic center. We yelled at the courthouse and at the new university president's house. We closed the town. We closed the university. We filled the streets, and blockaded the highways again. So you might say we took State City. Then it became a matter of keeping ourselves from dispersing. In a way we needed counterattack to make it interesting. There was plenty.

State cops came. The sheriff called in other sheriffs and deputies from rural counties. He deputized guys from the Construction Workers Council and the local teamsters. Altogether they had somewhere around two hundred men, some with guns, all with clubs and Mace and helmets.

It was very fluid, a lot of trashing and running. Then they would try to establish something, like a line blocking us off from Former Territorial. Then we'd bust their goddamn line, just with numbers.

We made a line. It was in front of the fire station, to keep them from getting the wagons out and setting up hoses. Mona and I were side by side in it, Vaseline on our faces for the Mace, and work gloves, which were being distributed. I assume they were stolen. We sat and retched, and wouldn't move, and finally the fire chief told the blue knights they couldn't have the hoses anyway. There were bound to be fires to fight. The blue knights went away, and we cheered, and danced on back to the big lawn in front of Former Territorial.

About six o'clock Mona began to get tired.

"I've got to stay with it, Mike, we've all got to," she kept saying, but she'd been up late the night before addressing protest mail with her good hand. Got up early in the morning to walk in the peace vigil that went on here continuously for over four years, night and day.

We were sitting on the lawn when the news came over a portable radio: Pricky was out of his head, wandering around Washington like a zombie, asking kids why they didn't like him.

That cheered us up. Things were getting quieter. People were settling down. We decided we'd better go check on Stoney and the baby.

We got back to the section and got flagged down by a friend. He was one of the ones patrolling the section, challenging strangers, and it tickled him to ask us the password:

"Halt there, Shapens. Who's your Vice-President?"

"Agnew very much," Mona said, with the required bow.

"You're welcome."

It was pretty silly, but it made us laugh, and our friend said: "It's okay about the car, isn't it?"

"What car?"

"The guy you told the password to. He said his car was needed, so we let him bring it in. Past the blockade. He's just gone out again with a bunch of boxes."

"Stoney," I said.

"He's taken Betty's things," said Mona.

"Never mind." I wasn't going to let anything like that spoil the political high. It was too much fun, hearing the guard say:

"Anyway, it's over. We've backed the Prick all the way down. You hear the latest? He went on the tube and said he's getting out, and he never meant to stay in Cambodia anyway."

We laughed again. The Prick could tell any petulant little television lies he wanted.

Mona said: "I don't care. I nevoo wanned to keep my sodjers in your old Cambody anyway, so there." We laughed. Anything could make us laugh. "Come on, Mike. The baby."

So we moved on, reached our corner, turned onto our street, and saw fire.

Stoney, you Lyndo-Nixo turd from Frisco, I wish you could hear me: You missed being your foster son and namesake's murderer by about five minutes.

The fire wasn't anything big yet, just some other little sad-ass State City landlord house like ours, burning down, but it wasn't far from ours, and we flew. I never knew Mona could run that fast. She started so quickly it was half a block before I caught up with her. Then I passed her, and ran into Crazy Betty's side of the house, and there was Rock Junior, crying quietly to himself in his basket because he was hungry, but not really squalling, because against the window he could see those pretty, dancing patterns of red and yellow from three doors away.

I grabbed the kid and ran out with him in my arms. Mona came up, sobbing for breath, and we waited for a minute till she recovered enough to hold the kid.

It was never established who set fire to the section. They blamed us, of course, but it was we who lost all our stuff in that part of the battle of Cambodia—all our people lost: their clothes and books and records and pots and pans. Whatever they owned. The only ones who stood to profit by the firing of the block were the State City landlords, who couldn't evict us and couldn't get their rent but still owned the lots and whatever they got for insurance.

Mona and I saw it start, anyway: The little piece of cardboard crap they called a house next door to ours caught fire next, and then the engines came, the same ones the blue knights had wanted to take out in the streets for riot control. The engines came, but they weren't anywhere near in time.

"It's going down," Mona said, holding the baby "Look, Little Rock, and clap your hands, it's all going down," and I ran back into Betty's side for a bottle of formula, and then over to our side for Mona's cello and part of Professor Lekberg's opera score I'd taken home to copy. By the time I came running out again, there was a huge stream of water going against the walls and windows of Betty's side.

I think they'd have drowned the baby before he burned up—nobody went in to check or asked us whether there was someone inside.

The only one who said anything to us was the guy holding the nozzle, who yelled at me:

"Stay right where you are, goddamn it. The police want to talk to you people."

I ran, not toward where Mona was standing with the baby, but across into the next yard, jumping around and clapping my hands at the fireman, kicking a garbage can, making a diversion. The fireman sent his stream after me, trying to knock me down, I guess, and I got a little wet, and another fireman ran halfway toward me and stopped. Then they both turned back to the fire, which had jumped onto the roof of our house, and by then Mona had slipped away with the baby, unnoticed.

I dashed around a little more, followed for a couple of yards by some blue foot knights who appeared suddenly and apparently decided I was the mad arsonist who burned his own house down. I crossed the alley and ducked into a house. A motorcycle went down the alley, very fast, and I remembered something about one of the State City landlords saying if the police wouldn't evict his tenants, he knew where to hire a motorcycle gang to do it, and I wondered about the fire, but it was more likely one of our people getting away from the knights.

I waited five minutes, hoping the fire wasn't coming toward the house I was in, let the door swing open, stood back in the shadows, and looked out. There was fire everywhere, but the alley looked clear, and I ran down it and into the A and P parking lot, where I knew Mona would be.

There were hardly any cars there at all. The store was closed. But there was a big semitruck that said Jane Parker on the side, which looked like the thing to hide behind. I skirted the outside of the empty lot until I was as close as I could get to it and then made my dash, hoping blue-car knights wouldn't happen to drive by and spot me. They didn't.

*

Mona and the baby were sitting in the shade of the Jane Parker semi.

"Hey, Mona Squeezya."

"What's next?"

"Here's your cello," I said. "I'll hold the baby, and you play us a tune." She didn't have much laugh left in her, but she smiled anyway.

"The truck's bigger than our house was," I said. "I wonder if we can get into the cab and lie down?" Mona needed rest.

I checked. The doors of the cab were locked, and the windows were up. Then I heard Mona call me.

I went around the truck to where she was, behind it, holding the baby. She was pointing to the black metal bar that held the loading door closed.

"Yeah," I said. "Padlocked. I wish I had something to pry it with."

"Look at the lock."

And damned if the key wasn't in it. Somebody'd been in a hurry to leave.

We opened the lock, lifted the bar away, and opened the door. There were all sorts of cases in there, stacked up, and an aisle going down between them. I took the baby, Mona crawled in, and I handed her Rock Junior.

"Mike, it's junk-food paradise. Bakery stuff and pop and chips."

"I'll be right up," I said, but before I went in, I let the air out of a pair of the big duals. They had the kind of valve caps that are notched on top, for use as a valve tool, so it was easy enough to take out the valves and throw them away. I didn't want someone starting up and driving off without our knowing it. I got in back and pulled the big door mostly closed.

We ate cupcakes and barbecue chips, dried beef from a jar, and a can of Portuguese skinless and boneless sardines. We drank warmish ginger ale and gave some to the baby, who loved it. We were very hungry, and the junk food tasted wonderful, and Mona went to sleep for a little while.

There was a constant sound of sirens, all the different kinds, bleepers and bloppers and wee-waws and wailers and frogs, in State City that day, but you didn't pay much attention unless some one kind was coming close. About an hour after we'd made our Jane Parker camp, several kinds came close. I stood up and opened the door a crack more, and a couple of ten-speed bikes came sailing into the lot, into sight and out again, and then thirty or forty kids came running. I recognized a couple and saw their dismay that there weren't cars to hide behind, and then I saw Crazy Betty. Her blouse was half torn off, but she looked wonderful, and it was as if the other people who came in were surrounding her somehow. I slipped out of the truck, swung the door almost closed, and ran over to her.

"Mike. Mike, they rescued me." I'd never seen her so exhilarated. Blue-knight cars were squealing, stopping, ready to charge into the lot now, and there weren't enough people to make a good line.

"Come on, Betty. Fast," I said, ran with her to Jane Parker, around the corner of the building, and got her in before anybody else knew it.

Then we decided to risk closing the door all the way, and kept very still. There was a crate of matches. We lit matches when we wanted light. Mona woke up, and was quite unsurprised at Betty's being here, and Betty took her little boy and found his bottle and began to feed him. The truck was insulated. We couldn't hear a thing from outside.

"There's a clerk at the police station," Betty said. "A fat, plain, country-looking woman. I don't know her name, but she's with us." She burped her baby and then fed him some more. "It was city police who took me in, but when we got to the station Lieutenant Fisher was furious. 'Goddamn if we're going to hold her here,' he said. 'We'll have the street full of kids, and I want you guys back out in your cars, not here guarding City Hall.' So he told the clerk to call the sheriff and tell him to come get his prisoner.

"The clerk was staring at me in an odd way, catching my eye; she gave a little nod. Then she made the call, and got up and went out of the room. There are phone booths in the lobby, but I didn't think of that then.

"About half an hour later, two deputies showed up. They took me into the alley. There was a private car and the sheriff and two more deputies in it. They put me in back, between two men, and then they all took their hats off, and started through back streets for the County Jail. I'd been listening for shouts when they led me out of the police station, and looking for a crowd when we drove out of the alley, but it was all quiet and I nearly cried. Nobody seemed to care enough even to break a window for me.

"We stopped on the street behind the courthouse. The three in the front seat got out, and then one of the ones in back, and they stood facing one another, making a little corridor for the last guy to push me out into. I'd been going to make them carry me, but I was tired and discouraged, and I thought there must be big action somewhere else and I was missing it. And no one cared. So I just stepped out, with my head down, and the sheriff said, 'Get moving, Betty,' and suddenly there were Indian yells and pig shouts and people bursting out of hiding places. It was an ambush. They were behind cars and shrubs, around the corners of the building, and they came charging out at us, John my tennis friend and some jocks, and people from the section, and kids I never saw before, jumping onto the deputies' backs, clipping the sheriff, piling on. 'Run Betty. Run Betty.' I was free."

*

It wasn't a long battle out there in the lot, outside the truck. From what I heard later, our people used their stolen Mace until it ran out, and then scattered, but some were busted of course.

We ate jelly doughnuts and Fritos and cashew nuts, and drank warm Pepsi-Cola, and stuck matches in Hostess Twinkies and lit them and said it was the birthday party of the Pepsi generation.

But we knew it couldn't last. Someone would notice the door bar hanging down, sooner or later, and we wanted to get the baby someplace safe.

It was evening by then, and we'd hoped to get out under cover of darkness, but they had big lights in the parking lot, and it was checked constantly because it was a known assembly point. After a while I slipped out, keeping behind the truck, to scout. There wasn't much to see, except a blue-knight car going by slowly, which I hid from, and some of the debris of the skirmish: work gloves, empty Mace cans, and one of the ten-speed bikes, abandoned.

I went back in and said: "There's a bike out there. I could try to get away, but I don't know what good it would do."

"I could try to get away," Betty said. She was smiling again. "And I'm the one they want."

We argued some, but her plan really was best. She'd go first, and try to get chased. It would go on the blue-knight network, and that might give Mona and me a chance to start with the baby for our only hideout, which was Henry Fennellon's farm.

"Mona can't," I said. "It's a six-mile walk."

"Mona can," Mona said. If I learned anything, it's that women go as far on determination and guts as men do on dumb endurance.

"You could go back to Former Territorial and find our friends," I said.

"That part's over. We've won that part. Anyway, you'd never get the baby across the bridge, and I can."

Betty went first. She slipped out of the truck, got the bike, sat on it behind the truck, waiting for a blue-knight car. Just as one went by the parking-lot entrance, she started her ride, getting up good speed, going across the lot, out the entrance, and overtaking the car. It was moving slowly. She slowed down too as she came up even, and when she got level with the windshield, turned her face toward the man on the right and waved. Then she shot forward and made a U-turn in front of the car and rode wildly off in the other direction. The cop car braked, squealed, U-turned, and went off after her.

Mona and I left, and walked toward the Seventh Street bridge. Mona'd been right. Except for the Crazy Betty hunt, wherever it was taking place, State City was quiet as night came. It was two encampments now. Opposing forces were occupying their ground, counting their losses, resting. And I thought again, as I'd been thinking all day, that we'd won; the Vietnam veterans were with us, and all the kids in the world, and even John, the tennis jock, was with us now. The only people left on the other side were the ones paid to be there, the mercenaries, and a few teamsters and creepsters. And house painters.

We called them collectively Sinatras, after the asshole of the same name.

*

So Mona and I started walking west, carrying the cello and some music manuscript and the baby through backyards and alleys, until we came to the Seventh Street bridge across the State River. There were blue knights guarding it, apparently to counter our having blocked off the big Bancroft Street bridge again, farther north.

"Can you swim the river?" Mona asked. "I can walk the baby across, and the cello. I'll just say we were burned out."

"It'll work, unless there's someone who knows you."

We slipped up close enough to identify the cars. They were sheriff's-department cars from Cedar County, brought over to help. So I let Mona walk up and over the bridge, saw her stop and talk with the Cedar County knights, saw her go along. But it was a long bridge, and a heavy baby. She had the cello in her damaged hand, and it had music manuscript packed in with it, which made it heavy, too. I knew what her arms were going to feel like by the time she got across, and thought:

Bastard knights, if you believe her, why don't you give her a lift?

I went through a fence and down the bank to the river. I took off my shoes and pants, made a two-bellied sack out of the pant legs, put a shoe in each one, tied it around my neck, and waded out into the river.

It's a filthy river, and it smelled terrible. The smell bothered me more than the coldness of the water, and though the current moved me downstream strongly enough so that I was relieved to get footing on the far side, it wasn't much fun crawling out over garbage and rusty cans and old auto parts to shore.

After that, the only bad thing was crossing River Drive, which was very brightly lit and absolutely deserted except for the patrol cars. Since they couldn't get by the student blockade, they were patrolling the strip that included McDonald's and other worthy franchises. I hid in a driveway going out of one of the automobile dealer's joints, and waited for a couple of criss-crossing cars to stop and the drivers to lean out and talk with one another.

Then I ran across into the Big Mac lot; the place was closed, but the lights were on, and I wished I had time to break some.

I met Mona, as we'd arranged, in a used-car lot off Seventh Street. It wasn't very prosperous and didn't have night lights. She was sitting in an open jeep back there, with the baby in her lap and the cello beside her. She was exhausted, and while she didn't say so, I knew her hand must hurt. She hadn't been up to physical therapy to exercise it for a week.

I was cold and wet. Mona was dry, but she was shivering, too.

"I don't know," she said.

"We can't go back. But you can. Go down to Bancroft, and wait for a chance to cross back east, to our blockade. Come on. I'll see you as far as I dare. Come on, Squeezya."

"No. We'll make it together. Mike? Leave the cello. Keep the opera pages in the case, and leave the cello."

"It's not that heavy," I said. "I can carry it."

"No. You have to take the baby."

"You're tired."

"Let me take it." She did. "I'll never play it. I know I won't."

There was a wonderful orthopedist working on her hand, and sometimes he had her believing she could use it again for fingering.

We started up the steep part of Seventh Street, ducking into yards whenever we saw car lights coming. The baby was crying, a thin little wail when we started, but after a block or two he went to sleep and didn't even wake when I shifted him. It was misty, so that there were halos around each streetlight as we went under them, and far away, in the center of town, our friends were marching, running, sitting.

But I told myself it was quiet now; I repeated that we'd won, we weren't deserting, only unavoidably detained from the victory celebration.

We went by ugly brick apartment buildings, the junk middle-class housing State City landlords build new with the money they get from the junk student housing they remodel. Then we got to the outskirts, out around the doctor's houses, and a sedan went by we couldn't hide from. It slowed down and backed up, but the people in it didn't do or say anything. They kept their car windows up, but we could see by the streetlight that they were Amish people, two young men and an older one, all bearded, in back, and two women with net headdresses in front. A very young boy with hardly any beard was driving. They just backed up and put their headlights on us and stared.

We came to a place where the pavement was all broken up, and it was there, stepping into a small pothole, that I turned my ankle. At the time I had the baby over my shoulder, hugging him with one arm, and the cello in my other hand, so I couldn't recover my balance. I threw the cello a little way trying, and managed to turn and go down on the side away from the kid, so I could hold him away from the pavement as I fell.

I sat up, doing the best I could to laugh at my clumsiness, but Mona wasn't misled: "Are you hurt?" She took the baby.

"I'm okay," but when I got up, the ankle did hurt quite a bit.

"Please leave the cello. Please, throw it in the ditch."

I wouldn't. It wasn't a great instrument, but Mona'd loved it for a long time. It was a piece of her. I walked along, trying not to limp, and Mona did laugh at me:

"I've seen people fake limping," she said. "But you're the first I ever saw trying to fake not limping."

She gave me a warm little kiss on the neck, and it was just then that another car came powering over the rise in front of us, and would have run us down if we hadn't got into the ditch. Fortunately, Mona was on the shoulder, and didn't actually have to toss the baby. She sank down and rolled, and I dived after her with the cello. We lay there, Rock Junior crying again, the three of us huddled together in tall spring grass. The ditch was around four feet deep, and wet at the bottom.

This car, too, came backing up, and I said:

"Maybe they'll help, Squeeze. They may have seen the baby and want to help."

I climbed, with the baby held in front of me, out onto the road again, and the car ran me right down into the ditch again. Then it stopped, and two men got out of the back and started throwing gravel and empty beer cans at us, and cursing. There were others in the car, who started laughing and yelling at the two to come on, and I figured it wouldn't be much of an idea to do anything but lie still. I just put the baby down in the grass, so I'd be ready to get up if they came for us, and I took my belt off—it had a pretty good buckle—to have something to swing.

They debated, and eventually went on. We climbed out of the ditch, and kept walking.

If we'd won, why were we retreating?

*

Toward the end of that walk, we'd count steps and trade the baby every hundred. We had to rest a lot. Six miles is a long way at night and afraid. We took no more chances with cars. Not many came along, but when one did, we'd hide.

There were no lights in Henry Fennellon's barnyard or in the farm-house; we'd have gone in anyway, but Henry's dogs sounded tough in the house.

We went over to the barn. We were both cold then, and dead tired. Poor little Rock Junior was too limp and cold to cry anymore. I couldn't find the light switch in the barn.

There was enough moonlight to see that there were sheep in a lambing pen. They woke, and stood up, and we could sense them milling gently in the dark. They smelled friendly, somehow, and warm, so I felt around for a bale of Henry's hay, and lifted it into the pen where the sheep were. Then I put in another, and a third, to make a bench with a back. I helped Mona over the rail, into the pen, and she sat on the hay. Then I handed her Crazy Betty's baby, and then I climbed over, too.

We sat very close together, and after a time the sheep crowded around us, soft and strong smelling, and Mona went to sleep on one of my shoulders, and the baby on the other.

　　＊

Henry came home about forty-five minutes later. I woke up when I heard the truck, but the sheep didn't. I pushed my way past them, climbed out of the pen, and called to Henry from the doorway of the barn.

He came over, and I told him about Crazy Betty being rescued and on the run or caught again, but maybe, I thought, heading here, too.

"I hope so," Henry said.

And that Mona and little Rock were in the lambing pen. Henry said he'd spent the evening in town, moving around, talking with county of-ficials, with farmers coming to town for the show, with some of the student leaders. All those groups trust Henry, though they don't all like him. He's a keeper of the peace.

He told me that a big group of state police had come in, and that they were a lot less jittery and more professional than the local ones and the sheriff's men. Things were pretty quiet.

"Your goddamn farmers," I said. "They ran us into the ditch."

"More likely farm kids," Henry thought. "Maybe some of the older guys, but a lot of the farmers are with you by now. These men have been out, too. On milk strikes and slaughter strikes. They've been jailed and beaten and rounded up. They aren't like this generation of union men." He sighed. "This generation of union men think they've been through hell when they're on strike if the bowling alley doesn't open till eleven in the morning. Let's get the baby."

"It was the warmest place," I said.

Henry cut on the lights in the barn, and the sight I had then of my wife was one I shan't forget soon. I think you'll agree that Mona is wonderfully pretty, but you'd have no reason to know how remarkably clean she is. Even in the State City landlord house, where it took half an hour to draw eight inches of warm water into the tub, and the shower head on Betty's side was clogged useless with lime, Mona always managed to be fresh and exquisite. But that night she was dirty.

There were smudges on her face and forehead, and she'd slumped down, so that her hair was full of hay. She'd put her jacket around the baby, and the white sweater she wore under it was grey.

Sheep were clumsily getting up, now that the light was on. They were crowded against her, one with its head almost in her lap; another had lambed that night and had gotten blood and a mucus on Mona's jeans. There was a smear of it on her face, too, and quite a bit on the baby's head. Mona's face itself was pale and puffy. The whole gleam that's Mona's basic appearance was gone out of her. She was a beat woman, ageless, hurt, and the baby she clutched a dirty doll that she held for comfort.

I'd never seen her anything like that before. I'd never loved her so much in my life.

She woke slowly from her exhausted sleep, and smiled a pained sort of smile. Her bad hand, I noticed, was pretty swollen again.

"Come on, Mona," Henry said. "Let's go in." He carried her, and I carried the baby. And the damn cello.

*

In the house Henry and I bathed and fed the kid and changed him, while Mona washed. Then she and Rock Junior went off to the spare bedroom to sleep.

Henry got ready for bed, came out in his socks and pajama bottoms, put his boots on the hearth, hung his pants on the firescreen and gave me a drink of moonshine whiskey. I was pretty tired, but I thought I'd better calm down and cool out before I got myself together for anything as energetic as going to sleep.

Henry had just sat down, and was smiling, his big head and handsomely lined face reassuring over the brim of the whiskey glass, when we heard the first automotive engine. It moved by us, along the gravel road, some heavy vehicle going slow, and before the sound died, there came a second. And another, and another, at regular intervals, same speed, same pitch.

Henry Fennellon got up, pulled his pants on over the pajama bottoms, and started kicking back into his boots.

"Twenty-five years since I last heard that," he said. "I hadn't expected to again."

"What is it?"

"A military convoy," he said.

He turned out the living-room lights so we wouldn't show up when we stepped outside. I stood in the doorway with him, and for a time we counted trucks, ten wheelers with canvas covers, full of silent men and rifles. A helicopter came overhead, not very fast, guiding on the truck column.

"National Guard, Henry?"

"Looks like the governor's called them out."

"Why this road?"

"Because it's a back road."

"Nobody's supposed to see them coming in?"

"Surprise is the textbook tactic. I don't guess we better let it work this time." He thought a minute. "They'll go to the Four-H fair ground. It's county property and just far enough out not to attract attention. They'll muster there, and be deployed in groups by morning, ready to break up the roadblocks."

"How can we stop them?"

"We can't. But we can take away surprise. If there's no surprise, there'll be no panic, and maybe no one will get hurt. Do you want to come with me?"

"I'll leave a note for Mona."

I needn't have, really. She slept for thirteen hours, Henry was there when she woke up, and by then I was back under arrest again.

*

On the way to town that night, after the convoy'd gone by, I tried to ask Henry something. "Do you worry about Betty?"

"Not as long as she's running and hiding."

"I don't mean now. I meant . . . sometimes Mona and I have wondered. We both love Betty." He didn't give me any help, so I blurted on.

"Well, she's been at the farm a lot. She needs someone . . . to worry about her. And we both like you so much."

He hesitated over that. First he just said: "Thank you, Mike." Then he said: "Men my age are often attracted to young women, aren't they?"

"I'm sorry. It's none of our business."

"Sure it is. Because you care, and so do I, but there's no proper way for me to continue this conversation. Nothing's happened between Betty and me, if that's what you want to know."

He sounded sad, and I remembered the night we'd brought Betty out to the farm, drunk, after her peace flag exploit, and thought I knew what it was he couldn't properly discuss. I wanted to ask, *When peace comes?*, but I didn't.

Then Henry turned on the radio in his truck, perhaps to end an embarrassing discussion, and we heard the news that National Guard troops had fired on and killed kids in Ohio, at Kent State University.

*

We spent the next day under the helicopter, fighting to try to keep the city closed.

The helicopter was used to disperse us. Whenever it spotted a large enough group, or was called to one by radio, it would move upwind and drop tear-gas.

Then the Guard troops would move in wearing gas masks as we broke and ran from the stuff, and occupy the ground we'd gathered on. But there were enough of us so that others would come moving in behind the Guard as the gas moved away, and the Guard and police would have to make arrests. And while that was happening, we'd rebuild a blockade, or raid somewhere.

Toward late afternoon, their organization and equipment, and the fact that most of us had been running and fighting for three days, began to work for them. They got the Bancroft Street bridge reopened, at least for a while, and the campus pretty well cleared.

There weren't any orders on our side, there was only the word, and somehow it came. Anybody that thought the bridge needed blocking was to lie down in Bancroft Street, cover head and eyes, and just stay there, under the gas. I knew that Henry was home, I knew that Mona was okay, so I went to Bancroft Street.

It worked for an hour or so. The helicopter came over and dumped, the gas was all around me and a couple of hundred others. It made you weep, and made your throat sore as hell, and smelled like beer puke. After I'd been there a while, I felt someone prod me to get up. I looked up, and there was a guy in a mask with a rifle. He was nudging me with the butt. I put my face back down. To hell with him.

I got picked up and thrown onto a truck and hauled over to the lawn in front of Former Territorial. It was hours since there'd been any jail space, so they'd put up a temporary fence with guards, but their first batch of prisoners had busted out. Now the fence was electrified barbed wire, three strands. I was dragged and rolled into the fenced area, with a number of others. Then they closed their gate, reconnected the wires, and had me.

I sat up. It wasn't bad to be resting. There was an outdoor command post near the gate, and some kind of colonel there and a state police officer. They had their radios and runners, and though they moved far enough away from the electrified compound so that our jeering wouldn't disrupt their operations, we could hear stuff coming in over the radio amplifiers, and sometimes it was bad news for them, and we'd cheer.

But we had an excellent view of the damn helicopter, working over Bancroft Street, and now and then new trucks would arrive at our compound with new people, so we had to realize the chopper was effective.

And Former Territorial stood there serene, off to one side, that lovely, calm, gold-domed antique building, with plenty of time to wait and see whose ideas and procedures would win it as a prize this time around.

*

There was a tall black guy in military uniform over near the gate. I figured it was one of the Guardsmen, posted inside our compound for some reason. The National Guard privates and lower-rank noncoms were mostly kids our age, and if their sergeants and officers were hardware-store and franchise Sinatras, playing soldier, the ones under them were mostly innocent draft dodgers, and could be shamed about what they were being made to do.

I figured as soon as I got some energy going, I'd go over and hassle the tall black. It was a tactic, like everything else.

After a while I stood up and walked over, and it wasn't a National Guardsman at all, it was one of our Vietnam Veterans Against the War, and it was Maury.

The last time I'd seen him was at a music-student farewell party for him, two years before, when he'd let himself be drafted. It hadn't been a very big party; a lot of people been surprised and dismayed that he let himself be taken, but Mona and I went, because Maury was our friend. And I thought I understood him: He didn't favor the war, he just didn't want to claim exemption from the crap the government was throwing. If there's a hundred people in a shit storm and ten umbrellas, ten guys will grab them, seventy-nine will fight, beg, or moan for them, and one of them will stand up to it and let what others want to crouch behind him.

Maury saw me as soon as I did him, and the bastard picked me up and squeezed me till my damn ribs cracked, and I beat on him as hard as I could with both fists. It was our standard form of greeting. He'd been in intelligence, doing interrogations mostly, and was on his way to Harvard for a semester, had stopped off to see his friends, and got drawn into the action here and arrested right away.

"Guard boys saw my ribbons, and didn't know whether to salute me or handcuff me," Maury said, and we talked. We talked ourselves thirsty, and there wasn't anything to drink, so we kept on talking anyway. I don't know where I'd got to, which battle, which outrage, which political figure—

"Hey, Mike. Tell me something."

"Sure."

"Suppose I'd just been drafted, and I was going, and there was a farewell party like before. You wouldn't go now, would you?"

"Sure I would," I said, and then I realized it probably wasn't so. "Things have changed."

"Things have?"

"Have I?"

"You were always a hard-ass," Maury said. "But you didn't talk slogans, and have dirty names for everyone. You've got a little bit rancid, Old Mike."

"Sorry," I said.

"Like a real, well-indoctrinated Cong, or a Johnny Wayner Greenhead."

"That bad, huh?"

He squeezed me again, hard, hurting enough so I'd be sure he still loved me in spite of my rancidness, and I got enough foot under me to whack him a honey with my elbow in the side, so he'd know I loved him in spite of his lousy perceptions.

"Has it happened to my little Mona, too?" he asked. I didn't take that so well, and stopped hitting him, and said Mona was fine.

The plane came at five o'clock.

＊

It came out of the southwest, out of the sun, but we heard about a plane first before we saw it. The news came crackling over the radio by the command post.

"Chopper One, to Barbershop Command," a voice said. *"Come in, Barbershop Command."*

The reply wasn't audible, but the first crackle from the helicopter had enough tension in the voice so that we all got quiet to listen. They called their State City invasion "Operation Barbershop" because some ace in the state senate had remarked, and been quoted in the papers, "What this country needs is a clean shave."

"Command, we got a civilian plane coming this way. From the Municipal Airport, looks like."

Maury and I stood up, close as we could get to the fence, and we could see the helicopter turning itself slowly toward the southwest.

"Damn-fool sightseers. Colonel Heskit? Or Captain Blass?"

We could hear it now. The airplane engine higher pitched and not intermittent, roaring above the outboard sound of the helicopter.

"Captain Blass, can you get ground control at the Municipal Airport, sir? Tell them it's a single-engine, high-wing—looks like a Cessna Skyhawk, but he's in the sun for me. Tell them to get his ass back down on the ground. I got cans to drop."

Maury grinned and said: "Your team got an air force, Mike?"

Suddenly I knew. I grabbed his arm. "Crazy Betty, I'll bet anything she's stolen a plane."

"I better go up a little. There's a lot of hippies underneath. Listen, get him out of here."

Then we heard cheering from the direction of Bancroft Street.

"Jesus Christ, Barbershop. Do something."

The helicopter dipped its nose, raised its tail, and began to move. Then it seemed to stop again and hover, indecisive. And then I could see the plane. It was flying head on at the chopper, from the same level or just a little bit below.

"Jesus Christ."

And I said: "Crazy, crazy Betty." And, of course, I was right.

She flew a straight collision course until it seemed there wasn't any chance left to avoid a crash, then veered left, banked right at about fifty degrees, and flew two fast circles around the chopper.

Maury chuckled. "That's a seven-hundred-and-twenty-degree turn."

The plane banked the other way, went out of sight for a moment. The engine sound receded, roared back louder, and we heard:

"Shit, it's coming back again. Shit, it's a goddamn woman."

There was a very brief interval. Then Betty came in sight on a new collision course, and the loudspeaker crackled:

"I'm on a mission here." And then: *"I'm not landing on any street, captain. I've been dropping gas on those hippies down there all afternoon."* And: *"Well, clear them with troops. . . . Jesus. . . ."*

Because it came again. The head-on buzz. The veer, the fifty-degree bank and the tight, seven-hundred-and-twenty-degree turn.

And she went away this time, withdrawing for her next pass, the voice said: *"Goddamn right I'll hang in."*

The next remark wasn't so certain: *"Captain, I can't move once she starts coming. I don't know which way the bitch is going to turn."*

She had him immobilized in midair as she made her third pass, and we were all cheering now. Three angry Guard officers came striding over to order us to shut up, they couldn't hear, they had to maintain communication, couldn't we prisoners see it was dangerous? So we cheered louder, Maury too.

The next thing over the speaker was sheer delight to hear, though you couldn't be sure whether it was petulance or panic creeping in.

"Well, where is Colonel Heskit?" And finally, *"I'm not in your command, captain. Did you ever hear of a Flight Evaluation Board?"*

Betty dived past his tail, just for a change, I guess, but not terribly close. She recovered, went out of sight, and, by the sound of it, turned again for another head-on buzz.

"Fuck you, captain. It's not your flight pay. I'm getting out of here."

And with Betty flying capers after him, the helicopter lumbered off, over the hydraulic plant, across the State River, and away.

She wasn't gone long, and, of course, we didn't know what might be happening at the command post. Probably they sent for other planes, because after dusk some came. It was just over by then.

For almost an hour after she turned away from her pursuit of the helicopter Crazy Betty, the rat flogger, patrolled Bancroft Street in figure eights, east to west and west to east, turning at River Drive, using the smokestacks at the hydraulic plant like pylons, coming over Former Territorial and over us sometimes, cheered by us and by the people at the blockade every pass she made. I wish she could have heard the cheers.

I don't know what she was thinking, up there.

She flew until sunset, too dark for the helicopter to resume, came over us for the final time, finished the turn, and went west, low, along and over the street, waggling her wings once to return the waves. Maybe she was fatigued. Maybe she looked down and back for a last glimpse of the blockade she'd defended. Maybe she even saw those Guard fighter planes on their way, and lost her concentration. Whatever caused it, I saw it was going to happen an instant before it did: her wing tip grazing the hydraulic plant smokestack, the plane rising a little past it, falling off, and then one slow spin across the setting sun as the little plane went down into the tumbling muddy water, below the power dam, of State River.

*

The sheriff's wife, who had the jail-matron franchise, also got to draw some county pay for taking care of abandoned children when there were any.

I was surprised that Mona was willing to let Rock Junior stay there at the courthouse apartment on his way to his grandparents. But Henry's farm wasn't equipped for baby care, and we had no home of our own anymore.

Sue and Davey Riding offered to put the baby up at their schoolhouse, and ourselves with it, but Mona didn't seem interested in the suggestion.

I did get her to go to the courthouse with me one day and see the baby. We had a few of Betty's things that had been left at the farmhouse to leave off.

The sheriff's wife was kind of nice.

"I liked Betty," she said. "Poor thing. Sometimes, when she was the only one in jail, I'd take supper to her and sit, and we'd talk." She told us her husband wasn't going to run again for sheriff. He'd had enough, and was going to move to the Ozarks and open a bait shop. "There's going to be a reaction, kids," she said. "I hope you've had enough, too, because I hear people talk, and there's going to be quite a reaction, after a while."

The building seemed very quiet as we left. I don't think there was a single cell door closed, or if there was, whoever was locked up must have been asleep.

I took Mona's hand, going down the steps outside.

"Never mind, Squeeze," I said. "We saved their ugly country for them."

"My hand hurts, Mike," Mona said. "Hold the other one."

17: Fats Say: Polly Takes One Fink. Hiss, Starey! Some Fang, Elf. Bite Yo'self.

Maury. Does his energy never wear down?

"Mike the Spiker." Lift, whirl, bear-hug, and out the door.

"Dick the Hick." Spar, grab, hairline rib fracture? Heave, and after Mike goes Dick.

"Daby, my baby boy. Jailed, bailed, and cottontailed." Pursues, catches, folds double, bears him off behind the schoolhouse partition. Sound of springs creaking as Davey Riding is dumped on the bed. Like a child experimenting with the flexibility of kittens, Maury is punishing his friends good night, at 4:00 A.M.

Having disposed of jailbird Dave, newsprung, Maury returns to the main room.

"Soufflé, Suefly, and you too, fly, Mr. Hoffman. Last but least, I'll take you to the State House here in a minute."

From outside comes the sound of Mike departing, taking bikeless Dick along.

"Hold on a minute, sir." Softly, to Sue. "Well, what's the matter now?"

"Don't bother, Maury."

"That's your husband in there."

"Yes, and the more I think about it, the madder I get."

"You do."

"He won't believe me. He doesn't want to believe I didn't know about those wretched paintings up there. He wants to think I'm involved, so he can lie in there smugly taking the blame to protect his dumb little chattel-wife."

"Pretty dumb."

"You want to do something for both of us? Go in and tell him to stop lying. I hate it."

"That's what I've been telling him, but I can't hate it."

"Maury, you're just as infuriating as Dave. I'm going to kick you out of here. Off my sofa. Come on, now."

"Pretty stupid, and supposed to be so smart."

"No, no. You're the smart one." Two hands to his wrist and tugs. "Maury, the genius. Never got less than an A in anything, from kindergarten through Harvard."

"Yes, I did." Allows himself to be tugged to his feet. "When I quit their basketball, got me a C in Physical Education. You ever get a C?"

"Please? Let me be? I'm sleepy and mad and worried, and I've got to be alone. Please?"

"You must be sleepy. We're staying just long enough to wake you up. You think Davey is trying to take this thing on to protect you, you don't know your man. He'd protect somebody needed it."

"I don't understand."

"Spelling time: C as in criminal. H as in half-assed. A as in artist. R as in recidivist. L as in grand larceny, third felony. E as in eight to twelve, mandatory, that's years. You beginning to get this, dumby? S as in State Penitentiary. That's for *Charles*. Now you want me to spell out Mr. *Riding?*"

"Maury?"

"R for risky. I for imbecile. D for devoted. I for iffy. N for nolo contendere and just maybe nol-pros. How about G for geste? Davey might lose six months, but he could get off with probation, first offense with restitution and apology. And that might just save Charles's ugly sanity."

She wavers.

"And I don't mind adding that you've given Davey every reason not to."

But her eyes are a little wet.

She bites her lip. She nods. She hugs Maury, sobs for a moment face against his chest, nails digging into his back. Pushes off, darts and stops, darts around the partition.

Meanwhile Hoffman, with a deep sigh, has stretched out and gone to sleep in Sue's place on the sofa.

FASHION

"Wake up, Billy Hell, and read the blackboard."

This must be a dream of Hoffman's, isn't it? Maury Jackstone isn't really standing in front of him, in the lifting light of dawn, by the Ridings' sofa, wearing Davey's rain coat, open like a robe over naked chest and jeans, bare feet wet from walking in the dew, with a long piece of chalk in his hand, with which he appears to have written an unusual sentence on the big old school blackboard behind him:

Ya can wrata evere werd en Inglish indirstinibli woth onlo ono uf thu vuwuls

"Your request is denied for sweet, sad Afro-American rhetoric, like: My father was a jump shot, my mother was the blues.

"Forget it, melodreama, you've just been on Channel One's court-rumor, first figment of the earling show.

The Trial of Horny Gus
#691

Judge Fats working, Tondelayo clerking, La Mère persecuting, Gabe yelling "Dee-fense, dee-fense," and Gus caught right in the middle between grin and squirm.

Courtroom like 16 miles between towns on the Interstate, Fats riding the median on a motorola elephant, Tondey keeping right except to pass, all in motion slicker than a daylight pig.

Gus tied face down, heels up, on a tinplate Lizzie worm, charged with:

TONDELAYO. A wall in Miami. Forney case. Blackface. Disgrace. One Kate Jackstone, of Mississippi descent. Checked out to Rear Admiral Maury Ginsberg, U.S.N., retired. Gus did herewith fabricate one unauthorized divine male fetus, number 691. Plead?

And Gus has got to ride his worm, guilty, with extenuated prostate, happens every six years, hard as Sardanapolis.

GABE. Never wanted to, can't help it.

FATS. Slice it any way you want, it's still Mahoney.

La Mère makes her horrid move, opens out her mothering arms, all she asks for is the fetus for Exhibit A, and let the deefense rest.

Gus. She'll throttle it and bottle it, like she did 690 times before.

Fats. Another outburst like that and I'll destroy Nebraska.

Here comes the jury to decide, twelve angels riding golden drome-daries, La Mère smiles but what's this? Blue-robed angels chewing cigars? No wonder Gabe is tooting, what a tamper, every angel turns into Billy Hell, you wink your twelve right eyes. *Objection* cries La Mère. *Subjective* rules old Fats. *Pretty Kate* says Gus.

That jury's stacked says La Mère. *No, but it sure is hung* says Gabe. And Fats winks back, pats a dromedary on her golden ear, *Ingot we truss.*

When I was born, in the hotel suite in Miami, the midwife blew her whistle, hollered "Double dribble," and slam-dunked me in the bidet.

"Lie down, Billy Hell."

It seems probable that Hoffman, having dreamed of waking, wakes again to dreaming.

"I've been watching Channel One all night, not hard to do, never starts till all the rest go off. Then you disconnect your set, hold tight to the plug with your right hand, antenna lead with your left, start walking and watch for the screen. When the stars start to move together to a single point of light, put yourself on vertical hold, turn up your amplifier, far as it will go. See?

"Often as not, Channel One's just a talk show, with Fats and Hearye Gus nutsying around with someone, but I generally find it interesting.

"Second figment. Storical, 1905, they were giggling over giving Jem the Lapsist first foresight:

Gus. Looka Shem, thunks he's writing a lather to blather Shaun the Papist.

Fats try to rede over Shames's shouter. Whet'see say? H'addessing Me? Can't spec My findacles.

Hooch McGooch wreats it. ". . . by the crucified Jaysus, if I don't sharpen up that little pen and dip it into fermented ink and write tiny little sentences about the people who betrayed me, send me to hell. After all there are many ways of betraying people. It wasn't only the Galilean suffered that . . ."

Tondelayo off stooge. We heard that.

Hoppy Scotch reeds slenderly. ". . . Whoever you are, I inform you that this is a poor comedy you expect me to play, and I'm damned to hell if

I'll play it for you . . ."

FATS sadly. The longest, most indifferent bone I put in man, the blasé femur.

HERBY JIST. ". . . What do you mean by urging me to be forebearing? For your sake I refrained from taking a little black fellow from Bristol by the nape of the neck and hurling him into the street when he spat some of his hatched venom at me."

FATS. What Maury doing in Bristol?

HALEY'S JEST. Hatching venom, it looks like. Mighty young for that. Minus forty-four. What you gointa do with Jumbo?

FATS. Prophecy and blindness, solo mio, head upon a blooming bladder. Pretty soon now, coupla books or five, he gonna wake and spew the newest tastey mint.

"Are you cold, Billy Hell? I would make you coffee if I could find Sue's pot, but close your eyes, inhale, dream of coffee. There, rapid nostril movement, turn the other shoulder, hitch the blanket, we are moving toward a future you will almost know, not quite, not quite, and the winds will blow on this hard journey.

"You're prepared. You see it so far, man of the stripped-down brain, the pattern of service in Vietnam, the brief obligatory connection with Harvard, the marriage to New England wealth and culture, even the reeteeveepair as a way far better than practicing mere human medicine to become a figure trusted and depended on in people's homes. Delegate to the convention where McGovern will be nominflated, the Sheriff's law and order hippie to be, but shortly we will see another transmission which will summarize the worldly career, and after that another showing its ambiguous, unworldly end. But the next figment.

"Sports.

"There's Gus again, in Miami again, but it's different business. He's in a press room, hovering near a linotype. The operator's leaving now, for his coffee break. Gus dumps the new galley into the hellbox, takes the stool. Watch his fingers go, watch the galley fill with new lines of type, stock press-room shot at triple-triple speed.

"Whooosh, the galley's filled again.

"Now there's you again, it's morning, early, you can't sleep. You buy a paper. Sit on a park bench. Light traffic. Kid eating a popsicle walks by. You open to the sports page. The scary headline shivers you to screaming:

"FISSION!"

"Slack-jawed with amazement, throats torn with shouting, a limp, incredulous crowd found breath for one more cheer at 10 P.M. last night to acknowledge the most incredible one-man performance in the annals of Miami high-school sport, as West beat East, 58–57.

"That one man was West Captain, Maury Jackstone.

"Sometimes called Mr. Poise, sometimes Captain Cool, always, once the intensity of a game is over, deserving the title Mr. Congeniality, the stylish leader leaves no doubt now that his true name is Mr. Courage.

"It was no secret to This Reporter, nor to many another, prior to last night's game, that the fix was in. Even Jackstone, it was whispered, knew it, saw his duty, reported to his coach before the game he'd been approached by gamblers, and was told: 'Boy, you trying to get someone hurt?'

"The word was: East wins this year, but keep it close.

"Payments to coaches were $200, to starting players a range from $75 to $150, and to lesser ones the sincere promise not to mash their thumb-bones with hammers.

"It can be revealed that when Jackstone, accosted in the playground where he was practicing, refused the bribe, a day before the game, he had literally to run for his life, escaping through alleys and then hiding until game time under the protection of a mysterious overworld figure known as Fats.

"Fats's advice is said to have been: 'Any time Slim says silver for losing, you got gold for winning, Black Sheep, three bags full.'

"Slim, a southpaw, could not be reached for comment.

"It was a tense, uneasy throng that watched the two teams take the floor.

"Then, on the opening jump, they saw Jackstone leap with the toss, high above his opponent, and spike it, volleyball style slam into the right cheek of Referee Tom E. Gibbons ($250), with sufficient violence so that Gibbons thereafter called a dazed but reasonably honest game.

"Recovering his own tip, Jackstone then drove for the game's first score.

"On a one-man press, he stole the ball almost immediately, as East brought it up the floor and scored again with a Cinderella lay-up.

"East countered, Higgins and Prouty holding Jackstone while East's Fitzperkins went in for an unopposed hook short, with an assist from West's

Weigmuller. On the following play, Jackstone stole the ball from his team-mates by intercepting a pass, evaded Weigmuller's attempt to trip him, and hit a jump shot from forty-five feet which seemed visibly to correct its aim with a slight change of direction in mid-flight.

"Unable to contain East's offense playing man-to-five within shooting range, Jackstone established himself in midcourt where he frequently seemed able to anticipate East's passes before the intention to throw one was formulated. When the ball was, on occasion, advanced to the key, Jackstone's pursuit and shot-blocking were so devastating that more than half East's first-half points were awarded as penalties for "goal-tending," as called by Umpire Alfie Rurick ($250). However, Jackstone's dribbling, a machine-gun like propulsion of ball against wood which actually splintered the floor in several places, kept seeking Umpire Rurick's feet, causing the delighted West supporters to break into a chant of "Dance, Ulfie, dance," whenever Jackstone came close. With 9:05 to go in the first half, after an outrageous hacking call, Jackstone pursued Rurick dribbling the length of the court, and ball met foot, producing a howling of pain and forcing the corpulent Umpire to retire to the nether caverns of the postulous duggerum, there to moan.

"With the score 29–29 and a second to play in the half, Jackstone took a rebound under his own basket, cocked his arm and hurled the ball over-hand so high it disappeared above the rafters, only to reappear moments later at East's end of the court, drifting bubblelike in the air currents, settling finally on the rim of East's basket, and then rolling gently into the net through which it worked slowly down. Fitzgerald, attempting to catch the sphere as it wafted floorwards, was knocked flat by its weight—East 29, Jackstone 31, and his teammates were gibbering like faculators as they left the floor . . ."

Look out! Too late. A purple-necked thug has snatched the paper out of your hands and is hurrying to other benches, grabbing up copies of that early edition. Trucks are skidding up to newsstands, confiscating all the stacks of early papers, substituting an identical edition except that Gus's story has been replaced.

It's all right. The tale is told, the world knows.

I lost count of the colleges that wanted to recruit me.

"But let us proceed to the next transmission, Billy Hell."

—Billy Hell! Wake down! Sleep up!—

FOX 'UM

"The 1984 commemorative panel on Channel One was less disappointing than you might imagine in view of the fact that Orwell himself was on a competing talk show on Channel Zip, which, while occasionally tempted, I do not, perhaps out of prissiness, perhaps wisdom, care to receive. It is, however, you will agree, interesting to conjecture what inducement the Zip people may have offered Orwell.

"Doubtless it was because I had allowed myself to be tempted that I received sound only on Channel One that earling. Since I was also a little late in tuning in, the first thing I heard was:

FATS. . . . so well you weaslecomb his gulf stream of conchiness, Fidel Castro. Howzit, Preem?

CREEM OF THE PREEM'S STREEM. . . . all cultura grande have the wilde barberio to haunts the border Kittyche. And drive him back does cultura as Rivera drive me when I am wilde. Comes barberio close and closer, overcome and become this cultura, but estados de la norte, which exterminate their beesteman in siglo diez y nueve are historia's great damn fool. Baberuthsize damn fool hit the genocide jonron on indio, at the same time, oh forgive me, Kittyche, my wilde sistabroth, bring in new wildemen in shipping loads. Hundreds and hundreds and hundreds new black negro wildemen and wildewomen for to breed they bring and in one hundred years turn loose. Turn loose! Inside the border is homegrow, maybe you say homebrew, barberio. Without any fight is there, inside, and growing all the time, a leetle riot here, burnababy, make the ugly face, and he win every city without fight Santo Louis Santo Jose Santo Los Angeles Santo Neuva York Santo Francisco. Never no beega battle, justa burnababy, Kittyche . . .

BLACK BARBERIO. 'We shall overcome.'

WASPISH HONK. You just did.

CREME DE LA STREME DE LE PREME. Cuban people all isolated now.

KITTYCHE. But where did you go wrong?

CLOTTED CREAM. My fine war with Jamaica, so necessary and glorious a victory did it seem, but what good? what good? and how much harm done? For a cup of blue moutain coffee, second category tobac, so bad a place for kindly Cuban tax collector. How can you colonize a place like that?

SUGAR FIELDS. By day they cultivate, by night they sabotage, oh my burning cane.

CUBAN PEOPLE. All alone under the Carib moon.

WHIPPED CREAM. Isolate from 'maica. Isolate from 'hama. Isolate from 'nidad and Jaiti. We are the longingtude and lassitude white country now, oh Kittyche, tween states unidos of the north and fearful Africa.

FEARFUL AFRICA. May the great earth pig eat you, Castro, you racist termite.

BUTTER CAY. I am the last white chance. Bring me the intelligence on President Jackstone.

THE INTELLIGENCE. Black president of a white country, Jackstone's political career has been created by the exploitation of paradox. First elective office, president of State City junior chamber, whatever that may have been. As county supervisor gained reputation for honesty and efficiency, while committing county funds massively to people programs, whatever that may have meant. In second term as supervisor served simultaneously as city councilman and mayor of State City, percentage of population black less than one percent, revamped park commission and renewed Urban; Urban is believed to have been a political crony, but this is the only instance of cronyism in Jackstone's record we can find. Entering state politics from this secure base, Jackstone showed himself so efficient at getting out the vote and handling crowds at rallies, by the magic of his singing of the songs we love so well and his command of rhetoric down at Maury's, that he was elected chairman of the state Democratic party. Gaining national attention as a unique political phenomenon—that is, a black leader with a white constituency—Jackstone was named to many national boards and commissions, he was offered a cabinet position as Hew. As the cabinet has been abolished, it is not possible to say what he might have hewn, but the word suggests internal security matters. Jackstone refused the cabinet maker, and ran instead for governor of his state, opposed by a Republican backlasher. His state having little to backlash from, Jackstone was elected. Though there were by then many black mayors, congressmen and several senators in Santo Washjington, Jackstone was the only one who could be advanced seriously as a Racial Peace candidate nationally. As leader of a white country, he would have a black army, a black urban and white rural population, a white financial structure and a black economy, and the need to balance black privilege with white civil rights. Consequently, he was the nominee for president of both major political parties, and neither the charge of 'Tomtokenist,' advanced by extremists on one side, or 'Cryptorastafarian,' advanced on the other, attracted sufficient votes to minority parties to give either one a majority, although in combination they had more than half the popular vote . . .

Old Buttermilk Cay. . . . ees the dumbest intelligence I ever hear.

Kittyche. Can you count on Jackstone against the Caribbean and Fearful Africa?

"What follows has often been rerun on the earling news, Billy Hell. President Jackstone reacting tough, putting the cities under martial law, destroying the new feudalism boss by boss. Then, as the war Castro predicted breaks out, putting his nation on full military alert, and on that pretext seizing the arms from the rural communes. 'There are strong passions in support of both sides among our population,' the President says one day, and this becomes the basis for what Fidel will call 'treacherous Jackstonean neutrality.' Jackstone will not like dumping poor Fidel, but he must. Then see his diplomacy neatly divide East from West Africa, Portuguese from Spanish South America, and incorporate them all until his hegemony extends to the edges of the great, air-conditioned Arabian dome on that side; includes the subsummation of the European ruin and Western Russia; and, moving in the other direction, ends only at the prickly Philippines.

"Have you understood all this?

"If so, you will understand why, overflowing with the emotions of the latest transmission, which I have been receiving all this night, I have been helpless not to invade your dreams."

FUSION

"Okay, buddy, what about the diphthongs?" Hoffman seems to hear a voice like his own saying, getting tough, before he is hustled off down gleaming, crooked corridors, insubordinate.

"Fæn, fœn." Maury's voice follows Hoffman's journey, passes it, reaches the turns in the corridors now ahead of the prisoner, so that the voice, echoing back, comes from in front of rather than behind Hoffman. "But language is too good to be true. The first word in any dictionary responsible enough to eschew the double *a* for representing that simple long *a* followed by *l* in proto-malayo-polynesian is, of course, that very *aardvark* poor Castro feared, the five-foot earth pig that eats ants in Africa. And unless you pick your dictionary at random, you will surely find the last word in it to be *zyzzogeton,* a South American leafhopper.

"When it is done in the Caribbean and we take the earth pig to South America, won't he eat zyzzogetons? So words eat words and what is left is what has happened.

"Billy Hell, in the last transmission I saw myself on the screen for the first time, and it was many years from now."

"What about the thorn letter?" Hoffman cries, defiant.

Maury's gentle voice corrects him: "We'll come to that, but Billy you're mistaken. The old thorn letter, pronounced 'th,' was never *y*. It looked like an italic lower-case *b* in runic, and as the runic typefaces wore out, medieval printers would substitute a *y* for it. That's all. Stop trying to divert me, Billy, please.

"There'd been a change in Fats. His Madison Avenue briskness was gone, and the prolixity of his language much diminished. I saw and heard myself ask about Horny Gus, finding Fats alone that way.

FATS. Retired, Maury. Said he'd come to visit, but he never does. Gabriel senile.

MAURY. I understand La Mère ran away and joined a convent.

FATS. Can't touch her there at all.

MAURY. I don't see Tondelayo.

FATS. Sleeping. Maury, I hear they're telling about a new God.

MAURY. Yes, Father.

FATS. You, well. Are you in touch with Him, Boy?

MAURY. Yes. Yes, we're in touch. Only it's a Her.

FATS. That's a joke, isn't it?

MAURY. Used to be a joke. Don't Gods start that way, as jokes? An example would be the primitive scatalogical explanation for rain and thunder, wouldn't it?

FATS. There's another possibility, Boy, ask Euhemerus. He says it's, Boy, is it, the new One, is it Mary?

MAURY. I'm not allowed to say. She's had a lot of experience, though, being prayed to. She doesn't forget to forgive.

FATS. Old Gods never die, Maury.

MAURY. I know, sir. I know.

FATS. Asses to asses, jest to jest . . . did I tell you about Mazda? Never mind. What did you want to see Me about, Maury?

MAURY. It doesn't seem so urgent now, but . . . Fats, I'm bigger than Alexander, holier than Rome. Can't I . . . call myself king?

FATS. I know, son. I know. You getting to it now, the crossward puzzle.

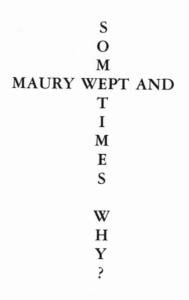

```
                    S
                    O
                    M
        MAURY WEPT AND
                    T
                    I
                    M
                    E
                    S

                    W
                    H
                    Y
                    ?
```

Ynd symytymys Y.

18: ♩ ⁊ ♪ ♩♩♩, You Know?

Hoffman. His lonely time has come. Time to be devious, time to overbear, time to stop trying to explain, time for treachery. Full, friendless Billy, absented from felicity awhile, looks inches taller, has acquired a presence to go with the absence. People notice him, without knowing why they do. Two weeks ago you could overlook him, like a small phone bill.

Snazzer Short empathizes. "His gut's twenty-four hours ahead of his brain, Ralph. He knows what he's going to do a day before he knows why."

Last night Hoffman heard the orchestra rehearse. Karen Jackstone sat with him, reading along the vocal parts so he'd know how the words fit horns and strings.

"Well. What did you think, Billy?"

"Loud." Hoffman prepares to negotiate with Ralph and Sato, over coffee at the State House cafeteria. "Can you give me any more time with Scene Two?"

"I would not be able to slow the tempo." Sato.

"How about a couple of big, mean, kind of farty pauses?"

"Certainly not." Ralph. "That is, I don't mean to be testy . . ."

"Yeah. Well, if that's the way it's gotta play."

"I'm sorry, Billy." Sato. "To retard musically changes the color so greatly."

In fact, of course, Hoffman is pleased with the speed of Scene Two, might even like it faster. Sato and Ralph are much too honorable to suspect this. Bad Billy tosses the next line back over his shoulder for luck. "Okay, then, if you can just hold the volume down for Scene Three, we got no other big problems."

"You believe the orchestra will be too loud even with three such voices as Marcel, Beth, and Henry?" Sato sounds surprised.

"It's right where we need those voices, all right. Every word, every single word's gotta be clear, or we lose the play."

Ralph, sorry to be testy. "Opera!"

"The audience understands all the words in Scene Three, boy, we can drive from there for a last-act curtain in Zulu with tomtoms. It's all visual after Scene Three."

"For heaven's sake—" Ralph begins.

Sato interrupts his friend pacifically. "I understand your concern, Billy. Of course. I believe we can be quiet enough."

"Yeah? What are you gonna do? Turn up the singers' mikes and tell the orchestra to take a walk around the block?"

"Please—" This time Sato begins and Ralph interrupts.

"You must trust Sato to make the singers audible, Billy. You simply must. It's not the first opera he ever conducted. Conductors know many ways of handling heavy orchestration."

"Yeah, I guess I'm being stupid." Tries for an abject frown, to keep from grinning. He's just gotten more authorization than he had any right to expect.

This table, in the State House cafeteria, is Hoffman's place of business now.

"Debbie! Sit down. Can I get you coffee?"

"You must not drink so much coffee, Billy. It's bad . . . such a dreadful little hat."

"Velour, huh?" It's a narrow brim, fuzzy felt number Hoffman dug out of his suitcase. Now he puts it on. "Listen, in Scene One. Halfway through, Pill wins a pot and says he's out for blood. Okay. Give me some blood in the lights there, will you? And keep pushing up the red."

She's too smart for him. Everybody's too smart for him. "So. Scene One is very long, now you decide to play it like two scenes."

"If you give me a little help, I do."

"You reblock and I must change my whole light book for Scene One."

"Just the second half. Hey. I'll give you my hat?" Takes it off, offers it to her. Debbie grabs the little thing and hits him with it. Beats him, smiling away her exasperation. Hoffman cowers.

Mostly wins by losing, but sometimes it's the other way around:

"Mona, hey. Over here. Hi. You already got some coffee, sit down."

"I don't think we can change the rehearsal schedule, Mr. Hoffman."

"Listen to that. All the ugly people in my show call me Billy, the pretty ones say Mr. Hoffman, you know? Why's that? No chance of getting the Scene Five people here, huh?"

"I'm sorry. I tried to call Beth first. She's already gone out."

"Yeah. Or maybe she's not back in yet."

"Well, maybe, Billy. Do you like that better? Maybe, because I couldn't get Johnny Ten, either."

"Let it go. Schedule's probably okay. What have we got?"

"Run-throughs on the telephone scene this morning, and polish Scene One, starting at noon."

"Tell you a secret." Wink. "We're gonna reblock the second half. I told that damn Debbie, and she stole my hat. What I didn't tell her, we're going to reblock Scene Three, too, you and me."

"Are we? Oh, how?"

"From here on, Mona, we're not doing an opera, we're not doing a play, we're not even doing a very damn good pantomime. Our people don't move that well. What we got is like a foreign movie with no titles. We've got to make pictures. Like in Scene Three, we're not going to be focusing on Beth's entrance. What's gotta be clear from the pictures is that Al really is indifferent to this great-looking new chick with the thrilling voice, you know? We gotta have Al with his back to Norah, Al paying more attention to anything else on stage, Al impatient for her to leave—and Norah plucking at him. I mean, Snazzer's got it in the words, but who's going to hear them? Norah just can't look like she's getting a flicker from him."

"Have you told Marcel?"

"That won't be hard, not much flicker to start with. I'm just giving you an example. Making pictures, you know? Here's the shocker, Mona. I'm sorry, but I changed my mind. Hughmore keeps his lousy beard."

"Mr. Hoffman!"

"I know. I know it's an issue to you. Me too, and I hate like hell to let the son of a bitch win one. But he's gotta to be a visual villain for us. Every minute he's onstage, that beard's his villain mark. I just had to decide he was right, I was wrong. Marcel, the noble pink balloon. Hughmore, the mean, pointed, pricky beard."

Her eyes go down. She won't reply.

"I heard the music last night. Now watch, you're looking at an absolute musical illiterate, but suggestible . . . Jesus, I'm like a baby crow. I try to imitate everything. Hey, you're really sore, aren't you?"

She shakes her head no, but won't look up.

"I have to get up in the middle of the night, anybody else'd be going to the can, but me, I've got to write some music. I mean, I can't read, write, play, or sing, but there I am, summarizing the whole pacing for the show as one bar of four-four. Look:" Grinning, draws a quarter note, an eighth rest, an eighth note, and three quarter notes tied as a triplet. "Five notes, five scenes: bammo, bam, bammabammabamma. Does that make sense to a musician?"

"Yes, Mr. Hoffman. I'd better go unlock Old Biology now."

As she walks away, Hoffman notices that her left hand, which she generally holds high and is often, as a matter of fact, exercising with Silly Putty (which she is supposed to squeeze out between the fingers, gather, and squeeze again) is hanging down, trailing along forgotten, at an odd, pathetic angle.

The time is 9:45 A.M., at Hoffman's cafeteria command post and only a fraction of a second earlier two miles west, at the Territorial Motel, where John Ten Mason, M.D., lets himself back into the room where he and Beth have spent the night. Though he has a place, and she a room at the State House, Beth just thought it would be fun to sneak off to a motel last night, naughty as a kitten.

He brings her a pot of tea, an order of cinnamon toast, and the morning paper, from the motel dining room. She is still asleep. He reads the paper.

Now in Old Biology, Marcel, Skeats, and Sidney are in place for the telephone scene, and Debbie is measuring Sidney once again.

"What we have for furniture will be zo girlish," Debbie says. "Like Little Abner's Daisy Mae. There will be a dressing table with pink ruffles, but the table is, you can see, this orange crate, and the ruffle put on with roof nails. A mirror, but with advertising for sewing machines, and a stool, also with ruffles, but a cow-milking stool, you see? You like to wear a short negligee, yes?"

If Sidney's seemly smile protests abashment, this is perhaps a reward for Dick Auerbach, the sole spectator, who sits stolidly, watching, having promised his lady to be on hand every time this lurid scene between Hugh-more-paws and Simple Sidney is rehearsed.

Hoffman says: "The phone rings, okay? You come on in ein so short negligee . . ." Debbie is trying not to laugh. "Und put ein knee on der milk-cow stool." Hoffman gets his hat back, right between the shoulder blades.

Beth's eyes open. The tea is cold. She smiles at Johnny Ten, murmurs, and holds out bare arms. The nightgown she kicked out of ten hours ago, under the covers, is still down there. There are two empty fifths of California champagne on the floor, and a third, half full, on the table beside the bed. Johnny's stomach and forearm muscles tense pleasantly. In an incredibly sensual night, during which he had more length, strength, and rebound than seems medically possible, he found himself yielded to so completely that the recollection now is almost embarrassing. Inch by inch, Beth's whole, generous body seemed to sensitize and give way to him, all its depths and expanses, the big, firm, glowing buttocks, sculpted back, hills and hollows, thighs and arms—the surprisingly neat hands and fine feet, the waist with its endearing little bulge of sloppiness to be kneaded and castigated, the entering places, all open to his touch and probe and most punishing stimulation. Like that of a delicate porcupine, all over tiny spines, his body, away from the sexual centers, seemed to fit Beth's pore by pore. Or they were like Velcro with nerve endings, overengineered to be redundantly held together, too, by one tender-coated, steel-cored bolt locked into soft, insidious nuts and washers.

Waking and reaching, she is still that wonderful, soft, sensual receiver. He descends on her, clothed and buttoned, and she makes immediate moans of pleasure, as if the night were just beginning now.

"Oh, you John, yes. Mmmmmm. Now. Give me that champagne, you John."

"It's flat, I'm afraid." He untangles himself and sits on the bed, watching her with a smile.

"Such a dear, skeptical Columbus, oh, I'm sure it's round." She drinks from the bottle, nudity emerging from the bedclothes. "Let's get dressed and get some more." Naughty.

Johnny smiles and shakes his head. "Got a rehearsal pretty soon, Bethgirl."

Some kind of dark, wicked, humorous gargle comes out of her. Sounds like: "dhull wuthut, John. Let's go to Rock Island."

"Can't do her, Bethie." But he is proud. Look at that. Listen to it. What in the hell hath John Ten wrought? "Tonight's coming."

"Soo'um-ay-ay." Grabs a finger formerly belonging to him and sucks it, making a strange, surrounding noise. Suddenly he would like to recover himself.

"You chick'm, John?"

"Reckon, Bethie. What's the game?"

"Janet's in Rockrock Island," God, she's got two fingers now, slides them down between her breasts, hunches her shoulders forward and makes a hugger.

"Margesson? She got a concert?"

"Nonono, she wants to see me."

Johnny Ten stands up. He means to do it lightly, not fall up onto his feet and stagger.

"Lotsa thingsyou doanno, innocent as clouds and pretty John." Transferring her caresses to the empty champagne bottle, she rolls it up and down her stomach, exposed now to just above the hip bones, tilts the bottle, disappears it under the covers.

"World's full of things I don't know." If he's so cool, how come he didn't realize all his weight had got onto one foot, throwing him slightly off balance?

"You'd like my Janet, yes, you would. Come see her with me, Johnnyjohn . . . owww." Jesus, what did she do to call forth that little sound of pleased pain?

"Yeah. Yeah, sure I would."

"She had this concert up in Madison and called, like a great glass trumpet, and said Rockabye Island, I said nonononownow, couldn't do it, mustn't, and Jan said, oh, I'll come there, Beth, my soft one, and big Beth got just a little panicky, oww, can you imagine people in State City if Margesson, even in disguise, sitting in rehearsal all dark glasses, purple veils, and swishy skirt and boots, oh, she has boots, John, come on, John." Sits up. Prims the covers. Kewpie grins. "She's waiting at Rock Island, and you've never seen anything like her."

"I guess that's the truth. Yes, ma'am."

"Oh, but poor Johnny has to rehearse, he does, and I don't. Not today, not till tomorrow afternoon, and I can drive."

Beth, I'd like it if you wouldn't. Can he say that? What kind of wiggles, moans, and metaphors would a line like that bring out of her? Well, there's only one thing for him to do: give her a kiss and a pinch on the bon voyage, and walk out lightly on the balls of his feet.

"Beth, I'd like it if you wouldn't."

"But, Johnny, I want you to be with us, too." Lets the covers slide off, throws one leg over the other and so off the bed, marvelous tawny flesh picking up alluring colors as she ripples in the morning light coming in through filmy motel curtains, down on her beautiful knees to him, arms around his lightly sweating thighs, cheek pressing against his groin, face turning toward and into it, breathing, kissing, and then rolling away, lying on the carpet for just a moment, stomach down, looking back at him over her shoulder, and rising away from him fluidly to her feet, which brings her to some draperies in which she slowly, turning, wraps herself, until all that Johnny sees of her are roguish, baby-goddess slanty eyes.

"Bethy, I might just be too square for a scene like that."

"Do what you want, beautiful John, Janet would, oh, I won't, won't, better not say what Janet." Her intentions toward the closet doorknob she is backing into, taking her drapes along as far as they'll go, are pretty damn imponderable. Bites her lip. "I'll call old Hoffman for you, say I've got to go to Rockie, not in shape to drive myself, and that's as true as milk and muffins, John, you know it is, he'll let you off, you can miss one rehearsal, not like you were being paid in rubies, oh, I'll make him let you offf."

Johnny Ten Mason doesn't know at this point how he feels. Things have certainly changed, yes sir. Is he furious, dismayed, scared, horny, goddamn? And what a male tail grail she's waving sans merci, himself with two such women, Jesus, Margesson! and anyway, he *is* alarmed for Beth. How can she operate a motor vehicle while intoxicated with her own juices?

However, there is only one possible thing to do—cool, neat, fastidious, independent: Walk away. Give her a smile, blow her a kiss . . . Christ, she has wiggled the door open and is disappearing into the closet . . . anyway, walk away. Out.

"Okay, Bethgirl." Yes, he walks. Into the closet.

"Marcel? Want to stick around a minute." Hoffman. "Hey, everybody, that was a good rehearsal. See you after lunch. Eat fast. Marcel?"

"Yes, Mr. Hoffman."

"Jesus, all the weak voices in the show call me Billy. The strong ones call me Mr. Hoffman. What's that for? Listen, you bail that kid out?"

"Oh, the painter. Yes. Well, the Ridings did, that is."

"He's okay, huh? Listen, you seen this thing next door?" He means the natural-history exhibit.

"Well, just glancing in. I haven't really taken time, sir."

"No, I mean. Come on. It's interesting." Hoffman leads the way, gesticulating, talking, stopping his tenor finally in front of a case of stuffed cormorants, mounted as if in flight. "Flying snakes, you know? Listen, Marcel. You got an irony problem."

"I'm not sure what you mean, Mr. Billy. I'm sorry."

"Okay. Irony on the stage is a simple thing. It's just what comes when the audience knows more than the characters do about what's going on up there. Audience knows Oedipus is marrying his mom, right?"

"Well, yes, sir. Yes, they do know that."

"Terrible thing. Awful. They know the gods are really going to crunch this kid. Chew him up good, right? Incest, boy. Worst thing a guy can do. Horrible. Repulsive. The way to really get your living guts laid open and fed to the celestial worms. Yeah, the audience knows that. But what does Oedipus know?"

"Well." This is making poor Marcel nervous. "He . . . he doesn't know it's his mother."

"Christ," Hoffman says. "He knows one hell of a lot. He's got more misinformation than the TV weatherman. He knows this lovely stranger in her late thirties is the most beautiful, desirable thing that ever stirred his young loins. Wow. Not only that, there's every possible advantage to getting married to her. Riches, boy. Power. Oedipus absolutely cannot believe his luck. He knows, not just feels, he knows this is the best thing that could possibly happen to him. And the audience knows it's the worst."

"I've never really, well, I do guess I realize that. I just never quite thought about it that way."

"I wonder which eats up more fishes, these cormorants or a pelican? Listen, what does Al absolutely know about Sally Anne when he calls up on the telephone?"

"Well, of course, he still thinks she's a very nice girl."

"No, Marcel. He knows it. With every goddamn atom of his lover's heart, he knows she is the purest, fairest, most wonderful person in the entire world. See what I mean? You can't play Al for pathos, you can't play him for a guy with a cause to mistrust women. He's triumphant. This phone call is a man's whole life working out right. He's really confident now."

Marcel doesn't look too happy. "Do you mean virile, Mr. Hoffman?"

"If I meant it, I'd say it. I'm a brutal bastard, boy." Brutal bastard Hoffman. "Know what I heard? I heard the Japs can train these cormorants to catch fish for them, only they got a collar around that skinny neck so the bird can't swallow."

Marcel, smiling. "That's irony, isn't it?"

"Huh?"

"For the bird. He must just feel that he's making his lovely dive and is going to get something lovely to eat—"

"Hey."

"—but the audience knows about the little collar."

"Okay, okay. All right. Look, I'm going to improvise a telephone scene with you. Who I am, is the director of the goddamn Paris Opera Company. You met me after I heard you sing, got it? I was flattering, all over you, but you've about given up expecting to hear from me, so the phone rings. Ready?"

"Well, I'm not sure I understand."

"It's okay. Answer the phone. Ting-a-ling, you know?"

"Hello?"

"M'soor Marcel St. Edouard?" Hoffman's burlesque French accent is a real vintage wince maker.

"Well, well, yes."

"Aha. Marcel. Mon ami. You are readee to come wiz me to Paree?"

"Paris?" Marcel's heart is in the case with the cormorants, at which he stares. If only the big one in the lead would complete the wing stroke in which the taxidermist has suspended it, power on, crash out through the glass, leading his flight out through the maze of animal and bird cases, crashing out the window, and on over the prairies west to California and the ocean, taking Marcel's heart with them. But he supposes the showcaseful of stuffed fish next over would reanimate, too, and the birds would stop and eat, and Marcel's big heart would drown in painted waves.

"In thees company we 'ave many parts for you. Debussy! Ravel! La-fayette! So you come, right away. On Air France I weel send zee first-class ticket. The champagne. The Beef of Wellington. We meet you at Orly, okay?"

"Why, yes, I guess so."

"Come on. Play it with me. We take you to the Reetz 'otel. You like the Reetz?"

"That will be fine. Sir."

"My board, they have heard your wonderful records. Let us talk now about salary, about clothes, about zee tour of Russia. When can you come to us?"

"Well, right away. I mean as soon as the ticket gets here."

"Ah, magnifique. How you feel about zis?"

"Oh, wonderful. Well, I . . . well, of course. Thank you, thank you so much, Monsieur. *A votre service!*"

"See how pleased you are? How you're strutting, calling your friends to tell them the good news, capering? Of course, the audience knows the son of a bitch has sold you to the Moscow Circus. Clowns will pound you when you try to sing. Acrobats will land on you for a net. You're going to wind up live meat for the trained bears, you see? That's what the audience knows, but you don't, do you?"

Beth bathes, perfumes. Sitting naked on the motel bed, she calls Janet Margesson, and they sing to one another, sort of, over the telephone. She hardly even feels like getting dressed, much less like calling Hoffman; who could sing to Hoffman over the telephone? Suppose the little man said no, it wouldn't be all right for darling John to miss this funny little rehearsal? Wouldn't that bring Beth down? But she'll be mostly good. That is, she'll get dressed, anyway. Lovely soft, fresh panties, comfortably skimpy bra, crisp pink broadcloth culottes and a stunning tailored piqué sleeveless blouse. Oh, she'll look cool. Oh, the foresight with which, last night, she packed her overnight case, on the lovely chance things might work out this way.

"Hey, Bethgirl. Looking great, you make that call to Billy Bigears, did you?" Kiss. "Let's play us some big hooky."

Tricky Hoffman. It's as if he kept forgetting to work on Scene Five, which, finally, they will begin running through tomorrow. He has held off in a way that seems almost like absent-mindedness to the cast, producing a certain anxiety in them, considerable anticipation, and maybe an uneasy sense that it is somehow their fault, that their tardiness in achieving perfection in the first four scenes makes it they who are guilty of not getting to the end of the story. Actually, Hoffman has no image yet of how he himself will direct them to end of the story. Needs something.

But he is ready to polish Scene One exhaustively this noon and expects everyone to be in a mood to work, pointing emotionally toward the resolution they will all start to realize tomorrow. Three complete run-throughs on One. The first will be very fast, without accompaniment, and with some new blocking. Then they'll sing it with the music. Then they'll really do it.

So one of his dumb actors doesn't show. Singers, yeah. Right. Naturally. The medical guy, the Texas leaguer, that sings Bert Tannenbaum. Dr. Here-I-am, Depend-on-me, Keep-it-clean, right? Just doesn't show. Just like that. Not a word. Probably struck oil in the hospital parking lot, and he's busy capping the well, huh?

"Okay." When you gotta rehearse, you gotta rehearse. "Okay, Mona."

"Places for the opening."

"Karen, you play the phrases when Bert sings, okay?"

"Mr. Hoffman?"

"Yeah, Maury?"

"You want me to, I know the part. I sing his and mine, too?"

"Yeah, okay. Places."

"You want me to sing both parts?"

"I said okay. Just take his lines from wherever you are. Let's get started."

There's always something you can work on. He runs them again and again through the middle arias, through the mounting tension in the second half, has to skip the closing tableau that precedes intermission and is built around Bert; skips to the swamp scene.

Maury has no trouble singing two roles, though the others get confused at times picking up their cues from him.

Most of the way to Rock Island, Beth sleeps, warm and throbbing against Johnny Ten as he drives the interstate, so that his whole right side is moist from it.

Once she wakes and asks, in his right ear: "Do you believe in ecstasy?"

"Now that is one hell of a question to ask a man at high noon of a Wednesday." Scruffles her hair.

In addition to the fond weight and warmth of Beth against him, Johnny is further immbolized by the open bottle of champagne held between his legs, under the steering wheel. Occasionally Beth will slide her head down, cover the mouth of the bottle with a mouth of her own, slip her hands onto its sides, and raise up gurgling. Occasionally, if there isn't a car too close behind them, John will accept the fat green fifth from her, and have a matching gurgle before he holsters it again.

Past the Atkins exit, about halfway to Rock Island, he pulls off onto the shoulder to open another bottle. There is an uphill grade here where the big trucks lose speed. Window open, cork loosened, Johnny waits for a Pacific Intermountain Express semi to come up alongside before giving the cork the final thumb, and dots the *i* on *Pie*. Beth grabs for the new bottle and gets foam on her face. This she presents to have the bubbles kissed off, and Johnboy's in the mood.

"Like old Cougar used to say, if you don't mean to put on the brake, pick up your feet. Old Hoffman mad, was he?"

Beth, in reply, takes his right hand, turns it palm up, pours a dram of champagne into it, and drinks from it. "Salty."

In Rock Island, Beth directs him uphill from the river, not to a hotel but to a handsome brick house, divided, it appears, into three flats. It's owned by the railroad, Beth says, and the apartments are used to house and entertain big shippers. There's a Continental convertible parked in front. John pulls Beth's little Ghia in behind it, rather pleased to be arriving in something reasonably fashionable, rather pleased with the appearance he and Beth make—he's worn his Brooks Brothers summer cord, a narrow tie, and his tan is right.

But, hey, the people who let them into the apartment are dressed as if they're about to step into rowboats—jeans, sneakers, and light shirts, all around—and not Janet Margesson alone, but that famous woman and another and a rather famous man, too.

John Ten Mason, M.D., with his sincere love of music and his good-naturedly acknowledged limitations in performing it, limitations as much sociological as physical, since he was unwilling to face a life with less than a surgeon's sure-thing income, loves musicians. He is not, with his Texas middle-class training, unimpressed by wealth. In idle daydreams, and never without chuckling at their shallowness, he has, he might confess to a roommate or, if he had one, sympathetic brother, sometimes seen himself traveling on yachts, sitting in European opera boxes, as good old country-boy friend and physician to the rich and musical.

How, then, can a missed rehearsal counterbalance walking into a luxurious, corporate-kept apartment with wonderful Beth Paulus on his arm, to join, for the afternoon and evening, Janet Margesson, Maggi Taro Short, and the man who pays the bills for this opera Johnny's singing in, Hervey Gandenberg?

"Mr. Hoffman?" Maury catches up with Hoffman on the street outside of Old Biology.

"Yeah. Hey, thanks, Maury. You singing both parts was a help."

"I enjoyed it."

"Anybody find out what happened to the other guy?"

"I haven't heard. You don't suppose he's out of it?"

"I dunno. If he is, I guess we get ourselves another baritone. Hey, don't get your hopes up, you know?"

"You think he'll be back tomorrow?"

"They generally are. With pretty good excuses. And when they aren't, some unexpected fat boy with a pretty face shows up and takes the job. I got that straight from Channel One, Maury."

"Excuse me?"

"Aw, come on."

"Whatever you say, Colonel. Tell me one thing only?"

"Ask it."

"Would it be all right with you, sir, if I got the promotion? Could you make it work in the show?"

"Excuse me?"

"Aw, come on, Colonel."

" 'Tenshun!" Maury jerks to attention. People on the street stop and look. "Present . . . h'arms!"

Maury salutes. Hoffman returns it, and bows to the people. Maury bows to the people.

"Beth beautiful." Janet Margesson looks strange in jeans. She is tall, straight, and has the high-cheekboned, planes and angles kind of face sometimes called patrician and, in Johnny Ten's mind, more accurately associated with American Indians. Oddly enough, she's freckled; she has straight, black hair. The eyes are guarded and the smile fast and dissembling; he has seen that on television often enough. It's characteristic of the wives of East Coast political figures. She uses her speaking voice like a magnet, pulling everyone toward her, but could as easily reverse it to repulse.

". . . and hello, John, at last."

Beth runs to her and they embrace, not as women do in public, feigning emotion, but as a secretly involved couple might, feeling and concealing sensual response. A brush on the lips, a brief pressing together of hips. "We must put some pants on her," Miss Margesson says, arm around Beth's waist.

Meanwhile Johnny's Texas eye totals Gandenberg's appearance at around twelve hundred bucks—razor-cut hair, Italian knit shirt, Levi's, German tennis shoes, wide alligator belt, solid-silver buckle, and a thousand-dollar watch.

"Herve Gandenberg." He offers a firm, trim, tanned hand, smiling cockily, a grey-flecked ball of fire, a man in motion. "These women don't believe in introductions. How're you, Johnny? Got time to shake hands, Beth?" Add another thousand for perfectly capped teeth.

"I recognized you, sir," Johnny says. "Your picture's on the music-department bulletin board, and from what I hear, we ought to have it on the wall at the hospital, too."

"Jesus, why? All I give is money." Gandenberg. "You guys make it count." Ran up the family million—John has seen the quote—on *the three B's: bellies, beans, and beets. Enjoy spending it on the musical B's, and wherever else it'll help.* Those are pork bellies, soybeans, and sugar beets. Gandenberg's enormous in the commodity market. "Maggi, come here—or do you know Johnny already?"

"If I did, would I be standing here with my hands in my pockets?" It's a hokier voice than Margesson's, from a prettier lady—wasp-nest teats, bumblebee waist, stung mouth, and hornet hips. This is no lady. This is what's buzzing Professor Short clean out of the orchard.

Beth is bulldozed by Margesson off into a bedroom, just as John was getting comfortable. Herve wants him to sit down and have a glass. They are drinking bullshots, made with beef tea from England and Polish vodka. The Polish vodka has buffalo grass in it. Johnny has a swallow, and it's like the grass went down and someone lit it. He can't keep his eyes off the bedroom door.

"Jan's just changing the baby's pants, Doctor Doll," Maggi Short says, mocking and amused. "This one's an actual Texas doctor doll, Herve."

"Yes, ma'am." Johnny's not without powers of recovery. "Wind me up, I turn into some kind of a arma-doctor-dillo."

Hervey laughs. "How does that kind of animal go on caviar?"

"Can't say they ever get the real stuff." Best thing to do to get the glass out of his hand might be to drink it empty.

Upon which, Maggi is beside him with a piece of toast spread with black stuff, and he didn't need a hand; she's going to feed him. Salty. "Good, Johnny Ten? That's what they call you, isn't it?"

"Where would you have heard that?" That damn glass is full again, and in his hand. Takes a gulp. "You've been gone, haven't you?"

"But not forgotten." Maggi, tragically. "Our thoughts must reach her, somewhere, for we remember her so much. 'Nother bite?"

"Not so fast."

" 'Nother bite!"

"Margesson food." Gandenberg. "When she's on tour, I have to have fish eggs flying after her all over the country. Mag, fix young John a plate of steak."

Before he has time to figure out what bothers him about the caviar information, Johnny Ten is confronted by a plate of raw chopped meat. Raw? He doesn't even like it rare. He makes a polite show of tasting it.

Best stuff he ever put in his mouth.

Hughmore Skeats, stuffily: "I'd have expected you to maintain professional rehearsal discipline here."

"Yeah, me too, you know?"

"Have you reached young Mason to demand an explanation?"

"No, I can't say I've tried to do that."

"May I ask why bloody not?"

"Better for him to reach me, isn't it?"

"I can't say I follow your ruckamacious reasoning, old boy."

"Well, there's three possibilities, huh? He got mixed up, he got detained, or he decided he'd rather play doodly squat. Either of the first two, what can we say but okay when he calls in, you know? But if it's the third, and we call him before he's got a story ready, then we gotta throw him out of the cast ten days before opening."

"Has it occurred to you we might replace him?"

"Could we, Hugh? You got some talent I don't know about? A fat boy with a pretty face, maybe—"

"I beg your pardon?"

"Look, the doctor closes the show, right? This moral figure, telling the pooky to get down on her knees and pick up the scrip, telling her it's eighty bucks' worth and she's got two good men lyin' dead because of it. Well, I think the doctor's going to look a little more authoritative doing that than your fat boy, Hugh."

"I haven't got a fuckamacious fat boy."

"That's what I mean."

Prettiest-colored wine he's ever seen.

"Pomerol." Maggi.

Herve. "Shall we open another?"

"I don't think your fiancée's in a rush to get to the church. Or even the next place, Herve."

Fiancée? That's what John caught, in the bit about flying caviar around: Then it's Gandenberg and Margesson who are a couple here. 'Fso, what about Margesson and Beth? 'Fso, where does Maggi Taro Short fit in? Wait. Grab the surcingle, cowboy, and look out for the horns. Aren't there buses back to State City? Then, to calm his apprehensions, Beth and Janet come out of the bedroom, Beth squeezed into jeans a bit too tight, and if raw steak tasted wonderful a minute ago, it tastes absolutely perfect now. They just weren't in there long enough. Were they? Probably Margesson watches herself around Gandenberg, come to think of it.

As if to confirm this surmise, Margesson kisses Herve hotly on the neck. Don't they go for the jugular, though? Maggi Short is fixing raw meat for Beth now, and a slice or two of cold roast capon, with which Beth won't have a bullshot, just some lovely red wine.

"You kids coming to Wisconsin, aren't you?" Herve.

"I'm afraid I'm ducking a small rehearsal right now, sir," Johnny says. "And Beth's got a big one tomorrow."

"I've got a plane." Hervey. "We'll be at camp in just a little over an hour. Come on, Janet. You'll explode if you eat any more of that."

She is finishing off the white jar of caviar, scooping it with the tip of her index finger and licking it away.

"Thirty-four dollars a lick," Maggi Short whispers into Johnny's ear. "Hmmmmm?" And she laughs without moving her lips away, till the old hearing organ wants to play chords and Beth in tight jeans slides into his lap.

"Let me give you a pair of jeans, Doctor." Gandenberg. "Thirtys?"

Hoffman. "We've done enough horsing, Mona. Dismiss them all but the ones in the swamp scene."

"Sidney, Marcel, and Mr. Skeats. The rest may go." Mona's wearing her left arm in a sling this afternoon. Hoffman decides not to ask about it.

The plane is a twin-engine five-seater, two, two, and one.

"You want to fly 'er, Johnny?"

"Haven't got past single engine myself."

"Check you out on this, if you like. Maybe tomorrow morning?"

"Be great. Thanks. I'd love that."

Puts Johnny in the single seat, behind, Beth and Maggi side by side in the middle, Margesson beside the pilot. Gandenberg flies carefully. Johnny feels confident, in spite of the Dom Perignon vintage Margesson opens and passes to her left. What the hell. Maggi, sharing a bottle of the same with Beth, hands the doctor one for his very own. He's doing the cork when he notices Beth's hand. It moves around under the seat belt, finds a buckle, and the seat belt flops away.

"Pants. Janny's pants too tight."

"Here." Good lord, Maggi is helping?

"Better." If it weren't for the motor noise, would one hear a zip?

"Best. Doctor doll, hand us up a rug?"

There are small, folded blankets on a shelf behind him.

Janet Margesson heard that. "Don't give them one."

Too late. He already has it in his hand. Soft. Tan. Reads the label as he hands it forward: 100% *Vicuña*

"Have to make Beth comfortable, Janny." Maggi. "Don't hog the champagne."

Johnny gives her his bottle. Champagne tastes sour to him now. He has a shot of straight buffalo grass, and decides to go to sleep.

In his half-dream, the plane lands smoothly at an airfield in cool, timbered woods, and he and Beth stroll over to a single-engine plane of Gandenberg's, are told they may fly it back to State City, and rehearsal is just starting. And in fact the plane does land, smoothly, so that there is a half-instant of elation until he sees, eyes fully open, that the airfield is in the midst of hot, cultivated fields. The vicuña rug is on the floor, Beth with the jeans belted but not fastened, is being handed out by Hervey Gandenberg, and Maggi Short looks smug and Janet Margesson looks fierce and Johnny Ten has got to scramble.

There is a station wagon there to meet them, a huge custom Chrysler, driven by a tall, moustached Mexican with huge, bare arms. Weird. Rich men in Texas have Mexican drivers.

Hervey makes the connection. "Make you feel at home, Doctor? Used to keep two families on the place up here, so there'd be enough of them to talk together. But I tell you—Galdencio, take the doctor's suit, will you, and press it for him?" Johnny hands over suit and shoes. "These east Wisconsin Germans around here. This is the bunch that sent Joe McCarthy to the Senate, about as mean and stupid as anyone can be. Threw a black man off a bridge here one day, all he was doing was fishing. And they weren't good to my Mexicans."

"How about Galdencio?"

'He's too tough to scare. Anyway, he married a local white girl and beats the crap out of her every day. The east Wisconsin Germans figure that makes him a regular guy."

It's a half-hour drive, away from the fields, along by woods, to a heavy, locked iron gate. Eight-foot cyclone fence, with three strands of barb along the top, runs from it five hundred yards in each direction.

The woods inside are thick.

Galdencio gets out to unlock the big gate, and Johnny says:

"You really don't like the locals, do you?"

"Oh, the fence is more to keep the dogs in than the people out," and as he says it, there is baying, and eight or ten Dobermans come bounding into view, up the graveled road through the pines.

"*Perritos,*" the Mexican yells. " 'Alt." And the dogs sit, their stubby tails wagging nervously as they wait to be released.

"Aren't they precious?" Beth wants to get out and pat them.

"Don't!" Gandenberg and Johnny together, and Hervey adds, "We could have Galdencio bring one over maybe, but all together they'd be a handful even for him." He slides under the wheel and calls out: "I'll take it in."

A quarter of a mile, and the trees open some. There's a lake out there, and then a house of redwood and glass, cantilevered over the water. A garage door opens on electronic signal, they drive in, and a moment later are walking past racks of fishing rods, cabinets of guns, on pile carpeting deep enough to lie down on anywhere. The big fireplace is filled with fresh flowers for summer. Outside the three walls of thermal glass that enclose the main room you can see nothing but water, as if the house were floating. Gandenberg, leading the way to the deck, calls it a cabin, and, standing with his guests out there, three feet above water, says:

"Lake Margesson. I own all the shoreline."

"Isn't it big enough to be public water?"

"Sure thing. Geological survey map shows a trail, beside my fence. But you try to follow it, you better be wearing pontoons. We blew a bunch of potholes."

"A castle and a moat." Beth.

There's a canoe, and a fast-looking inboard tied to the deck. Back inside, there's a kitchen, three bedrooms, three bathrooms, and a glass gallery looking back into the woods and opening onto the land side.

Out in the middle of the lake is a float plane, bobbing in the sunlight.

"There's something I could fly."

"Not unless you brought your motor with you." Hervey laughs. "That's a decoy, or just the opposite, John. Had some guys in a float plane land out there to fish one time, so we bought us that old shell. It's painted," wink, "kind of game-warden colors from the air. Stays in the boathouse through the winter."

Johnny's not so naïve as to ask what the local game warden thinks of it, though he'd kind of like to know how much Christmas present it takes.

Beside him, so casually that he's almost too late to notice, one of the world's more beautiful women is taking off her clothes: Maggi Taro Short, remarkably firm in the bosom, given her age and size. In spite of his professional indifference to nudity, John has himself an eyeful. Then he looks, as male manners require, at the man beside him, for the conventional exchange of looks of wonder or delight, and to his surprise Hervey Gandenberg is paying no attention at all. He's picked up a canoe paddle and is looking at that instead, critical of the faded varnish.

Maggi dives into the water.

"Swim. That's all she does up here. She may or may not cross the lake and back."

"She's a gorgeous swimmer," says John, watching, and hears a grunt and Gandenberg say,

"Hey."

Janet Margesson, slipping up behind her fiancé, has seized the canoe paddle from him, and is now stalking Beth with it. Beth's got jeans around her ankles, got one leg up to pull them off, when Janet Margesson lets her have it with the paddle, up and smartly across the bottom. Whack. Margesson wears panties, nothing more. Smallest breasts in camp.

"Janny, owww." Tears in the big eyes.

"Bad."

Whack, tears, and then Margesson drops the paddle, rushes, grapples, begins to wrestle her victim toward the water.

"No. Janny. Please . . ." In goes Beth, one leg free, the other still in jeans, a blue, short-sleeved work shirt ripped open and floating around her shoulders. Splash.

"I'll get you, bad little Beth." Margesson dives a clean dive into and past Beth. By the time she has swum back and is ready to commence ducking action, Beth does have the jeans all the way off.

"Please, my bra," Beth cries, and Margesson holds it up, then flings it behind her into the lake. Ducks her.

"Bad, bad little thing. Drown it." But now Beth has made it to the edge of the deck, grabs, desperate, and John can reach down a hand and help her up.

Sidney is pensive. "Wasn't it all right?"

Hoffman shakes his head. "I could hear you singing, but I couldn't get the words up there." He has just listened, from back in the balcony, to the swamp scene during which Sidney sings from the deepest part of the stage. "Don't worry about it."

"But with a big orchestra, Papa Hoffman, in a big hall . . ."

"We'll get you a big microphone, you know?"

Buffalo grass. Buffalo Bill. Buffalo John Ten Mason clings to the Polish vodka bottle, as if the austerity of drinking this in preference to the Dom Perignon, of which everyone else has a bubbly bottle, might keep him straight and manly.

It's déshabille time. Miss Margesson wears a man's bathrobe now; sure looks like more of that genuine vicuña. It's Herve's robe, and the tan of it is marvelous with her strawberry-flecked copper skin. Yes, sir. Maggi, however, now that she's done swimming, has on part of a swimming suit. Bikini bottom, you might say, exposing a dimple at the base of her spine, just before she cleaves, which a medical gentleman might recognize, but never remark publicly, as being really the scar from a neatly excised pilonidal cyst. Good piece of whittlin'. Now around her shoulders she wears, this Hollywood-type lady, a square of aquamarine silk, yes she does, and with the points of this she plays what you might call teat-tac-toe.

As for Bethie, she looks a little bit baby-fat, lying around with the two hard, grown-up females, still in her baptismal costume of underpants and a man's blue work shirt, but with, of course, the bra deep-sixed. The shirt, while open, has its tail tied, sometimes, across the pudge diaphragm.

Hervey, like his fiancée, and what the hell is going on around here anyway? wears vicuña, bathrobe, but maroon. Which would John want, anyway, maroon or tan? How could a fellow choose? Drinks. Johnny has Herve's jeans back on, rather pleased that the waist is clearly loose; barefoot, barechested Texas John. Okay.

Hervey sits with Beth, defying Margesson; the game is that he's protecting Beth from meanness. Shouldn't it be John protecting Beth? Hell, it is all he can do to protect his grass from the buffs.

Maggi, slowly, rolls over in the deep pile carpeting, onto her back. Margesson, beside her, eating with her fingers again yet another white porcelain jar of caviar. Takes a dab, considers it, smiles, leans over, and blows the tip of the aquamarine scarf away from Maggi's right nipple. Blows the right one clear. Puts her dab of caviar on it. Dabs the other nipple black, careful, deliberate, covering. Maggi smiles. Margesson eats the caviar.

Things aren't weird enough. Margesson looks directly at Buffalo John, and says in the voice you obey: "Put the bottle down, baby, and have a nip." And somehow, in the drift and roll of late afternoon, with a warm sunset over the pure, pine-bordered lake, Johnny Ten finds himself prone on the floor, tasting caviar for the second time in his life as the great diva, never hurried, spreads two canapes for him.

I mean, what's good manners now? Do you eat the right one first or the left? He catches deliberation, intently begins to roll each tiny egg off its quarter-inch, circular, hard, pliant, live, pink platelet with the tip of his tongue, feeling too the caviar-sized bumps of horripilation, gooseflesh, correct, with the tongue tip, hooking in caviar, egg by egg, crunching each globule between two front teeth for the oily spurt of salt, and when the nipple is clean, after achieving a creditable nirvana, taking it into his mouth to get what taste of fish egg clings.

Then, feeling slim, strong fingers slide under the waistband of the jeans and down his belly, turns his face for a good-natured look at Margesson and sees, over the freckled shoulder, the disappearance of Gandenberg with Beth.

He would rise and righteous around some, though not ill-naturedly of course, but there's something really enervating about buffalo grass, apparently, and the hands of Margesson are firm, their intention not disintriguing from the standpoint of a young fellow with a half shelf of Margesson records back at his apartment in State City. What the hands intend is to take the doctor's pants off.

Down over the innominate bones go the pants, why nameless?, each consisting in its consolidation of an ilium, an ischium, and a pubis and connecting to the socketed acetabula, fused above at the upper base of the sacrum and culminating inferiorly at the pubic symphysis, it tickles. What tickles? cried the queen. Testicles, cried the king. Maggi's eyes, he notes, as the hands urge him over onto his back, look past him into Margesson's, and there is a faint smile there.

Maggi's face now comes slowly over his as she turns, lowers from the left side, and begins to kiss his mouth, meanwhile playing twiddle with his own damn-fool, vestigial, hell, responsive nipples. Down below and cut off from sight the pants seem to have reached the right patella and left femur, and it is interesting to note that in birds the true femoral region is hidden by the skin and feathers of the body, while some ornithologists, who should know better, persist in so denoting the segment below, containing the fibula and the tibia. What is happening to the man's cock? She pinched it! Now Maggi is soothing, holding him down for her partner, probably didn't mean to hurt, ouch! She bit it!

"Owww."

Now he is subdued, and they are pacing themselves as they work him over, mouth-to-all-points resuscitation, yeah, they got him just about resuscitated all over, have they worked together before? Mrs. Short, wife of the well-known bon vivant and littérateur Rigby "Snazzer" Short, now begins to loom. She looms like a slowly rising, out-of-focus blimp, face mounting his face—and oh, those hands, they are removing Mrs. Short's bikini bottom—shoulders rising over his chest, her partition separating the thoracic cavity from the abdominal cavity hovercrafting above his belly button—and those most famous coloratura hands have moved a sofa cushion or something under his semivoluntarily rising rump.

And Maggi mounts him. She is having him. Coming into focus up there in the middle distance as she straightens is a tender smile. For her partner, whom she kisses. And now the partner's freckled face descends, and turns into busy tongues and goddamn hundreds of teeth, and swarms of opposed thumbs and fingertips, hopping over him, nipping, sucking, all the vulnerable places, the armpits, inner thighs, the very rectal crease and pubic seam. It is a matter of control, of course. They work him toward orgasm and tweak him away, attention suddenly diverted to the place tweaked, then directed to return by synchronous massage. Buffalo John. As his prostate finally unloads, in a final pitch and ague, Margesson covers his face completely with her crotch, and in the smothering darkness thus created he cannot see, of course, but knows that the braves who have butchered him are embraced and kissing up there.

Snazzer Short. "No. Still no answer, Billy."

Maggi Short. "Relax, baby."

Hoffman. "Let's check around. The Gump, the schoolhouse. Maybe somebody knows something."

Margesson. "Thank you, Doctor."

Short. "Come on. We'll take my car."

Maggi. "Be right back, lovers."

Hoffman. "I gotta have those kids tomorrow. Look, no offense, Snazzer, okay? You better let me drive."

There is no postcoital cuddling, nuzzling, or further conversation. Margesson lies back. John rolls away, hitches onto a low foam sofa, and looks at Janet. Maggi returns, and there begins something he has sometimes felt he'd like to watch, but he's in no great shape to enjoy it now. They are done with him, unaware of him, have rolled away together, abominably embraced. Margesson's on top when they come to rest, her black hair covering Maggi's face, hips thrusting like a man's. Then there is a heave, and turning over, and now Maggi's the man, grasping something in her hand, moving it with her hips in and out of the famous diva's internationally celebrated ringdangdoo, as they murmur, kiss, get excited, and John has seen several models of dildo before, passing as they do around the medical school, obtained by direct mail only, for educational purposes, "the orangutang," "the Viennese warthog," "the Pike's Peak," but gentlemen, there is no recorded technical or scientific name for the implement we are observing at present, other than its common designation, a bratwurst.

There is a hiatus. Beth appears during it, quietly, and sits on Johnny Ten's foam sofa, raising his head into her lap. He finds this cloying. Someone, Hervey probably, puts the Polish vodka bottle in his hand. He finds this uncloying. It's about too dark to see what anybody's doing in the room, but probably no one's doing much of anything. Except restless Hervey, can't sit still, has removed the flowers from the fireplace and is building a fire. Buck naked. Buck naked Johnny drifts off to sleep. Then, last thing he hears is Janet saying to Hervey,

"What on earth were you two *doing* in there?" This is such a nutty, practically eerie, thing for her to say that he can feel a smile on his lips as he moves into sleep.

"Billy?"

"Yeah. Yeah, hello Mike. Come in, huh?"

"You were asleep. I'm sorry."

"Kind of tired. At least you didn't call me Mr. Hoffman, huh?"

"Billy, what did you say to Mona? I'm sorry to wake you."

"I don't know. What do you mean?"

"Her arm. Or her hand. Sometimes it gets paralyzed, but there's no physical reason."

"Yeah. Well, I guess I took something away from Mona, Mike. I'm sorry."

"What? I guess I know."

"A little victory. We all need'm, Mike. I'm sorry. Well. I had to tell her I was going to let Skeats keep his beard."

"I wondered if that was it."

"I knew she'd mind. I hoped it wouldn't be all that important, you know?"

"Have you told Mr. Skeats yet?"

"No."

"Could you change your mind again?"

"No, Mike. I couldn't do that."

"I didn't think you could."

There is a dream of stimulation without humiliation, and a piece of Johnny's head is eager for him to wake to it, and another piece is opposed, and the ayes have it. Maggi Short unmouths him and sits back, grinning, on her heels. The others, sitting by the fire, are laughing, and Maggi says:

"Time for school, darling. Rise and shine."

The others laugh, wink, gurgle, and Johnny's pride of flesh humbles down fast, used, resentful, but he has enough preservation balls left to break off a bark of laughter with them, and say:

"What's for breakfast, Mummy? As if I didn't know." Saying that, getting a guffaw out of Hervey, makes him feel better, soberer, able to concentrate on revenge.

"Now, you must all close your eyes." Marcel lights the brandy, pours it on the cherries jubilee. "Voilà!"

"Marcel!" Sidney.

Sue Riding. "How beautiful. Oh, that's lovely."

Davey. "God, I've never eaten such a meal." Marcel's dinner party at the schoolhouse for the Ridings, Sidney, Dick, and the Jackstones, has climaxed. He is exhausted from the shopping, the fuss of cooking, but he loves it and he loves his young friends. A shame the Shapens couldn't come, but he beams.

"Cherries jubilee." Maury. "Now wouldn't that just make old Pablo P. Castle break his paintly brush?"

Somebody's going to get it; Johnny pulls on his pants. Which one? Beth's an adversary now. He'd like to punch Maggi. But Margesson's the one he really wants.

In a street fight there is always one guy you really want, whatever it costs, one particular bastard you need. If you can get to him, break a nose, cock a tooth, bust an eardrum, then the fight's okay, never mind what licks you have to take. Okay, Miss Margesson. Cunning makes him sit by Beth, turn his back against hers so they lean comfortably into one another, sticking his bare feet out away from the fire.

Sure. If Maggi messed with him, if he appears close to Beth, then Margesson will have to go after the toy, won't she?

She does. She's after his toes and ankles, caressing.

He takes a slow count of twenty, then pulls his feet away. She gives him a level look. He returns it, narrows his eyes, doesn't move. She scrootches toward him, ass along the carpet, thin, long, loose, planes and angles, reddish, teats like tennis balls. When her nose reaches his knee, she raises one hand, and he takes it. It's like sitting close to a wood stove. He turns slightly away, puts his other hand on her neck, pulls sharply, and raises her onto his lap, her head into his shoulder. Her face turns up, and he kisses her mouth, hard-lipped, pushing her lips against her teeth. Her mouth opens and becomes infinite, but it's the first kiss from above he's gotten into all evening. He squeezes on a tennis ball, gets control of her weight by wrapping his other arm around her hips. She'll take what she gets, folks and injuns, but don't misunderstand. Texas John wouldn't hurt the lady. What he would do is lead her to a bedroom, and give her as hard, honest, thorough, and normal a man-on-top screwing as ever lady did submit to, make her like it, and leave her just a little bit, well, not sore, but disinclined for further action, right? Why isn't that fair enough, ringsiders and apaches? This'll be the final action for ol' John's practically-six-shooter, too, counting last night and a few hours back—it's been silked, milked, and bilked, it's got its own tender spots, but there seems to be one left in the chamber, and she'll be a while squeezing on the trigger before it goes off.

No doubt she responds to the linear quality of his intentions toward her, for Janet is close and complying, but what about Beth, leaning in, back meshed with his, shoulder blades lapped and rubbing. Johnny thinks for an instant, almost like regretting lost youth, of the innocence with which he fantasized, way back this morning, some kind of great, hellacious two-chick-and-a-stud scene with Beth and Janet Margesson. Is that what's supposed to come next? Not on your high E, Margesson, forget it, even if Beth is still, adversary or not, his *pro forma* girl, at least until they have time to figure out how they feel toward one another after all this is over. He recalls with astonishment waking up in the motel, going out for tea and cinnamon toast and a paper, and wondering about marriage. Marriage!

Hervey is fixing, and Maggi serving, something yellow in glasses with shaved ice. Janet takes one, so Johnny, hanging on to her with one hand, does too, matter of wanting their mouths to taste the same. He has a taste. It's like alcoholic licorice ice cream.

"You like licorice, Johnny Ten?" Beth asks, back there behind his head. Matter of fact, he's not crazy about licorice and decides to drink it down and get it over. Big swallow.

"Careful, man," Janet Margesson murmurs. "That's absinthe."

"Thought that was against the law."

"What isn't?"

Maggi big-eyes him. "Hervey gets it in Tarragona, Spain. Still made by the Pernod family, but invented by a doctor, Johnny, Doctor Ordinaire."

He big-eyes her right the hell back, drinks it down, tightens his hands on Janet, and rises, pushing her up and out in front of him. Submissively, she leans back against him, back to his front. She is almost exactly his height, but bends her knees a little.

Maggi laughs, probably because he chewed his licorice candy instead of sucking it. Or could Janet be making a face? He gets her around the waist, steps closer, moves her toward a bedroom door, ignoring Maggi, Beth, and Herve. They may not, of course, ignore each other, that's as may be, what's got to be done has got to be done.

And suddenly Herve, sheepish in his nudity, blocks their way. "Another frappé?" Is the man imploring, holding out his two little glasses?

"No thanks, Herve." John holds firm to naked Janet's waist and elbow, wearing the pants around here. *Don't mean to abuse yer hospital'ty, suh, but I reckon you had your wick dipped in my lamp, there, didn't you now? Little change of whale oil made the old flame bright, didn't it?* Grabs fingers full of blubber, under the rib cage. *Didn't make the rules here, Ahab, but I've chased me down a whale, reckon I'll do the harpooning.*

"But I'd like another. To take in," Janet says. "Is it all right, John?"

Noblesse obliges; Lord Ishmael releases her to step away from his side, follow the disconsolate skipper toward the cabin, where they have inaudible words. Perhaps she is insisting? Then Janet moves back past him, tossing back her curiously entrancing head as she goes by, turning her eyes to meet his, and glides graceful, rippling, nude into the bedroom. She leaves the door almost closed, and Johnny's almost to it, when Herve takes his elbow.

Johnny's mind is made up, of course, which allows him to smile. If this son of a bitch tries to stop things now, no matter how humbly (*"Please, we're engaged, you see.")* or with what lie (*"Miss Margesson asked me to say she's tired."*), or with threats, or with bribes, Johnny's going to give him the same answer. He's going to deck the bastard. He picks the spot where he'll hit, just under the point of the jaw, for maximum snap. He sets his weight, fingers curling in, hand slightly behind him. It's going to be a left uppercut, up from the pocket, taken off a hitch step with a small head fake so that Hervey won't see it coming at all. He may literally never know it wasn't the absinthe that hit him, and if the first shot fails to produce a clean knockout, Johnny will have the right-cross, left-hook combination ready to follow, all aimed at chin point to snap the head first one way, then the other.

"Johnny, listen." Whisper. "Janet's never taken two men at once. You game?"

"Uh."

The fingers uncurl. "Come on." His host looks mischievous, trotting off into the dark room. Johnny is confused. He tries to block out Maggi's voice, saying delighted things to Beth, so that he can concentrate. What he wants to decide is that Hervey's move is the cuckold's last craven resort—if he's to be horned, mayn't he please be present and participate? But what are the mechanics of this thing going to be, anyway? Well, Ishmael, old buddy, how could it be but fore and aft? The room is almost dark, but he can see the whiteness of Margesson covering the shorter bulk of Gandenberg, on his back, underneath. John hesitates. Was he set up for this, too? Are Ahab and the whale in cahoots, Moby Dick an old and practiced lover of the double shaft? Isn't there another book by Melville, *Pierre?* The ambiguities.

Sea images fade. Knee on the bed, finding himself surprisingly capable, it all at once becomes a medical matter. Let's play, doctor. The procedure'd better start with dilation, obviously, and his fingers know the task well enough.

"Ahhh," says Janet Margesson. The facile radiation of the sphincter implies prior muscular conditioning. Lubricant lacking but perhaps unnecessary. He hoists a leg over, adjusts position, and penetrates quickly. There is some resistance in the lower part of the passage, a request ("Easy, darling"), in reply to which he inflicts a thrust both deft and uncompromising. ("Oooch.") And what he feels, after an impulse of triumph, is Hervey Gandenberg, on the other side of the rectovaginal septum. Over on his side of the wall Gandenberg, for Christ's sake, is getting a massage; quickly, before the idea nauseates him, Johnny calls up an anatomical cross section of what's between them: There's, Gandenberg, vaginal mucosis, muscle, fibrous tissue, membrane in the middle, fibrous tissue, muscle, rectal mucosis. Jesus, what's the membrane called? All he can bring to mind is the voice of a lecturer comparing it to Saran Wrap. Thrusts, trying to concentrate on what Margesson's sensation will be. Not high sensitivity, just pressure. Suddenly begins to laugh at himself, internally, pressurizing her Saran Wrap; what the hell kind of gratification; Hervey's? Something in the mind?

His text becomes an old filling-station joke: *Hey, Johnny, know what a McGuimp is?*

No, what? Check the oil, Cougar?

Naw, changed it yesterday. Look, in a whore house sometimes they get busy, they got to get out an old, tired one to take care of the rush. Just a dollar's worth, Johnboy. Whoa. A McGuimp's the guy who lies under the bed with his feet up again' the mattress, movin' her up and down.

Got me a job like that, old Cougar, but a bit more complicated. Call it, call it a scarlet McGuimpernel. He rides, rumbles, and rolls off, gulled again, amused, wishing he weren't, because amusement is one long step toward corruption, nostalgic for his anger.

"Drink, Sato?" Snazzer Short.

"I like your little son's cornet. A sweet tone." Sato can play anything.

"You have lip for once more?" Debbie is at the Shorts' piano.

"No. Enough, I'm afraid."

"Drink, Debbie?"

"For me, yes. For you, I have something." Reaches for her big old bag, gets out the second section of the day's paper. "Did you see in the paper?"

Snazzer. "What?"

Sato. "What is this you have?"

"They have twelve questions. If you answer two by yes, you are becoming, you should be careful, an alcoholic. I save it for him, Rugby."

Sato. "Let us see."

" 'Do you feel you need a drink at bedtime, or you will not sleep?' This is one."

Sato. "Well, no. I enjoy a nightcap at times, but I think it tends to keep me awake to enjoy the evening a little longer. I read, then, a little while, if I am alone."

Debbie. "For me, I am afraid the answer is sometimes yes. I like to go to sleep maybe. I am becoming alcoholic? Here is the second one. 'Is there a regular time of the day when you feel you need, not want, but need a drink?' Here I will say no. Maybe I am all right. Sometimes I go many days. You?"

Sato. "Now this I cannot understand. To *need* a drink. That would interfere so much with work. No, not at all. But perhaps the next?"

Debbie. "I think you must say no this time, too, I bet it, Sato."

Sato. "Let us read it."

Snazzer, almost aside. "Yes. Yes. Yes. Yes. Yes."

John Ten Mason has him a real drink. He will have no more of absinthe, champagne, or buffalo-grass vodka. In the kitchen is a bottle of plain, down-home, millionaire's bourbon (Jack Daniel's Black), suh, sane as water.

In the living room, Beth, Janet, Maggi, and Herve are messing with something in front of the fire. He doesn't know what. He prevents himself from caring. Janet suggested he might give them shots, amphetamine apparently, but he begged off fast, before she could tell him what, not doctor-disapproves beg off, only said his hand was far from steady. Wanted to feel distance from them. Does. So they are doing something with ampules instead, little glass vials of something volatile that they twist and inhale. It's because they expect him to be interested that he isn't, not at the moment. He needs first some kind of instruction from his past to clarify this present, and perhaps he'll find instruction in a belt of Daniel's Black.

Takes a good one, and knows, immediately and too late, that it was a mistake. Or perhaps it wasn't. Whichever. It makes him drunk, really drunk, fall-down drunk. Hand against the wall for balance, he moves into the dark corridor to the first bedroom door, attracting no attention, leans against the door, is grateful that it opens. Totters into the room, feels a mattress against his shins, and collapses.

Beth screaming wakes him. A deep, terrified, throbbing scream, like that of a mortally injured horse, somewhere in the house.

He catches fear from it and is trembling, his mind almost sober. Then he slides past fear into the need to answer an alarm and tries to push up from the bed on which he fell how long ago? He manages to get up on one side, and his legs seem to work. God, for a pint of saline intravenous, all in a rush! He gets the legs over to the edge of the bed and under him, and the screaming starts again. He gets a foot down onto the floor and then the other, puts his hands down, one on either side, and pushes. Hard. He's up. A scream. He fights it with all his will, but his legs sag away, and he's down, now, elbows forward on the floor.

He tries to yell, but it's a croak. There's a light on out there, at an unfamiliar bearing. The gallery. The glass gallery. He crawls. There is another scream, and then laughter, crazier and more evil than any sound he has ever heard before, high enough, high enough in pitch and volume to fill an opera house! Margesson. At the door, he pulls himself up, hand over hand, on the frame. Sways there, snapping his head from side to side, to his right sees Gandenberg sleeping peacefully by the embers of the fire in his maroon vicuña. Left. Left the gallery lights are bright, and the sound of breaking glass, another scream, another laugh. And another wild sound, pouring in now through the break in the glass. Excited dogs, barking and baying, outside the gallery, maybe on the concrete walk that joins it to the garage. Leaping?

Wants to retch, swallows it, wrenches himself away from his doorjamb and lurches toward the gallery, feeling stronger with each step. He thinks he saw Gandenberg's eyes flick open, mildly curious. There is a louder, higher scream, and Margesson's voice, full of shove and strain, speaking obscenities.

Makes it across the hall to the gallery opening, and the bright light. In it, at the glass door, one panel broken outward, Beth is jammed against the corner, naked, cut, Margesson naked, heaving at her. And a kitchen knife on the floor.

Finds coordination with the sight of dogs outside, crouching, pawing, rushing glass and falling back. Margesson has Beth almost to the door. Johnny flings himself, clubs Janet Margesson hard across the kidneys with his left forearm while his right goes around her neck and hurls her back. Margesson screams.

"Hey, what are you doing to her . . . ?" Gandenberg, but apparently he has not finished saying it before he sees. "Janet!"

"I was just . . . I wasn't . . . Beth's dirty."

Beth's crying. Margesson sits on the gallery floor, splayed out, legs and arms here and there, chin in her chest, awkward.

Whatever was in those glass ampules, a wave of irrationality seems to hit Gandenberg, for now he starts to laugh, a high, tittering screech.

And in comes Maggi Short, wet, nearly sober, from the lake, out of breath. "I heard the dogs. What is it? What is it?"

Johnny goes to Beth, is looking at her cuts. There are two shallow knife-tip cuts in the skin of her back, over the ribs.

"Come on, Beth." She is shivering violently. He gets her to the living room, and the tan vicuña robe over her.

"Margesson?" Maggi asks him, coming in. She's grabbed a towel.

"Get her in bed, cover her up. Give her a sedative," Johnny says. "Something mild, just restrain her. She doesn't have to go to sleep."

He sits weeping Beth on the foam sofa. Watches Maggi helping Margesson up, sees Margesson suddenly attack and welts appear on Maggi's flesh. "Your fault, bitch, horrible Maggi bitch."

"Jesus, help me with her."

Hervey can't. Johnny runs to the two women, puts a full nelson on Janet Margesson. Humps her along the gallery floor into the bedroom he just left, hurls her onto the bed, and with Maggi's help, covers and holds her down till she subsides. "Better just lock her in till that ampule crap wears off. What was it?"

"I don't know. I just pretended to take mine." They move outside the door; there's no lock, but they prop it shut with a chair. "It made a lovely little burst of flame when I threw it in the fire."

"Then what happened?"

"Nothing special. Grabassing. Beth went to sleep. Hervey was nodding. I went swimming. I heard the dogs and swam back."

"Where the hell's Galdencio?" Hervey is having one of his flashes of sobriety. "Shut the damn dogs . . ."

Johnny stares into the fire, getting his breath, thinking but not replying: *probably drunk like the rest of us. Bright mind, no information, trying to make observations: dogs, lights, knife, cuts, welts.* Hears Gandenberg ask:

"What was she trying to do?"

Maggi tells him. "Feed Beth to your dogs, darling. A special treat, so good for their coats."

"Oh." Hervey is fighting for rationality, even attempting briskness. "Yeah. That's terrible. Listen, take Beth into a bedroom, John. Go on. Lock yourselves in."

"No, suh."

"We've got Janet locked in, lover. All snug as a rug in a bug. House."

"You going to be in any kind of shape to fly in the morning, Herve? This girl's got a rehearsal at noon. What the hell was that stuff you sniffed?"

"I can fly. I . . ." Titters. Something's come back to get him.

"You're flying right now." John to Maggi. "How far's State City?"

"Four hundred miles."

"You know the time?"

She goes far enough to glance into the kitchen. "Three fifteen."

"Cities in the road?"

"Dubuque, if you go the short way."

"I can make it. Help get Beth dressed?" Beth's asleep and weirdly smiling. "Herve! Hervey! Got a couple of Dexamyls?" He feels terrible, but the pills will help.

Hervey's back. "Sure. Sure. Shouldn't she sleep first? I'll charter you a plane."

"You sure? In time?"

"I don't know . . . what's sure? What's it matter? Her health, listen . . ." The man's trying, anyway, say that for him.

"I don't want her waking up here. Get her away, she might forget it. Can I have a car?"

Johnny still has on Gandenberg's jeans, his suit and shoes gone perhaps for good. Jams his small feet into Margesson's sneakers. Borrows a T-shirt, and is ready. Maggi's got Beth into panty hose, loafers, a sweater, and the maroon vicuña robe. It looks almost like a belted dress.

"Wait, that's, that was a present from . . ." Hervey is confusedly protesting the taking away of the robe. "I'm sorry."

In the garage are a Mercedes and the huge Chrysler station wagon. Johnny regrets the German car, chooses the American. Beth can stretch out.

"Maggi. Mrs. Short. You want to come?"

"I won't say I'm needed here, but I'm fascinated." God, she can mock her way through anything.

John's behind the wheel. Feels, for a moment, natural. "You better both get back in the house before I open the garage door. Dogs'll rush in. Hervey? Call your Mexican, will you? Meet us at the gate."

"Gate key on 'nition." Gandenberg is already retreating, or rather Maggi herding him back. Okay. Johnny starts the car, hits the radio control, the door swings up, the dogs close toward him, and he floors the gas pedal, Beth lounged away in back. The wide wheels spin, spurt, and he's out and away, the dogs wheeling to run after him, exuberant and deadly.

Halfway down the lane, going forty, his headlights pick up the man Hervey won't reach even if he tries, Galdencio, coming toward him at a trot, carbine swinging in his right hand. No sense stopping to explain. Seeing the boss's big station wagon being driven off by a young stranger, the boss not in it, Galdencio could only make them go back to confirm that it's okay. Down goes the pedal, sway goes the car into overdrive and past the watchman, throwing gravel at him, from forty to sixty and around a curve, dogs distanced, gate in sight. Galdencio won't shoot. He doesn't know if the boss is in or out. The dogs will be here first, anyway. Johnny hits the brakes, swerves right, backs up fast, swinging right again parallel to the gate, and pulls out the ignition ring, the car still unscratched. The gate key comes to hand first as he lowers the power window, sticks key into the padlock, everything working right. Lock open, backs up again, straightens, and smoothly out the double gate, using the front bumper to push it open. Galdencio can close it, and worry about getting his damn dogs back. Johnny in the Chrysler is off like an elk.

Sometime around dawn, hurtling through central Wisconsin on his second Dexamyl, using road signs to Dubuque to save stopping for map reading, his concentration is disturbed by Beth, crawling up from the back to slump fuzzily into the seat beside him.

"Mmmmmm." Face into his side, she couldn't sound happier. "Was it a lovely orgy for you, Johnny?"

"Hey, Beth." Doesn't want to think. "Go to sleep."

"Was it, though?"

"Well, I learned something. Learned you can't have a real orgy without slaves."

"Oh, but Johnny." Sits up. Knows something herself. Almost indignant. "I'll bet the orgy slaves were the proud ones, proud as herons. So intimate with the masters. Oh, very much better than the slaves who were only athletes or philosophers."

"Tell me what happened. I mean, do you . . . ? Tell me what happened in the gallery."

Giggles. Giggles! "Oh, I don't know. Just, oh, lovely. Wasn't it?"

"Did you know Margesson was mad?"

"Oh, yes, at Maggi Short. Oh, yes. She's moving in, bad as glaciers, taking my Janny goose away from Mr. Gander. . . . isn't Janny lovely?" Head against his side again.

"You don't remember, Beth. Go to sleep. Sometime I'll tell you. Do you want to get in back?"

"Poor Johnny Ten." Beth says this as if she were very much older and not a little wiser than he, and goes to sleep.

Hoffman arrives outside Old Biology in the bright morning. Snazzer Short and Debbie Dieter Haas arrive with Sato. Marcel and Sidney arrive together, singing cues back and forth as they come. Skeats arrives. Henry Fenellon, whose most important scene is Scene Five, which, finally, they will sing for the first time today. Skeats with Ralph. Mona, Karen, Mike. And, though they are not in it, Dick, Davey, and Maury.

"Welcome to Scene Five," Maury calls. "Right this way, folks."

Still outside, almost reluctant to go in before their group is complete. "I don't know, Maury." Hoffman. "You the ill-omen bird or something? Or has anybody seen our alto and her boyfriend?"

"Johnny Ten called me." Mona. "They'll be here."

"Called from where?"

"He was calling from a gas station off the interstate. He said they'd been shanghaied. To Wisconsin."

"Ah, jeweled lakes." Skeats. "Ah, tinkling brooks. Ah, pine needles up the old bazookum."

"Pretty up there, huh?" Hoffman is waiting for Mona to unlock the door.

"What do you plan to do about it?" Skeats.

Snazzer. "Really, Hugh. Let's wait and see."

Hoffman. "Right now, I'm going to wait here and hope they don't get a flat tire or something, you know?"

Mona has the door open, Mike helping, but not conspicuously, so that his wife won't appear one-handed, when a great, strange vehicle appears, slowly rounding the corner and coming toward them—an enormous, shiny station wagon, sailing as smooth and deliberate as a yacht.

"I say." Skeats to Ralph. "Isn't that Hervey Gandenberg's auto?"

It moves ponderously parallel, dipping in a little toward them, and stops, rocking gently back when braked. A tinted power window slides down, and Dr. John Ten Mason looks out at the group, pale of forehead, wrinkled, red of eye, uncombed.

"Be right with you," he croaks. "I got to dock this Cris Craft."

Skeats trots around to the other side of the steel cabin where Beth is emerging, and helps her down. Ushers her around the back of the wagon. Anxiety eases; her eyes are clear. Her clothing is strange, some sort of robe, but she looks rested, and her hair is brushed.

"Hello," she sounds delighted to see them all. "Thank God for Johnny Ten everyone. We made it."

The Chrysler is disappearing slowly now around the corner, where parking meters start.

Hoffman. "Your friend didn't exactly make it yesterday, Beth."

Beth, hand to his chest. "Oh, Mr. Hoffman. But that was so my fault. I told him he didn't have rehearsal. Oh, I lied and said the schedule, so naughty. But I thought maybe he even didn't, vague as cucumbers, Mr. Hoffman, and I'm sorry but it is my fault, yes."

"Well." Hoffman good-naturedly. "Next time you want to have a picnic in Wisconsin, check with the stage manager, you know?"

They go in, except for Snazzer Short. Short waits at the door for Johnny Ten.

"You all right, Johnny?"

"Sure." Not much more than a whisper. "I'll be okay."

"Friend Maury sang your part yesterday."

"I got the girl back, didn't I?"

"You look like a zombie."

"I got your singer back."

"Can you rehearse?"

Johnny Ten shakes his weary head. "I got no voice. Beth should be all right. She slept almost all the way."

"It's Scene Five."

"I know."

"It's just those few lines, at the end. Tell me what happened. So I can tell Billy and Skeats and Debbie. And Sato. Let me help."

Johnny looks at Snazzer. "Nothing happened. I missed a rehearsal."

"Please, John. Give me the story. Let me tell it. I want you in that part. Bert Tannenbaum's couple of lines close the show. It's got to be strong, not weird."

"There isn't any story, Mr. Short. It got your singer back."

"Maybe he'll let you just read today," and they go in.

Inside Mona is calling places for Scene Five.

"All right." Hoffman has them up there. "First we'll read and go over the blocking. Then we get to hear it. Karen?"

The piano begins. The cast walks through the scene, saying lines they have long had memorized. Everybody's out of book. Everybody's ready.

But when Johnny comes on at the end with Mike, his speaking voice is inaudible.

They finish. They take places again for the opening of the scene. Marcel and Beth, in the hotel, watching for Pill and Sally Anne. Karen starts to play.

"Wait a minute." Hoffman. "What about it, Doctor? You going to be able to sing it?"

"I don't guess so," Johnny whispers.

"Sing it for him, Maury." Hoffman.

19: To Whom Mrs. Short May Concern

Hoffman's ears are litmus by the first day of the final week of rehearsal. Everybody notices.

"When they droop nicely, and are kind of pinky-mushroom, then we're being good." Sidney.

Marcel. "When they grow rigid and turn red, mah frens, beware."

"And when they flare and flame . . ." Davey Riding. "Man the lifeboats."

"I think it's because he's lost the power of speech, and it's gone to his dear ears." Sidney, pensive. "Yes, Bitsy, beer, please. Today I said, 'Mr. Hoffman, am I the kind of girl that would, well, *consider* Al's offer just a little, or am I plain evil?' And he looked at me and said, 'HUH.' "

Marcel looks at Sue Riding, and says: "HUH."

Bitsy comes with the beer, and Sidney says: "HUH, Bitsy."

Bitsy says forty-five cents, please.

Today there were three complete run-throughs, tomorrow morning one more, then first rehearsal with the orchestra. Tomorrow afternoon, polishing of spots on the new stage. Wednesday morning, orchestra. Wednesday afternoon, technical rehearsal starts and will continue through Thursday. Thursday evening, one time through with orchestra, lights, and costumes: dress dress rehearsal. Friday all day, polishing, coaching, sewing, laundering, prayer. Friday evening, dress rehearsal. Saturday, all day off, until the six-thirty call for the eight o'clock opening.

Hughmore Skeats gets a phone call.

"Well, Hervey, it's damned hard to say what the blighter's doing."

Gandenberg's crisp voice. "He hasn't announced it as a cast change yet?"

"No, just as rehearsal's starting, old Billy-balls'll bloody-mumble something, and it turns out to mean he wants us to stay as we were yesterday."

"Let me be clear. You mean, with the black boy singing the featured part and Dr. Ten Mason doing the Second Poker Player? How does the cast feel about that, Hugh?"

"Bloody hard to say, Hervey. Funny bunch."

"How about yourself?"

"Black boy's got the bigger voice, no doubt of that. Shouldn't necessarily call it the better voice. He's a cheeky devil, young Maury."

"Suppose you were directing it, Hugh?"

"Perhaps I'd let them stay as they are. Matter of discipline? Does look a bit odd, of course, Maury being so tall and blasted blacko."

"Suppose I were to tell you quite confidentially that the doctor's in no way to blame for his absence the other day? I happen to know that. He behaved very well, and really isn't at liberty to explain himself."

"Then he ought to have his part back?"

"It's an injustice if he doesn't. Frankly, I like him."

"Me too."

"Can you deal with Hoffman?"

"I should think I can, and smartly if it's as you say."

"It's exactly as I say."

Skeats seeks out Hoffman. He's no longer to be found at the Gump, with the cast. Nor even at his once-familiar table, drinking coffee and consulting in the cafeteria. Hoffman's by himself, in his room.

"About this cast change, Billy-o."

"Yeah."

"It's been a bit awkward for you, I know, wanting to keep the strong gripper. Right, of course. But I've some rather good news."

"Yeah. Good."

"I've learned it wasn't Ten Mason's fault, missing rehearsal. He's a very nice bloke, you know, and fetching the girl back, well. It may just have saved our grand old opry, mightn't it?"

"Sure."

"I'm not at liberty to explain further, you see, but you can take my blistering wordo, can't you?"

"Sure, you know."

"Right, then. He's rather a friend of mine. May it be I who tells him?"

"Tells who what?"

"Dr. Ten Mason. Our Johnnyboy. That he has his part back."

"Yeah, well. I thought you saw it the other way."

"I've just been explaining . . ."

"Let's ride it this way, okay?"

"But you just said you'd take my word."

"Yeah. No problem there. But let's just ride it."

"See here, Billy. Casting's been my responsibility. Now then, put it on me if you like. Call it producer's decision or something, eh?"

"We got a horse. Let's ride it."

"Do you mean to say—"

"Yeah."

"Can you give me a reason, please?"

"Well." Shrugs. "I dunno, Hugh."

"I hope you don't suppose you've heard the last of this?"

"No." Irritating bugger.

In the morning the irritating bugger charges Sidney: "Al makes her so goddam mad she'd like to take out after him with a hatchet, you know? Listen." Sidney is astonished. She's more or less forgotten having asked a question about it yesterday. "She's been coming on, sure, to amuse herself. What the hell? Dumb cluck, he's a pastime, you understand? And it makes the two or three other girls in town green, listen, it's a goddamn small town. They're like sisters that she hates, Molly Crampton, Peggy Frampton. Okay, Al's good looking, he's a professional man, single, they could use him. So Sally Anne's gotta put him in the manger, but it's a finger exercise for her, right? Look what Mister Dumb's offering. Siddown. Go hang out at a university with a bunch of creepy students, get down in some new tropics with the scary foreigners, sit around and wait for him to come out of the jungle with itchy arms and yellow eyes, huh? Thanks a lot, Al. What a wonderful offer. What this chick wants is a little sophistication. She could run through a year or two of what Pill's got to offer, Miami and Vegas, and then be on the boat to Rome, you know, going to fashion openings, letting Prince Rainier sell her used Mercedes cars from behind that spic moustache, okay? She's ready to learn fast, and Al can't teach her a goddamn thing."

Attacks her like a drunk after a hostile lamppost, but his ears don't stiffen and color. Still, it would have been better not to get him started.

After the run-through Debbie takes him into the museum. They stand in front of the walruses. The walruses are getting a bit faded, but they still seem to be enjoying their fish.

"Billy, I think this time about the doctor you could giff in, all right?"

"I dunno."

"It will be best."

"Yeah, I suppose so."

"For the show, and for you, and for me." But he won't look at her. The walruses have his attention. Wrapped.

"Things are kind of balanced now, you know?"

"This is not why."

"Ah, you're too smart."

"What you are doing?"

"I dunno. Listen, we got to go over to the other place. The orchestra, huh?"

"You will not change back?"

"Come on. Let's go over to the other place."

But he hangs back, letting her leave alone and puzzled. Outside the museum, in the hall, Debbie meets someone who has returned.

"Maggi! So you have returned."

"So I have. Aren't you rehearsing in Janscombe?"

"In what, please?"

"The new auditorium."

"Now we go. Until eleven the workmen screwed the chairs."

"Oh. Sorry." It takes her another moment to stop laughing. "God. Is Mr. Hoffman at Janscombe?"

"He is in there, at the walruses. His big friends. You come?"

"I'll catch up, Debbie."

Maggi goes into the museum room.

"Hello again."

"Huh? Hello, Mrs. Short."

"How come all the beautiful men call me Mrs. Short? The ugly ones say 'Maggi.' "

"You been learning my lines."

"I've been learning everything about you."

The idiot blushes. She wishes this weren't going to be so easy.

"Walk you to Janscombe?" She puts a hand on his arm. "If I have your permission to watch rehearsal, Mr. Hoffman?"

Half an hour ago there were fiften people involved in rehearsing this opera in a dusty, underused building, on a worn, old stage. Now, in a vast auditorium of 2700 seats, no one of which has ever been sat in before, smelling of metal polish, glue, paint, soap, and wax, over a hundred are preparing to rehearse, with sounds of the orchestra tuning, Debbie's technical crew testing microphones, lights going on and off, scraping of furnishings on stage, and the sound of voices calling, talking, laughing.

Maury Jackstone lets the excitement come in, sees Hoffman walk by with Maggi Short, claps his hands, points to Hoffman, who smiles at him, and whirls to face Dick Auerbach.

"I'm about half-scared to go up on that stage." Dick.

"You are now going up." Maury needed an invitation to get physical. "I shall place you in its exact, umbilical center." Dick runs. Maury chases. The only way to run is through the small door at left, and once they're through it, they're in the big scenery shop, where Maury won't let Dick go left again. Enter Dick Auerbach, from right, pursued by a bear.

Of the hundred or so there is one who was, that half hour ago, central to the whole rehearsal effort and who is now passed by. She sits by herself and watches quietly, omitted from the excitement, a little depressed by it, Karen Jackstone. Oh, she'll play in another rehearsal or two, but her time of intensity is over; the rehearsal accompanist and piano coach, without whom . . . oh well. She watches Hoffman. At Old Biology they were as close as two antennae on a grasshopper. Here he probably doesn't even know where she's sitting.

"Karen?" Someone equally quiet is behind her, hands on the seat back.

"Hello, Johnny." She is grateful, though it's awkward having to turn her head and look up. The surgeon pats her shoulder and smiles nicely, the best-looking man in the cast.

"A little rest for you, at long last."

"Oh, I know. Johnny?" Shyly covers the hand on her shoulder.

He still smiles.

"I don't think it's at all fair. About your part."

"Seems to suit your husband."

"But it isn't Maury's doing. Oh, he wanted to sing Bert, of course, but it's all Mr. Hoffman. Why don't you ask Mr. Hoffman? He's thinking about so many things, it might just—"

"He knows what he wants. Hoffman's not overlooking."

"Please ask him. Or . . . or let me?"

"I don't ask for things like that. Floors don't feel good under my knees."

Mona Shapen calls: "Places, everybody. Places for Scene One."

Mona holds a nylon bandanna in her right hand, squished up, doesn't seem to know what to do with it. It's been her sling. She tosses it to Mike to put in his pocket. Mike grins, winks. "Places."

"See you later, Karen." Squeezes the shoulder. "Goddamn, look at that Marcel."

Though Marcel is without costume or makeup, the stage lighting and Sato's gathering together of the orchestra with his baton, seem to have affected the big tenor's physique. It's as if the impending music could turn fat to muscle, make puffiness solid. He no longer feels bulky, and awkward, he's a trifle more compact if anything. The overture begins, the orchestra color a surprise to him, but its message is pure confidence.

Sato moves now into a condition in which he will remain through Saturday's premiere, a condition like perilous illness, and the bypassing of mind that some call clarity. He is, as he draws with his black stick the first chords of the overture from the musicians who face him, neither man nor musician but seventy-eight instruments. He is twenty first and ten second violins, a dozen cellos and violas, six big contrabasses; and not the whole instruments, either, but their two hundred thirty-two assorted strings and their fifty-eight sounding chambers. His mouth is reeds and mouthpieces, his skin tympani, his bones cymbals, glocks, and triangles. There has been, though perhaps no one can see a thing so well contained except Debbie, a ten-day, accelerating working frenzy, growing to inner, always discreet, hysteria, preceding this beginning of sustained delirium, and in this condition Sato has simply turned into an orchestra. Now the overture is over, the stage manager calls "Curtain," and Sato cues the first singer, and is voices, too.

And Ralph Lekberg, hearing what he has fantasized, then spent three years writing down as symbols, become sound at last, is thrilled to tears. His wife, Josette, sitting by him, sees the actual wetness of his cheeks and knows better than to touch him now.

Debbie Dieter Haas is in a working frenzy of her own, but it will not become delirium, rather the opposite, something near total sanity, nor will it start till technical rehearsal, Thursday, when she begins to see her designs, her costumes, her sets transformed by light. Now she sits at the light board (but it is not turned on), going through the score, checking her cues, imagining her way through the illusions to be produced, for the final time before realization.

But Debbie's capacity to achieve intensity, lower than Sato's in any event, does not prevent her from noticing with mild irritation that Hoffman still has the black boy singing Bert Tannenbaum. Ah, well. The papers for Billy to sign accepting his appointment as associate professor of drama are in the mail by now, and Debbie does not regret it. She expects, she looks forward to, many professional disagreements with Billy Hoffman through the years, and if the consequences of this one may be a little awkward, what consequences are not?

And there is the black one, singing beautifully, she must admit, singing to conclude Scene One: " '. . . How much on four thousand dollars? Jesus Christ.' "

Final chord. Sato nods down there to Mona, and Debbie can hear the girl calling, "Twenty minutes, everybody. Twenty minutes."

"Mr. Hoffman. Billy. Billy." Mona taking him aside during the break. "I think you're wonderful."

"You do, huh?"

"I just want you to know. Last night I talked to, well, I talked or called up, all the student members of the cast. And Sidney, too. About you giving Maury the part. We appreciate what you're doing for us."

"I'm not doing anything for anybody."

"Well, we voted. Sort of. And we're all behind you."

"Jesus, Mona. This is no democracy. You know better than that."

"But there's pressure, isn't there? Look, Sato and Mr. Lekberg are waiting for you. I just thought you'd like to know."

His ears turn pink.

"Debbie, I believe, is upset with your cast change." Sato.

"Yeah? How about you, Ralph?"

"Oh, I like the voice." Ralph. "I think Snazzer may have some objections, Billy. But I don't want to interfere."

"Sato, you're the conductor, you know? You can overrule me."

"One week ago, I decided the direction was in very good hands. And the vocal coaching was equally outstanding. At that time . . ." At that time hysteria was starting, but he says: "I was pleased to know that I could cease to concern myself with the staging of the opera and the teaching of the singers."

"You two supporting me?"

Ralph shrugs. "It's between you and Snazzer."

Sato. "We are not overruling. We are not supporting. There is Debbie and there is Mr. Skeats."

"What about the soprano?"

"Excuse me?"

"I was sitting back thirty rows. Can anybody hear her?"

"Oh, dear." Ralph.

In the swamp scene they listen for it, and midway through, Sato stops the orchestra.

"My dear, sing from the front of the stage, please? We do not have the microphones right as yet."

In Scene Three Beth's in a dither. Marcel is singing so beautifully, it's wonderful to set her voice against a real orchestra again, and kind Henry Fennellon is such marvelous support, but Maggi's out there. Maggi Short. Beth saw her. She'll phone Janet. Of course. To say how Beth, how Beth. How Beth blows a line, starts singing something from Scene Five! To say how Beth stumbled! But, oh, it's really horrible Mr. Hoffman's fault, everyone is so upset, dear Johnny has been replaced by horrible Mr. Hoffman, horrible as carrots, with his ears, the way he glows at a person in the dark, what are they all to do? Janet says Hervey is furious, dear Johnny hasn't called, no wonder, so upset.

At the final curtain of the first rehearsal with orchestra Sidney is in tears, hiding, wanting Hoffman to find her. But Snazzer Short is hanging in, feeling just a little grim, waiting for Hoffman, too.

"Come on, Billy. Take you to lunch."

"Maybe I oughta see the soprano. Too much orchestra for her, huh?"

"Come on. Let's eat."

"You hungry?"

"Come on, guy."

"Let's just get coffee, okay? I couldn't eat. Whatever you want."

"Let's get coffee, then."

They walk, without conversation, from Janscombe to the State House cafeteria, both knowing what's on Short's mind. They get coffee.

"Something on your mind?"

"Listen, guy. You got my libretto so I hardly recognize it already, you know?" Hearing himself using Hoffman's turn of phrase irritates Short. He'd have thought he'd outgrown that kind of imitation. Tries to change his voice, and feels as if he's coming out like Marcel: "I really think the sight of Maury as assistant foreman is too much, Billy. It simply isn't credible. Have you a reason?"

The ears go pink, but this word *reason,* with its interrogation point, has had its day to work against the dam, now; Short is braced for the flood of words. "Yeah, well. I know, Snazzer. I used to know, here it is, this painter, okay? Woman painter, I mean. Well, to be frank with you, I knew her pretty good—Christ, one night I was sleeping there, and she just very quietly opened up the fly on my pajama pants and painted my, you know, dong, with body paint? How'd you like to wake up with a red and purple dong?"

Snazzer Short stares at the man, somewhat disbelieving.

"So I used to watch her splash on the paint, you know, and maybe I'd say something like, 'Paint me something for breakfast, Monica. Paint me a couple of eggs, over easy.' And she'd laugh, and maybe start sketching in the hen fruit, right? And pretty soon she'd have an accident, make a mistake. And then she'd get interested in the mistake and paint it, you know? That's really where she got her ideas for paintings, making mistakes. People thought she was a hell of a painter, too, boy, five grand for the big ones."

"Jesus, I don't follow you."

"She had this gallery guy, he'd call up—"

"Let's keep it simple. Maury's black. The scene is southern. I don't care about discipline or feelings or politics. I want the show right."

"Yeah, I guess you do."

"Will you give the doctor his part back?"

The man doesn't say no, but the ears are getting redder. The end of his nose is so low it's practically dipping into his coffee when he shakes his head negative, but not so vigorously as to make waves on the inky surface.

Sidney is apprehensive. Since Hoffman didn't come to reassure her, he's probably going to scold, but it's nothing she can help; they've got to get the microphones right for her. She wishes she hadn't taken the part, supposes she got it because Skeats had cute ideas, considers sitting by Skeats now, and oh, oh, here comes Billy. The cast waits in the first two rows, spread out. She sits by the bearded Australian, and says:

"Oh, look at them now."

The ears. They're so red they have white specks this time. Maybe it's Beth he's mad at—she blew her scene. Yet when he starts, he sounds quite mild. "I was looking at this rehearsal schedule last night, you know? Said we were 'sposed to polish spots this afternoon? Sounded pretty good, didn't it, like when you're polishing, you're sliding down the back of the hump, about to sail off over the camel's tail and home to the oasis, right, eat a couple of dates, pour a few barrels of oil out on the sand and watch it soak in. Fun. Well, this guy gets a job as a dishwasher, you know? It's a really fancy house they got, they got butlers, first, second, third, fourth, and fifth. They got housekeepers like platoon sergeants, every one's got her own squad of house-maids, and there's even a substitute squad so, like, if one comes down with the knee, they can call in another one off the bench. They got meat cooks, pastry cooks, bakers, egg cooks, salad chefs, so this guy doesn't just get hired as a plain dishwasher. I mean they got the platooning here, the special-ists, and he gets hired to do the silverware, I mean, it's beautiful stuff, you know?

"Okay, so this guy Hoffman, the silverware specialist, reports to the big chief dishwasher. I mean, Hoffman's new on the job, he's been working his way up in dishwashing for years, right? It's his big chance, he doesn't want to blow it, and he says, 'Okay, chief, where is it? Where do you want me to start? Let me show you what I can do.' So the big chief, he's an Ital-ian, right? With the nose veins from too much vino, and the garlic hand-shake, he hands Hoffman a can of silver polish about the size of a medium wastebasket, right, and says, 'Here-sa da polish. Polish heem oop.' So this Hoffman grins. He takes the long walk, down to the other end of this enor-mous dishwashing room, with the columns and a hundred marble sinks, and all the other dishwashers are watching, some are jealous 'cause they wanted the job, and others hope Hoffman can make it 'cause he's a spunky little bas-tard with the soap and towels, and so Hoffman gets to the ten-foot stack of sterling, all jumbled around, and lays out his polish rags, and opens the big can of polish, and rolls up his sleeves, and picks up a fork, right? My God. Good Jesus. Egg yolk! Egg yolk between the tines! He can't believe it. He picks up a spoon. Bitcham'l sauce, boy. All over the back. Gummy. Tries a knife, it's half rust and half old cheese. Reeking. Smells the smell coming off that old silverware, and it's terrible. Awful, and he yells: 'I CAN'T POLISH. It's not READY. I gotta CLEAN IT UP FIRST, YOU HEAR ME?'

"Anybody got any questions?"

Maggi is almost entranced. She wonders how many times he's bulldozed a cast with this bizarre speech, how many times elaborated it. If she were in the cast, her mocking spirit would move her to applaud.

His voice gets quiet. "I want you to sit right where you are for half an hour. Mona's gonna give each one of you a copy of the script, and I want you to read it through to yourselves, okay? The whole thing. And remember where you are and what you're doing line by line, I don't care if your're off-stage, think where you're going to be offstage, what you'll be doing there. Don't talk about it, just read through, okay?"

Maggi watches him go sit on an aisle seat by himself, brooding, not like a man but like a hen. A hen squats on eggs, waiting, because instinct tells her to, and if she does, then the right thing, whatever it is, will proba-bly happen.

Karen Jackstone is at the piano, dutifully reading through the score to herself, feeling almost reprieved that there's to be another rehearsal in which to work, and here in Janscombe, too. This is the big Steinway, the one that Horowitz will play, and other great men and women in the months to come. She supposes she may be the first to perform on it publicly, sort of, and that's rather pleasant, even though the people are not exactly an audience and her performance will only be accompaniment. But she fantasizes that maybe Mr. Hoffman will ask her to play the overture, and though there's no piano transciption for it, no need for one, maybe she will be able—as Maury would say, or Mike—to fake it. Karen almost giggles, using a word like that to herself about music; at her home in Boston music and capitalism are sacred things, and if her young sense of social justice has brought her to despise the latter, her feeling of holiness about the former is perhaps corre-spondingly deeper.

Please, Mr. Hoffman, ask Karen to play the overture.

"Hey, Karen. You know what?" He's whispering. "We're going to put this crowd through the wringer, you know? Next thing we're going to do is make'm sing it, whatdya callit?"

"A cappella?"

"Yeah. Without the old musical crutch."

Insensitive Hoffman yells now at his stage manager: "All right, Mona. Line up your turkeys." And he's grinning, and the ears look normal.

"Fast," he says to them, and for reasons none of them understands, they respond with pleasure to his sudden access of mischievous geniality. "This show runs sixty-eight minutes, not counting scene changes. Got that up there? Okay? Sixty-eight? Now, when we play it Saturday night, I want it down to sixty. Sato wants to take some of the *Sprech* stuff faster, and Mona can hustle the stage crew like their pants were on fire. So right now, I want you to do it in forty."

Gasps. Laughter.

"Get ready. Get the stopwatch ready, Mona. Okay. This is agacabelly, right? I'm your accompaniment. If you slow down, I yell. Sing as fast as you can, move as fast as you can. Sidney, you got no time to sit down there watching. Your entrance is gonna be here before you know it. Let's go."

"Places."

"Ready, Pill?"

"Ready, Bill-o."

"Go."

"Fouradimensninospadestenaclubs—"

"Faster."

"Twoheartsnothertenfidealerfirstenbets—"

"Dumdiddy dum." Hoffman.

"Checkaten," sings Dicks in a rush, and they're off.

"Yay. Go. Yay."

He's like a bloody ridiculous cheerleader, capering about, but it's rather exhilarating to be challenged this way. They race one another through the first scene in eighteen minutes, and finish breathless, almost hilarious, to hear Hoffman yell:

"Clear the stage. Scene Two. Keep it moving." And Marcel, hovering just offstage, runs back on as best he can, feeling big as a cloud, but laughing.

When it's all over, all five scenes, Hoffman has soaked his shirt through so thoroughly leading them that he can be seen to shiver in the air-conditioned chill.

"Forty-four minutes, Mr. Hoffman." Mona.

"Karen! Hey, Karen. Come on. Now we'll run through," he says. "Then we'll polish."

He trots away, out through the scenery shop. Then they see him reappear on the floor and sink into his aisle seat to watch.

Mona goes after him and hands him the legal pad on which he makes notes. Somebody, oh yes, Mrs. Short, has written something on it for him. Mona doesn't exactly mean to read what, and anyway, it's pretty harmless:

See you at Ralph and Josette's — I'll bring the medium-sized wastebasket — You bring the soap and towels —

M —

They are all there at the Lekbergs' for dinner, the older ones: Ralph and Josette, will you welcome Debbie and Sato, Maggi and Snazzer, Hughmore, your gentle neighbor, Henry, and unpopular Billy H.?

Henry Fennellon is not exactly anxious about this dinner party; anxiety is not a state of mind he permits himself. But Josette has roasted a baron of lamb he gave her, from the first of this year's lamb crop; it's just back from slaughter, and only when he tastes it will he know if it stayed long enough on lamb starter, if the grass was right, if the locker did a good job of killing and cooling and hanging. No worry about the cutting, Henry did that himself, and it does look like fine lamb this year.

It's superb. Josette's a Basque patriot, but concedes that it's the Catalans who have a way with lamb; she has made a pinkish sauce, with garlic and almonds, roasted traysful of whole green onions, there is a wonderful *crema Catalan* for dessert, and the company disposes of four bottles of Inglenook Pinot Noir and most of a fifth.

Lighting his after-dinner pipe, Henry is pleased to think about how food and wine, taken together, can soothe disharmonies among people, and have through the centuries. There is none of the antipathy left that seemed to flare and suspend during the long day of rehearsing. When he hears Hughmore Skeats say to Hoffman, "Expect a communication, Billy my boy," Henry Fennellon is pretty sure what that means, and decides to take a hand in the matter.

It is still quite light out. "Billy, have you ever seen a prize-winning ram?"

"Yeah? What'd he, win the county fair, you mean?"

"He's a national reserve grand champion. Worth about the price of a trip to Europe."

"Gold hooves, huh? Like that Brooks Brothers sheep they put on the label. You got him here?"

"He's Josette's. He's penned right now, to keep him away from the ewes."

Hoffman gets up. "You mean a sheep like that doesn't stay in the house, with his own room? Let's have a look."

They excuse themselves and stroll out, into the warm June evening.

Halfway to the barn. "I admire what you're doing. I'm not sure it's worth it."

"Huh?"

"I took the liberty of talking with Maury about it this afternoon. He didn't seem disposed to question it, if you want to revert to the original casting."

"He didn't, huh?"

"Actually, he was quite amusing about it. I think he looks on whites rather paternally, as unhappy children with odd, irrational folkways. 'Let him close the show,' Maury said. 'And put M.D. after his name in the program, so they get the picture. Doctor like that, wears a white robe, green face mask. Covers up his hands with pink gloves, and there in the outer room, with all the knives in bubbly water, they bend down, all golemn solemn, and do the X-ray pray.' "

"Yeah. That's Maury's stuff."

"Whichever way you decide it, I just wanted you to know that I admire you."

"Where's this fancy sheep kid, Henry?"

Skeats has excused himself and left early by the time they return. The party settles down, listens to Sato play modern jazz on the piano. He's okay, but Maggi notices Hoffman starting to nod.

"Hey."

"Yeah. Hi, Maggi. Got your note."

She says it very softly and very distinctly. "I will pick you up in front of State House at twelve thirty tonight." He is trying to return one of his dumb, uncomprehending looks, so she pinches him pretty hard in the soft flesh under the ribs. "Don't you pretend you didn't hear me, bubble-ears."

By eleven Snazzer is drunk and asks Maggi to take him home. He has a feeling there was something he wanted to say, to get settled tonight, and there was even a time when he felt he could be brilliantly persuasive about it, advance incredible new arguments, but Hoffman was out at the barn at the time, and then the sogginess began for Snazzer.

Maury Jackstone, waiting in his car on the road, listening to a blues tape on the deck, watches the Shorts come out, thinks it's rather nice the way Maggi helps her husband, tucks him into the car. He waves to them as they drive by, and waits.

Sato says, "Debbie, it is now time for women to drive men home. All right, Billy?" Hoffman came with them. He stands, and nods.

Debbie wants a final glass of brandy with Josette, with whom she has been talking about vegetables.

Maury watches Henry Fennellon come out the door, stand there a moment saying good night to people Maury can't see, and stroll out the drive.

" 'Lo. Maury?"

"Waiting to see Mr. Billy Hips Hoffman."

"Why don't you go on in? Josette would be happy to have you."

"Hips is the terror of State City. Don't believe I could take him in Mrs. Lekberg's living room."

"Good luck. Good night."

That Henry Fine Fennellon, walking away, he's like reading a long-ago back number of a very good, once-was magazine. The writers and the artists you're reading and looking at don't know they're dead, don't know they're gone, they don't know dust from dynamite, how could they?

"Billy, sir?" Hoffman has come out with Debbie and Sato, and Maury moves over there. "Would you let me drive you in?"

"Sure, I guess so, Maury."

Puts his man in the car, closes the door solicitously, goes around, gets under the wheel, and starts. Turn down the music.

"Hey, Mr. Billy. Don't get civil rightsy over me."

"Huh? Oh. Oh no. I won't."

"I am nobody's symbol, Mr. Billy Hope-of-man, not yours, not any-body's."

"Uh-huh. No, you're not."

"I want to step down from the part. You got a bad case of politics, we better let that doctor cure it."

"Yeah?"

"Yeah."

"Get off me, willya? Uncle, okay? Look, what do you want me to say? I hate niggers? They smell bad? Okay? Now will you sing Bert for me and get off me please?"

"He wants me to sing Bert."

"Yeah."

"I think he really does. I don't know why. But he is the director." Maury feels some kind of joy.

"Go on. Take a look up in the sky, and say you'll do it."

"Hey, Mr. Billy." Flings an arm around him, hugs him. "I'll do it. I'll not do it. Anything you want. I'm your own bad-smelling boy."

"Lemme go, willya. Jesus, you got an arm on you. Anything else the goddamn management can do for you tonight?"

Marcel sits with Beth, as she asked him to, in the lobby of the State House. She is very tense, and he is trying his best to be chatty.

"I'm sure it'll be all right, dear. I just know it will. Tell me about your costume. Is it ready?"

"Oh, Marcel."

Here he comes. Marcel stands.

"Mr. Hoffman? Beth and I would like to see you, may we?"

"Yeah. Okay."

"Beth?"

"Tell him. Tell him what you said."

"Why, I make it a principle never to question a director, or a conductor . . ."

"Yeah. That's good."

"But if Maury, I mean, he's a wonderful boy. But I've been thinking of the final curtain there. You know, they say in jazz, what's important is starting good and endin' strong, and what's in the middle doesn't much matter. And, well, of course, I'll be just terribly dead lying there, but if Maury. You know about black people and southern women, well, won't it make a wild kind of a way to end?"

"Yeah."

"Well, if it's discipline, well, Beth has something to say now, don't you dear?"

Surely he must be persuaded by Marcel's marvelous speech. Of course he is. Beth is so grateful she puts a hand on each of Billy's wonderful arms. "And it was my fault, Billy. Every bit, naughty as a lamb in someone's garden."

"That's all right."

She could kiss him.

"And we've been, oh, I hope we still are, such friends, Johnny Ten and I, and you saw, with the orchestra, I got so upset. Oh, I know it will help me be good Saturday if I knew Johnny Ten isn't unhappy because of naughtiest Beth."

"Yeah. Well, don't worry about your performance, Beth. You either, Marcel. I got things all muddied up, I guess, but you two are going to save me, willya?"

They watch him go to the elevator.

"What did he mean?"

"I think he meant he wasn't going to change it. I'm so sorry."

"He looked so tired, oh, but he's horrible, isn't he? Horribly tired."

Maggi decides to let him off.

Arriving down front for the late date, feeling high-schoolish about it but not displeased with the feeling, she sees immediately that he isn't waiting. It hardly occurs to her to be irritated. She leaves her car, rings the night bell, gets herself let in by a clerk from the desk, and asks briskly for Hoffman's room number.

She knocks on his door once, then knocks again.

He opens it. "Huh? Oh, shit."

She can see immediately what happened. The poor goof changed his shirt, sat in the chair by his bed to wait for twelve thirty, and went to sleep.

"I mean, not you. Me. I was trying to stay awake, tuh, tuh meet you. Like you said."

"Hey. Hey. Don't wake up." Takes his shoulders, turns him around. Pushes him toward the bed. "You silly drunk, you're work-drunk, aren't you?" Kisses the back of his neck, but so lightly he may not feel it. Murmurs: "Silly, passing-out work drunk. Wouldn't do a lady any good at all, tonight. Move it, little buddy." She has him to the bed. Puts him onto it, his eyes glaring at her, his ears turned off altogether. Takes his shoes off. Holes in both socks. Kisses the foot through each hole, so lightly. Moves along, puts her cheek by his, her arm under his head. Astonished at how really tender she feels. "Tomorrow's soon enough, so's Friday, Saturday, the bills keep coming, pay them when you can, now go to sleep."

And, in a minute or two, slips her arm away, withdraws on tiptoe, turns out the light, closes the door. That little rat, he's got her trembly.

Okay for him. Boy, will he get the full-court press tomorrow afternoon, about six fifteen.

The toughest course in the Theatre Department at State University is Professor Dieter Haas's Stage Lighting: History and Theory (optional for undergraduate majors, required for graduate-degree candidates; required as preliminary to Advanced Stage Lighting). The first lecture covers aeons, primitive theatre, the use of fire for night productions in ancient Greece, of torches and oil lamps by the Romans, particularly in the theatre of Plautus.

Then the centuries slow down into periods, then eras, decades. Finally the course is moving from year to year. Here are some final-examination questions:

I.

(Essay, 1 hour. Choose one.)

Discuss the importance of Sebastiano Serlio's *Second Book of Architecture* (1545), with particular reference to designs for placing of torches behind glasses of colored water, dimming, and reflecting devices. You may illustrate with drawings.

or,

Garrick and de Loutherbourg are usually credited with the introduction of concealed footlights, wing ladders, etc. What was to be accomplished by these innovations to replace chandeliers? Do not neglect to mention other technical contributions and contributors of the period. You may illustrate with drawings.

II.

(Identify briefly six of ten, 1 hour.)

1. Kokman.
2. Argand burner.
3. Jublachkov.
4. Welsbach mantle.
5. Limelight.
6. Irving.
7. Arc lighting.
8. Davy.
9. Fresnel.
10. Isenhour.

III.

(Essay, 1 hour.)

Compare and contrast the theories and achievements of Gordon
Craig and Adolphe Appia.

That's the first day. The questions for the second are more technical. The
wise student will be particularly versed in the third question, and, while
being fair to Craig, incline a little toward Appia, the Swiss theoretician of
stage design (1862–1928), on whom Debbie wrote her Ph.D. dissertation.
The brilliant student will recall material not in the books, like Debbie's recollection, described each year in class, of the terrible smell from the primitive dimmer in a back-country theatre she once worked in in Wales. It
consisted of a water barrel of weak brine, by which the current could be
diminished by raising one metal plate through the brine away from another
on the bottom.

Under the circumstances it is evident enough that Debbie should have
been the delight of the architect who designed the great new lighting system
for Janscombe Auditorium, and the terror of the engineers who installed it.

Sitting now at the console, in its own soundproof room, mezzanine
rear, she looks with pleasure at the sculpted ramps and levels of her out-
doors-at-night setting, down on the big stage, for Scene One, which the
singers already love for the way it enhances all the movement Hoffman has
insisted on. It is 9:00 A.M.

She throws a switch. The anteproscenium banks come on upstage left,
center, and right; then the downstage pools; she switches on the balcony rail
banks and then, all at once, the boomerang spots from the sides. They work;
they all work. She cuts all the switches, and the humming stops. She speaks
into the intercom:

"Ready now." That's for Mona backstage, Hoffman on the floor.

Glances at Karen, with her in the console room, with the light-cued
score.

Mona's voice: "Ready, Mr. Hoffman? Ready, everyone?"

The singers, costumed and made-up, are at their places. Now Debbie's
hands dance to the switches, and the first line sounds:

"Stop." Technical rehearsal has begun, a day of joy for Debbie, slog-
ging for Hoffman, incredible tedium for everyone else concerned. Sato,
knowing the process, is away rehearsing his orchestra. Ralph and Snazzer

watch for an hour or so; when they leave, the rehearsal has just gotten to Sidney's first appearance, in the power-shovel cab, and Debbie and Hoffman are once again debating over the intercom:

"On 21 through 25, I have surprise pink. You want more bastard amber, I must bring in from the first pipe."

"Let's try it. . . . No, I like it the first way. How about you?"

"The first way, too, but I can give you flesh from the left.

"Let's see that."

Thus. Repeating, going over, changing, changing back, over and over till lunch break; until three; until four; until five; until ("almost through for today, people") six. At six, when they break, they have finally finished with Scene Three.

Maggi is waiting for Hoffman at the back of the auditorium.

"Come on."

"Hey."

"Let's go get a drink. Or have you forgotten me again?"

"I'd never forget you. I told you. Listen, I gotta—"

She smiles, and watches his wax run.

"You gotta come with me, bubble-ears, you know?"

"Yeah. Okay."

They walk out to the parking lot. It's vast, and nearly empty. Students pass on foot along the sidewalks west and north of it. Maggi's car sits by itself.

"Get in."

He does. So does she, under the wheel. "We goin' to your house?"

She takes his cheeks, pinching lightly, one between each thumb and forefinger.

"No."

"Hey." He moves away from her fingers. "Hey, come on. I'm the biggest pullover in town, you know? I got no toes at all. Now, what do you want?"

She laughs, turns away, and starts the car.

"Maybe I'm just horny, and you look willing."

"No, no." He indicates a group of students strolling by to the west. "Look, you got a world of little boy tail here. Cute, curly-headed, big, and little, some got beards. Or if, you know, you want the mellow stuff from the smorgasbord, with some age on it, there's professors, doctors, I bet, football coaches—it's ass paradise, isn't it?"

"Go to hell. Maybe you're my great love."

"That's probably it, all right." As they reach the street at the end of the parking lot and wait for traffic: "You working for Snazzer?"

She takes the car out of gear, sets the handbrake, and turns toward him. "Once I did Zhakesbeer, with Debbie directing *Kink Lear*. It was wonderful, a sort of Lear the Absurd. And she was wonderful, Debbie ought to direct more. Every now and then she'll say something you never forget. 'Now Gordelia, you giff 'im a great big giss on der strumpeter.' How'd you like a poke in the strumpeter, bubble-ears?"

She operates the gear shift, pulls out of the lot, and turns right.

"You do parts here? I didn't know."

"Did once. When we first came back from Snazzer's year in Hollywood. We had nice ideas. An acting company. Something happening, Snazzer would write and organize. There was another good director, besides Debbie. Some interesting students." She drives, she shrugs. "A place. This university, this town, this state. Support . . . good work, Hoffman."

"The town's all right, huh? What happened?"

"Rigby Short had a drinking problem before we met. Not a big one. In Hollywood he hardly drank at all. Then we got married, and came here—"

"Boy meets girl, yeah."

"No, the plot starts before that. Boy meets bottle, boy loses bottle, boy finds bottle. It's probably my fault."

"Yeah. So what are you going to do?"

"You'll see."

"Yeah, but I mean, after I see, huh? You leaving?"

"I don't know. Maybe find a rich man and marry him?"

"Any prospects?"

She glances at him, thinking she got a little careless there. "Maybe." *Hey, Maggi-beans, don't underestimate him.* "Maybe you're him. D'jever think of that, chump?"

She turns in at the State City Holiday Inn, drives around to one side, and parks, gets out, and waits for him to follow her into the room. He hesitates. Then she can see the grin start and the ears light up, and he gets out of the car.

She pulls him into the room and lays him fast, getting rid of the easy one—wiggling out of her clothes, pulling him onto her on the bedspread, getting his pants down, her legs around him, popping him into her and bringing him off in a few breathless moments.

"Hey. Wow."

She hangs on. "That was your dues, buddy, for making me wait." Hangs on. "Now you can have a drink." Hangs on. Once in Hollywood she knew a girl who laid guys for the F.B.I. *You don't bargain for the first one,* this girl said. *Unless the guy's an absolute jerk, he'll turn off; if he's a jerk, he'll tell you anything. Out of his head. So you make sure he's got time, get rid of the easy one, and get him rational. Then you open the bottle.*

Maggi turns loose.

"Hear you're a Wild Turkey drinker, turkey," she says.

Hoffman rolls off her and sits on the edge of the bed.

"You're really great with the sweet nothings, aren't you, Maggi? Hey." And as she sits up to move past him, his arm catches her, he pulls her against him, and pushes his face into her shoulder, and his own shoulders seem to be heaving slightly.

"Crying?" She can't believe it. Her arms go around him almost without volition. "Baby?" She holds him. Can't let go. "Hoffman?" Can stand, after a moment, pulling him up to his feet where he'll be as tall as she is, and there they cling together, behind her, out of mind, the Wild Turkey bottle, the ice bucket, the glasses, the bottle of pure spring water, the tan vicuña robe.

She leaves him there asleep with his ears folded at 2:00 A.M.

She sits close to him while they finish technical rehearsal next morning, but two rows behind so he won't be too much aware. She celebrates with him, letting him take her to supper after dress dress, which goes pretty well.

Dress rehearsal. It goes as dress rehearsals go, even for Hughmore Skeats, who never makes errors, dying a line before his time so that he has to resurrect himself to sing his final notes. Dr. John Ten Mason is an unexpected bright spot. Good-naturedly resigned, he volunteers, after Scene One, to help Debbie and Karen at the light console, where he is very good, very cool. Karen, without the security of a keyboard under her hands, was getting flustered.

Saturday morning Hervey Gandenberg has a conference call that lasts forty-five minutes, with an Undersecretary of Agriculture, a man on the State Department Caribbean desk, and a White House aide. It has to do with sugar beets, next fall. Saturday morning's a good time to talk with government guys.

He decides, when it's over, not to return a call from Janet Margesson. He talked with her twice yesterday, once to tell her he would not take her to the opera opening in State City tonight, the second time to ask her not to attempt to go to it by herself. Janet is too damn crazy.

With State City on his mind now, he gives his secretary half a dozen names there to call, and goes over his notes on the beet sugar thing as she locates the people, one by one.

"I'm sorry, Mr. Gandenberg. I can't get Mrs. Short."

"Okay, Becky. Here's the last call. And get me the weather, and make sure the flight plan's filed? I'll go to lunch after this call, and then straight to the airport." He'll fly to the state capital, drive back to State City with the governor, and have his plane ferried back to Wisconsin. Galdencio is already on his way to State City in the Mercedes, so he'll have a car.

He picks up the phone and listens to Becky: "Mr. William Hoffman?"

"Yeah. Billy."

"Mr. Hoffman, can you hold for a call from Hervey Gandenberg?"

"Sure."

He waits for Becky to buzz him. Then he says, "Yes. Mr. Hoffman?"

"Billy Hoffman here."

"And how are you, sir?"

"Well, you know how it is, you know?"

"Of course. Jitters?"

"Sure."

"I've been in close touch with your project. I'm grateful for the way you've taken hold."

"Thanks, okay."

Articulate, isn't he? "I'm certainly looking forward to this evening. Looking forward to meeting you. People in State City are very much impressed."

"That right?"

"Mr. Hoffman . . . is Billy okay with you? . . . Billy, I think you probably know that I've done whatever I could for this, this premiere."

"Sure. I don't guess there'd be one without you."

"No. I don't flatter myself that much. People like Debbie Dieter Haas and Hughmore Skeats know how to get things done, whatever it is they have to work with. I may be able to help them hire a Sato Murasaki, or a Billy Hoffman, but they'd find a way if I didn't. Billy, I owe you an explanation."

"No, No, you don't."

"Excuse me?"

"I mean, I'm the kind of guy nobody owes. They look at me . . . I was a kid, I had this newspaper route, I used to have to take my mother around to help me collect Friday evenings."

"Mothers are wonderful people. . . ." Wait a minute. "Billy, I called to make a confession. It's embarrassing, I'll be grateful if it goes no further, but I know enough about you to be fairly sure it won't. This is about two members of your cast, Beth Paulus and John Ten Mason."

"Yeah."

"Frankly, they've been protecting me. Here's the situation: I'm a pilot. I flew them up to northern Wisconsin for a party last week. I was indiscreet about my drinking, and it became clear to the doctor that I'd be in no shape to fly them back for their rehearsal. I'll even tell you that he borrowed a car, somewhat against my wishes, in order to drive Beth back. I admire him for that. He's a courageous young man."

"Yeah, that's good."

"Hell, Billy, I was drunk out of my mind."

"Yeah?"

"Look, in all justice, he ought to have his part back tonight. I'll certainly enjoy your show a lot more if he's singing Bert Tannenbaum."

"Yeah. Well, it's kinda late, you know?"

"I anticipated that. I've talked to him this morning and I've talked to Maury Jackstone. A very reasonable boy. They've agreed that they'll abide by your decision, and that either one can do either part. I've talked with Sato, Ralph, and Snazzer. No problems. Debbie has agreed to talk with your stage manager and the rest of the cast, if you decide to make the change. Jackstone said that he'd talk to the others, too, to keep it from becoming a divisive issue. I liked him. And Hughmore seems very emphatically in favor of it. My impression is that it would be the kind of last-minute morale boost for everyone concerned that might make the opening really go, after what was apparently a pretty rough dress rehearsal last night."

"Oh, yeah. Well, don't worry about the dress rehearsal, you know? Listen, can I ask you something?"

"Of course."

"Listen how come all the pressure about this thing?"

"Aside from its being a matter of justice? All right. It's correct politically. Music and drama get a great deal of support from the medical school. Read the list of thousand-dollar donors to the new complex, you'll find that most of the local ones are on the medical faculty there. Dr. Mason is a very popular young member of that faculty."

"Huh. I didn't know that."

"But let's not talk about politics. What I want to say is that no one is challenging your authority. No one. But everyone who knows that libretto and knows theatre, feels that logic requires Mason in that part. Mrs. Short, for example, in addition to the others I've spoken of. And frankly, I have no expert knowledge at all, but they've convinced me. I hoped I could convince you."

"Well, yeah, You make a helluva case."

"Do you agree? That it's logical?"

"I dunno."

"Well, Jesus Christ." There is a counterfeit of anger used in negotiating of which Gandenberg knows himself to be a master. When to use it is a matter of timing. "You're the goddamn director, Billy. If you don't know, who in hell does?"

Slowly. "Everybody else, I guess."

"I admire a strong-willed man—"

"Yeah. Me too."

"—but even more, I admire a man who can admit he's wrong and change his mind."

"Hell, I do that all the time, huh? I even change it sometimes when I'm right."

"Let's stop bullshitting each other. You're going on intuition. I've done that all my life. Sometimes it works. But when it's wrong, it's dead wrong, isn't it?"

"Sure."

"All right. Let's cut this short. Are you willing to go back to the original casting for the premiere?"

"Well, you know. I got all day to think about it."

"Will you?"

"Yeah."

"You're lying to me, aren't you?"

"Yeah."

# 20: Canterbury

Mona and Mike Shapen arrive at Janscombe at six. There are already cars in the parking lot, people going to the box office to ask if the premiere is really sold out, activity. The stage entrance door is unlocked. Mona props it open.

"Feeling, honey?"

"Butterflies," she says. "Isn't that silly? You're the one who's in it."

They go through the corridors, turn in through the shops, and walk together out onto the dark stage. There are house lights on, and someone sitting there, out front by himself. A big man, with a pipe in his mouth.

"Henry?"

"Hello, Mike. Hello, Mona."

"You're so early." Mona.

"So are you two."

She goes back across the stage and out through the small door, onto the floor. Mike follows.

"I thought you'd be the last to get here. You have the latest entrance, and the farm . . ."

"Hired the neighbor boy to do the chores. I just felt like being here." He is wearing a suit and tie. "Sitting." He pauses. People wait for Henry Fennellon's pauses. "Sitting with the star of the evening." The pipe is unlit.

"What are you talking about?" Mike.

"This, this theatre. This hall. When you read the papers tomorrow, our opera will come third. First the reporters will describe this auditorium. This theatre. And they're right. Shows will come and go, but having a place like this here will change the university, and the town. Like the Coliseum changed Rome."

"Is that good?" Mona.

"I don't know. But I'm glad you and Mike came along. I wanted to say it to someone."

"What comes next in the stories tomorrow?"

"The audience."

"You figure that's correct, too?"

"Mike." Mona takes her husband's wrist. "Let's go make sure the dressing rooms are open. And check the props."

She pulls him away. When they reach the shop, she says softly: "I wonder if he's thinking about Betty."

"Crazy Betty?"

"I think about her sometimes. At a time like this, when she . . . isn't here."

"I know you do, Squeeze."

"Or about his wife?"

"Let's see about the dressing rooms."

They are open, but someone is already in one of the cubicles on the women's side.

"Who is coming?" Debbie's voice.

"It's Mike and Mona."

"So." She steps out of the cubicle, smiling, in a wonderful, old-fashioned evening dress.

"I have my dress for the party, but now I put on my working clothes."

"Can I help you, Miss Dieter Haas?"

"No, Mona. You do your props now. My dress is too funny?"

"Oh, no. I love it."

"Like a madam it makes me feel, in Berlin, in the time of Brecht." She smiles. "And I have never been in Berlin."

Sidney and Beth have not become friends during rehearsal, but they arrive together in Beth's car, from State House.

"We tried to bring Mr. Hoffman, but he wanted to take a shower." Beth.

"It's a very long shower." Sidney. "He's been taking it for hours. I'm going to do my makeup. Mona, will you help with hair?"

Mike strolls off. The men aren't due for another half hour. Beth goes by him, looking anxiously at doors.

"Something I can help with, Beth?"

"Is there a practice room, to warm up in?"

"There are a bunch of them." Mike is glad enough to have something to do. "I'll see if I can find a janitor, with a key."

Maury arrives, carrying a suitcase. "Karen's score, with the light cues. She here yet?"

"Haven't seen her. She didn't come with you?"

"Own car tonight. Independence night."

"You two fussing?"

"Karen doesn't fuss, she recedes. And gets out her car. But she left the score in mine. Anyway, her family's in town."

Skeats arrives, rather boisterous, with John Ten Mason, quiet but smiling. Then the roar of Dick Auerbach's motorcycle, coming almost in the door before it cuts off, and Dick comes in with Davey Riding, who rode behind him.

The men's dressing room is getting crowded. Sidney is alone on the women's side. The instructor from Dance, who's in charge of makeup, is late. That suits Sidney. Doing her own reassures her, but she wishes Beth would come back. Then she hears a kind voice:

"Sidney, sweet, may I just come in for a minute?" It's Marcel. "Heah. For you and Beth." He has flowers. She could cry. There's no vase, but they fill a little wastebasket with water. It's barely big enough for the long-stemmed gladiolas and irises. And then a telegram! And more flowers with it: a wreath. *Lots of luck, to lovely ladies. Hervey Gandenberg.*

Now some more women come in, musicians in the orchestra, dressed to perform, but needing to leave wraps and purses.

The telegram man is back: "Who's Beth Paulus? These are for her." It's a spray, this time, of orchids, and the orchestra women go half-crazy when they see the card: *Call me after the show. Wish I could be there. Janet Margesson.*

"Oh, yes." Sidney to a violinist. "Beth's quite close to Miss Margesson. She'll be very pleased."

There's a good deal of noise, now, in the backstage corridors. Karen hurries in, feeling herself to be late, though she isn't. Her parents have come to State City for the opening; she was getting them settled at the State House. She is not so much cross as disappointed in Maury; she understands that he didn't want to visit with them before the performance because he is so keyed up, that he's quite willing to see them with her afterward, but she wishes he'd at least have come to say hello. Luckily Mr. Skeats, who is loads of fun, and Johnny—Johnny—were having supper together at State House when she went in with Mother and Father, and they all sat together and had a jolly time, after all.

Hoffman leaves his room.

He takes the elevator down to the lobby, is relieved to see no one he knows in it, and steps out into the midwestern June evening. It's a little moist. He walks slowly around to the river side of State House. He can see the new auditorium across the river, the incandescence of the parking-lot lights, the thousand headlights of cars moving in under them from the feeder streets, and a blaze from the tall lobby, where people he can't see must be hurrying in now. He moves slowly toward the footbridge across State River, starts to cross it, and pauses in the middle to lean on the rail and look upstream at the lights, thinking with some solemnity about opening nights. There must have been a hundred in his life by now, and every one somehow solemn to him, like some stupid fucking form of prayer.

Relights his cigar.

There are none of them that he regrets and none that he'd relive, if he could; who wants to pray the same prayer twice? Yet he thinks it is his real weakness as a director that he has cared about them all equally—all the *Seventeen*s, and *Time of Your Life*s and *Arsenic and Old Lace*s, as much as the few Shakespeares, the one, off-Broadway *Uncle Vanya,* the Sophocles at Yale. Because, he thinks, it is not the play alone he cares about, but the play and the people in it, the amateurs no less than the professionals, and the audience that sees it, and himself, joined invisibly with them, but having let go his control—his discomfiting metaphor continues—in some kind of worship. Or celebration. Or to hell with it.

Throws a pretty good half a cigar into the river. Spits after it. Pulls himself up straight and as jaunty as five feet eight can jaunt, and is off across the bridge, putting out of his mind the youth in which he did *The Adding Machine* in Philadelphia and Saroyan during the war with an army cast in Liverpool before he was willing to settle for stepping back into invisibility, to give up the once indispensable hope of being known in his time.

Hoffman then, joining the line moving toward the ticket taker, with one body and two tickets (he only asked for one), the body dressed in the cleaner of his two suits, the shirt clean from the launderette, but who ever saw the collar of a drip dry crisp? And a tie whose only spot is perfectly well hidden if he keeps the suit jacket buttoned. Almost immediately he is out of himself, feeling the audience. He likes it. A dressy, animated audience. He knows where his seats are, main floor, back row, last two on the right. He'll take the one on the aisle. In a minute. Now he stands behind it, watching the concertmaster and the music librarian put out music, down front in the pit. Musicians are entering it, finding seats. In tails! They didn't wear those at dress rehearsal; Hoffman is surprised and pleased. Their uncased instruments shine. The women are in long, black dresses, with touches of white. They visit, shift chairs and stands, adjust, begin to tune up.

The entering audience is not a stream now but a flood. The ushers, new at this, are hustling, forgetting sometimes to give out programs, having to be called to it by the head usher, girl ushers in short evening dresses, boys in dark suits, music and theatre students.

Audience of women in cocktail dresses, mostly, men in suits, but several groups, enough not to be conspicuous, coming along together, very gay, in dinner jackets and long gowns. In one are Ralph and Josette Lekberg, with a couple Hoffman thinks must be the liberal-arts dean and his wife; Snazzer and Maggi are supposed to be with them, aren't they?

A rowdy group, noticeably in jeans and odd jackets, or corduroys, not student age but older guys with sporty-looking wives, strutting together.

"The painters," says a squeegee voice behind Hoffman. "From the art department."

He turns and it's Snazzer, in dinner jacket and soft shirt; Maggi is with him, and two scrubbed kids, and Hoffman remembers that the Shorts were planning to stop at home, after the dinner party, to pick up Snazzer's children. And that Maggi can't have children.

"Hello," he says, and Maggi gives him the look. It's over with Maggi, he thinks, after last night. Like it's over with the opera, after tonight. Neither one his any more. No more shaping, no more learning; celebration now, expiation, and then. On to the next thing, you know?

The hum gets louder. People are looking left and talking about what they see. Hoffman rises onto tiptoe. It's six people, not as formally dressed as the Lekbergs and the Shorts; the three women are in evening gowns, but the men in business suits. It must be the president of the university, the governor, Hervey Gandenberg and—who did Hoffman hear? Some political lady. A judge? He wonders which of the men is Gandenberg.

In front of him the house has filled up. He sees, not far from where he's standing, Sue Riding, with an empty seat beside her. That seat was supposed to be for Charles, the painter, he heard, but Charles seems not to have showed. He considers sitting with Sue, but Hoffman never sits with anybody at an opening.

There will be standees. Hoffman, feeling a seam in the floor through the thin sole on his loafer, decides that he'll stand, too, right where he is. It's a good-luck seam, there under his foot. He'd better not leave it. Suddenly, a delayed take, watching Snazzer, proud of them, maneuver his two kids toward their seats, and wavering only a little. Hoffman remembers the comic voice in which Short said, "Painters"; Hoffman laughs. *Ch-ka. Ch-ka.* It sounds like a crow with a sore throat.

The student girl standee next along the rail to him, looks over at this alarming noise. "You alone, miss?"

Her face shows slight distaste. "I'm with my friend." There's another girl next to her.

"Here." Hoffman hands her his ticket stub, and the ticket that hasn't been torn yet. "Take those two." Points to his seats. The girl shows them to her friend, they look at Hoffman, back at one another, nod, squeal, and dart around to get seated.

They become two shiny heads, close enough to put his hands on. Vaguely he thinks they could be the right age to be his daughters. His daughters could even be living in State City, for all he knows. He shakes his head. The sound of tuning up, like zoo birds at feeding time, diminishes, as if, one by one, the birds are fed.

The house is noisy; the lights go down to half, and the noise increases. People saying whatever the last thing is to say before it happens. The lights go down to a quarter. A hush begins in the front rows and travels back. The pit lights brighten. The podium light goes on. Sato, slim and serious in tails, comes out the stage-door at left, goes out of sight into the pit, and reappears at the podium.

Applause.

Sato's arms go up, but he does not turn to bow. The applause stops gradually; six thousand eyes, sitting or standing in the dark, focus now on the tip of a black stick. The tip gleams. The stick descends, slowly, moves right, moves left, rises again, goes firmly down and, as it moves again, draws music.

The Overture to $4000. It begins, is played through, collecting the audience, but Hoffman is suddenly too hollow in the stomach, too empty in the head, to be collected; all he has left is a tiny will to pit against this gathering.

Applaud, you bastards, applaud, clap your hands bloody, let my cast hear it back there, applaud. And they do, a tumult, even a few cheers, but immediately he thinks: *Sure, but they're clapping for themselves for being here, for their fine clothes and the new building.* He watches the two polished heads of his two daughters (*Cut it out, Billy, you know?*), one turning to say something to the other as they clap, and the curtain goes up:

Yeah, it's a bunch of poker players around a table. Yeah, that's real construction machinery. Yeah, the tableau's right, the men look brawny, the hard hats look hard, and Skeats, opening the show as Pill, sounds menacing as a bull:

Four of diamonds. Nine of spades. . . .

They're going. Dick with a line. Tough little Mike, okay. Big Maury. Skeats again. All okay, all sure of themselves, all through the first moments, and now Hoffman waits for it to happen, waits for them to make him start forgetting their names, convince him they're a construction crew, playing cards for too much money. When it happens, it takes him by surprise. They're only a couple of dozen lines in when Al—not Marcel, not a double-chinned, childishly sweet, blushing fag with a great tenor voice—but Al, a big, rough, clean-hearted engineer, does it with an off-rhythm line:

That information will cost you a hundred bucks.

Hoffman grins hard, and would have said he didn't vocalize Pill's nasty reply:

Call him, damn it. Let's find out.

But if Hoffman didn't vocalize, why does one of the shiny heads turn into eyes looking up, under his elbows, and into a mouth forming the sound of shush?

In the wings Sidney is waiting to go on. She has sucked in her cheeks so hard, chewed on them so much, that they're raw. She knows her problem in flashes, and forgets it in others. It's a simple one, of strength, like Dick and Maury leg wrestling. She's got to put down that seventy-eight piece orchestra out there, make it lie down so she can hurl a voice over it—bass fiddles taller than she is, brasses that outweigh her, massed like a grinning army out there between her and the people. She fills her diaphragm. She'll reach them. She will. Her voice will soar, she'll pound them. Come on.

Just let the extra mike concealed in the shovel cab be right. She hears her cue:

PILL: There's fourteen hundred dollars in that lousy pot.

Time for *trompe l'oeil.* While the action Hoffman composed—poker players rising, glowering, shoving one another right—diverts, Sidney goes lightly and quietly, midnight cloak against a midnight sky, face turned away until the machinery hides her, onstage and up the short ladder of steel-like rungs, into the cab of the shovel and stands very still.

Now begins Marcel's solo, "I only know I think about her all the time," and even though he's singing out and away from her, Sidney is astonished at his volume, the big baby, and his accuracy, it makes Sidney mad. Which is what she needed, to be ready for the lights to come up, now, in the cab where she stands with the demure cloak held together, madonna-like, looking out over the boys with a serene, ambiguous smile, hooded, knowing that no one out there can be looking anywhere but at her, knowing they are waiting only until her first notes ("Whither thou goest . . . ") for the audience's adoration of her to be as complete as dumb Al's for Sally Anne. She is sure she hears them gasp.

There is sustained applause for Marcel's aria, and she waits through it, watching Sato's baton, but is the mike on? She snaps it lightly with her fingernail, and hears a little *chuck* sound.

Marcel leaves his applause for the poker table, resumes singing, sits down:

Soft, sweet . . . living in my trailer . . .
POKER PLAYERS: Come on/Let's play poker/Deal the cards.

Sidney raises her chin for attention, eyes still on the baton, gets her cue, plants her feet, and lets them have it:

"Whither thou goest, I will go. And where thou lodgest, I will lodge, and thy people shall be my peo-

ple." You see, I went to Sunday school and know
those pretty words.

Yes. Yes, she has it. It's all right. The adoration of the unseen and the
volume to command it, for they are very, very quiet as she pumps it at them,
word after tumbling word, Sidney triumphant.

Sidney wrong. Hoffman, standing at the back of the main floor, can
make the words out only because he has them memorized. She has lost. So is
he. If Hoffman had a gun, a beautifully silenced machine pistol with excellent sights, he could now commence shooting two out of every three
musicians in the orchestra. Shoot a couple, listen, a couple more, until he
had that sound down to where his audience could hear his soprano. Lost,
lost, the show is gone. He looks down at the shinyheads, and sees one turn
to the other and turn back again without having said anything, and then
the other turns, and they whisper:

"What's she saying?"

"I don't know."

If only he could tell his daughters now.

Dutiful applause of an audience let down.

Skeats knows. Skeats may not be big-time, but he knows audiences. He
can feel the lapse of attention, the puzzlement, even though Sidney's voice
sounds clear enough to him onstage. Skeats can respond, take charge, help
out. When she's done, and the time comes for him to do his own first solo,
he can tell the audience what she was saying, can't he? Not the other bloody
poker players. So he sings it out straight:

If I was goin' after it . . .
[*Jerking his thumb at Sidney with a sweep of the arm*]
It wouldn't be for playing *Tarzan* in the *jungle*.

A thump on the chest, a short swing on the old vine. He gets a laugh on
that, a light one, but it encourages him to keep improvising gestures as he
sings about how those little shoulders could wear mink. Now he decides to
go back to something they tried once, in rehearsal, something he suggested
and Hoffman discarded. Moves upstage, singing, back to where Sidney
stands posed on the boom.

Her cloak is cast off now. She wears a two-piece bathing suit, and a
sequined beauty-contest ribbon; and he directs her now, with hand signals,

into bumps and grinds, while he sings—Pill going Al one better, not just describing his vision but demonstrating it. Old audience bleeding loves it, boyos, eats it up. Comes to a pause. Holds out his arms, and she's got it, takes a dance step—that's all right if she's upstaging him for now—slides into a sitting position on the shovel boom and down into his arms. Hooray.

Still singing, whirling completely around once, he begs Sato with his eyes for just a slight ballocky retard, and gets it, enough to carry Sidney straight to front stage center, where he sets her down, turns away, and struts back to the table, indicating with gestures that she's still up there on the boom.

Gets the biggest hand of the evening so far.

POKER PLAYERS: Come on/Let's play poker/Deal the cards.

Skeats winks at them, all round the table. Perfectly timed, wasn't it? Let's see what Billy Bigboy has to say to that one.

Sidney doesn't stop to question how she feels, knows where she is, catches the spirit of Skeats's maneuver, and going into a vulgar go-go step, she sings. Belts it out. Debbie finds her with a light. Loud, long applause.

As for Billy Bigboy, he's at first delighted merely to find her close to audible. He feels an absolutely ferocious grin on his face now, a grin like a big hard-on, full of a mixture of gratitude to Skeats, disgust with Skeats, and a subliminal judgment that what Sidney is giving them now is better than the nothing they were getting, that if she can't do it as a singer, she's not too bad as an entertainer.

The two shiny heads, instead of turning to one another, lean forward now, catching words. Okay. The loud applause now, of relief. Only one pair of hands in the crowd not responding, those of Ralph Lekberg. Ralph's appalled, his subtly comic music here, a piece of writing he loves, perverted into honky-tonk, and he hates them all, Sidney, Skeats, Hoffman, Sato, Debbie. Conspirators. Assassins.

Onstage no one knows quite how to get reorganized. Marcel has the next line, but the girl in front has no inclination to leave while there's still clapping going on. She ought to hustle off. She won't. He hears his music for "What's your bet, Pill?" and instead of singing it, looks at Sato over the cards he's holding, sees Sato motion Sidney offstage, sees Sidney finally respond, and takes the speech four beats late, confident that he has the vocal power to give this error the sound of authority.

What's your bet, Pill?

And they're going again, Sato adjusting, everyone adjusting to Marcel, and the shaky time is over. They've got through it, and the exhilaration of being back in stride communicates, picks up the audience, relieves Hoffman, a little disinvolved now so that he watches two minor individuals, John Ten Mason and Maury.

You gotta give if you're gonna get. This is what Hoffman gave, and he hopes it won't show up to anyone else as clearly as it now does to him. Second Poker Player is a sycophantic little assistant crook; the young doctor's nowhere close to that, can't act it, doesn't have the meanness, inclination toward dishonor. And Bert, now sung by Maury, is straightforward, dedicated to fair play, courageous. But the image, this way, of Bert standing up to Pill, wanting to fight him, is way out of character, too. What you've got is a big, physically dominant young black guy backing down a smaller, middle-aged white one. Instead of things being stacked unfairly against Al, the way it ought to seem at this point, so the audience would be rooting for him hard, things are almost stacked against Pill. Hoffman shakes his head, and sighs; he'd have said he didn't vocalize that sigh, either, but one of the shinyheads looks up, and Davey Riding, paymaster, comes on, and Hoffman's big worry turns into a small fret: Did he make this thing about scrip visual enough so the students here, who never heard of the stuff, can understand it?

. . . How much on four thousand dollars? Jesus Christ.

The curtain lowers, the music stops, Scenes One is done, ragged, barely held together, values a little off—Hoffman is astonished at the volume and enthusiasm of the applause. Audience rising? What for? Then he grins, a let-off grin this time. It's still applauding itself, he thinks; they brought a mood in with them that's carried them through Scene One. Okay.

Sidney has the only costume changes in the opera, from cloak and bathing suit, to negligee for the telephone scene, to a dress for Scene Five.

She decides to go to the negligee now, put the cloak back on over it for her offstage voices in the swamp scene. It isn't necessary, really, she'll have time during Scene Three, but it's something to do, and something to keep her mind off the whole scary, awful subject of offstage singing.

Maybe if she could have a hand mike for the next scene. Who can she ask? Where is Hoffman? Where is Debbie?

It was fun being carried downstage, front and center, but she realized even at the time that Papa Skeats wasn't doing it for fun, that she was wrong, her voice hadn't been carrying out over the orchestra. Will somebody please knock on the dressing-room door—she is out of the bathing suit fast and into underclothes—Hoffman, Debbie, even Mona? Or why doesn't Beth come in?

Somebody knocks.

"Oh, come in." She reaches for the negligee, and has it on but not fastened up when Hughmore Skeats enters, grinning.

"You were smashing, knocked 'em utterly, old girl."

"Oh, Papa, thank you, thank you for the ride. Do you think—" Finally she has the damn, zo zhort necklijay, tied together.

"—Don't break a ribbon there."

"—could I have a hand mike or something for the swamp? Do you think I could?"

"Bloody orchestra was loud as thundereeno, luv, let me give you a hand. Here now, we better redo these bows."

"Will Sato make it quieter?" She submits. The bows are across her bosom.

"They're all out there in the bumpery hallway now, shouting their heads off over it. Ooops. . . ."

"Oh, please."

"Sorry, old girl." But he gives her a squeeze on the left one, too, before she slides away and gets after her hair at the mirror. Fetching piece.

His report on the hallway scene is somewhat true.

"If we could get some balance," Ralph is pleading. "It was sixteen bars before you had the orchestra and singers back together."

"I believe we were lucky to have it that quickly." Sato. "Marcel it was who saved us. How shall we adjust now?"

"All that signaling from the stage . . ." Snazzer. "Where's Hoffman?"

Mona's bringing him. They arrive.

Ralph. "It must be played as it's written, Sato. Let the singers recover as best they can. If we lose the girl's speeches, we lose them. That's all."

"Listen." Hoffman. "Listen, guys, first scene's done, you know? What do you want to do with the next one?"

Sato. "If I reduce the sections?"

Ralph. "No, no, no. The people have a synopsis to follow."

Hoffman. "Never mind, okay."

"And your black friend . . . ?" Snazzer.

"Sato, take the soprano into the pit. Look, we put her dark cloak on, see, just lead her out with you and stand her up in front of the band, huh?"

"Allow her to concertize?"

"Yeah, I think so. Put her so they don't see much of her, okay. The scene's short, Debbie's got a busy set for'm to watch, just let the soprano lines float up with the rest of the music instead of coming from behind, okay?"

Snazzer. "You tried that in rehearsal, Billy. Nobody liked it, including you."

"Yeah. Nobody's gonna like it now, including me, but let's do it."

Ralph. "Sato?"

"Yes. That might be best."

Hoffman. "Hey, Mona. Hey. Hold the curtain five minutes. Where's Sidney? Which dressing room?"

Big Dick Auerbach, First Poker Player, through singing for the evening, is standing a respectful distance away, listening, concerned for Sidney as he always is.

"This way, Mr. Hoffman." Dick the wrestler.

Hoffman. "Hold it, Sato. I'll bring her." Hoffman follows quick Dick down the hall, is right behind him as Dick pushes open the door, and comes upon a steamy little scene: Sidney in negligee, looking in the mirror, Skeats behind her, pressed against her, arms around and hands fondling.

It's as if they were rehearsing for the telephone scene, only they're not. Sidney is standing for him, Hoffman knows at once, not because the hands are welcome but because the caresses of the voice are needed, the voice telling her how bumping well she sang, how glorioso she is going to be.

Dick Auerbach is across the room in two strides, and knocks Skeats away from Sidney, straight-arm to the shoulder.

"Let her alone."

Hoffman moves after him fast, grabs Dick, "Never mind, never mind. Listen, Sidney."

Skeats. "What in hell, chums?"

Hoffman, moving around Dick, standing between him and Skeats, close to Sidney. "You were swell, Hugh. That was a great move, you know? Jesus. Listen, Sidney. Get your cloak back on, okay? Hood up, everything, okay?"

Dick picks up the garment, holds it for her.

Hoffman. "We ain't got balance, we can't get balance, maybe tomorrow. Listen, take her out to Sato, Dick. Sidney, Sato's going to have you in the pit. You'll be in front, right under the podium, try not to let 'em see you."

"Not . . . ?"

"They wouldn't see you this time anyway, right? If you were back behind the scenery. There'll be a mike there for you, it's all fixed up, don't worry. Come on, we got a real show goin' here." Grinning, shoving, cajoling. Dick takes her out, and Hoffman turns to Skeats, who's rubbing a sore shoulder.

"Bloody hell."

"Don't take it hard, Hugh. Listen, as far as I can find out, those two kids were married and still are."

"Still are?"

"Yeah, I think so." Puts an arm around Skeats's shoulders now. "Got it from the outraged husband, did you, Hugh?" and Hughmore throws his bearded head back and laughs.

"Smashing ningleberries, eh? That's one on me, then."

"Look, you got an entrance. Find Marcel, will you, tell him what we're doing?"

Jesus, Hoffman hopes no one has copped his particular standing place along the rail, with the lucky underfoot seam, above the shinyheads.

Nobody has.

Swamp music. Enter Al, tiring; shoos a water moccasin. Reclines, singing, and looks back into the foggy distance of the set, where a drifting twinkle of light indicates the place from which Sally Anne's envisioned voice should come. When, instead, it comes from out in front of the orchestra, Marcel is visibly startled; apparently Skeats didn't reach him with news of the staging change.

The tenor almost flips over toward the unexpected sound direction, *Ch-ka, ch-ka;* but it isn't funny. No one else laughs, certainly not Hoffman's daughters. They seem quite intent. And, in a dumb way, Marcel's move probably works, particularly since Marcel now rises—probably not improvising staging, probably just getting his feet under him, and when the soprano voice sounds again, wanders toward it, probably just wanting to be a little more downstage, but it could be seen as a search through the swamp for the will-o'-the-wisp. He's an actor, and the scene's okay, and Hoffman for the first time finds himself taken into the music itself, the swampy, spooky music, full of night sounds and mist movement. It settles him. It settles the audience. They are quite sure of what's going on by the time Al leaves and Pill stomps in, quite intent, and Pill even gets a gasp of disapproval in response to his terrible speech about killing a sergeant during the war.

Debbie keeps the lights down, and Sidney gets off inconspicuously during the applause.

Inconspicuous, and a little miserable, she slips through the stage-side door and is in the shop, where Dick is waiting for her.

"Don't you want to watch out front?"

"I wanted to wait for you."

"That was sweet."

Scrims and flats are moving up and down. Furniture goes by on silent wheels. Then Marcel, not noticing them, to his entrance.

Music, lights, curtain. "Cindy."

"Shhhh."

Hand on her neck, lightly. Whispers "Cindy?"

"Shhh, Dick. Listen." Actually puts her hands over his mouth. Whispers. "It's Beth."

Glory, sheer glory of sound now, out there on the stage. If in rehearsal Beth's voice was great, now it's transcendent; Sidney finds herself moving toward it, Dick after her, close as they can get to the stage, finding a line of sight that lets them watch her.

"God," Dick says, and suddenly Sidney—or maybe Cindy, for the last time in her life—is holding his hand, squeezing it hard.

What town? When things are open here, the town's still closed.

Incredible noise of applause. Cheers. And then Marcel, overriding the end of it as he should:

Yeah. Worms don't do much to liven up a place at
that.

And the two of them are off, out there, in their complex duet, joy, passion,
sensuality, complaint hurled back and forth, flirtation and refusal, but the
music of those voices is more than the meaning, and there are louder cheers
when the duet is over. Dick and Sidney can hear the audience get up, knows
they are standing, like people at a tense moment in a football game, as
Henry Fennellon goes past and onstage, adding his solid, bass boom to the
tenor and alto; then,

I'll see you in the morning, buster. Pleasant dreams.

And Henry is back with Dick and Sidney, whispering: "They're standing.
The audience is on its feet." As Beth and Marcel resume, maneuver, kiss,
and Beth, despairing, delivers the solo, Ralph's most lyrical music, which
begins:

Kiss me, and I'll believe you.

And by the end of it there is so much cheering and applause that Beth is
singing out over it, totally unconfined, a duet almost with the audience,
until the curtain comes down.

The show has come alive. Hoffman catches himself bouncing up and
down on the balls of his feet, caught up in an excitement he didn't know
about before. In all the hundred shows, there's never been a voice like this.
It's past belief. Marcel, given someone to sing with, was past belief, and
Henry a foundation in a soaring spire of sound, and when he exited, it was as
if the spire was cut loose, not to fall but to ascend. Billy Hoffman cheers as
loud as anyone, cheers like caws, his arms virtually flapping. The applause
that started in the middle of the scene never really stopped, did it, growing
and growing with the singers to the end?

The shinyheads, up on their feet like everyone else in the theater, are
hugging one another.

"Want me to put your cloak away?" Dick.

"I'm going to scoot to the dressing room, and check my face. Go on
out front, Dickie."

"Sidney, your mom and my folks are out there. They brought Sam
down. He's with a baby-sitter at the motel."

"Yes. Okay."

"Shall I say you'll see him tonight?"

"Oh, Dick. He'll be asleep. It would break my heart." Sidney starts off. "But what about Skeats?" Dick cries.

"I'll make him behave." She's at the door.

"Tomorrow? Shall I tell them tomorrow?"

She disappears from the shop.

Skeats is at the dressing-room door. She needs him now. She presses up against him briefly, says, "Wait, now," rushes into the dressing room, sheds the cloak, looks herself over, and struts back out to join the baritone.

"Come on, let's get 'em, Papa Bear." She grabs his arm, and they trot. They reach the wings. The telephones are in place, front stage left and right. Of course she'll be heard. She's got herself charged now.

The curtain rises on Marcel, across the stage, picking up his pay phone, dialing. Big hunk of physiology, look at the lung capacity. She leans back into Skeats standing just behind her, a hand on her waist. Giggles, but she's mad. Mad at Marcel's size.

"Now don't get us arrested out there, Papa Bear."

Walks out with a wriggle, and picks up the telephone on the dressing table, right after the second ring. And shouts:

This is Sally Anne, speakin'.

They heard that all right. Someone say they didn't. Al replies, Pill comes in behind her, rough, fondling, and she plays off his excitement. To hell with the rest of it, the pitch, the intonation, the musical subtleties; she does the whole scene in a voice she knows is strident, keeping to her best range, ignoring the musical line when she must, singing it out and away. Finds, loud and lucky, a note somewhere she never heard herself sing before, concentrates on making her whole voice sound like it. And she's getting, from Skeats, some kind of complementary vocal performance, she knows; maybe they're both raucous, but for sure they're being heard. Sidney is back in the show.

In the wings at right Beth frowns softly at Mike and Maury, and says: "Poor darlings." Which is accurate. To the singers listening professionally the exchange between Skeats and Sidney sounds awful, full of concession and effort. It's with great relief that they hear Marcel's wonderful voice come back, take the scene away and end it.

Offstage, at left, Skeats keeps a hand on Sidney's arm. He has gotten the bloody girl through it. He frowns. He knows as well as any of the others what they've had to give away in quality to make that scene intelligible. He smiles, bitterly, cops a feel on 'er kiss-me-Charlie. Still married, is she? Ralph won't have liked that rendition a bit, but bloody Hoffman better thank him again.

Bloody Hoffman is beyond thanking anyone, blaming anyone. Being called back briefly into authority between the first scene and the second, forced to decide, was unwelcome to him, an interruption. Beth and Marcel and Henry, in the next scene, gave him his role back, as this production's passive, not its active, lover. He can be ravished or seduced, treated brutally or mocked, made ashamed or proud, but he no longer controls or wishes to. What he made happen must happen now to him. He was aware, of course, of the contrast, the difference between the brassy, superficial singing of Sidney and Skeats now being somewhat routinely applauded, as compared with the great musicality and passion of Marcel and Beth. But Hoffman's awareness is helpless by choice, by propriety, and by tradition. He would not go backstage again for anything; it will all come together now, or it won't, as the curtain goes up for the fifth and final scene.

Marcel opens it with Beth, a Marcel more and more inspired by his own voice with every note—"leaps followed by runs followed by leaps, and all the same voice"; that phrase, from some forgotten music critic, shines in his head as he sings to Beth, loving her voice equally. Catching, he thinks, something of what she has and he finally lacks, the willingness to expose all that emotion, spend it as if it were inexhaustible. He lets her bring it out of him, too, knowing he has never sung as well with anyone else, beyond his own expectations of himself, and when Sidney enters, Sally Anne, sugar-voiced and enticing, Marcel simply will not let her lower what they have. He has watched Sidney and Skeats across stage, at their telephone, been embarrassed at the vulgarity, and now it's as if he were taking her away from Skeats and from cheapness, and Sidney, too, knows that her first notes to Al in Scene Five are the first right notes she has sung tonight.

Then Norah, accosting Sally Anne, all vocal power and shimmering words, and Sidney's transfiguration becomes complete from sheer competitiveness. She will not be cut by Beth, face to face, toe to toe, and Sidney too sings as she never has before, reaches back inside for power she never knew she had or had to have. Flinging words now at Beth, hearing words flung back, she destroys her own consciousness, loses herself finally in a great, musical scream of,

Pill! Hurry, Pill!

It is not in Hughmore Skeats to reach the level of these three young singers, and he knows it. But he can sustain, with acting and exaggeration, some of the frenzy they have entered into, and he bounds onstage, snarling, sneering, facing Al, but really looking for the vocal help he must have in the confrontation, knows that it's coming, and it does. Enter Ray Applegore, most sinister of all, rock-solid Henry, and there are four singers with Skeats, and Sato is responding with the orchestra, picking up tempo slightly, daringly, moving the whole damn thing to crescendo—Knife! Norah's scream! Al's yell! Gunfire. Fallen bodies. Death. Horror. Damnation and Catharsis.

Snazzer Short believes. Sitting straight and forward, gripping his young son's shoulder, he sees his corny knife and gun fight, of which he's been a bit ashamed, grade-B TV stuff, purified by music, glorified by performance, made real.

Stop. Down music. Hushed pause. Here comes, flanked by his short, tough henchman, a strange Horatio with a shotgun. Snazzer does not see Maury there, nor a black, but a dark-gold avenging angel, blazing in some combination of lights for which it does not occur to him to credit Debbie— majestic, with the authority of a puppet master entering to bless the unbreathing bodies and chastise the living, the pale and greedy girl in a voice like thunder pealing:

Both of them meant for you to have it. Pick it up.
Down on your knees and pick it up. Go on. It's two
cents on the dollar that they're paying, girl. Easiest
eighty bucks you'll ever make.

Audience to its feet, cheering, as the curtain falls.

Shinyheads obscuring Hoffman's view. Hoffman limp at the power of it, vindicated, resting his head on the rail, *ch-ka*-ing weakly at the effect of the final tableau he fought for, illogical as it was, full of bad sociology and distorted history: incongruities made harmonious, the preposterous accident of art.

21: Bag and Dog. Calls...
Calls...
Calls...

Bustling weakly, Billy Hoffman opens the door to his room at State House, goes to the bed, sits on it, and feels the last bubbles of bustle drain out of him fast, like someone pulled the plug.

"Ah, shit," he whispers to his suitcase. "Gurgle, you know?"

There is a cast party, but Hoffman doesn't go to cast parties anymore. He stopped for a minute at the president's reception in the Green Room at Janscombe, shook hands with the president and Mrs. President.

"You're joining us, Mr. Hoffman. I'm very glad." Pres.

Hoffman grinned like a dog.

Mrs. Pres. "There's so much you can do here." She seemed very nice. So did Pres. "I think you'll find State City can be a good theatre town." Then. "Governor, this is William Hoffman. He directed the opera, and he's joining our faculty."

So Hoffman dogged it some more, shaking hands with the governor. Then he got carried off and hugged by whooping Maury, and patted by purring Sidney, and kissed by Beth, and gave his paw to Marcel and did the other tricks for the other people in the cast, and as for Snazzer and Maggi and Ralph and even Debbie and Sato, they must have figured he was going to see them at the cast party, at the country club, your host, Hervey Gandenberg—which one was Hervey Gandenberg?

Maggi wants to marry Hervey Gandenberg, you know?

So he slipped away, making the slip look like a bustle, and didn't meet Ganderbag, Maggi's Skanderbag. So Bag will be your host, your director maybe, at the big party at the club, to which everybody breathless is going. Dog doesn't know everybody breathless anymore. They aren't Dog's people anymore. Maybe they're Bag's people now.

All Dog wanted was to feel the plug suck and lift and drain, so he did the bustle, and here he is, and it's starting to feel better. He pats his suitcase, a canvas and leather affair, next to him on the bed, and whispers to it:

"How's tricks?"

On the table by his bed is a document. It is a letter of appointment from the university president, whose hand Hoffman just shook. He can't quite remember what the man looked like, twenty minutes ago, so he concentrates on trying to think how the hand felt. It was a big, firm, dryish hand. Hoffman guesses he must have been looking at the hand, not the face, of the president of the university.

Then Hoffman stops guessing and sits, hearing, but attaching no importance to, a crisp knocking at his door.

The knock comes again. Hoffman shakes his head at the suitcase, not a big movement, just enough to draw the suitcase into the conspiracy of silence. Suitcase is not to say a word.

The door opens. Shit, he didn't lock it. He thinks maybe it will be some of the kids, looking to leash him off to the party, and is framing an amiable sentence about resting a coupla minutes and then calling himself a cab and coming over, you know?

"Hello, Billy Hoffman."

It's a short, straight, ruddy, salt and pepper man, in a gorgeous dark suit and silk tie, with a goddamn real Havana, a Monte Cristo by the shape and color, by the unmistakable brown and white band, in the middle of his shapely face.

"I'm Herve Gandenberg."

Hoffman nods. The grin is back; he can feel it. He can't keep it off his long-eared face. But he can find something to say, can't he? Something courtly.

"Where'd you get the Monte Cristo?"

"A friend brings them in from Paris. But they're cheaper in Spain."

"How much?" Dog.

"Two dollars each in France. About sixty cents in Spain." Bag.

There is a pause, and then Bag says: "Look, Billy."

"Will you take two bucks for one?"

"Oh, for God's sake." Hervey Gandenberg shakes his head, reaches inside his jacket, gets out a case, and gives Hoffman a cigar. Hoffman looks at it, rolls it gently, can't believe it. A Monte Cristo. How much for a match? He nips off the end, sniffs the length of it, licks the length of it, puts it in his mouth, and the match is there. Puffs once lightly to be sure it's going, and then, filling his lungs with the incredible smoke, watches Gandenberg take a step to the bedside table, put the burnt match in the ashtray, and pick up the document, Hoffman's letter of appointment from the president. It offers Hoffman a tenured appointment as associate professor of drama at $14,500 a year plus benefits. Gandenberg reads it as if he had every right to, puts it down, and ponders.

Then he smiles. "You did a marvelous job with this opera, Billy. That's the important thing."

Hoffman thinks about that and eventually nods consent. That's the important thing to him, too, isn't it?

"I'd planned to do this at the cast party, but then when I realized you weren't coming, I hated being deprived of the pleasure, so I came over." Hoffman stares at him through the fumes of the great cigar. "I made some inquiries"—it's starting to come out like a little prepared speech now— "and learned you'd been having difficulty in State City finding a place to have your shoes repaired. Well, we may not have shoe repair handy, but we've got another solution to too much walking." From his pants pocket he takes out a key ring, two shiny little keys on it. "These are the keys to a brand new Chevy Monza Towne Coupe. It's in the parking lot of the club, and it's all yours." The set part is over, and Gandenberg says, more naturally: "It's still up there, I'm afraid. I didn't want to ask anyone to drive it down with me, figuring you wanted to be alone."

Hoffman smiles back. "What am I, the most valuable player, huh?" He's leaving something out, you know; what? "Hey. Thanks. Thanks."

"Some of us wanted to do something for you, anyway." Gandenberg continues to hold the keys. Hoffman doesn't know whether to reach for them or not. "Mind if I sit?"

Hoffman waves the cigar at him. What was empty in Hoffman is illusorily full, now, of sweet, intoxicating, insubstantial Cuban fumes. Levitation seems possible. He'd better say something.

"Yeah. Have a chair, you know."

Gandenberg sits down in a straight chair by the bedside table and picks up the letter of appointment.

"Billy, let me be frank. I'm not sure Debbie's as enthusiastic about this appointment as she was when she made it."

"She tell you to say that?"

"I appreciate that you're tired. I'll make this as quick as I decently can." The dark suit is silk, like the necktie. Shimmery, huh?

"Hey, I heard you were buying her a new curtain. Seven grand."

"Yes. It's been ordered. I want to support music and theatre here as much as I can. I want to try to raise money, too, or rather help Debbie raise it. That's something successful department heads do, you know, and she'll be very good at it. She's shrewd and practical, she has her own kind of charm, and she's not afraid to ask."

"Yeah."

"What I plan to do is to get her to some of the alumni who are eager to buy this university basketball and football players, to talk about investing in actors and singers and technicians. I want to see her have the best theatre department in the country, and I believe she can."

"Yeah. Great. That's great."

"You're a blunt man. I'll be blunt. I think she's making an error appointing a man of your qualifications to a tenured job. Her tenured people ought to be theatre scholars. Men and women who can cut it academically as well as do studio work. I think she should have a good, big special budget to get the straight professionals, like yourself, in whenever she has a show for one. And at a hell of a fee."

"So the car. That's to travel in, huh? The Monza."

"Let me finish. We both care about Debbie. I assume we both care about theatre in this country, even in this state. Can we agree on that?"

Hoffman looks at the man and nods. "You want me out of Maggi Short's britches pretty bad, don't you, Mr. Gandenberg?"

That stops him. Hoffman goes on.

"I got news. The britches aren't my size."

Gandenberg recovers. "Rough son of a bitch, are you? You don't want to talk with me about a theatre department?"

"Maybe Debbie doesn't want the best theatre department. Maybe she just wants to do good shows."

"What are you, a negotiator? Look, I'm not negotiating. I'm going back to my party and just forget the hell out of you." He stands up. He puts the car keys down very deliberately, next to the letter of appointment.

"You're supposed to understand motivation. Sit there, will you, and try to figure out how motivated I'd be to help Theatre if people make dirty jokes out of my serious opinions and advice. Here." He hands Hoffman another Monte Cristo. "This will help you think about it."

"I already got the appointment."

"I'm aware of that. You don't have to accept it."

"Maybe I oughta take that and the car, too."

"I'll let you judge."

"Yeah. I'm aware of that." Where did Hoffman get that phrase from, anyway? "Hey, here Mr. Gandenberg." He has thought of something dirty to do. If he weren't tired and empty, he wouldn't do it. If it made a damn bit of difference, he wouldn't do it. He slides a hand into his worn pocket. The pocket won't hold change anymore—little hole in the corner. It'll hold halves, but not dimes and quarters. He pulls out his billfold, and from it a five-dollar bill. Hands it to Gandenberg. "For the cigars, you know?"

"Jesus Christ." Gandenberg takes the bill, smooths it, folds it neatly, all of this somewhat automatic, and puts it in his own silk pocket. "You dumb asshole."

With which incontrovertible summation of Hoffman's character he leaves. Hoffman is still on the bed. Hoffman addresses the closing door, softly.

"You owe me a dollar," he says. "Two cigars is four bucks. I gave you five."

Now he lies back, swings his legs up on the bed to enjoy the rest of the cigar. He lifts the rather light suitcase to the bed beside him, his traveling companion.

The suitcase was packed yesterday afternoon, just a few minutes after the mail brought him his letter of appointment from the president.

The letter came, and Hoffman grinned over it, and loved it up a little, and made a call to Philadelphia. Collect.

"Yeah, I'll accept charges from Mr. Hoffman."

"Hey, Don. You know?"

"Don't horse around. Long-distance costs money."

"For twenty-five percent of all I get, you can stand a little horsing."

"What do you want?"

"That California thing still open?"

"Jesus, yes."

"Can I have it?"

"It's street theatre. All spades. You sure?"

"*All* spades?"

"Yeah. We had a coupla spade directors interested, and they both skipped, right? Everybody wants boogies, that's the hod commod. One's going to Princeton, for Chrissake, he's never done a show in his life outside of boys' camp. The other one fell into a big budget off Broadway, maybe you saw his picture in the *Times*?"

"No."

"So how'd it go out there, Billy? What was it, a musical, right?"

"Opera, listen, I'll do California, then."

"We oughta have a boogie."

"I'm your boogie."

"It's like Watts, baby."

"I never worked southern California. Two hundred a week, huh?"

"No. Hang on, that was if we got them a spade. They'll go a white if they have to, but it drops to one and a quarter."

"What for?"

"When I tell you, you'll say no, and I'm glad you will. Seventy-five is for a gorilla to guard your bod."

Hoffman had hesitated, then he'd asked: "You rippin' your twenty-five percent off two hundred or one and a quarter, Don?"

"All right." They like one another, though Hoffman knows Don thinks his kind of theatre old-fashioned. "We'll take it off the one and a quarter. That gives you ninety-three seventy-five a week, net. It's a fee, so there's no withholding. Maybe you can get your gorilla to cop your joint when he's not busy banging heads."

"How many weeks?"

"Four or six. How it goes. Protest shows. Set up on a flatbed truck, you got it?"

"I've done it before," Hoffman had said, and took down the names and numbers in L.A.

So he was going. He is always going. He fills himself with smoke, arm across his canvas and leather friend, wishes he'd had time to get the other suit cleaned, wonders if he'll have to buy sports shirts in L.A., wonders what color car Gandenberg was trying to give him. He could take the keys, you know, call a cab, and go on up to that club, find the Monza Towne Coupe maybe, hey, drive it out to L.A. He lies still, smiling at the unreal thought.

Then he smiles at the dilemma of the maid who comes to do this room in the morning. She'll have her choice between a new car, won't she, or bein' an associate professor of drama. Maybe she'll take both.

Then he takes his shirt and shoes off and drifts toward sleep, no sense getting all the way undressed, there'll be a 5:00 A.M. phone call. He rehearses himself mentally for getting up, putting on his shoes, shaving, remembering to put his wet razor and toothbrush on top of the clothes in the packed suitcase, and making it down to the airport bus. Limousine. They still call it limousine out here. By limousine, to answer the calls: the next show, the next people; the next place. Otherwise he could stay here and grow old.

Neither Hoffman nor a hobo is allowed to grow old, for they are mendicant friars and born to go where the roads go. Sometime in his life sleeping Hoffman learned all he'll ever really need to know about that: The American road never ends.

Empty Hoffman sleeps like he's been hit over the head with an ax until, at 3:00 A.M., not 5:00, there comes a knocking at his door. He's a long time coming out of sleep to hear it, and would not answer except that he hears, along with it, oh, come on, willya? Sobs, female woman sobs.

He lies there, bare-chested and stocking-footed, dazed, and finally grunts that he is coming, gets up, puts on a thin, terry-cloth robe he stole once from a Turkish bath in Memphis, goes to the door, and opens it.

Standing there in tears, her plain face puffy, blonde hair limp, and yet with a remarkably clear smell of sex about her, so that the impression is more distraught than distressed, is Karen Jackstone.

"Can I come in, please? I'm afraid. I'm afraid of Maury."

He stands aside to let her in. "Jesus Christ," he mutters. "I'm afraid of Maury, too."

She falls in a dumpy but not altogether unstylish blonde heap in the one large chair, so Hoffman sits back down on his bed and looks at her.

"My mother and dad are here, too, but they won't let me in their room."

"Yeah?"

"I mean, they said, isn't this funny?" She's getting comfortable on him. "They were so against the marriage, but now they said, 'Maury's your husband, Karen.' And they liked Johnny so much, but they said 'Maury's your husband. You can't come in.' Billy, I'm afraid he'll kill me."

"No. Not Maury. I doubt he'd even biff you one."

"Billy."

"What'd you do, make it with the doctor?"

Gives him a look, and looks away.

"Like a goddamn revenge play," Hoffman says, realizing as he does how little he is able to care. "I gotta go to sleep, you know? Make yourself comfortable." Has enough chivalry to consider offering the healthy young woman the bed, while he takes the chair, but not enough energy, maybe in a minute. Keeps the robe on for modesty, lies back, pulls the bedspread over him, and turns off the light. He hears Karen go to the bathroom. Then, oddly, for he has expected to have trouble getting back to sleep, he corks right off, and is waked again by the black plastic telephuck ringabanging at his very balls.

He rolls around, finds the thing, and says into it: "Shit."

"Mr. Hoffman, is Karen Jackstone there."

It isn't Maury's unmistakable voice. He doesn't care whose unmistakable voice it is. "Probably. I'll look around, huh?"

Anyway, he can see Karen's unmistakable bulk rising out of the chair. "For me?"

Drops the dreary thing on the table in the dark, turns away from the conversation, not bothering to listen, and is halfway asleep when she leaves the room.

A ring again at five, but this time it's the desk, waking him so that he can be ready for the airport bus. He feels like a dried-out fishing worm, you know, one of those ones that crawls out onto the pavement in a hard rain and lies there shriveling as the impenetrable surface dries.

There are two other passengers in the dark of the minibus. Hoffman doesn't look at them. He hopes they won't be people whom he's met or who might recognize his shriveled self. He may be able to sleep a few minutes more on the bus, or anyway, lean back with his suitcase clasped and his eyes closed.

Eyes. Closed. Churlishly he refuses to open them when, instead of the bus starting, he hears a voice he knows say to the driver,

"Just a minute, lover. I'm changing seats."

And even if he didn't know the voice, he'd know the perfume and the charged air and the waft of warmth as Maggi Short moves in beside him.

"Open your eyes, fool."

"Is Gandenberg here too?"

"Are you going to open your eyes or not?" She drops a hand into his crotch in the dark; there isn't much there to squeeze, but she manages.

"Cut it out." He opens his eyes.

"That's what you call it?" She hooks an arm around his neck and is whispering. "Your cuddidout, Hoffman? Hey, you want to hear gossip?"

Suddenly he remembers—he had actually forgotten—that Karen Jackstone sat in his room awhile last night, and anxious, guiltless, wishes they were going faster. "Am I in it?"

"Well, not that I know of—oh, you pig. What have you been doing?"

"Trying to get some sleep. Hey, Maggi, you're seeing me to the airport at five A.M. Hey, that's nice. You been to bed?"

She smiles and strokes his neck.

"Someone's about to get his cuddidout mangled if he doesn't tell nice Maggi."

"The rich girl from Boston. Karen. The vocal coach, Maury's wife."

"Hoffman! You weren't in that?" She laughs with delight.

"Yeah, like I'm the neutral embassy. Three-o'clock refuge."

"So that's where. I'm impressed. I'd say I didn't know little Karen had it in her, except of course she did. They leave the party about midnight, and the eyes of I-hate-Texas are upon them, Karen fairly drunk and very cross because Maury won't leave our clubby scene to call on her parents. Maury phones the parents, urges them to join us at the club, but Karen's mother is reported tired. So Maury says:

" 'Will you rather I don't come down disturbing until morning?'

"Seems that's capital with Karen's popsi, they'll have a nice family breakfast, but Karen won't believe it.

"Maury says, 'Call them yourself, dear wife, here's a dime for the pay phone, and a penny for being a good girl.'

"Bam. Karen whacks him, to the delight of all good drunks assembled, and grabs the nearest strong young arm—which just happens to be that of the doctor in the house, he's got some answering service, that one.

" 'Take me to my mom,' says Karen.

"With which Snazzer the Matchmaker Short gives me a meaningful punch on the arm, only it lands low on the hip. Snazzer's walking pretty short by that time of the evening.

"All right? Maury's friends are alarmed. This might be serious. Mike, Mona, Davey, Sue, Dick—it's their theory Maury needs Karen for stability, and they're cheering him on: Heal that breach, man, go.

"I'm appointed to go with Maury, and Mike's appointed to go too to keep an eye on us, so we pick out two bottles of Mr. Gandenberg's medium-good champagne, suitable for younger casts and office parties, and we buzz on down to State House.

"Oh, Hoffman, you dirty bastard, you don't know how I longed to just stay on the elevator after they got off and take my bottle of champagne to your room. But there was Snazzer and, for all I knew then, Hervey too, with their eyes on the clock, back there at the country club.

"So. I knock at the door, my genteel but imperious Katharine Hepburn knock, whence we play a scene of utter indignation, confusion, and embarrassment—Popsi and Mom were sound asleep, and no sign at all of stout John and horny Karen, and it's Maury's foot in my mouth and mine in Mike's and Mike's in the cuspidor, if only they had one.

"What ever happened to cuspidors, Hoffman? You pig, I'll bet you've got hundreds in your luxurious bachelor apartment, back in Philadelphia, don't you?

"I used to pride myself on having the dirtiest mind ever created, but I swear it never occurs to me that Johnny Ten and Karen mean to pull the wool out of Maury's Afro over all our eyes.

"But he's great, Hoffman. Maury's some ridiculous kind of great man. Aren't all great men ridiculous? Was there ever a bigger nut than Thomas Jefferson?

"Maury apologizes to the Karen parents, Maury says: 'Guess that doctor prescribed her a Texas transfoo-type A-voosion, let's go save the party before it dies some dead and awful death.'

"God, Maury and Mike and I whang back into that party like holy rollers, git up, drink up, dance, come on. I tell you, he's a great man, Maury, but it's Karen who's the nut.

"Do you know that she cried all night, one night last week, because it didn't occur to you to ask her to play the overture to the opera on the piano at some rehearsal or other? Mona told me that.

"We're back at the club. We're swinging and singing, and a tiny little thing happens to divert my fascinated attention from the main show. Mona pulls me away from a dance with muscles Dick Auerbach, I'm having such a nice time coaxing him into feeling silly, it's the telephone. Mr. Hervey Gandenberg's number-one fiancée, a certain Ms. Janet Margesson—"

Hoffman. "No kidding? Margesson?"

"—calling Mr. Gandenberg's number-two fiancée, my gorgeous self.

" 'Janny,' says my gorgeous. 'Where are you, darling?'

"She was not sober. 'Rock rock Ilse lum,' she says, meaning Rock Island.

" 'And did you want to speak to Hervey, darling?'

" 'Maggi. Maggi. I want Beth.'

"Now Beth, at the moment, is engorging Mr. Hughmore Skeats Fourth by dancing down his throat, apparently under the impression that he is at least Ezio Pinza and more likely Feodor Chaliapin. And dirty-minded though I am, I am working around to telling Janet Bethie isn't there, but Beth's hi-fi, Hoffman. She receives it all. I think you could twiddle her left kneecap and get Singapore police calls on the ankle.

"I'm still giving my friend Janet the subtle, when all of a sudden Bethie's in behind me, breathing louder than most people scream, saying,

" 'Jan. Oh, it's Jan, isn't it? For me.'

"She takes the phone, melts it into a puddle of plastic, croons for a minute, drops the receiver instead of hanging up, halfway knocks me down with a hug, looks around, and says, 'Johnny Ten?' Everybody else in the room knows he's gone and with whom. Not Beth. She looks mischievously pleased. He isn't there. Imagine. Next thing poor Hughmore knows, his dancing partner is out in the parking lot, revving up her Ghia, without so much as having stopped to pick up her brand-new pink, purple, and gold eight-foot handwoven Siamese-silk stole.

"It's a gorgeous thing, Hoffman. Gandenberg gave Beth and Sidney each one at his awards ceremony, shank of the evening. Do you like it?"

"Huh?"

"Beth leaves it, leaves everything. Oh, she'll get it back, pig, but I love wearing it for now. I run after her with the damn thing to the car, as a matter of fact, but Bethie's on her way by now, and all she says is, 'Tell Johnny the Banjo Man's cabin, Maggi, You come, too.'

"An obese opportunity, my friend, hey, by the way. You're featured at Hervey's award ceremony, Billy Hoffman, did you know? Of course you do. You got a car sitting up at the club parking lot, my man. And Hervey announced his sadness, you were moving on."

"That's how you knew, Maggi?"

"So where are the car keys, lover?"

"Oh, yeah. Well, I left them, you know? Sort of a tip for the maid."

"And there was a letter of appointment—?"

"She was a damn good maid."

"I wonder what her first play will be? *The Admirable Crichton's* got a butler in it."

Jesus, Hoffman's having a good time. "No, I think she'll do *She Stoops to Conquer.*"

"Bad pig, of course she will." Gives him a nice kiss on the cheek, a squeeze on the shoulder. Rests her pretty head against him.

"And the Ridings got burgled, no, wait a minute. That comes later at the big police scene. Where was I, Hoffman?"

"Beth runs off to see Janet Margesson and some guy that plays the banjo? And you got Hughmore standing there with his mouth open and his pants around his ankles, and I dunno if I believe a word of it."

"Cross my heart, if I can find it, oh, listen." The wicked woman straightens up, sparkles. "Marcel's little friends. There were three of them at the party whom he hadn't asked at all. He was terribly concerned because they'd crashed, and poor Marcel, he kept asking me if Mr. Gandenberg minded, but they were exquisite. The prettiest things there, and one especially, I wish you could have seen it. Long, soft taffy hair, and a lovely pants suit from Neiman-Marcus—I know, because I ordered one just like it from the catalogue last week, worn with just a little tiny bit of ambiguous padding here and there, very light makeup, perfume. My he's turned himself out nicely. I absolutely do not suspect until we happen to walk down the hall toward the ladies' room together, and there at the door the vixen gives me the most brazen wink and darts on to the men's."

"Are you tellin' me Skeats—?"

"Oh, yes, my dear. Yes, I am. It isn't fifteen minutes after Beth floats off before Skeats has the fascinating pants-suit charmer in his arms. 'Oh, Maggi,' says Marcel. 'Please tell him. Mr. Skeats. Do you think he knows or not?' Am I the world's worst, Hoffman? I wouldn't have told Skeats for anything, but I pat poor Marcel and say don't fret, and the dance is barely over before Hughmore bears the dazzling creature off into the tender night. Such a lovely evening, Hoffman."

"Jesus, you got more to tell? I suppose Henry Fennellon is doin' the rhumba with Ralph Lekberg's wife, next, huh?"

"No, and they never will, poor darlings. No, Henry was comforting Ralph last night. When the three go out, someone always has to leave early so the farms won't be unoccupied too long. Do you know there's still cattle rustling and pig stealing out here, pig? With the price of meat; they use a portable loading chute, right in the pasture, and then to the interstate and clear out. Anyway, Josie says it's the men's party, she'll take the turn on watch. She goes off home, and I think she has in mind that Ralph may need Henry's strong shoulder. Ralph's in a funny state. For one thing, he's terribly disappointed you aren't there at the party, he feels very grateful and keeps saying, 'But I want to shake that odd little fellow's hand.'

"He's got a poor head for liquor anyway, and the excitement of seeing his opera softens it just a little more. He's talking with Henry and with Mike and Mona Shapen, they're Henry's special student friends.

"Ralph is fifty-two, and feeling it. They're sitting at this little round table at the club when I go over to ask Mona, 'When is Billy Hoffman coming?' Love, it's much earlier in the evening. And I stay to hear Ralph say:

" 'Three score and ten. That's seventy. But I may not have eighteen left to work in, and I never thought about that till tonight. That anybody's career is finite, isn't it, but when you're young, you never realize you have to choose which work to do. You say yes to it all, and then the years come down to where you have to choose: say, one more symphony. And one more opera, and finish some chamber work, and maybe that'll be it.' He's not pitying himself. He's just trying to get himself rescheduled, and Henry says:

" 'When I was a kid, I did sports casting, Ralph, on local radio. First job I ever had. I was covering our minor-league club, and they were in a play-off that year. The starting pitcher was an old guy, older for his job than you are for yours, named Rootsie Seller. I'll never forget him. Bowlegged veteran, he'd been on half a dozen major-league teams through the years, and then down through the minors, level by level, till he wound up here. They had a lot more minor-league teams then in the small American cities. I was a kid, and I'd just learned the phrase *game plan,* so when I interviewed Sellers before the game, I said: "Rootsie, what's your game plan for this one?" And he said: "It's a high sky today, Henry. Heat's not gonna help. But I'll stand up there and throw everything I can, and when I can't, I'll sit down." '

"Ralph loves it, and he keeps saying it over, and telling it to anyone who'll listen. Old Debbie comes to chat, and Henry's up, doing his duty dance with Mona Shapen, and Ralph tells Debbie the story. And the punch lines comes out, 'Hot weather's going to help. I'm high as the sky. I'm going to throw everything I can at them till they sit down.'

"Debbie says that's beyoodeeful, she's pretty sauced up and speaking pigeon, and, oh, Hoffman, I can't resist. I'm so bad. I say Debbie has to come right now and tell it to Sato, before she forgets. So Debbie mangles the story gorgeously, of course, I'm not sure whether Rootsie was playing baseball or basketball, and she gets to the big line, and pauses, and delivers: 'Ve must trow effryting ve kon at der vons who sit in der sky.'

"And Sato listens in that beautiful, attentive, smiling way of his, and suddenly he looks quite serious, and says: 'Yes, Debbie. That is what we must always do, I believe.' "

"Yeah. You believe that, Maggi?"

"If you do, Hoffman." But it isn't really time yet for an affectionate silence between them, so she says: "Furthest adventures of Maggi Short, girl troublemaker, but I'm just a cameo in the next scene. The party's getting late, Short is crawling from table to bar, Ralph will work till he's eighty, Debbie is the chick singer out in front of the little orchestra Hervey hired, on her fourth chorus of 'Good Night, Irene,' and all the kids are larking.

"I'm dancing Marcel around, he stays about three feet away, and I'm trying to work him in to two feet. Marcel is saying that he must work with Beth again, he must try to get her something in Hollywood, and I'm agreeing, no way that girl's not going to be a star, as long as she doesn't regain consciousness, when in comes young Doctor Calm, J. T. Mason, to our drunken midst.

"Maury sees him first, leaps up into the air like a cheerleader, and yells: 'Come on, students. Gather round. The doctor's here.'

" 'Karen's with her parents at State House,' Johnny announces, as if Maury'd asked. That must have been when they wouldn't let her in, and she knocked on your door, pig.

" 'Doctor's going to demonstrate his greatest operation, the spousectomy, and I'm the patient. Doctor, I got me this turr'ble spouse here in the side, right where the rib fell out, can you fix it for me?'

" 'I thought maybe you'd want for you and me to have a visit, Maury,' Johnny says.

"Maury claps his hands.

" 'Seems he might not be ready here this evening, so I'll show you what the doctor does. Nurse!'

"Maury calls me over. I take a step toward him, and nod.

" 'Prepare for surgery. Razor.' He slaps his hand as if I'd put a razor in it. 'Aftershave . . .'

" 'You don't care to have a private talk, Maury?'

" 'Now, John, can't you see I'm operating? Nurse! Deodorant. Call of the Wild Perfume. Ruffle shirt. Nex ties. Shepherdy plaid suit.' Johnny turns and is walking out. Maury capers after him. 'Shoeshine. Clockedy sockedy orchidy corsageliss the bliss the kiss'—turns to the orchestra—'Play it, boys. "Stardust"!'

"That's the last we see of Johnny, and as the orchestra plays 'Stardust,' Maury slumps onto a leather sofa, and I run over to him.

" 'Maury.'

" 'I didn't want to fight him. I'm not mad. Just wanted Johnny good and mad.'

" 'Maury.'

" 'I'm sorry for the way I had to do it. You think he'll understand if I apologize tomorrow?'

" 'He might. I won't.'

" 'I had to cut her loose. I didn't ever even want that boy's part, but he's so right for her.'

" 'I always thought Karen was pretty right for you,' I say.

" 'She couldn't come where I'm going. She'd have lost her mind.'

" 'Are you exaggerating?'

" 'Been crying a lot of tears lately, Karen has.'

" 'Where is it that you're going?'

" 'Wherever the country's going, Maggi. *Sauve qui peut.*'

"We got a last act coming, Hoffman, and an epilogue, are you with me?"

"Gandenberg? Let me guess—goes off with Sidney?"

"You are a very brilliant pig this morning."

"It's not that hard, you know? She's had her little pink whaddya call it? What they cut trees with?"

"Chain saw."

"She's had her chain saw idling here for three weeks, looking for some timber tall enough to cut."

"She cut it, but she may have a little trouble getting it to stay cut. Herve has his car and driver waiting outside all evening. When the time comes, he sends her out to it first, so no one can be quite sure what's happening."

"Yeah? What about Dick?"

"Oh, you infuriating—if you keep guessing my story, I'm going to stop telling it."

"Don't stop."

"What do you know about Dick?"

"They're married. I even got a hint they have a baby."

"Oh, I didn't know about the baby. How lovely—Hoffman, Hervey thinks she's virginal. That's a type Hervey speaks of, not a physical condition, he regrets to say.

"The party is breaking up, anyway. Maury has gone to drive the Ridings home—"

"You said there was a burglary?"

"Wait a minute. Maury and the Ridings have left. Mike and Mona and Fennellon and Ralph are going. Sato and Marcel went off to have a quiet drink together—I think it may be something quite nice for Marcel that Sato has in mind. Are you glad? I am. There's Debbie and me and Short, the orchestra is packing up, and Gandenberg and Dick, and Sidney goes fluttering out the door in her eight-foot Siamese-silk stole. I'm sorry I don't have that one too, the colors are lovely.

"Herve makes a great show of hand shaking all around, yawning, well, he'd better be off, he supposes, strolls out casually. Poor Dick. He's been waiting for Sidney to get ready, expecting her to ride on the back of his motorcycle, I suppose, maybe change to slacks for it. Suddenly Sidney's gone. He looks around, bewildered. Wait. Gandenberg. Dick reaches the parking lot as the Mercedes is purring out, and leaps on his bike. And the moment the driver hears that motor, Sidney must say something, because the purr goes to a roar, and the car leaves a hole behind it in the dark. Into which Dick plunges, revving like a madman, and the chase is on.

"I know I'm not going to keep up with it, but I want to make sure the kid gets through town safely, so I jump into the Volvo, Short yells that he and Debbie will walk, and I whisk away through town and out toward the interstate.

"The state police had Dick before he even reached it. You know why?"

"Uh-uh."

"Come on, pig, you're such a brilliant guesser this morning, tell me why the state police were there, one car in front and one behind?"

"Oink?"

"Because Gandenberg has a shortwave radio in that car, lover, and he calls them. Oh, little Hervey can get things done. Now guess, no, don't bother, how I *know* that Hervey calls them. Because Maury receives police calls in his car, and he is on his way back from leaving off the Ridings, and he hears it."

"Hey, what about the burglary?"

"You've been very dear and patient, and such a good guesser, so I'll tell you. Maury is waiting at the county jail when Dick's brought in, and then I come along, and he tells me: a friend who lived with the Ridings apparently. Instead of attending our opera with Sue—he was supposed to come in their van and meet her—he loaded the van with everything he could stuff into it and off he went."

"Oh, shit."

"Not Davey Riding's attitude at all. Maury isn't to report it even. 'Let him go. A lot of bad goes with Charles, and very little good'—now how in hell would you have an actor read a line like that?"

"Jesus. I dunno."

"Davey's already on probation for taking the blame for something this friend did, you know about that? Okay. It's almost four in the morning, pig. You're lying in your sack at the hotel, aren't you, snoring and grunting, and letting young women in and out the door—oh, hell, where's that cuddidout?"

"All right, quit. Uncle."

"Now it's your uncle? Really, Hoffman. All right. Maury and I have almost got the cops talked into reducing the charge for Dick. I'm giving them the fine young man, just off a big performance and a slicker runs off with his wife. They want to believe me, and they all know Maury and like him; he's giving them ghetto jive like he'd never in this world talk normally, and it makes his cop friends feel like a bunch of sociologists.

"And Dick, this big handsome farm animal, I know he'd win a ribbon at the Four-H fair, is sitting there, looking like a crushed petunia. He's none too sober, among other things, but they've agreed to let him off the blood test, we're going to get a reduction of charge to speeding, and Hoffman, there comes a boozy yell from the doorway:

" 'Let him alone, you cossacks.'

"Snazzer Short, with Debbie, and a pair of gendarmes walking them in. Seems they'd been walking back from the club along the county road, Short with a bottle of champagne holstered in his belt and another in his drinking hand. Debbie's letting him pass it to her so he won't drink too much and get in trouble, when trouble comes along with its big red spotlight.

"Public intoxication is what's going on, and the two deputies stop and get out, they often check the club about closing time, and my Snazzer's going to fight all fifty of them to protect Debbie's honor or something. So instead of a warning and a ride home, they've been hauled in. Debbie says one of them whacked on Short a little in the back seat, and he was indeed a mess, but still full of jumping beans when they burst in on us.

"Ah, there are screams and curses, charges, countercharges, confusion, and alarm. Debbie is strong, insisting she'd seen Short get hit while handcuffed, and for a while that's the only point that our side has. But then, gradually, after listening and smiling and waiting for the shouts to moderate, Maury starts sorting us out and taking charge. I can't exactly describe how he does it—Henry Fennellon has the same quality, in a totally different man—you do it, Billy, but not till the third week of rehearsal. Authority. It's like charm, only strong. There's someone everybody's willing to listen to, not because he's saying anything different but because it's him saying it.

"So Maury gets his honkies settled, we get our two drunks released—listen, I think Debbie is as smashed as Short and Dick, but she carries it like a queen. Maury takes Dick, and drops Debbie; I take Short, drive him home, I wash his face, put on his pajamas, tuck him in. Asleep with a smile on his face, he breaks my heart. And then, I look at my watch, and the time is five, and I think, 'Nope. Sorry, Snazzer.' I think, 'Hoffman wants me if no one else does, because Hoffman's my great love.' Listen, pig, you say no and the next sound you hear is going to be you screaming."

That hand, but Hoffman is chuckling too hard to say no, or yes, or anything. There's something about this outrageous creature that just tickles him.

"You coming with me?"

"You haven't asked me."

"Come on."

"Okay."

"It won't last two weeks."

"I'll bet three."

They shake.

Maggie wins. It's in the third week that an actual, no-kidding Los Angeles private detective knocks on the door of their closetdoor-bed, refrig-and-hotplate room.

Maggi's been very good one-room company. She's a clever cook. She's taken care of Hoffman's clothes, even to picking up half-pockets at the dime store and sewing them in the pants. She's been funny and faithful, loving, lively, cheerful, never anything less than an absolute pleasure to look at—and more support than a stumblebum director can use, getting the black theatre thing on the trucks. Can a Hoffman kinda man really get what the only first-rate woman he ever knew in his goddamn life has to give? Can a country fiddler get the good out of a Strad?

They live on the edge of the ghetto. Maggi doesn't go out except in the middle of the day. A couple of times she's been over to Beverly Hills, to see people she used to know in the movie business. But she comes back shrugging, with a couple of new jokes.

So Hoffman looks at the kid in the trench coat. He's got a pimple in the nose wing, which puts Hoffman on his side right away, and it's an imitation trench coat, you know, and kindly Hoffman says:

"Yeah?"

"You William Hoffman?"

"Billy."

"I want to talk to you."

"Who are you?"

"Jud Jarvis." He flashes a card, a license.

"Hey, Maggi." Hoffman couldn't be more pleased. "C'mere. We got a private eye."

"I'm an investigator, ma'am. From Confidential Services."

"Well, sweetibeans. Come in, come right in here this minute."

"Yeah." Hoffman. "No. Wait, wait. Hey, Maggi. He's gotta punch me in the jaw first, so I'll talk, doesn't he?"

Maggi. "There's ways to make guys talk."

"Listen, Bridget." Hoffman. "Maybe you play me for a sucker. Maybe you don't."

Maggi. "Maybe I just play you for a punk, punk."

The youth. "Excuse me. Did you say Bridget?"

"It's an alias, shamus." Maggi. "But whaddo I care? This punk with the ears like Valley Forge in April. He's got a three-nine-one hanging over his head, back in Dago."

"You gonna listen to her?" Hoffman. "It's a four-seventeen. And it's in Santa Barbara. Aw, come on in, kid. What d'ya want to talk to us about?"

The boy comes in, accepts a cup of coffee, and says he is looking for Mrs. Rigby Short.

"It's all over." Hoffman. "The jig is up."

Then they both laugh idiotically, because Maggi's been saying "the jig is up" every morning when Hoffman's black bodyguard, a noisy man on the stairs, arrives.

"I'm Mrs. Short," Maggi says. "What can I do for you?"

"I don't know." The kid. "I'm just supposed to report if I can find you or not."

"How odd." Maggi. "I've talked with my husband two or three times from here."

Hoffman. "Tough case."

"I suppose your client's name is Gandenberg. All he had to do was phone my home in State City."

"I don't know. This was a referral from our Philadelphia office, ma'am."

"Anything else we can do for you?" Maggi likes to get Hoffman to bed early. He's working with two different groups, kids in the morning, adults when they get home from work.

They show their visitor out, and Hoffman says: "Yeah?"

"Yeah."

"You did it, Maggi."

"Yes."

"Leaving when?"

"Tomorrow. Okay?"

"Sure, you know?"

Fall comes and goes. Hoffman's ghetto people like him. They're very serious about their acting, hard to teach, but once they've got something right, they never do it wrong. Pretty soon Hoffman's known, partly for what he does, even more for who his protectors are. He doesn't push it, doesn't go out alone at night, but in his usual places he's recognized and welcome. His people get a grant. Now they want him to stay and do Christmas plays at churches with their kids. They want a directing class, pay him an extra twenty-five a week for it. It has three students, a Haitian, an Alabaman, and a copper-red young woman who grew up around the corner.

Sometimes they talk about the election, but it's a joke to them—McGovern's a flake, they say, and Nixon's like a crooked cop. Anyway, they're revolutionaries. Hoffman doesn't vote, though he thinks about it.

Without quite meaning to, he slips into something with the copper-colored woman, who's nineteen and beautiful as a snake. Nobody raises objections, but he feels uncomfortable with it. He thinks he'll leave after the Christmas plays. Lila, the young woman, is personally defiant about it, but makes Hoffman nervous when she describes how prejudiced the other men she knows are about her sleeping with a white. The ones he knows are carefully tactful, maybe willing to make an exception with Hoffman, maybe just polite.

He gets questioned by an FBI man one day, asked to identify revolutionaries. He says he doesn't know any, says he just puts on plays with people and gets a fee for it. The FBI man wonders whether a fee paid weekly really ought to be exempt from withholding tax, and if that's how all Hoffman's income is received, and whether Hoffman would mind talking to someone from Internal Revenue about it, and if Hoffman's sure he doesn't know any revolutionaries. You know?

So the suitcase is out again. There's a job near Portland, Oregon, a suburban community-theatre show.

On December 29, 1972, there are some clean shirts back from the laundry to go into the suitcase, and Hoffman gets a phone call from Henry Fennellon.

"Henry who?"

"Fennellon, from State City, Billy. I was in the opera last summer."

"Oh, yeah. Sure. I'm sorry, Henry."

"I want to talk to somebody. To you, I mean. May I? I've just gotten back from Hanoi."

"Jesus."

"I remembered you were out here. I phoned Maggi Gandenberg, and she was nice enough to give me your number."

"Maggi Gandenberg."

"You did know about that?"

"Not directly."

"She asked me to give you her love. May I come over?"

"Yeah. Sure."

"It won't be an imposition?"

"Huh-uh."

"What may I bring to drink?"

"Whatever you want. I'm sorry, I got no booze right now. I was packing, as a matter of fact, to go up to Portland."

"Bourbon?"

"Anything you want."

"You sure you don't mind?"

Jesus, what's wrong with the guy? How many times do you have to say okay? "Come on over, Henry. Be great to see you."

The big older guy with the nice, deep voice, right?

By the time he arrives, Hoffman's got Henry pretty clearly remembered.

Henry wears a real trench coat. He looks jittery.

"Come on in, Henry. Jesus, I love that coat. It must go back thirty years."

"This really is an imposition, but thank you for letting me impose."

"Sit down. You look tired."

"I'm too big to be comfortable on airplanes; the Pacific's a long flight." He sits, and sighs. "Oh, my God."

The phone rings.

"I'm not here." Rings again. "I'm sorry. I don't mean to be abrupt."

"Why would someone think you're here?" Hoffman answers the phone. An operator says: "Mr. Henry Fennellon, please."

"Who?"

"Mr. Henry Fennellon. The Washington *Post* calling."

"Tell Mr. Post we're fresh out," Hoffman says, clicks the receiver and leaves the phone off the hook. "Newspaper calling you, you know? Where would they get the number, anyway?"

"The hotel switchboard would have a record of my calls, I guess. Dumb of me. I should have used a phone booth—Billy, it might be a newspaper. It might not."

"Who?"

"Spooks."

"Huh?"

"Intelligence people. The newspaper men met my plane. TV crews. But you can always figure some of the men with notebooks are not really press."

This sure is what Hoffman needs right now, along with the FBI interest in his working with black militants, and maybe Internal Revenue curious about his fees. Ah, to hell with them.

"Hanoi. I'll be damned."

"I'll talk with them, of course. The press, the intelligence men. I don't mean to avoid it, and I shall be as truthful as I'm able. But it seemed important to me to tell it once first freely, without having to be careful. To a friend, if I'm not presuming. Do you remember Mona Shapen?"

"My stage manager, sure. The little beauty with the bum left hand."

"Mona was killed in Hanoi Christmas Eve."

"Oh, Henry. No."

"That's what I want to tell you about. Unguardedly. May I? Before I begin to tell it formally to the authorities. And the newspapers. And Mike."

"Oh, yeah." Hoffman is pretty empty of emotion, with the shows all done here, but thinking of Mike Shapen hits him pretty hard. "Mike, the little bass. Yeah."

I am not a partisan of Hanoi. Nor of Washington, as it is these days. But I am a partisan of what the best of this country's people have tried to make it, very much one.

I take being a citizen seriously. It's a privilege so basic that we almost always forget it, like forgetting we have lungs and hearts, but there come times for acting as a citizen. That's why I shall cooperate with the authorities, bad as they are these days, and give precisely the same information to the press.

About three months ago I had a call from Mike. He'd got a job, just as school was about to begin, teaching music in a New Jersey high school, not far from Mona's home and not far from New York. He and Mona were very pleased about it and wanted me to know.

Mona came on and talked mostly about a radical pacifist organization they had joined. I asked about her hand and about her music, but she said she could not think about those things while Kissinger and Nixon still had their war going on. Although there were negotiations in Paris, she did not trust Kissinger. I thought she was wrong, but of course it was I who was wrong.

When the Shapens first arrived at State University, before the protest movement got started, Mona was the finest cello student they had ever had. She was strong enough to play with the faculty string quartet during a time when its regular cellist was in the hospital. When Mona gave her junior recital at the university, something all students have to do and which is ordinarily attended by teachers and a few friends, there was so much interest, it was moved from afternoon to evening and held in an auditorium instead of a small recital room. She filled it. There was coverage in the newspapers, and her picture appeared in several music magazines.

In 1967 she filled the same room for her senior recital, but that year, instead of playing an encore, Mona made a speech. In 1968 her hand was injured, and though she continued her graduate-school registration, she stopped going to classes.

The following year she was not registered.

She and Mike often came to the farm, and I grew very fond of both of them. Sometimes they sought and took my advice, but although I got Mona to begin working with an orthopedist, who was quite optimistic about the chances of her playing again, Mona's progress with it followed the changes in fortune of the movement that absorbed her.

By last summer she had begun again to do the exercises prescribed, but Mike admitted there were days when the headlines were discouraging, and on those days he did not believe that Mona worked on her hand.

Two months ago, you perhaps recall, about ten days before the election, Dr. Kissinger made the announcement: "Peace is at hand."

That evening Mona phoned me and was so jubilant I could not say what I privately felt to be the truth, that the announcement might more easily be a highly cynical campaign device than an accurate report of diplomatic progress.

Mona proposed to return to State City, to be reexamined by the orthopedist. I longed to invite her to stay with me at the farm, but since Mike was not coming, did not suggest it, and she stayed with Sue and Davey Riding.

The orthopedist, in addition to having her do squeezing exercises, designed and had made a glove for her in which the fingers could be flexed open and spread against tension provided by elastic cords, running from the fingertips to the palm. It cost almost two hundred dollars to have made, but at my request the doctor told her there would be no charge because the device was still experimental. The doctor and I shared the cost.

She finished at the hospital just before Thanksgiving. Just a month ago. Mike flew out, and we all spent Thanksgiving at the farm. The Ridings joined us for dinner. It was a very warm occasion. I was so fond of all of them.

In a secret way, and I have never told anyone this before and shall not again, I loved Mona Shapen. Perhaps I should say repressed, not secret, because I learned about my feelings from my dreams. I have frequently, in the past few years, had sensual dreams about Mona, and sentimental dreams with fearful little twists.

I had one yesterday on the plane, returning from Hanoi, and the reason I did not sleep from then on was because I would not risk having another.

During the Thanksgiving visit I learned that Mike and Mona planned to spend Christmas in Hanoi. Mona's group had raised enough money to be able to designate a couple to join a large party, chiefly older radicals, that would leave for North Vietnam at about the time Christmas vacation started. They were sending four students as well, but particularly wanted Mike, who is quite a good photographer, and Mona because she photographed so beautifully.

December 7 is a date of which, like most men my age, I am always aware, because Pearl Harbor did so mark our lives. That was the date of Mike's next phone call from New Jersey, asking my advice. That would have been three weeks ago. The trip to Hanoi was still scheduled, but his own situation had changed. The school wanted him to take his band to a holiday band contest, for which he had not expected his students to qualify. But they had worked hard in response to his teaching and won their way through several eliminations. He felt that he could face his superintendent and the school board, but there were some decent people on it whose public support might be damaged by Mike's leaving his band to go to Hanoi, giving the school board right-wingers the sort of cause they were looking for.

Mostly, though, he hated to let his students down. I said I thought he ought to do whatever he had given his word to do when he took the job.

Mike said in the tough, teasing way that meant he would take it, that that was good, solid bourgeois advice. Then he stunned me by asking if I would go in his place.

Mike said it was shamefully chauvinistic of him, but given the intensity of Mona's temperament, he would feel badly about her making such a journey without him unless I were to go. He even admitted to feeling some anticipation of physical jealousy, given the circumstances of the trip.

I couldn't tell him I immediately felt the same wretched anticipation in my older, bourgeois way. I found I wanted very much to go then. I left my profession as a reporter some years ago, but I did not leave my reputation for veracity, and I told myself that a true report from North Vietnam, for which I knew I could get a national hearing, might, as the New Year began, be some kind of contribution to peace. I said I would go if I were permitted to pay my own passage and if my intention of relying and reporting solely on my own judgment were acceptable to Mike and Mona's sponsors.

My name is not current, but it is not unknown. The sponsoring group was pleased, and used the funds regained to add yet another student to the group.

Mona and I stayed mostly with the students. There were some political celebrities along, but they made up a higher level of our total group, and actually we did not all travel together. We arrived in Hanoi on different days and stayed in different accommodations. That suited me quite well, because I felt I wished to see what the North Vietnamese showed the younger, less imposing people. I felt the presentation might be more cursory, a less polished public relations performance, and perhaps it was. We went sometimes with the full group, sometimes with our own guide, whose French was better than her English. We did attend the interviews with the well-coached few American fliers that were, I understand, widely reported here. The poor men were parrots, and although our hosts put the best face they could on it, North Vietnamese life was squalid and cheerless as we saw it.

But I did not wish to be offensively cynical. I kept my own counsel pretty much, I took no notes, and was allowed to take few photographs.

Mona's response to it was of a kind to inflate my repressed tenderness almost to bursting point. She gradually and, to my eye, glowingly moved away from the poison vocabulary and stereotyped thought patterns of the hard-liners to what I thought was her simpler and more genuine way of being; she seemed every day to be less a radical and more one who loved peace for its own beautiful sake. She talked to the people through our guide, whose close and instant friend Mona became; she hugged children on the street. She worked with her Silly Putty and her special glove.

Neither Mike nor I need have worried, of course, about her wanting to celebrate victory with one of the hot-eyed youths. What we were seeing wasn't "victory" to her. Just peace. Just people not killing other people.

Two of the students in our group had brought guitars along. She borrowed one and could play simple things on it, the first music she'd produced in five years. Mona was twenty-four. That had been a fifth of her life.

The day before Christmas, at about five in the afternoon, I got back from having a drink with some British correspondents I used to know, at their hotel, to find Mona sitting outside our quarters. We were in a dormitory formerly used by medical students before they moved that kind of training away from the city. Actually Mona and I were assigned to a room together, because word had not got through that the man with her would not be her husband. But there were two small cots in the room and a rather pretty Oriental screen of flowers painted on silk, so we could stay there modestly enough, not that Mona wasn't capable of crossing heedlessly to my side of it, less than fully dressed, to speak of something that excited her. I am pleased that I never gave her cause to know with what agony I ached for her at those times.

When we dressed for official ceremonies, as happened thrice, she would cross to my side to have her dress zipped, turn, rise onto tiptoes, and kiss me lightly for it. Each time I'd have to send her out to wait for me with the others, pretending I'd decided on a different necktie or something of the sort. That was to allow myself to blot my eyes.

It was after the third of those receptions that I stayed to have a Christmas Eve drink with the British correspondents, but only one drink, for I didn't think that I could handle very much more Christmas cheer.

When I got back to the medical-school dormitory, Mona was sitting outside in the dusk by herself. Some children had been with her, she said, but they had all gone home to supper. She had been singing Christmas carols to them and wished she had thought of borrowing the guitar. Perhaps she would tomorrow, for Christmas itself.

Then she stood to go inside, and I watched her walk away.

It came just before midnight, out of the clouds, that flight of American bombing planes, bring *Donner* and *Blitzen.* Some came low to increase the terror.

Mona was in the lounge, talking and laughing with the students, and I had gone upstairs to get undressed and read. I was reluctant to spend so sentimental an evening close to that lovely young presence.

I heard the motors and could not believe it. I heard the sirens and tried to tell myself it was a mistake. Then I heard the bombs.

I grabbed my coat, turned off the light in our room, and ran barefoot out into the corridor, down two flights of stairs, and along another corridor to the lounge.

The lights were going out all over the building, it hadn't been especially well blacked out. Our kids and a Scandinavian group and some young North Vietnamese who'd come to entertain were crowding to get out the door and over across the street to an air-raid shelter we'd been shown. I found Mona outside, holding herself away and back against the building beside the doorway, with the others going past her. For an instant I thought she'd waited for me, and was grateful. Then I saw her face, that beautiful face, open-mouthed with shock and hate, staring at the sky.

There were flashes and explosions, incendiaries, fragmentation bombs, heavies. I seized her arm and urged her to hurry. She came for a few steps, in among the other young people running for the shelter, and in the crowd I lost my hold on Mona. I ran on for thirty yards or so, believing she was running near me in the same direction. There was a lot of confusion, and some screaming up the street where a small bomb had exploded among people coming to this same shelter. I stopped to look that way. There was a bomb flash, and I saw Mona in it, walking away from the rest of us, her face still tilted toward the sky. She was already sixty or seventy yards away. I had pushed my way through the people and was halfway to her when the next bomb landed, out in front of Mona, but close enough so that the concussion knocked me off my feet.

The same concussion killed Mona. It must have picked that small body up and thrown it sideways, because I spent ten or fifteen minutes looking and calling in the dark before I found where it lay, crumpled. The bombing had moved away by then, to another part of the city. I had a flashlight in my pocket, and I searched with that. The body wasn't marked very much. No wounds. I think the back was broken in several places, and there was no life in her at all.

I picked her up. She was very light. I carried her back with me to the barracks and into the lounge. It was closer than the shelter, and by the time I got there, the body seemed unbearably heavy.

Henry Fennellon is silent, diminished, pulled away somewhere inside his trench coat. Hoffman can't say anything either. He can reach for the brown paper sack, open the bottle of whiskey Henry brought, and finally mutter:

"Yeah, hey, Henry? Want a drink?"

Getting no answer, he can pour some whiskey into water glasses, look for ice, remember he's neglected to fill the ice trays, hand Henry the straight bourbon, and taste his own, not liking it much. First drink he's had since Maggi left.

"Oh, lord," says Henry. "What have we done to our children?"

"Nothing they won't do to theirs," says Hoffman softly, and there's a knock on the door.

"Goddamn it." Henry roars and rises, glass in hand. "Am I not allowed to have one drink in peace with a friend. Here come the goddamn vultures, Hoffman." He drinks his whiskey off, a savage grin coming onto his face, strides to the door, and yanks it open.

But it is neither reporters nor spooks, but Hoffman's copper girl, beautiful as a snake, worried because she's tried to call him several times, gotten a busy signal, asked the operator, learned the phone was off the hook, and come to see if Hoffman is in trouble.

Fennellon in his trench coat moves out past her, tossing the water glass onto the sofa, looking from behind like who? With his height and his hair still dark—like Cary Grant or Gary Cooper, on his way to danger.

"Who was that?" Lila's innocent young ferocity will not let her ask the question kindly. Everything she says challenges.

"An old white man," Hoffman tells her. "Who was hurt at Selma."

"Where?"

Hoffman on a bus, traveling again. Hoffman on his way to Portland, empty again. Ready to be filled with stories, again. To make stories, again. Old Billy Bigears, with an empty seat beside him: Take it. There's a story you could tell to pass the time as the lovely, polluted California seascape passes. So could we all, every man his own Homer, blind, caught in the endless wonder of the words, of the cries, of the shouts, of the laughter, of the tears of the things of the stories of our lives. There we go.